Albion Winegar Tourgée

Hot Plowshares

A Novel

Albion Winegar Tourgée

Hot Plowshares
A Novel

ISBN/EAN: 9783743305908

Manufactured in Europe, USA, Canada, Australia, Japa

Cover: Foto ©Andreas Hilbeck / pixelio.de

Manufactured and distributed by brebook publishing software
(www.brebook.com)

Albion Winegar Tourgée

Hot Plowshares

A FATEFUL SEARCH.

"She came in, went straight to that desk there, raised the lid, and appeared to be hunting around for something she could not find." —p. 525.

HOT PLOWSHARES.

A NOVEL,

BY

ALBION W. TOURGÉE,

AUTHOR OF "A FOOL'S ERRAND," ETC.

NEW YORK:
FORDS, HOWARD, & HULBERT
1883

PREFACE.

FICTION is the handmaid of Truth. Imagination is almost always the forerunner of fact. History gives only the outlines of the world's life. It tells us what was done, who did it, when and where, and, in a general way, the reason why it was done. It traces the movements of races, nations and parties. It is concerned chiefly with nouns of multitude, taking no heed of the individual save when he becomes connected with the general result in the relation of cause and effect. Rulers and leaders are noted as types of great events; the man—the human atom—is only an incident. History tells what the army did, and gives the general a place in its pages simply because he commanded the army. Of the motives that inspire the rank and file it takes as little note as of their individual acts.

Biography both supplements and obscures History—supplements by showing the relation of great events to a particular individual, and obscures by magnifying his causative relation to them. If we accepted the verdict of the most conscientious biographer as veritable truth, we should soon be hopelessly astray. Biography covers the whole area of History with private landmarks. Every great event is pre-empted by a thousand claimants, each of whom asserts his individual right to be considered its originator. The rivalry of the dead is even worse than that of the living. Men who wrought and fought side by side while alive against some common enemy, are no sooner dead than they are pitted against each other in a never-ending struggle for the laurels of the victory they have jointly won.

Fiction labors under no such disadvantages. It fills out the outlines History gives, and colors and completes its pictures. It shows what manner of men they were who wrought its great events. It vivifies the past of which History only furnishes the record.

Twenty-two years ago a great nation was broken in twain in an hour. There was no splintering of the parts, no strain, no lesion. The cleavage was sharp and smooth. The day before there was no sign of severance. The day after there was no trace of the union that had been. The one republic became two without a ripple in the daily life or relations of the people. Governors, judges— all officers, state and federal—continued to perform the same duties under the new as under the old organization. The two hostile powers were as far apart as if they had never been united. Before the sword was drawn the separation was as complete as if the ocean rolled between. Some of the border states were held by Northern power and occupancy. They were, so to speak, over-laid by Northern life. The soil was held, but their life, their sympathy and the bulk of their strength went with the South, of which they were a part.

What made this sudden severance possible—not only possible but inevitable? It was not ambition nor partisan malice, nor the lust of power. It was because the two sections had grown apart—had leaned steadily away from each other, farther and farther every year for a generation.

The separation was not effected by any act of secession or declaration of independence. That was but the sign of the fact. The mutually repellent forces within the respective sections had completed their work. The North clung together because it was homogeneous in sentiment. The South was solid for the same reason. War followed naturally. Which was right and which was wrong, abstractly, is of little moment to-day. That all who were actors in that mighty drama should understand and appreciate the sentiments and motives of those who stood opposed to them is, at least, desirable. That our children should understand that the great cataclysm was sprung, not from passion, greed or ambition, but was based upon the deepest impulses of right and honor, is essential to that homogeneity of sentiment on which our future prosperity and happiness so much depend.

We are accustomed to speak of "the results of the war." It would be more logical to speak of the results of the years of peace that preceded war. The peculiar relations that still prevail between certain classes at the South are less the result of war than of the system which was overthrown by war. There are many problems which the past has left unsolved. Some of them are of the gravest possible character. Their peaceful solution makes the fullest comprehension of the pre-existing influences and developments a prime necessity on the part of all.

Many years ago the author conceived the idea that he might aid some of his fellow-countrymen and countrywomen to a juster comprehension of these things by a series of works which should give, in the form of fictitious narrative, the effects of these distinct and contrasted civilizations upon various types of character and during specific periods of the great transition. Beginning their preparation in 1867, in the midst of the fading glare of revolution, on the very spot where one of the great armies of the rebellion surrendered, he has worked patiently and honestly and zealously to complete his analyses of the representative groups of character. By birth and education he became intuitively familiar with Northern life. Born upon the Western Reserve, the impressible years of boyhood and youth were almost equally divided between the East and the West. They were years of fruitful though unconscious observation. From the close ot the war until 1880 he resided continuously at the South, and studied with the utmost care, and from a standpoint of peculiar advantage, the types of the expiring and the coming eras.

The present volume is the last of the projected series. It is designed to give a review of the Anti-Slavery struggle, by tracing its growth and the influence of the sentiment upon contrasted characters. In the main, it does not concern itself with the promoters of this struggle. In no sense does the work profess to give a *history* of the movement, but only a truthful picture of the life upon which it acted, of the growth of its influence and its character as a preparation for the struggle in which those whose thought had been moulded by its sentiments were destined to engage.

The period covered by the now completed series of six volumes extends from twenty years before the war until twelve years after it. By the public, they have been persistently designated as "historical novels." The term is true only in that they have been endeavors to trace the operation of sentiments which have arisen from, and been instrumental in producing, historical facts. In chronological order they would stand as follows: "Hot Plowshares," "Figs and Thistles," "A Royal Gentleman," "A Fool's Errand," "Bricks Without Straw," "John Eax." When the series was begun the author had little hope that it would be completed. Now that it is finished, he is almost sorry to bid adieu to a subject that has engrossed the better portion of his active manhood. It is believed that it constitutes the most serious attempt ever made to portray the various phases of a climacteric era, by successive pictures of the various forms of life developed thereby. For the favor extended to the preceding volumes the author desires to render renewed thanks.

A. W. T.

PHILADELPHIA, May 2, 1883.

CONTENTS.

CHAPTER   PAGE

    I. The Shadow of the Storm, . . . 7

   II. President-Making, ... 20

  III. "Arise, Sir Knight!" 31

  IV. "For Wounds, Balm," 43

   V. "A Defeated Joy," 62

  VI. The Clue to the Labyrinth, . . . 66

 VII. Between the Pillars, ... 75

VIII. On Guard, ... 86

  IX. Hargrove's Quarter, ... 95

   X. Merwyn Hargrove, ... 110

  XI. "Gay Castles in the Clouds that Pass," 125

 XII. Partners, ... 136

XIII. A New Day, ... 158

XIV. The End of the Law, ... 163

 XV. "For the Glory of God," . . . 170

XVI. Brackish Waters, ... 192

XVII. What Waked the World, ... 215

XVIII. A Weekly Post, ... 231

XIX. A Momentous Question, ... 246

 XX. "He that Is to Be," 258

XXI. A Subterranean Myth, ... 278

XXII. A Free Institution, ... 291

XXIII. For the Amendment of Divine Error, . 297

XXIV. By an Unpracticed Hand, . . . 311

XXV. A Punic Peace, ... 319

CONTENTS.

CHAPTER   PAGE

XXVI. The Reconnoissance in Force, . . 329

XXVII. Not Without Honor, ... 338

XXVIII. Bridging the Chasm, ... 349

XXIX. A Hard Bargain, ... 355

XXX. A Good Investment, ... 370

XXXI. On the Divide, ... 379

XXXII. Possessio Pedis, ... 397

XXXIII. A Nineteenth Century Buccaneer, . 400

XXXIV. A Change of Base, ... 413

XXXV. Blindfold and Barefoot, . . . 429

XXXVI. Born of the Spirit, ... 446

XXXVII. The Freemasonry of the Oppressed, 456

XXXVIII. Out of the Toils, ... 469

XXXIX. The Church Militant, ... 480

XL. Cleansed from Blood-Guiltiness, . 502

XLI. The Proof that Healeth Doubt, . 520

XLII. The Effect of a Side Light, . . 535

XLIII. That Nothing be Lost, . . . 546

XLIV. Facing the Ordeal, ... 563

XLV. A Masked Battery, ... 576

XLVI. Clamor in the Home Nest, . . . 583

XLVII. A Flickering Lamp, ... 588

XLVIII. Bits of Gossip, ... 598

XLIX. The Harvesting, ... 606

ILLUSTRATIONS.

*Designed by A. B. Frost.   Engravings by G. P. Williams
and Edith Cooper.*

	PAGE
1. A FATEFUL SEARCH, ...	*Frontispiece.*
2. THE RUNAWAY, ...	42
3. THE CHRISTENING OF AMITY LAKE, . . .	109
4. PARTNERS, ...	156
5. THE VINDICATION OF THE LAW, ...	288
6. AT BAY, ...	409

HOT PLOWSHARES.

CHAPTER I.

THE SHADOW OF THE STORM.

It was the fifth day of November, in the year of Grace, one thousand eight hundred and forty-eight. A man and a boy were husking corn in a hillside field overlooking the valley of the Mohawk, a valley once so celebrated for wealth and fertility that the early pioneers looked upon this favorite hunting-ground of the Iroquois as the *ne plus ultra* of a farmer's desires. To be of the Mohawk valley, even during the present century, was to occupy the most enviable of agricultural locations. Of varied soil, pleasantly undulated, richly wooded—the forest giving place to the most succulent herbage which grew under the settler's feet whenever his axe let in the sunlight—it is no wonder that the Dutchman cheated Skenandoah and the Yankee looked with covetous eyes from the rocky hills of New England upon its milk-and-honey flowing slopes. Principalities were carved out of its rich acreage. The landmarks of the Livingstones, the Schuylers, the Van Renssalaers, bounded realms worthy of a Palatine. Towns and cities grew up within them. Lesser farms filled in the uneven jointure of their borderings. To own even the outskirts of the valley was enough to make the possessor envied. The first Puritan owner of the tributary valley in which the field of which we have spoken was situated, had seized a precarious foothold between the duchies of two contending families and gleefully named his insecure possession Paradise Bay. There was no bay at all and the neighborhood was anything but paradisaical to the intruder. He was in the valley, however, and content, he and his descendants, thinking there was nothing more to be desired until the wonder-working To-day rushed by them, lifted the gateways of the West, and under the setting sun revealed marvels which dwarfed with daily facts the wildest fancies of the Orient.

The time of which we write was near the waking from a long slumber. The canal which stretches from lake to river was still the main avenue of transit eastward and westward through the Empire State. Beyond that the steamer and the stage-coach held sway. The grosser products of the West consumed themselves before they reached the Eastern market. The cattle and swine stretched away in endless droves across the States lying eastward of the Mississippi. The sustentation of these while on the way to the Eastern market enriched the farmers along the route more than those who reared and drove. Cheese sold at the ports of Lake Erie then at three cents a pound. That very year tens of thousands of fat sheep were slaughtered in Ohio for the hides and tallow—only the hams and tongues being saved for food. The West was open; was known to be full of possibilities. It teemed with food but yet was poor. The East was at its zenith. Every industry was quick. Labor was in abundance and yet in demand. Wages were low and so were supplies. There were few centres of population and still fewer unoccupied arable regions. Life and labor were evenly spread over the whole country. The land was a bursting hive—a magazine of possibility.

We were still a nation of hand-workers. There was not

a mower or harvester then in existence. No house contained a sewing-machine. The telegraph had begun at Washington and ended at New York twelve months before. The land was lighted with candles after nightfall. The spinning-wheel and shuttle sounded in every farmer's house. Butter was unmarketable a hundred miles from the dairy. The steam saw-mill had just begun to devour the forest. From East to West was the pilgrimage of a life; from North to South a voyage of discovery.

The migratory fever that New England breeds made the valley the great highway of the seekers for the sunset. The Yankee overran the Dutchman, and the great thoroughfare transformed him. Along the Mohawk ran the line of the homogeneous. It linked the East and the West. The Dutchman became first an innkeeper, then an immigrant, and then the Clutes and the Van Slaicks were lost in the great sea of American life that knows little of its origin and cares less. The great estates, the lordly landowners, remained, but the towns and villages and the hillside farms were stamped with the impress of New England life. It was a sort of half-way house.

Beyond was the West and possibility; here was fruition. The rich were lavish in an abundance which was not yet coveted by the keen eye of commerce. The poor had enough, and in the comforts of life were almost on a par with the rich. The lord of a thousand acres sat with his harvesters at dinner. He who counted his possessions by the square mile kept open house for the wayfarer. The epoch of haste had not come. The sun rose quietly and set at leisure. A day's journey was a serious matter. The canvas-covered wagon was the ark of trade. The saddle was the emblem of speed. Men slept yet in their beds. The day began with the dawn and not with the train's arrival. The turnpike was still the great artery of trade. The highways were dusty and populous. There was time to live. Brawn and brain went hand in hand. Every life touched nature. Like Antens we felt the earth beneath our feet and were strong. We had vanquished Nature and sat by the Indus of Time weeping for other worlds to conquer.

It was not long to continue thus. Already the footsteps of the prince were at the portals of the silent palace. The age of miracles was about to dawn. Within a year the gold of California; within a decade the railroad, the telegraph, the mower, the thresher, the sewing-machine, petroleum, gas—ah! so many wonders that they that wrought before forgot their cunning and learned anew to guide rather than do, to stand by and direct the goblins whom science had evoked from earth and air and sea to do their bidding.

The man and the boy still wrought together in the field. The corn stood in serried shocks between the rows from which it had been cut. The outer, weather-beaten leaves flapped brokenly in the wind. Here and there a yellow ear peeped out. The close-bound top and the wide-spread base made an extempore rick that promised a sturdy defense of the treasures which it held, even against winter storms. But the farmer had no idea of trusting his crop to this protection. To husk and house it properly was the greater part of his "fall work," as it was called. It was hardly past the period of the Indian summer yet, though the maples were almost bare; the birches showed their white arms on the hillside; the beeches had grown brown, and the seared leaves were whirling in weird dances down the hollows.

One of the shocks of maize ("stooks" they were called upon the Mohawk) had been thrown down and the band that confined the top loosened. Upon one side of this knelt the man; upon the other sat the boy. Each held in his right hand a sharp skewer of buckhorn which was fastened by a leather thong about his middle finger. With the left hand he drew toward him the dry rustling stalks, quickly seized the ear and thrusting the buck-horn "husking-pin," as it is called, through the dry shuck, stripped down the husk, first upon one side, then upon the other; and then breaking off the ear with a quick jerk threw it upon the golden pile which lay where the shock had stood. As the stalks collected, each husker put them beneath his knees and so advanced toward the other through the rifled shock.

The man was in the prime of life, smooth-shaven as was the custom of the time, strong, heavy-browed, with a prominent sharply cut nose and a mouth whose mobile under lip and flexible corners showed a mental activity clearly indicated also by the rapidity and certainty of his physical movements. He was clad in a blue frock with overalls of the same material, and wore also a sort of leather garment like a smith's apron, except that it was cut open below and strapped about each leg. His black felt hat, straight-brimmed in front and slightly upturned behind, showed marks of use but still more evident marks of thrift and respectability.

The frock open at the throat revealed a bit of white linen and a black silk tie, somewhat out of keeping with the rough outer habiliments but thoroughly in harmony with the strong, earnest face above. His hands were broad and strong but deft and supple. His eyes rested intently upon his work, but the movement of his lip and the quick humorous flash of his eye showed that his thought was busy elsewhere and that the quick play of his hands was half unconscious. It needed but a glance to tell that this man was of that class unmatched in any other land, the American Farmer—Gentleman and La-borer in one—Servant and King. This man, husking maize upon the hillside, might sway a senate or lead an army as easily as he fought the battle of life with na-ture. He was a good type of that democracy which

always surprises the world when the strain is put upon
it. Unconscious of any rank above himself and compas-
sionate of any that may be below, he seems born to
self-reliance and success. Content to do what he finds
to be done, respectful of himself and mindful of the
rights of others, his real power is unknown even to himself until occasion places some new burden on his shoulders and then the world wonders that it has found an
Ajax. He is the Cromwell who comes from the fens
to grasp the "fool's bauble" from the hands of weak-
lings.

The boy was a type, as well as the father. His dozen
years might have been more or less, so far as one could
judge from appearances. Small, weazened in look and
feature, and of the sallow dullness of complexion so
often found in the American farmer-boy, his countenance was redeemed from the commonplace by the keen
blue eye and the full red lips which, even when puck-
ered into a whistle, showed character and life. Instead
of kneeling by the shock, the boy had rolled one of the
many big yellow pumpkins which were scattered over
the field, to his side of the shock of corn, and sat upon it
with his legs stretched out contentedly under the stalks.
He worked neither with the energy displayed by his
father—for the relation was manifest—nor with the list-
lessness of the hireling. Sometimes he husked ear for
ear with his father; then he would sit and watch him
dreamily or dawdle with some peculiarity of the ear his
hands laid bare. More than once he amused himself
by throwing bits of stone or nubbins of corn at a small
dog, a long-haired mongrel with bright eyes, whose
fleecy coat had become matted with cockle-burs and
Spanish-needles until it was hard to say what might have
been its original color. The dog had dug for moles in
the cornfield, yelped after rabbits in the alders that grew
along a little brook that intersected it, barked at gray

squirrels in the wood above and now sat beside the heap of slender twelve-rowed ears of yellow flint (to which the father added an ear with every second almost with the regularity of a pendulum stroke), with his tongue out and his muddy nose pointed toward the house below, as if suggesting that his day's work was done, and done to his own satisfaction.

It was getting toward nightfall. A wind had sprung up from the northwest. The sky grew dark and leaden. The boy began to shiver. The horses which had been quietly hitched to the wagon at some distance feeding out of the box, began to whinny and grow restless. All at once the man seemed to waken from his preoccupation. His hands lagged at their work as he glanced up at the sky and noted the signs of the weather with a quick, shrewd intelligence.

"Hello, Martin," said he, "what's this? Vow if it don't look as though 'twas going to snow. If it was two weeks later I should think we were going to have an old rouser from the nor'west. It's getting cold, too. Makes you shiver, does it?"—noticing the boy's quivering chin. "Well, I don't wonder. Let me see," he continued, drawing a large silver watch from beneath his jacket and consulting its face, "I wanted to finish this row of stooks, but it's now four o'clock, and to-morrow is 'lection day. We'll do this one, pick up the corn and quit work for to-day. Come on, let's have it done with in a hurry."

The boy who had listened with evident pleasure to this conclusion added a few ears to the pile with unusual alacrity and then began to scrutinize the sky himself.

"Father?"

"Yes?"

"What made you say you thought it would snow?"

"Looks like it"—not raising his eyes nor intermitting his work.

The son was silent for a moment. Then he said hesitatingly:

"I don't see how you know."

"Why there," said the father stretching his arm toward the north, "off there in the northwest, where the wind comes from, don't you see that dull heavy bank of clouds?"

"Yes"—doubtfully. "Is that snow?"

"Well, it may be. If it hadn't been such a mild season or was a little later I should say it was. Besides if you look across the valley you can just see the steeple at Rockboro. In good weather you can see the whole town though it is most ten miles away. That is sure to mean a storm and a big one too."

There was silence for a moment, except the rustling of the cornstalks. Then the son:

"Father?"

"Yes?"

"If it storms *very* bad will they hold the 'lection just the same?"

"Just the same. It's one of the things that's never put off for the weather, my son, though I 'spect it makes some difference in the result. At least they always claim it does."

"What difference?"

"Well, fair weather may be better for one party and bad weather better for another."

"How many parties are there, father?"

"Three—Democrats and Whigs and Barnburners."

"What do they mean by 'Barnburners,' father?"

"That's the new party. Barnburners is a nickname that's given them. They call themselves the Liberty party and Free Soil party. Other folks call them Abolitionists, sometimes."

"You're a Whig, ain't you father?"

"Well, yes, I s'pose so;" (musingly,) "I've always voted that ticket an' s'pose I will agin'."

"Which party is it that's for General Taylor?"

"That's the Whig party."

"I hope they'll win, anyhow."

"You do?" glancing at him with an amused smile. "Why?"

"'Coz he fit the Mexicans!"

"Ha! ha! ha!" roared the father in hearty sonorous tones, which echoed over the valley with singular clearness owing to proximity of the coming storm. The boy's face flushed.

"What makes you laugh? Ain't that a good reason?"

"Good or bad," said the father, still laughing, "it's the only one anybody has yet been able to give. So I s'pose it will have to do."

They finished the shock as he spoke, and as he rose he showed himself a man of powerful frame. He glanced at the clouds again and said:

"Get the baskets, Martie, while I bind up these stalks and we will be out of this in a jiffy."

The boy ran for the baskets—great bushel measures—and came back warmed by the exercise. The corn was piled in one, shaken down and heaped up, and the father, perching it lightly upon his shoulder, carried it to the wagon, a few rods away, while the son filled the other. The afternoon's husking was soon loaded, and they drove away to the house and in upon the threshing floor of the great red barn that flanked the house upon the hillside below. As they were unharnessing the horses the boy asked, in a tone that showed his doubt as to a favorable answer:

"Father, may I go to the 'lection to-morrow?"

"Go to 'lection? Well, I don't know," said the father, thoughtfully, as he rubbed the horse he had unharnessed with a handful of straw. "What do you want to go for?"

"Just to see how it's done, sir."

"How what is done?" asked the father, looking at him thoughtfully.

"How a President's made, I s'pose."

."How a President's made, eh?" with a twinkle in his deep gray eyes. "That's not so bad, Martin. That's about all the makin' they get. Yes, you may go and see how a President's made and who makes him, and all about it that you can learn by looking on and listening. But remember, my son, that you must not ask questions nor get in the way, nor be any trouble to any one. I shall most likely be busy countin' the votes, and you must come home in good time to do the chores."

"I will, sir," was the glad reply.

Martin Kortright dreamed all night of the mystery of mysteries which he was to unravel on the morrow.

The boy had been in bed an hour. The clock struck nine. The farmer put away his newspaper; his wife laid aside her knitting and brought the Bible and laid it on the table before her husband. He read a chapter, gravely and solemnly but in tones that echoed through the silent house thrilling with the tremor of a strong man's earnestness. Then the husband and wife knelt in prayer. Her head was bowed upon the low, cushioned rocker on which she had been sitting, while his hands grasped the heavy wooden "Windsor" chair he had occupied, and his strong face showed over its back as he prayed. Harrison Kortright was a positive man in all things, but in his religion, especially so. If he had ever been troubled with doubt, it had long since been exorcised. That he meant to walk with God no one could doubt who looked at him. He was not soft and loving and sweet of temper, but he was in earnest and would have fought for his faith or died for it without a

murmur; though he would have much preferred the
fighting to the dying. His earnestness somewhat im-
paired what we are accustomed to term reverence. The
God he worshiped was an approachable, every-day
being. In his prayers he spoke to this Omnipotent face
to face, and was quite unabashed by the fact. He was
not ashamed to come before the throne of the Eternal,
for he felt that he came by virtue of a divine right. The
God to whom his family altar had been builded was the
One, Almighty, Invisible Eternal; but then he had been
bidden to come before him with boldness and he came
in simple obedience to that command, and poured out .
the desires of an earnest, honest heart. Outside, the
snow fell upon the window-ledge, silent and soft. The
great flakes came noiselessly against the pane. The
heaps grew higher and higher upon the sash. The voice
of the worshiper went beyond the walls—out into the
snowy night which muffled its tones to a soft murmur.
The candlelight shone upon the white flocculence and
made a golden pathway upward from the window-seat
toward the sky. As he prayed, a face looked in at the
window—gave a quick startled look—then another, a
close keen glance—at the bowed woman's head and the
man's face, calm and strong. The snow fell between the
watcher and the window, but the light showed that
it was a woman's face. The prayer ended, and the
face disappeared. The worshipers arose. The woman
passed her hands over her hair smoothing it down
toward the temples. She began to put back the chairs
against the wall. The man put the Bible he had
read upon the mantel near the stove and passed out
into the hall. The whirring of wheels was heard as he
wound the old Dutch clock. It was the last of the day's
duties. When this was done he would cross the hall
into his bed-room. His wife had taken up the candle to
follow him when there was a knock at the door. She

started, then stopped and listened, as though uncertain. She thought she heard a movement on the porch. There was another knock.

"What—who's there?" she asked, in startled accents.

The question was not answered. The door opened and a woman entered. The two gazed at each other a moment and then, as though there had been a mutual recognition, the farmer's wife approached her unseasonable visitant, asked a question, and in a moment more the new-comer was sitting by the stove and the good wife was ministering to her comfort.

An hour later, Harrison Kortright left his house with the stranger, who had meantime eaten heartily, snugly wrapped up beside him in his buggy, while his wife held the flaming candle at the end of the porch.

"Don't set up for me, Martha," he called as they drove away. "I shan't be back afore midnight, anyhow, and like 's not it'll be later 'n that."

It was later, for the clock in the hall had struck two before his step sounded again on the porch, and, stamping the snow from his feet, he entered the room where his wife sat awaiting him.

"All right," he said in reply to a look of inquiry; "but I've had a hard time—an awful hard time. The snow's above knee deep and I had to leave the buggy at Smithson's and ride home horseback, an' without a saddle, too. Even in that way it was hard to get along. I've had to walk half the way, for fear the horse would give out. As good luck will have it, it ain't very cold; if 't had been I don't know how I'd ever got through."

He shook off the snow and removed his hat and coat. His wife lifted the coffee-pot from the stove, and set it on the table where she had already spread a lunch. Then she approached as he sat tugging at his soaked boots, and laying her hand on his head exclaimed:

"Why, how wet your hair is!"

"Wet! I guess if you'd seen me wading through this snow and towing the horse after me for five miles, you wouldn't wonder. I'm just as wet as if I'd been in the river. Don't believe I ever had such a job. If it keeps on this way I don't know how anybody'll get to 'lection to-morrow."

"I don't think it makes much difference whether they do or not," said the wife briskly. "'Twixt Whigs and Democrats and Locofocos and Hunkers and Hards and Softs, and what not, I don't see much difference."

The husband sat gazing intently into the fire a moment with one of the boots he had just laboriously drawn off still in his hand, before he answered:

"It really does seem, Martha, as if the Lord was takin' a mighty queer way to establish righteousness in the land, but I guess He'll do it. Oh, dear," he exclaimed, rising from his chair and stretching his arms above his head, "I'm too tired to talk about it—I'm just done out."

He evidently spoke truly. After a sup or two of coffee he declared that he could eat nothing—he was too tired. And almost before the words were fairly uttered, with his wife's help he had staggered off to bed. She returned presently and hung his wet clothes by the glowing stove and then herself retired. It was almost three o'clock when silence and darkness fell upon Paradise Bay that night. The silent flakes were still falling without. The clouds that hung above the valley when the sun went down were outspread upon the earth when it arose. The clouds that hung above the land waited till the sun of a generation had set before they burst.

CHAPTER II.

THE morning showed that the promise of the evening had been more than fulfilled. Snow had fallen during the night to a depth almost unprecedented even in that region of deep snows. There had been no wind, and the fleecy coverlet had fallen evenly and softly upon hill and dale alike. It was as though the earth had been blotted out by magic, and a white, boundless sea had usurped its place. Fences and walls were hidden from sight. The roofs were laden with the clinging mass. The trees, still bearing half their foliage, bent beneath the spotless burden. Highways there were none. The flocks were buried from sight. The cattle fought their way with difficulty through the snow to the barns. Two feet and more in depth it lay upon the level, soft and heavy as if it felt ashamed of its untimely coming and longed to melt and run down the hills and into the unfrozen rivers, and flee away to the unfreezing sea. The sun shone bright; the dogs barked; the cattle lowed; the cocks crowed incessantly and all nature seemed determined to regard this sudden onslaught of winter as a jest. But for the mass of snow, the day would have been a balmy one. At the lowest the thermometer had hardly touched the freezing point, and the sun shone out at once with a warmth that showed his resentment at this unexpected intrusion of Winter.

That day the freemen of the Republic were astir early. To get to the polls at all required an effort. If the slothful and laggard were not urged and transported thither, the ballots would be few.

At an early hour, on every road leading toward the polls was to be seen a company of men engaged in breaking the way thither. A half-dozen pairs of oxen were yoked before a great sled with a score of men and boys in attendance, some riding, some driving, some carrying shovels to dig out the deepest places, and all laughing, jesting, snow-balling each other and enjoying this first surprise which Winter had given them, constituted the advance guard of this jolly army of patriot rulers on their way to the universal *witenagemote* of the Republic. Following in the wake of this pioneer snow-plow, perhaps coupled to it, would be another sled or two, then horses, sleighs, cutters, and, after all of them, a rabble still on foot following along the track beaten smooth and hard by those in advance. Every house that was passed contributed its quota to the procession. Every one was good natured, as people generally are in cold weather, and this election day promised to be even more of a holiday than the occasion usually is.

Such a cavalcade it was that about nine o'clock that morning stopped before the residence of Harrison Kortright. The house was a tidy white one, standing a few rods back from the road, with green blinds, a bit of porch over the front door, and two dark evergreens flanking upon either side the walk that led down to the gate. It was a dwelling somewhat more pretentious than the most of those in the neighborhood, yet by no means betokening wealth or luxury. Half way between the house and the gate was our little friend Martin, shoveling manfully away at a path, the level snow being almost even with his shoulders, and the piled-up masses which he had flung out on either side reaching above his head. He paused in his work as the procession came into view from around the side of the hill, looked and listened for a moment, and then sturdily resumed his labor while the tears showed themselves under his dark lashes. It was evident the storm had spoiled the holiday of which he had dreamed.

"Halloa, Martin," cried the foremost driver, who, clinging to his ox yoke, half walked and was half dragged through the deep snow. "Halloa, Martin, hain't you got your path dug yet?"

"What's the matter on ye, boy?" said another. "Snowed up so't you didn't know it was day till just now?"

"Hi, you little Barnburner," cried a third; "you'll have to wake up earlier'n this if you are going to make your namesake president. How's 'Matty Van' anyhow?"

"He has got a worse road than that before him," said another.

The crowd stopped before the gate, and still kept on badgering the patient boy.

"Why didn't you let us know you were snowed in?" said one of them. "We would have come over and dug you out long afore this, if you'd told us on 't."

"The Barnburners will be snowed in worse than that before night," said another.

"Oh, you let the Barnburners alone," retorted one evidently inclined to that persuasion. "They will take care of themselves and clean out Whigs and Democrats both, first you know."

"Say, sonny," cried a young man who wished to show his age by displaying his impertinence, "is your name 'Matty Van'?"

"No, my name ain't Matty Van," shouted the boy, setting his teeth close and shaking his shovel at the crowd, while the tears coursed down his cheeks. "And I ain't no Barnburner neither, and you know it, too.

You had better jest go 'long and mind your own business, and not stay here makin' a fuss and a noise 'round where folks is sick."

"Sick? Who's sick, my son?" spoke half a dozen with ready sympathy.

"My father is,—that's who," said the boy, beginning to sob. "And that's the reason the path ain't dug out, too. There wasn't nobody else to do the chores, and a boy can't do everything in a minute if he is twelve years old."

"Sick? The Squire sick? Why, I declare, we hadn't heard a word on it, son," said an elderly man who stood on the foremost sled, while the whole crowd was hushed at once into respectful silence.

"Here you fellows, a half dozen on ye," he continued. "Take hold here and help shovel that boy's path. What the dickens you doin', anyhow? Such a lazy unmannerly crowd ain't got together every day. One would think you hadn't got nothin' better on hand than just to stand 'round and holler and worry a boy because he is at work. What's the matter with your daddy, son?"

"I don't know nothin' about it, sir," sobbed the boy, now fairly broken down, as he leaned upon the handle of his shovel and gave vent to his grief. "I don't know nothin' about it. He was jest as well as could be last night when I went to bed, and this morning the first I heard he was just groanin' and takin' on like he was going to die, and I tried to get Ma to let me go after the doctor, but she said the snow was too deep. I'd a had him here before now if she'd just let me gone."

"There ain't a doubt about that, my son," said the elderly man. "Here you, Orrin Coltrane on the horse yonder, can't you go for the doctor for the Squire?"

"'Tain't no sort of use to try it, Squire Ritner," said

the man addressed. "There ain't no horse in the world can plow his way through that depth of snow. Better just let the oxen go on as fast as they can, and I'll send the doctor back just as soon as we get there."

"Well, it's too bad," exclaimed Ritner. "Squire Kortright's lived right here, man and boy, nigh on to fifty years now, and I don't believe he was ever in bed a day in his life before. If there's any man in the whole valley that is always up and 'round and a stirrin', bright and healthy and willin', that man's been the Squire, always. I don't know how on earth we'll get along without him at the 'lection to-day."

By that time, twenty willing hands had dug away the snow and made a broad, clean path from house to gate.

"I guess, boys," said the man who had acted as spokesman, "I guess you had better go now and dig out the paths around the house, to the barn and the well, and the like, and I will step in and see how the Squire's gettin' on. Won't you come in with me?" he said, to some of the older men in the company.

Three or four, who were evidently the men of most note in the procession, walked up to the house with Squire Ritner at their head, stamping their feet upon the red brick walk that had just been cleared, brushing the snow from their clothes, clearing their throats and seeking to make themselves presentable for the sick room with no little noise and ostentation. As they were about to ascend the steps of the porch Ritner turned and said to those in the road:

"You may as well drive on as quick as you have shoveled out the paths here. Pick up all the men folks as you go along, and we will overtake you after a little, or foot it the rest of the way into town, just as it happens. 'Tain't a great way, anyhow, and it's time somebody was gettin' through and lookin' after things there."

Martin, drying his tears with his woolen coat sleeve, sobbing and red-eyed, opened the door for the neighbors, ushered them into the family sitting-room and then went to inform his mother of their arrival.

Mrs. Kortright, a snug, tidy matron, whose hair was just beginning to be flecked with silver, very soon entered and saluted them each by name, evidently much more composed than they had expected to find her.

"Martin said the Squire was sick, Mrs. Kortright."

"Yes," responded the lady in a matter-of-fact tone, "for once he was not able to get up when the clock struck six."

"Nothin' serious, I hope?"

"Well, he's sufferin' a good deal. It's rheumatiz, I guess. He's easier than he was, though. I got him to take some boneset tea and put a bag of baked hops to his back and fixed him up the best I could, because the snow was so deep, Martin couldn't go for the doctor, nohow."

"It's monstrous sudden," said one of the men, "and I don't see how we're goin' to do without the Squire for clerk at the 'lection."

"That's just what I told him this mornin'," said the matron, briskly. "Says I, 'Harrison Kortright, it's mighty queer that the first time anythin' is the matter with you, since you and I was married, twenty odd years ago, should be just the very day of this election; and in my opinion,' says I to Mr. Kortright, 'it's just a judgment on you for bein' so hard-hearted and unreasonable as to be aginst the Abolitionists and in favor of keepin' the poor niggers in slavery year after year, and you free and forehanded, and doin' as you're a mind to 'round here on your own farm, and with your own wife and babies, under your own vine and fig tree,' says I."

"Babies?" said one of the neighbors, quizzically. "I didn't know"—

"Oh, pshaw," said the matron, blushing brightly and putting her arm over the shoulders of the sturdy boy who stood beside her. "Well, Martin is rather big to be called a baby, but you see I was improvin' the occasion, Mr. Sullivan."

"Oh, that won't do, Miss Kortright," said the leader. "You shouldn't be takin' advantage of a man when he's down that way. Besides that, we can't allow you to make a Barnburner of the Squire, if he has got the rheumatism. You know he is just about the mainstay of the Whig party here in Skendore Township, and so many of our best men have been a droppin' off and runnin' with the Abolitionists lately, that its just nip and tuck we can muster enough to take care of Shields and his crowd of Democrats. You haven't got the Squire converted, have you?"

Squire Ritner gave a quiet chuckle and winked quizzically toward one of his companions as he spoke.

"Well, I don't know 'bout that, gentlemen," laughed Mrs. Kortright. "But I can tell you one thing. If last night didn't convert that man, there ain't much hopes of his ever turnin' from the error of his ways, it's my opinion."

"Do you think it would do for us to see him?"

"Oh, certainly, gentlemen, certainly. I don't 'spose it's anythin' dangerous, though Bub here's been cryin' about it all the mornin', and Mr. Kortright certainly does take on a good deal whenever he moves hand or foot."

The cheerful dame led the way into the sick room of her husband. Hers was one of those enviable natures that never go forward on the path of life to meet trouble. To do all that lay in her power to relieve suffering was instinctive with her, and the very act kept her mind too busy to admit the shadow of apprehension. To such a wife, an attack of rheumatism seizing upon her husband after twenty years of the most provoking robustness, was an opportunity not to be neglected. Pain without serious danger of a fatal result, then the popular idea of this disease, was the very perfection of occasion for the display of the qualities of the nurse. This opportunity Mrs. Kortright had fully improved. It is doubtful if in her heart she was not half glad to find, when awakened by her husband's groans at daylight, that the doctor was an impossibility for many hours. At length she had a chance to minister to her husband in his weakness. To her alone he should owe relief—perhaps even restoration. She had fully justified her reputation as a nurse and had brought into play all her housewifely knowledge of herbs and simples to relieve the fierce attack that wrung the strong man's frame. In this she had in a great measure succeeded. The self-constituted committee of condolence found their stalwart neighbor propped up in bed, wrapped in many drapings, with the smell of pungent herbs filling the room. Already his pain had been greatly modified, and the moisture of the hand which he extended in welcome promised quick recovery.

"How do you do, Squire?" said Ritner heartily, shaking his hand. "I tell you we're sorry to see you in this fix. I was just a tellin' Miss Kortright that you was about the last man in the neighborhood that anybody'd have expected to hear of bein' sick."

"Oh, it's nothing," said Kortright half jestingly. "Just a deep cold that I've got, on account of this storm, I guess. I expect to be about before the snow's off."

"I don't know so well about that," said Shields. "It's goin' mighty lively. This hot sun and south wind is just takin' it off almost as fast as it come. Just the teams that went along breaking the road packed it down smooth and made right good sleighin'."

"It'll be mighty bad for 'lection though," said another.

"Wal, now, I don't know 'bout that, Mr. Van Wormer," said the sick man, disputatiously, the instinct of the partisan getting the better of his pain. "I don't know about that. I've always noticed that 'tain't the pleasantest days that brings out the biggest vote. If what Shields says 'bout the roads is true, it's my notion we'll get a bigger vote than if it hadn't snowed at all. It's my idea that if a man wanted to get out the very biggest possible vote, and had the makin' of a day to suit himself, and had watched 'lections as long as I have, that he would have a big storm in the morning and the rest of the day bright and clear."

"Wal now," said Ritner, "I had never thought on 't in that light. There's bound to be some folks stay at home on 'count of the storm."

"No doubt," said Kortright, "a few on 'em of course. But then you know, neighbor, the loafers will come out anyhow."

"Of course—and the Democrats. That's the reason Shields got started so early," said Van Wormer, mischievously.

"Oh, well, now," said Shields, shutting his thin lips firmly, "you needn't trouble yourself about Shields. He was raised a Democrat when Democrat meant the people's right, afore Hunkers or Barnburners was ever heard on, and about the first thing he learned from his father was that votin' weren't a privilege so much as it was a duty, and he always has voted, whatever the weather, and he always will, too, as long as he can get to the polls. I guess the Squire'll bear me out in saying that's what a man ought to do, too."

"Yes," said Kortright, doubtfully, "I believe it is.

I've always voted myself, and always expected to as long as I lived, as you say, but I guess I shall have to score a miss this time.''

"Oh, no," said Ritner, quickly. "A man that's been clerk of the 'lection board as long as you have ain't a goin' to be sick right handy by the village here, and not have a chance to vote. The poll-holders 'll have to come and bring you the box, so 't you won't lose your vote. We can't afford that, this time, anyhow.''

"Wal, now, I don't know," said Shields, banteringly. "We'll have to argue that pint, and see whether the poll-holders have got any right to be carryin' the box around the country for folks to vote in, just here and there and everywhere.''

"Oh, you know that's customary," said Ritner, in a conciliatory tone. "Always been done, no matter what set wanted it—here in Skendore, anyhow. Whatever the law may be, that's what we've always agreed to, and there hain't never been no objection. Ain't that so, Squire Kortright?"—appealing to the sick man.

"Well, yes," answered the Squire, smiling. "That's always been the custom here, and it's a good custom, too. I don't know if it's exactly strict law, but it's good sense and good neighborship, that's certain. However, you needn't mind about doin' it for me, for I'd made up my mind not to vote, if the day had been ever so fair and I'd been as well as I ever was in my life.''

"Not vote!" they all ejaculated in surprise. "Why, Squire Kortright!"

"Ah, gentlemen," said Mrs. Kortright with a triumphant smile, "what did I tell you?''

"You don't mean," said Van Wormer in surprise, "that you have turned Barnburner, Squire?''

"Well, no, not exactly that; though I'll tell you what I do mean, gentlemen," said the Squire, suddenly sitting bolt-upright in bed, and speaking in a voice rendered almost tragic by its solemnity and the suggestion of his surroundings. "I do mean that I won't never cast a ballot for any man that holds a slave, nor for any man that thinks another ought to hold one, nor for any man that is willin' the law should let any man be another man's slave, so long as I live. So help me God!"

There was an instant's solemn hush in the sick room, as they listened to the burning words and looked upon the flushed face and upraised hand of the speaker .

A shriek pierced the stillness.

A child's voice.

"Ho!" A sharp, shrill shout. Another.

"Help! Help!"—a man's hoarse, agonized appeal.

CHAPTER III.

"ARISE, SIR KNIGHT!"

WHEN the party of neighbors went into his father's room, Martin strolled out upon the porch. There he stood in the bright sunshine, gazing longingly after the procession, now almost lost in the distance on its way to the village, which lay nestling under the hill two miles away.

To the boy's thought, the earth's axis ran through Skendoah village. It was only a little hamlet, consisting of a church, a tavern, two stores and a few dozen houses, and he knew that there were great cities and towns beyond. He himself had once been to the city with his father, and in the long winter nights he had listened with wondering delight to the story of marvels which his father had seen. For Squire Kortright in his youth had been a wanderer; although he was born in the valley, his veins were full of the bluest and liveliest Yankee blood; go somewhere he must. The migratory instinct was as strong within his heart as in the barn-swallow that brooded under the eaves of the great red barn his father had built, not only after the Dutch style of his neighbors, which he readily recognized as superior to that prevailing in New England and accepted with the true adaptiveness of his race, but also of a size and conspicuousness to make it a landmark in the valley. He did not go West. He was the youngest of many, all of whom had flitted early from the home-nest and with sturdy hands had let in the sunlight upon many a forest home in the westward-stretching wilder-

ness. He was the last, and the mother's heart yearned
over him and could not let him go. So it was early
understood that he should remain at home, and in consideration of his having thus ignored the blandishments
of fortune and the Great West, should inherit the paternal acres. But he had no thought of waiting quietly
for his patrimony. He must work, and work for himself. His father, yet hale and strong, with the aid of a
hired man in harvest could manage the farm. He must
go East and work. He did not know exactly what he
would do—he hardly cared. To do something, to earn
money, to match brawn and brain against gold—that
was his animating impulse—an inheritance his parents
had given him before they thought of bestowing Paradise Bay upon him. It was not an ignoble desire. It
was not for money as an end that he wrought. It was
not mere greed of possession, but the nobler lust of accomplishment. It was the grand egotism which has
been the whip and spur of American progress, the undying aspiration to do, to excel, to work miracles for the
mere sense of power that goes with a completed task.

So, while yet a youth, he had bidden his parents good-
by one summer morning, and gone with a drover to
New York in the place of one who had sickened the
night before at Rockboro. He had been at another time
one of the crew of a canal-boat as far west as Lockport,
and told with vociferous laughter of the funny "boom"
in values that occurred in that almost forgotten borough, when the canal first reached it and developed a
water power which many fondly thought would make
the little village a metropolis. He had gone there,
touched by the mania for speculation, thinking to invest
a little money profitably; but finding the excitement so
great that the prices dismayed him, he came away with
his money in his pocket—a fact he never failed to mention with great satisfaction.

He had been to the Eastward too. With another
Yankee instinct, he wanted to see where his forebears
came from, to survey for himself the surroundings that
had been made familiar to him by the fireside tales of
his parents. He had found the place far up on a rugged
mountain side—a little patch of open land, green where
the rocks gave the grass a chance to grow; a little
mountain lake glancing the morning sunshine into the
humble doorway; a pretty brook, full of speckled trout,
gleaming among the alders as it hied away to its work
of weaving and spinning and turning and forging in the
valley below, where it was fretted with dams, imprisoned
in locks and finally beaten into foam over groaning
wheels. It was one of those places where, at the best,
subsistence must have been an endless struggle, yet
one whose quaint charms so impress those reared among
them, that generations of prairie and forest-born Western descendants hardly release themselves from its mys-
tical enchantment. Ah! sweet mountain home-nests of
the nation's fairest life. In the homes of the Mid-west
the farmers' children dream to-day of the fairy-land
of which their grandparents tell. The herder on the
plains looks toward the East, and feeds his fancy with a
picture of "the old place" which perhaps his father
never saw. When he makes an unusually "good thing"
on a shipment of cattle, he will leave his "traps" at
Chicago, and go on to visit this Mecca of his dream. He
will return disgusted. Then the thread of tradition will
be broken. Laughter and ridicule will take the place
of loving glamour, in telling the story of his origin, and
from thenceforth New England as an active inspiration
will pass out of the western stock; thenceforth they
will be true and loyal children of the plain, and will turn
toward the Occident when they pray for happiness, as
well as when they offer sacrifice to Mammon.

The boy who stood upon the porch knew of the world

that lay beyond the field of vision by this tradition, so much more real and inspiring than the printed page could be. His father had seen and felt the life of the city and the mountain ; had wrought in the mills of the East for a season ; had made at least one trip on salt water, and had seen the bright-bosomed lakes of the West. He knew that the world did not revolve around the village of Skendoah, yet it was to him the sole gate- way to the life that lay beyond. It was the world *in posse.* He had been strictly reared. The father had worn out the vagrant humor early. When he settled down to the duties of life on the paternal farm, there was no fur- ther thought of unrest. His life-work was before him ; and he took it up. Curiosity was smothered in that hour. So too with ambition, change and hope for bet- terment. Hereafter there was no holiday in his life. The hillside farm was his tabernacle, from which he had no desire ever to go forth. He wore a silk hat on Sunday, and was called Squire before his thirtieth birth- day. He was a solid man. But the virus of unrest that was in his blood he had transmitted to his son, who saw the gay procession of road breakers disappear around the bend of the hill with tears of bitter disap- pointment.

Martin had been to the bleak, hill-side school-house every day it had been open since his seventh birth- day. He was a good scholar—all the teachers said that, and a good boy, all said, too, except one who called him mischievous. He knew all about the hills and woods and springs and brooks in the neighborhood. There was not a wood-chuck's hole within a circle of half a mile, that he had not visited and speculated on the dislodg- ment of its occupant. But his world was getting too small for him of late. He wanted to go through the Gate Skendoah into the World Beautiful. Of course he went to the village to church and Sunday-school. But he took his home-life with him there—father and mother. He went now and then to the village store, but he always had some errand to keep him company and repress his enjoyment. He wanted to go alone, and at least peep out at the boundless. He had been to Utica, once, when his father was drawn a juror in the court there. If he had been alone, he would have learned a great deal. He longed to know, to realize, to subjugate for himself, the kingdoms of this world. The inquisitiveness of the Yankee is proverbial. He is said to be prone to ask questions. It is perhaps true, and it is certain that he will also pick up more facts with fewer questions than any other mortal. Occidentalism always impels humanity to learn, to acquire, to do. The world-life in our veins is stirred into a fever which can be appeased only by action, knowledge, achievement.

The boy was just beginning to feel this New-World disease. His father had seen it in his eye when he asked to go to the election the day before, and had shrewdly determined to indulge rather than attempt to suppress it. The problem of government was already before the boy's mind, and his reply to his father had been perfectly sincere, when he told him he wanted to see "how a President was made." Of course, he did not exclude from his anticipation the meeting of boys from all parts of the township, or the luxury of "doing" Skendoah all alone for a whole day. His dream had come to naught. The election day had dawned and would set and he would not see how a President was made. It would be four years before the chance would come again. He knew that. The political ferment that was just taking hold of the American mind had left its impress on his. He knew the times and seasons of our government far better than the city boy of to-day knows them. Four years—he wondered how big he would be then—what he would have done, learned and seen, by that time. The loss of his holiday meant almost an eternity of delay to him.

He had not told his mother. He knew his father's illness made it impossible that he should be absent, and he would not add to her care by acquainting her with his disappointment. As he brooded over his ill luck, his eye fell upon one of the evergreens that stood beside the path. They were his mother's trees. She had planted them soon after her marriage, and they had grown to overtop the house. They were of a kind then very rare in the country, and passers-by often stopped to wonder at them. The seed had come from over the sea—aye, even from that side the earth that lies below our feet, and the name told the story of its origin. It was written on the little packet of seeds, which was all that the letter contained which had come so far to the young Squire's wife—"*Cryptomeria Japonica*, or Japan Mourner." She had kept the bit of paper, with these words written upon it in a fine, manly hand, "so as not to forget the name," she said; but she had once told her boy a curious story of a friend of her girlhood —a bright-eyed but poor boy, who had romped and roamed with her about the hills and valleys, until childhood's feet had touched the borderland of Youth; who had then gone away to the East, on foot and alone, not to seek his fortune so much as to find the knowledge for which he thirsted. He had promised to return when his task was accomplished. But the years went by, and the girl heard no more of her boy-friend. She grew to womanhood. He did not come. He was almost forgotten—quite forgotten, by all in the valley save the girl whom he had made his special playmate. Even to her, his memory had grown dim. Harrison Kortright had wooed and won her. She only vaguely wished that Dawson Fox might know her good fortune, when one day a stranger came to her mother's house—tall, fair-haired, laughing-eyed. Her heart leaped in half recognition when she saw him, but she shook her head, and said "No, she did not know him." When he told his name, and stood looking as though he would clasp her in his arms and devour her with those hungry eyes and quivering lips, she coolly gave him her hand, and in light, even tones, asked him to sit down. She talked of everything but the old times, until he could bear it no longer. Then he burst out with a story of boy-love, effort and conquest, and told her he had come back a man to perform the vow of the boy.

The woman's lip trembled, as she told the story to her son on a summer afternoon, sitting on the porch. "But he was only thirteen," she added, "when he went away. Who would ever have thought he would remember me?"

He was not rich, he said. She knew that, without the saying. His was not one of the natures that grow rich, except in love and good works. He was not rich, but he had worked hard, had studied diligently, had graduated from an Eastern College, was now an ordained minister of the Gospel, and had been called to go as a missionary to the heathen of the old, old world beyond the great Pacific, and had come to ask her if she would go with him—be his wife. She told him she was to marry the prosperous young farmer whose acres joined her father's land. She did not tell her young boy what he said in reply, but only that he preached in the village church the next Sunday, and then went away, and she had never seen or heard from him since, except by the little package of seeds that came a year afterward, to let her know that he had arrived safely in the strange land to which he was bound, on what seemed a vain attempt to bring God's word to those who would have none of it.

"He was only thirteen when he went away!" said the

boy to himself, as he glanced up at one of the drooping evergreens which served to keep alive the memory of a dead love. As he looked, he saw that the mass of clinging snow had weighed down one of the long, slender branches, until it had split off from the trunk, and was now left clinging to the tree only by a shred of bark and a tough splinter of wood fibre. The outer end, thrust forward by the fall, was lying on the floor of the porch. The boy seized it, and by a sturdy pull detached it from its socket. Then he shook out the snow, and held the long green branch above him like a banner, while he marched to and fro up and down the porch. The banner was large and the knight was small, but his plain face was flushed, and his eyes burned with a light as pure and steady as ever shone upon the face of one who sought for deeds of high emprise.

His dreams were high—dreams of valiant well-doing in the manhood which he panted to enjoy. The great green banner taxed his strength to bear it upright on his shoulder, but he struggled bravely with its weight. Its tip brushed the ceiling of the porch. Its lower limbs dragged on the floor. It was in ludicrous disproportion with himself, but to his dream it was the pennon of a knight. He was a squire who waited but an opportunity to win his spurs. His step was springy and his muscles tense with longing for life's battle. The dead present was but ashes beneath his feet. His disappointment was forgotten. How a President was made concerned him not. In his dream-thought there was no doubt. He was the peer of him who rode the gray horse and "fit the Mexicans." Fancy's fiery chariot upbore his feet—the gateway of the future that should never be swinging back, and his eyes feasted on glories that only the pure in heart may see when they dream dreams of self-forgetful wonder-working.

He heard a cry, and glanced swiftly toward the window of his father's room. His dream had cast out fear, but the spectre of disease thus suddenly recalled by the thought of his father's sickness blanched his young face. As he looked toward the valley he saw the doctor's horse and cutter coming past the school house. His face lighted with joy, for he remembered his father's pain and thought relief was at hand.

Another cry—now shrill and clear. Turning to the left, he saw rushing down the hillside road a pair of dark blood-bays attached to a light sleigh that only dimly showed above the wall of snow bounding the track the road-breakers had beaten down. Their sleek coats glistened in the sunshine. The richly-mounted harness sparkled as they moved. Their black manes flew back from their high-arched necks in tossing waves. On they came at full speed, the loose reins flying from side to side as they ran. The richly caparisoned sleigh bounded back and forth in the narrow track. One robe hung over the dash-board; another had fallen out, and its red lining showed like a stain of blood on the white track behind. A young girl clung to the back of the sleigh, her blanched face turned with the fascination of a mortal terror toward the frightened animals which whirled her onward to destruction. Shriek after shriek went up from her lips. Far behind them, making frantic gestures and uttering hoarse cries for aid, a man was running, so slowly in comparison with the flying steeds that it seemed as if he were standing still.

The boy stood an instant as though petrified. Over the white expanse he saw the frightened runaways come with long swift strides down the gentle declivity toward the spot where he stood. Now he saw their outstretched heads as they came straight on; then, as the course changed, their gleaming sides with the tossing cockle-shell behind and its clinging white-faced occupant. The light of his dream was in his eye; his teeth close shut and nostrils spread while his hand clutched nervously the great dark bough upon his shoulder.

Ah, boyish squire, thine hour has come ! The prayer of faith unsyllabled, the aspiration of a heart unsmirched by sin has won from fate the golden opportunity. Thy budding manhood hath its devoir. Do or die ! Stake length of days against thy dream !

He stood still, gazing at the furious beasts, each striving to outdo the other in a mad race from some imagined danger. They were scarce twenty lengths from the end of the pathway that led down to the road. He could see their black eyes, the white foam that hung upon their lips and splashed with light their dark sides. He saw the sunlit steaming of their nostrils ; he heard their sharp snorts of terror as they looked back at the sleigh, transformed by their fears into a threatening pursuer.

All at once the boy sprang into life. "Whoa !" he shouted, sharply and imperiously, as if the terror-stricken animals must obey his command. The green banner was upreared once more. He dashed down the steps and along the path where lately he had stood weeping with vexation. He did not think—there was no time to think ! The banner showed above the heaped-up bank of snow ; the knight was almost hidden in the trench. "Whoa !" he cried again, as he reached the roadway. There, almost upon him, were the straining steeds. Their red nostrils shone, braced and quivering. Their breath came, hot and spumy. "Whoa !"

The off horse saw the little objector and his quaint forest banner burst from the snow almost beneath his feet, and shied with fright. The movement threw his mate against the snowy wall beyond. At the next stride he landed in the soft, clinging mass. The boy saw his advantage in an instant. His eyes flashed fire. The light of battle glared in his face. He set the bush in rest as though it had been a lance and charged on the

horse nearest him. "Whoa!" he shouted through his
set teeth. The brute flinched and pressed his mate
farther and farther into the snow. Both were flounder-
ing in the white, untrodden depths. The boy dropped
his bush and sprang at the bridle of the nearest. His
right hand caught the bit, and the left shut close upon a
lock of flying mane. The frightened beast reared upon
his hind feet and tossed the boy about as if he had been
a feather. The cruel iron-shod hoofs struck against him
but he kept his hold. The near horse floundered and
fell. The one to which the boy clung stood upright,
staggered, fell across his mate. Half-buried in the
snow, both struggled with a wild frenzy that was deaf
and blind to everything save an all-possessing fear and
the untamable instinct of self preservation. Underneath the struggling, heaving, snorting mass, half hidden by the tossing snow, beaten, bruised and crushed,
was the boy. The overturned sleigh stood on its side.
The little girl, thrown harmlessly against the yielding
bank, had scrambled up, and half-way to the house, stood
gazing at the half-buried pile of writhing limbs and
straining forms. The air was full of shrieks and cries.
Squire Ritner and his fellows came rushing from the
house. The mother flew shrieking down the path. The
Doctor lashed his horse into a run to reach the scene of
the encounter he had witnessed. The drooping runner
was but a few steps away. The horses, one above the
other, struggled and fought to rise. The boy, now here,
now there, then hidden underneath—could it be he was
alive?

Willing but cautious hands seized bit and rein. Martha
Kortright with a woman's instinct caught the frightened girl in her arms and stood moaning with short unconscious breaths. Suddenly, her husband, risen half
clad from his bed, shot past her. His unshod feet
hardly seemed to touch the snow. Before any one could

cry out to prevent, he had the off horse by the bit ; had forced him back with an iron grip, and reaching down, had seized with his right hand the boy, in whom his father's heart was wrapped up, had drawn him half-way from beneath the other horse, when the one he had by the bit reared again, again fell across his mate, throwing the father headlong beside the son and holding both beneath him.

But in the place of Harrison Kortright stood now a man who was even his superior in strength. Younger by some years, broad shouldered, with a square, firm-set jaw and dark flowing beard, he was still panting for breath, but his face was aflame with passion. Seizing the uppermost horse by jaw and nostril he suddenly twisted back his head with relentless strength until with a cry of pain the animal rolled upon his back down the slope of yielding snow, into the beaten track. Harrison Kortright rose with the limp, insensible body of his son in his arms. The doctor leaped from his sleigh. The neighbors assisted the father into the house. He would not yield his son to any other arm. The doctor ran by his side, feeling for the boy's pulse, and giving calm directions as to his carriage. Mrs. Kortright followed, bearing the little girl in her arms. The stranger, blown and flushed with exertion, stood beside his horses, both of which had risen and stood looking curiously at the havoc they had wrought.

THE RUNAWAY.

The neighbors assisted the father to the house. He would not yield his son to any other arm.—p. 42.

CHAPTER IV.

"FOR WOUNDS, BALM."

HARRISON KORTRIGHT staggered into the house, and laid his insensible son upon the chintz-covered lounge in the dining-room. His own face was as white as the pinched and weazened one that looked up from the pillow, but he waived aside the friendly hands that would take him away, until the doctor, looking up from a hasty examination of the boy, caught sight of his pallid countenance and said quickly :

"It is only a faint, Squire."

"You think he will live?" gasped the white-lipped father.

"Undoubtedly. He is in no danger at all; but you—"

He did not finish the sentence. Had not a friendly arm supported him, Kortright would have fallen to the floor. As it was, he sank down upon a chair, his teeth chattering, his white lips drawn, his face pinched and wan, and his eyes wild and unsteady. The reaction had come. The excitement that had enabled him to forget pain and overcome weakness had departed, and in its place was an ague-fit which told that the disease, which had momentarily relaxed its hold, had seized him again with redoubled violence. His nervous power, which had been strained to the utmost, had given way. His mind wandered. The events of the past twenty-four hours were strangely mingled in his fevered fancy, and his disconnected words were only half comprehensible to the listeners whose willing hands assisted the doctor in the vigorous measures which he at once adopted.

"Marty, Marty, my boy Marty!" moaned the sick man. "They've killed him! They've killed him! Kidnappers, did you say? Kidnappers! There ain't no kidnappers here. God wouldn't allow it! Marty! Marty! Whoa! Why don't ye kill 'em! Get away; let me get at 'em! I'll kill 'em! Let me go; they've killed my boy! The kidnappers have killed my boy!"

Mrs. Kortright, who had been utterly overwhelmed by the catastrophe that had happened to her son, released the little girl from her arms immediately on entering the house, and then stood, weeping and wringing her hands, beside the couch on which he lay. No sooner, however, did she perceive the condition of her husband, than the instinct of the care-taker returned. Instantly she was at his side, her perceptions sharpened by her love, the most efficient of aids to the physician. In less time than it would require to state in detail what was done, the sick man had been taken to his bed, a vein in his arm opened, masses of moist snow packed about his head, his feet and limbs swathed in hot cloths and chafed by strong and willing hands, and powerful remedies administered. Under this treatment his symptoms rapidly subsided. His mutterings ceased, his eyes closed, the nervous twitching of the face disappeared, and his breathing became regular and natural, in place of the stertorous and labored suspirations of an hour before. The physician felt his pulse for the hundredth time, passed his hand over his face, pulled down the lids of one of his eyes and then of the other, peered into the unseeing orbs, and then drew a long .eath of relief.

"I guess it's over," he said.

"You don't mean—!" Mrs. Kortright exclaimed in frenzied tones,

"I guess he'll pull through," replied the physician, glancing keenly at her as he spoke, "but we mustn't spare any exertion till the circulation is well established. He's better, but he needs care. Everything depends on that, now. Keep on rubbing him awhile longer, gentlemen. Are those flat-irons at his feet warm, Mrs. Kortright? Couldn't you get some more bottles of hot water to put about his limbs?"

Mrs. Kortright became at once the obedient and careful nurse again. She left the room to obtain what was desired. When she had closed the door the physician's countenance relaxed.

"He's doing all right, gentlemen, but it won't do to let her know it just now. I've known her all her life. She's a mighty capable woman, no mistake about that; but this thing's been a little too much, and if she ain't let down easy there'll be another faint here. Just keep on till I tell you to stop. 'Twon't do any harm, and will help her to pull up easy. By the way, I wonder how the boy is getting on. Gad! gentlemen, that was a plucky thing, and he had a narrow escape. I thought, when I saw him swinging by that brute's head, that he'd be past my help by this time. It was the snow that saved him—and his father, too, for that matter."

"This has been a bad day for the Squire," said Ritner, with kindly sympathy.

"It might have been worse," said the physician seriously. "If he had had to wait for treatment, he'd have been past help before now. I tell you, gentlemen, Squire Kortright's always been a lucky man—'specially since he married Mattie Ermendorf—and his luck hasn't left him to-day."

The doctor had been washing blood-stains from his hands, wiping his lancet and turning down his sleeves as he spoke. Mrs. Kortright entered the room as he concluded, with a bottle in either hand wrapped in a towel. There was an anxious look in her face, but the strained, apprehensive expression had disappeared.

"Can't you go and see Martin, now ?" she asked, glancing up at the doctor's face.

"Certainly, Martha," he answered, with the familiarity of an old friend ; "but don't you have any trouble about him. If a boy ain't killed off-hand, you needn't be afraid but what he'll come out all right. Young bones are tough," he added, in a jovial way. "Here, by the way," he continued, pouring something into a glass, and adding a little water, "you just take this."

The woman obeyed.

"Now," said he, taking her by the arm and leading her to a large, old-fashioned rocking-chair, "just you sit down there and cry. You'll feel better then. These gentlemen will take care of the Squire and I'll look after Martin."

Mrs. Kortright sat down with a look of remonstrance in her eyes, from which the tears were already flowing. Ashamed to display her weakness, she threw her apron over her head, and only her convulsive sobbing attested the relief which the tears brought. The physician nodded approval and left the room.

When they had started for the house with Martin and his father, the owner of the runaway team—for it was he who had released Kortright and his son from their perilous position—shook his head to Shields, who seemed to halt in regard to his duty, whether to go with the others or stay with the stranger, and said, sharply, "You take care of the Doctor's rig, there, and then go into the house. You may be needed. I'll look after these brutes."

The horses had risen, and now stood with the melting snow dripping from their steaming coats, the broken harness dangling around them, and gazed with startled surprise at the confusion they had caused. They had not yet recovered entirely from their fright, and the sight of the overturned sleigh caused them to snort and shy as they sought to turn and examine it.

"Whoa!" cried the master, as he caught them both by the bits and gave them a savage pull that brought them to their haunches in the deep snow where they stood. "Whoa! you infernal fools! You've done enough for to-day. I wish you and the cursed idiot who caused all this trouble had been dead before I ever set eyes on either of you. There's been nothing but bad luck in my life ever since George Eighmie left me his inheritance of folly and I was dunce enough to accept it."

He jerked the horses savagely about, until the fear of the master overcame the fright under which they had been laboring, and they stood, trembling and apprehensive, while he tied up the broken harness, righted the sleigh and secured them again in their places. Then he drove back along the road by which he had come, secured the scattered robes and cushions, picked up his whip and applied it furiously to the horses, which he held and managed with the ease of an accomplished horseman. Arrived again at Kortright's house, he drove into the yard, hitched his horses to a post near where the Doctor's sleigh was standing, carefully spread a buffalo-robe upon each, did the same with the Doctor's horse, which Shields had left unprotected, and then knocked at the side door, which opened into the family room. His knock was answered by the little girl, who looked out with a blanched face, and eyes distended with horror at the scenes she had witnessed.

"Oh papa, papa!" she cried, and, leaping into his arms, she laid her head upon his shoulder and burst into tears.

"There, there, Hilda dear," he said, soothingly, as he kissed her tear-stained cheek and smoothed the dark curls that clustered about her head; "there, there, don't cry. You didn't get hurt, did you?"

"No, papa," the child answered quickly, raising her head and hushing her sobs, "but the poor little boy, papa, do come and do something for him. I've done all I could."

"But his parents, child, where are they?"

"Oh, his papa was hurt just awful, and the little boy is hurt, too, only he won't say a word, but just lies there and cries about his papa. Do come, papa," she continued, as she slid to the floor and drew him forward by the hand, "do come; he is a real good little boy."

"Yes, indeed," said he, "I am afraid I should have had no little Hilda now if it had not been for his bravery."

The child shuddered and hid her face against him. The father lifted her up, kissed her again, and passed through the door.

Martin lay upon the lounge where he had been placed, with the cushion from the chair by which his mother had knelt the night before beneath his head. The girl's hood and rich furs were upon a chair beside him. Left alone with him, her childish instinct had led her to seek to comfort him, as soon as she saw that he was conscious. She had accordingly dried her tears, put aside her wraps and sat down by his side. After a while she smoothed the hair back from his forehead, wiped his face with a handkerchief, the delicate perfume of which came like a breath of Araby the blest to the boy, unaccustomed to luxury. Then she asked him tenderly if he was hurt, and was not deceived by his stouthearted denial. She gave him water, inquired if she should not call his mother, and when he refused to allow her to do so, had returned to his side, weeping for his pain, her soft caresses soothing him more than she knew. The woman's admiration for courage had

already developed in her little heart, and the great
brown eyes looked with an awe born of reverent worship upon the white face that lay before her, as impenetrable as the sphinx in its resolute endurance. For
the first time in her life she looked consciously upon
a hero. The impress her young mind received that day
was one that years could not efface.

In every respect the two children were the opposite
of each other. The one, as we have seen, was blue-
eyed and fair, unused to luxury or the display of affection—a tough, wiry lad, whose life, while without hardship, had been familiarized only with the harsh, every-
day plainness of a farmer's home. He had been loved
but never petted, save now and then when his mother's
half-concealed caresses had gladdened his heart. His
father's love he had taken for granted. Careful, grave
and undemonstrative, he had never realized, until he
felt the firm grip that dragged him from beneath the
horses, what intense love burned for him in his father's
heart. His own heart was very tender, and he almost
forgot his bruises, as he lay there gazing at the beautifully clad girl and thinking of the father whose love
he had just discovered, and whose condition he had
revived sufficiently to apprehend before his removal
to the other room. He thought that he had never seen
anything so beautiful in his life as the brown-skinned,
dark-eyed little girl, whose hair clung in abundant ringlets about her head, as she alternately gazed out of the
window at her father, and bent over him in sympathetic sorrow. Unconsciously she did the very best
thing that could have been done for her charge. She
told him what her father was doing, how he struck and
jerked the horses about in anger at their misdeeds;
how they reared and plunged and were drawn back and
beaten still more severely; till his mind was diverted

from his own and his father's woes to the sympathy of a born horseman for a fine animal.

"Are they your father's horses?" he asked.

"Oh yes, indeed, but he will sell them now. I know he will. I shall never ride after them any more," she answered, warmly.

"Why not?" in surprise.

"Because they are so bad—because they hurt you."

"Pshaw! That ain't nothing. They didn't mean to hurt me. They was scart; that was all."

"Well, I don't want to see them any more—the hateful, mean old things!"

"Your father must be very rich?" meditatively.

"I don't know—why?"

"To have such nice horses. I wish I had them."

"You? What for?"—in amazement.

"To drive, of course."

"Why, they would kill you. I should think you would want them killed too. I do."

"That's because you are a girl," with quiet contempt, despite her beauty.

"Would you really like to have those awful, bad, wicked horses?"

"Of course I would. If I was a little older, I wouldn't be afraid of them any more 'n your father."

"Well, you shall have them," with quiet decision, "when you get well and have grown up. I'll ask my papa to give them to you. He always does what I want him to."

"What is your—your father's name?" He tried to say "papa" as she did, but could not, somehow. He had never said "papa" in his life. To him, as to all of his class at that time, his father and mother were known by no other names. He had read of the other titles in books, and had thought them very pleasant words. He had even wished sometimes that he might use them, but had never dared to do so.

"Why, don't you know my papa?" said the girl, with evident pride. "He's Captain Hargrove, and we live at Sturmhold."

The boy looked up at her with a sort of awe. He knew the great brick house, built on a ragged spur of the upper Catskills that overlooked the valley for twenty miles up and down, and, though ten miles away, was only hidden from view by the wooded crest of a range of hills that skirted an intervening tributary. The owner of Sturmhold was accounted fabulously rich, but was thought by his country neighbors to be a man whose past life would not bear scrutiny. He had built the house some years before, lived lavishly, it was said, kept a large retinue of colored servants and fished the mountain streams for trout; but had no relations with any of his neighbors and did not encourage any approaches on their part.

"It must be mighty nice to live in such a grand house," he ventured.

"Oh, it is so lonesome," she said, wearily; "only when papa is at home."

"Why, ain't your—your mother there?"

"My mamma is—is—dead," said the child, with sudden moisture in her eyes.

Martin would have apologized, if he had known how, for the painful reference he had made. He had never said "I beg your pardon," or uttered any similar form of polite regret in his life. His father had once whipped him for half an hour to compel him to ask his teacher's forgiveness for some piece of mischief of which she had made complaint. He had yielded at last, and repeated the humiliating ritual the next day, but the words had left a bitter taste in his mouth. Fortunately, just at this time her father knocked at the door, which she ran to open.

Captain Hargrove came at once upon his daughter's entreaty to the side of the lounge, and said in a softly modulated voice, while he looked down into Martin's eyes with thoughtful keenness :

"Are you hurt, my little man ? I hope not, for you saved my little Hilda's life, and I should feel very badly to know that you were injured in so brave an act."

"Oh, 'tain't nothin', sir," said the boy, his eyes filling with tears, and his cheek flushing, more at the contrast between his own rough speech and the evenly-spoken, well-chosen words of the gentleman, who sat down as he spoke, and taking his arm felt for his pulse with a hand as soft as velvet.

"Where are you hurt, my boy ?" he asked. "I am not a doctor, but I have had some bruises myself, and seen smart of broken bones, first and last. I hope you have had no such mishap, though." He spoke pleasantly, and smoothed his long dark beard with one hand while he held the boy's wrist with the other.

Martin looked into his deep dark eyes with wondering surprise not unmixed with admiring distrust. He remembered that some people believed that this white-handed gentleman had been a pirate in his day. Some even surmised that he still made a trip, now and then, on a fast-sailing sloop that had been known to come up the Hudson, take him on board, and, spreading its white wings till it seemed like a great cloud, speed away in silence to the sea to return again after many months, and leave him—always after nightfall, and always disappearing again before the morning.

Captain Hargrove skillfully disarmed the boy's suspicion, which he no doubt mistook for bashfulness, and learned that his left arm was the chief seat of pain. Carefully examining this, he found that one of the bones below the elbow was broken. Taking a knife from his pocket—the boy noticed that it was pearl-handled and had many slender, bright blades, and wondered still more at the luxury that clothed the most ordinary things of life with such lavish splendor—he opened it and cut away the sleeve so as to leave the arm bare. He did this so gently and deftly that the boy's confidence was won without reserve, and he told him of every ache and pain he had experienced since he was dragged from beneath the struggling horses.

"There isn't anything else the matter with you, my little man," said the stranger briskly, "except bruises, which of course, must be expected by any one that undertakes so tough a job as stopping my bays when they once get away from their driver."

At this moment the door opened and the physician entered.

"Ah, Captain Hargrove," said he, "this is a bad day. I hope your horses were not hurt."

"Unfortunately, no," said Hargrove. "I wish their necks had been broken instead of this brave boy's arm, —I do indeed."

"What! his arm broken?" said the doctor in incredulous surprise. "That's a fact," after a quick examination of the injured member, that brought a groan from the close-pressed lips of the resolute lad. "Well, well, my son, this must be looked after."

The fracture of the arm was soon reduced, the hand and forearm bound so as to prevent the dislocation of the parts, and Martin, relieved from pain, sunk away into a quiet sleep. Mrs. Kortright, her equanimity restored, became again the careful housewife, and took up the task of attending to her two invalids with her wonted cheerfulness. It was agreed among the neighbors that one should stay until night, when the others were to send watchers, and the doctor consented to look out for a girl to assist in the housework. At this point in the discussion, Captain Hargrove advanced, and said to Mrs. Kortright:

"I beg, madam, that you will not leave me out of the arrangements made necessary by my carelessness. I have a servant who is a most experienced nurse, as well as a most capable manager of a household. I insist, madam, on placing him at your service. He is entirely reliable, strong and untiring."

"I am much obliged," said Mrs. Kortright, "but—"

"Madam," said he earnestly, taking his little girl by the hand and leading her forward, "Madam, this is all I have to love in the world. Your brave boy saved her life. Have I not a right to testify my gratitude?"

Still the feeling of independence that is innate with the class to which she belonged withheld the woman from a frank acceptance of the proffered aid. Perhaps this feeling arose in part from the manner in which he spoke of the one he desired to send, as—"a servant." Somehow, the word was very repulsive to the ears of the great masses of the North, and every possible periphrasis was employed to avoid its use. Perhaps it was a relic of the great revolt of the Occident against the Orient that separated the New World from the Old in manners and customs, even farther than in laws and institutions.

"Thank you," she repeated, "but the neighbors—"

"Beggin' your pardon, Mrs. Kortright," interrupted Shields, with the incisive bluntness that characterized him, "the neighbors 'ud think you wa'an't fair to yerself or Captain Hargrove, either, if you didn't let him do as he proposes. Don't ye say so, Squire?" turning to Ritner, who assented with a nod.

"Besides," added the doctor, as he stood with his hand on the latch, "a steady, trained nurse, as Captain Hargrove's man no doubt is, would be vastly better for your husband than the best of watchers, coming and going from day to day."

Mrs. Kortright could not resist this appeal to her love, and she turned toward Hargrove with a gesture of assent.

"Consider it settled, then," said he. "I will send Jason to-night. I must drive into the village to make some inquiries upon a matter that caused my unfortunate drive in this direction. By the way," he added, turning to the men who were just passing out, "perhaps one of you may be able to give me some information."

"We'll be glad to do anything for you that we can, Captain," said Ritner, politely, but not over-cordially. There was something in the manner of this man, frank, bold and tender as he seemed to be, that was so different from the people among whom he lived as to awaken suspicion in their minds at once.

"Some time last night," continued Hargrove, "a servant woman left my house, and wandered off into the storm. She had been in my service for a long time, seemed perfectly contented, and, indeed, had no reason to be otherwise. She was my housekeeper, and had almost absolute control. I am afraid she must have been seized with a sudden hallucination, and fleeing from some imagined difficulty, met with her death in the storm."

A knowing look passed around the little circle as he spoke.

"Was she a colored woman?" asked Ritner, gravely.

"Certainly," answered Hargrove, with a smile. "I have always been accustomed to colored servants, and should hardly know how to get along with white ones."

"Most likely not," said Shields, with the trace of a sneer in his tone.

Insensibly the little group had grown suddenly cold. Hargrove and his little girl stood in the midst of them, but were not of them. The northern jealousy of personal freedom built a wall about the man who was believed to hold his servants in subjection by a terror they could not resist.

"I hope the fact that she is colored is no reason why I should not seek to find and save her from death, if possible," said Hargrove, answering the tone rather than the words.

"Sartin not," said Shields, "if that's what you want to find her for."

"If!" said Hargrove hotly, looking from one to another, and for the first time fully realizing the suspicion they entertained. "If! By Heaven, gentlemen, I am not always in a mood to endure such imputation; but after the events of this morning, I cannot quarrel with you. I suppose you think that because I have slaves under my control in another State I regard the whole African race as mine, 'to have and to hold,' as the lawyers say?"

"Wal," said Ritner, apologetically, "the Free Soilers are havin' so much to say about slavery, jest now, that I s'pose we're gettin' to be a little unreasonable on the subject. You mustn't think hard on us, Captain, we don't mean no harm."

"I do not think you do," answered Hargrove earnestly, "and you ought to know that if I intended any evil to the girl I would not ask such men as you for aid."

"There's sense in that, certainly," said the Doctor, with the instinct of his profession to make matters smooth.

"I assure you," said Hargrove, "that I am more anxious than I can express in regard to her safety. She has been very tenderly raised and is utterly unfitted to protect herself in such a storm."

"Oh, there ain't no danger of any one suffering in so thickly settled a country as this," said Van Wormer, the youngest of the neighbors, who had hitherto taken no part in the conversation. "She's all right. You'll find her at some neighbor's house, probably."

"That was my opinion, too," said Hargrove, "but my servants and myself have been visiting the houses in every direction, since early morning, when her absence was discovered, and we find no trace of her. I fear that in an insane apprehension she may have been even afraid to ask for aid."

"Wal, wal," said Shields suspiciously, "that's a queer story."

"No doubt it seems so to you," said Hargrove with evident annoyance. "She was my housekeeper, and I should almost as soon have expected my child to run away."

"Perhaps you did not pay her enough," suggested Van Wormer.

"Pay her?" ejaculated Hargrove. "I never thought of such a thing. She had only to ask for money to receive it. I have often left large sums in her possession and never thought of asking an account of what she spent."

"Hain't you any idea what made her take such a sudden start?" asked the Doctor.

"My overseer arrived from the South yesterday," responded Hargrove, "and I think her fears, awakened perhaps by meddlesome parties who did not know as much as she ought to have known, were excited that she might be returned to slavery. I had kept the record of her manumission with my own papers, lest it should be lost, and she no doubt distrusted my intentions."

"'Twouldn't be onnateral ef she did," said Shields grimly.

"Perhaps not," said Hargrove, "but I never thought of it. It is hard to get over the habit of regarding one who has been your slave as, in a sense, still under your guardianship. So I never thought of handing her

this bit of paper, which shows she is as free as you
or I."

He drew a folded document from his pocket, as he
spoke, and handed it to Ritner, who examined it curiously.

"Well, I can't say I blame her," said Shields, squint-
ing his eyes toward the document that Ritner held.
"Ef my freedom depended on a bit of paper like that
'ar, and somebody else hed hold on't, an' kept holding
on to et, too, I must say I should be mighty apt to cut
out fur a country that wasn't healthy fur kidnappers."

"Kidnappers! What do you mean?" asked Hargrove,
turning impetuously upon him.

The hatchet-faced farmer did not quail before the
flaming glance or clenched fist of the angry gentleman.
His slender fingers worked nervously, and his gray eyes
had a dangerous light in them as he said:

"'Tain't no use to try any Southern swagger here,
Captain. My words wa'nt hard to understand, and I
hain't got nothing to take back, neither."

"There, there, gentlemen," interposed the doctor, with
something of authority in his tone; "this is not the place
for any such talk as that."

"I beg your pardon, madam," said Hargrove, turning quickly, and bowing deferentially to Mrs. Kortright.
"With my anxiety about this poor woman and the mis-
haps I have been so unfortunate as to bring upon this
household, I am hardly responsible for what I do or say.
Come, Hilda, let us go."

The child, who had clung to her father's hand during
this conversation with tearful eyes and quivering lips,
now inquired: "Won't we ever find my mammy,
Papa?"

"I will try, my child," answered Hargrove huskily.
"Good morning, madam."

"Mr. Hargrove," said Mrs. Kortright, as he moved

toward the door, "was the woman you are hunting for named Lida ?"

"Yes, indeed," answered Hargrove, turning eagerly toward her. "Do you know anything of her, madam ?"

"Oh! have you seen my mammy? have you seen my mammy?" cried the little girl, running to Mrs. Kortright and seizing her hand. "Do please say you know where she is, and that she isn't lost and dead under the cold, bad snow." She burst out sobbing as she cried this and hid her face in the woman's dress.

Mrs. Kortright fondled the child's head soothingly, as she replied :

"A woman who said her name was Lida, that she had been livin' at Sturmhold, and had run away because the kidnappers were after her, came to our house and asked for shelter and protection. She said she was 'colored,' but she was just as white as I am, for all I could see."

"Oh, that is my mammy! I 've found my mammy!" shouted the little girl in ecstasy.

"And she is now—where ?" asked Hargrove, eagerly.

"Captain Hargrove," answered the farmer's wife, gazing at him keenly, and speaking very slowly, "I do not know ; and, I will be fair with you, I would not tell you if I did."

"You did not turn her out into the storm, I hope ?" —angrily.

"Into the storm, sir!" said the woman, proudly; "nobody was ever refused food or shelter at Harrison Kortright's house, and never will be, in fair weather or foul."

"Pardon me, then she is still here, madam ? I was only anxious for her safety. If she is safe, it is all I care for. I am sorry she chose to leave us, but it is her undoubted right to do so."

"She is safe," answered Mrs. Kortright, with significance.

"You'd better be contented with that, Captain," said Shields. "You can't git yer nigger back, an' 'tain't no use a-tryin'. When once they git loose up in this country, up north of here, there ain't no more use of follerin' 'em than of huntin' a fox on skates—not a bit."

"Gentlemen," said Hargrove, with lofty dignity, "I perceive that it is useless for me to appeal to your reason. You will persist in misinterpreting my motives. I am a slaveholder because the law permits me to be. The same law gives a manumitted slave the right to be free, and I would help to tar and feather a kidnapper just as quick as the hottest abolitionist that ever howled about what he knows nothing of. There are reasons which I cannot explain here, why I am especially interested in this woman. I would not interfere with her freedom, however, for the price of a king's ransom."

"Captain Hargrove," said Mrs. Kortright, extending her hand to him, "I believe every word you say."

"Thank you, madam," said he with emotion, as he clasped her hand. "You will never regret your confidence in my integrity. You will then inform me of the whereabouts of this unfortunate woman?"

"I cannot, Captain. I assure you she is safe. My husband took her through the storm last night to the house of a friend; but I can tell you nothing more until he is well enough to permit of my consulting with him."

"You are entirely right to act with caution, madam. Meantime may I make you my agent to transmit to her this document," said Hargrove, taking the record of manumission again from his pocket, "and also this money for the supply of her present needs. Whenever she may require more, you have but to inform me of the fact, and I will gladly supply any reasonable amount."

The sum which he laid in the honest woman's palm was such as to cause her breath to come quick with amazement.

"Come, Hilda," said Hargrove, cheerfully. "Good morning, madam. I will send Jason over as soon as I get home. Good morning, gentlemen."

Passing out of the door, Merwyn Hargrove unhitched his horses and drove back to Sturmhold, with a look upon his face that showed how genuine had been his anxiety.

CHAPTER V.

"A DEFEATED JOY."

THE neighbors followed Hargrove out of the house and stood peering at the bright sunshine from the little side porch, while the master of Sturmhold hastily stripped the robes from his horses, unhitched them from the post, and, with sharp, stern words of command, started them upon their homeward way. The noon sunshine was undoing the night's work with wonderful rapidity. Bright streams trickled from the eaves of every building. The softened snow slipped from the bowed branches of the trees, which leaped up to their proper places with sharp sighs of relief from their burdens. Avalanches swept down the sloping roofs. The beaten paths yielded beneath the feet as if a sea were hidden under the dripping whiteness that overspread the earth. Boreas declined the gage of battle and left his chariot to be melted by the wrath of the conqueror.

"Going fast," said Ritner, looking at the sun and the torrents pouring from the eaves.

"Which?" asked Van Wormer, glancing roguishly from the eave spouts to Hargrove, then just stepping into his sleigh.

"Wal, both," answered Ritner, with instant but solemn appreciation of the jest.

"Jest as they come, too," added Shields, dryly, losing nothing of the humor of his companions, but fitting his own caustic wit to their pleasantry, "without invitation and for mighty little good."

62

"Queer that he should have run across the woman's track right here," said Van Wormer.

"He didn't make much off o' Martha Kortright, anyhow," said Shields.

"That's how the Squire got his rheumatism last night!" said Ritner, inclining his head knowingly toward the room they had just left.

"And that," said Shields, nodding assent and raising his finger for emphasis, "that's what made him a Free-S'iler this morning, too."

"Well, gentlemen, can I take one of you down to 'lection?" asked the Doctor, briskly, as he passed them on the porch and began to untie his horse. "What say you, Shields? I don't often take a 'Hunker' to the polls, but we couldn't get along without you."

A ripple of laughter greeted the Doctor's joke.

"Wal, no, thank you all the same, Doctor. I ain't a bit proud, an' having come this far with a 'Silver-Grey'"—glancing at Ritner—"I wouldn't mind going the rest of the way with a 'Woolly Head;' but I bleeve I won't vote to-day. I ain't sure but Squire Kortright is about right. Anyhow, I'll pair off with him this time, an' try an' make up my mind 'bout some things that I ain't exactly sartin of now afore 'lection time comes 'round agin."

"So you're going to let the country go to destruction without trying to stop it," said the Doctor, as he settled himself in his cutter and took up the reins."

"Wal, yes," answered Shields, deprecatingly. "I know I ain't doin' right, an' it's my fault, too, but the fact is, I don't exactly know what I ought to do. I'm at a standstill an' can't determine whether I ought to be for the woman that run away in the snow or for the man that followed after in the sleigh."

"That's my idea exactly," echoed Ritner warmly, "and that's about all there is in our politics when you

git to the bottom on't, too," he continued meditatively, "though everybody keeps swearin' that politics
hain't nothing to do with Slavery or Freedom."

"Good Heavens, Doctor," said Van Wormer, "did
you ever see such a nest of Abolitionists?"

"Well," said the Doctor, cutting the snow with his
whip as he spoke, "I'm in about the same predicament;
but I've made up my mind to run betwixt and between,
as we have to do sometimes when we can't exactly make
out what's the matter with a patient. There ain't no
chance of the Free Soil party winning *this* time, and
yet it seems to me to be bottomed on the right idea. So
I believe I'll give them a vote this once, just to encourage them."

"It amounts to jest the same thing," answered
Shields. "We both own up that we don't know the
river, as we used to say in raftin', an' so we give up the
steerin' oar to them that thinks they do."

"That's so," said the Doctor, tightening his reins.
"Well, won't either of you go?" looking at Van Wormer
as he spoke.

"Well, no," said the younger man, "I believe not. I
guess I'll go home with these two 'Barnburners' and in-
troduce them to their families. They've changed so
since they started out that nobody there would recognize them."

The Doctor drove off with a laugh, while the others
walked homewards over the soft and splashing roadway they had helped to make a few hours before, more
thoughtful if not wiser men.

As Kortright had predicted, the vote that day was an
unusually heavy one, though the storm had extended
into several States, and when the boxes were closed as
the sun went down, "the man that fit the Mexicans"
had been "made" President of the Republic. For the
first time in the history of the nation the lines between

Slavery and Freedom had been sharply drawn, and Liberty had achieved its first victory, though its advocates but little understood the significance of that day's work, and did not realize until many a day had passed that a defeat which mocked them with apparent hopelessness was but the shadow of coming victory.

CHAPTER VI.

THE CLUE TO THE LABYRINTH.

THE sixteenth Presidential election was really a turning point in American history. For the first time, the Anti-Slavery sentiment then became an actual power in American politics. The growth of this principle and the conflict between the two opposing claims of right—the right of the Master to hold and the right of the Slave to be free—must long remain the most interesting phase of our history, as for more than a generation it was the most absorbing question of our national life. So deftly was the ebb and flow of this mighty thought concealed beneath the waves which the gusts of party passion stirred upon the surface, that many of the most prominent actors in our destiny little dreamed that they were borne on to victory by its power or drawn down to oblivion by its undertow.

It has been too much the custom to regard this great conflict of ideas as simply a series of partisan successes and defeats. In truth, no great principle ever gained a foothold in the polity of a republic so independently of all party influence and favor in its growth and development as the movement in the United States for the abolition of slavery. For many years it was outside of all parties, yet underneath every political organization. It had few professed advocates ; yet it colored with its intensity every public life. Long before it had become a recognized political power in the nation, it had entered the pulpit, the home, the school, and had stimulated thought to a point never before paralleled in history.

The struggle it inaugurated was pre-eminently a conflict of ideas, and the field on which it was fought covered almost the entire domain of human knowledge. Every physical scientist, from Agassiz down to the half-taught quack of the country cross-roads, had an opinion by which he was ready to stand or fall as to the comparative capacity of the African and Caucasian races. In defense of his special theory was always arrayed his professional pride and not seldom his professional spite.

The archæologist exhausted the lore of history, tradition and scientific guesswork to prove or disprove the negro's capacity for self-direction and self-control. The political economist faced his fellow-scientist in the struggle to show that Cotton was King, and that the king could be made regnant only by the slave's labor. The theologians hurled tomes of learning at each other's heads, proving and disproving more doctrine from Scripture than the most inspired of the prophets had ever forecasted.

Its growth was not only extra-political, but it grew in spite of parties. It is probable that when the first petition in regard to slavery was presented in the House of Representatives, the number of people who were distinctly opposed to it—who actually regarded it as a wrong toward the slave—was very insignificant. It has been said that there were five thousand such in the State of Massachusetts, but it is doubtful if there were that number in the whole nation. There were many who believed it an evil to the white race, and others who thought it only a choice of evils; but the number who actually regarded the negro as a man, entitled to all the rights and privileges attaching to white manhood, was excessively small during the last quarter of the eighteenth and first quarter of the nineteenth century.

Both parties shunned the mighty problems it in-

volved. Even the splendid powers of John Quincy
Adams were sufficient only to make the right of petition an uncertain and dubious issue. The one party
not only openly declared against the assailability of
slavery, but in the main, insisted that it was the necessary and normal condition of a considerable portion of our population. To this party the Anti-Slavery
movement was wrong in theory as well as in practice.
On the other hand, the opposing party, while deprecat-
ing slavery as an evil, deprecated still more all movement looking toward its extinction. The one denounced
the very existence of the movement; the other hesitatingly courted its support and thought its advocates
unreasonable when they demanded more than bare tole-
ration at its hands. The one actively proclaimed and
advocated the rights of the slave-owners; the other
mildly questioned the extent of them but stubbornly
refused to recognize any right attaching to the slave.
Each party fought the other manfully on most questions,
but joined hands in putting down the heresy that a
black skin ever afforded lodgement for inalienable right.

The South was "solid," even then. It had two parties, but only one political creed. Each party had a
"Southern wing," and, so far as this question was concerned, they might have swapped "wings" and the difference hardly have been perceptible. Instead of being
the creature of party "Abolitionism" was the *bête noire*
of all parties. The one declared that such an idea was
treasonable and dangerous; the other that it was impracticable and absurd. Between the two the choice
was not great. The one favored slavery and the other
would not advocate freedom.

A like anomaly presented itself in the church. One
ecclesiastical body undertook to enforce the doctrine of
its founder as a vital element of Christian faith, and
was rent asunder in the convulsion that followed. Other

bodies of a less homogeneous character displayed the most amazing contradictions of dogma. In the same town, one pulpit thundered in behalf of slavery and another, of the same faith, promulgated the doctrine of human liberty and equality.

Commerce, as usual, was with the majority, and favored the *status quo.* Cotton was King, on 'Change at least, and he who spun and wove bowed obedient to its mandate. Trade seeks peaceful highways, and the trafficker avoids every element of uncertainty that can be eliminated from his estimate of the future. So Commerce joined hands with Politics and Religion and threw obstacles in the way of the new movement.

Yet still it grew. There is nothing more wonderful in history than its growth. Despite its burdens of predicted disaster, of irreligious tone, of commercial distrust, of scientific absurdity, of political animosity — despite all this, it grew like the oak hid in the acorn and pressed down by the rock—silently, imperceptibly, none could guess in what direction, but always toward the light.

Strangely enough, too, it grew in streaks and spots. It did not follow geographical or State lines. It took root on one side of a mountain and never found lodgement on the other. One bank of a river was anti-slavery in sentiment, while that a bowshot away was bitterly hostile to the last. One end of a street was for and the other against the dogma. So, too, one could judge nothing from the antecedents of parties in regard to their course upon this question. The New England Brahmin and the nameless shoemaker's son struck hands in advocacy of the doctrine. Here would be found a community devoutly in earnest in the battle for liberty, while all around it sneered at the notion of right attaching to ebon-hued humanity. The most trivial incident turned men who carried with them whole communities. A traveler by chance saw an assemblage of men and women refused admission to a public hall, because they proposed to discuss the doctrine of human liberty. He offered them his house as a refuge of free thought, rode all night to prepare for their coming, and from that day the voice and pen of Gerrit Smith rested not until slavery was no more.

Its early advocates were men and women of profound convictions. The opprobrium attaching to the name of Abolitionist had no charm for the demagogue. The man who declared his adhesion to the odious dogma must needs have the courage of his convictions. Even the South, which honestly and naturally regarded this movement with hate and horror, could not but admit its sincerity. They accounted it fanaticism—cruel, harsh fanaticism—but they could attribute no selfish or unworthy motives to its advocates. The only approach to such imputation was the frequent claim that fanaticism was fanned by envy—that the ease and abundance of the South stirred the envious hate of the half-starved New Englander. But this was the raving of ignorance. The truth is, that upon no public question in the world's history have a whole people ever been so intensely sincere in their convictions. Upon no other hypothesis can the intellectual phenomena of that day be explained. Of course, both sides misunderstood and misappreciated each other. The Anti-Slavery leaders thought, spoke and wrote ; were beaten, incarcerated and maligned, until they could not conceive that those who advocated the preservation and continuance of an evil that grew blacker with every ray of light thrown upon its real character, could be moved by other than base and selfish considerations. The slaveholder, on the other hand, who looked upon slavery as upon any other incident of his accustomed life, regarding it as an institution not altogether perfect or in all respects admirable, but

infinitely superior to any condition of society likely to
be formed of the same elements, considered the mere
agitation of the question as an unlawful infringement
of his sacred right of private property. To his mind,
the nation was a simple confederation which he had
entered clothed with certain powers, among which was
the right to control and manage his own property in
such manner as he chose. This was in his eyes a guaranty which all the land had pledged its honor and
power to sustain. That the slave had a right that
might conflict with his he did not dream. His father
and his father's fathers, back to the dawn of history, had
held slaves or been slaves. He was right, too. The
weight of authority was with him. Leaving aside the
New Testament, the literature of personal liberty was
very light when Garrison dipped his pen in fire for its
advocacy. Even in this, the lesson of comfort given to
the poor "doulos" was, by interpretation, made to over-
weigh the vision of the "common and unclean" that
came to Peter, the declaration of Paul that the Christian idea recognized neither "bond nor free," and the
whole lesson of the Master's life. The whole doctrine was an innovation. One little island, in its rebound from the pains of foreign thraldom, had given to
its soil the magic power to dissolve the fetters of the
slave by instant contact. But even her dependencies
were yet ruled by the lash, and the slaves' labor yet
filled the coffers of her merchant princes. Aye, it was
from her that he had received his heritage of bondsmen
and the right to hold and use them as he chose. Confirmed by generations, extending over one-third of the
Republic, and affecting not only every one who owned a
slave, but every one who dwelt within the zone where
the African race constituted a considerable proportion
of the population, it is not to be wondered at that all
efforts to change this established relation or interfere

with the right confirmed by a prescription which might
well defy the law's severest test, were regarded as incendiary, and, lacking a selfish motive in their promoters,
were thought to be inspired by a fanaticism "moved
and instigated by the Devil."

There are some phases of this struggle for which it is
almost impossible to account. Among these was the
intensity of the odium attaching to the advocacy of
anti-slavery principles at the North. There was no personal interest to excuse or justify this. The mere *vis
inertia* of the public mind, which is of course opposed
to change, is not sufficient to account for its rancor. To
be an "Abolitionist" was to be regarded with distrust
in almost all localities, with clearly-expressed disfavor
in a majority of cases and with absolute hostility in not
a few. Men and women were mobbed in quiet country
towns hundreds of miles away from the northern verge
of slave territory, for simply avowing the belief that
slavery was an unrighteous and an evil thing and should
be abolished at the earliest possible moment. This was
done, too, by quiet, earnest, moral people, who would
have looked with horror upon the denial of the right of
private opinion on any other subject.

As the struggle grew more general it became also
more bitter. The feeling in its favor grew stronger year
by year, its adversaries more numerous and the war of
words more universal. Despite the protests and clamor
of parties, the question began to color all political controversy. Without ever having been distinctly recognized,
it was the underlying motive of almost every political
act. The growing army of Abolitionists was made up
of men whose convictions made them valuable allies and
dangerous enemies. They had little regard for party
lines and still less for party platforms. Their one idea
swallowed up all others. To this they subordinated all
other political considerations. Whatever moved the

wheels of progress toward the goal of liberty by even a hair's breadth, that they favored. Whatever stood in the way of the accomplishment of their one desire, that they hated and opposed.

So it was that they formed strange alliances. In one State they aided the Whigs and in another the Democrats; but, whatever the specific result, in all cases they gained something by the continuous discussion of the question which controlled their action. As a rule, the Whigs were supposed to lean toward the party of liberty and the Democrats to incline themselves toward the supporters of slavery. The official utterances of the former were intended to conciliate the Free-Soil element without offending any more than was unavoidable the Pro-slavery wing of the party. The latter sought to achieve success by conciliating the Slave Power, as it was then called, and stigmatizing in the severest terms the Abolitionists. Yet in its early struggles the Anti-Slavery movement was very largely reinforced from Democratic ranks, and perhaps the greater number of its political leaders came originally from that party.

The great leaders of it as a moral and intellectual movement—those who planned its campaigns among the people and fought its battles in the forum of conscience —belonged to no party. To them individual liberty and its proper guarantees were above all things in importance. They had no other aim, no ulterior purpose. They rightly named themselves in their first party convention—a weak and beggarly affair so far as numbers or great names were concerned—the Liberty Party. One great thought absorbed them. Outside of this they were nothing. Already their names are falling into obscurity. Their work accomplished, the world has no more use for them. They are the worn instruments which the Master Workman lays aside when they have served His purpose.

To the whole land, however, this struggle was the great impulse to thought.   No mind could slumber in the fever heat it brought.   Every soul was wrought up to its best and brightest in assault or defense.   There was no middle ground.   Those who stood by and faltered were ground to powder.   The greatest was as the least before the onward sweeping avalanche.   One moment's hesitation, and the greatest of leaders was trampled in the mire.   One moment's inspiration, and a pigmy was thrust over the heads of all into the leader's place.   Men were nothing—the one great thought was all.

CHAPTER VII.

BETWEEN THE PILLARS.

On the day when Harrison Kortright's friends stood upon his porch and debated as to their duty, the Anti-Slavery movement, having cast off the fetters of political thraldom, had just laid hold upon its first opportunity to make or mar—to lift up and to cast down in the Republic. Four years before, there had been a fierce struggle in the Democratic party. One of its great leaders had been thrown aside by a combination of many lesser ones. For twenty years and more Martin Van Buren had been the strategist of his party. Its victories had been won under his direction, if not through his apparent leadership. He was to Jackson what Hamilton was to Washington, and even more. Not only had his brain conceived the successes of his party, but he had generally proved himself capable of warding off the perils resulting from the stupidity or stubbornness of others. Weighted through the entire period of his own administration with the blunders he was powerless to prevent his predecessor from committing, (the resulting effects of which were fully developed only during his own presidency) probably no candidate ever offered for a re-election under equal disadvantages. His defeat was overwhelming, but his management in saving his party from demoralization and dissolution in consequence of this defeat was most admirable. During the four years that followed this overthrow of the Democracy after a brilliant series of uninterrupted successes, it was his masterly skill and unequaled sa-

gacity that transformed the shattered and defeated mob
of 1840 into the triumphant host of 1844. He was the
head of his party in defeat as well as in victory. This
most trying of all rôles to the partisan chief he filled,
not only with success, but with a peculiar dignity that
enabled him to enter the next convention of his party
with an undoubted majority at his back. Perhaps so
difficult an achievement has never been successfully performed by any other American party leader. Its difficulty was greatly enhanced, not only by the fact that the
defeat came after a political life of unusual duration
and activity, but also by the further fact that there
were in the ranks of his party a large number of aspir-
ing veterans whose service had been nearly equal to his
own in length, and whose successes had been only less
conspicuous. To the ambition of each of these the
lapse of another quadrenniate was fraught with danger.
With so astute a leader as Van Buren, the success of
the party was assured. Their antagonists, the Whigs,
demoralized by the defection of Tyler, and weakened
by the rivalry of two great leaders, each of whom considered the party a simple machine for his own personal aggrandizement, were indeed rather to be despised than feared, even with the name of "Harry of
the West" upon their banners.

The number and efficiency of the lieutenants Van Buren had attached to himself was marvelous. In his four
years of retirement he had managed, none knew how, to
make himself again the autocrat of his party in his own
state of New York. It was not from any fear of failure
under his leadership, therefore, that his name was re-
jected by the convention and that of an unknown Tennessee politician substituted in its place. Two causes
were at work. Each of the leaders who stood next him
in rank thought it possible that such defeat might mean
his own selection. Having combined to effect this re-

sult, they found that the defeated statesman had still sufficient power to prevent any one of them from wearing the laurels that had been snatched from his brow through their conspiracy. The best they could do was to acquiesce in the selection of a man so obscure and of such conspicuous weakness as to leave the matter of the succession open to a free scramble four years later. This course suited well the baffled giant, who was no doubt even then meditating his revenge.

The lot fell upon a Southern man, quiet, scholarly, narrow-minded, and, in all that affected the South, a bigot of the extremest type. Strangely enough, he lacked all the characteristic attributes of a Southern politician except good family. He was neither a brilliant orator, an astute manager, a magnetic personality, nor any other thing that is supposed to characterize the successful leader. He was merely James K. Polk, of Tennessee—a good enough man, a fair lawyer, a sound State-Rights Democrat, cold-blooded, precise, suspicious and weak—a man morally certain to organize no following that would enable him to be or to name his own successor. At the same time, he was regarded as a docile, manageable man, whose administration would probably be one of those even, unmarked periods, not at all dangerous to the success of a party whose strongest guarantee of power was its unswerving adhesion to the established order.

Probably no character in our history is so hard to analyze as that of Martin Van Buren. The secret of his power seems to have died with him. He was not renowned as an orator, and yet must have possessed great powers as an advocate. He is not usually credited with having devised any great public measures, yet, during the most important epoch of his party's history, every measure to which it owed success not only required his approval, but showed

his shaping or modifying touch. He was not eminent
in debate, but was always a leader of his party in
legislation. He is said to have been personally calm,
self-poised and unconfiding. He heard every one's
opinion, but took no one's advice. He was accounted
shrewd and cunning, but never was accused of personal
treachery. He was cautious to the verge of timidity
and, at the same time, confident to the verge of rashness.
He never exulted over victory nor whimpered at defeat.
He had few personal friends, but an amazing popular
following. In theory he was the broadest of democrats;
in practice the most exclusive of aristocrats. None of
his associates seem to have regarded him with affection
and few of his opponents looked upon him with animosity. Perhaps no political life in our history shows
so few mistakes. In no single instance did he fail to
make the best of the occasion, viewing it from his own
standpoint; unless it were the last and greatest of his
life—the opportunity to lead the movement that eventually transformed the nation. He seems to have had
all men's regard, but to have given none his trust.
By his opponents he was called cunning; by his followers sagacious. More justly than almost any other
politician he may be said to have achieved his own
successes. Living, he was the envy of all who would
succeed; dead, he has been the model of unnumbered
failures. Few statesmen would covet his fame; fewer
still do not envy his success. He is the Sphinx of our
history—the hidden hand in many great events—a man
in whom the elements were so deftly mixed that no
friend knew his heart and no enemy ever came within
his guard.

In that knowledge of the public heart on which is
grounded the power to forecast political events he was
admittedly unequaled by any man of his day. Another
characteristic also none ever denied him—the most

unruffled courage. IIis course once fixed upon, nothing could swerve him from pursuing it to the end. Public clamor or private cabal he regarded with equal indifference. Friend or foe he met with equal urbanity. In a time when personal collisions were frequent and factional strife was hottest, he was on terms of personal familiarity with all. No insult disturbed his serenity, yet no affront was ever forgotten. IIe never clamored for revenge, and never failed to obtain it. To those who aided his plans he was a faithful ally ; to those who openly opposed, a dangerous but yet pleasing enemy ; to those who sought to undermine and betray, a power that never failed to countermine and crush.

With his great contemporaries he offered a strange contrast. While John Quincy Adams scourged and distrusted all, he spoke ill of none. To Jackson, turbulent, boisterous, impulsive, and stubborn rather than determined, he was a rudder unseen, quiet, often unshipped, yet in the end preserving him from the disaster he invited. To Calhoun he was a calm, unruffled mirror, in which that clamorous and ambitious controversialist read his doom of defeat and mortification. To Webster and Clay he was a fate that disarmed their eloquence, thwarted their schemes, detected their ambition and defied their disappointment. In short, he is the one man in our history who always stood alone and yet for a quarter of a century was a leader of the majority. IIe was called " the Little Magician," and the genius which transformed the country tavern-keeper's son into the most successful of party leaders justified the title.

In 1844 this man met with a disaster which he knew was irretrievable. IIis knowledge of public sentiment, wider, keener, more accurate than any other of his day possessed, told him that he had no hope of re-establishing himself in the seat of power. Age had already left its impress upon him, though he was yet erect, his step elastic, his eyes undimmed and his tones as even and decisive as ever. For almost forty years he had been in public life, filling perhaps more positions of honor and trust and discharging more varied and responsible duties than any other citizen of the republic has been called upon to perform. His was that ripeness of knowledge and intellect that is an invaluable adjunct to any fixed purpose. As a statesman he was the best trained of his time. As a diplomatist he was unmatched at home or abroad. As a politician he was the envy of friend and foe alike. This man, in the ripeness of his powers, was relegated to the private station partly through the envy of his inferiors, and partly through the operation of a cause that remains to be traced.

The State of New York was really the theatre in which the first political battles of the Anti-Slavery movement were fought. It is true that New England has generally claimed the leadership of this movement, as, in a sense, she very well deserves to do. But the Empire State was that in which it first became an active and important political factor, and there, chiefly because of its co-operation with different cabals in the Democratic party. In that State the old Republican party, and its successor in doctrine and *personnel*, the Democratic, was not only very strong from the beginning of the century until the time of which we write, but the State had also produced a surprising number of political leaders of that faith. The success of several of these had been such, not only in the politics of the State but in the councils of the nation, as to inspire in them a just and reasonable desire to become the candidate of their party for the highest place. Each had his particular followers, and this struggle for the leadership of the Democracy of the Empire State offered the first practicable opportunity for the new doctrine to obtain lodgment inside of established party lines. She gave it a foothold that seems surprising when we reflect how few outspoken advocates it had among her recognized intellectual leaders. Already, in 1840, when first a vote was cast for Anti-Slavery candidates for President and Vice-President, there were almost twice as many in New York who were willing to accept the odium of "Abolitionism" as in Massachusetts, and these two States furnished more than half of the seven thousand voters of the "Liberty" party. By 1844, this number in New York had increased from three thousand to fifteen thousand, still leading Massachusetts by fifty per cent. of its vote, and furnishing one-fourth of the entire following of the new party.

This was the situation of affairs when Martin Van Buren received his death blow as a political leader in the Democratic Convention at Baltimore. Samson was shorn and blinded. In the silence of retirement he meditated his revenge.

The State of New York has always been noted, not only for the struggle of factions within the great political parties, but also for the nomenclature that has been adopted to designate them. In this respect it has been in striking contrast with the New England States, which, except in a few instances, have hardly ever departed from the orthodox designations of the national parties. Considering the general reputation for humor which attaches to the New England character and the contrasted repute for phlegm which has been attributed to the citizens of the Empire State, this is somewhat remarkable. Especially is this true when we consider the grotesque and ludicrous epithets that have prevailed in the latter State—"Locofoco," "Hunker," "Barnburner," "Silver Grey," "Woolly Heads," and many others of equal insignificance at the present time, but each constituting at the time of its adoption a nickname that expressed some actual or supposed character-

istic of the faction to which it was applied. Some of
these are said to have been self-assumed. Others were
adopted by the parties in defiance of the ridicule attempted to be conveyed by them. Some, as "Locofoco,"
spread beyond the boundary of the State and became
accepted party designations in other states. This one
is said to have ·been derived from the use of matches—
then a luxury just beginning to be common in the
land, displacing the ancient flint and steel, which was
not entirely dispossessed until the century had almost
reached its meridian—and called by their supposed
inventor "Locofocos." These matches, much more
strongly charged with sulphur than the modern match,
are said to have played a prominent part in one of the
meetings of the faction, which thence took its name.
Another faction was compared by a wit to a farmer
who burned his barn to rid himself of the rats who
devoured his grain. Thence they were termed thereafter "Barnburners," a name which for a time bade fair
to usurp the place so long held by that king of denun-
ciatory epithets, "Abolitionist." "Silver Greys" and
"Woolly Heads" were epithets applied to Whig factions, corresponding very nearly with the "Hunkers"
and "Barnburners" of the Democracy, and representing respectively the conservative and liberal elements
of the parties. In the period between 1844 and 1848
this epithetic warfare was at its height. The struggle
of factions seemed constantly intensified during this
time by some unseen power which never rested. No
sooner was one breach healed than one even more
dangerous discovered itself. The acknowledged leaders
of the Democracy became mysteriously estranged. Apparently Van Buren did nothing, but accepted as his
quietus the defeat he had received. There were some
who professed to see his handiwork in this distracted
and warring condition of the Democracy. Others saw

in it only the lack of his fostering care and marvelous tactical skill. The one counted it as due to his
active machinations; the others attributed it solely to
his indifference. It was tacitly understood that he no
longer felt himself bound to bear true faith and allegiance
to his old party. During the Presidential campaign that
followed he remained loyal to his party colors, or if he
did not co-operate in the election of Polk, he at least
refrained from any overt act that could be accounted
bad faith in a defeated candidate. That election, however, loosed his bonds. He had been defeated by the
Southern wing of his party. They had opposed him
solidly, and, by an alliance with the followers of Cass
and others of less note, had adopted the two-thirds
rule, which made Van Buren's nomination impossible.
This was charged upon Cass as an act of bad faith, and
the events which followed seem to sustain the imputation.

It had been alleged against Van Buren that he was
not true to the South, and that section, always jealous
of those whom it favored with its support, under the
inspiration of some whose motive was no doubt partly
that of revenge, declared against him. How far the
charge is true it is hard at this time to determine. That
he was impelled by his sagacity to be progressive there
is no doubt. He knew human nature well enough to
understand that men could not always be kept fighting
over and over again the same old battles. He knew
that the successful leader must always be fecund of
new issues. In his own State he had won and held his
leadership by originating and adopting various new
departures. Upon assuming the presidential chair he
had at once devised a new method of evincing his sub-
serviency to the slavery power by declaring in advance
his purpose to veto all measures affecting that institution in the District of Columbia. Excepting his oppo-

sition to Calhoun, there is little if anything in his career to justify the inference that he was ever lukewarm in his support of slavery.

The Democratic Convention of 1848 was held in May, and Lewis Cass was its nominee for President, receiving the almost undivided support of the Southern members. The time was therefore ripe for his revenge. The Southern wing of the Democracy, which had deserted from his standard, was now united in interest with Cass who, he claimed, had betrayed him, while Marcy and other great leaders of the North felt in some degree the sting that rankled in his own breast. In August thereafter, a "Free Soil" Convention was held at Buffalo. · It was the old Liberty party under a new name, and in it was a new element. Martin Van Buren was its candidate for President, and when the votes were counted, at the close of the day of which we have written, a hundred and twenty thousand of the freemen of New York stood where four years before there had been but fifteen thousand. Almost one-half the Free Soil strength was found within her borders. Zachary Taylor was elected and Lewis Cass defeated by thirty-six electoral votes—the electoral votes of New York. The shorn and blinded Samson had pulled down the temple on those who mocked at him.

Four years afterwards, the Free Soil vote of New York had fallen back to twenty-five thousand. By a comparison of the votes of 1844, 1848 and 1852, it will be seen that in New York Van Buren not only received the full strength of the Free Soil vote, but also carried to it fully *one hundred thousand votes from the Democratic party!* There is little in his previous or subsequent career to justify the belief that he accepted the principles of the party whose cause he apparently espoused. Indeed, he can hardly be said to have expressed approval of them at all. He merely engaged to carry them into effect if elected, which, as he had no hope of an election, was a promise cheaply made. He indulged in some platitudes with regard to the danger of Slavery as an element of our national life, which hardly any one would have presumed to question then, and which he lived to see fulfilled in a way that astounded him so greatly as almost conclusively to prove that his utterance of these warning words was merely a perfunctory recognition of a growing public sentiment and not a positive conviction. That he secured the unhesitating support of a party to which he had previously been peculiarly obnoxious, and at the same time, after two defeats, carried so great a portion of his own party into the camp of their bitterest opponents, without patronage, without hope of success, and without faith in the future of the movement with which he was identified, is a testimony to his power such as few men have ever received. To have detected the underlying tendency toward freedom in the hearts of his own followers who had hitherto been the professed allies of Slavery, is also a proof of that marvelous sagacity which marked his career.

CHAPTER VIII.

ON GUARD.

MRS. KORTRIGHT was not long left alone with her two invalids. The wives of the neighbors, who had unexpectedly returned home at midday, no sooner heard the story of the strange happenings at Paradise Bay, than they were clamorous in their reproaches of the carelessness manifested by their respective husbands in leaving the good woman to care for her sick ones, even for an hour. The snow had hardly time to melt under the feet of the sympathetic dames on their way to supply their husbands' delinquencies. The story spread through the neighborhood, and from every one came offers of assistance. Willing hands and kindly hearts crowded to the house of pain, with that earnest alacrity that prevails where men are not so thickly crowded together as to care nothing for the well-being of those that live beyond the barrier of a party-wall. At that time, our American life had not become so distraught with the events of the world outside as to forget the duties of good neighborship. The lightning which brought "the uttermost parts of the earth" to our doors, also put far away from us the joys and sorrows of the vicinage. The world's life comes into our hearts with the morning sunlight. We know the woes of India and feel the throbbing of the great guns that pour their iron wrath upon Alexandria. We know how all the peoples of the earth are faring, almost hour by hour. From Irkutsk to Zululand, not a heart bleeds or a frame suffers with heat or cold, famine or pestilence, but we know its ill before the going down of the sun. Our sympathy reaches out and gathers in the whole world. "Who is my neighbor?" is no longer a conundrum. Our charity embraces the world, and humanity is the boundary of duty. Yet the old-fashioned neighborhood is no more. Beyond the threshold of the front door, all the world is alike to us. Printing-press and telegraph and telephone—steam and light-ning—have annihilated time and space. To be face to face is naught; to be eye to eye is a useless luxury. The world's heart-beat comes through the ear or pulses along the printed page. Contiguity is nothing. The street puts asunder as far as the sea. San Francisco is nearer to New York than the hill-top and the valley were when Martin Kortright, bruised and sore from crown to sole, lay moaning in his troubled sleep and dreaming of the enchanted castle, ten miles away from the house which could never more prison his life within its walls. His banner-tree from far Japan had made him a true knight-errant from the hour when he had borne it so gallantly to his first joust with evil-working force—the griffin that sought him in the hour of his self-abnegating watch.

In that day, the meanest dweller in the Valley could not feel the touch of sickness without knowing the ministry of willing hands and the cheer of kindly faces and hopeful tones from those who honored the then unfor-gotten name of neighbor. When Martin awoke, there-fore, he found the house full of friends. There was a superfluity of care. Many hands made light the house-hold work. He was urged to eat and sleep, to keep silent, and to talk of the day's adventures, almost at the same time. His lounge was transformed into a bed by being turned front to the wall and piled high with downy feather beds and swelling pillows—the store of provident generations of exemplary housekeepers. All was bustle

and confusion in the living-room where the bruised boy
lay, but at the door which led to his father's room the
kingdom of silence began.   There none entered but
his mother, to whom the restful gloom was a needed
refuge, and the nurse who had quietly installed himself
in charge.   Now and then there appeared at the door
a dark face, and a tall form came forth with noiseless
steps, the appearance of whom at once hushed the chatter of the neighbor women, who did nothing but watch
his movements until he returned to his duties at the
Squire's bedside.   This was Unthank, the butler or
" head-man" of the servant household of Sturmhold.
Captain Hargrove had not exaggerated his capacity as a
nurse, and his efficiency on this occasion was greatly
enhanced by the fact of his color.

Though hardly a generation had passed since the abolition of slavery in the state, the number of blacks was
so few in many of the rural districts that they were
looked upon, especially after the anti-slavery crusade
was well under way, with a strange mixture of pity
and dread.   The quick imagination clothed every dusky
face with the romance of oppression and suffering.   To
have been a slave was to be a hero.   To the wide eyes of
the neighbor women, well-read in the literature that was
already becoming a part of the daily food of the Northern mind, Unthank—who had been a slave and might
be a slave again for aught they knew—was the impersonation of the woes and wrongs of all his race.   His
kindly, dark brown face was to them a mask behind
which all the evils of slavery were hidden.   A scar
upon the temporal angle of his broad brow, a slight
limp in his gait, were to their teeming fancies texts
from which a woeful history was woven.   The careful
quiet of his movement, the lightness of his slippered
footfall, the noiseless opening and shutting of the door,
his softly modulated tones that seemed to die away as

soon as they had passed his lips, the instinctive order-
ing of every breath and movement to meet the need
and comfort of another—all these were evidence to
these watchful eyes of the servitude which had warped
his nature and made him as different from them in
character as in appearance. Then, too, his language,
though not the broad dialect of the plantation, was
unmistakably Southern, and had a charm for their unaccustomed ears which, indeed, no familiarity can destroy. So they answered his inquiries nervously and
hurriedly, shrunk from the accidental touch of his
hand with a shiver which brought with it a blush of
shame, watched him wonderingly, but kept away from
his peculiar domain—the bedside of the sick man.

The Doctor came again toward night, nodded approval of what had been done, left new directions
and more medicine, cautioned Mrs. Kortright to take
abundant rest, and went away promising to come early
in the morning. For the boy he predicted swift recovery; of the father he said little. A daughter of one of
the neighbors had consented to come and "do the house
work" as long as her assistance should be required.
A neighbor volunteered to look after the stock until a
man could be hired. So the struggle with disease began.
The lad recovered speedily. Young flesh soon forgets
its bruises. The sudden snow had hardly time to flee
away before he had left his improvised couch and caught
a glimpse of the stained whiteness here and there in
sheltered nooks. The broken arm had hardly time to
lose the charm of oddity before he almost forgot its
existence. He was kept a prisoner still, but a most
unwilling one. With the master of Paradise Bay, the
case was different. His room was kept dark and silent.
The nurse passed noiselessly in and out. Low moans
were sometimes heard within. The Doctor came and
went, till he grew to be an accustomed presence. The

neighbors gathered and in hushed tones inquired of the sick man's condition. Mrs. Kortright grew pale and anxious-looking. The spring sunshine had started the sap in the maples on the hillsides before the doubtful issue was decided.

A week after "the great snow-storm" the Indian summer had resumed its interrupted sway. Unprecedented mildness followed the sudden irruption of winter, but the gloom that pervaded the household was beginning to tell upon the spirits of Martin Kortright. He began to grow peevish and discontented. His mother's preoccupied anxiety was a serious deprivation to him. He had been her pet in a quiet way. Now she seemed almost to have forgotten him, or remembered him only to weep over him. Harrison Kortright had not been a demonstrative man in his household, but he had been its head in a most emphatic sense. He had ruled it not by conscious assertion but with unconscious power. Theoretically, his wife had sometimes differed from him ; practically, she would as soon have thought of attempting to live without air as of failing to anticipate his wishes. He was the king of Paradise Bay, not because he wished to rule, but because he was one of those men who cannot help ruling. He had impressed himself upon the house, the farm buildings, every rood of land and every rod of fence and wall. To take him out of its life was to remove not the steersman but the rudder. The boy felt this all the more keenly because of his own weakness. It hung about his spirit like a nightmare. He forgot his joys and anticipated only sorrow.

One morning he was gazing out of the window in this mood of restless discontent, when all at once his pale face lighted up and he forgot his troubles as he cried out to his mother, who chanced to be preparing something at the stove ;

"Oh, mother, mother, here they are again!"

"You don't say!" she said, catching his tone—glad in spite of her sorrow for the joy it betrayed—"and who might 'they' be?"

"Why, the Captain—Captain Hargrove and—and the little girl and—and *the horses*," responded Martin, with an admiring stress upon the last words, which showed unmistakably that the prancing bays, whose glistening coats gave no hint of the rough usage of a week before, eclipsed in importance to his mind the other personages he named.

His eyes danced with joy as he stood gazing at them and the carriage which, though by no means magnificent, seemed to him the very perfection of luxury. It was only a double-seated phaeton with the top thrown back, light and bright save where some splashes of the autumn mud attested a sharp drive over the country roads. On the front seat was a colored driver, while the owner and his daughter sat behind wrapped in robes; for the weather, though bright, was bracing at that hour. The Captain smoked a cigar. The driver wore gloves. The harness was richly mounted with silver. So intent had the boy been in observing these things that he hardly had noticed Hargrove spring out, throw away his cigar and come quickly along the porch, until he heard a light knock at the door and saw his mother hasten to open it, somewhat flushed, wiping her hands upon her apron and giving a hasty touch to her hair, with the feminine instinct of making herself presentable, on the way between the stove and the doorway.

"Good morning, Mrs. Kortright," said the visitor, removing his hat, bowing and speaking in low tones which of themselves expressed sympathy and consideration. "How are all this morning?"

The emphasis implied that he knew how they were yesterday, and brought to the hearers' minds the fact that every day since the accident a messenger had come from Sturmhold to make this inquiry on his behalf.

"About the same, Mr. Hargrove," answered the comely matron, who still felt somewhat abashed in the presence of this man, who seemed to belong to a sphere · of life with which she was unfamiliar. She was not at all oppressed with any sense of inferiority, but only embarrassed by the ease of his address. "Won't you come in ?" she added, as she threw open the door and stepped backward to bring a chair.

"Ah, here is our little hero," said Hargrove, as he entered. "How is he ? I am glad to see him up, at all events."

The boy hung back at first bashfully, but there was no resisting the dark-bearded stranger, who took him by the hand, spoke so pleasantly and had such a charm of mystery about him. He drew the boy toward him as he sat down and kept holding his hand afterward. Martin noticed the contrast between his own hand, even after a week's sickness, and the soft, firm palm in which it rested. There was nothing effeminate about the man, whom he watched furtively as he stood beside him. He had heard during the days he had been confined to the house astounding stories of his strength. It was said by the neighbors, who witnessed the rescue of father and son, that he had thrown the horses right and left as if they had been sheep, instead of the finest span of high-bred roadsters within a circle of fifty miles at least. So the whiteness of his hand was all the more amazing to the boy, who contrasted with it his brown fingers with their irregular and grimy nails.

"I am afraid he is not much of a hero to-day," said Mrs. Kortright, reproachfully. "He has been fretting and teasing ever since he woke up."

"Just what I expected, and that is why I drove

around this way," said the Captain. "Wouldn't you like to take a ride, George?"

"His name is Martin," said the mother.

"Martin, eh? That's a good name, but it should be George—after Saint George of England."

"I had rather be named after George Washington," said the boy sturdily.

"St. George of America, eh? Well, either one. They were both born knights, and need not be ashamed to give their names to a boy who does what you did."

"Now, now, Mister Hargrove, don't," said Mrs. Kortright deprecatingly. "I'm afraid they're going to spoil the boy with praise."

"Do not fear, Madame. Praise that is honestly earned is not apt to do harm."

He touched, as he spoke, the gray end of the fingers that peeped above the wrappings of the splinted arm. His look was reverent, and his touch was a caress. The mother was moved by his earnestness, and said, apologetically:

"You don't know, sir, how much has been said about it. I am afraid it will make him vain."

"Not as vain as you are of him," said Hargrove, glancing archly up at her.

"I?" she asked blushing, but now quite at her ease.

"Yes, you. But what about the ride? Would you like it, George—Martin, I mean?"

"Oh, mother, may I?" he asked in pleading tones, seeing her look of dissent.

"Really, I am much obliged to you for thinking of it, but "—

"Madame," said he earnestly, "please do not make me feel that I can do nothing but harm in the world!" His face grew sad as he spoke, and Mrs. Kortright hastened to say:

"Indeed, sir, you have been very kind. I am sure

nobody could have done so well as your—your man, Unthank. If—if, when *he* gets well"—nodding toward the sick room, while the tears sprang to her eyes—"he will tell you how grateful we all are for your kindness."

"Do not say so, Madame," Hargrove answered huskily, rising to his feet to conceal his emotion. "But let me take this boy for an airing. It would give my little girl great pleasure."

The mother could not resist this earnest appeal. Martin was soon ready and took his first taste of luxury, as he reclined against the strong man's breast upon the back seat, the dark-eyed Hilda sitting face toward him on the front one, and was bowled along over the undulating roads by the horses, whose very hoof-beats were music to his ears. The bright sky, the soft swinging carriage, the even-voiced, black-bearded man of mystery, the balmy air, the autumn colors mixed with the dark hemlocks on the hillsides—all made it the perfection of bliss to the convalescent boy. He wondered if Elijah was happier in the Chariot of Fire.

When they returned, the Doctor was at Paradise Bay, and added his approval, almost his command, to Hargrove's request that he might take the boy for a time to Sturmhold. The mother, with much doubt as to what "Father" would say, finally consented, and after dinner Martin was whirled away again, the first time he had ever left father and mother for a night. The day's excitement had been rather too much for his weakened frame, and his mother's kiss was hardly dry upon his cheek before, lulled by the easy motion of the carriage, he fell asleep in the arms of his strange new friend. When he awoke it was in wonderland.

CHAPTER IX.

HARGROVE'S QUARTER.

MERWYN HARGROVE was of a notable if not famous ancestry. His father, St. John Hargrove, was one of the most deserving officers of the infant navy of our young republic. His family was of the old colonial day, and their plantation, bordering on one of the sounds that indent the Southern coast, had long been noted for the hospitality and sturdiness of successive generations of the rugged English stock who had become possessors of many a square mile of alternate swamp and intervening level, long before the third George had trouble with his Occidental dependencies.

On the bank of a beautiful inland lake, and within bow-shot of one of those deep and narrow streams that lazily wind in and out among the gray-bearded trees that line its banks, and loiter about the arching roots of the surrounding cypresses as if they had forgotten which way they should run, stood the old family mansion. Twenty miles away, across a shallow bay, and beyond a low range of hills through which a narrow channel, known as Hargrove's Inlet, gave a dangerous passage in and out, the Atlantic showed a long, low line of lazily-bursting waves in fair weather, and in storm a mile in width of yeasty billows that left stretches of bare sand between pursuer and pursued, as they chased each other inward toward the line of shifting hills which the ocean's wrath had piled up to defeat its progress. The Sound—a river balked of its will and spreading itself up and down the coast for half a hun-

95

dred miles in search of an outlet—was barely a mile
away. The water of the lake and of the shallow wells
dug here and there upon the plantation, was sweet,
though not without a yellowish tinge and a flavor that
spoke of the swamp and the cypress. The land was
of astonishing fertility, a black, loamy sand, lying just
above the water level, full of peaty fibre which burned
like punk if it happened to take fire in the dry summer
time, and told the story of its creation as plainly as if
written with a pen. Out of the marshy shore the sea
had builded its own barriers. The sandy, undulating
ridges had once been barren hills like those that
stretched along the shore beyond. The reedy levels
had been transformed to rich alluvial beds. The prisoned river had thrust itself between the ridges in search
of an outlet. The tributary streams had followed the
same windings. The swamp had come and fenced the
waters from the land with its clinging growth. Then it
caught the sands with its rootlets; balked the winds
with its yielding branches; crowded back the sea and
staked off the channels of the rivers. With the water
in the estuaries it fought a constant warfare until deep,
dark channels only were left to them. What the sea
threw up in scorn the earth received gladly and transformed into an impassable bulwark against the assault
of her enemy.

Here, early in the history of our country, one Dobson
Hargrove had fixed his habitation, which, after the
fashion of that region, was thenceforth known as "Hargrove's Quarter"; none knew by what right, and he did
not care. It was vaguely understood that "sixty-nine
miles wide from sea to sea" had been given to one of
England's nobles under the broad seal of the realm, to
hold forever, subject only to a yearly tribute of "twelve
ears of Indian corn and twelve choice beaver skins for
the royal robes." This principality unquestionably in-

cluded the tract on which the original Hargrove first made settlement. But there were few at that time to report the trespass, and fewer still who cared whether the King's favorite or the King's yeoman enjoyed the soil.

So, year after year, the occupancy of Hargrove extended. Despite its beauty and the fertility of the soil, the situation was not one to attract neighbors. It was a minutely divided delta. Between swamps and channels and estuaries, where the balked tide rose and fell almost imperceptibly, lay arable levels of sand and peat which had once been the bottoms of lagoons. Here and there a little bank of crumbling, sand-mixed clay showed above the level—the foundation of some old-time bar, behind the shelter of which the waves had deposited the sandy tribute of ages. The cypress and the water oaks held the swamps and borders of the channels. The pines grew dense and close above the sandy reaches that lay between. Some scrubby oaks and dogwoods crowned the rare banks of clay. The channels were many and devious; the sandy reaches narrow. The corn was gathered with batteaux. Broad ditches joined the inlets and made the roadways of the Quarter.

The log house which Hargrove built commanded the little lake which was the key to the situation. The trough in which it lay had been burned out by fire, and the clayey filter through which its waters came kept them sweet and fresh. Year after year, the squatter "took in" more and more of the pine levels, and by implication extended his sway over the swamps and estuaries that intervened. A few cattle occupied an enormous range. He waged war on the wild beasts that disputed his dominion, and the barriers he built against them, in time, were transformed into muniments of title which the lord of the manor himself could not overthrow.

This sturdy English settler could not have helped

being a fisherman and a hunter. On the point which
jutted into the sound, at the mouth of the narrow river
that ran by the Quarter, had been an Indian fishing
camp of much repute among the aborigines. Indeed,
for almost a hundred years after the first Hargrove
settled at the Quarter, they were wont to come, even
from the mountains, two hundred miles to the westward, in the season when the shad and herring ran, to
catch and dry their stores and market the winter's
peltry. The woods were as full of game as the waters
of fish, and the settler was too wise a man to waste his
time in cultivating a soil that supplied nearly all his
wants without labor. The little that he grew was for
luxury rather than need. It was only when he became
the owner of slaves that the hunter-fisherman was transformed into a planter.

Little by little the dug-out in which he had been wont
to visit the settlements up the river and along the coast
grew into a more pretentious craft. A clumsy shallop
took its place, and this in turn gave way to a sloop not
overly trim in her rig but whose lines displayed the skill
of her northern builder, and whose performances, both
on the doubtful waters of the sound and in the roughest
seas outside the bar, soon made her master's name justly
famous in the coastwise traffic of the day. Before the
third generation had been gathered to their fathers
"Hargrove's Quarter" had become a busy hive. The
owner's one sloop had increased to a little fleet that plied
back and forth between the West Indies and the settlements of all the Southern colonies—sometimes engaged
in legitimate traffic, but more frequently setting at defiance the laws of the realm. Then it was that they became not only navigators but cultivators, too. Slaves
were cheap in the Indies, often indeed a drug in the market, and the shrewd Carolinian not only found his advantage in introducing the new laborers upon the mainland,

but thereby also secured an abundant supply for himself. The Quarter became a barracoon which supplied the planters who dwelt along the river above. Overseers and drivers and an array of subordinates, who did his will ashore and afloat, gathered about the occupant of the Quarter, so that when the lord of the manor sent the king's officers to dispossess the intruder, to spoil his improvements and to tear down the house he was building of bricks brought from France by way of Martinique, they found a host ready to oppose them, and came away the worse for the affray they had provoked. The buccaneer planter was ready to hold by force what he had taken without leave. Then the powers that were became his enemies. For a time he even was an outlaw by formal proclamation of the judges of the assize, held far enough away to be safe from his reprisals—though it is reported that once, in a jolly mood, he found two of the king's judges crossing the sound, and compelled them and their attendants, the peripatetic barristers of that day, willy-nilly to come aboard his sloop, brought them to the Quarter, and kept them for a week's carouse, during which the rum of St. Croix flowed by the tierce and the wine of Madeira by the tun. At the end of that time, his sloop took them by night to the town where they should have entered an appearance a week before, and they were left asleep upon the porch of the Ordinary, to awake in the morning dazed with their long debauch, afraid and ashamed to confess their delinquency, and so unable to account for their absence. This very delay was afterwards solemnly recounted as one of the grievances which the colonists averred that they had suffered at the hands of the king's servants. Tales of wrecks and spoils are told to this day of the owner of Hargrove's Quarter. It was believed that sometimes on the Spanish Main his vessels carried the black flag. A strange, rough company gathered around him. Half the popu-

lation of two or three neighboring towns were really his
retainers. Every squatter in the piney-woods was a spy
in his pay and interest. No bailiff could come nigh
by land or water without warning being given of his
approach. When he went into the towns he had a following about him that forbade his arrest. "Hargrove
of Hargrove's Quarter" would probably have been
hanged at the yard-arm of some one of Her Majesty's
men-of-war, had not the opportunity occurred for him to
exchange the rôle of a buccaneer for that of the patriot.

That the Hargroves grew rich goes without saying.
Every time that one of their staunch little coasters drove
her smutty nose through the chopping waves of the tortuous inlet that made through sand-hills and surf just
below the long, low cape that masked the entrance, and
was warped to her hidden berth in the narrow river
that flowed by the "Quarter," it brought new stores of
wealth. They were not merchants, yet they bought
and sold for half the planters round about. The rivers
and the sounds were then the sole highways between
these low-lying principalities. The dug-out and the bat-
teau brought produce and took away merchandise to the
"up-country." Even the sea was in league with them.
If argosies foundered upon the coast, the best of all the
waves cast up found its way to their storehouses. Strange
stories are yet told in the cabins of the "sand-hill-
ers" and "hog-hunters" in the piney-woods, of a horse
that was trained to bear a lantern up and down the
rolling dunes that formed the cape, when the storm
drove to the northwestward, to lure passing ships upon
the breakers. Perhaps men whispered it to each other
at that time, but they said nothing about it to the master of Hargrove's Quarter. Some may have disapproved
his methods but few hesitated to profit by them. If
the wine he sold was rich and old, they asked not how
it came into his possession. If tea was cheaper on the

inland river bank than in the harbor of Charleston, they did not discuss the cause. If his rum and molasses were of the best quality, they did not ask to see his invoices.

The Quarter grew populous, but it was all the property of the master. He built no docks; he invited neither partnership nor competition. The cypress-lined river still hid his craft, which rarely came or went by day, and only stayed to discharge and receive their cargoes. They belonged, nominally, to other ports. They traded between city and city. They were simple coasters beyond the bar. They ran in and out without making any entry in the log of the variation from the accustomed track. It was an easy thing. There were few to watch and few to go astray in those days. The wind's wings were the swiftest messengers then known upon the earth. Twenty miles to the westward, the highway from the South to the already more boisterous and adventurous North crossed the river, whose swollen surface made the sound. Couriers sometimes came express to Hargrove's Quarter by that route, taking boat at the town. Gentlemen left their carriages sometimes, and came in the same way to enjoy his hospitality. The little lake lay in the heart of a wondrously fertile plantation now. Road there was none leading into this checkered domain. The driver's horn mustered slaves by the hundred when he wound it at daylight. There was hunting and fishing and lavish hospitality.

Yet, despite their power, the Hargroves were not on terms of familiarity with the planter aristocracy whose residences dotted the river banks above, though not one in twenty of them could show a tithe of his substance. After a while, there came a time when this fact galled the hereditary prince of the "Quarter." He determined to conquer his neighbors as his ancestors had conquered the obstacles that beset them. So his only son was

educated to be a gentleman.   He was sent to travel
through New England.   He made the voyage to Europe.
The revenues of the Quarter were placed at his disposal.   His lavish hand and cultivated manner obtained
him entrance to homes and hearts.   The semi-feudal
aristocracy of Virginia received him.   He became familiar with that strange group of democratic exclusives,
whose burning eloquence held the Southern settlements
to a movement utterly inconsistent with their development, but which grew as naturally out of the animating
impulse of the Northern colonies as the flower comes
from the bud.   Away from his home, the young Hargrove was welcomed by the best and esteemed of all.
At home he was only the heir of the Quarter—the son
of old Nathaniel Hargrove, the hard-working, hard-
drinking, hard-headed master of princely revenues, but
of ill repute.

From his son the father caught the fever of the time.
The thought that was working like yeast in the hearts
of the colonists just suited his adventurous spirit.   To
defy power of any sort was to him a luxury.   All at
once he became a leader.   When a meeting was held a
hundred miles away to consider what the grievances of
the people were, and what remedies ought to be adopted,
he summoned his henchmen and appeared upon the day
appointed at the head of a following so considerable
that the officers who were commissioned to disperse
the assembly counted it the part of prudence not to
interfere.

When the Congress met in Philadelphia, one of his
sloops was lying in the Delaware, and when the Declaration was signed, his son sent him word by sea and
Jefferson sent couriers by land to announce the great
event.   From that hour Hargrove's Quarter lost its evil
name.   Patriotism sanctified both its surroundings and
its antecedents.   Interest and inclination ran hand in

hand. Successful rebellion meant to the Hargroves security of title and undoubted position. The best families of the colony were nearly all rebels, many from motives hardly less questionable than his. They were all outlaws together, and he was most esteemed who could do most to promote the common unlawful end. The practical sagacity and boldness of the master of the Quarter made him a leader in their counsels. The son trod the quarter-deck of a letter of marque. The change was more apparent than real. What the rakish coaster was reputed to have done before the privateer now did openly. There were many adventures both by sea and land. The son was captured and confined in the prison-ship at New York. One privateer was cast upon the beach as she sought to make the inlet heavily laden with spoils. Tarleton burned the Quarter. The slaves died by the score of a strange sickness that broke out among them. Yet Nathaniel Hargrove never faltered. He gave as long as he had. Then he pledged his credit, which was almost unlimited. The new government's promises to pay were never dishonored by his non-acceptance. Robert Morris wrote him a letter of thanks for his sturdy co-operation with him in maintaining the sinking credit of the infant nation.

When the war ended, he had great store of Continental currency, a good title to the lands he had held before by sufferance, a burden of debt, and unbounded faith. Patriotism had not paid so well as his old trade, but he was not discouraged. He began at once to rebuild the Quarter. He bought new ships and began to trade again with the Indies. His son had won fame and died in the prison-hulks. His grandson, though only a lad of fourteen, had been with Paul Jones on the *Bon Homme Richard* and shared his captain's glory. For a time it seemed as if he would rehabilitate his shaken fortunes. The new States were not swift to offer remedies to the creditors. Nathaniel Hargrove shirked nothing. He believed in the dingy paper piled up in boxes, and barrels even, in the rude cabin that served him for an office. When it finally became worthless by express repudiation, his hope failed and his heart broke. He died, leaving the Quarter to his grandson, greatly reduced in acreage and sadly encumbered with honest debt.

St. John Hargrove, when he thus became the heir of the shattered fortunes of his family, had just donned the uniform of the navy of the young republic. His pay was meagre, but the prospect of glory was bright. Already another war was imminent. He left the Quarter in charge of an agent to redeem itself. When he was thirty-five, he had seen service in every sea, risen to a captaincy, married a young wife in a Northern city, and sailed away to return no more. A year afterward, when the widow went South to take possession of her dower in the Quarter, she bore a son in her arms whom she had christened Merwyn, after his uncle who had died in the prison-ship during the war for liberty.

Chastine Elverson was a Quaker orphan of small estate and of a soft and tender beauty, when she left the Meeting to marry that son of Belial, St. John Hargrove, the red-handed officer of a man-of-war and reputed owner of vast estates and countless hosts of slaves in one of the Southern States. Perhaps her husband knew nothing of this magnifying of the Southron into a nabob, which has always been characteristic of the North, and which led her almost unconsciously to suppose herself the wife of a magnate rather than a poor officer whose fortune was his sword. Perhaps he hesitated to disturb her silly dream. At all events, he did not undeceive her. It is true he did tell her he had no living relatives; that the old plantation was terribly run down, and that he had not seen it in ten years. What he did not tell her was that he had pinched and saved all he could from his pay as a naval officer to discharge the interest on the mortgage that hung over it. So the young widow was greatly disappointed when she came to view the place her fancy had pictured as the seat of a luxury such as the bleak North could hardly match. The agent who had lived at the Quarter had done little else. The incumbrances that overhung the estate had grown greater rather than less. Her own little dowry and the modest pension allowed her would do little toward discharging the debts that rested on it, but to this task she addressed herself with the utmost devotion, for her son's sake. She had the shrewdness and self-reliance of her sect and people, and saw in the Quarter possibilities which its founder had not discovered.

Colonel Peter Eighmie, who owned a plantation a little up the river, heard of this Quixotic resolution of the fair young widow, and, after many sneers at her folly, concluded to go and give her his advice, or, as he phrased it, "send her back to her people, where she belonged." In pursuance of this resolution, he had himself conveyed to the Quarter, and found the lady he sought supervising some repairs she was having made in order to render habitable for herself and immediate family a part of the unfinished mansion the old patriot had begun. The Colonel was past forty, long a widower and childless. The widow was twenty-four, and very fair. The Colonel's mission was one of pure charity. He had never seen his new neighbor, and only thought of her as a young woman who was going to do a foolish thing. It was not the claim of a vain, boasting plantation life to be called patriarchal. The man who for years had swayed the destinies and cared for the woes and ills of scores of human beings, became accustomed to looking after all his vicinage as a matter of course. It never occurred to this plantation king that there could be any impropriety in the step he was taking, nor did he dream that the foolish woman would for a moment think of rejecting his counsel. He went to scold her as he would a wayward daughter, and expected her to obey with equal readiness. Yet as he came briskly up from the old neglected landing, and saw her standing in the soft autumn sunshine directing the workmen with a quiet resolution in her young face, he was smitten with unconscious respect for the fair dunce he had come to reprove. He advanced, however, and addressed her courteously, introducing himself by name.

"Ah, then you are my neighbor, though you do live miles away ? I am so glad, for it is getting to be lonely already, though the people on the plantation have been very kind," was her reply to his greeting.

"You do mean to live here, then ?" The Colonel drew down his heavy brows and bent his deep gray eyes upon her, as though she had committed a deadly sin by thus presuming to contravene his will even before knowledge of its terror.

"Oh, yes," nervously; "I hope to get it habitable before spring."

"You've plenty of money, I suppose."

"Oh, dear, no. Just enough to fix up a little and furnish supplies for the next year."

"You've got niggers, and stock, and boats, and all that's needed for a plantation that hasn't fed its hands, or hardly more, in twenty years ?"

"Bless me, no sir ; but a friend in Philadelphia has agreed to advance me something on the crop, and I hope to get through somehow."

"Yes—yes," sententiously. "So you will—*somehow.* Do you know, Madame, that this plantation can't be made to bread the hands necessary to work it for the next five years ?"

"Oh, you don't mean it !" she said starting and looking across the lake, incredulously, yet not without perturbation. "Surely, it cannot be true."

"Cannot, eh? Madame, will you please to make inquiries as to Colonel Eighmie's character for truth? And while you are at it, perhaps you may as well ask what he knows about running a plantation."

"Oh, I beg your pardon," she said quickly, turning her great brown eyes upon his face with a plea for mercy. "I know already that you must be both honest and capable, or you could not be Colonel Eighmie of Mallowbanks."

"Thanks, Madame," he answered gravely, bowing acknowledgment of her earnest compliment, "I believe I have earned the reputation you have heard. I am old enough to be your father, ma'am, and came here to advise you for your own good."

"I am sure, sir," she replied, "I shall be very glad to have your advice in redeeming my son's inheritance."

"Meaning this old run-down plantation, I reckon?" sarcastically.

"Of course," quietly.

"How much is the mortgage?"

"About twenty thousand dollars, I believe."

"Well, let me tell you, Madame, it will take twenty thousand more to make it sell for that money."

"Well?" she said quietly, as she looked away from his face across the little lake to the scraggy, half-grown-up fields, which years of neglect had spread where thrift and neatness once had been.

"Well?" he echoed in surprise. "Well? Are you going to undertake such a task?"

"I have twenty years to do it in," she answered absently, still looking across the lake as if she saw the changes she would make, and beheld her son entering upon his unincumbered heritage. "It will be twenty

years before *he* will come of age, and a great deal can
be done in that time, even little by little."

Her look grew fixed and hard as she spoke—more to
herself than to her listener. The fair young cheek
seemed to lose something of its bloom; her lips shut
close, and her hands clasped each other tightly, as she
thus consecrated her life to a harsh duty.

The Colonel looked at her in amazement. He read
the fixed look of self-sacrifice upon her face, and removing his hat, he said in a voice full of respectful
homage :

"Pardon me, Madame, you are right and I was wrong.
You will do it; and it is worth doing. Allow me to
place my poor services at your disposal."

"Oh, thank you, sir," she said brightly, extending her
hand in frank recognition of his sincerity. "Then
please tell me what I ought to do first."

"By all means, change its name."

"Why? Hargrove's Quarter is"—

"A poor name to conjure with," he interrupted.

"But what difference does it make ?"

"Your son's inheritance will be worth a great deal
more if it has a good name. It takes time to change the
style of a plantation, and in this country it is best done
when a change of ownership occurs."

"You think I should mark my coming by giving the
Quarter a new name."

"It will be of great aid in what you have undertaken. The power to name presupposes the power to
hold and control. Your neighbors will esteem you all
the more highly for it."

"I see ; but what shall it be called ?"

"The ancients were accustomed to give names de-
scriptive of some incident attending their first sojourn."

She was silent a moment, looking up into his kind,
strong face. Then she said :

THE CHRISTENING OF "AMITY LAKE."

The Colonel steadied his little hand as it poured a wine-glassful of water on the soil.—p. 169.

A.B.FROST.

"The first good thing the place has brought me is your friendship, sir. Might I call it 'Amity'?"

"You do me too much honor, Madame," said the Colonel, bowing low, with a hint of a flush upon his face at this unexpected reply. He was unaccustomed to the directness which marked her Quaker breeding.

So the young heir was brought out from one of the cabins where he had been left in care of a nurse; the mother held him up; the Colonel steadied his little hand as it poured a wine-glassful of water on the soil, and with much quiet mirth the plantation was re-christened "Amity Lake."

And such it remains, even to this day.

CHAPTER X.

BEFORE Merwyn Hargrove attained the age of two years, "Amity Lake" was joined to "Mallowbanks" by the marriage of Colonel Peter Eighmie with the widow of St. John Hargrove. A year afterward, a half-brother, George Eighmie, was born, and the death of his mother followed close upon this event. Thereupon the twice-widowed gentleman became the legal guardian of Merwyn, and devoted his life to the training of the two boys his wife had committed to his care with her dying breath. No trustee had ever a more scrupulous and tender conscience than Colonel Eighmie. The interests of the heir of Amity Lake were looked after with an exactness greatly exceeding that bestowed upon his own estate. Not only did he insist upon the utmost scrutiny being given to his dealings in this fiduciary capacity, by the Orphans' Court to which he made report, but he even went farther and assumed the responsibility of using his own funds in the betterment of his ward's estate. Between his son and his ward, it was remarked, he never made the slightest difference in his demeanor. Both seemed in an equal degree to be representatives to him of the wife whose memory he adored. The short span of married life which he had passed with her had been to this strong, tender man a foretaste of heaven. Despite his mature years, he seemed only to have begun to live when he first met her. She had awakened him from the lethargy such as is apt to supervene upon years of continuous plantation life ; had given

110

a purpose to his existence and made him again a man of action. Had she lived he would no doubt have been known in much wider fields of influence. His young' wife, demure and staid as she seemed, was yet ambitious, and her love for her children, already stimulated by the fame which her first husband had won, demanded an equal legacy of renown for those that might bear the name of one whom she loved not less deeply and whom she must have felt to be even more worthy of her devotion. Her death, however, put an end to all such aspirations on his part. Thenceforth he had no thought but to promote the welfare and happiness of her children.

To secure this he spared no pains. They grew up together twins in his love and care. Between them, also, subsisted the warmest affection. They were so different in character and temperament that their inclinations rarely clashed, and the sports of the one always supplemented the pleasures of the other. In force and vigor of constitution and character there was much more difference between them than their years would imply. Merwyn, the scion of the unknown yeoman stock that had stolen a piece of the New World and held it in defiance of the laws of the Old, was a sturdy, resolute boy, whom nothing could daunt. Before he had reached the age of a dozen years he had become a fearless navigator of the Sound. Indeed, his little sail-boat had more than once danced about in the disturbed waters of the inlet, and once or twice had even thrust her nose into the blue waters beyond, only to come scurrying back when she reached a point even with the breakers on either side, beyond which the boy had promised his father never to venture alone. The buccaneer instinct early showed in his nature. Not only did he feel quite capable of defending himself, but no show of force could deter him from insisting upon his own right or that of his younger and weaker playmate.

On the other hand, George Eighmie, the heir of the name and blood of a family which, in the person of a brave knight, had come out of Normandy across the Channel with William, and had afterward been famed for deeds of high emprise in many wars, sending at length to the New World a cadet to found a rival house when kingdoms should supplant the forest, was weak in body and timid in mind. He followed his more rugged playmate with the most unquestioning faith. Wherever Merwyn went he was willing to go also, but he never led in any physical sports. In their studies, however, he was easily first, and in the drawing-room and the society of strangers, to which the Southern child is accustomed at a much earlier age than the Northern boy, he was far more self-possessed and accomplished than his sturdy elder brother. These differences grew more marked as the boys grew older, and their mutual devotion also increased. They were almost inseparable; the younger became a hunter and fisher of no mean skill, while the elder grew to be more of a scholar than he would otherwise have become, in order that they might not be separated.

This difference between the two lads did not escape the attention of the watchful man who had been a father to both alike. If he regretted the fact that his own son was of a less rugged type than the elder brother he never expressed his sorrow to either. Prudently refraining from any attempt to change their natural inclinations, he adapted his favors and gifts to their diverse tastes—a horse or a hound to the one and a book or a picture to the other. Amity Lake bade fair to become a hunting lodge; Mallowbanks a scholar's retreat. To the tastes of each the father ministered with equal wisdom and equal pleasure, as it seemed. Yet there were not wanting those who believed that the dead hero's son had a stronger hold upon the doting second husband's heart than his own offspring. This was not strange. He had his mother's great liquid brown eyes and her calm, unshrinking gaze, that looked into the eyes on which they rested as if they saw and read the soul that lay beyond. George, on the other hand, had the gray eyes of his father, deepened into a blue that attested his affectionate tenderness of disposition, but gave no promise of ambition or achievement. The former had one of those restless spirits to whom the world's life offers an irresistible charm. He must do and dare. Without adventure, life to him would not be worth living. His brother might sink down into the sloth of a planter's life. ; he might avoid responsibility and enjoy the repose of a cultivated gentleman of large estate—what his life would be depended very greatly upon the forces that surrounded it. What Merwyn's would be depended more on the character of the task he undertook to perform. If he sought the Northwest passage he would find it—or a grave. He would give his life to a purpose, great or small, with a steadfastness that could not falter. The one might be a dreamer; the other must be a doer. The one might do himself an injury, or even others, from lack of power to resist evil. ; the other would never question the righteousness of anything which he once undertook. Obstacles that would dishearten George Eighmie would only stimulate Merwyn Hargrove.

When Merwyn had reached the age of sixteen these differences had become so palpable that his thoughtful guardian saw it would not do longer to defer the selection of a profession adapted to his temperament. Though it was like parting his heart in twain, Colonel Eighmie could no longer conceal from himself the fact that the best interests of his step-son demanded that he should adopt the profession which his father had honored, and to which the whole family seemed to have an instinctive inclination. It was no difficult matter to secure for the son of St. John Hargrove a commission in the service his father had adorned ; and the young midshipman bade adieu to his home, the brother he loved, and the father whose prescient love had in nowise failed to banish regret for the father he had lost, with a sorrow greatly lightened by the longing of the instinctive sailor for the roll of blue water under his feet. Before he left, his guardian informed him fully of the condition of his estate, showing him that upon arriving at majority he would become master of a plantation not only unencumbered with debt, but yielding a revenue almost equal to its entire value when it fell to him by descent. The skill and care of Colonel Eighmie had transformed the run-down plantation into one the fertility of which he frankly confessed had proved a surprise to himself.

"No one knew, my son," he said in tremulous tones, "no one knew, in that day, what Amity Lake was capable of but your Ma. She, poor dear, saw it all, and shamed my experience with her faith and instinct. She always said that Amity Lake would make you an inheritance equal to any in the State, and it'll nigh about do it, my son ; nigh about."

He gave him a complete inventory of all the personal property in his hands, with a map of the plantation showing the use of the different parts, and requested him to keep these by him and write very fully about his affairs, so that he might become accustomed to the management of his estate through an agent while yet his guardian had it in legal charge.

On the day that Merwyn reached his majority the Colonel filed his final statement as guardian, and transmitted a copy with a letter requesting his ward's instructions as to the selection of an agent, to a distant port, where the young sailor was expected to be about that time. It met and passed in mid-ocean a letter from the young ensign, inclosing a release in full to the guardian, executed on his birthday before the consul of the port, and also an unlimited power of attorney continuing in his hands the management of the estate. The noble old man, still erect and vigorous, though he well knew the end could not be far off, wept tears of happy pride at this exhibition of his step-son's trust in him. He filed the release in the Orphans' Court, calling especial notice to the date as identical with that of his final statement and the fact that it was executed in the port of Fayal—half the world's width away—and proudly desired it to be noted on the record that he consented to the withdrawal and cancellation of this release should his ward at any time see fit to question any of his acts or accountings as guardian and trustee of his estate.

The young officer had little desire to return home. The adventurous life and arduous service of that day suited well his inclination, and it was not till he had passed the age of twenty-five that he came back, browned by exposure, with the regulation bit of whisker just reaching below either ear, and the stiff navy stock rising squarely above shoulders on which rested the epaulettes of a lieutenant. His service had been an honorable one, and the brevet rank in a higher grade, which he had won by special coolness under fire, gave almost as much joy to the fond old man who awaited his coming, as did the dark-eyed little wife whom he brought with him from abroad to be the mistress of Amity Lake. At her solicitation, united to the importunity of his step-father, Merwyn Hargrove quitted the navy and gave himself to the care of his estate, the enjoyment of domestic life, and the solace of the last years of him who had been more than a father to his orphaned state.

For some reason Colonel Eighmie had become estranged from his own son, and, on Merwyn's return, he was still domiciled at Amity Lake, while George resided at Mallowbanks, the use and revenues of which his father had given up entirely to him. Between the two there had not been the slightest intercourse since the son had come of age. Some unpardonable offense had frozen the father's love, and he never mentioned the name of the quiet, studious occupant of his splendid riverside plantation. Merwyn learned from others the cause of the estrangement, and tried to effect a reconciliation, but was at once commanded by the stern old man never to allude to the matter again. He visited his brother and found him leading a quiet, luxurious life—his plantation entirely in charge of the overseer—seeing and desiring no society. The old regard for his elder brother was undimmed by the latter's absence, however, and he entrusted to him fully his version of the difference with his father. Merwyn tried to persuade him to yield the point of controversy, but, on this alone, found him to be inexorable. It was useless to consider the question. He had no ill-will toward his parent—indeed, he wept as he spoke of the estrangement; but he could not yield. Merwyn's wife, Rietta, also conceived a most unconquerable aversion to the luckless George, and did all in her power to persuade Merwyn to cast him off. In this, however, she failed, and her failure became a potent element in the results that followed.

Thus a few years passed away, and the old man sank peacefully into the grave, the idol of the household at Amity Lake, but never reconciled to the quiet, gentle scholar who dwelt at Mallowbanks. People wondered at the father's firmness, but denounced in the most bitter language the scandalous obduracy of the son. He came, indeed, to attend the funeral of his father, but the fiery Italian blood of Rietta gave him a welcome such as he did not care to face again. With the death of Colonel Eighmie, her dislike of the recluse of Mallow-

banks ripened into a hate which did not hesitate to
ascribe to him the death of the father, who had yielded
to only seventy odd years of life's wear and tear.
Then, too, the antipathy against him among the neighboring planters began to increase. With his elder brother alone he remained upon terms of confidence and
affection. Captain Hargrove, as he was now called,
seemed somehow to blame himself for all the moral delinquencies of his weaker brother. When the good
people of the vicinage expressed their disapproval of
his life and conduct, and proposed to visit their wrath
upon the recreant son, they were amazed to find that
the young officer had constituted himself the defender
of his brother. He had always been his protector, and
still felt called upon to assume that rôle. He did not
pretend to justify his brother's course—he did not expect the neighborhood to approve it; but George Eighmie had a right to do as he chose, and no one must interfere with that right except on peril of an altercation
with Merwyn Hargrove. The result of this was that
Merwyn and his young wife were soon included in the
social condemnation visited on their brother, and Amity
Lake was placed under the ban pronounced against
Mallowbanks.

It was because of these things that Captain Hargrove
became the forerunner of that class of ocean-wanderers
known in our day as yachtsmen. To remove Rietta from
the petty annoyances of life at the plantation, and at
the same time minister to his own enjoyment, he procured a noted Boston shipbuilder to make for him a
small sloop, which, while thoroughly seaworthy, should
still be fitted up in a style of luxury worthy of the
bright-eyed queen whose floating palace it was designed
to be. This costly toy was regarded as a marvel of ele-
gance in those days, and the frequenters of the Northern watering-places, where she now and then folded her

white wings for a few weeks' rest, thought the master and mistress of the jaunty little craft must be nabobs of very great wealth.   During one of these summer cruisings they had sailed up the Hudson, and, mooring the sloop in the bay that lies below the Kaaterskills, had started in a carriage to explore at their leisure that region, then in its quiet rural beauty the richest the land afforded, and to-day not excelled in the rare views which are to be seen from its mountain peaks.

Unknown to her husband, the capricious beauty had made up her mind never to return to Amity Lake, and was quietly looking for a new location for the Hargroves of the future.   Though of good family in her native land, the profusion of her planter husband had been such as to impress upon her mind the belief that his resources were inexhaustible.   Accustomed to the blue vistas of the Piedmont, it was but natural that she should weary of the level richness of the plantation. Her lively nature was struck, too, with the greater apparent vivacity, life and energy of the Northern people. Her father, who had become an exile for having plotted for Italian liberty before its day-star had arisen, had infused into his daughter's heart, during their years of refuge in England's sheltering arms, such an intense devotion to personal liberty that her whole nature revolted at slavery.   Her experience at Amity Lake, where the wise and kindly Colonel Eighmie had permitted only its best features to take root and grow, might have lulled her antipathy to slumber, perhaps, but her relations with the master of Mallowbanks did not permit its most offensive features to be forgotten, even for an hour. Rietta Hargrove had therefore determined that her husband, through his love for her, should be induced to transplant the family tree from Carolina to such portion of the more free and enterprising North as she should select for a permanent abiding place.   With this in view,

she had persuaded him to sail up the Hudson, in that
day the paradise of elegant American leisure, whose
picturesque heights and umbrageous valleys had already
been dedicated to luxury by the most intellectual and
scholarly of the fortunate children of the great metropolis. Its jutting headlands were crowned with castles,
fresh and garish enough as yet, and in many instances
somewhat too frail to furnish sightly ruins even in age.
Hidden under its leafy groves were the homes of more
than one of the writers of our classic age. The villas
which fashion is now deserting for other haunts which
the railroad has brought near, were then the summer
rendezvous of all that was best and brightest in the life
of that marvelous little island that lies between the
rivers and rests upon the sea, through which the nation's life-blood flows in a throbbing, ceaseless stream.

These had pleased her fancy well, but she wished to
see the interior before revealing her secret plan to the
husband who, she believed, could deny nothing that she
asked. They traveled leisurely, stopping to climb the
heights that promised the best outlook, comparing all
that they saw with those of their kind in her childhood's
home. The sky was not so blue; the silence and the
brightness of the eternal snows were not there. The
ravines were not so dark nor the valleys so narrow.
But ah, the verdure! The grand umbrageous woods
upon the slopes! The bright waters that ran down between and mingled and grew into placid streams! The
sense of thrift and peace and home! These Piedmont
never knew. The shadows on her hills were as dark
as the sad fate of Italy—torn, distracted, trampled,
bleeding beneath the feet of contending ravishers. This
was an Italy on which English peace had smiled and
where only American abundance dwelt.

It was upon the third day after they left the sloop
that they climbed by a devious path to a wooded table

land, terminating a spur of the mountains which shot out into the valley of the Mohawk between the waters of two of its tributaries. It was a balmy day of early summer. The little plateau on which they stood was carpeted with fragrant verdure. To the eastward, the long range of rugged hills that shut in the level trough of the Hudson showed their western slopes under the morning sun, aflame with the glory of the mountain laurel—billows of rosy light. Beneath, the triple valleys met and stretched away, until the northward limit was lost in distance, while the far western sky was indented with a line of purple heights. Behind them, the mountain rose sharply many hundred feet, its rugged face screened and softened by the dense foliage of low-branching trees that clung to its rocky sides. The valley was a scene of peaceful life. Sleek herds cropped the green pastures. Farmers wrought busily in the fields. Tidily-dressed women passed in and out of the snug homes, engaged in their household labors, and the voice of song came faintly to the ears of the wanderers who from the hill-top first beheld the quiet scene. The roads wound in and out among the hills and through the fields and groves. The sun shone brightly. The bees hummed in the clover at their feet and in among the branches overhead. As they stood there, a storm swept in turbulent wrath down the bed of the western tributary, and melted into a laughing shower in the sunshine of the broader valley.

Rietta watched it all with heaving bosom and with eyes aglow with rapture.

"Ah, Heaven!" she cried, as she clasped her hands and looked over the vale the shower had kissed. "Here would I live! Here would I die! Here is Italy! Here is Ameri-*ka!* Oh, Merwyn—my Merwyn, here must we live—here die! We, *caro mio*, we and—our children!"

Her will was law. Amity Lake was sold, and Sturmhold arose upon the table-land from which they viewed
the summer storm.

It was in the flush times just preceding the great
crash of the Jacksonian era, when speculation ran wild,
and the old Hargrove's Quarter, transformed by Colonel
Eighmie's wise and prudent management into a plantation notable among the finest of the South Atlantic
slope, produced a sum which would have amazed his
buccaneer ancestors even more than it did Merwyn Hargrove. Taken as a piece of business, merely, the impulse of his Italian wife was a most fortunate one.
Sturmhold and the picturesque domain that surrounded
it absorbed but a small proportion of this sum. Of
the remainder a part was invested in the China trade,
with which his foreign service had made him familiar,
and a still greater part, with the timidity of a man but
little accustomed to business, or perhaps with the inherited instincts of his race, he transmuted into coin
and secured in the strong box whose secret hiding place
and mysterious lock were only known to himself and his
faithful servant, Jason Unthank.

So the Southern planter was transformed into the nabob of that portion of the valley. When the crisis
came, a few years later, the master of Sturmhold, instead of being in the least harmed by it, found the pur-
chasing power of his hoarded coin trebled and quadru-
pled. It was then that the commercial instincts of the
people by whom he was surrounded first took hold upon
him, and he bought farm after farm, to right and left
and up and down the tributaries, until his domain
rivaled in extent the possessions of those who had taken
by virtue of the King's grant or by pretended purchase
from the aborigines. Then, too, his swift-sailing sloop
lost somewhat of her holiday neatness and made long
trips, whose destination and purpose none of his neigh-

bors knew, always with the master of Sturmhold on board. In all this, however, Merwyn Hargrove preserved the characteristics of the plantation even more than those of his profession, and the two united formed a combination which his new neighbors were utterly unable to analyze. His agents were his servants, and his servants were trusted more than the most confidential of agents. Of his neighbors he asked no advice and sought no assistance. He neither courted their good-will nor deprecated their resentment. He seemed unaware of their existence and unconscious of their strictures. His wife felt this sort of isolation even less than he. Accustomed to the social life of Europe, where every class is absolutely shut out of all ranks above and below itself, it seemed to her by no means unnatural that they should dwell among a people whom they did not come near in their social life. Plantation life had deepened this impression, and she made no effort to become a part of the people among whom they lived. She was happy because of her beautiful surroundings, the elegant mansion in which she received her many friends from the great city, and the belief that she had transformed her husband from the king of a plantation into a citizen of the world. In truth, they had brought the plantation with them. They had superimposed Amity Lake upon Sturmhold. In name, they had become citizens of New York; in fact, they still remained Carolinians. This impression was greatly aided by their having brought with them a retinue of colored servants— all manumitted slaves, as was carefully given out— favorite servants from the plantation; but the fact that some of them had disappeared, without leaving traces that could be followed beyond the master's sloop, led many to conjecture that they had been inveigled again into slavery.

The mistress hardly lived long enough to enjoy the

triumph of her love. Perhaps, if she had, she would
have discovered her isolation, and, with her keen in-
sight and ready sympathy, have found a way to open
the hearts of the rugged farmer-folks about her and
have made Sturmhold the focus of the region's life and
her husband the exponent of its aspirations. Almost
before the lawn had lost the trace of the builder's work,
however, the rigors of the climate took hold upon her.
She laughed at her husband's fear of the cough that
rang through the elegant halls of the new home. When
the spring came the hectic showed upon her cheek. She
was taken aboard the yacht, and its white wings bore
her again to summer seas. It was in vain. When the
autumn had painted the hills with his magic touch she
was brought back to the place she loved, to die. She
left behind her daughter, Hilda, then scarcely three
years of age, asking but one thing to be done in her
memory, and that was that her husband should keep
Sturmhold as the family seat and not return to the South
and its institutions. Her opposition to these was intense and peculiar. There was very little of the humanitarian element in it. She did not pity the slave
so much as she deplored the effect upon the master.
She believed that bondage was degrading and unjust,
not merely to the oppressed, but to the oppressor even
more. Her keen perception taught her that the time
must come when the unnatural relation must be dissolved in blood. She saw that liberty and slavery could
not long co-exist. She feared a servile insurrection and
desired to remove her loved one from its scope.

Her husband did not share these feelings or prejudices
of his wife. To him slavery was not only a natural
state of society, but the only social organization which
was possible where a strong race and a weak race dwelt
together. However, he had little to induce him to leave
Sturmhold, and he assented without hesitation to his

wife's request.   From the time of her death he grew still
more reserved with all about him.   His sloop made
still more frequent trips, and he seemed to desire to
conceal his movements from his neighbors.   Year by
year the dislike became more and more apparent and
intense.   Evil rumors were current in the region, and
Captain Hargrove had a constantly growing ill-repute
until the day when he brought misfortune to the home
of Harrison Kortright.

CHAPTER XI.

"GAY CASTLES IN THE CLOUDS THAT PASS."

"GOOD MORNING, little boy."

Martin Kortright opened his eyes, sat up and looked about him in amazement. He found himself upon a wide, high-posted bed above which hung a canopy of pale blue silk, the curtains of which fell about him, making a tent, and reminding him of the summer sky at twilight. These were drawn back in front, and through the opening he saw a spacious room, high-ceiled, and frescoed in blue and gold. Heavy silken window-curtains matching the rest in color shut out the sun-shine, save here and there a ray that shot between their folds. The furniture was rich and massive beyond any that he had ever seen before, while just in front of him a mirror that reached almost from floor to ceiling multi-plied the magnificence a thousand-fold to his astonished eyes.

"Don't you know where you are?"

The words were followed by a merry, rippling laugh. Martin looked in the direction whence the words and the laugh came. Standing just in front of him, one arm upon the coverlet and the other on the great white pillow she had pulled down so as to get a sight of his face before he awoke, was the dark-eyed little lady who had filled his dreams of late. Her bright face hardly showed above the coverlet. A colored nurse stood holding back the curtain and laughing at the child's impatience.

"La, chile, don't be so fractious-like. Do let the little boy git awake afore you bothers him so."

"He is awake. Aren't you, little boy?"

Martin rubbed his eyes again, and said candidly, "I —don't—know."

"Don't know?" laughed the sprite. "Don't know when you're awake? Oh, you're too funny for anything. Where do you think you are?"

"I don't know," said Martin seriously. Then glancing around the room he added solemnly, "In Heaven, I guess."

"Oh, you queer boy. No, you ain't in Heaven. You are here at Sturmhold, and you have been asleep, oh, ever so long. I thought you would wake up when we got home, but you didn't, and papa brought you here and put you on the bed himself. Oh, he's awfully good, my papa is. Don't you think so?"

"Well, well," said a brusque voice at the foot of the bed, and Captain Hargrove stepped forward with a smile on his face and a twinkle in his eyes. "Is that the way you treat your guests, Hilda—wake them up to catechise them on your papa's merits and demerits?"

"Oh papa!" cried Hilda with tones of rapture, bounding into his arms and kissing him again and again.

"There, there, dear," said the father, checking her caresses; "save some of them for to-morrow morning. Let me speak to your little friend, won't you?"

"Oh, papa, he doesn't know where he is."

"I'm not surprised at that, puss, if you waked him up."

"Oh, I didn't kiss *him*," she said, glancing shyly at Martin under her dark lashes.

"Indeed! Why not, I should like to know?" he asked quizzically.

"'Cause"—she said, dropping her head still lower and putting a finger to her pouting lips—" 'cause I—I couldn't get at him."

"Ha! ha!" laughed the father heartily. "A very good reason, indeed. I suppose you would have kissed him if you could, eh?"

"He's a good little boy," said the girl sententiously.

"That's true, dear, and how is the good little boy this morning, George—I mean Martin?"

"Pretty well," answered the boy, simply. The affectionate by-play between father and daughter had been almost as great a marvel to him as the enchanted palace in which he found himself.

"That's right," said Hargrove, patting the boy's cheek and noting the temperature and tone of the skin as he did so. "Yes, you are all right. Does the arm ache?"—looking at the fingers the surprised lad was unconsciously bending back and forth to remove the feeling of uneasiness which the night had brought to the splintered member.

"A little," said Martin.

"Sorry," responded the master of Sturmhold, "but when you have had breakfast and a ride after the bays I reckon you'll feel better, won't you?"

"Oh, yes!" said the boy, waking into life at the mention of the horses.

"Well, well," said the Captain, laughing at his enthusiasm, "William will come to help you dress presently, and we will see that you do not get drowsy again, before night at least. As you could not wake your prince with a kiss, Hilda, you might as well give him one to disenchant him now. He is evidently under a spell of some kind.

He held the child over and she put her arms about Martin's neck and kissed him on the cheek. The boy drew back doubtfully, while the Captain tossed his daughter up and bore her laughingly away. The kiss burned on Martin Kortright's cheek with a strange warmth. Could it be that the wonderful being, the

very sight of whom had soothed his pain on the day of
his misfortune, had kissed him ? There was something
so strange so wonderful, so fairly-like about her that he
could hardly believe himself awake. He thought it must
be all a dream, and when the colored servant came,
he submitted to be washed and combed and dressed with
a half belief that he would yet awake and find that the
castle had crumbled. But when he saw his rough farmer-boy shoes nicely blackened and the careful servant
brushing his clothes, which, though his very best, yet
seemed coarse and out of place amid the grand things
that were about him, he began to experience a sense
of depression and awkwardness that destroyed all the
glamour, and made even the magnificent surroundings painful and oppressive. When he was ushered
down to breakfast and sat beside the little Hilda, whose
eyes seemed deeper and softer than ever, and remembered
the kiss upon his cheek ; saw a repast, really plain, but
appearing to his unaccustomed eyes of regal richness,
served by watchful servants who moved about with
noiseless steps, and spread upon a massive table, in
dishes of rare delicacy of form and material—china and
silver and glass, with the glint of gold in the lining of
some of them ;—when all this burst upon him, the sense
of unreality returned. He wondered if the missionary
who sent the seeds from which had grown the two evergreens before his father's door ever saw such splendor
in the far-off Orient. Then he glanced shyly at the
master and wondered if he were as bad a man as was
whispered around the country-side.

And all that day, and for many days thereafter, the
sense of dreaming unreality remained. The Knight had
found his Lady-love and was imprisoned with her in the
castle of Indolence, at the portal of which a terrible
giant stood guard, and such was the enervating effect of
the magic spells that rested on him that he no longer

dreamed of doing great things, but wished that he might live on forever in this abode of luxury and ease.

The days grew into weeks, and still Martin Kortright remained at Sturmhold. Captain Hargrove, by some occult influence it would seem, had persuaded Mrs. Kortright to allow him to remain for a few days, and, by sending him every day or two to receive her caresses and inquire of his father's condition, had finally reconciled her to this partial separation ; so that when the convalescent father was inclined to complain at the boy's absence, she even undertook the task of proving to him how much better it was for the lad than that he should be shut up at home during the severe winter weather, and succeeded so well that Martin was allowed to remain and share the sports and tasks of the little Hilda, with the hearty concurrence of his parents.

It was not strange that they consented. The one desire of their hearts, cold and undemonstrative as they seemed, was the happiness and interest of their boy. His good was the motive of all their acts and the chief element of all their plans. Already they had ceased to look forward to a future of their own. They thought they had attained the limit of their growth and development. What they were to be they had already become. They might gather somewhat more of wealth, though they hardly desired to do so except to lift up their son. To put him higher in the scale of being than they were ; to make him one of the Presidential possibilities, not by wealth nor by chicane, but by giving him a chance to make himself felt among his fellows ; to be all that he might—this was the one thought of their fond, silent hearts ; for this they labored, watched and prayed.

That it would be for the child's good to remain at Sturmhold for the winter they had little doubt. Not because the master was a rich man—there was in the sturdy couple none of that spirit that courts the rich for favor. They were not poor themselves, and would have scorned the thought of allowing the son to improve his chances in the world by becoming the favorite of another. It was not of benefit from Merwyn Hargrove that either of them thought in assenting to his proposal, but of advantage to be derived from a style of life Martin could never look for, even in the house of his well-to-do parents. They meant him to be something more than they had been, if it pleased God to favor their plans, and they thought it nothing less than providential that he was privileged while he was yet young to become familiar with that life which they hoped he would some time adorn.

"It's a good thing," said the Squire, talking over the proposal with his wife, "to get used to the ways of the world early. It comes awkward to a man after he gets grown up an' has reached the top of the ladder the Lord has set afore him to climb, to be brought in company with those that were born somewhere about the top rungs. It must take a deal of trouble to get used to servants and forms and ceremonies, then. But they're the very things a man's got to know—and not only know, but be used to, if he's going to get on in the world."

"Marty is a well-behaved boy," said the mother, half resenting the idea that any training could be better than that of Paradise Bay.

"Of course he is, mother, and he's got good stuff in him, too. But he's like my Sunday boots. There ain't no better made boots in Albany than them—good stock and good work, every stitch on 't. And they're all right for church here at Skendoah meetin' house, too. But you jest ought to have seen them boots when I went into the Governor's house to present that petition we sent up 'bout the bank. I thought they were jest the meanest, awkwardest, cheapest-looking things a man ever wore. I'd had 'em blacked at the hotel, but they wa'n't used to it, you see, an' it didn't take well. They squeaked an' hollered; stuck out at the side an' up at the toes an' were run over at the heel, till I thought every one in the room must be lookin' at them; an' when I sat down I hustled 'em under my chair jest as far as I could get 'em. But there was the Governor, jest as homely a man as ever looked over a stump fence, with feet as much as three sizes bigger'n mine; great, long, flat mud-splashers, the biggest I ever saw, except Henry Clay's—I never shall forget his. As I say, the Governor sat there among all them great ladies and gentlemen with jest the commonest kind of boots, not more 'n half blacked and a patch on the toe of one on 'em; but I tell you, Martha, they looked as if they'd jest grown there. They were used to it, you see—used to it. That makes the difference, and jest about all the difference, Martha, whether it's with men or boots."

"It does take you to see things nobody else would ever think of, father," said Mrs. Kortright. "But I've often thought that it makes more difference where a man's been than what he knows. Now, there's Captain Hargrove; I don't s'pose he really knows any more 'n the ordinary run of the neighbors."

"I wouldn't be afraid to bet," interrupted Kortright, "that half the men that rent farms from him read more pages, year in an' year out, than he does."

"I shouldn't a bit wonder," answered his wife. "He seems to be real kind of rough like, sometimes."

"Been a sailor, you know, or at least an officer of the navy and seen a good deal of roughness there, I s'pose."

"Well, whether 'twas there or somewhere else, I don't undertake to say," said Mrs. Kortright, with a determinedly non-committal air; "what I say is that there are streaks of roughness in him, now and then, yet no one would ever think of his being the least bit awkward or embarrassed, even before kings and queens."

" That's so," assented Kortright.

" Besides that," said Mrs. Kortright, "it is a good chance for Martin to have the advantage of learning without goin' to school, after havin' his arm broke. You know boys will be boys, and Martin ain't strong, nohow."

" Never was sick a day in his life."

" That's so; but yet you know he don't grow and seem stout like."

" Well ?"

" Now you know Captain Hargrove has Miss Barber, the minister's daughter, from Loweboro', up to Sturmhold in his carriage every day to give that little girl her lessons ; and he says Martin can jest go on with Hilda an' not cost a cent more nor be a mite of trouble. In fact, he says it'll be a great advantage, 'cause it'll make the little girl work harder to keep up with him ; for it seems that our boy's ahead of his girl, if he hasn't had more'n half her chances."

" That would be handy for Marty, and, as you say, save any danger of gittin' his arm broke agin."

" Yes, and then you know this rheumatiz may hang round you all winter, and I don't think it's good for children to be shut up in the house where sick folks are, too much."

" Well, no ; and besides that, as the Captain says, it would keep the girl chirk and lively while he's gone. An' there's where Jason agrees with him. You know he always said the little girl wouldn't do nothing but mope an' mourn when the Captain was away."

" So he did. One wouldn't think to see her, though, that she ever did anything but laugh and carry on."

" She is a bright little thing," assented Kortright thoughtfully. "But they say that's jest the kind that suffers most when they do have trouble."

" I s'pose that's the fact," said the cheery matron, as

she rocked back and forth, her needles clicking as their bright points gleamed in the candlelight. Her husband glanced at her with a half smile as he thought how well she illustrated the converse of his remark. Trouble had never worn Martha Kortright and never would.

Harrison Kortright had left his bed and occupied now during the daytime the lounge on which Martin had passed the early period of his disability. Yet he was none the less an invalid. His thin and wasted face, over which, as he spoke, passed twinges of pain every now and then, testified to this fact as clearly as the cramped limbs and the pair of stout canes that lay beside his couch. As if his pain had reminded him of the fact, Kortright added after a moment:

"I don't more'n half like lettin' the boy stay there, after all's said and done, but we can do no less after what the Captain's done for us, that's certain. I don't know how you'd have got along, or I either, if it hadn't been for that man Unthank. There must have been a month that he scarcely slept a wink at night. And come to think on't, the Captain wa'n't a particle to blame about it. I'd have had the rheumatiz, any way."

"But you got it takin' that woman away that he was goin' to kidnap."

"That's so; that is, I got it that night before the 'lection," assented her husband. "'Bout the kidnapping, I ain't so sure."

"Didn't she say that he was planning to take her back to slavery, and that was the reason she ran away?" asked his wife in surprise.

"She certainly did; but I've been thinking about the matter since I've been lying here, and I can't make it out."

"I should think she ought to know," said Mrs. Kortright.

"So she ought and perhaps she did," responded the Squire; "but I can't make it out for all that. If he'd wanted to kidnap her why didn't he do it before, or in fact what did he bring her here for at all ?''

" Why, to nurse his little girl.''

" Couldn't he have hired that done just as well without risking such a piece of property here ? And don't the girl need her just as much now as ever ?''

" Well, really, one would think you were sorry for what you had done,'' said Mrs. Kortright.

" Not at all,'' said he stubbornly. " The woman wanted to go and had a right to go, and I took her. That's all there is of that. But I don't believe Captain Hargrove had any more idea of kidnapping that woman than he has of kidnapping our Martin.''

" Oh, mercy !'' exclaimed Mrs. Kortright, with a start.

" There, there, mother,'' said he soothingly. " I hadn't no idea of putting such a notion in your head. What I meant to say was that he hadn't no more notion of running off that woman than—than of eloping with you.''

" Now, Harrison !'' said the comely matron with a blush and an arch look at her husband.

" Well, well,'' said he with a laugh, " I couldn't hardly blame him for wanting to do that.''

" There must have been something wrong at the bottom of it.''

" There ain't no doubt of that, but I ain't at all sure that Captain Hargrove was at the bottom on't.''

" Perhaps not.'' The good dame was busy picking up the stitches she had dropped. After a time she said : " Did you ever think it queer what Jason told us about all the servants at Sturmhold except himself being paid off and sent away at one time ?''

" No ; and I don't see anything queer about it now. I s'pose rich folks change their servants, sometimes.''

" Of course ; but ain't it strange they should change all of 'em at once ?''

" Well, I don't know but it might be."

" And that such a man as Jason Unthank should never see nor hear from any of them again ?"

" It does seem a little odd, now you mention it," assented Kortright gravely.

" And that, you remember, was just before this woman Lida came, too."

" And after his wife died."

" And before he brought his daughter home."

Kortright drew a long breath.

"It's all so, Martha, and there's something wrong somewhere. I don't doubt that. But it ain't in Captain Hargrove. If he ain't a good man and an honest one, then I don't know anything about a man. That's all."

" Well, it's somebody," persisted the wife.

" I ain't so sure about that," rejoined the Squire. " I'm half the notion that it's just a bad system that's made the Master a slave and the Slave a victim."

CHAPTER XII.

LITTLE by little the farmer-boy was transformed. His blue cap gave way to fur ; a rich cloak and bright red tippet made him appear a fit companion for the little Hilda, with whom he rode every day. While his external appearance was thus changing he underwent a not less striking mental transformation. The ways of the great house were no longer irksome or unfamiliar. The retinue of servants no longer awed his unaccustomed eyes. The little Hilda lost none of her spiritual charm in becoming a sweet, familiar fact. Her morning and evening kiss were like honey-dew upon his lips. The child had led a lonely life, and the absence of her accustomed nurse had left her hungry for companionship, even in the crowded mansion. The "good little boy" had taken a hold upon her fancy, which the father gratified as he would have gratified her wish for any other toy. Besides, the boy had done a brave thing. He liked him. There was an unflinching straightforwardness about him that not only amused but interested. Mr. Hargrove was desirous of recompensing him somewhat for what he had suffered. So Hilda was allowed her own sweet will with her new plaything. She had persisted in giving him the room next her own, and treating him in all respects as her brother. She consulted his wishes in all things, and, to the surprise of the servants, yielded readily her will to another besides that of her father. The simple sincerity of her conduct was met by a corresponding openness and earnestness on Martin's part. He knew so little of the world which he had entered that it never once occurred to him that there was anything unusual or peculiar in his position. All around him there was an apparent lavishness that made the sums expended in his behalf seem trifles not worth considering. Why should not a man make gifts who seemed to spend his money freely in every other conceivable method? For to this country boy's unsophisticated mind there was nothing wanting in the appointments or surroundings of Sturmhold. Besides, he had felt himself somewhat ill at ease with Hilda while the coarse habiliments of his home-life seemed to mark the distinction between his lot and hers. So he accepted the good things that fate threw in his way, became the companion and protector of the little lady, and, unconsciously to all, soon shared her throne and ruled with her the retinue, and through her the master of Sturmhold. Hardly had the injured arm been released from the sling and the rôle of the invalid ceased, ere he had become an accustomed and welcome presence in the picturesque but lonely mansion. Sharing the pleasures and the tasks of Hilda all constraint was soon forgotten. That age

> ". . . 'twixt boy and youth
> When thought is speech and speech is truth,"

makes a smooth pathway from heart to heart. The farmer's boy lost nothing of his self-respect; the nabob's daughter never dreamed of condescension. He never questioned why he found his new surroundings sweet; and it never occurred to her that they were any fairer than he had always known. She had been so accustomed to luxurious environments that she never thought of regarding them as exceptional. He had never known want, and so had no envy of wealth. Her pictures, books and toys were as rich a treat to him as if a fairy had brought them at his wish. She never tired of the stories of his rustic sports, and soon grew almost

as anxious as he for the day to come when they should
visit Paradise Bay.

So it happened that, before Christmas time, it seemed
as if each home had gained another child. Squire Kortright and his wife had become devotedly attached to
Hilda, and Captain Hargrove manifested more affection for Martin than he had exhibited toward any one but
Hilda since his wife's death. Mrs. Kortright had been
to Sturmhold on the master's invitation, and saw with
a fond mother's delight all that made her boy so bright
and happy. It was observed with many wondering remarks by the servants that this was the first time that
any of the neighbors had been invited to the precincts
of Sturmhold. Up to the day that Martin had come
into the life of the mansion the utmost seclusion had
prevailed. Not only was no one asked to visit the premises, but precautions had been adopted to prevent even
accidental intrusion. Hilda's teacher had always been
driven back and forth each day, no matter how unpro-
pitious the weather. But since Martin's laughter had
wakened the echoes about the silent house, she had several times been invited to stay for the night, and once
had been kept prisoner, half against her will, for several
days. A change was noted, too, in the master. It seemed
as if a burden of care had been unexpectedly rolled from
his shoulders. Before, he had appeared moody, absorbed and care-worn. Since his wife's death he had
hardly smiled on any one but his daughter. Now he
was full of humor and seemed to take almost as much
pleasure in the sports of the children as they did
themselves.

"I declar' for't," said Jason Unthank, in conversation
with one of the servants soon after his return from
Kortright's, shaking his head solemnly, "I declar' for't,
Bre'er William, I don't know what's a-gwine to happen.
I'se knowed Marse Hargrove ever sence we was boys

together, down at de Quarter, an' I'se been with him almost every blessed minute sence I come on, jest atter Miss Retty died, an' I don't 'llow thet I'se ever heard him laugh, enny more'n jest a sort o' chuckle dat he swallowed 'fore 'twas half out, till this blessed day. 'Pears like he's done turned boy agin', sence I'se been away. I do declar ef he ain't for all the world jes like de young Marse Merwyn down on de ole Carolina plantation."

"Been so most ever sence you went away, too, more or less," said William, earnestly. "We've all done talked about it over and often."

"I can't understand it," said Jason, shaking his head seriously. "I'se afeard it don't mean no good. I'se always heerd 'twa'n't no good sign when anybody turns right round from t'other to which that way—cryin' one minute an' laughin' the next, or *wice wersy*, with no sort o' reason for changin' that anybody can find out."

"An' I b'leeve it," said William, with a look and tone that attested his sincerity.

"I hain't got no call to deny it," said Jason, as he passed on to his duties, with a non-committal air that befitted his position as the trusted head of the household retinue.

After a time, however, the master of Sturmhold became again preoccupied and moody. He ceased to take any part in the children's sports, and, indeed, became apparently almost oblivious to their existence. Hilda, used to such moods, after vainly trying to divert her father from them, gave her attention still more to Martin, who, after a day or two of uneasy wonder at the changed demeanor of the man who had so completely captivated his fancy, became accustomed to it, and the twain almost forgot his existence for days together.

With many misgivings, Mrs. Kortright invited Captain Hargrove and the two children to share the Christ-

mas dinner at Paradise Bay, and greatly to the surprise
of all the invitation was accepted. It was a red-letter
day in the calendar of the two young lives. They went
in the crisp brightness of a winter morning. All day
long, after their arrival, the hero-boy showed the wondering girl the scenes of his early achievements. The
great red barn, with its dark corners, dim passages,
great mows and cobwebbed roof, decorated with the
mud-daubed homes of summer swallows, was explored
from purline to basement. The broken arm, grown well
and strong, was quite forgotten by the boy, who was
only preserved from even more serious injury by the fate
that watches over boys; but it was not for a moment
absent from the mind of the girl who beheld his ex-
ploits. She held her breath in terror at his daring
familiarity with the horses, oxen and cows. The reck-
lessness with which he climbed the ladder, walked the
great beam and took a flying leap of a dozen feet down
upon the cut side of the haymow, not only commanded
her admiration but awakened her amazement. Sturmhold sank into insignificance beside this silent play-
house of the sturdy boy, whom she was daily coming to
regard as a hero of more than knightly mettle.

Within the house a different scene was enacted. From
early morning a fire had been burning in the parlor—
that strangely isolated portion of the American farm-
house of a generation ago which was never used except
on great occasions, and, with its inseparable parlor-bed-
room, was sacred to company, consumption and death.
Fortunately, the physician had been informed of the intended festivity, and had enjoined that a fire should be
kept burning in this prohibited sanctuary all the previous day. His injunction had been strictly fulfilled, and
before the Captain's arrival the Squire had been installed
in this spare-room to entertain the visitor until the
dinner hour, which, with especial reference to the con-

venience of the visitor, was put at three o'clock, thus splitting the difference between the dinner hour of the farm-house and that of the mansion. During this time the mysteries of housewifery demanded the attention of Mrs. Kortright, and the two men were left to themselves.

There could not be a greater contrast. The Squire, thin and pallid from his two months of suffering, occupied the plain chintz-covered sofa. His beard had not been cut since his illness, and formed a grizzly stubble over his chin. His hands were white and skinny and the left seemed drawn and weak. One leg was flexed and the toes incurved by the force of the disease that had racked his frame and only spared his life at the price of his activity. It was a heavy ransom for a man of his stirring habit to pay for the bare privilege of existence. He was beyond danger—at least the physician thought so—but he was rigorously commanded not to venture beyond the threshold until the summer sunshine had opened the doors and equalized the temperature within and without. Even then it was doubtful if he would ever walk erect and without the aid of a staff again. He would live—confined to a chair, hobbling about on crutches or chained to a staff—a life that had little charm to one who had been accustomed to bid defiance to nature, whose strength had been the pride of his youth and the boast of his manhood. He felt the bitterness of his lot as he saw Captain Hargrove, in the glory of his prime, broad-chested, round, full-limbed ; a flush upon his dark cheek ; his eye full of fire, and his step firm and elastic with something of the tendency to "brace" which is almost always perceptible in the walk of one accustomed to a sea-faring life. It was with something of envy, therefore, that he said as soon as Mrs. Kortright had withdrawn :

"I'm afraid ye'll find me mighty dull company, Captain."

"On the contrary," said the Captain, "a chat with you is just what I would have chosen had it been left for me to say how I would like to pass the day."

"It's very good of you to say so, Captain," said the Squire, not without surprise, yet evidently pleased at this hearty speech, "but it will be hard to make me believe that a man who has been upon his back for two months with this miserable pain racking him most all the time, can be very good company for any one."

"I suppose," said Hargrove, as he seated himself in a large rocking-chair near the fire, "this is one of the very reasons I want to talk with you. If you were well and busy you would have no time to think of what I want most to say, and perhaps I might not care about trusting you, either."

"If it's that woman Lida you are referring to, Captain, I may as well say at once that I don't know anything more about her than you do."

"Nor half as much, Mr. Kortright. I am well aware of that, and you have reason to be thankful for the fact, too."

"How so?"

"No matter. She has no connection with what I wish to speak of now, at least not directly, and it won't pay to spend time in discussing her."

"Well, just as you please," said Kortright, evidently not pleased himself that the other did not intend to pursue the topic he had introduced.

"Not that I would be unwilling to tell you all I know of her, but the story is a long one, and I hardly feel like undertaking it to-day."

"I 'spect not," said the other, with a caustic dryness of tone that did not escape the attention of the visitor, who laughed quietly as he said:

"Queer, isn't it, that a man should be regarded with suspicion because of his good deeds, while perhaps his evil ones bring him only respect?"

"I don't know 'bout that," began Kortright argumentatively.

"Nor I, as a rule," interrupted Hargrove; "neither do I care whether it is generally true or not. I was only speaking of my own case. I never thought of it till lately. Somehow, since your boy has been with us I seem to myself like one just wakened out of a long sleep."

"I hope he hasn't disturbed you," said Kortright, with a twinkle in his eye.

"Disturbed me? Oh, no; he fits in as if he had been the missing link between Sturmhold and the world."

"Martin is a good boy."

"Ha, ha!" laughed Hargrove, "that is just what my Hilda is always saying. By the way, Squire, it is marvelous how those two children seem to suit each other. They haven't found a point of difference yet, and seem to grow fonder of each other every day."

"I'm glad on't, Captain. The little girl must have had a lonesome life afore he came."

"Well, I suppose she did; though I never thought of it. The truth is, Mr. Kortright," he added solemnly, "I have had a burden to bear ever since her birth which no one could share with me, and which has left me very little opportunity for other things."

"Yes," said the Squire, as Hargrove paused, not because he meant to assent to what had been said but because he did not know what else to say.

"I wish I could tell you or some other good man all about it, but I can't. That's the trouble of the matter. I undertook to do a good thing—at least I thought it was good and kind, but it has brought a heap of sorrow and misunderstanding. There's that girl Lida, now; I set her free, gave her a home, and shut all society out of my house that she might be undisturbed, and now am regarded with horror throughout the valley here, because she ran away."

"There is some feeling about it, certainly," said the Squire.

"Feeling! Bluebeard was an amiable man in comparison with me, taking my neighbors' estimate."

The master of Sturmhold laughed pleasantly as he spoke, as though the neighbors' opinion of him was not a matter of grave importance after all.

"Well, he continued, "the girl Lida made me a deal of trouble when she left, but it was nothing to the trouble she had made by staying. I hardly realized it before; but when she was gone and your boy came, I seemed to have lost a load that had been on my shoulders so long that I had almost forgotten how it bent me down."

"I confess, Captain," said Kortright, "I can't understand the matter, an' as you don't seem inclined to tell me all about it, perhaps you'd better not say anything at all, an' so not start my curiosity."

"I've no fear of that, sir," answered Hargrove. "If it was my secret I'd tell it in a minute, but it concerns every one else whom it touches more nearly than it does me; and yet I am the only one that knows the whole of it."

"That must be unpleasant, anyhow."

"Unpleasant! It has made me a hermit and built a cave about me. No wonder Hilda was lonesome, as you say. I never thought, when I undertook this job, that she would come to need anybody but a nurse. In fact, I didn't think of anything."

"That's the way mostly with what folks go into for the pleasure of the present minute," said the elder man severely.

"Oh, but I didn't go into this, Squire, at all. It just spread itself over me without so much as saying 'by your leave.' I wasn't even indiscreet, except in picking up a load heavier than I could carry."

"See here, Captain," said the Squire energetically,

"you and I ain't much more'n strangers, but I want to say to you plainly that I don't want to know anything about the matter that you're referrin' to. I'm just as sure as that I'm lyin' here that it's somethin' growin' out of slavery, and I don't want the responsibility of carryin' any of its sins."

"There's where you're wrong, Squire," said the Captain, with a touch of triumph in his voice. "All the trouble in this case has come from liberty instead of slavery. There would have been no burden on my back if I had not tried to make a slave happy by giving her freedom."

"Aye, that is your logic," said Kortright almost bitterly, "because a day of freedom does not heal the evil of generations of slavery, you say it causes the ills it only drags out into the light of day so that they can be seen."

"I don't know about that," responded Hargrove curtly. "I believe that negro slavery is a better thing than negro liberty. Abstractly, I dislike slavery as much as you or any one else. I have seen a good deal of it in one country and another, and honestly wish we had never had it here. But then I should want to be rid of the African, too."

"He wouldn't be here if he hadn't been brought," said the other significantly, watching Hargrove keenly as he spoke.

"True," said Hargrove carelessly, "but here he is, and here he is likely to stay. The only question—if it is a question—is *how* he shall stay."

"He can't stay here much longer as a slave, that's certain."

"I cannot see why you think so. A few fanatics make a great deal of noise, but slavery has grown stronger every year since the formation of our government."

"The steeple's kept gittin' higher, that's a fact; but how about the underpinnin'?"

"I don't see but it stands on just as good a foundation as the government itself."

"That may be—that may be," meditatively.

"If the government stands I don't see how slavery can help standing with it. That is my view, Squire, candidly. I wish we had never had slavery, nor the negro, either; but having the negro, I don't see how we can get along without slavery. I hope you understand me."

"Yes, I guess I do," said Kortright, raising himself on his elbow and looking at the other with eyes that burned like live coals in the ashen pallor of his face, "and I want you to understand me, too. If we've got to have slavery in order to save the nation, I don't see any use in savin' on't. I'm sorry, myself, that the negro is in the country, but bein' here, I'd rather try to get along with him as a free man than see the country go on heapin' up wrong, year after year, by the wholesale, as we are doin' now."

"Well," laughed Hargrove, "there's no mistaking that. You would rather the country should perish than slavery live."

"I would rather see the best machine man ever devised broken to pieces than made the instrument of oppression and wrong."

"Well, well, we can never agree upon that subject, so we need not discuss it."

"I s'pose 'twould be a waste of time. You look at it one way and I another, and we're both a little set in our way, probably."

Harrison Kortright smiled grimly as he settled himself upon his couch again. The younger man looked at him with amused expression for a moment, and then said:

"I reckon, Squire, you would be surprised to know that at this very time I am in very bad odor in Carolina because I am considered a dangerous enemy of 'the institution.'"

"You?" lifting his rugged brows and surveying the man who sat before him, critically.

"Yes, I."

"I think I should," emphatically.

"Then listen."

Hargrove drew a newspaper from his pocket and read :

"Facts which have come to our knowledge warrant us in cautioning the people of Clayburn County against one of her sons who has turned traitor to the South and her institutions. People thought it strange, when, some years ago, a certain gentleman sold his plantation in the vicinity of Amity Lake and removed to the bleak hills of New York ; but no one supposed that a man who owed his fortune and his place in society to the chivalrous watch-care of Colonel Peter Eighmie could ever become a renegade to the land of his birth. There was some comment on his folly in taking with him to a free State and there manumitting a considerable number of his most valuable negroes, but, as they were his own property, no one was inclined to regard it as anything more than the harmless freak of a wealthy planter. Indeed, it was generally attributed to the influence of his foreign wife, who had imbibed a foolish prejudice against the patriarchal institution. So, although there had never been any reason to suppose that her husband shared her folly, no one believed it possible that when he became the executor of the son of his benefactor he would either squander the estate through his abolition fanaticism or attempt to meddle with the domestic relations of his neighbors. It was known that there had been an unusual number of runaways from that vicinity, but no one suspected that one who had been an officer of the United States navy would ever descend so low as to become a kidnapper of his neigh-

bors' slaves.   By the capture of a. gang of runaways, in
Hurricane Swamp last week, however, it was learned that
they were waiting to be taken North in his sloop.   It
seems that she has hardly ever crossed the bar without
taking a stolen cargo.   It has been learned almost to a
certainty that on the last trip he took one of Colonel
Granby's most valuable house-servants, a likely woman,
who had taken up* with a negro named Unthank, the

---

* This term, "taken up with," was one of the unconscious testi-
monies of slavery to its own demoralizing tendencies.   It was used
to express the relation, as nearly as might be, of husband and
wife existing between slaves.   "The fact," said the Chief Justice
of the Supreme Court of the State in which our story is located,
"that two slaves have *taken up* with each other, no matter under
what pretended ceremony of marriage, and have lived together
as if in the marital relation, in no sense constitutes them husband and wife, nor clothes them with any' of the rights and privileges of that relation."   The influence of this doctrine is no doubt
distinctly visible in the morals of the race to which it was applied.
Unquestionably this doctrine is absolutely indispensable to the
peace of society where the relation of simple chattelism in man
is maintained.   The thing—mere property, cannot at the same
time be clothed with the rights of a husband and father.   The
chief difference between American slavery and that which the
world has known in other lands and ages was that it did not
pass through the intermediary stages of serfdom in its downfall.   The American slave was transformed into a freeman
without development, without instruction ; one day a slave,
the next a citizen—changed in the twinkling of an eye.   Hitherto the road from slavery to freedom has always been a harsh
and rugged one.   One right after another has been won with
difficulty and danger.   Blood has flowed and generations of struggle have engendered a fortitude worthy of the liberty that came
at length as its reward.   This is the universal history of European
development, and out of these struggles grew up the peoples
that make what we term the civilized world of to-day.   Whether
the sudden transplantation that marked the downfall of our
American system, lacking, as it did, all that opportunity for
gradual growth which serfdom and feudalism afforded, will show
like beneficent results, is a question which only time can answer.
It is not yet decided, and the claim of the Southern white man of
to-day that two races, so distinctly marked in outward habit of
body and so widely separated by previous development, can only

body-servant of this man before he was taken out of the State and freed by his fanatical master. This man Unthank is known to be a very impudent and dangerous negro, who has been coming to the State in company with his former master, in open defiance of the law that forbids free negroes to come into the State. We learn that the people of that part of the county are justly incensed at these facts and have organized to give both Unthank and his master such a welcome as they deserve, should they ever dare show themselves in that region again."

"Meaning you?" asked the listener on the chintz-covered lounge, gazing in undisguised amazement at the reader.

"Undoubtedly, meaning me," responded Hargrove, with a quiet laugh at the other's surprise. "You see I am bound to have the name of kidnapper, wherever I go. It must be something in my face that condemns me, or perhaps it runs in the blood. The Hargroves of a few generations back are said to have done a land-office business in that line."

"You are sure it ain't in your actions, I suppose?" said Kortright dryly.

"Well, no," said Hargrove in a tone of candor, "I am not. On the contrary, I am half of the notion that I'm guilty of the charge in Carolina."

---

live together in a relation in which one is subordinate to the other, and controlled by it, is a dogma that will be sneered at only by the fool who is too dull to read the past and too blind to fear for the future. We may hope—we must hope—but that very hope should teach us that simple liberty is not all that is required to transform the slave into a freeman. The African of America must have time to learn very much and to forget still more before the Proclamation of Emancipation will have become effectual. On this fact depends the duty of to-day. The Slave may be emancipated; the Freeman must be developed. We may believe in a result consonant with liberty and our ideas of justice; but the fact that such an outcome is not demonstrable should teach the people of the whole land that the end of duty is not yet,

"What!"

"I think I am guilty of kidnapping, as charged in that paper, and you, too."

"I? How do you make that out?"

"I have reason to believe that Unthank has been bringing one or more of his friends back on the sloop, every time I have been down there for a year or more, and I suppose you have been helping him away with them."

"That's where you've shot mighty wide of the mark, Captain. I don't mind saying that I would do it in a minute, if the chance came; but, as a matter of fact, I never did help a runaway, even with a meal of victuals, till the night before the 'lection. That woman's story made me an Abolitionist."

"So? And what was her story, please?"

"No matter, Captain. I'm willing to give up that you didn't want to kidnap her; but that you didn't mean her harm of any kind I'm not quite so sure."

"You think a Southern man cannot deal fairly with a man or woman having a black skin?"

"Well, it don't matter what I think. What she said to me I suppose she told in confidence, and I have no right to go and repeat it to one she was afraid of, to say the least. You see that yourself."

"You are quite right in that," said Hargrove, "but knowing the girl's history as well as I do, I had a curiosity to learn how much of it she would tell. I assure you, Squire, that girl has a story well worth hearing, without any fiction being added."

"The one she told me changed my politics, and I ain't sure but it colored my religion just a trifle."

"And the real story has changed my life," said Hargrove, as he rose and walked moodily up and down the room. "I suppose I kidnapped her, too. Confound it, Mr. Kortright, do you believe in a devil?"

"It's the one thing I never had a doubt about," answered Kortright doggedly.

"Oh, I don't mean a mere theoretical devil; I mean a being that cannot help doing evil, even when meaning to do good—one whose acts are all cursed with the venom of destruction, no matter how well intended."

"I don't know. I suppose that must be the very way the devil is situated."

"And that is the way it is with this girl, Lida. Poor thing! she's had a hard time. I don't think she ever meant any one harm, but her very presence is a curse. I never did her anything but kindness in my life, but she brought a curse with her into my house, and I have not been so happy in years as since she left it."

"Well, she ain't likely to trouble you much more, and, as far as I can see, you're both very well rid of each other."

"That's the trouble, Squire," said Hargrove, stopping short before his companion. "I am not rid of her, and cannot be for many a year. She is hung around my neck like a mill-stone. Even now, I am compelled to go away in a few days to face any amount of danger and trouble on her account."

"Well, Captain, I'm sorry for both of you—you and the woman, I mean; but if you won't tell me what it's all about and I won't tell you what she said, what sense is there in our talking around it all day? To change the subject—your speaking about mill-stones brought it to my mind—you know that farm of yours just across the creek, to the east of my land?"

"Yes."

"Wouldn't you like to sell that tract?"

"I don't know. Why?"

"Well, you see, the doctor says I'm not likely ever to be of much use on the farm any more—may not be anywhere—but at least must look for some sort of busi-

ness that will keep me out of the weather. Now, I
never had any turn for merchandising; and there's the
big fall in the creek there, I've always thought would
make somebody's fortune, some time. I ain't rich, but
I've a mind to try and build a mill there, if I can get
the property on easy terms and long time. The dam
would back the water up on my meadow, anyhow, so
I've got a sort of an interest in it, you see."

"Yes," said Hargrove, still pacing back and forth
across the room, "I've thought such a thing might be
done, myself. How much power could be got there?"

"Power? I don't know. I ain't a mechanic, exactly, but if a good dam was put across that narrow
place, there ain't a water-power in this region to compare with it. Why, it would run anything."

"Have you money enough to develop it?"

"Not as it ought to be done; but I'd do enough to
hold it, make a living, pay the interest and wait for a
chance to do better."

"Suppose you had the money?" pausing and looking
down at the man on the lounge.

"If I had the money I'd make that tract worth more 'n
all the land you've got up and down the valley."

"Yes," slowly resuming his walk.

"I don't know exactly what 'twould be, and I wouldn't
be in no great hurry to decide neither; but, if I had the
money, I'd put in a dam there that wouldn't be in no
danger from high water, and then I'd look around for
something for it to do. No fear but I'd find something.
The only trouble would be to determine what would be
the best."

"Do you think you would be able to attend to it?"

"Well, Captain, I don't never expect to be well again,
I s'pose I'll be a sort of half-cripple the rest of my life.
I won't be able to *do*, but think maybe I'll be able to
look after what others are doin',"

"A much more important thing. The great trouble with all of our American work is that there is not enough overlooking. The laborer, being a peer of the employer, naturally resents supervision, and so he is told what is to be done and left to do it in his own way."

"It's a good deal so," assented Kortright.

"How much money would it take?" asked Hargrove.

"Oh, that depends on how much is done. It might take ten thousand, and five times that might not be too much."

"Squire Kortright!" stopping suddenly in front of him.

"Well?" quietly.

"I am a rich man."

"I s'pose so."

"And I believe you are an honest one."

"I'm glad you think so," dryly.

"I do, and I will furnish you all the money you need, on one condition."

"What's that?" asked the Squire cautiously, betraying no more emotion than if he had merely been offered the most ordinary of daily favors.

"I came here to-day to make a proposition to you of another sort. Your suggestion opens a better way. As I said, I am a rich man, to-day. But I have undertaken an enterprise which is full of peril. If I should die to-morrow, it is quite possible that my estate would be swallowed up in the litigation that would ensue. I have only my daughter to care for. She will be my only heir. But, if I should die while she is yet young, she might have no estate when grown to womanhood. Now, I want to provide against contingencies, and I will tell you what I will do. I will sell you the land at a nominal price, and will give you twenty-five thousand dollars to expend in its improvements, on condition that

my little girl shall have a half-interest in the business
when she comes to be twenty-one years of age.''

"Meaning little Hilda, I suppose?"

"Of course."

"And you want I should give you what sort of a
bond?"

"None at all. I want your word that you will transfer
this interest to her, if you should be living at that time,
and that you will leave it to her by will so that she
might not lose it in case of your death."

"What!" exclaimed the Squire, sitting up, regardless
of his ailment, and looking at the Captain in amazement. "You mean to trust me with all this and take
no instrument of writing?"

"I have been entrusted with much more, and merely
expect you to be as faithful as I have been."

"Oh, I can't take it, Captain. I can't take it. I did
think of borrowing it from you, if you could let me have
good clean money, but I could not take it in this way;
I couldn't do it; I couldn't do it. I'm much obliged—
ever so much obliged—but I couldn't do it, nohow."

"What do you mean by 'clean money'?"

"Clean money? Well, you must excuse me, Captain,
but—but I meant money that wasn't made in—in any
way—that—that "—

"Kidnapping, for instance?" sharply.

"Well, yes," responded the Squire, his self-control
at once restored by the other's tone—"that or anything
else that—that a man of my convictions couldn't approve of."

"I'm afraid you couldn't take this, then. I inherited
a part of it from the Hargroves of Hargrove's Quarter,
who were a tough lot in their day—worse than kidnappers, I'm afraid—buccaneers—pirates, perhaps."

"Slave-holders, at least, and perhaps slave-traders
too," said Kortright,

"Both," said Hargrove, resuming his seat.

"And you—how have you used it?" asked Kortright severely, looking under his eyebrows at the other.

"Me? Oh, I took a little that I had left after building Folly Castle, up there, and put it into the 'China trade.' It has grown from a little to a good deal, and I thought I would draw out while there was something to be had. But that was strictly moral," he added, with a laugh. "We took tea and opium one way and missionaries the other."

"I s'pose that's the way of trade," said Kortright with a sigh.

"Squire, I don't often share your peculiar notions, but have never tried to change them; still I do think you are carrying them a little too far. I wouldn't like to take money that was the direct result of crime, myself; but can you follow up each piece of gold, and refuse it if a scoundrel's hand has touched it since it left the mint?"

"No, I s'pose not. Perhaps this very dollar," he added, drawing one from his pocket, "has helped pay for cutting some man's throat. Yet I don't know. Somehow, I've never known money that was made in a wrong way to bring much enjoyment to them that had it."

"That's what they say about the 'nigger-trader's' gains in my country," said Hargrove.

"I should think that would curse the purest gold that ever was minted!" said Kortright vehemently.

"Yet you were willing to borrow money of me that, in its origin, was, as you fully believed, stained with this very traffic."

"That is so," said Kortright meditatively. "That is so. Perhaps I was wrong. I s'pose I must have been. You see, I'd been thinkin' of this, day after day, as I lay here, and had kind o' got my mind set on having the money, somehow, and doin' this thing that I

s'pose has been lyin' in my mind, I don't know how
many years. I must have been wrong, though," he
added humbly, " for why shouldn't it be just as wrong
for me to borrow such money as for another to use
it ? "

" There's this difference, Squire, and I think it makes
all the difference between ill-gotten gains and 'clean
money,' as you called it. If the doer of the wrong uses
the money, the curse of his evil may very naturally at-
tach to it ; but I do not see how by any justice or reason the innocent holder should be affected by it."

" Perhaps not, perhaps not," sighed Kortright. "I'm
sure I don't know." He sank back on the lounge and
was silent for a little while and then said, " You want
to do this for your little girl ?"

" Yes."

" And I want to do it for my boy."

" Then why not make them partners ?"

" How ?"

" If you must have an instrument of writing to witness the trust, why not make yourself a trustee for them
jointly, binding yourself to convey to them equal moieties
on coming of age ?"

There was a moment's silence.

" I'm a good deal older than you, Captain."

" But will very likely outlive me. Whether you do
or not, a reasonable support will be secured to the child,
whatever may be the result of the complications that
now threaten me."

" I'll do it, Captain !" said Kortright, sitting up and
reaching out his hand to clasp that of the other. " I'll
do it, if Martha hasn't any objection. I didn't think I'd
ever be mixed up with slavery or its results. I didn't
want to be ; but this seems kind o' thrust upon me.
My boy and your girl shall be equal partners, and I will
be a faithful trustee for them. May God so deal with

PARTNERS.

"*I'll do it, Captain!*" *said Kortright, sitting up and reaching out his hand.* —p. 156.

me as I shall deal with them," he added, solemnly looking upwards.

So the matter was settled. The bell rang for the Christmas dinner. The children came rushing from the barn, their clothes sadly rumpled and not without stain and rent, but with glowing cheeks and ravenous appetites. The company that gathered round the farmer's table was a happy one, despite the infirmity of the master of the house. Even he, thought his observing wife, was more cheerful and like himself than he had been since his sickness, and her heart was made glad when she saw Captain Hargrove enjoying the results of her labors with a gusto that was unmistakable. So the day was a happy one, and the Christmas blessing rested upon all. The Squire had a new lease of life in the prospect of doing what he had long dreamed of as a possibility, but never quite expected to realize. The master of Sturmhold had the look of one who had accomplished a cherished purpose, while the good mistress of Paradise Bay rejoiced in the happiness resulting from her scheme. The present had been made bright. The future fortunately cannot always fling its shadows before.

The two "partners," after a day of rollicking fun at the old homestead, went back to Sturmhold at night, ignorant of the eventful crisis in their lives which it marked.

CHAPTER XIII.

THE weeks passed by, and still the master of Sturm-hold delayed the departure of which he had spoken in his conversation with Kortright. The arrangement which had been then agreed upon had been fully consummated. The tract conveyed was much larger than the Squire had dreamed of in connection with his project, and the sum placed in his hands greater than he had asked. In return for this confidence, Harrison Kortright had included in the property thus held in trust all of his own lands, except a small tract about the homestead.

"I couldn't put this in, you see," he said to Har-grove apologetically, "because—well, there's no knowin' what might happen, and I wouldn't like to be entirely out of a home, nor have Martha feel, if I died, that she was only a trustee in her own house."

"Certainly not," replied Hargrove. "I had no idea of your doing anything of the kind. Indeed, I thought that your care and attention were fully equal in value to my investment, and I was very willing to leave it in that way."

Mrs. Kortright, however, was opposed to the reservation her husband's caution had made in her behalf. The project seemed to have captivated the good woman's fancy in an unusual degree. For the first time in his life her husband had risen beyond her highest ideal of manhood. The boy-lover who had gone to the heathen as an emissary of that Divine love—prototype of the earthly bliss that had been denied to him—shrank to nothingness in her esteem in comparison with the man

158

who, in mature years, could make a bed of pain the birth-
place of a new life. She had always respected her husband's sturdy will, his inflexible integrity, keen and true
judgment and unfailing self-poise in all the events of
common life. He was a man that filled to perfection her
definition of a husband. Kind, careful, thoughtful for
every need of his family, respected by all, and year by
year rising higher and higher in public esteem—she was
proud of his manly completeness, and had almost unconsciously yielded all care into his hands, confident that he
was entirely sufficient for all the earthly needs of the
denizens of Paradise Bay. She had lost her own self-
reliance, or rather had transferred to him the faith she
once had in herself. If she still spoke with some independence and had her "notions," as she was wont to
say, it was only in accordance with a suppressed intuition. She was positive only where she knew that her
husband's convictions would not run counter to her preferences. Otherwise, no matter how keen her impression,
she was sure to await an expression of his opinion.

All this had been a matter of growth with Martha
Kortright. The marriage which bound her to her husband had not been completed with the ceremony that
made the twain one flesh. She had grown toward the
nature which she at first only half understood, and had
contentedly yielded to its power, little by little, until
Martha Ermendorf had been quite forgotten in the wife
of Harrison Kortright. In all this, however, there had
been no enthusiasm and very little pride. She was, of
course, in a sense, proud of the confidence and esteem
her husband had won among his neighbors, but the romantic element in her nature was not stirred by his
character or achievements. What he did was either so
commonplace, or done so much as a matter of course,
that she never thought of him as a hero. Dawson Fox,
the missionary, was the hero of her past ; the boy Martin

was the hero of her future. Even in the tragic scene of the election day her husband's part was quite forgotten in comparison with her son's daring and Captain Hargrove's dramatic gallantry. Martin's brave attempt came ever to her mind as the key-note of a life of matchless heroism. The Captain, as he hurled the rearing steed back upon its haunches, seemed a king of men. But the husband, half-clad, pallid, his face wrung with agony at the son's danger, was only a matter of course —an instrument of duty. It was all right that he should do as he did. She could not imagine that he would do otherwise ; but it never occurred to her that there was anything uncommon or heroic in it. She had lived so long in intimate relations with his thought that she had no idea that the transparent soul hid heroism under the simple guise of duty.

His plan for building a busy city out of the foam of the great waterfall that had dashed and roared by the sleepy hamlet of Skendoah for many a day, unheeded by those who saw and heard, awakened her at once to the consciousness that her husband was of no common clay. She listened to his plans, grasped his idea and for the first time realized that the companion of her life was indeed heroic. He had been husband, father, lover, in a sedate and solemn sense, these many days ; now he was more—the one man to whom her womanhood bowed in adoration. So she was stirred to rival his noble idea by a self-sacrifice that should show her trust. It was a sort of unconscious penance which she set herself to do for the sake of this man, her husband, whom she felt she had robbed of half his due. Wiser counsels prevailed, however, and through the aid of a lawyer, it was finally arranged that Harrison Kortright should hold and manage the combined property, receiving himself one-half the yearly income—or more, if that did not amount to a certain sum—and reserving the remainder with the principal for Hilda and Martin, in equal moieties, to be given to each at majority and to be held by them as partners thereafter until they should elect to terminate the relation.

With the spring, new life came to the prisoner of the winter at Paradise Bay. The world was in the light of a new dawning. The great West had been made greater. There was a rumor of gold in California. A few enthusiastic outcasts had groped their way across the dun sandy swells to a new Land of Promise under the shadows of the Rocky Mountains. The world was waking, and the telegraph began to stretch its web up and down the land, annihilating distance and making time a jest. It was then that Harrison Kortright undertook the work for which he had been fitted by years of silent thought and that self-reliance that comes only from isolation and self-communion. The dream of his life was now about to be realized. He almost forgot the grip of disease upon his distorted hand and the finger of pain upon his flexed and dragging limb. The flesh could not weigh down his buoyant spirit, and the voice of his nightly prayer was fuller of triumphant thanks than of supplication for strength. He had dreamed of the waterfall from boyhood and now had his hand upon its boisterous strength. That he would make it do his will he no more doubted than did Cromwell the issue upon Marston Moor.

The time was favorable, and as the tidings of his project spread, every one who heard wondered that it had not been undertaken before. Success ran to meet him in his new endeavor. Skendoah awoke from its slumber, and waited in expectancy for the coming of new feet and a new era. When the spring buds burst into flower Martin bade adieu to Sturmhold, the new life that had enchained him and the Princess who had awakened him with her kiss, and returned to give the aid of quick eyes and nimble feet to his father's enterprise. There were tears and kisses at parting. The farmer's boy found Paradise Bay exceeding dull without the bright eyes and ruby lips that wept and sobbed for him at deserted Sturmhold. The grief of both was assuaged only by the promise of frequent meeting and of a future reunion when the torrent had been tamed and the master of Sturmhold should go no more away from its delightful surroundings.

CHAPTER XIV.

THE END OF THE LAW.

A TALL, stately man of middle age, with a mien of
peculiar grace and dignity, called at Sturmhold one day
not long afterwards, during a brief absence of Captain
Hargrove, and was shown into the library to await his
return. In person the visitor was one who would anywhere have attracted attention. Fully six feet in height,
well-knit and muscular in frame, with a noble, well-
proportioned head set on broad shoulders, he was a fine
specimen of self-reliant manhood. Add to this an ex-
pressive face, strong features, a large, brilliant, kindly
eye, a musical, sonorous voice, and you have a fair picture of the stranger who waited patiently for Hargrove's
return. To him entered Hilda, restless from the loss of
her companion. It was not long before she yielded to
the fascinations of a manner which few could resist, and
gave her fullest confidence to one whom no man had
ever presumed to doubt. When Captain Hargrove returned he was handed a plain card, on which was written
the name, "Jared Clarkson." It was a name well
known in that region, as that of a landholder whose
acres were numberless, scattered over half a hundred
counties of the State. Equally noted as an orator, a
philanthropist and a financier, he was a man of remarkable character and of great personal power, but so
given to what were deemed impracticable vagaries as
to be held in very trivial esteem in any public capacity,
while the regard for his private character was unbounded. Hargrove had often heard of him and had
163

no little curiosity to meet him, but chance had never thrown them together. He wondered what this man, who was chiefly known as the leader of the most advanced ideas upon social and political subjects, could want with him—the one man in all that region who was credited with the most active opposition to these ideas. Knowing his eccentricity, however, it occurred to Hargrove that perhaps his visitor had come to Sturmhold on an evangelizing tour, and proposed to accomplish nothing less than a conversion to the dogmas to which he was attached. It was with an amused smile, therefore, that he proceeded to the library. His amusement changed to amazement, therefore, when, opening the door, he saw this radical reformer seated on a low stool before Hilda, who was perched upon the highest chair in the room, with an open book in her lap, over which her eager face expressed only undoubting wonder.

"Yes," continued the excited child, "and the bears got after him !"

"Bears ?—the Great Bear and the Little Bear, I suppose ?" with the hint of a smile at the corner of his broad mouth.

"I reckon so," she responded, with an uneasy feeling that she was being laughed at. "Of course there must have been little and big ones, for there were twenty thousand of them."

"Twenty thousand !"

"Well, perhaps it was only ten thousand ; but it was a great many, *anyhow,*"—the last word with great positiveness of emphasis.

Mr. Clarkson bent in apparent absorption, while his tawny beard almost swept the page and his genial face was aglow with delight. It was the story of the adventures of Baron Munchausen, of whom Hilda was discoursing as she turned the pages and explained the engravings which illustrated the text. It had been a favorite with Martin, and so a part of her repertory of the wonderful.

"And this," she said, didactically, "this is where he went to the North Pole."

"You don't tell me!" said her auditor, in a soft, melodious voice. "Well, what did he do then?"

"The Baron? Oh, he was all right. He always was. He climbed the Pole!" in a voice of triumph.

"Climbed the pole? Was it a bare pole?"

"Yes—well—I don't know. But they were polar bears, you know."

A rich, full laugh rang out at this unconscious sally. The stranger caught Hilda in his arms, and turning met the surprised and amused glance of Captain Hargrove. Without putting the child down, the visitor advanced and said:

"Captain Hargrove, I suppose?"

"That is my name. This is Mr. Clarkson, I presume?"

"Yes. I wanted to see you a moment on business, and while I waited made the acquaintance of this little girl. She is very entertaining."

"For a wild girl, she does well enough," said Hargrove, smiling. "She has always lived alone, except when I have been here now and then for a while, and, though she has had a teacher, seems to have had her own way and taken her own course. I am thinking of sending her to school, now that she is getting so large."

"Indeed?" looking inquiringly at the child.

"Yes; I have to be away so much that I cannot look after her, and the servants are spoiling her, I am afraid."

"I don't know," said the stranger, seriously. "Nature is a great teacher—a great teacher, sir, and the grandest of nurses. I always pity the child that has to give the freedom of a life such as she has known for the *tyranny* of the school-room." The sentence was given with oratorical precision, a graceful outward wave of the left hand as he referred to the surroundings of Sturmhold, and a heavy, queer emphasis upon tyranny, the first syllable of which was pronounced with a long *y*.

"Well," said Hargrove, "I don't know which is most to be pitied, the child that has nature and misses the school, or that has the school and misses nature. But how can I serve you?"

"Oh, I just want to talk with you a little," replied Clarkson. "There, run away, my dear." He kissed the child, and lowered her to the floor as he spoke, and she left the room without further words. Hargrove motioned to a couple of chairs that stood in the embrasure of a window at the end of the room overlooking the valley, and they sat down. The visitor looked at the prospect without for a moment, turned and cast his eye over the well-filled shelves and rich adornments of the room, and then surveyed his companion from head to foot with careful scrutiny. Everything apparently pleased him, for he said:

"You have a fine place here, Captain Hargrove."

There was something in his tone that conveyed a deeper meaning than the words. Hargrove smiled quietly as he replied:

"You did not come all this distance to tell me that, I suppose, Mr. Clarkson?"

"Well, no," said the other, frankly, "I did not. I came as the representative of Mrs. George Eighmie."

"Indeed!" said Hargrove, lifting his eyes.

"You are surprised, perhaps?" he asked, with a smile.

"At your coming, no; at the title of your embassy, yes," with a light laugh.

"So? You object to my credentials?"

"Not at all. If you are satisfied with them, I am."

"You no doubt know to whom I refer,"

"I am sure I have not the slightest idea," replied Hargrove, with significant blandness.

"George Eighmie was your brother, I believe ?"

"My half-brother."

"Yes, of course. You were his executor ?"

"There is such a record, I believe."

"And the guardian of his children ?"

"You say so," smiling.

"I ask you, Mr. Hargrove; I ask you as a man, sir," turning upon him a grave, earnest face, half-flushed with anger at the levity of tone and manner of his listener.

"You have the right to ask, Mr. Clarkson, and I have an equally indubitable right to answer or not, as suits my pleasure."

The visitor regarded him with surprise. He was one of those men who are accustomed to overbear those who converse with them by the mere force of their own directness. Subterfuge was rarely attempted with him. He was sincerity itself, and not only expected, but almost compelled sincerity from others. That one should think of refusing to answer such an inquiry was a thing most preposterous to him. So he said :

"I am a plain man, Captain Hargrove."

"They call me blunt, sir," said the ex-officer in a tone that fully justified such a description.

"And I ask a plain question," said Clarkson severely, ignoring the other's interjection.

"When you do so you will get a plain answer, sir," was the emphatic reply.

"Humph ! Will you tell me, then, whether you were the guardian of your half-brother's children ?"

"I will not."

"You will not ; why ?"

"Because I do not choose to do so."

Clarkson rose and walked quickly once or twice across the room.

"Mr. Hargrove," he said, finally, as he paused near his former seat, "I came here in a spirit of friendship and conciliation to induce you to do justice to an injured and outraged woman."

"Am I to infer that you show your conciliatory spirit by accusing me of the injury and outrage?" asked Hargrove, with a smile.

"She is your brother's widow," said the other, hotly.

"So you have said before."

"And you have not denied—you dare not deny it."

"I do not feel called upon to deny it."

"You have taken her estate and left her in penury. You have separated her from her children and—"

"That will do, Mr. Clarkson. I do not question your motives, but you must remember that I am in my own house—a fact which I may forget if you do not use milder language."

"I beg your pardon, sir," said Clarkson. "The wrong of which this woman's life is only one sad chapter always stirs me to the very marrow. The law which permits such outrages is a vile and infamous thing."

Hargrove made no answer. Clarkson turned away, and, after a moment, returned and said:

"If you do not mean to comply with our demands, Mr. Hargrove, why not say so plainly?"

"You have not as yet made any demand. When you do so I will certainly reply distinctly."

"Very well, I will proceed now in form," said Clarkson, resuming his seat. "Here is a power of attorney from the relict of George Eighmie, late of Mallowbanks, planter, whose half-brother and executor you admit yourself to be."

He handed Captain Hargrove a legal document as he spoke.

" Well ?"

"By examination you will see that I am authorized by her to demand from you a share of the estate of her late husband and the custody of her children. Now, what have you to say ?"

"Only, Mr. Clarkson, that the law has decided that George Eighmie left no widow and no legitimate children. Through failure of these, his estate fell to me as his heir. What I shall do with it as such is a matter for my own conscience alone. If, as executor of his will, I am in the least in fault, the law offers a remedy."

"Yes, the remedy which the poor have against the rich —the weak against the strong," said Clarkson with a sneer.

"Pardon me, Mr. Clarkson," said Hargrove, rising to his feet, "that is not so. If the woman you call George Eighmie's widow had not you for her friend— the richest man of all this region of wealth and thrift— she still has me, and knows very well that I would not see any wrong done her by any one, much less be guilty of it myself."

"Yet you hold and enjoy the estate which should have been hers, while she is obliged to seek refuge among strangers."

"Pardon me again, sir," said Hargrove, "the woman of whom you speak is in no need. Whatever I have she is welcome to enjoy. Even now my house is at her disposal, my servants subject to her control."

"Yet she fled from this house in a frenzy of terror."

"A silly, baseless fear, yet one which her sad experience made it not unreasonable that she should entertain. She is a weak, foolish woman at best, and has been made doubly suspicious by the snares into which she has fallen through her own folly and the love of a weak man."

"Perhaps your own conduct gave her ground for suspicion."

"I have reproached myself with the thought that it may have done so, Mr. Clarkson," said Hargrove frankly. "I am free to admit that I do not like her. I never did. She is a vain, selfish, querulous thing, who never had anything but a pretty face to make her attractive. Then, too, I have never been able to forget the woe she wrought in my poor brother's life."

"Was it not his fault rather than hers?" sharply.

"Oh, no doubt; but you see, Mr. Clarkson, I loved him, and it is always the one we love who is wronged by misfortune."

"But if you do not want her in your house, why do you not let her have the estate—or a widow's portion of it, at least—give up the children to her charge, and leave her to care for them and herself as she chooses? Certainly you have enough without it. Or, if the law gives it to you, you might at least yield a moiety to her."

"Mr. Clarkson, your remark shows how easily we are misled by our prejudices and prepossessions. If this woman had not been, at one time, a victim of the evils of a system which you regard with peculiar horror and aversion, you would not look upon her case as one of hardship. A good home here or a good support elsewhere—anything in reason, and in fact a good deal more than reason, I am ready to provide."

"But, still, what should have been her own is withheld from her."

"You think so? Let me tell you the facts. When I shall have disposed of that estate according to the wish of George Eighmie, it will have consumed itself and half as much more, and will leave me still to provide out of my own estate for this woman and her children."

"You might at least allow her the control of her own children."

"Your opinion differs from that of George Eighmie. That is all there is of that matter," answered Hargrove.

" He left two children to my care. His own relation to them was complex and peculiar. Whether I received them as executor or as guardian is yet an undetermined question, legally. As his brother, however, I have thus far strictly followed his injunctions in regard to them, and intend to do so hereafter, no matter what the consequences."

" Where are they now ?"

"Mr. Clarkson, the woman whom you represent knows very well that one of them, the boy, was stolen from my possession, and I have since been unable to find any trace of him. As for the girl—well, she is properly cared for."

"She is about the age of the child I made the acquaintance of here this morning, I believe ?"

" Very nearly," said Hargrove, with a smile.

" And resembles her in appearance, too ?"

" Perhaps," the smile deepening as he spoke.

"Mr. Hargrove, why is not this mother allowed to see her child ?" Clarkson asked the question with deep feeling, and then proceeded : " Put yourself in her place, my dear sir. As you say, her life has been a sad one. She seems to have known poverty and wealth, love and hate ; and now to be debarred from her children's caresses is surely a hard lot."

"No one realizes that more than I," rejoined Hargrove with emotion. "I greatly misdoubt the wisdom of my brother's plan ; but I pledged him my honor to carry it into effect, and I mean to do it to the letter, if it takes my fortune and my life."

" Surely his plan did not contemplate any such cruelty toward the poor woman who had been his wife—at least in the sight of Heaven."

"I think, sir, that his plan was devised simply with a view to securing the happiness of the children. The law had dealt very harshly with my poor brother's foibles, and he wished to save them from its scath,"

"The law—the law!" exclaimed the other hotly, "do you call that *the law*, which separates husband and wife? It is sacrilege, sir! Such an enactment is no law. It is an instrument of iniquity—an outgrowth of that 'league with hell,' the Constitution of the United States!"

His eyes flashed fire under his heavy brows, and his strong face worked with excitement as he spoke.

"That may all be, Mr. Clarkson. I do not pretend to know where the law cuts the line of right too sharply to bind the conscience. This I do know, that George Eighmie enjoined it upon me on his death-bed to do for these children as he would have done had we exchanged places. His purpose was one that my conscience approves though my reason may not. I am doing now what you would do, what any honorable man would do. What his purpose was, I have never revealed to any one. Should I live to see it accomplished, no one will ever know it save from such rough guesses as you may make. If I die before that work is completed, I will leave it in good and honest hands. Mr. Clarkson," he added, suddenly laying his hand upon the latter's shoulder, "If I should die before the youngest of these children arrives at maturity this trust will devolve on you."

"On me?"

"Yes, on you. I have long been thinking of one whom I could make my successor, and our conversation to-day has brought me to this decision."

"I will not touch it, sir, I will not touch it!"

"I think you will, sir. No honest man will ever refuse another honest man a just and reasonable request. At least, if you will not act yourself, you will select some one to act in my place."

"I refuse, sir, I refuse, utterly and absolutely, now and forever," said Clarkson, moving toward the door,

"You will not, sir, when he who asks is dead."

"I will not hear of it! If you think you are doing right, go on. I shall not trouble you. But what shall I say to—to this woman?"

"Tell her that George Eighmie asked me to provide for her every reasonable comfort, and that not one syllable of what I promised him shall ever fail while Merwyn Hargrove lives."

"And if she wishes to return? You will make her welcome, I suppose?"

"No; I have no welcome for her. I wish she might elect not to return; but, if she insists on coming, my house is open, and she shall have no reason to complain of any lack of respect while here."

"And the little girl, she will be allowed to assume her old relation to her, I suppose?"

"To Hilda? Oh, yes; though she is getting past the need of a nurse, which is about the limit of her capacity."

"But you will not separate them?"

"Not unless she abuses my confidence. In that case, of course, I shall lose no time in ridding myself of her presence."

"Of course. Well, I will tell her. I think that is the best she can do."

"I should prefer, Mr. Clarkson, that you should say what is a reasonable allowance for her and let me pay it into your hands."

"No, sir; no, sir; I drop the matter from this moment. It is evidently one of the accursed secrets of slavery, of which I have already heard too many. By the way, Captain Hargrove, I am surprised that, with the sad experiences which you have known, you should still be an advocate of the system which produces them."

"I do not know that I am an advocate of it; but I was born where it prevailed, and, while I appreciate its evils, I do not see how they can be remedied."

"The remedy is freedom!" said Clarkson, enthusiastically; "make the negro a man and he will soon take care of himself."

"Pshaw! Mr. Clarkson. I have seen the negro at home and abroad, free and slave, and I know the people of the South. I have myself set free more slaves than all the Abolitionists in the State of New York."

"You?"

"Yes, I," he repeated, in a contemptuous tone, "and I have now no particle of interest in a slave, except through the will of George Eighmie."

"Indeed?"

"Yes, and I don't mind saying that I don't want any more slave property. I believe I would rather be poor than have it. Yet, I am not sure that slavery itself is a sin, and I am not surprised at a man who inherited slaves along with his family Bible hanging on to them just as strongly as he sticks to that."

"Yet that does not make it right."

"Granted. Neither does the fact that liberty is abstractly right make universal freedom desirable."

"I do not see why."

"You do not? Why if, by a miracle, the slaves were freed to-day, they would be re-enslaved or annihilated in a week. It is impossible and absurd to think of. Freedom cannot be where there are two races, almost equal in numbers, one of which has been the master and the other servile. It can never be—never, sir, unless the spirit of the one is broken and the manhood of the other developed. The path from slavery to freedom must always be a long and hard one. I do not see how the American slave can ever set his foot in it. Slavery has been a hard master, but it has taught him much. He is infinitely above his congener on the African coast, but he is not yet able to go alone. Isolated from the white race, he lapses into barbarism without fail. The problem, which seems so simple to you, Mr. Clarkson, is a terrible and bloody one to me. You may, perhaps, set the slave at liberty. It looks now as if the time would come which my Rietta was always prophesying, when the land will be riven by the conflict, and slavery be drowned in blood. It may come, and you may live to see it, though I do not think you will. But, if you do, remember what I tell you to-day. A slave may be freed in an hour; a free man cannot be made in many a day."

The two men stood gazing earnestly into each other's faces. They were splendid types. The one dark and swarthy, with a hint of Southern sunshine in his eye, his long beard and a certain litheness of form distinguishing him from the other, who, not less stalwart in frame, had a tawny tinge in his beard and a clear light in his blue eye that told of generations that had looked up at frozen winter skies. Of the two, the latter was by far the more carefully dressed. He was graceful without the languid ease of the other, and more readily awakened to engrossing interest, though perhaps less intensely excited when his interest was once aroused.

"You may be right," said Clarkson, earnestly, and extending his hand as he spoke. "I can appreciate your feeling, though I do not share your apprehension. To my mind, you omit one important factor—indeed, the most important."

"What is that?" asked Hargrove, as he took the proffered hand.

"God!" said the other, in a tone of the utmost solemnity. "I can only see the evil that is, and hear a voice calling me to tear it down, and trust Him to provide a remedy for that which shall come after."

They looked at each other for a moment in silence. Then they parted, each to ponder the thoughts the other had expressed.

CHAPTER XV.

" ' FOR the glory of God—for the glory of God '—I declare, Captain, I don't know. I thought of it when you first brought me that will, but, as there wasn't any opposition—that is, no *caveat* filed, though there was considerable talk of one—I didn't give it much attention. Since that, I 've kind of thought it a settled matter—not exactly *res adjudicata*, you know, but a question not likely to come up again, till now this new claim of the heirs that Gilman is pushing, and I 've had my mind turned to it again, and I declare, Captain, I 'm more 'n half afraid on 't."

The speaker sat in the library at Sturmhold beside a table on which were numerous papers, while on the other side sat Merwyn Hargrove, his face flushed and his brows knitted close above angry, impatient eyes. It was at night, and a shaded lamp left the two men half in shadow, while the papers, inkstand and the stubby hand of the lawyer, who held a quill pen with the back of it downward while he spoke, were in the circle of white light about its base. Just beside it, too, stood a silver waiter, on which was a decanter, a small pitcher, a sugar-bowl and spoons. A glass, half full of liquor, stood at the speaker's right hand, while an empty one stood at Hargrove's elbow. The clock upon the mantel struck a soft, mellow chime as the speaker paused. Each of the listeners counted stroke by stroke, mentally wondering what would be the result. It was eleven o'clock, and they had been there since seven. Neither thought

176

so long a time had passed. It was the conclusion of an important consultation. The man who had spoken was Mr. Matthew Bartlemy, the legal adviser of Merwyn Hargrove in Carolina. Mr. Bartlemy had been the attorney of Colonel Eighmie, and his devoted friend as well, and had naturally been intrusted with Captain Hargrove's affairs for that reason, if for no other.

But there were not lacking other reasons why one charged with delicate and important duties should seek the aid of Matthew Bartlemy. He was one of the men who had come up from the lower ranks of Southern life to the highest pinnacle in his profession. The fact that one of this class rises at all is evidence of his unusual power. Even at the North, the capacity to come up through superincumbent social grades without the aid of money or friends is not regarded lightly. The man who achieves success from nothingness is apt to look back upon his past with a peculiar complacency, and boast, directly or indirectly, of being a self-made man. He may be wrong to feel so. It is a matter of grave doubt whether a good brain is not often hampered with the accidents of wealth and position rather than given any advantage thereby. It is a question whether the paucity of opportunity which poverty brings does not favor that intensity, concentration and self-reliance on which, in the main, success depends. Many a plant would have grown rugged and strong on the bleak mountain side that, prisoned in a hot-house, is dwarfed and weakened until it falls a victim to hordes of parasites who could not have pierced its bark in its wild estate. So many a man, who would have grown strong and grand in wholesome poverty and risen out of obscurity into eminence under the ceaseless sting of dire necessity, fades into insignificance under the influence of wealth, opportunity and the lack of an unrelenting need.

But if such a career at the North be regarded as creditable, what shall be said of it under the social conditions of the South of that day? That such instances were not infrequent speaks volumes for the strength and vigor of that unconsidered class who constitute the majority of the Southern whites—the "common liver," "crapper" or "poor white" class.

From this class, unesteemed and, in many respects, undesirable, has been constantly repaired that vital waste which slavery produced in the ruling or aristocratic class. By a principle of selection not less certain than the survival of the fittest among the lower forms of life, there rose out of this neglected, ignorant and ofttimes degraded class, year by year, the strongest, bravest and toughest—the best and the worst—into the ranks of the ruling class, to take the places of those whom luxury, leisure and vice had weakened and destroyed. From this source came the new blood that kept the old families up to the level of ability their names implied. Solitude, nature and poverty were the inheritance of such. The pine trees crooned their cradle songs. Rocks and rivers were their playground and *academia.* They were so near to nature that they had almost the toughness of the savage. Their needs were as simple as the slave's. The woods and waters furnished half their subsistence without labor. They looked forward to be to-morrow as they were yesterday. For their children they asked no more than they had themselves. The public school was so rare as to be a curiosity and so poor as hardly to merit the name. If knowledge came to such it was by accident, or as a reward for a perseverance that of itself guaranteed success. This life strengthened, however, and toughened its best specimens, while the inferior ones shriveled and rotted. Strong-willed, thick-skinned, tough-fibred men came out of this class and conquered places in the aristocracy. They mated with its daughters. They won its estates by industry sometimes, not unfrequently by fraud. They won their way by overmatching in brain and power those that boasted of hereditary gifts, and took their places in the caste they had conquered. It was by this means that new families grew and old ones were kept alive at the South. It is for this reason that the individuals who stand at the head of Southern affairs, who dominate its political life, are very rarely the blue-bloods which the sycophants of the North conceive them to be. One needs only to run through the list of Southern statesmen, present or past, to discover the fact that their marvelous strength, individuality and energy, is due, not to their old families and aristocratic descent, but to the nameless herd whose very memory is spurned by the leader whom the same hardships have toughened for conflict. Therefore it is that the Northern man is apt to boast of having overcome poverty, while the Southern man extols the wealth and social rank of his kindred, it hardly matters how remote. The Northern man who rises exults in his victory. The Southern man is often humiliated by the memory of really humble origin. Indeed, it is rare to find at the South a strong man who is, on both sides of his family, two removes from that peculiar substratum which is the really distinctive feature of Southern life, and on the elevation of which the future of the South must depend. What called itself aristocracy was a pleasant thing. It had its uses in the past, no doubt. Indeed, it has a use in the present—it is the dead trunk, smitten by the fiery bolt, but yet erect, about which the living vine of the scorned and unconsidered lower class will cling and climb.

The ancient aristocracy will serve as the mould in which the manhood of the South will in a measure be shaped, but it is in the undertow that its strength, its

enterprise and its destiny must be sought. From this
class, even in the past, have come its best and strongest.
Jackson, whose birth is still a mystery, against whom
stands yet the record of the hostel that he left without
paying his bill, came out of this class. A President of
questionable parentage, who learned the rudiments after
his marriage ; a Senator whose first shoes were worn
when, according to tradition, he fiddled at his mother's
first marriage ; Governors and Judges and generals by
the score, whose names are accounted of the proudest
among the living and the dead, derived from this class,
which they have too often made haste to disown and
contemn, the strength that gave success. So, while
the strongest of those below conquered their places in
the rank above they were in turn overcome by the
caste to which they aspired, which, as a condition of
recognition and acceptance, demanded that the fact be
forgotten. So the aristocracy preserved itself and yet
renewed its strength by constant accessions from the
ranks below. The gradations in society were preserved
with a distinctness impossible at the North. The poor
white remained poor. The aristocrat still boasted of
his proud descent. They kept the pride of the great
families alive, and the son whose sire was of humble
origin flaunted his mother's family crest. Even the
bar-sinister was not always allowed to interfere with
the pride of descent, and instances are to be found
of great men who have sunk the pride of self-achieve-
ment to boast the unsanctioned kinship of a great name.

Ah ! do not sneer, good Puritan. The results of this
social system are not lightly to be condemned. While
the system which you deem incomparable has tended
more and more to crush out individuality, to furnish a
Procrustean bed for all, this has developed the reverse.
Before *you* boast of material results you must remember
that you have taken the choicest blood of the world to

repair the waste of life your follies have entailed. Half a million lives a year have brought fresh blood to inject into your veins. You have been the Canaan of the world's hope—the highway of its aspiration. Europe's life, from the frozen ocean to the steaming sea, has mingled with your life. Good and bad have come alike. The evil have come to ravish as well as the good lawfully to enjoy. But all have brought strength and kindly nature has chastened the evil with her amenities, and developed the good with healthful antagonism and abundant reward. Babel has been builded at every four corners. Every churchyard is polyglotic. Who are you, and whence? How many peoples mingle in your veins? How many ancestral languages make up your speech? You have wrought wonders on the face of the earth. Is all that you have done good? Can you forecast a cloudless future? You claim to be the perfection of the American idea—to be yourself American. Is it true?

With the South how different have been the conditions! Her people are all the children of those who dwelt within her lines when the Revolution ended. The world has run past her borders. Her children have poured out of her limits, but none have returned. She has peopled her own West and flowed over into your Northwest. You have builded factories and cities and marts. She has grown men. She has given of her life by millions to make your life-blood richer. You have grown too rich to raise children ; her homes are swarming with them. One system may be better, but neither is bad. Perhaps the best may lie somewhere between. At least, O, boastful Northman, remember this: what thou hast achieved has been with the world's help. What the South has done she has done alone—because she willed to be alone, no doubt, but yet the fact remains. The world has not come into her life. The English stocks that settled on her eastern coast have

filled her borders and overflowed them, too.   There is
little admixture.   The immigrant has been excluded ;
the African is afar off across the abyss of darkness.
The one life has grown out of itself ; the other has
sucked the veins of the world.

Mr. Matthew Bartlemy was of the stock of common
livers.   His father had been an overseer ; his grandfather
a "crapper"—good, honest people, as are the most of
their class.   They ate and drank with content.   For
them there was no morrow that gave promise of more
than to-day, and little fear of any that should be worse.
The place of the rich and favored was too high for them
to aspire to, and below them was only the slave, who
was separated from them a world-wide distance by his
color.   They were poor.   They did not feel it deeply.
Their people had always been poor.   They expected
nothing else for their children.   They were poor but
honest and—white.   Of these two things they were
justly proud, and of these alone.   There was nothing
else in their past, present or future, so far as they could
foresee it, to justify pride.

They were coarse, rough people ; hardened by generations of want.   They did not murmur.   They were as
well off as their neighbors.   The pride and luxury of the
rich did not gall them.   They were only poor folks ; expected to be treated as such ; had no idea of being anything else, and had no quarrel with fate over what they
deemed inevitable and irremediable.

Some of these attributes the good people had transmitted to their descendant.   He was neither sensitive
nor retiring ; and he was ambitious.   He could not see
why others should have what he did not possess.   He
was not especially desirous of fame, but wealth, success,
power, he coveted with an unquenchable desire.   Whatever lay between him and these he early determined to
overcome.   He was not scrupulous.   What others hesi-

tated to do he performed with alacrity if it promoted the end he had in view. By stubborn persistence he gained an education. An old field school, the kindness of a clergyman to whom even the pittance he could pay was an object, and the place of a beneficiary at college, together with his indomitable energy and tireless application, put him on a level, in acquirement, with the most favored. He had brain. Everybody had learned that before he graduated. He was not brilliant, but he was solid. He did not know everything, but what he once learned he knew forever. What he needed to know he was sure to find out. For what he did not need he had no care. He chose the law; gave himself to his client; was faithful, tireless, shrewd and hard. He had few intimates; avoided politics; served his profession and made it serve him. Before he had reached middle life he had the leading practice in his circuit, and was known and feared as an opponent even in the capital of the state. Now, in the fullness of his years, he stood at the head of his profession, the aspirations of his youth more than fulfilled—the lord of many a plantation, the owner of hundreds of slaves. He had steadily put aside the honors of his profession, and gathered only with untiring zeal its material advantages.

The habits of his life were so strong upon him that he still labored as assiduously as when spurred by necessity. Colonel Eighmie had been his patron in his early days, and he never forgot a service rendered to himself. Merwyn Hargrove, thus commended to his attention, had further commended himself by being a very profitable client. Matthew Bartlemy had served him faithfully, and never dreamed of relaxing his watch over the interests that had been committed to his care. He would not have scrupled to demand half the estate for an emergent service; but, having undertaken that service, he would not for a thousand times that amount have failed in any duty attaching to the relation he had assumed. He gave to the affairs of every client not only reasonable care but the utmost diligence. As a man, he was not altogether admirable. As an agent, he was the perfection of vigilance, sagacity and fidelity. As Matthew Bartlemy he was feared, hated, and sometimes loathed. As M. Bartlemy, Esq., Attorney-at-Law, he was trusted by his clients, feared by his opponents and envied by the entire bar of his state.

"You don't mean to say that you really have any doubt as to the validity of that will?" said Hargrove, taking a paper between his thumb and finger and holding it toward the lawyer.

"Well, I don't know. Gilman has been feeling round on this matter a right smart while, and now he has got all the collateral heirs to agree and is going to bring suit for them to the Fall Term. There ain't any doubt about that. Now, Gilman isn't the sort of a man that stakes on a play he don't think has a fair chance of winning, and I may be allowed to say I am hardly the man he'd try to bluff on a weak hand. Whatever else may be said of Matthew Bartlemy, it's pretty well settled that he don't scare easy."

The short, erect figure that sat opposite Merwyn Hargrove just moved as a low chuckle escaped the lips. The small gray eyes peered keenly over the gold-bowed glasses on his nose as he passed his hand over the round solid forehead that rose like a dome springing from the red face and gray, furzy brows below. The trim old man, whose head seemed to rest almost upon the massive shoulders, so short and stout was the neck that upheld it, was the very embodiment of courage. Hargrove laughed, despite his evident vexation, at the grim humor of the old man's allusion to his well-earned reputation. Bartlemy laid down his pen, emptied his glass, and, turning toward his auditor a little more squarely, raised a silver-headed cane that had rested against the arm of his chair, crossed his hands upon it, and, still sitting bolt upright, continued :

"Now, Gilman thinks he can overthrow that will, but he isn't sure about some things. If he'd been entirely sure he wouldn't ever have come to me with a proposition of compromise. He would have brought suit and waited for me to go to him. He ain't in any hurry. He knows you're good ; but there's something in the way. I know him so well that I can tell his state of mind almost as quick as he can himself. He thinks he sees his way through that will, Captain Hargrove. There ain't any other way to his end. If that will is good the collateral heirs of George Eighmie have no more claim to his estate than the King of Timbuctoo— not a bit."

The old man stamped the floor with his cane, raised his glasses to his forehead and leaned forward with flushed face and burning eyes as he uttered this conclusion at which he had arrived.

"But why ?" queried Hargrove. "There is no doubt of its being George's will, I suppose ?"

"Not a bit," said Bartlemy. "It has every element of a valid holographic will, which was duly ascertained when it was admitted to probate. Besides, that question cannot be raised by these heirs. Every one of them had due notice, and that question is decided."

"What, then, can be their ground of action ?"

"That's just what I set myself to find out. As I said, I know Gilman. There's just this difference between him and me : he ain't afraid of anything he can see, and I am not troubled about anything I can't see. So I set out to find first what sort of a hole the damned rascal had found in that will to make him think he could drive a cart and oxen through it ; and, in the second place, what there was behind it to scare him after he got through; and I've found out both, Captain Hargrove!"

"You have?"

"I have. The hole he's found in the will—or thinks he's found—is that piece of sentimental foolishness, 'for the glory of God.'"

"What?" inquired Hargrove in surprise.

"'For the glory of God,' sir, 'for the glory of God;' that's it. If ever Gilman or any one else gets past that will, that's just where he'll drive through."

"I don't see how that can affect it."

"That's just what the idiot thought who wrote it. Confound the fool, if he had just let me draw it, there'd never been any such chance. Religion hasn't any place in a will anyhow, and I shouldn't have wasted any in that way."

"I presume not," said Hargrove, with a smile "though I cannot see what harm George's weak attempt at piety can do."

"That's it—that's just it. The man was a coward. He hadn't pluck enough to do what he wanted done himself, and so naturally distrusted you."

"I do not see that," said the other.

"You don't see it? Why, he had some sort of an understanding with you, and so made you his heir, with a secret trust that you should do some particular thing with his estate, didn't he?"

"Yes," responded Hargrove. "He had talked with me very freely of what he wished done, and I had promised him repeatedly that, if he left it to me, I would not take a cent of it for myself, but would—"

"There, there," interrupted Bartlemy, striking his cane on the floor and stamping so as effectually to drown the other's words, "haven't I told you a hundred times that I don't want to know anything about that? A secret trust ought to be kept secret, and especially must not be inferable from the terms of a bequest. Now, if he'd been the kind of man you are, Captain, he'd have trusted you without any doubt to do just as you had promised."

"Why, so he did, Mr. Bartlemy," interposed Hargrove.

"Did, eh? Then what did he put in that confounded 'glory of God' clause for?"

"Why to remind me of my promise, I suppose," said Hargrove.

"That's it—that's just it!" said Bartlemy, springing from his chair, and beginning to pace up and down the floor. "He thought he must prick up your conscience by some sort of a hint that you alone would understand. The infernal fool! That's always the way with a man that hasn't pluck enough to get a lawyer to draw his will, but sneaks off alone and writes it himself, and leaves a court to find out whether it is legal or not."

"Still," said Hargrove, "I do not see how this hint, as you call it, can affect the validity of his will."

"I don't say it does," retorted Bartlemy, "but it may. It depends entirely on whether a court holds it to be a hint, and, if so, what kind of a hint they think it is."

"Don't almost all wills have a similar clause, 'In the name of God, Amen,' or something of the sort?"

"Oh, yes; and if we can only make the court believe that this is a sort of amen clause, or a mere pious ejaculation, it will be all right. But that's the trouble. Scholar as he was, George Eighmie wasn't over-inclined to piety. He wasn't so desperately given to religious exhortation and you weren't so badly in need of it, especially from him, that he would be very likely to send you a sermon in so short a will as that. Here, let me read it."

The old man caught the paper from Hargrove's hand,

thrust it down into the circle of light near the lamp, worked his eyebrows up and down with a quick twitching movement that brought his eye-glasses down upon his nose, and read :

"I give and bequeath all my real and personal property of which I may die seized and possessed, and all my negroes—"

"That is all right," said the old man, gesticulating with the head of his cane in his left hand. "He might have left out 'real' and 'personal,' but they do no harm ; and, having used them, it was well enough to mention 'negroes' particularly, too, for they are hardly one or the other—a sort of 'chattel-real,' the courts have sometimes called them." Then he read on :

—"to my half-brother, Captain Merwyn Hargrove,"

"If the fool had only stopped there I should not have been coming up here on any trumped-up story about seeing a New York doctor, especially as I haven't had any call for a doctor at home in sixty odd years. Now here's the trouble :"

—"to hold and use according to the dictates of his conscience and for the glory of God."

"There it is, just as plain as black and white can make it, that he meant to constitute you his trustee and not his heir. At least it seems so to me, and I am afraid will appear so to the court."

"Well, what of it ?"

"What of it ? Well, there is a good deal of it. In the first place, if that is admitted, the court will want to know what sort of a trust it was, and whether it was a lawful one or not."

"Hasn't a man a right to dispose of his property as he chooses ?"

"We sometimes say so, Captain, but it isn't true—not by a great deal. Let us suppose now that this trust your brother hinted at was that you should use the proceeds of his estate to build a school or a college, or any similar charity. Then it would be all right."

"The purpose was certainly a charitable one," said Hargrove.

"Tut, tut! I don't want to know what it was. Remember that. But now let us suppose again that it was given to you in order that you might take care of that woman he called his wife and the children he had by her."

"Well."

"Or suppose this was only part of it, and the rest was that you should free his slaves and use the estate to make them comfortable and help them make their own living."

"That would be a very reasonable supposition from what I have done," said Merwyn with a meaning smile.

"I'm afraid it would," rejoined Bartlemy, "and if the court should be of that notion I 'm afraid the will would be in a bad way."

"How so?"

"Well, you see, just a few months before George died the Legislature passed an act declaring that slaves should not be set free by will. You see it was getting to be a common thing for a man to hold niggers as long as he lived, and get all he could out of them, and then, just at the last minute, set them free, without any provision for their support or anything of the kind. This 'free nigger' population, scattered all through the country, is getting to be a dangerous element, corrupting the slaves, encouraging them to steal and run away, and really disturbing the peace of the state. Very often, too, it worked great injury to creditors. A man would perhaps get trusted on the strength of his slave property, set them all free, die, and leave his creditors to whistle for their money. Now, to cure this evil, the

Legislature enacted that a slave should only be manumitted by leave of court and when the owner was not indebted to any considerable extent. Besides this, the owner was required to give bond for the negro's good behavior, and to provide for his support and keep him off the county. This didn't quite meet the evil, and so they cut off testamentary manumission in express terms."

"But that is not this case, even according to your supposition."

"Not exactly; but you see I am afraid the principle of the law that don't allow a man to do indirectly what he is forbidden to do directly may come in. If he could not set his niggers free by will, could he by will make you his agent to do it for him? Honestly, Captain, I don't believe he could. So, if the court should think it showed a trust, and should infer that it was this particular kind of a trust, I'm of the notion that the collaterals would recover."

"Yes, yes," said Hargrove, rising and walking thoughtfully across the room, "and what about the woman?"

"That's the very question I came here to ask you," rejoined the lawyer. "I want to know all that is known about that woman Lida; and I want to see every scrap of paper you've got or can lay hands on that in any way relates to her. I'm satisfied that, in some way or other, she's the stumbling-block that is in Gilman's way. It isn't in the will, I'm sure; and after that's past I can't see anything but this woman and her children to make him shy. You see, if the will is set aside, the estate goes to the heirs-at-law, and the next question to be decided is—'Who are the right heirs of George Eighmie'?"

NOTE.—The chronological sequence of legislation and decision upon the points embraced in this chapter it has not been attempted to preserve. In most of the Slave States a part of this legislation was of much earlier date than that given in the story, while the remainder was a few years later. In nearly all of them, however, these laws were enacted. Indeed, they may be said to have grown unavoidably out of the necessities of the institution. To one accustomed to regard the slave as a *man* they seem harsh and cruel; to one accustomed to regard him as property they appear only reasonable requirements to prevent fraud and avoid the growth of a population, of necessity dangerous to property endowed with the power of locomotion and a natural inclination to escape from the restrictions of another's will. Generally, the owner of slaves could manumit by will, if the will provided for the removal of the persons thus freed from the state. Even this was not, however, permitted in some states toward the last years of the existence of the institution. The condition that invalidated the will of George Eighmie is copied from a reported case in a Southern Supreme Court. It sounds queerly to unaccustomed ears, but is unquestionably good law under the conditions which slavery imposed. The increase of the free negro population being counted against public policy, and the slave himself not having any right to be considered, the conclusion was logical and just.

CHAPTER XVI.

BRACKISH WATERS.

"HER story is a sad one, Mr. Bartlemy. If it was not for the wreck she made of poor George's life I suppose I should pity her even more than I do, for, though I don't like her, I must say she has had a hard time."

"So I suppose," said the lawyer, lightly, "though I can't say I care much about that. What I want to know is just what her relations may be to this estate."

"Well, I suppose you know the main features of her history," began Hargrove.

"Don't suppose any such thing," said Bartlemy, sharply. "I may have heard a great deal, but I want facts. Just tell me all you know of her, directly or indirectly, from first to last."

He pushed his spectacles high up on his capacious forehead, clasped his hands on the head of his cane and leaned back in his chair to listen. Now and then, as the story proceeded, he reached forward, and, lifting the glass to his lips, took a sip of its contents.

"Alida Barton, as she was called," said Hargrove, when he saw his listener was ready for him to proceed, "was certainly a pretty girl when George first became acquainted with her. It was while he was in college, and she was supposed to be the daughter of a poor Methodist clergyman, who officiated at that time in the little town where the college was located. She was a lithe, coquettish creature, whose jet black hair clung in close, clustering curls about her head, while her sparkling eyes, full, but finely-shaped lips, and cheeks that showed a ruddy bloom through a dark, soft skin, formed a peculiarly piquant and pleasing picture."

"You needn't mind painting her portrait," growled the lawyer; "I don't want to buy her; and, if I did, she's gaunt enough now, I'll warrant."

"I was only excusing George, sir," said Hargrove, apologetically. "I loved him, I reckon, as well as man ever loved a brother. There was never a word of unkindness between us, and the poor fellow never saw the day he would not have given his life for me. Say what they may of him, I haven't found any better man since his father died. And, for that matter, though the old gentleman did cast him off, I doubt if he would have acted differently, under the circumstances, himself."

"You don't mean it!" said the other in surprise.

"Every word of it," said Merwyn warmly. "If there ever was a true-hearted, honest, clean-souled man, his name was George Eighmie!"

"I thought him a kind of mean-spirited dawdler, who let this woman lead him by the nose," said the lawyer.

"He was a quiet, studious fellow, who loved his ease, and the peculiar troubles that he encountered made him a hermit; but he never had a low thought and could not be driven or hired to do a mean thing."

"I thought, as he had broken with the Colonel and taken up this woman, there must be something wrong about him. Of course, I never knew much of him. I was the Colonel's counsel, and not his, and, as you know, Peter Eighmie wasn't given to talking of his affairs, even to his lawyer, unless it was actually necessary."

"George worshipped this woman. There is no doubt of that," continued Hargrove, not heeding the other's explanation, "and I must say, after all she has suffered, she is a woman to attract any one's notice. He came home from college engaged. His father was prejudiced against her from the outset, not so much on account of her rank in life—for she had been fairly well educated, and her manner, saving a sort of pertness that grew into pride and suspicion when trouble came upon her, was certainly that of a lady—as because of some difficulty that he had once had with a man of her name, who was, I believe, a distant relative of her father."

"The name was what, did you say?"

"Barton — Charles Barton, originally of Mecklin County."

"You don't say? Well, go on," said the lawyer, with apparently renewed interest.

"His father's opposition was a serious thing to George, but as it was based on nothing more substantial than the opinion that there never was a Barton who was not a mean-spirited, low-down cur, he did not feel bound to allow it to influence him."

"Right, too," interrupted the lawyer. "My mother was a Barton on the mother's side."

A half-smile crept under Hargrove's moustache, and his eyes twinkled as if he thought the reason not altogether conclusive. He went on, however:

"So they were married, and came to Mallowbanks to live. His father, though not entirely satisfied at first, was soon won over, George wrote me, by the spirit and brightness of the young wife, and everything promised a life of quiet happiness for them. George's letters to me about this time were in one ceaseless strain of satisfied delight. And it is no wonder. His wife, his father, his home and his prospects seemed to be all that man could ask. I, who had never met my Rietta then, and was just a roving, jolly young lieutenant, who had no thought of love or home—I even envied him his blissful prospects. Poor fellow! I have thought of it many a time since with shame for my selfishness.

"Well, things went on in this way for something like

a year, when one morning, while they were at breakfast,
Salathiel Jenkins, the nigger-trader from up the country, came with a couple of men and asked for George.
They were shown into the old keeping-room, which you
remember at Mallowbanks, that overlooked the river
and opened off the dining-room. George and his wife
were at breakfast, but Colonel Eighmie had not yet left
his room. George went to them at once, and as he
came into the room they could see Lida sitting at the
head of the table. Jenkins told him he had come to
reclaim a nigger gal of his that was 'harboring' on
the plantation. George promptly replied that he had
no slaves on his premises except those that had always
been there. You know it was the boast of the Eigh-
mies that they never sold a slave and never bought except in families. He was sure they must be mistaken.

"'Oh, not at all,' said Jenkins, with that infernal
leer that drew the scar on his face almost up to his
eye and made him look more as the devil ought to be
painted than any man I ever saw."

"Jenkins wasn't any beauty," chuckled the lawyer,
"especially after that fight with Grinstead. I happened to see it myself. It was at Martinburg court.
They were both young men, and Grinstead had sworn
that he would kill him on sight, as I reckon he ought to
have done. They met just at the court-house steps and
both drew their knives. There was some pretty spar-
ring for a moment, and then Grinstead got his point in
just at the corner of Jenkins' right nostril and drove it
back with all his might. It ripped Jenkins' cheek open
clean back to the ear and left a mark there's no mistaking. But while Grinstead's arm was up doing it,
Jenkins give him a slash across the middle and he
never stood straight afterwards. Luckily for him it
wasn't deep enough to hit a vital part, or Jenkins
wouldn't have lived to trouble anybody else. Grin-

stead's brothers never would have let up on him till they had shed the last drop of blood in his veins."

"So I have heard. Well, Jenkins said there wasn't any mistake, because he had seen his nigger since he had come into the room.

"'Seen her? Where?' asked George.

"'In the dining-room,' answered Jenkins.

"'There is no one there but the regular servants,' said George, 'I have just come from there.'

"He felt so sure, he told me, that he would not go to the door to look in.

"'Oh, yes, there is,' said Jenkins—'sitting at the table.'

"'Why, that is my wife, sir!' said George.

"'That may be what you call her,' said Jenkins, 'but I know she is my slave!'

"'Jenkins!' said George, 'this may be an honest mistake on your part, but a man cannot intimate such a thing of my wife, either in jest or earnest, without answering for it.'

"Jenkins wasn't a coward, and besides, he had two men with him; so he did not flinch at George's words, but said very coolly:

"'Mr. Eighmie, if you will call that woman in here, should she not recognize me and own that she's my slave, you may shoot me on the spot.'

"'Very well,' said George, 'as you seem so sincere in your belief, I will convince you of your mistake, and you shall answer for it afterwards.'

"So he called Alida in, and, leading her forward on his arm, he said:

"'My dear, do you recognize either of these men?'

"She looked at them carelessly, and answered in the negative.

"'See here, Lida,' said Jenkins. 'You don't mean to say you've done forgot me an' your mammy, that yaller girl, Sophy, that I bought of Dr. Gant? Oh, no,' he continued, with his usual grin, and hitching nearer to her on that one short leg, 'Oh, no! It's a right smart while ago, and you was only a bit of a gal, but you hain't forgot that nor me either.'

"It's a wonder George didn't kill him in his tracks," said the lawyer.

"It's what he ought to have done," said Merwyn, emphatically, "and what he would have done, if his attention had not been turned to his wife."

"What did she do?"

"She looked at Jenkins at first in surprise. Then her eyes distended in mortal terror. She threw up her hands, and shriek after shriek rang through the house. She fell in spasms just as Colonel Eighmie entered the room."

"Wh—e—w!" said the attorney with a long low whistle.

"There wasn't any doubt about the facts when they came to investigate them," said Hargrove, not noticing the lawyer's interruption. "Jenkins had a bill of sale for the woman Sophy and her daughter Lida. Lida herself confirmed the trader's report, though she persisted in declaring that Sophy was not her mother. Though she was not three years old when separated from her, she has always asserted that Sophy declared she was not her child, but that hers had died, and she had been given her to nurse. To this day she declares that Sophy used to cry for her own baby, and tell her that she was the daughter of a great lady."

"It's queer how many pretty quadroons get that notion," said Bartlemy. "I suppose it is the natural revolt of the white blood against slavery."

"It did not seem to have any good foundation in her case," said Hargrove. "Dr. Gant and his wife were both dead, and left no children; but the neighbors remembered Sophy, who was a bright young mulatto, belonging to him; also the fact of her having a child and being sold.   There was some laugh about his wife's jealousy being the cause of the sale, which fixed the fact in their memory.   After his wife died, according to Jenkins, and others, too, the Doctor tried to trace the girl, and was especially anxious about the child.

"Jenkins, on his part, said the child was a puny thing —that he had no idea it would live.   The mother was a strong, handsome woman, and the care of the child, as well as its sickly appearance, was likely to affect her value.   As he was on the way to New Orleans, where such stock always sells high, and had besides a large gang, he concluded to abandon the child.   So, after she was asleep he took her to a house near where they were camping for the night, and left her upon the porch.

"It happened to be the house of the childless itinerant, Charles Barton.   Owing to her complexion, which was even more misleading because of the pallor of disease, there was no thought of the child being of colored blood and especially no idea that it was a slave.   People are not apt to abandon slave children, and ever in this case it seems to have been just a trick of that scoundrel Jenkins.   I suppose he hardly liked to kill her for fear of consequences, and probably had no thought that she would live.   There was some inquiry made, but nothing elicited as to the parentage, and so the good couple took the little waif into their homes and hearts as their daughter."

"My God! that was rough on George and the Colonel, wasn't it?   What did they do?"

"What could they do?   The Colonel bought the girl of Jenkins at his own price, and then told him he would shoot him on sight if he ever came into the county again, or if he ever breathed a word about the matter to a living soul."

"No doubt he meant it, too."

"Of course; from that day until his death he never went off the plantation without carrying a pistol to 'shoot that d——d scoundrel Jenkins.'"

"And George?"

"His father gave the girl to him—"

"There was a deed, I suppose," interrupted the lawyer.

"Yes, a deed of gift under seal."

The lawyer nodded.

"His father advised him to take her North, set her free, buy her a comfortable home and give her a reasonable support."

"Very liberal, by God! as the old man always was, and just what George ought to have done."

"With our notions, yes, but not with George Eighmie's. In the first place, he loved the girl better than his life; and, in the next place, he did not believe there was a drop of colored blood in her veins. So, what does he do but bring her to New York, manumit her in due form and marry her again."

"The devil! You don't tell me?" said Bartlemy, springing from his chair. "I never heard of that."

"Here are the papers. These are copies—Lida has the originals—of the deed of manumission, the license and marriage certificate."

"Well, I declare!"

"Not only that, but about this time a child was born —a son, who, by the way, was cursed with the exact duplicate of that scar of Jenkins,—and so anxious was George to put him on a legal footing that he formally legitimatized him according to the laws of the state. Here is a copy of the record."

"Good Lord!" exclaimed the lawyer, "was there any other foolish thing that idiot could do?"

"Oh, yes. What he did next was a deal worse. He

went back to Mallowbanks and presented himself and *family* to Colonel Eighmie.''

"No!" roared Bartlemy, striking the floor with his cane. "He didn't dare do that?"

"He did that very thing."

"And the Colonel?"

"Turned on his heel; went down to the landing; was rowed over to Amity Lake, and never looked on his son's face again."

"Served him right, too, just right," exclaimed the lawyer almost gleefully.

"Did the only mean act of his life, sir," said Har-grove gravely.

"What, sir! do you mean to justify such an outrageous thing? Would you associate with a man who marries a nigger?"

"That is not the question," rejoined Hargrove. "George married the girl without any deception on her part. Her memory of the trader and that of her 'mammy,' as she no doubt called the girl Sophy, was only of a horrid man who had taken her and her nurse from home. All she knew of her past life was that she had been told that her mother was a 'great lady.' This was the account she gave of herself to her foster-parents. Being so fair and so young—she could not have been over three years old—I do not suppose the idea of slavery had ever entered her mind, at least in connection with herself. The kind people with whom she had lived afterwards had made an idol of her. George had made her his wife, so far as intent could go. She was the mother of his child. Her kind foster-mother was dead—died of grief at her calamity. Under these circumstances, George thought it his duty to share the misfortune that had fallen on the woman that he loved, be it more or less, as you lawyers say, and I honor his memory for having done it. I might not have had the pluck, and of course you wouldn't," he added with a slight smile, "but I 'll tell you what, sir, when a man loves a woman well enough to go to hell with her rather than to heaven without her, he 's bound to be very much of a man !"

"There 's a good deal of truth in that," said the other thoughtfully.

"That 's why I say Colonel Eighmie was wrong. He ought to have stood by George because he had acted with a manly motive, and at the worst hurt only himself. If he had done so, and sent them West at once, there never would have been any trouble about it. But he was like most Southern men—he never could realize that there was a world beyond his own horizon. He never dreamed that a reputation shattered by an indiscretion at home might be healed and cured by a life of honor abroad."

"There's where he was wrong. He ought to have remembered that one of the greatest men the State ever produced had to leave, it is said, because of a little mistake about some money. He went West and never came back until he was one of the foremost men in the United States Senate. If he had been a lawyer, Colonel Eighmie would never have made that mistake. If he had confided in me I should have told him the best way to get rid of a son he didn't want to see was to send him out of his sight. It seems just natural, though, for a planter to think that there isn't much room in the world outside of his own possessions. That life does narrow a man's ideas wonderfully."

"Yes; that is so. Well, the Colonel never thought of that or anything else, except that George had disgraced him. So, while he let him live on the plantation and enjoy its revenues, he yet gave him no right to the least thing, and refused all intercourse with him."

"Well, what was the upshot of it ?"

"Just what you might suppose. While there was of course an effort to suppress the facts, they had somehow leaked out—partly known and partly guessed at, no doubt. I question if ever a word would have been said if his father had stood by him. After that, you know the scorn and insult that was heaped upon them. Of course, it drove him into solitude. I think she would have faced it and braved it down, but he couldn't. IIis hands were tied, he had no means, and could not get away ; and so, for years, he never left the plantation. I came home and took his part, but it was too late. I never dared speak to Colonel Eighmie about it, and my wife loved him so well that she hated George as only one of her blood can hate. I think this family shame was more than half the cause of her hating slavery as fiercely as she did."

"She was an Italian, I believe ?"

" Yes."

" You married her abroad ?"

" In London."

" Yes ; I saw her once ; a very pretty woman."

" She was accounted a beauty."

" I never knew you had a child until to-day."

" She was born while we were on a cruise—at Kingston, where I had taken Rietta in the hope that a Southern winter would do her good. Because of her weakness, she was persuaded when we sailed to leave the child with the family of an English clergyman, who cared for her until she was nearly three years old."

" I thought she had seen hotter sunshine than you get up here."

" Oh, yes ; Hilda is at least semi-tropical, both by birth and descent."

" I see. Well, is there anything more about this woman Lida ?"

" Oh, yes ; her troubles were not ended with the estrangement of her husband from his father and the public sentiment that marked them and their children as the most degraded of pariahs. After a time the Colonel died, and a surge of wrath swept through the community, as if they had been guilty of parricide. Perhaps, in his later years, the heart of the father had softened toward his unfortunate son. At least, he made no attempt to disinherit him, and, dying intestate, his property descended to George. What the son had suffered had not only made him a hermit, but he had also become one of the most rabid and fanatical Abolitionists that ever breathed."

"An Abolitionist! That is all that was needed to complete the picture that you have drawn," said Bartlemy, with evident disgust. "There was more sense in his being such, however, than any of these rabid fools that howl and foam through the North about what they know nothing of, and in which they have no interest."

"Well, George was an Abolitionist, right or wrong, and made up his mind as soon as Mallowbanks and its slaves fell into his hands to set them free without delay and then go himself to some part of the great West where he thought slavery would never come. Unfortunately, his estate was not large enough to permit him to do this just out of hand, without impoverishing himself. The plantation had reached that stage, by reason of the increase of its slave force, that it was almost impossible to make any great profit out of it without reducing the consumption by disposing of some of them. He determined, however, after due consideration, to devote the net proceeds of each crop to the creation of a fund which should be sufficient not only to remove the slaves to another state when freed, but also, with a portion of the proceeds arising from the sale of the plantation, to give each family a comfortable start in the new life which he proposed to bestow upon them. He told me all his plans, and, though I regarded them as visionary, I could not but respect his earnestness and admire the sagacity he showed in their execution,

His new purpose transformed the listless recluse into the active and unresting business man. He calculated that five years would be sufficient for the purpose he had in view, and he allowed himself no luxury and spared himself no labor tending to its accomplishment. Soon after he undertook this task another child was born to them —a daughter whom the mother called Heloise. Her birth seemed to arouse the hatred of the people even more than all that had gone before. He and Lida were indicted for living together illegally. The matter dragged along for several terms of court and nothing was done, at least no trial took place. I suspect, from what has since occurred, that the collateral heirs may have been at the bottom of the prosecution, fearing, perhaps, the accomplishment of his purpose in his lifetime."

"It's more than likely, for I've heard myself of his having that fool-notion among others. But, no matter, go on."

"At length, just as it was about to come to trial, George suddenly died. I was not there at the time, and, queerly enough, Lida did not know where to find his will. I knew he had made me his executor, and he had told me, in connection with his plans, where he kept his will, and I knew just what he expected me to do. It was to carry out his plan with regard to his slaves and to see that his children grew up entirely unconscious of the stain upon their birth. In regard to this latter he was very emphatic. The question of administering on his estate arising before my return, Lida showed splendid pluck in urging her claim as his widow to be appointed administratrix. She also claimed dower and her year's provision."

"Pluck? Do you call that pluck, Mr. Hargrove?" cried the lawyer, impetuously. "I call it d——d impudence."

"Well, whichever it may be, it saved her and the es-

tate both. I came just before the matter was decided.
The court below had pronounced her marriage illegal
and the higher one had it before it on appeal. I found
the will—and the rest you know."

"I know that you proved it and entered into possession, and all that touches the legal history of your administration. I can now understand why you did, from
time to time, certain absurd things which I advised you
not to do."

"Yes; I freed the house-servants in order to run the
plantation more economically, and so increase the fund
more rapidly; but it has already taken me longer than
George expected, chiefly because I determined to make
the slaves pay for their own freedom and save the estate
intact for Lida and her children. Then, too, the search
for the boy—"

"Yes; I want to know about that."

"There is very little to tell. About the time we
offered the will for probate the child was missed from
the house one evening, but his mother was not greatly
alarmed at first, as she supposed him to be over at the
quarters, hardly half a mile away. Upon inquiry,
however, it appeared that no one on the plantation
had seen him since noon. His mother was sure that
he had been kidnapped, but we thought that being
so peculiarly marked it would be no difficult matter
to trace him. It never entered into my head at the
time that he might be put out of the way entirely.
I at once removed Lida and her daughter to the yacht,
which was lying in the sound, and sent her to New
York to get her out of harm's way. Then I set myself
to find that boy. I had every slave-market watched;
offered a liberal reward, of which every slave-dealer in
the country was informed, and was just about to give
up all hope, concluding that the boy was dead, when,
after he had been missing two years, I heard of a poor

white family in Western Carolina, away up among the mountains, who had a child answering my description. Before I could reach there, however, they were gone. By dint of careful inquiry, I learned that Jenkins had been in that region not long before their flitting, and from some facts I gathered had no doubt that he had something to do with their departure. He probably learned that I was on the scent and spirited away not only the child, but the people who had him in charge, to avoid discovery. I have been on a constant hunt for the child ever since, but have not found the least trace of him, or the people who had him. My agents have gone through every state of the South upon the search for him in vain. There is no doubt in my mind but some of George's cousins kidnapped little Hugh and intended to do the same with the daughter, in order to induce the mother to forego any further claims to the estate."

" That 's more than likely, and it chimes in with my theory that the woman and her children are the stumbling-block in Gilman's path," said the lawyer. "Though the inferior court decided, on her petition for dower and leave to administer, that she was not the lawful wife of George Eighmie, I 'm not exactly sure that it was right. The first marriage was no doubt void, because she was a slave. The effect of the second one it is hard to determine. If they had been married in Carolina the presumption would have been against its legality. Having been a slave, she is presumed to have at least one-eighth of colored blood. As her descent is unknown, I hardly see how this presumption could be rebutted. So I think the second marriage would have been held to be contrary to the law of the state regarding intermarriages between whites and free blacks if it had been solemnized there."

" But the marriage was in New York," said Hargrove.

"So I understand," answered Bartlemy, "and that makes a queer state of affairs. The marriage would be illegal here, I reckon—it would in most Northern States —if the woman was actually colored. But here the presumption is right the other way. It would be necessary to show colored blood in her veins affirmatively, before she could be adjudged a negro and the marriage invalidated. So, I take it, the marriage would be held lawful in the State of New York."

"If lawful there, where it was contracted, I suppose it would be held lawful in Carolina ?" said Hargrove.

"Well, no," responded Bartlemy ; "that doesn't follow. It has been decided in our state that if parties who are prohibited by its laws from marrying go beyond its limits, and contract marriage according to the laws of another state, and then return there to live, that it is in fraud of the law, and void."

"So she must have been his wife in New York and not his wife in Carolina," said Hargrove in surprise.

"That 's about the situation. The same principle applies to her manumission. It has been held that if a man take his slave to another state, and set him free under its laws, and then bring him back into a state that only permits a slave to be set free by order of court, it shows a purpose to evade the law, and the foreign manumission is void. In such a case, it was held that the slave was not free at all, though the former master had always regarded and treated her as such, and in his will made her a specific bequest, but was still his slave, and passed to his heirs as a residue of his estate, with respect to which he had died intestate."

"So," said Hargrove, rising in excitement, "I understand you to say that that woman was George Eighmie's lawful wedded wife in New York ?"

"That is my opinion."

"And that she was, at the same time, lawfully held as his slave in Carolina ?"

"My dear fellow," said Bartlemy, "you ought to have been a lawyer. That is as near as I can figure it out, and I couldn't have stated it better myself."

"Then, Mr. Bartlemy," said Hargrove, bringing his fist down upon the table vehemently, "George Eighmie was right. There was never any other land in which the master could not make his slave free at pleasure, nor one in which marriage, duly solemnized, did not make free. George was right. An institution that permits and renders necessary such things, is not fit to exist in a Christian land."

"Sho! sho! You are not going to turn Abolitionist just because the institution of slavery is not perfect, I hope?" said Bartlemy. "Just think what we should have if it were swept away."

"That is where I have always stood," answered Hargrove. "It is not long since that I told one of the foremost Abolitionists here in this very room, that I thought it a choice between negro slavery and negro liberty, and that the latter was far the more dangerous."

"You were right, too," said Bartlemy; "entirely right."

"I was a fool!" said Hargrove impetuously. "George Eighmie was right when he told me, the last time I saw him, that one such experience as his outweighed the argument from convenience and necessity a thousandfold. A system that permitted and compelled such horrible monstrosities ought not to live a moment."

"Why, why, my dear sir," said Bartlemy; "one would think you were really going to come out a howling Abolitionist."

"I am going to come out that most earnest of all the opponents of slavery—a Southern Abolitionist!" responded Hargrove. "From this hour, for George Eighmie's sake, I will do all I can not only to secure the rights of his wife and children, but to carry out his wishes as to his slaves. Every one of them shall be set free if it takes the last dollar I have on earth !''

"But—but—Mr. Hargrove, I—I—protest ! As your counsel, I protest against any such rash course on your part," said Bartlemy. "I—I—indeed, sir—"

"Never mind about it, Mr. Bartlemy," said Hargrove promptly. "I want your aid to carry out my purpose ; not to instruct me what I ought to do."

"But I refuse to act as your counsel with such an object," said the lawyer petulantly.

"You have already become my counsel with a tacit knowledge of the trust I had to execute."

"I knew nothing about it, sir ; nothing about it."

"Not in words, perhaps, until to-night, but by unavoidable implication you well understood what it was," answered Hargrove. "However, if you wish to discontinue your relation to me as counsel you have only to present your bill."

"Oh, no, no, no !" said the lawyer, waving his hand back and forth and shaking his head deprecatingly, "by no manner of means. It wouldn't do to act hastily in such a matter. Gilman might get an advantage if we did. Of course, you must follow your conscience. It's really none of my business. But I do hate to see a good estate squandered on a lot of niggers that haven't sense enough to appreciate what is done for them."

"Well, Mr. Bartlemy, that was George's affair, and not ours, and it's his estate we are administering and his money we are spending."

"I'm not so sure of that," growled the lawyer.

"Well, the rest of it is mine," said Hargrove positively.

"At least it isn't mine," said the lawyer, "so we

won't quarrel over it. Now tell me what has become of
the other child."

"The other child ? Oh, yes—Marah," said Hargrove
meditatively.

"I thought you said her name was Heloise," said the
lawyer quickly.

"Heloise ? Yes, so I did. That was her name, but it
should have been Marah, for if ever a life was doomed
to bitterness it was hers."

"She is dead, then ?"

"No," said Hargrove, walking meditatively back and
forth.

"Then where is she ?"

"Mr. Bartlemy," said Merwyn, stopping before him,
"my brother desired that his children might never know
the curse that a possible drop of colored blood in their
veins might work in their lives. I alone know the secret of the child's existence. I have already provided
that in case of my decease before everything is settled,
one other man should be informed of it. That is quite
enough to know what is intended to be a secret. Should
I live to see the entire matter concluded, as I hope to do,
no one will ever know the truth as to that child's birth or
be able to trace her parentage."

"Just as you choose," said Bartlemy, with something
of pique in his tone. "I suppose there is nothing else
I need ask about ?"

With a parting drop from the decanter, the lawyer
bade his host and client good night. It was late when
he arose the next morning. After breakfast Captain
Hargrove said to him :

"You will no doubt set me down in the same category
as my brother, but I think you told me that Lida was
unquestionably George's wife by the law of New York ?"

"Beyond the shadow of a doubt."

"She returned this morning, and will remain here as

his widow hereafter. Would you like to speak with her ?"

Upon Bartlemy's signifying his assent, Hargrove led him to the sitting-room, where a slight, dark-eyed woman, who was plainly dressed in black, sat listening to Hilda's prattle. Her face was pale and thin, and a nervous tremulousness about the lips, as well as a startled, hunted look in the eyes, showed how her sufferings had wrought upon her life. After introducing the lawyer, Hargrove took Hilda and left the room. An hour afterward Bartlemy came to him and said :

"There isn't a bit of doubt about it, Captain. That woman and her children are just what Gilman is afraid of. If he had them in Carolina, they wouldn't give him a minute's trouble ; but being here in New York, he's afraid of them. He hasn't any more doubt about the will than I, but he's afraid that this woman, living in another state, might set up her claim through the United States Courts ; and he is in a good deal of doubt what the Supreme Court at Washington would do in such a case, and I am not very clear about it myself. There's one thing I want to tell you, though. You have long since settled the estate of your testator. Your only interest in the state now is as the owner of the property devised you by George Eighmie. Now you keep out of Carolina. If they have to sue you here, the chances are all in your favor ; if you let them sue there, they are all the other way."

"But I must atttend to the property," said Hargrove dubiously.

"By an agent, yes," said the lawyer with a smile.

"Very well, I will remember your advice," he assented.

"Another thing, Captain," Bartlemy began hesitantly.

"Yes ?" said Hargrove in a tone that invited him to proceed.

"It is about those children."

"Well?" responded Hargrove, still expectantly.

The other looked at him doubtfully a moment and then blurted out:

"Why don't you tell that woman all you know about her children?"

"I have."

"No, you have not."

"I have told her of my search for the boy, and that I have put the girl in good safe hands where she is well cared for."

"But that is not what she wants to know. Why don't you tell her where she is?"

"Because I am carrying out my brother's instructions. He had made up his mind to put his children away from him, and have them reared and educated under assumed names. She would perhaps have trusted him, or he might have trusted her; but he warned me that the children must be put beyond her reach, or at least beyond all possible knowledge of her relationship to them."

"By Heaven! Captain, I am not much given to sentiment, but that is hard. Can you be cruel enough to carry it out?"

"I must. I have been tempted a thousand times to give it up, but thus far I have stood firm."

"Do you know she suspects you of having sold the boy?"

"No doubt," said Hargrove sadly. "There is no end to her wild fancies so far as the children are concerned. Her love for them makes her life a constant torture. I am the only one who has befriended her since George's death, but I think she has lost the power to trust even me. I discharged all my servants except Jason when I brought her here, so that there might not be the least suspicion of the facts, yet she fled as soon as my overseer set foot in the house, thinking I was preparing to abduct her. She is a weak, silly woman, whom I cannot trust with a knowledge of my purposes lest she should unintentionally betray them.''

"I see, I see," said the lawyer, "but how you can resist her piteous appeals and those great eyes with the tears running over the lids down on that sad face, passes my comprehension. I 'm pretty tough, but I swear I couldn't stand that."

"You can guess what I have suffered then," said Hargrove, ruefully. "It has been a terrible task, but I pledged my honor to do it, and no one shall ever say I failed through weakness or lack of diligence."

"Do you know that she thinks Hilda her daughter?" asked the lawyer, with a keen look.

"She has hinted such a suspicion," answered Hargrove, with a smile.

"And what was your reply?"

"That she might think what she chose, so long as she did not breathe a word of her suspicion to the child."

"And if she did?"

"That she should never see her face again."

"You think you would know it?"

"Hilda could not hide it from me for a moment."

"So you hope— ?"

"To keep Lida quiet and prevent her life from being entirely miserable."

"It 's a great risk—a great risk, Captain, and for very little good, so far as I can see. What is the use of all this secresy?"

"Simply to fulfill a brother's request. If you had heard him implore me to save his children from the curse which the knowledge of one drop of colored blood entails, you would not wonder at what I have done. Only think, sir, suppose your child—suppose my little Hilda should come to believe that the blood of that unfortunate race flowed in her veins—that she was branded with the mark of degradation and shame—what evil would not be counted light in comparison with it? She would pray for death, sir, and I would rather see her dead than know her thus accursed."

"Well, well," said the old lawyer, shaking his head. "Perhaps you are right; but I am glad it is you and not I that have this thing to do."

CHAPTER XVII.

WHAT WAKED THE WORLD.

TIME fled. The world moved faster than ever before. The telegraph was beginning to unify thought. Like a giant centipede, it crept over the land. It murdered sloth and ran ahead of time. It stole the merchant's secret and sold it to a rival a thousand leagues away. It made principal and agent one. It fed brain with fact and gave to mind the ubiquity of the Infinite. It made every man an Adam and marshaled the world's life before him.

The curtain of darkness was rent in twain, and beyond the Mississippi a boundless empire was revealed. The Golden Gates were uplifted, and the traditions of the Orient were beggared by the facts of the Occident. For two hundred years the world had hungered for gold and found no new supply. The temples and palaces of India had been ravaged by ruthless hands to satisfy the greed of civilization. The jewels of her gods shone in the royal crowns of Europe. Brave men wore with pride the gems that valor had won from heathen hands. The wives, the sweethearts and the courtesans of Christendom flaunted upon snowy arms and billowy bosoms the pillage of the unbeliever.

But, alas! the supply was almost exhausted. The lands that Cortez and Pizarro ravaged, stripped of the wealth the Aztecs and the Incas had amassed in the unknown centuries before the robber's torch shed light upon their stores, lay barren and unheeded under the torrid sunshine. When the chance for plunder passed away the light of civilization fled. Mexico, Potosi and Coquimbo gave a steadily decreasing output. All the rest of the world was guessed at a beggarly ten millions yearly of actual gain of the world's lucre. When Begums and Rajahs became pensioners rather than victims of legalized plunder—when the East called for aid, instead of offering an unlimited chance for looting—then the romance of India was gone, and it became only a refuge for parsimony and thrift, which were content to endure exile, discomfort and long delay for moderate gain.

The wall that encircled China had been broken down, but only the paltriest tribute could be wrung from a people whose economics stupefied even the thriftiest of Europeans, and demanded for their expression a coin a hundred times less in value than the meanest that ever boasted a queen's face.

The world was base and man was greedy. For a hundred years the supply of the precious metals had steadily diminished. Commerce had increased meanwhile a thousandfold. The accepted basis of exchange had grown less and less sufficient for the world's need. Already the human mind was busy devising substitutes. Production was limited, not by demand or by capacity for supply, but by the difficulty of transport and the paucity of an indestructible measure of value. "Gold! Gold! Gold!" was the hopeless cry of all the world. It was generally believed that the earth was virtually exhausted of precious minerals, and no one supposed that the supply would ever be materially enhanced.

The width of a continent transformed boundless wealth into pitiable poverty. Where nothing was expected, infinite possibility uprose. Fifteen years before a Congressional report had said: "No man will, after a moment's reflection, suppose that the country beyond the sandy prairies in the West and North can ever become members of this Union. They are scarcely less distant than the coast of Africa, and are separated from us by a breadth of continent requiring more time and expense to traverse than the ocean itself." A noted politician, who yet lives to laugh at his own folly, said, in a public speech upon the acquisition of California, holding a well-worn pencil up before his auditors, "I would not give that pencil-stub for all the gold that will ever be found there;" and his hearers applauded his wisdom.

No wonder the world woke with amazement from such dreams and ran wild when golden plains and silver mountains outspread themselves before its famished eyes. All Christendom felt the throb of an insatiable greed. The lust of sudden wealth thrilled peer and pauper. The desert that lay between was robbed of fear. The tropic sun blazed down in vain upon the reckless way-farers. The glint of gold outshone the stars. Distance could not dim it. Difficulty could not quench desire. A grain of yellow dust inflamed a hundred hearts. A single nugget fired a thousand souls to new exertion. Men who would have died clods lived to be envied of princes through the lust born of a gold-streaked lump of snowy quartz shown in a shop window. Thousands failed. Thousands died. The highways to the land of promise became endless charnels. Dead men's bones pointed the way to those who came after. The sharks of the southern seas grew fat on frequent corpses; yet over the dead all the more greedily pressed the living. For every one that fell there were a thousand that sprang up. For every one that went there were ten thousand that sought to go. For every one that came back laden there were a million who dreamed that they might some time know a like good fortune, and, because of this dream, wrought more earnestly, saved more persistently, and so achieved more richly than they otherwise would have done. Thus Science and Greed stirred the world into new life.

Wherever trade went the fever flew. Gold flowed through the world like water, in comparison with the dearth that had been. Half a decade yielded more than half a century had given before. "Dust" and "nuggets" grew familiar to all eyes. The slang of the mining camp crept into the world's speech. Palms that had only known shillings were gladdened with crowns. The child leaped from his cradle to join in the struggle for gold. The peasant's heart grew big and his arm waxed strong as he saw a possibility that he might yet be richer than his king. Mammon gave his right hand to Democracy. The yellow, molten torrent undermined the throne and made the crown look dim. The highways of empire were opened to the humblest feet. The doors of kings' palaces were unbarred, and unwashed feet poured through the sanctuaries of power. Wooden shoes gave place to golden sandals. Miracles were multiplied. Where one had risen a step before, a thousand were to reach the top thereafter. Rank was cheapened ; manhood magnified. Those above were not dragged down, but those below were forced upward. The world was started on a race which grew more fierce and headlong as the years went by. The past was swept away as with a burning besom. The future bloomed with hope. A flood-tide marked the century's zenith.

In that same hour Freedom and Slavery cast their eyes upon the new domain. Both were inspired by greed. The free North demanded that at least a part of the fertile plains, the golden sands and the silver-veined heights should be held as an arena wherein every man might struggle with his fellow for the prizes of life without let or hindrance from another's will. The South demanded that the institution most favored by the

Constitution, and especially nourished and protected by the laws of the states in which it had taken root, should also be protected in the territories of the United States not yet organized under municipal forms or erected into self-governing states. They claimed that the government which allowed the citizen to hold a certain species of property under the laws of certain states of the Union, was bound to protect him in the enjoyment of that property upon its unassigned domain, of which he and his fellow slave-owners were joint proprietors in common with the non-slaveholding citizens of the Northern States.

It is not enough to say that this claim was a specious one. Not only has it never been fairly answered, but it is not susceptible of logical refutation if its premises are granted. The argument against the *right* of slavery to exist, to be defended and to extend itself, was always incomplete and unsatisfactory when it was based upon the written word of the Constitution. To hold that instrument sacred above all things else and yet deny the slave-owner's legal right to his human chattel was impossible. Many a lover of liberty and righteousness tried to do it and failed. To doubt the one was sacrilegious. To admit the other seemed little less than sin. The Constitution was admittedly inspired. To question that was treason. A curse too fearful to be uttered rested upon any one who should query its lightest word. All that it contained was not only just and true, but there was nothing of governmental justice and truth that it did not contain, if not in the full ear of explicit declaration at least in the fecund germ of necessary implication. Tried by the declaration on which it rested, there could be no slave beneath its ægis. But the "person held to service or labor in one state, under the laws thereof, escaping into another," could be nothing but the slave fleeing from bondage toward the hope of freedom. Men gravely argued that this *might* mean apprentices. The quibble

was never worthy even of the contempt poured upon it,
though it found favor with minds that nothing but the
desperation of dilemma could have induced to harbor it.
In very truth the argument was all with the slaveholder when it was once admitted that the Constitution
was infallible. Standing upon the "person held to service or labor" clause, slavery was impregnable. Right
or wrong, the Constitution covered it by unavoidable implication.   Grounded upon that, who should assail it?
Had not the blood of the fathers sanctified its provisions?   Did not Washington commend it to our jealous
care?   Had not every patriot whose memory we cherished regarded it as the talisman of our liberty—the sacred scroll on which our destiny depended?

But for this single clause in the Constitution, slavery
would have withered before the glare of conscience long
before even the time of which we write. The bulwark
of the Constitution was its moral as well as its legal
cover from assault.   A thousand quirks and quibbles
were devised to avoid the potency of this claim which
had the merit, unusual among political dogmas, of never
being tinctured with doubt in the minds of those who
put it forward..   As to his moral right to buy and sell
and hold human beings as slaves, the Southern man
might doubt—many of them did.   As to his legal right
there was never any question.   The Northern mind
conceived innumerable pleas against it, chiefly based
upon a specious use of the word "man," meaning in one
part of the argument a slave and in another premise a
free man.   The impetuous logic of the South was right
when it termed them all makeshifts and evasions. If the
Constitution meant anything it guaranteed in the most
emphatic manner not only the right to hold slaves, but
to hunt them.   If it gave that privilege in one state it
was a right of property, which the citizen was entitled
to carry with him and exercise in the national domain,

This was not contemplated by the framers of that instrument, because they were affected by human conditions and could not foresee the future. It followed, however, as certainly and indefeasibly as the right of the merchant to offer his wares, of the tradesman to exercise his calling, or of the farmer to till the soil—admitting always that the Constitution is the complete compendium of political truth. These quibbles served only as excuses for feeble brains and timid consciences. There were those who did not stop to speculate on the absurdity of picketing state-lines against runaway apprentices, or who easily overlooked the fact that Benjamin Franklin, himself an absconding apprentice, signed the instrument. There were others who, halting between their reverence for the sacred charter and the dictates of conscience, needed only a formal quibble to satisfy them that their convictions of right did not contravene the letter or the spirit of the Constitution. From first to last the Constitution was the Gibraltar of slavery, and the reverence felt for that instrument was the last stronghold, which its opponents were never able to storm until its advocates had thrown down its walls upon themselves.

Their first step in this direction was when they sought to make of this shield of the "peculiar institution," as it was called, a weapon of offense against their aggressive and persistent enemies. For nearly sixty years there had been a law upon the statute-book regulating the recaption of slaves and their return to captivity. Stung, however, by the defeat which their candidate had received through the power of the Anti-slavery idea, the Southern leaders determined to stamp out this political heresy for all time, by the assertion, in the most irritating and offensive manner that could be devised, of the constitutional principle on which they rested. The theory on which was based what is known as the Fugitive Slave Law, was that it was sound

policy to demonstrate so clearly that none could evade
or deny it, the constitutional sanction on which slavery
rested secure.   For this purpose not only were the rights
of caption and removal reasserted, but it was made the
duty of every citizen, under an express penalty, to aid
in such removal.   It was this pinning upon every
man's conscience a constitutional duty which was intended to destroy all opposition to slavery, that ultimately wrought its overthrow. The right to retake existed ; the power to summon a *posse comitatus* no doubt
resided in the officer of the court, and the duty to obey
rested on all good citizens before this statute was enacted.   But the old law had become almost a dead letter.
Its machinery was imperfect, since at that time (1793)
there was no tangible hostility to slavery.   It was
merely a machine for carrying out an unresisted and
unquestioned provision of the Constitution at the best.
The reassertion and elaboration of these features, however, coupled with some others of peculiar offensiveness,
stirred the heart of the North as if shackles had been
put on the hands of its first-born.   For a time, the
supporters of the Anti-slavery movement were overwhelmed with discouragement.   Many who had begun
to pay court to its adherents, and for political advantage sought to be numbered with them, fell away.   Some
who had stood in the forefront of public regard thought
they saw in this the end of a disturbing conflict, and for
personal advantage favored it covertly or openly.   Of
these, some were amazed when the earth opened and
swallowed them up, and others made haste to recant
when they saw the tenor of public feeling.   Instead of
being weakened, the Anti-slavery cause was strengthened a thousandfold.   Many gave up to the stupefac-
tion of despair, but many more had their moral responsibility for slavery and its fruits brought home to
their own doors so that they could not evade it longer.

Every enforcement of this law, which was eagerly seized upon by slave-owners, not only as a means for enabling them to recover valuable property but also of teaching the people of the North the strength of their position, only added fuel to the flame of hostility against its provisions and awakened a stronger doubt as to the infallibility of the Constitution on which it rested.

Parties were eaten to the core with discontent. This law was the solvent which released Whig and Democrat alike from the bonds of party fealty. Webster was buried in shame—relegated to that death in life which is of all things most horrible to a man who has helped to move the world—pitied and despised at length by those whose admiration for his genius had made them blind to his faults. Sumner was uplifted in glory from his bed of martyrdom to mark with the utmost emphasis the disapproval of the great leader's cowardice, and the emphatic indorsement that Massachusetts would give to the heroism of her youngest representative.

What had been before a mere vague generality now assumed a personal and individual aspect. Men of conscience rebelled against what they before had only dimly regarded as evil, now first plainly realizing its true nature and their unavoidable responsibility for its existence. Men of spirit arrayed themselves against the law because of its offensively dictatorial character. It enhanced the horrors of slavery by cutting off even the little chance there was before of escape, and thus confirmed the Anti-slavery sentiment of those who were feebly halting on the absurd plea that slavery would soon die from natural causes; although it increased in numbers twice as fast as the ratio of increase in the surrounding populations. These were now convinced that only positive measures would ever cure what they deemed a wrong against humanity. Many worthy men, who had never violated the law before, counted themselves honored forever when permitted to aid in the escape of a fugitive.

A thrill of angry apprehension passed through the whole North. People knew that a great crisis was at hand, but none could trace its outcome. A few were confident that liberty would triumph. Others counted slavery the victor, and yet sullenly resisted; while still others thought the whole matter ended, and looked for the old parties to muster their hosts again on the old familiar grounds that had been fought over quadrennially for threescore years or so—the means of raising revenue, the appropriation of the public domain, and other questions of method in administration only.

Instead of this chaos ensued. Before the sentiment produced by this measure had time to crystallize into organic form a Presidential election came. Party bonds were dissolved. The Democracy, by reason of its close alliance in doctrine with the pro-slavery faction, suffered less than the opponent at whose hands it had suffered defeat four years previously. Yet it had many defections, and, in almost every state, those who left its ranks were men of remarkable strength and character. It is easy enough for even a weak man to be left by his party, but it takes a strong man to be able to break away from life-long associations on a question of principle that does not even promise success.

The Whig party crumbled like shattered clay. Claiming liberal principles and covertly seeking the aid of the Abolitionists, whom they sought to hold to their support upon the plea that only through their success was there any hope of ultimate triumph, the leaders had shown themselves utterly unable to read the temper of the times and, as a rule, too cowardly to defend the views they secretly professed to favor. To avoid giving offense to the South, they trifled with the convictions of the better element of their party at the North, and found at length that its intelligence, conscience and courage had renounced allegiance to a party of cowardice and hypocrisy.

But as yet it did not appear what would be the result. The doom of the Whig party was sealed. Insurrection against the folly and recreancy of its leaders had made any further success under its banners impossible. Its two greatest names had been smitten with the madness that destroys. Drunk with envy of each other, mad with the lust of power and filled with disappointed ambition, they had forgotten all but themselves. For thirty years they had been the rival leaders of their party. The voice of adulation had become as the breath of life in their nostrils. They had forgotten that the worship of admiring followers was a poor test of truth. They had so long been hailed as gods that, like drunken Alexander, they had come to believe in their own divinity. The party whom they once served had, in their minds, degenerated into a mere personal following. Its declaration of principles was to them only a formulation of the ideas of which they were the incarnation. They no longer remembered that they had grown to greatness by faithfully serving those whom they represented. They both ignored the fact that it was not Clay nor Webster that the people had followed, but the ideas that each had wrought into the fibre of his life. They made the mistake, fatal to party leaders in a republic, of first placing the party above the nation and then themselves above the party. The people, through whose choice they had been called to the foremost places in the councils both of party and nation, had shrunk to nothingness in their eyes, which beheld only the greatness at which they had themselves arrived.

A considerable number of the Whig leaders who stood next to the highest in rank were among the malcontents. Some of them for many years had held their allegiance

but lightly. Others had marked the tendency of public
sentiment, and not only put themselves in harmony with
it, but while yet recognized as Whigs, had become really
the leaders of a movement which could no longer be reconciled with the policy of the old party as dictated by
its acknowledged chiefs. Then, as in all such crises,
the claim was strenuously made that this was not a
party question. However vital it might become in the
opinion of the voter, it was urged that it was not, could
not properly, and never must be allowed to become a
party question. It was a moral question, a social question, a religious problem; but a political question—an
idea upon which parties should divide—it could not be.
It lacked all the features of the regular stock-in-trade
political issue. There was no element of taxation or administration in it. Its decision did not involve any
change of governmental form, internal economy, or
foreign relation. It was merely a great moral idea, affecting directly the people of those states in which slavery
existed, and only by the remotest indirection those who
gave it aid and comfort through the "held to service
or labor" clause of the Constitution. However wrong-
ful it might be, parties could not legally interfere with
it. Whigs might bewail its unrighteousness; Democrats might mourn its iniquities; all alike must regret
its abuses; but nothing more could be done. Moral influences might be exerted. Perhaps, indirectly, legislation might do something to prevent its spread and
growth; but beyond this no political party would ever
dare to go. Beyond this line was only a violated Constitution, a broken pledge, a divided people. What
politician scheming for place and preferment could
dream that a people's conscience would ever drive them
so far? Who would imagine that the pangs of remorse
for an evil done by the fathers, would ever induce the
children to violate a compact solemnly made binding

upon them and the heirs of their honor and glory forever, simply from a deeply-rooted conviction that such agreement was unjust, unholy, oppressive and therefore void ?

Already Seward and Wade and Giddings and Chase, and a hundred others of the coming men of both great parties, had declared this issue to be paramount, and their constituencies had not only approved their course, but unmistakably indicated a willingness to follow them beyond party lines. Very few of them had, however, ostensibly severed their relations with existing parties. The people clamored for leaders, for organization, for progress. The politicians paltered and schemed; sought for substitutes and preferred excuses. Parties sprang up like mushrooms. A thousand visionary projects were broached. Secret political organizations that grew up among the people, none knew how, confounded the estimates of the demagogue. The professional politician was at sea in all his calculations. No man knew how his neighbor stood on any political question. Blind leaders thought they led blind followers, but found themselves deserted at the last moment. Chaos reigned in politics. Each one was seeking for a new and sure way out of the labyrinth. The recreancy of some of the old leaders produced suspicion of almost all.

The blame which attached to the Whig chiefs extended also to the recognized leaders of what had been known as the Liberty, or Free-Soil party. The nomination of Mr. Van Buren, though it resulted in an immense increase of the vote previously polled by that party, was by no means regarded with approval by its rank and file. They were earnest men, who had been tried as by fire, and they had no faith in the sincerity of the candidate's weakly-worded professions. They regarded it very generally as a matter of bar-

gain and sale between the leading members of the
Free-Soil Convention and Mr. Van Buren, by which, in
consideration of their lending the party name and
strength to aid his plan of personal revenge, he formally
consented to carry out their principles in the unexpected contingency of his election. It was freely charged
that the leaders of the Free-Soil party had made this
bargain with a defeated Democratic aspirant in the interest of the Whigs. The result of the election and the
immediate abandonment of the party and its tenets by
Mr. Van Buren, as soon as it had served his individual
purpose, gave color to this charge. By reason of this,
the Free-Soil party was tainted even in the hour of its
apparent success with the seemingly well-grounded suspicion that it was a party not of principles, but designed
only for the sale and delivery of votes in the interest of
certain leaders. To the men who composed this party
no charge could be more galling. They despised chicanery. Not one in a hundred of them believed at all in
political management, as it is called. They were brave,
honest men, who feared God, loved liberty and hated
wrong. To ally themselves in any way with the great
parties who had paltered, lied and finally betrayed
the great principle which overshadowed all others,
was, in their view, the blackest treason. The party
had thitherto been distinguished from all others in
that it did not seek for power, was wedded to the fortunes of no man or set of men, but was simply a standing protest against a national evil. Those who had
been prominent in its councils were the martyrs of
its cause. Steadfastness in the midst of persecution,
hope in the midst of discouragement, and a willingness
to serve " without favor, reward or the hope of reward,"
had been the qualifications of its standard-bearers.

For the first time, in 1848, these simple, earnest, single-hearted men were subjected to the artful wiles of

ambitious, self-seeking, political tricksters, with the president of the convention at their head. The brilliant scheme, like many another which he lived to evolve for his own elevation to the Presidency, while promising well for immediate success resulted in ultimate disaster, by producing almost universal distrust of those who were regarded as the promoters of this act of barter and sale. The schemer had secured for himself the Senatorship at which he was then aiming, and to obtain it had renewed again his allegiance to the Democracy. He had, indeed, opposed the measure which had now become of paramount interest to the advocates of personal liberty for the slave, but he was still regarded by the mass of the Democratic party with insuperable distrust. The suspicion which attached to him extended to many of his former associates of the Free-Soil party, and even to the name which had been adopted by them. It is rare that such swift and universal execration follows on the breach of an implied trust. If all that was done then had been *bona fide*, the party, in 1852, would have been tenfold as strong as was indicated by the convention which met at Pittsburg, and, under the name of the "Free Democracy," sought to rally its scattered voters back to the support of "equal liberty for all men" as the cardinal principle of political life. Its votes on the day of election were only one-half as many as four years previous, but its power was many times greater. It had purged itself of the taint of fraud, and was ready to enter with clean hands into the climacteric struggle that was rapidly drawing near.

In the midst of this seven-times-heated furnace of popular thought Martin Kortright laid the foundations of his manhood at the academy in the neighboring village of Rockboro. There Jared Clarkson's open door invited the oppressed to share a welcome that took no note of color or condition, but evidenced forever the sincerity of his devotion to the cause of liberty and equality of right for all. The eloquence of his words was excelled by the eloquence of his example. Skendoah felt the new life that came with western gold, and hammers rung and forges glowed amid the roar of its prisoned waterfall. The trustee of the young partners had already become a magnate in the surrounding region. Hilda was exiled to a New England seminary, whose cautious principal disapproved all agitation of the question which, despite objection and protest from the best and wisest, was swiftly coming uppermost in the minds of all. There were those who uncharitably hinted that the good lady's dread of all discussion touching slavery was stimulated by the lusty term-bills of her Southern patrons. Sturmhold's master went and came, apparently undisturbed by the conflict which he watched with a quiet, puzzled interest. Among the people who lived near, he was regarded with less of aversion and distrust than when he was considered as in some sort a legitimate successor of the Patroon—a nabob who dwelt in their midst and fed upon their life. His intimate connection with Kortright had brought him nearer to his neighbors, and the young people of Paradise Bay and the Castle of Folly (as it was sometimes called in jest) upon the hillside, were already looked upon as lovers, of whom all wished only good. A sad-faced woman, whose hair was blanched to a soft and piteous white, sat at the board and wandered about the rooms of the great mansion, waiting patiently for the light that came only with the recurring vacations of the distant seminary. The master went sailing but little of late in his yacht, which only left her moorings now and then in charge of the faithful Jason. So the years went by and the world's life fled faster than the years.

CHAPTER XVIII.

A WEEKLY POST.

It was in the fall of 1854 that Merwyn Hargrove sat in his spacious library with the weekly packet which, even at that day, was all the service the Post Office Department could give to the chain of little inland villages, the route between which Sturmhold overlooked. Turning over the pile of letters that were placed before him, he selected, for his first assault, one which was directed in an irregular, girlish hand, the sight of which brought a tender light to his eye. He broke the seal and took out a many-sheeted letter, written across and around after the manner dear to the feminine heart.

I. A SCHOOL-GIRL'S LARK.

BEECHWOOD SEMINARY, }
BURLINGDALE, MASS., —— ——. }

My Dear Papa :—Miss Hunniwell has sent me to my room to write a letter to post with hers enclosed. She always does so when she has to send any unpleasant word to the parents or guardians of her scholars. The girls say it is in order to save postage, but I don't reckon that is the real reason. Anyhow it is all true what she says about our running away, Amy and I, but we only did it for a lark, you know, just as boys do in college. Miss Hunniwell says it was just awful, so improper and unladylike and—and—everything that it oughtn't to be, and I suppose it was ; but, Papa dear, we didn't mean anything bad, only to have a little fun, you know. So you won't scold us too hard, will you, dear Papa, that is me, because Amy she hasn't got any papa, nor mamma either, and she don't know who her guardian is, only he sends her nice presents

231

and such lots of money and things through the bank for her holidays. Isn't that nice? Only it must be lonesome not to have any dear old papa to go to see and to ride with and have all to one's self in the long vacation. But she won't have to write any letter of explanation, as Miss Hunniwell calls it, because there ain't anybody to explain to. Oh, I am real sorry for Amy. She is such a jolly girl, and her name is Hargrove, too, and we are "sin twisters" as we call ourselves in sport, that is, twin sisters, you know. The girls called us that because we were together so much, and we put it the other way for short.

But Miss Hunniwell says I must tell you all about it, and I am to stay in my room all day and have my supper sent up to me, and it isn't to be anything either, only just some "cambric tea" and cracker, and I know I shall be just as hungry as can be. Well, to begin at the beginning, I don't know how it did begin. Amy was in my room or I was in hers, as we most always are together in one or the other, and she proposed, or else I did, that we should have some fun. It's just awful dull staying here in the house all the time, unless when we go out with some one along to see that we are just as "proper" as can be. I go riding sometimes, but not very often, because I am the only one that has a pony, and I think it makes the girls feel a little —just a little, you know—well, if I could take one of them along sometimes it wouldn't seem so bad—I know I should hate a girl who had a pony if I didn't have any. I lend him to one of them sometimes, and then I get a good nice ride afterwards, because I feel then that no one will think that I am selfish, you know.

Oh, dear, where was I? I don't get along a bit in my "explanation." Oh, yes; we were in my room, because that looks out toward the west, and I always like to watch the sunset there, and think of you at dear Sturmhold, and of Aunt Kortright and Mammy and all of you.

("So she leaves Martin out, eh? Writes his name and then erases it," said the father, as he paused in his reading and glanced with a loving look up at his daughter's picture that hung opposite him upon the wall. After a moment of dreamy scrutiny, he resumed.)

So we were sitting looking out at my window, when Amy moved and I seconded it, as they said at the meeting, or else I moved and Amy seconded it, that we should have some fun. And then I proposed one thing and she another, until finally one or the other suggested that we should go to the meeting that was to be held in the town hall that night. You see from my room we can go right out on the roof of the wing the kitchen is in, and from the kitchen roof down on the wood-shed roof, and the back end of that is right against a big rock that one can get on with a pretty long step, and just walk down by scrambling a little. So, if we put out the light and lock our doors, Miss Hunniwell thinks we are not well, and have gone to bed early. She is a great believer in sleep, and is real kind and good, Papa dear, only sort of notional sometimes, as I don't see how she could help being with so many girls to invent "improper" things to do to torment her, as they must.

There was to be a big meeting in the town that night—what they call an "Abolition" meeting—and a woman was to speak, and a colored man, that was a runaway from slavery, and had a reward offered for him; and a little girl was to be there, not as old as I, who had been a slave, and was bought and set free by a kind gentleman in Boston, who was just as white as any one—the little girl, I mean—and it was all so dreadful, and so—so—like a circus, Papa, only more so—more exciting, you know—that we couldn't resist the temptation. We didn't dare ask Miss Hunniwell, because we knew she wouldn't let us go. Just that morning at prayers two of the big girls, the best ones in the graduating class, real ladies, you know, they asked her if they might go, and you just ought to have heard her go on at them. I never thought she could talk so—never. She said the Abolitionists were just the worst people; they wanted to steal and rob and stir up strife and—oh, I don't know what all, but it was awful—perfectly awful. And I thought of Mr. Clarkson and Uncle Kortright, and I told Miss Hunniwell that they were Abolitionists, and I knew they weren't bad people and didn't want to do anybody any harm, and I wouldn't have them abused, there! Then I cried. But when I called Mr. Clarkson's name, half the girls they just clapped their hands and waved their handkerchiefs, and the other half they hissed—just like a lot of horrid, ugly boys—and Miss Hunniwell she put up both hands and shook her head till her gold glasses slipped almost off her nose, and one side was tilted up and the other hung down so that she looked at me over one glass and under the other, and—I couldn't help it, you know—I burst out laughing, and then both sides stopped cheering and hissing and we all laughed till we cried, and Miss Hunniwell she stamped and screamed, and I got sent to my room for being bad. But I couldn't help it, Papa. It was just too funny for anything.

Well, that night—last night, you know—we were sitting here in my room looking for the stars to come out, and seeing them light the town hall in the village below, and the people going in, men and women and children, when one of us proposed that we should go and see the fun anyhow. "The weight of the meetin'," as the chairman said after he put something to vote last night, was "in favor on 't." So we locked our doors, without lighting the candles, and put on our hoods and wraps and crawled along the roof and went to the meeting. Oh, Papa, it was such fun—I mean it was so sad, you know. The black man that had been a slave was as big as our Jason, and he told, oh, such horrible stories of how they cut and walloped him. I held my fingers in my ears, it was so terrible. But I could hear every word just as plain as could be. And then he told such awful things about his masters, and called the slaveholders such bad names, and stamped his foot and looked as if he was going to swear. But he didn't, only kept on abusing all the masters just

too bad to think about, till I just hated them, just as bad
as he, I do believe, when all at once I thought that you
were a slaveholder, and grandpa, and grandma, and Uncle
George and all the relations. I was so angry at that man
that I forgot where I was, and I jumped right up there in
that meeting, where it was just as still as death, only for
the man that was talking, and said, "It ain't any such
thing, sir! My Papa is a slaveholder, and he isn't any
bad man. And I think you must have been a pretty bad
nigger, too, or you wouldn't have got walloped so much!"
Then there was an uproar. Some cheered and some
hissed, and I heard them ask, "Who is it?" And then
some one said, "It's one of Miss Hunniwell's girls," and for
a minute all was confusion. The man stopped speaking
and held up his hand with the palm toward us, and just
shook it a minute, and everybody was just as still as the
grave. It almost frightened me, there was such a hush
came over that crowded house. The palm of his hand had
that queer yellow look that made it seem as if he was sick.
It trembled, too, and he looked, oh! so changed and tender, as if the tears were going to overflow the eyes that
had burned so hatefully a minute before. I cried as
soon as the people made such a clamor about what I
had said, but I had to take my handkerchief down to look
at that man. So I sat and bit my handkerchief and cried
and watched him. He came out to the very edge of the
platform and said, "Will my little Missy let me ask her
forgiveness? I was wrong. Anger made me unjust.
There are good men and women who are slave masters
and mistresses, and, thank God, there are good little mistresses like her, too." Then I was ashamed, and hid my
face while he went on to tell of his master's little girl,
who was so kind and good to him that he never thought
of Heaven without thinking that she would make it lighter
and sweeter by her presence. Oh, it was just lovely the tender things he said, and the soft, low tones in which he spoke.
I heard the people on each side of me sobbing and sigh-

ing, but I didn't cry any more. I just kept my head in my hands and wondered to myself. I kept saying over and over again, "Can this be a black man? Why should he be, and why should he have been a slave?" Though, for that matter, I think I should rather be a slave than be black; and if I was black it don't seem to me I should care much what else I was. I got to thinking about that so much that I didn't notice what went on afterwards.

The woman spoke, I remember, and she brought out the little girl who had been a slave and was sold on the block. And, Papa, it was a fact, she was just as white as I. Then the woman spoke some more, but I didn't mind what she said or what went on, till, all at once, I heard the strangest voice I ever listened to, and looking on the platform I saw a man I can never forget. He looked to me like some one out of the Scripture dressed in our every-day clothes. He had a full, broad forehead, from which the hair grew away of its own accord all around in heavy waves. His eyes were very wide apart, and looked so straight out from under his heavy brows that they seemed to see right through me. They did not flash, but seemed to burn with a steady, clear light. His face had a hard, stern look, and his wide mouth shut so close that I could hardly see the color of his lips from where we sat. He was a tall, straight man, and wore a good dark suit of clothes, which seemed to be new and not quite what he liked to wear. His voice was not exactly loud, but it seemed to come directly to one as if sent for a special purpose. I didn't think of anything else while *he* was speaking. I couldn't. I don't remember what he said, only that he was "glad that slavery was coming out of its shell. It could not be killed with honey. Instead of smooth words it would take hard blows. The cry of the poor in bondage was for help. The rich and powerful must be taught to respect the weak. The master must be brought low before the slave could be lifted up. He had no feeling of revenge. He did not hate the master. He pitied the mistress and little ones.

But the will of the Lord must be done. He had built up in mercy, He would tear down in wrath.''

He did not say very much, and what he did say does not seem very remarkable to me now, but then somehow it seemed as if he spoke with authority. I did not weep or tremble as when the other man was speaking, but I could not help thinking that this man knew all about it and was saying what was the very truth. I could never have interrupted him even if he had abused you by name, dear Papa. I should just as soon have thought of interrupting Elijah if I had heard him cursing the priests of Baal. He seemed just as much a prophet. Just before he sat down he said : "I want to tell that little girl who spoke up for her father to-night that I am sure no one meant to hurt her feelings. I am sorry her father is a slaveholder, and hope she will persuade him to let the oppressed go free.''

Then there were some resolutions, and just as they were going to adjourn this man came down the aisle and asked me my name, and when I told him he said, "Hargrove? Hargrove? Where from ?''

I said, "Sturmhold, near Skendoah.''

"Yes. Merwyn Hargrove,'' he said as quietly as if he was looking right at you, and he asked me about Jason and Mammy, too, as if he had known them all his life.

Then he went back on the platform and said with a queer smile : "I want to say that if all the slave masters were like this young lady's father there would be no more call for such meetings as this.''

Then everybody looked at me, and I was too surprised to mind it at all. What did he mean, Papa? Everybody cheered and seemed to think that I was entitled to a great a deal of consideration. There was a great company going by the Seminary when the meeting was over, and they insisted on paying us attention, so that we couldn't slip away to climb up our rock and get back into the window. Indeed, two of the young men walked up to the door with us, and one of them sounded the knocker before I could get my wits together to stop him. After a long time the door opened and there stood Miss Hunniwell. You should have seen her. But the letter she sends will tell you all about it, I suppose. We must have been very bad, though I don't see what harm there is in it. If you say there is any I will not do so any more.

Oh, dear Papa, I want to see you so much! I want to tell you something that I don't know how to write. You know you told Miss Hunniwell she was never to open my letters, and you told Martin, too, that he might write to me and I might write to him twice every month. It was very kind of you, dear Papa, and it has been a great pleasure to me, but I am not certain that you meant that he should write as he has done lately. He wants to be my lover, Papa. You may not think it right, though I hope you will not be hard on Martin, for I do love him, Papa—though I have not told him so, and will not until I have your permission. Perhaps I am too young to think of such things, but it seems to me as if I had always loved Martin ever since he stopped the horses when they were running away. Then he has been with me so much at home that it seems just as natural to love him as to love you, only it is different, of course. I never thought of it in that way until he wrote, and am sure I ought to let you know. You are such a good papa that I know you will do just what is right, and you may be sure your "little Hilda" will obey your wishes. Please do not be angry at Martin if he has done wrong. I inclose you his letter. When you read it just think you have me in your arms with my face hid in your bosom and the blushes burning my cheeks as they do now.

Your loving daughter,   HILDA.

P. S.—That strange man is named Brown—John Brown. Do you know him? I suppose you do not. He is only a common working man I should say from appearances, perhaps a farmer, but I think John the Baptist must have been just such a man. Amy thinks he was perfectly horrid,

and all the rest of them, too. She just hates them, she
says, and doesn't see how any Southern man's daughter
can endure them for a minute. She is the *Southernest*
girl in the whole school. I think, though, that if these
people and Uncle Kortright and Mr. Clarkson are a sample
of what Abolitionists are like, Mr. Brown was about right
when he said last night that he had been "accustomed
to move in the best society for twenty years —the society of
fugitive slaves and Abolitionists." II. II.

P. S.—Please return Martin's letter and write very soon,
won't you? That's a dear Papa. II.

P. S.—I forgot to ask if you think my explanation is
sufficient. If it is please write and tell Miss Hunniwell
that I am your spoiled Hilda and must be allowed a few
"improprieties."

The father paused a moment when he had finished
this long epistle, and looked up to the portrait in tender
thought. Then he opened one of the enclosures. It
was written in a coarse, sprawling hand, that almost
made its fervid words ridiculous. The father smiled at
the careful request for its return that Hilda had repeated
on the letter itself lest it should escape his memory.
Then he re-read a part of his daughter's letter; walked
up and down the room a few times, and glanced at the
letter of the principal of Beechwood Seminary, which
was full of regrets and excuses for the corruption of
mind to which his daughter had been exposed despite
the care of the teachers. Miss Hunniwell was no doubt
distressed and alarmed at the escapade of the rich man's
daughter. He answered this in a few curt sentences
requesting that his daughter have full liberty to go
where she chose among the good people of Burlingdale
whenever her time was not required for the performance of any school duty. As to what she had done,
he did not see anything reprehensible in it except
the deception practiced upon Miss Hunniwell herself,

which he thought would never have been attempted if instead of being watched she had been trusted. As to its being an Abolition meeting, he saw no reason why she should not attend this as well as any other. She had to form her own opinions, and this was one of the questions on which she might yet be called to act, and he should prefer that she should act intelligently.

The good woman's amazement knew no bounds when she read this reply. Was it possible that a slaveholder could doubt upon the question of slavery? The question itself almost disturbed her own faith in the Scripture which saith "Servants, obey your masters."

II. A WISE MAN'S WARNING.

The next letter that Merwyn Hargrove opened was written in a cramped, close hand, but every character was clear and perfect, and the mind of a strong man shone out from the closely-lined page.

OAK RIDGE, Oct. 24, '54.

MY DEAR CAPTAIN :—If you are still bent upon carrying your Quixotic scheme into effect, it is no doubt necessary that you should remove the slaves from the country entirely. In the first place, they would not be safe anywhere in the United States should the collateral heirs ever obtain a decision against you, as they are nearly certain to do if they ever get you into court here. The passage of this new Fugitive Slave Law was a great piece of folly on the part of our Southern Congressmen. They meant well enough, but were mighty short-sighted. Anything that keeps up the agitation about slavery is bad policy. We had a deal better just have submitted to the loss of the few slaves that get away and said nothing more about them. After a negro has once been in a free state a little while he is good for nothing more anyhow. He may do to sell South and work on the sugar plantations, but the chances are .that he'll keep on running away till he gets himself killed or so torn by dogs that he is good for nothing afterwards. This law will just encourage all our people to spend twice the value of a slave getting him back, and keep the North in a constant tumult till somehow or other they will find out a way to set the last one of them free. I don't know how it will be done, but I'm clearly of the mind that this law will be the death-knell of slavery inside of fifty years—perhaps inside of twenty. It's the biggest piece of folly I've ever known.

If Gilman had his judgment against you, though, he wouldn't lose any time in getting hold of those negroes you took to Ohio. It would be the same anywhere in the Northern States. Besides that, it is simply a refinement of cruelty to take a negro to that climate, set him free and expect him to make a living. With all that you did for those you emancipated, I'll wager you've had to help support them ever since. The great philanthropist who offered that immense tract in the Adirondacks to negro settlers gratis, might just as well have given them a quarter section each in Nova Zembla. No humane master would be so cruel as to send a slave there. I suppose it will make a big transfer station on the Underground Railroad—a sort of harbor where they can stop on the way to Canada, and perhaps they may get so strong after a while that a marshal will not care to serve process among them. But I think if you will do it, you should send them to Liberia. If a negro is not going to be a slave he has no business to live among white folks. The greatest nuisance in the world and the most dangerous element in the land is the free black population of the Southern States. I say Liberia, too, because it may be that the Colonization Society would pay part of the cost of transporting them there. I do not know. I hear they are very full this year, and they may not have transportation for any but those paying full rates for passage. The only objection to this is its

cost. And right here let me ask if you have fully considered what it costs a Southern man to be an Abolitionist?
Our Northern friends talk about it very glibly ; and well
they may. It costs them nothing but fine words. Now
take your case. There is first the value of these seventy-
six or seventy-eight slaves and the twenty-one you sent to
Ohio. It is not a cent less than eighty thousand dollars.
Then the cost of transportation is a hundred dollars apiece,
if they go to Liberia. At least that is the estimate I find
made in an old Congressional report by the chairman, who
seemed to know what he was talking about. It would
take, I suppose, as much more to set them on their feet and
give them a fair start toward getting a living there. This
will make it at least $100,000. It is not much wonder
there are so few Abolitionists among our planters. If they
thought slavery was wrong not one in twenty of them
could afford to be right.

But in your case this is only half the loss. You lose
the slaves like any one else, but if the collaterals should
get a judgment against you, as they certainly will if they
ever get service of process, you will have to pay for the
last one of them, and pay for the use and enjoyment you
have had of them, too. You are, I suppose, very wealthy.
Amity Lake and the negroes you sold with it gave you a
good send-off, and I hear you dropped into some very good
investments afterward. They tell me you are selling off
your land, which is a very good idea. It will never be
worth any more than now, when everybody has gone wild
over California and dreams of having gold as plenty as
pewter in a few years. I'm not so sure about it being a
wise thing to put the money into telegraph poles and
wires, as I hear you are doing. However, that is your
lookout. Fortunes are easier made now than in my day,
when they only came by hard work. However rich you
may be, you can hardly fail to think twice before risking
any such sum as this. Let me advise you once more to
abandon all idea of doing it. To my mind, you are carry-

ing a point of honor too far when you imperil your own estate just to carry out your brother's silly notions. If you should lose Mallowbanks and have to pay for the slaves you have already liberated, George Eighmie's bequest would be a very costly one to you even now. He certainly cannot have expected you to use the proceeds of the slaves you sold with Amity Lake in order to set his Mallowbanks negroes free. But all this is for you alone to consider. As to whether there will be any difficulty in getting them away, I should say it would have to be done very expeditiously. The idea seems to have gotten out that you are going to free them, and you might have trouble if you tried to take away so many at once. Of course, it won't do for me to have anything to do with it, and I can think of no one you can trust with such a delicate business. You might get a Northern agent—but his lack of knowledge of the ways of the people would make his success doubtful, and his presence of itself would awaken suspicion. If there were not so many of them, the best way would be to take them out by the Sound; but there are more than your little schooner could carry, I suppose. However you proceed, be very careful. If you will let me know when it is to be done I will be in that region to help you if you get into any trouble. If the Colonization Society will take them it would perhaps be better, as their agent would then attend to the removal. You may as well make up your mind to this. However, you will never get those negroes out of the county if your intention to remove them is known two hours before the start is made. However you may attempt it, count on this to a certainty. I think that boy of George's is in Virginia; but I am afraid there is no doubt the mother is colored. I had a notion something might be learned to the contrary, and went myself to investigate. There is no room for doubt. She is a quadroon. It's a pity, too, for I don't know when I have seen one I felt so much sympathy for. Poor woman !

If there is anything further I can do, you will please command me at all times.

Yours very truly,

MATTHEW BARTLEMY.

III. "GOOD LORD AND GOOD DEVIL."

The next letter bore the heading of an institution especially characteristic of those times.

OFFICE OF THE AMERICAN }
COLONIZATION SOCIETY. }

DEAR SIR: I am sorry to inform you that we have carefully examined the status of the seventy-six negroes named in your application for transportation to Liberia, and have fully determined to decline receiving them as colonists. Our Society is not designed in any degree to interfere with the institution of slavery. With its right or wrong, lawfulness, humanity, extension or continuance we have nothing to do. The removal and colonization of free blacks on the western coast of Africa at their own desire, or at least with their full consent, is our sole purpose. The first requisite in all cases is that they should be free—free beyond a peradventure. As the usefulness of the Society depends in large degree upon the hearty co-operation of slave owners as well as those opposed to the institution, we could not think of interfering in any case where there was a doubt, even, as to the freedom of the parties offering as colonists. In this case, while you no doubt consider your right to manumit the slaves in question to be indisputable, yet we are informed that it is not only questioned but is likely to be controverted by parties who imagine that they have a much better right to the possession and control of this property.

In such a case it would be manifestly indiscreet for the Society to allow itself to be in the remotest degree concerned. I enclose you a report of the proceedings of our last annual meeting, with the speech of Mr. Clay, and other documents, from which you will gather our purpose as an organization more fully. It is now some twenty-five years since Mr. Clay, with that lucidity of statement peculiar to him, expounded the doctrine on which our Society is founded, and to which it has steadily adhered since its first institution, to wit, the removal of that greatest of all nuisances to civilization, the free black. We do not interfere with the slave or slavery, *pro* or *con.* We are neither for nor against it. The free black in the midst of a slave population is an element of danger and corruption; in the midst of a free white population he is cheated and oppressed, and can never occupy an independent position or acquire a healthy development. He is an excrescence on the social body. We confine all our attention to this one evil. We seek to remove the free man of color to a soil and climate where, unrepressed by the power and prestige of the Caucasian, he may develop and grow into a manhood such as his capacity may warrant. We not only do not receive for transportation cases in which there is any doubt as to the right of the master to manumit, but we could not allow them to land as colonists if transported thither at your expense.

Regretting the necessity that compels a negative answer to your very liberal proposition, I remain,

Yours very truly,
A—— M——, Secretary.

There was a knock at the library door as the master of Sturmhold finished reading this letter, and in answer to his invitation Martin Kortright entered.

CHAPTER XIX.

A MOMENTOUS QUESTION.

THERE was a flush on the face of Martin Kortright as he advanced quickly across the spacious library and exchanged greetings with the grave, easy-mannered man beside the heaped-up writing table, and who welcomed him with something of surprise. After shaking hands with his visitor, Hargrove motioned to a chair that stood opposite to his own and scrutinized the young man somewhat more critically than usual as he sat down. This was his daughter's suitor—her first suitor, and, judging from her words, likely to be the last, if only the impulse of her heart was to be regarded in the decision. He could not blame her. Martin Kortright, at eighteen, must have been confessed by the most casual observer to be a very proper young man. In his person the father's ruggedness had been softened by the mother's fullness of outline. The keen, blue eyes and massive brow of Harrison Kortright were happily blended in his countenance with the richer complexion and rounder oval of Martha Ermendorf. His lips were as mobile as his father's, but had something of the fullness and color that still made his mother's smile so sweet.

Ever since his first visit there, Martin Kortright had made Sturmhold his "other home," as he had been wont to call it. "Martin's room" had been one of the permanently appropriated apartments of the mansion. It was never occupied by any one else, and was always kept ready for his coming. The life of the hillside mansion had become in him inextricably interwoven with that of the humbler home in the valley.

To Hilda he had been as a brother. Neither had any other intimate associates of their own age. Between them there had never been the least restraint, and in all these years no serious estrangement. Mr. Hargrove had come to love the sturdy boy almost as a son, all the more easily because of his young daughter's evident fondness for her playmate and protector. Then, too, the boy had made his way like a conqueror into the affections of the whole household. Jason, the faithful butler, had long known him only as "Marse Martin." Hargrove could not have resisted, if he would, his frank intrepidity.

He had not planned that Hilda and Martin should love each other. In fact, the simple words of his daughter had brought to him that feeling of jealous surprise with which a loving parent always learns that the life he has cherished is to be dissevered from his own. Yet, while he had not purposely designed to promote this result, he had more than once contemplated it as a possible contingency, and he was not unwilling that it should occur. He remembered that in the very moment when he said to Harrison Kortright, "Let them be partners," it occurred to him that it would be an odd instance of our American conglomeration of races and peoples if his Hilda, sprung from the buccaneer, the planter, and the exile of sunny Italy, with a dash of Quaker steadfastness in her veins, should mate with the child of the Dutch Yankee, the offspring of chill New England and phlegmatic Netherlands. After all, he thought, it would only be Yeoman Hargrove and Yeoman Cartwright striking hands across the centuries in the persons of their children, whose English lives had subjugated the currents of foreign blood that swelled their veins. It was strange that he should quietly have con-

templated this contingency. He was not without pride
of birth. The father and the father's father, whose
portraits looked down from his library walls, were not
men to beget offspring who could be otherwise than
proud of their name and achievements. There was not,
it is true, the warmth of attachment between him and
the other branches of the Hargrove stock that one is
accustomed to find among kindred in the South. Indeed, he hardly seemed to have any kindred in the
sense of near relations. The owner of the "Quarter,"
in the old days, had been *the* Hargrove of that region.
His kinsmen had lacked the inherent force necessary
to enable them to rise above the rank in which they
had been born. As the family grew rich and strong
they gathered around and shared its prosperity. They
were rather privileged henchmen than kindred and
equals. So, too, the family alliances had not generally
been with the very best of the vicinity. The taint of
yeoman origin, as well as the somewhat rough manners
of the early owners of the Quarter, had prevented that.
His father's Northern marriage had been seriously resented by the connection when they found that it was
not sufficiently lucrative to restore the lavishness of the
old régime. They had looked very coldly on the young
widow who came to face the prospect of penury on the
encumbered plantation, and never quite forgave her for
capturing the heart of Colonel Eighmie and, through
his aid, avoiding the fate that apparently awaited
her. It is very hard for people to permit themselves to
be forgiven. So when he himself returned with his fair
foreign bride he found the consanguineous Hargroves
green with envy at the good fortune that had fallen to
his lot. They had, too, the distrust peculiar to that region, of those who come from abroad or whose habits of
life and methods of thought are not formed on their
peculiar models. When, therefore, he espoused his

brother's cause against a public sentiment, than which nothing could be more intense and bitter, they were but too glad to disown any responsibility for his conduct and to withdraw from him not only their approval but also their society. Absorbed in each other and the gay life they met at the Northern resorts which they visited, Merwyn and his Rietta had cared little for such conduct on the part of those who, though relatives by blood, had been only strangers in fact. His devotion to his wife, whose foreign birth and education separated her somewhat from society, tended even more to secure their complete isolation. Till her death he had wished for nothing more than her presence. To please him was the aim of her existence; to be with her the height of his desire. Their very fitness to adorn society had, in a sense, shut them out from it by making each sufficient for the other's pleasure. The presence of others was a restraint to them—an intrusion into that paradise which they held sacred to each other.

When his wife died there was nothing living that he loved. Even the child she left seemed a stranger to him until years had passed and her pretty ways began to recall her whom he still mourned. Added to these circumstances was the duty imposed upon him by his brother's will. It was neither light nor congenial. Remembering the aversion with which the public mind had regarded his intercession in that brother's behalf, he naturally expected a similar sentiment to obstruct the execution of his dying wish. The difficulties in the way seemed insuperable. He would have shirked his duty could he have done so with honor. But honor was his king, and his love for the dead brother was intense. He had brought from Mallowbanks the books of the student recluse, which he had been especially requested to keep for himself. The shelves of his library groaned under them. Through them he still communed with the gentle

spirit who had loved them. His own estate would not
at that time have sufficed to discharge the task he had
undertaken. But, while he waited in sorrowful seclusion, it had grown many fold greater, and he looked
upon this unexpected enrichment as a token that he
must perform to the letter the strange trust confided to
his hands.

By all these things he had been excluded from the
usual circle of association, and therefore, no doubt,
looked with more equanimity than he otherwise would
on the possibility of marriage between his daughter and
one not her equal in birth or station, and separated by
the whole width of the world's life from the traditions of which she was the natural heir. So, when
the children played together as boy and girl, and he
thought that they might some time be partners indeed
in the game of life, he said to himself, "Well, why
not?" and then half thoughtlessly brought them nearer
and nearer by the strong bonds of his own unconcealed
affection.

Merwyn Hargrove could not be termed superstitious,
but there was something about his relations to Martin
Kortright and his father that seemed to him to partake
of the mysterious to a degree that unquestionably influenced his conduct not a little. At the time of their first
unfortunate meeting he had decided to proceed at once
to execute his brother's wish. He was not ignorant
either of the danger to himself or peril to his estate
which such a course would entail. Living, he had no
fear of the result. Should he die, he felt that in serving
the interests of his brother's children he might destroy
the inheritance of his daughter. After much study he
had determined to adopt the very course that his brother
had pursued, except that in his case, he would, while yet
living, select a trustee, who should hold a certain fund
for his daughter in such a manner that the law could in

no event divert it from the purpose designed. Casting about for one on whom he could safely devolve so delicate a trust, he could fix upon no one except Jared Clarkson. He had never met with him personally, but from all that he had heard of him in the region where his name was a household word, he felt that he could rely upon both his judgment and integrity. It was well known that the most cautious financier in the land had not feared to intrust him with hundreds of thousands of dollars, without even so much as a written receipt for it to bear witness of a transaction then almost unprecedented in amount between private parties. He seemed to have inherited the same rugged faithfulness to his plighted word or implied promise that Hargrove recognized as an element of his own nature. The very fact that he lived up to his convictions upon the subject of slavery and the rights of the Negro, without regard for the clamor and vituperation of others and in defiance of a public sentiment which regarded any step toward the social equality of the races with peculiar horror and animosity tended, no doubt, very strongly to strengthen the conviction of his especial fitness for this trust. At that time, as we have seen, Hargrove had no sympathy with Clarkson's convictions upon this subject, but only by accident had found himself charged with a duty that seemed in harmony with them. Negro slavery as an institution seemed to him less dangerous than negro liberty. He was not in favor of emancipation from any point of view. He was simply an instrument of another's will. He could not but recognize the fact, however, that faithfulness to conviction was but another name for duty, and that one who did not shrink from obloquy in the advocacy of political principle was most likely to perform a private trust. Knowing that Kortright was familiar with his character and history, it had been the purpose of his Christmas visit to Paradise Bay to make more specific inquiries in regard to Clarkson. Kortright's sturdy independence, thorough integrity and the boldness and practicality of his scheme to render tributary to his will the unused waterfall in which both had an interest, had turned him from his purpose, and it flashed upon him like an inspiration that here, in his very presence, was the man for whom he had been seeking—a man whom no difficulty could daunt from a task once undertaken, and whom no temptation could swerve from the path of rectitude.

The plan Kortright had conceived was a bold one. At some period in the remote past the brawling mountain torrent, on its northward way to the Mohawk, after passing through a level valley where the hills retreating on either side left wide stretches of fertile bottom lands, had met across its pathway a rugged chain of granite-founded hills. Through these it had wound in a narrow, tortuous passage, till at length it burst through a last stubborn ledge and tumbled foaming and raging to the plain beneath, thence to pursue its way unheeded to the wider channel which it sought. It was traditionary lore among the Indians that the level region to the southwestward had once been a lake of several hundred acres in extent, before the Great Spirit had cleft a passage for the pent-up waters through the hills. The fall had been utilized to turn a grist-mill almost ever since the white man's occupancy. There was a tradition that the stones first used in it had been brought from Massachusetts slung across a horse, supported by a pack-saddle specially devised by the enterprising pioneer miller for that purpose. It seems an almost incredible tale, but when one has looked upon one of the veritable stones themselves, or what the "picker" has left thereof, as vouched for by tradition among those whose feet have trodden upon it year by year since its grinding days were over, and has noticed what a tiny thing it was be-

side the great burr-stones that crush our modern harvest, he begins to grow more credulous. And when he
looks upon a letter in which this sturdy pioneer recounts
his experience with the twain millstones and the gray
horse, whose strength he had wrongfully misdoubted
at the first, as they picked their way with difficulty
through the Blankshire hills to the little settlement whose
need he aspired to supply, doubt vanishes. Without
such "sensible and true avouch" the writer hereof had
never credited the story which he tells.

This mill, together with the lands above, had come
into Hargrove's hands in the manner before described.
Kortright's plan was to rebuild the barrier and re-cre-
ate the lake. The task was not one that would be
called stupendous at this day, but it was bold enough
to make most men of that time hesitate. As to its
results, when once accomplished, there could be no doubt.
The supply of water and the resulting power would be
practically unlimited. That this man of mature years
should have had the self-control to nourish this idea in
secret, with hardly the remotest prospect of its final accomplishment, marked him, to Hargrove's mind, as in
some sort extraordinary. To Kortright himself the wonder always was that he revealed his secret at all. Only
the enfeeblement of disease, he mournfully asserted, could
have so weakened his resolution as to have induced him
to complain of disappointment or condescend to ask for
aid.

The result of the confidence Hargrove had been thus
strangely led to bestow upon Squire Kortright had inclined him still more to the son. It was not the father's
success, but the power to succeed in so difficult an undertaking, and one so apparently at variance with the
training which his life had given, that had year by year
increased his respect for the self-centred man whom
neither pain nor difficulty could daunt. Neither Martin

nor Hilda had the remotest idea of the strange relation they were to sustain to each other and toward the prosperous enterprise that had transformed Skendoah from the sleepiest of hamlets into one of the world's most bustling hives. The blandishments of fortune had not changed Harrison Kortright. His nervous, firm-shut lips were like a barrier of iron set to guard the gateway of his thought. All knew that he had prospered marvelously. None knew the secret that underlay his prosperity.

The crisis in his affairs which Merwyn Hargrove had long expected, had at length arisen. The collateral heirs of George Eighmie had delayed action for two reasons. First, because of grave doubt as to an ultimately favorable result to themselves, and, secondly, because they were advised that, as the word "heirs" was not in the will, the property would revert to them in case of the death of Hargrove before converting or consuming the estate. As his fortune, outside of what he had inherited from his testator, was ample to satisfy all claims against him for rents and profits, should he be adjudged to have held the estate wrongfully, it was believed that the wiser course was to allow matters to remain pretty much *in statu quo* until he should make some further attempt to carry out what was believed to be the secret understanding with George Eighmie. By some means or other the impression had gotten abroad that this was about to be done. The collateral heirs were moving. The case of "Sherwood Eighmie *et al. vs.* Merwyn Hargrove, as executor, and Merwyn Hargrove individually," had been instituted and was being pressed. Matthew Bartlemy did not fear the action against his client as executor, but the designation served to give the plaintiffs a place in court and to justify a continuance from term to term in the hope of obtaining personal service of process. His opponents were right. The time had

come when Merwyn Hargrove had at length decided
to perform, without further delay, the trust his brother
had laid upon him. The son of the man to whom
he had intrusted her dower had come to ask the hand of
his daughter. Had the trust he had bestowed upon the
father only prefigured the greater confidence he must
now extend to the son? The whole household had long
regarded him as heir-apparent to the daughter's love,
as he had already become her partner in the father's
confidence—all save Lida, who, with the inconsistency
of a jealous nature, had long regarded him with an aversion that had finally extended to his parents. Since
Hilda had been at the seminary, her distrust of Hargrove had returned also, and she had more than once
absented herself from his house for considerable periods
of time. On such occasions, Jared Clarkson, whose faith
in Hargrove's sincerity had become almost as strong as
his pride in his own honesty, had generally managed to
inform him of her whereabouts in order to remove any
apprehension as to her safety. He did this all the more
easily because of his connection with those organized
enemies of slavery—or more properly, perhaps, friends
of freedom—whose joint efforts to promote the escape of
fugitives from slavery constituted what was quaintly
known as the " Underground Railroad," an institution
the importance of which, as an element in the great
movement of the time, has perhaps been somewhat magnified by the many startling incidents connected with its
operation.

Martin Kortright had come to the verge of manhood,
never doubting his father's kindness or his mother's
love. He had seen himself transferred to college after
his course at Rockboro' Academy; had rejoiced at his
mother's pride in his progress and success, but was profoundly ignorant of any plans that might have been
made as to his future life. His father was one of those

men who cannot yield their confidence to any one except under an irresistible compulsion. No hint of his purposes as to his son had ever reached the boy's ear. With the natural instinct of the American youth for self-direction, therefore, he had laid out for himself a path in life and a part in the world's great conflict that accorded strictly with the influences and ideas of the time in which he lived. Neither the quiet life of Sturmhold nor the bustle of Skendoah's restless wheels and hammers altogether suited him. He did not realize the suffering of which the former was the mellow fruitage, or the deeper life that underlay the latter. The world's thoughts had entered into his heart, and it throbbed with a wild desire to do some great thing for humanity—for liberty—for the right. His love for Hilda, instead of being a check, was only a spur to this desire. He loved her so well that he was even willing to die in order to be worthy of her. Everything was to him an impulse toward the heroic. His father's stoicism; his mother's half-secret bursts of effusive love; Hilda's undoubting confidence in the presage of greatness that he felt within; even the quiet and apparently insignificant life of Mr. Hargrove—all were to him unresting impulses to do. The spirit of the unfailing succession of inborn knights-errant was upon him and would not let him rest content with what others had done. Rose-leaves were not soft enough for his limbs to rest upon. Only laurels, plucked by his own hand on the rugged heights where fame and valor alone may come, could satisfy his soul.

So, as he sat opposite the grave, quiet man, in whose beard the threads of silver were showing more and more with each recurrent year, his thought was busy with the future—his future—the world's future—when he should help to shape its destiny. His flushed face, swelling nostril and lips, close shut yet tremulous, told of an unusual excitement. The man noted his excitement, and not doubting as to its cause, was well pleased to see this boy-suitor for his daughter's love so impressed with the importance of what he had come to ask. He had half feared that the love that Martin had professed was rather a matter of course—a something born of propinquity and the habit of years rather than the absorbing and self-forgetful passion that sways and dominates a life once for all. Now there could be no further doubt. The face of the young man plead for him with the father's heart, and before his lips were opened his cause was won. Very kind was his tone, and his countenance invited the utmost confidence as he asked:

"Well, Martin, what is it that brings you back from college so unexpectedly?"

He knew, of course, but it would not do to betray his knowledge. He wondered in what words the young man would clothe the announcement that had been so simply made by the daughter, who had never learned to doubt either her father's love or his wisdom. There would be a turbulent storm of words, he did not doubt, when love broke through that painful restraint which the young man had put upon himself. For this he was prepared, but he was not prepared for the words that accompanied the look of pain and entreaty which overspread Martin's face as he said, in tones that quivered with sorrow and apprehension:

"Mr. Hargrove, *do* you believe slavery is right?"

CHAPTER XX

"WHAT?" exclaimed Hargrove, in amazement.

"Do you believe that slavery is right?" repeated Martin, with a look of anxious entreaty in his eyes.

"Martin Kortright," said Hargrove, leaning forward and peering anxiously into his face, "are you crazy?"

"No, indeed, sir; but I am in earnest."

"So it seems."

A smile that might have been pitying or scornful crept about the corners of Hargrove's mouth as he spoke.

"I came only to ask that one question," said the young man, with tremulous eagerness.

"Indeed? All the way from your college?"

"No; from Skendoah."

"Ten miles for one question! What a pity! Why did you not prepare a longer catechism?"

The sneer was too apparent to be unheeded even by the preoccupied mind of the young man. He started like one suddenly awakened, and looking at the man before him saw his eyes flashing and his lips quivering with suppressed anger.

"I—I hope," he stammered, "that you are not offended?"

"Oh, not at all," said the other; "I am delighted. Such diligence in the pursuit of knowledge is very commendable. My daughter, I am sure, will be charmed."

"You have heard from Hilda then?" asked Martin, while an ingenuous blush overspread his countenance.

" I received a letter from my daughter this morning," said Hargrove, coldly. "By the way," he added, turning over some papers, and handing Martin's letter to him, "she enclosed me this. As you have apparently forgotten all about it, I may as well give it to you now, and save her the trouble of mailing it."

"You—you—do not approve of it then?" said Martin. A sudden pallor succeeded the flush upon his face. The words seemed to choke him as they came forth. He took the letter as he spoke, and sat looking at the other with a sort of dull, hopeless agony in his eyes.

"Oh, about slavery?" said Hargrove, lightly. "Well, I don't know. You seem to consider my opinion upon this question of great moment."

"It is of the utmost possible importance to me, you may be sure, sir," answered Martin, choking down the emotion that threatened to overcome him, "or I would never have troubled you with the inquiry."

"No doubt you think so, sir," said Hargrove, rising in uncontrollable anger. "There seems to be no bound to your assurance. The fact that you were seeking covertly to win my daughter's love you no doubt thought gave you an unquestionable right to catechise her father. You need not have any further anxiety, sir. Your relations with her are ended, and my opinion upon any subject can be of no further moment to you. I bid you good morning, sir."

Hargrove bowed with mock politeness, and waved his hand toward the door as he spoke. Martin had risen, too, and stood gazing at the master of Sturmhold with a look in which surprise and pain were blended.

"I do not understand, Mr. Hargrove," he said, with quiet dignity, "in what I have been so unfortunate as to offend. I did love your daughter, and always must. I did not suppose that you were ignorant of the fact, though I had only lately found it out. I wrote her

frankly in regard to it, and had no doubt she would con-
sult you. If I did wrong, I did not know it."

"But you made the mistake of not first inquiring fully
what were my views on the slavery question," sneered
Hargrove.

"My inquiry had no connection with your daughter,
or my love for her," responded Martin.

"Indeed!" exclaimed Hargrove. "Am I to understand that you would have condescended to acknowledge
a father-in-law whose views upon that question were not
entirely sound ? I am sure I am very much obliged."

"Captain Hargrove," said the young man, straightening himself up until his eyes flashed proudly into the
flaming orbs before him. "I do not understand your
allusions, but it is evident that I have made you angry.
Allow me to say, however, that my relation to Hil—to
your daughter—did not in the least affect my interest in
the question I asked. If there is any reason why I
ought not to press it, of course I will not, but it is still
a matter of vital interest to me—perhaps all the more
that you regard my love for—for Hilda as a matter of
presumption."

Hargrove looked at him in amazement.

"Do you mean to say that you still desire to know
whether I consider slavery morally right ?"

"I do, indeed, sir."

Hargrove's brow relaxed as he gazed upon the sad
but earnest face before him, and unconsciously his tones
softened somewhat as he inquired :

"Will you please tell me how my opinion upon this
political question can be of any interest or importance
to you now ?"

"If you will allow me to explain, sir, you will easily
see. I came home last night to ask my parents' permission, or, perhaps more truly, to inform them of my determination, to do a certain thing. Both opposed my

wish, and my father especially forbade it, giving as his reason that you were in favor of slavery, and that our relations to you were such as to forbid my doing anything that might displease you."

" It is natural that they should consider conduct that would be displeasing to me inconsistent with your position as my daughter's lover."

" But they had no knowledge of—of any such thing."

" Did they not know you had written that letter ?"

" They did not."

" Nor that you intended doing so ?"

"Nothing of the kind."

"Indeed. Then I do not see how my opinions became important."

"My father said we were under obligations of no common character to you."

" Of course he explained their nature and extent ?" Hargrove smiled sarcastically.

" He did not."

Hargrove's smile deepened to a sneer as he said :

" And you did not ask him ?"

" I did not," said Martin, with something of pride in his tone. " I know it is useless to ask my father what he does not choose to tell."

" That is true ; that is true," mused Hargrove. " Then you do not know to what he referred ?"

" I only guess that you assisted him in his enterprises. I remember that he was only a well-to-do farmer. I know that he is now a rich manufacturer," answered Martin.

" Yes," said Hargrove meditatively turning away for a moment, only to come back for a still sharper catechism of the young man, who stood as if dazed by the unexpected turn the conversation had taken. " But you knew, sir," and he shook his finger at Martin angrily as he spoke, " you knew the relation you desired to sustain to Hilda."

"Of course," simply.

"And you thought Hilda would disapprove?" asked Hargrove eagerly, "or you feared to offend her father?"

"I am afraid," said Martin blushing and stammering, "I am afraid I did not think of her at all."

"You did not? I declare, you are a singular mortal. With the ink of the letter declaring your love, hardly dry, you forget her existence when deciding a matter so important that you call it vital. Pray what did you think of?"

"I tried to determine my duty."

"Oh, it is a question of conscience, then. You never thought Hilda might have a conscience too?"

"I should doubt my own if hers did not approve."

"But you took her approval for granted?"

"I should not have been worthy of her love if I could have doubted her approval of the right."

"You were right, too; just right," said Hargrove, with sudden heartiness, "a true woman's heart never indorses what is wrong. But will you tell me now why my opinion became important in the settlement of this question of conscience?"

"What I wished to do would probably be displeasing to one who believes slavery to be right."

"Well?"

"If you disapproved I had determined to abandon my project."

"For your father's sake?"

"Because I would not offend one whose feelings he felt himself under such obligation to consider."

"So, if I were your father's creditor you would cut your opinions to suit my notions?"

"No; but if you had done my father a great favor I would not express opinions that would be displeasing to you, if I could avoid it without loss of self-respect."

"Oh! this is one of those questions of conscience

that are binding at one time and not at another. I declare you are becoming quite a Jesuit."

"Not at all, sir," said Martin simply. "The question for my conscience was not whether the act itself was right. That I had already settled. The question that remained was whether it was my duty to do it or not."

"And you decided— ?"

"That if it would occasion you annoyance I must leave it to others ?"

"And that is still your purpose ?"

"It is."

Hargrove paced the room for a moment with his head bowed in thought. Then he came back and said in a tone very different from what he had used before :

"Pray be seated again and tell me what is this thing you wish to do that might offend me as a pro-slavery man. I hope you do not wish to preach a new Abolition crusade. I was afraid that Jared Clarkson's influence would turn your head, but I thought you had too much common sense to become clean daft on the subject. You must remember that what is tolerated as a harmless absurdity in a man of his peculiar temperament, becomes altogether a different thing in one not blessed with his idiosyncrasies. He does and says a thousand things which would not be tolerated for a moment in another. It is not because he is less sincere, or is so regarded by others, but only because he is in every respect exceptional, peculiar—eccentric, as it is termed. Whatever is pronounced and striking in his opinions or unusual in his conduct, therefore, is accepted as a legitimate outgrowth of this eccentricity. Of all the men who agree with him in regard to slavery, he is allowed the most license and regarded with the most tolerance, not because he is more deserving or more consistent than the others, but because of his eccentricity.

Such a man is very apt to charm the fancy, but is always dangerous to follow. What he may do with impunity, it would be ruin for others to attempt. He is no more of an Abolitionist than your father; indeed, not as much, since your father, having once reached a conclusion, would accept all its consequences, no matter how terrible. Clarkson, with all his hatred of slavery and all his willingness to cripple and destroy it, yet shrinks in horror from the bloodshed that would inevitably attend any attempt to carry his pet ideas into effect. He is a good man, a sincere and kindly gentleman, but not one who is fit to lead, nor indeed one whom it is safe to follow."

"Yet he is one of the leaders of public thought," said Martin.

"Not one of its leaders, but one of its mouthpieces. He is one of the exponents of an idea that just now dominates the public attention. The leaders of public thought are men of an entirely different mould."

"The leader must be exceptional and is often accounted eccentric, is he not?"

"Undoubtedly. 'He hath a devil,' was the popular verdict as to the Christ. John the Baptist, Peter Hermit and a thousand others, whose words, translated into deeds, have shaken the world, were no doubt eccentric to the very limit of what we call sanity. They were men of one idea, which they followed to the exclusion of all others. They were men whose souls could feel but one emotion. The intensity of their one thought shriveled all others like a furnace-blast. They were of the 'Leave-all-thou-hast-and-follow-me' type of the exceptional. They repeated one cry until the world heard and believed. They had no time for argument, expostulation or entreaty. From the means to the end was only a step to them. All between was a desert. Objections, excuses, fair promises, everything between them and the

result which their intensity made not only possible but
real, was as stubble before the flame that burned within
them. The pioneer is always one who gives his marrow
to light the lamp that shows the way—a man whose
mind is perhaps only large enough to grasp one phase
of a single thought. Such are they whom the world
follows. Others come after them, expound, amplify,
reduce everything to due proportions and set up the
thought the leader brought to light in its proper place
in the temple of human life. The few mark eras; the
many make history."

"Whom then do you consider the true leader of the
anti-slavery movement?"

"I do not know that it has one. The real leader—
the pathfinder of human thought—is one that never
doubts. The end he seeks is always clear before him,
and he goes straight to it, over whatever obstacles may
lie between. He may not reach his goal—rarely does—but
he shows the way to others, who clear the undergrowth,
level the hills, fill up the valleys and complete the thoroughfare that leads to the terminus of his inspiration.
But I hope you do not aspire to be such a leader?"

"No indeed. I only hoped to be a very humble follower," said Martin, resignedly.

"You need not sigh. The lot of a leader is not an
enviable one. He who swerves humanity from the
beaten rut must generally stand alone. Now and then
there comes one of such deft and subtle power as to
flex almost without its knowledge the world's life.
He switches the train of thought from its accustomed
track at so slight an angle that it is hardly perceived until the space between grows to be a yawning,
impassable gulf. Such a man is never thought of as a
leader at the time he does his work. The world looks
back on him afterward and wonders that his power was
not recognized before. Such a man must always come

from the ranks. He must be of the people, and only think their thoughts more clearly than they. He must translate into words and deeds what the dullest and meanest dimly feels. No high-bred masquerader in familiar garb can ever win the place, save by renunciation of his birthright and a consecration by the laying on of persecuting hands."

"But a man cannot be a leader who is not recognized as such by his followers."

"That is the very mistake that is usually made by those who desire to be leaders. They are not *his* followers. They are simply the creatures of the idea that animates his life. The real leader—he who shows a new pathway of progress—is more frequently considered an obstructionist in his day. He stands squarely across the old way and compels human thought to take a new road. He will not let the world go on in peace. He may be trampled down by the blind herd behind, but his stiffening finger will point the new pathway which the feet of those who come after must follow."

"But if Mr. Clarkson is not a leader what would you term him? He certainly seeks new ways."

"Yes, he is an experimenter—one who makes trial of new ideas for the benefit of others. He is one of that more numerous class who benefit mankind chiefly by demonstrating how great things can *not* be done. They are the skirmishers who skirt the flanks of the army of progress and develop the obstacles that lie before it. They draw the fire of the enemy ; unmask his batteries ; make him define his position ; show the path the forlorn hope must take, and what must be overcome when the grand assault is made. Their fusilade attracts attention because the world is still. The rattle and flash of their fire thrills the heart of every one that listens to the mimic contests of the outposts ; but when the army advances along the whole line, they will be drowned in the roar of the conflict, and when it is over will be almost forgotten. The work of such men is no less valuable than that of the greatest; but it is subordinate thereto and has no independent, permanent result. Such men are doomed to double misconception. At one time they are thrust into undue prominence and at another lost in undeserved obscurity. The scout is rarely a general. The partisan ranger's work is brilliant and romantic, but is not the sort of work that wins battles and achieves results."

" You think Mr. Clarkson a political ranger ?"

" Undoubtedly. He desires the abolition of slavery. He thinks it essential to national peace and prosperity, as well as due to justice and humanity. Across the road that leads to this result he finds an enemy, organized, alert, and, it would seem, impregnably entrenched. What does he do ? Does he lay down the grand strategic lines ? Does he mass the forces at his back and determine to carry the position at all hazards ? Not at all. He seeks for some weak point in the enemy's line. He dashes along his front; tries to turn his flanks; annoys him with unexpected attacks; makes brilliant dashes and quick retreats; fires colored rockets; explodes harmless mines; in short, does the work of scout and skirmisher for the general who shall finally direct the campaign. That is what Mr. Clarkson's work will be if the Anti-Slavery movement ever ripens into an organized aggressive force, successfully directed to the accomplishment of a specific purpose. I very much doubt if that time will ever arrive or that leader will ever appear."

Hargrove resumed his meditative walk back and forth across the library. He seemed almost to have forgotten the young man's presence, as he had apparently forgotten the starting-point of their conversation. He was unburdening himself of thought which long study and close

observation of the men and events of his time had forced
upon him in his semi-isolation. Untouched by faction ;
remote from the conflict of parties ; almost equally at
variance with every phase of the prevailing political
thought of his day, yet bound by an infrangible chain
of events to that institution whose continuance or destruction was the great question to be decided by the
gathering conflict, it is not strange that his views should
differ from those of the partisans who shouted, amid
the heat of the struggle, some for this brilliant political
champion and some for that.

"At any rate, I think he deserves to be called a
knight and not a scout," said Martin, with a touch of
pique in his tone.

"Aye, aye, so he does," said Hargrove, stopping
shortly and raising his finger to enforce his words. "So
far as gallantry, devotion and purity of heart are concerned, he is a very flower of chivalry. But unfortunately for him, perhaps, it is not knight-errantry, it is
not the display of personal prowess and skill of fence
that moves the world. The progress of thought in a
republic is the advance of a grand army. The knight
is a central figure when the march begins and swords
are first crossed in some casual affray ; to-morrow he
will be a scout, and when some Cæsar with his Tenth
Legion, or Napoleon with his Old Guard shall have won
the great battle, he will be remembered kindly and
lovingly by the few who remember how well he did his
part and forgotten by the many in whose minds his
achievements will be blended with, and subordinated to,
the grand assault, the leader of which has not yet appeared and—is not likely to appear."

"He will come," said the young man, whose close-
shut lips, flashing eyes and hand nervously clasping the
back of the chair by which he stood, showed how his
blood was stirred by the thought of conflict. "He will

come!" he repeated in a tone that rang through the silent room like the presage of victory.

"So?" said the other, as he paused in his walk and looked with a half smile upon the young face flushed with enthusiasm. "So the time has come when 'Our sons and our daughters shall prophesy,' eh? You may be right. But you said you wished to be a follower. Of whom—Clarkson?"

"No. Now that you point it out, I see that he cannot be a leader in the accomplishment of great events. I am sorry, too, for he is a splendid type of man, and, in most respects, I must admit that I share his views in regard to slavery."

"Just so. It is not at all surprising that you should. The only wonder is, that passing your youth in the full glare of his manhood, you should have retained individuality enough to modify your indorsement by that cautious phrase, 'in most respects.' When the truly great man puts his impress on such plastic material as your young life there is no doubt as to whose mark it is. If the leader ever comes you will follow him without any 'if' or 'but.' If I am not mistaken, you spoke of wishing to do something now. What was it?'

"I wanted to go to Kansas, sir."

"For what?"

"To help the 'Free State Men.' "

"You are anxious to fight the 'Border Ruffians' then?"

"I wish to see freedom prevail."

"Exactly; and you supposed my sympathies might be with slavery?"

"My father was of that opinion."

"He could not have made a greater mistake."

"What?" exclaimed Martin in surprise; "you think slavery wrong and yet own slaves?"

"You probably think Jared Clarkson very sincere in his belief in its unrighteousness?"

"Of course he is."

"Undoubtedly. But what he only accepts as an evil fact upon the report of others, I know by my own observation and experience to be infinitely worse than he conceives. If I own slaves it is because it is a hard thing for a man in my position to know how to avoid one evil without committing another."

"Yet you do not agree with him."

"Very far from it. He hates slavery, and adores the enslaved race. I hate slavery, and almost abhor the Negro. Not that I have any ill-will toward him, or would treat him with cruelty or injustice, but I believe his presence among us is an unmixed evil to the white race. Mr. Clarkson and those who agree with him are opposed to slavery for the sake of the slave. I would destroy it for the sake of the master. The white race has suffered more from slavery than the colored people ever can. I should dread their freedom among us even more than their enslavement. In short, I am a Southern Abolitionist as Mr. Clarkson is a Northern one. Both are humanitarians. He bestows his sympathy upon the slave; I save mine for the master. He would count his work ended with freedom of the slave; I would not rest until he was transformed or transplanted. He thinks freedom would cure all the ills of slavery; I fear that if the races remained together it would only enhance them."

"Yet you prefer colored servants?" said Martin, in surprise.

"Very true. Whether it is the force of habit or because of their peculiar adaptedness to the servile relation, I do not know. Certain it is that I do not like to be served by a white person."

"Why should you apprehend evil consequences if the

slaves were freed, and remained as the paid servants of the white race, instead ?"

" Because the two races can never commingle, and, living side by side with each other, jealousies and dissensions and conflicts would be the least of the evils to be expected. But that will never be. The Negro must be removed from among the whites or remain forever a slave. If they were emancipated to-morrow by some sudden stroke, they would be reduced to bondage again before a month had passed. The law of nature is an inflexible one : that where two races, separated by some physical barrier that prevents universal admixture and unification in the course of time, dwell together, the one must rule and the other must serve. They can never live equally and amicably together."

" But those who are among us here occasion no trouble," said Martin, with the unwillingness of a believer to abandon his creed.

" Ah, you misunderstand me. It is not because I think the Negro is any more depraved or vicious than any other man at his stage of development. It is not because he is bad, ungovernable, or even incapable that I believe this, but simply because he is not white. He is separated from us by the extremes of color. Nature has divided us. She has made two classes that can never be made one. Where there are clearly marked divisions there will always be discord, which must sooner or later ripen into conflict. The fact that such conflict has not arisen here is easily accounted for by the very small comparative numbers of the unassimilable element."

" It is strange how near you and Mr. Clarkson are to each other in your conclusions, and yet how far apart in your premises," said Martin, musingly.

" We agree only in one thing—the detestation of Slavery. To him it is obnoxious, because of its injustice and inhumanity to the negro, whom he considers an equal and of equal right with the white man ; as he has so often said : ' prejudice against people of color is a quarrel with God.' To me it is hateful, because it has brought the negro among us, enfeebled and corrupted the white race, and cursed the soil which it has touched."

"He sees no danger in emancipation and you no hope in it."

" Very true."

" And yet you are both sincere."

"Yes. He shows his sincerity by taking the Negro to his table ; I mine by giving my fortune to return him whence he came. He laughs at the distinctions between races. I shudder at the thought of their admixture."

" Yet how can this race, if naturally servile, weaker and less numerous than the whites, in any event work us harm ?"

" Ah, it is not the amount, it is the character of the mischief. It is the one fly in the pot of ointment. One drop of colored blood is enough to degrade. What would induce you, if it were possible, to wear the insignia of that race ? For how much money would you consent to be a negro or have in your veins a drop of African blood ? If you would test the idea of race-prejudice, as it is called, that is the fair way to do it."

" Candidly, Mr. Hargrove," said Martin, "I think I would rather die."

" Of course you would. It is not the Negro's fault. It is not our fault. It is simply a fact of our nature. Yet every year that the races remain together ten thousand, twenty thousand, perhaps a hundred thousand lives are cursed with this ineffaceable stigma. Only think of it! All the whippings that a generation of slaves can suffer are as nothing to what the mere suspicion of such admixture has brought upon Lida. And her children—God knows if any care can save them for generations from this blight!"

Martin shuddered and Hargrove resumed his walk to and fro across the room. Presently he returned, and, laying his hand upon the young man's shoulder, he smiled down at him and said :

"I presume this has relieved you of all fear as to my pro-slavery tendencies."

"Entirely," said Martin gravely. "Yet I am by no means sure that you would approve of my purpose."

He looked up inquiringly as he spoke.

"Perhaps not," said Hargrove. "Let us first dispose of the matter for which I supposed that you had come. You love my daughter?"

"As my life!" said the young man, rising and gazing earnestly into the other's eyes.

"I do not question your sincerity. I had just received your letter from Hilda when you entered and thought you had come to ask my sanction of your suit."

Martin's eyes fell and his face flushed.

"I suppose I ought to have done so, sir," he said submissively, "but it seemed so much a matter of course that Hilda and I should love each other that I never thought of any formality."

"Oh, I excuse you fully, now that I know all the facts. The young man of the North at best is not given to formalities in matters of the heart, and Mars and Cupid are poor joint-tenants. If one gets possession the other is sure to be locked out for the time."

"I did not forget her," protested Martin.

"Oh, I understand," said Hargrove ; "the fever of the public mind possessed you. The rage of battle was upon you, and the very fact that you loved made you all the more anxious for an opportunity to attest your manhood."

"It must have been so," said Martin, still abashed at

the awkwardness of his position. "I hope you will pardon what must have seemed the most inexcusable presumption."

"It made me angry, as you saw," said Hargrove. "All the ideas peculiar to a Southern man are so persistently misapprehended by the people of the North that even they who desire to vindicate us are apt to do it upon false grounds. For myself, I have been so generally misunderstood by those about me that I have become sensitive in regard to such questions as that which you so unexpectedly propounded."

"Why do you not let your opinions be known?"

"Because my neighbors cannot understand them. They are foreign to their own thought—the sentiment developed by the life of another people. The inklings I have given have caused me to be looked upon as a kidnapper, if not as a pirate. Yet I have freed a goodly number of slaves, and have reason to believe that Jason sometimes makes Sturmhold itself a station on the 'Underground Railroad.'"

"I am not surprised that you were angry," said Martin, "but I hope that you will not forbid my correspondence with Hilda."

"As to that, my son," said Hargrove, taking his hand, "I shall leave you entirely to Hilda's mercy. What you shall be to each other you must yourselves determine. She is worthy of the best, and I believe you will be worthy of her."

"I will try, sir," said Martin huskily.

"I know you will, and I see no reason why you should not be as happy together as my Rietta and I were in the few bright years she was mine. Hilda is sensitive and impulsive, but there never was a braver or more trustful nature. I hope to see your children making Sturmhold again as bright as your own childish lives made it but yesterday. I shall be glad to say, 'God bless you, my children,' when you come to make it your home.''

Hargrove fancied that he heard a low moaning sob in the hall without. He released his hand from the clasp of the young man, who was trying to express his thanks ; crossed the room, opened the door which was ajar, looked out, and then closing it securely, walked back to the table and sat down.

"And now,'' said he, as Martin also resumed his seat, " about Kansas.''

"I hope you are not offended at my desire to go.''

"On the contrary, I am very glad you have it. With your views, the conflict there is one between right and wrong, and I am glad that you were willing to sacrifice your own ease and comfort for what you deem the right. You were a brave boy, and I hope you will be a brave man.''

"Thank you, sir,'' said Martin, blushing. "I could not love Hilda and be anything else.''

"What put this into your head ?''

"The conversation of a man I met at Mr. Clarkson's the other day.''

"What was his name ?''

"Brown—John Brown.''

"Indeed,'' said Hargrove inquiringly. "What is he like ?''

"Just a plain man, sir. A farmer, who cannot stay upon his farm because men are held in bondage.''

"A great talker, I suppose.''

"No,'' said Martin reflectively. "Now that I think of it, I should say he talked but little. There was a great deal said, and it seemed as if all that was worth saying came from him ; but he used very few words. It did not seem to be so much what he said as the way he said it that made the impression.''

"How was that ?''

"Oh, I cannot tell you. There was such an air of conviction and authority about him that even Mr. Clarkson could not argue with him."

"That is remarkable."

"Oh, he cut everything short with just a sentence when they tried to reason with him—a sentence that cut up the root of all the argument, however. There was a man there who has written books and poems who was discoursing on the Constitution. He said that the clause 'No person held to service or labor shall,' etc., was meaningless and would some time be so decided by the courts. 'It has been so decided,' said Brown. 'Indeed,' said the other in surprise; 'by what court?' 'By the Judge that sits upon the Great White Throne,' answered Brown, as reverently as if in prayer. The conversation had been very animated before, and there was much difference of opinion, but none seemed to wish to carry the controversy farther."

"It was a stinging rebuke to those who admit the moral wrong of slavery but make excuse that the Constitution shields it," said Hargrove. "What does he propose to do?"

"Just go to Kansas and, as he says, 'help the poor that cry.' He has two sons there now."

"And you wish to go with him?"

"While I listened I felt like those disciples who said, 'Did not our hearts burn within us while he talked with us?' And afterwards I could not get rid of his ideas."

"And you would still like to go?"

"I wish to do all I can for liberty and the right."

"I would not have you do less, and your own conscience must be your guide. Every man owes it to himself, his country and God to do the most good that he can. I may be wrong on this matter. The others may be right. You that are coming to the front now must decide. It is a question for to-morrow. I will offer no objection."

"Thank you, sir," said Martin exultantly; "somehow, I thought father was wrong in thinking that you would."

"But I would like you to think of one or two things before you decide."

"With pleasure."

"The struggle with slavery will not be ended in a day."

"You have made that plain already."

"Your father is a very wealthy man."

"Well?"

"The management of his estate will devolve on you at his death."

"Well?"

"Wealth is an engine of great power, for good as well as evil."

"Of course."

"A brave boy is one thing; a strong man another."

"Yes?"

"Which is worth the more to liberty and righteousness—Martin Kortright, single-handed, immature, one of a disorganized crowd of squatters, half scout and half freebooter; made an outlaw, perhaps, by the imperious necessity of organized government—or Martin Kortright, matured, developed, clothed with intellectual mail and armed with the power to lead a thousand whithersoever he may choose?"

"I see," said Martin, after a moment's thought, "and I will wait."

CHAPTER XXI.

A SUBTERRANEAN MYTH.

It was October. The maples blazed upon the hill-sides. The river flowed between banks of gold and bronze and under arching canopies of shifting flame. The busy inland city was set in painted squares. The trees that lined the streets paved the ways of commerce with purple and gold, and sent troops of airy fays in the glowing garb of elf-land dancing in the sunshine up and down the dark green lawns, and in and out among the borders where dahlias and asters and coxcombs showed the deep rich lights in which summer says adieu. The smoke drifted lazily away from the tall chimneys. The sportsman's shot echoed from the distant hill-sides. Troops of children chased the dancing leaves or sought for nuts beneath the pictured heaps. By the long low sheds beyond, the autumn sun shone down on many a steel-like mirror, and lighted heaped-up piles of snowy crystals which seemed like mimic forerunners of the white drifts that soon would cover hill and plain.

The year had been a full one. The earth had ripened golden harvests. The prosperity of the nation in that year had been unparalleled by anything in its previous history. More gold had been minted than the world had ever gloated over before in a twelvemonth. The new Occident promised inexhaustible wealth. The looms were busy; the diamond-pointed spindles flashed and whirred through daylight hours and on into the night; the hammers rang; the barns were bursting; the orchards bent beneath their burden. The land waited to

278

give thanks for unmeasured bounty. Peace was in the air. The sunshine was the harbinger of blessing. The land was ready for repose. Those burning questions that for years had agitated the popular heart and threatened the peace of our Israel, had all been settled.

Slavery had conquered. "Held to service" had been defined by statute to be that servitude which the framers of our fundamental law meant , to protect while they shrank from using its name in an instrument purporting to be the charter of liberty. The arm of the law had been strengthened and the bonds of the slave riveted more securely than ever before. The great Whig leader had shaken hands with the master-spirit of the pro-slavery element, and responded heartily to his joyful prediction that for a hundred years at least the question of the slave's freedom or bondage would trouble the statesmen no more. The Puritan-descended expounder of the Constitution had given the weight of his corrupted intellect and surrendered his debauched conscience to the slave power. By his aid, the Samson of free thought had been securely bound. The Constitution was supreme. Slavery was paramount. The political horizon was clear. No cloud even a handbreadth wide was to be seen. The nation had but to eat, drink and be merry, with no fear of the morrow. In this very city, in the heart of the Empire State, the vibrant tones of the great Whig leader had but recently proclaimed the conflict ended. He had pointed out that the time had come when the law must prevail over personal inclination, and private conscience must bow to public necessity. The guaranties of the Constitution must be redeemed by the children of its framers. The rights of those who were parties to the great covenant through those from whom they held, must be regarded. "Held to service or labor" was to be no more a vain form of words. The nation had put the baton of power into the master's hand, and the ægis of its authority was above his head while he sought diligently for the wanderer whom the North Star drew like a loadstone toward its chilly realm. It had given him leave to go and search and take. It unbolted the sanctuary's doors that he might take the "held-to-service" from the altar of prayer. It opened the palace and the hovel ; it tore down the freeman's castle to render up the slave. It smote the hand that dared resist and scourged the feet that loitered when commanded to bring aid.

It was all over. For sixty years the murmur of remonstrance had been growing louder and louder, and the signs of contumacy more frequent. It was high time that the nation should speak. Its former utterances had come to be unheeded. The pledge of the fathers was well nigh forgotten. Men openly offered asylum to the runaway. They made null and void the pledge of the Constitution. The vanes upon the churches pointed toward freedom. Men offered public prayer for the fugitive from bondage. They put money into the hands of the destitute. They hid the affrighted in their hearts. They gave aid and comfort to the oppressed—food and raiment to the bondman who fled. It was time that the nation spoke.

And here, in the Valley of the Mohawk, on the great highway along which the East had run to meet the West, and along which the West came back with heavy laden hands full of rich offerings to the East, the tide of discontent ran high. Here Jared Clarkson lived and gave—for to him life was one continuous opportunity to give. A land-owner whose possessions would dwarf an English dukedom, he gave with lavish hand the soil itself, and openly maintained that a restriction upon the ownership of land was a prime essential of free institutions and general progress and prosperity. Forgetful of himself, he was so ambitious for the good of his fellows that no disappointment could dampen the ardor of his devotion. Hating all forms of caste, he sought not to drag the highest down, but to lift the lowliest up. He was of such chivalric honor that when he had once promised a gift he would not recall his charity, even when he had found the object unworthy. Counting all men as his brothers, he felt the wrongs of each as if they touched the marrow of his life. A patriot of passionate devotedness, he sought excuses, not always consonant with reason, for the acts of the fathers. Hating oppression for its own sake, he scrupled not at the means by which he wrought for freedom. Worshipping law, he counseled and practiced openly and boldly the evasion of unjust statutes and resistance to them. Asking nothing, giving everything, inconsistent only in the reasons with which he sought to maintain beliefs too high for meaner men to appreciate ; ready always with helpful words, and putting to shame even his own high ideals by the conduct of his life; it is not strange that the magnetism of his example should inspire men to a feeble emulation of his vaguely understood nobility. He was not, as Hargrove well said, a leader. Erratic in all things, his light was meteoric and marvelous, yet uncertain. What he would believe none could tell. That he would advocate at all hazards what he believed right none ever doubted. In matters of conscience he astounded the dull and shamed the evil-minded. Beside the corrupt and selfish he stood like an archangel clothed in light. He saw life's weakness, meanness, misery ; and pitied it. He saw every wrong that scourged humanity, and hated it. He sought out every good cause, and helped it. He was an Arthur among the knights-errant of his time, and held a diamond-edged excalibar, with a hand never soiled with dishonor and a heart never tainted with ambition. Yet he was not a leader—only an exemplar. He did not combine and organize his fellows, and, above all, he lacked that stability which gives a life to one purpose— that steadfastness which puts aside what is of less importance until that which is paramount has been achieved. He was like the comet among celestial bodies—bright, glowing, wonderful, upon which all gaze with admiration, but none set their watches by its movements. Yet within the scope of his personal acquaintance his influence, though somewhat uncertain, was great. The worst of men felt impelled by his example to do good. Around him centered a thousand vagaries of theory and endeavor, all of which he promoted because he thought they were based on good intent. He was a forerunner who prepared the way for him who should come after. He kept the public mind awake, waiting and anxious for that light which he was not. So it was that the region where he lived had become one in which the ideas of law and obedience were strangely confounded with those of abstract justice and ultimate right.

It was time that the government spoke; not only in the words of the statute but by the mouth of its most illustrious representative. The spring sunshine was upon the hills and meadows of the valley when the great Expounder stood before the listening multitudes of the growing inland city, and with the threatening aspect of a Jove that does not know his power has fled, proclaimed the law, and warned the people that from their busy streets would yet be taken the man-beast—the "*homo sed non persona*" of the civil law—"held to service or labor" by another. It was a strange prophecy, made with exultant bitterness by the child of the Pilgrims, who had sold his birthright for a vain ambition—an ambition that was to be foiled again by the very spirit over whose downfall he then blindly exulted. Sad hearts listened to his prediction.

Angry eyes hurled back the defiance of his threatening orbs. Groans and hisses mingled with the applause that greeted the words of the orator. He smiled in sorrowful pity as he heard them. The statesman's duty ran hand in hand with the foiled leader's thirst for revenge. The stroke he gave was for the nation's safety, but was aimed at an enemy who had balked his will.

The autumn had come, and the prophecy was about to be fulfilled. An awkward youth loitered curiously about the streets. He watched, with a singular furtiveness, those whom he chanced to meet. There was something slouching and uncertain in his gait. Meeting another, he stepped almost off the pavement and half removed his hat, with a timid, apologetic look as he did so. He was well dressed, but his clothes seemed somehow not to fit him, or rather he appeared not to be at home in them. He was evidently a stranger, and a stranger ill at ease. He saw a crowd of people going into a public hall, and drew near and watched them curiously. He was well built, but his face had a dull, sallow look. There was a red mark like a scar upon his right cheek and running back toward his ear. His darkbrown hair was cut close, but yet showed in rich brown waves upon nape and brow. The hands that showed below his white cuffs were large and strong, and deeply browned by exposure. His blue eyes were full of watchful wonder. All at once he started, gazed quickly around and hurried away from the place where the crowd were gathering. Two men, who seemed to be casually passing by on the other side, walked leisurely in the same direction.

Within the hall five hundred people had met together, a little company of evil-disposed malcontents. They were of strangely contrasted types. No band of conspirators against the law and the established order in a civilized land ever showed a greater medley. Men and

women, old and young, black and white, high and low,
were there. On every face, in every eye shone the
light of a great common purpose. Even children who
had come with their parents were hushed into a solemn
intentness. A Quaker woman, with a placid, motherly
face, sat upon the platform busily knitting during the
proceedings. A swart, lean figure walked to and fro as
fierce invective and scornful epigram fell from his lips.
A dark face, with eyes that flashed fire beneath overhanging brows, with pointed beard and lips whose quivering smile brought Mephistopheles to mind, told of the
slavery he had tasted in his own person. Ah! terrible
were the words of wrath, and more terrible still the
forebodings of despair, those stout-hearted men and
women uttered. They were few where they had hoped
to be many. The last great blow had been a terrible
one. It had decimated their ranks. The faint-hearted
and the hollow-hearted had fallen off. But to those who
remained the stroke had been as that of flint upon
steel. The fire flashed out of their hearts in hotter
words and fiercer resolves than ever before. They said,
these wicked malcontents, that "the enactment of the
Fugitive Slave Law, and the general acquiescence in it,
under the influence of devil-prompted speeches of politicians and devil-prompted sermons of priests, give
fearful evidence that this is a doomed and a damned
nation."

Their language was not only incendiary, but it was desperate. The prayer which opened their deliberations was
full of burning maledictions aimed at the best, the most
illustrious and most respectable citizens in the land.
One who listened to their counsels would have thought
that religion and civilization were only invented for the
sake of the poor and the oppressed. That all men
should be free seemed to them the end of aspiration.
Beside this all else seemed to them mean and trivial.

Diverse in all other things they were agreed on this. One grave man, from whose face the dark hair rolled back in billows, when the storm of angry, despairing words grew calm for a moment, rose and said in a voice and with a look that made every heart flutter with apprehension :

" We have had words enough. Why is not something done ?"

" Done ? Ah, me, what can be done ?"

So fluttered every heart in the sigh that swept over the audience. The grave man answered solemnly :

" We can die !"

Then Jared Clarkson spoke. Words of hope and cheer, —bitter denunciation of the enemies of liberty and scathing criticism of its friends fell from his lips. He could not be discouraged. Nothing could hide from him the light. Victory and defeat were alike to him in bringing always nearer the desired end.

" What can we do ?" he said. " We must take away the shield of the Constitution ! The Abolitionists of the North must insist that it shall not sanction such a compound of robbery and murder as slavery. The Federal Constitution must be strictly construed. In terms it does not sanction slavery. The word was purposely excluded. The slaveholder will be strong so long as he can plead law for his matchless crime. Take from him that plea and he will be weak. We can do it !"

" Not without blood !" said the grave man, interrupting.

A black-robed woman, sad-faced, gray-haired, rose suddenly, threw her black-gloved hands above her head, showing white, slender arms, and wailed in agonized tones : " Blood ! blood ! More blood ! The land is soaked with blood ! How long, O Lord, how long ?"

Her dark eyes rolled wildly. Her face, which showed the wreck of beauty, was ghastly in its pallor. A strong, motherly woman who sat next her drew her down and clasped the shapely head to her broad bosom. "I see it! I see it!" cried the Sybilline figure, half starting up again, and pointing toward the old man in the aisle. "Rivers and seas of blood! Great billows of blood, and he rides upon them! He rides upon them!"

The man smiled. The knitter on the platform forgot her work. The women shuddered and wept. The strong woman in whose arms she was drew her down again and soothed her like a child. The man in the aisle sat down. A low murmur of pity swept through the hall. Clarkson essayed to speak, but tears choked him. "If we were not a nation of atheists," he said at length, "we should tremble as if we heard the words of prophecy."

A shiver ran through the audience. The door was half opened and a scarred face looked in upon the absorbed and breathless assembly. The wanderer upon the street gazed in wonder on the malcontents. There were no evil or debauched faces among them. Sincerity, benevolence, uprightness had set their seal on every brow. They were bad men and women—dangerous men and women—conspirators against all existent good—the enemies of Heaven's unalterable laws—yet only in one thing had they sinned. Besotted license had no representative there. Pure lives stood behind their blasphemous words. Charity, kindness, unbounded love, devotion to the right, as they saw the right, marked every life. Albeit, they were all the more dangerous to the nation's peace. Had they only been bad in other directions also they could have been put down ruthlessly, but their clean lives and unselfish devotion protected them from martyrdom, and made the virus of their mistaken dogmas all the more malignant. The youth with the scarred face listened for a time, then glancing backward, turned and departed hastily. Across the way two men watched for his reappearance. The one pointed him out to the other as he came forth. They crossed the street toward him. Another joined them on the way.

Clarkson continued within:

"But who talks of blood? God may demand it for the blood that has been shed—He may require it for the remission of sin; but it is not for us to think of it as a means. Ours are not the weapons of violence. God has given us the Constitution with which to fight the battles of the oppressed."

"It is the shield of the oppressor—a league with hell," hissed the black Apollo through his set teeth.

"Oh, but there are two Constitutions," said Clarkson—"the literal and the historical. The literal is the charter of liberty. The historical is the sheet-anchor of slavery. The historical has prevailed."

"The literal is a dead letter," said the gray-clad knitter who sat beside him on the platform, with quiet sententiousness.

But Clarkson would not heed. His exalted chivalry would cast no blame upon the fathers. To him the words were separable from the spirit. He would save the Constitution from stain and redeem the slave from bondage also. His friends were annoyed at his stubbornness. They accused him of inconsistency. He was blind and deaf to remonstrance. "I have helped the slave to flee," he said. "I have paid the master to let him go free. If men are dying of pestilence we do not stop to ask the cause, but give relief at once. If tyrants hold my brother in bondage shall I not ransom him because they act unrighteously?"

There was a cry upon the street. Two of the men who dogged the footsteps of the youth had seized him and were taking him away, when he wrenched himself loose and fled. They pursued and caught him again. They wore badges of authority. They were the guardians of the law, and this struggling, panting, manacled thing they dragged between them, covered with mire, bruised and bleeding, to the temple of justice was the man-beast—the human chattel—the "held-to-service" under the "historical" Constitution.

While Clarkson argued a bell tolled solemnly. It was the signal agreed upon beforehand—the knell of Liberty murdered by Law. The little company of malcontents knew that the statesman's prediction had been fulfilled. The law had come into the midst of them to rebuke their lawlessness. Then fled doubt and fear. There was no more argument. Five hundred firebrands rushed out among the people. In an instant the streets were thronged with angry men. Scowling faces filled the forum of justice. Women stood at the gateways and wrung their hands and wept. Children clung to their mothers, hushed and pallid with a nameless terror. Men ceased their labor, asked the cause of the tumult, cursed the law's cruelty, and sullenly wrought on. The swift formalities were hurried through. Jared Clarkson pressed forward to speak for, and to, the man the law was about to transform into a thing. In vain! The judgment was quickly rendered by willing lips. The man-chattel was hurried along the street to prison, under the guard already provided, there to await upon the morrow transportation to the master's home, to whom his "service and labor" were rightfully due. The brown, sallow face was streaked with blood and full of sullen determination. "I will die," he said, in answer to the master's look of triumph, "but I will not be *a slave!*" He had been a petted servant too. But the law was vindicated, and the malcontents were shown how strong its right hand was, in that it plucked from the midst of them one whom they had unlawfully enticed to flee.

. . . .

The harvest moon looked down upon the city. An

THE VINDICATION OF THE LAW.

"I will die," he said, in answer to the master's look of triumph, "but I will not be a slave."—p. 288.

angry crowd was gathered at the prison gate. Jared
Clarkson's voice commanded that the doors be broken.
Three thousand angry freemen surged against the walls.
The keepers of the prison quailed. The captors of the
chattel fled. The doors flew open. The chains fell off.
The man-beast fled away toward the Northward. The
malcontents had answered the statesman's challenge.
Brave words had ripened into braver acts, and when the
law asked who had violated its safeguard, Jared Clarkson proudly answered "I." But no man dare lay hands
upon him.

As the carriage bearing the man-chattel whirled away
through the city's streets, the glare of a solitary lamp fell
on the scarred, pallid young face within. A woman by an
open gateway saw it—a dark-eyed, gray-haired woman.
Instantly her eyes lighted. She sprang away from the
embracing arm that was about her and sped after the
flying vehicle.

"My baby! My boy!" she shrieked as she ran.

Kind friends followed quickly—men and women, who
guessed her grief and saw that it had made her wild—
some who had heard her story; many who had witnessed
her woe. They followed fast, but not as fast as she
fled, and hours had passed away before strong but kindly
hands brought her back to the mansion from which she
had fled, bedraggled, moaning, chattering, crazed. Tender hands received and nursed and soothed; but when
the morning dawned Alida Eighmie held a rag-doll to
her bosom, and smiled and cooed as she clasped and
kissed the shapeless mass.

"My boy, my baby! Hush! hush!" she said to those
who spoke to her, "do not waken him! I've just found
him after ever so long—ever so long!"

.   .   .   .

The next day after these events the malcontents met
again and still further blasphemed the gods of our na-

tional Olympus. Unanimously these earnest, peaceful, kindly-hearted people resolved that " the Satanic Daniel Webster " was a " base and infamous enemy of the human race." It was a fearful accusation to leave upon the tablet of history against the ambitious giant who paltered and parleyed and perished—the grandest intellect of his day chained to the weakest conscience, and attested by the most meagre showing of good results. He was not what their words painted him, but when men believe a truth so fervently as to forget themselves, their words are not always measured with precision. The malcontents were all the harsher judges, because themselves unselfish. They stood in a seven-times-heated furnace, and their words were as fire. It was not brain alone that spoke, but soul that cleft to the joint and marrow. In behalf of the poorest and meanest they dared to denounce the highest and strongest. The storm that was expected to destroy served only to srengthen them.

CHAPTER XXII.

A FREE INSTITUTION.

AMONG the institutions which arose out of the fact of slavery, there are two so peculiar and distinctive in their character that no tracing of the thought of that day in its influence upon the formation of character would be at all complete should it omit to consider them. One has passed into history under the grotesque and ridiculous name of the "Underground Railroad." It was really not an organization or institution at all, but the simple voluntary co-operation of individuals to promote a certain end. When we reflect how deep-seated and earnest had become the hostility to slavery, and how many there were in all parts of the North who were willing to defy the law and imperil their own personal safety to aid in its overthrow, the wonder is, not that the "Underground Railroad" became so effective a method of assisting the runaway slave, as that it remained to the last so completely disorganized and fortuitous in its work.

It had two basis principles: first, that to assist a human being to achieve his personal liberty was a divinely ordained duty, and, second, that the institution of slavery itself could somehow or other be broken down by a system of attacks upon it in the shape of continuous and concerted escapes from bondage. So, too, it had two specific methods of operation, the one to assist fugitives who, of their own motion, had undertaken to escape, and the other to arrange for securing and expediting the escape of individuals and parties who were about to attempt escape. The difficulty and danger of such enterprises can only be dimly understood at this time. The whole South was in fact an armed garrison. Every port was guarded, and every vessel outward-bound was required to submit to the most rigid inspection ; every train and depot was closely watched for fugitives, and, beyond that, almost every important point in the North was infested with mercenary spies, who were always anxious to secure the rewards offered for the detection and detention of fugitives. In almost every city of the North these persons, very frequently under the direction and control of professional men of influence and position, regularly consulted the files of the Southern papers for the description of escaped slaves, which were clipped and studied as carefully as a Western cow-herder studies the advertised marks of a strayed or stolen steer.

The difficulty of traveling through the South without exciting suspicion and the danger attending all attempts of this character, can only be very faintly understood by those who do not understand the organization of Southern society in those days. Every slaveholder was, of course, bound by his own interest to exercise the utmost vigilance, not only over his own, but over each one of his neighbors' chattels-real. At the best, the slave was a species of property that demanded the utmost vigilance. His longing for freedom was irrepressible, and the more intelligent and valuable he became, the more intense was this longing. The mere journey, alone, on foot, and unaided, from the Gulf to the Lakes, was no small undertaking for the stoutest-hearted man. But when we reflect that this journey had to be made almost always by night, in the midst of watchful and suspicious enemies, and with the ineffaceable brand of color upon the brow of the fugitive, without money and without scrip, we are struck with amazement at the thought that any should have attempted it. This statement, however, only feebly shadows forth the difficulties that beset the path of the fugitive. The States of the South were really military camps. The system of patrols made necessary to prevent combinations and concerted movements among the slaves, carefully guarded every highway. The slave could not leave his master's premises without a written pass, without danger of arrest and punishment. The master was not only an owner, but an officer of a vast military organization, whose duty it was to watch the roads, bridges, ferries and other avenues to freedom in order that none should escape. Also, the law forbade all meetings of slaves, so that assistance and concert of action were made possible only by the utmost diligence and in defiance of danger. A secrecy that is almost inconceivable to one who has not studied the conditions of that society with care, was necessary at every step of such a venture.

Besides that, the danger to be encountered was by no means slight. In every Southern State the punishments for inciting slaves to escape, or aiding or abetting them in so doing, were of the severest character: whipping, branding, and in most cases, for the repeated offense, hanging. Then the penalty incurred by the slave himself, not only from the wrath of a master, who had in some states the actual power of life and death and in none stopping very far short of it, but also from the law itself, was something terrible. In South Carolina, for instance, for the first attempt at escape he was liable to be severely whipped; for the second to be still more severely whipped and have an ear cut off; for the third to be branded and lose the other ear, and for the fourth to have the tendons of the right leg cut at the heel or be hanged, at the discretion of the magistrates trying him. Through all this array of obstacles, however, men fled toward liberty and the North Star, and despite all laws they found men at the North to aid and protect them. In some cases, as between certain accessible points, there came to be well-known places of rest and refuge. Men were found who risked and lost their lives in inducing slaves to undertake the peril of a tedious flight. Men cheerfully gave time and money, endured imprisonment, faced obloquy—in short, became martyrs, willingly and gladly, simply from devotion to the idea of the sacredness of personal liberty as an "inalienable right" of "all men." Ship-owners brought away cargoes of human freight. Husbands and sons, in some cases even wives and daughters, went into the jaws of death to rescue their beloved ones. Strangers shared the risk and burden. White men and women worked side by side with free blacks in this singular crusade against an institution that did them no harm save as it held their fellow-men and women in bondage.

It was a strange movement. From the Atlantic to the Mississippi, almost every mile of the frontier line between freedom and slavery bore the track of a fugitive or was stained with his blood. Prices were set upon the heads of many prominent men for aiding and abetting such movements. They were indicted by grand juries, and in some instances attempts were made to take them to Slave States for trial. The number actually engaged at any one time in this movement was very small as compared with the whole population of the North, but the number who sympathized with them was very great. Perhaps the very element of danger added a strange zest to the undertaking. Men of the most diverse characters and positions were engaged in it. Of the most numerous and active of these, Jared Clarkson was a fair type. Earnest and sincere beyond all question; self-sacrificing to a rare degree, but yet greedy of praise and approbation, and having an insatiable love for notoriety; with a nature erratic if not inherently eccentric and unbalanced, he was a leader among those who spoke and wrote, a constant aid to those who wrought and an impracticable ally of those who sought to use other and more moderate means for procuring the same end.

As a means of abolishing slavery the "Underground Railroad" was ridiculously insufficient. In no single year did the whole number of successful escapes equal the gain in an average county of one of the Slave States. Even had the entire population of the North favored it, it is doubtful if it could ever have made any visible inroads upon the institution. Its chief value as a character-forming element of the times was in its marvelous record of heroic attempts, and in the facts with reference to the mysterious region lying to the southward of Mason and Dixon's line which it constantly brought to light. That the blood of martyrs is the seed of the church was never more beautifully illustrated in history. The furnace-blast of persecution made heroes of the merest clods, and lifted into a most glaring prominence men who would otherwise have died in obscurity. The strange charm which undeserved hostility gives the victim was thrown around the advocates of abolition. Men went to their meetings to revile and persecute, stayed to applaud, and came away with the mark of the beast in their foreheads. Then, too, there was mystery and daring and unlawfulness to charm the brave and pique the curious. The colored orator was in his own person at once a show and an argument. The woman, who stood by her husband on the platform while dangerous and offensive missles flew about his head, was, of course, a heroine. The tragedy was so deep that no one could withhold his sympathy from the victims. The hopelessness of the old Greek drama was in every hour of the struggle that marked the decade of which we write. The slave was an Edipus whose woes were forever enacted within the sight of all. The old saw and pitied. The young heard and shuddered. The nation's heart echoed his moans. The nation's life leaned daily more and more to his relief. Hourly the conflict of ideas grew more intense. Momently the decisive struggle grew nearer. While Time lagged in his flight, men and women were growing up in whose hearts liberty was enshrined above all other thought. The conflict that then raged was but a forerunner of a mightier revolution ; the slave who fled to freedom but an antitype of the slave to whom liberty should come almost as an unsought boon. The uprising of freemen against an unjust law was but a precursor of the wrath that should sweep away the foundations of that law. Time mocked at the Stateman's wisdom and justified the folly of the Malcontents.

CHAPTER XXIII.

FOR THE AMENDMENT OF DIVINE ERROR.

THERE was another institution of that time which, indeed, has striven hard to survive the chaos that has since intervened, and is, perhaps, more instructive as a historical study than any other of the institutions that owed their origin to slavery. It did nothing to shape thought, and, so far as the character and destiny of the country was concerned, it was utterly futile and insignificant. It neither led nor followed public sentiment. It was neither for nor against slavery. Fixing at the outset upon a middle course, it led a life of queer indecision, apologizing first to one school of fanatics and then to the other, and always protesting to both that, while not for their respective conflicting dogmas, it also was not opposed to them. In its case, the Scripture rule was plainly reversed—the negation of favor did not establish a presumption of hostility. The difficulty of this position may be better understood when we consider the fact that the subject-matter of which the institution treated was so closely connected with the two extremes of thought as to be inseparable from either. As they were concerned with the African in bondage, so this institution was anxious and careful about him in his freedom. It was called The American Colonization Society. As slavery brought the African to this continent for the purpose of enslavement, this society took him back to Africa for the purpose of liberation. For the millions in bondage it had no regard; for the few thousands who were free it had a watchful interest. It

297

had two basis principles; first, non-interference with
slavery, and, second, the removal of the freed black
from the land. These two ideas attracted to its support
the most diverse and incongruous elements. It afforded
a neutral ground on which the leaders of two mutually
destructive principles met upon a platform strangely
insincere in fact and yet perfectly consistent in theory
and letter.

This society held that on the Western Continent
the African in a state of freedom was a most potent
influence for evil. As to the African in a state of
bondage it was entirely non-committal. Its prime
object was to remove that demoralizing and disturbing element, the free negro. Its ulterior purpose was
to build up a black republic on the shores of Africa.
It placidly assumed that the Divine will was directly
and palpably thwarted when the African was brought
to America. · It was clearly the purpose of the Creator
that Africa should belong to the Negro—so the society
believed—and America to the White man. This natural
distribution having been interfered with by the slave-
trade the first great duty of the Caucasian to himself
was, by the creed of the society, to put an end to that
trade, and then, as rapidly as possible, to restore the
freed blacks to the continent "prepared for them from
the foundation of the world."

These peculiar doctrines, in connection with its equivo-
cal position in regard to slavery, had the effect of uniting
under its banners some curious extremes of thought.
In the North, very many were captivated with its ideas
under the belief that they offered a peaceful solution of
the problem of slavery. It was fondly hoped that, as
the years went by, the society would grow strong, the
foundations of the new African Republic be securely
laid, the slave-trade rigorously suppressed, and the
capability of the African for self-government clearly de-

monstrated; that the conscience of slaveholders would become enlightened and that they would crowd the docks from which the Liberian packets were to sail, in earnest rivalry with each other to obtain passage for their late chattels, now gladly freed and restored to Africa, Christianized and civilized, to aid in uplifting the "dark continent." It was a beautiful theory, and the tender-hearted humanitarians who already, in 1817, had come seriously to moot the question of the nation's right to uphold and protect slavery, seized upon this beatific vision with the utmost alacrity. To them it was the natural antidote and appointed remedy for slavery. There was another class, too, strong, clear-headed, practical men, who realized the ills and iniquities of slavery, but who saw the guaranty in the Constitution, respected the claims of that instrument, and could see no means by which slavery could be assailed or overthrown and its provisions still be honestly regarded. To them there seemed a remote possibility that the African republic might develop in the course of generations into something that might exercise a repressive and modifying influence upon American Slavery. At least, they could see nothing else that could be lawfully and properly done that gave any promise of the amelioration of the slave's condition, and so gave their sympathy and support to one of the most singular and absurd theories that ever·affected an intelligent people.

The sentiment that whatever could be done for the colored man ought to be done, as a sort of indirect atonement for the crime of his enslavement, was the mainspring of all the support this society received at the North. Of the colored man as a "free negro," in the sense in which that word was used at the South, the Northern man knew little and cared less. In no Northern State was this population in the least troublesome or in any degree dangerous or offensive. It was only in the hope that it might exert a reflex influence upon slavery in the Southern States that the Northern man gave either money or prayers to Liberia and the eminently respectable but yet Janus-faced Society by which it was founded. It was difficult for a Northern mind to understand the real relations of this movement to slavery. The South and her institutions have always been *terræ incognitæ* to the average Northern mind. Already, while these lines are being written, slavery has become a myth which the younger citizen of the North finds it hard to realize.

"Is it a fact," asked an intelligent young lawyer of the writer within a week, "is it a fact that men and women were actually bought and sold in those days?"

"Certainly."

"Were they attached and levied on, mortgaged, sold for taxes, stolen, sold at auction, and all that sort of thing, just like cattle?"

"Of course; why not?"

"I don't know, only I cannot realize that such things ever were."

A like incapacity to "realize" what actually was the state of slavery which they so very generally deplored, affected the people of the North in that time. They did not dream that the Colonization Society could by any possibility be of the least advantage to slavery or the slave-owner. To them it was a matter of great surprise that the master should favor its purposes at all, and this fact was for a time regarded as an indication of a general desire on the part of a considerable portion of the Southern planter-class to co-operate in any feasible and peaceful method of abolishing slavery gradually and quietly. There were some throughout the South who no doubt entertained these views. The names of very many of that remarkable class who may properly be termed "Southern Abolitionists," are to be found upon the rolls of this society. They were men who, like Hargrove, were opposed to slavery for the sake of the master race. They sometimes admitted its injustice to the negro as well, but their view of the African was, as a rule, hardly more favorable than that of the advocates of slavery themselves. They were willing to labor for emancipation, if the manumitted slaves could at once be removed from the country; and their idea of universal emancipation was of a time when not only no slave but also no negro should be found upon the continent. They were earnest, sincere, just-minded men; but if the alternative had been presented to them of freedom with the negro to remain in the land where he was born a slave, or the continuance of slavery, it is probable that by far the greater part of them would have preferred the latter. These men heartily and loyally espoused the cause of the Colonization Society as an entering wedge for peaceful abolition. They even urged national appropriations in its behalf, and uttered glowing prognostications of the time when freedom should come to the slave with a steerage ticket to Liberia and compensation to the owner—all the act of the national government.

A quarter of a century before the time of which we write, grave, thoughtful men, even aspirants for the Presidential chair, seriously argued in the Senate of the United States the question of the purchase and transportation to the shores of Liberia of two millions of subject souls. The reasons given for the movement were its humanity, justice and the ultimate well-being of the white race. Even in that day one clear-sighted man urged that course as cheaper than a civil war, which he declared must result from the continuance of the institution. He was laughed at almost as much as that Polish patriot—the friend of

Jefferson—who, dying, left his modest fortune to accumulate, and its proceeds from time to time to be used in the purchase and liberation of slaves. Fortunately, the law held such a gift invalid, and the wisdom of a later day laughed down the foreboding fool who dared to speak of war in connection with the patriarchal institution.

With these various classes in its ranks the society from the outset boasted a most amazing array of great names : presidents, chief justices, senators, congressmen, governors, scientists, literati, bishops, ministers, men of wealth and men of note, abolitionists, slaveholders, political economists, philanthropists—in short, almost all who had a handle at either end of their names, or a call to make the world better in any particular respect, were added to its numbers and gave to its proceedings a sense of dignity and propriety which was painful to contemplate in connection with the meagre results obtained. Its annual meetings were held at the national capital, and were occasions of unlimited pompous declamation and indirect electioneering. Year after year the great Whig leaders, Clay and Webster, vied with each other in alternate laudation of the purposes and designs of the institution. Within sight of the slave-pens of Alexandria they declared again and again that its purpose was not directly or indirectly to interfere with slavery, but only to offer a means for the reestablishment upon the soil of the continent the Divine will had appointed for them to occupy, of all Africans who might chance to become free within the limits of the United States.

By-and-by another class of men began to accept this doctrine. They were those who did not desire either the immediate or gradual extinction of slavery, but desired rather its continuance and prosperity. They saw that the removal of the free black made the slave more secure, more contented, more industrious, more peaceful and more hopeless. To this class the Colonization Society was an especial boon, and many of them espoused its doctrines with alacrity. Gradually the extreme Abolitionists of the North began to comprehend this fact, and thenceforward they denounced the society as a movement in the interests of Slavery. Another class of Southern men, however, reasoned that whatever recognized in any degree the self-directing capacity of the negro was in fact an enemy of slavery in disguise, and they were equally fierce in their denunciation of the society as a device of the Abolitionists, and designed to be simply a forerunner of compulsory emancipation: So it was both upheld and denounced because it opposed slavery and because it favored it, neither of which things it did or proposed to do. In trying to please every one it succeeded in displeasing all, and by declaring its absolute neutrality it bore the burden of the sins and errors of both extremes of thought. It held to the last its array of great names, but the tumult of the gathering conflict drowned its appeals, and long before the struggle reached its climax the people had almost forgotten this institution for which at one time the churches had so devoutly prayed—it being one of the few things of that day which the pro-slavery and anti-slavery Christians could unite in heartily commending to the Divine favor. As a historical fact, it is chiefly valuable as marking the almost universal admission, directly or indirectly, that slavery was unnatural, hurtful and unjust. It was a weak, blind effort to save the Constitution and yet find a way for securing the downfall of slavery. It was an attempt to do indirectly what the fundamental law forbade to be done directly.

It was to this institution that Hargrove had appealed to aid him in carrying George Eighmie's will into effect. Its refusal was strictly in the line of its policy.

This eminently respectable body was, in the strictest sense, all things to all men. To the Abolitionist of the North it held out the alluring hope that through its peaceful and benign influence slavery would yet melt and disappear. To the Slaveholder it painted the delights of a paradise where all the freemen were white, and all the blacks were slaves, into which should come no free negro serpent to tempt, corrupt and annoy. It represented in his eyes, in a peculiar degree, "the peace of God and the state," since the slaveholder was thoroughly convinced that the supremest beatitude of society was one in which there were only masters and slaves. He would willingly have dispensed with the non-slaveholding whites also in order to secure this blissful condition. If by any means the great men that avouched the society's respectability could have devised some method by which the poor whites also could have been transported, whether to Africa or elsewhere, the slave-owners would have hailed it with unmixed rapture, and as slavery ruled the land there would have been no question as to appropriations and governmental favor. It was a favorite doctrine among the most pronounced of the slave-propagandists of that day, that the free blacks and "poor whites" were the great enemies of the "institution." They little thought that the day would come when the landless whites would pour out their blood like water in its defense.

It would not do for such a society as this to risk its character for non-interference with the "institution" by furnishing transportation to slaves freed by a master about whose title there could be the slightest doubt. Already the Abolitionists of the North had sounded the alarm that it was the friend and ally of slavery, and its supporters in those states had either grown lukewarm or had fallen away entirely. It still had its list of great names and eminent respectabilities there. Men who feared every new movement, who thought the safe ground was always midway between the two extremes of thought, still clung to it. They gave to its revenues but sparingly, as is the nature of such minds, which are usually as frugal of pelf as of faith. The churches at the North, that once gave with enthusiasm, now received its periodical appeals with coldness. Jared Clarkson, who had mistakenly endowed it with a free hand aforetime, now denounced it bitterly. All who agreed with him not only regarded it as "the hand-maid of slavery," but also despised its hypocritical evasion and double-faced appeals to conflicting senti-ments. The society had come, at the time of which we write, to look to the South for its chief support. The conscience of the dying slaveholder every now and then bequeathed to it not only the slaves he could no longer hold, but also the means for their removal. At one of its anniversaries, about this time, the great Kentucky orator, appealing against a prejudice which had begun to obtain in some of the Southern States against this too frequent freeing of the slave by bequest, and the stringent laws that had been enacted to prevent it, as well as hostile resolutions of some of the legislatures in states where the Southern Abolitionists were propor-tionately numerous and active, had said :

"Why should Southern men fear the action of this society? A vast majority of its members and supporters are not only Southern men, but slaveholders also."

So it would not do for the society to give offense to the majority of its supporters. It not only declined to aid Hargrove, but through the information that its agents gave with regard to his designs, awakened the alarm of the adverse claimants of the estate of George Eighmie and inspired them to renewed activity. His next letter from Matthew Bartlemy contained this in-formation :

The enemy have finally moved in earnest. Yesterday they procured an injunction restraining you from removing any of the slaves. I suppose, if you do not appear and answer, their next motion will be for the appointment of a receiver. While they cannot obtain personal service of the writ of injunction, you must remember that it is one of those writs which are self-executing, and a knowledge sufficient to sustain a reasonable belief of its issue is sufficient to render you liable for its disobedience. I have no doubt that the plaintiffs will adopt measures to have you fully informed of it, and take it for granted that you will now make no attempt to remove the negroes. We may as well fight it out here, and I should advise that a suit be begun against you immediately by the woman Lida, for herself and her children, in order that the question may be taken to the court of highest resort.

Upon receipt of this letter, Captain Hargrove wrote to Jared Clarkson as follows:

The time has come when I must select some one to be the recipient of the trust conferred upon me by the will of my half-brother, George Eighmie. You know in general terms its character. Both as a man of business and as a philanthropist, you are peculiarly fitted to carry it into effect in case of my death or inability from any cause to do so. This is especially urgent, from the fact that the woman Alida, whom you were kind enough to shelter and care for in your home at the outbreak of her unfortunate malady, is beyond doubt hopelessly insane. It is true there are half-lucid intervals, but the better part of the time she is sunk in a despondency from which she cannot be aroused. Her delusion seems to have taken the form of fancying that a child, who was cruelly stolen from her in his early years, has been restored, and to her crazed and bewildered brain, the rag-baby to which she so closely clings is that child. The boy is no doubt dead or hopelessly lost in the labyrinth in which slavery hides its victims. He may be in the swamps of Louisiana or the cotton-fields of South

Carolina; but, wherever he is, the oblivion that hangs over the nameless existence of the slave as effectually hides him as if the grave covered him. For the sake of her daughter, however, as well as for my own protection, perhaps, it is necessary that a suit be brought against me in her name and as a resident of this state. This can only be done by an inquisition of lunacy, and the appointment of a guardian for her as a lunatic. This suit, while apparently hostile, will in reality be in my interest. It is possible that the will of my brother may be declared invalid, and in that case I become responsible of course to the heirs for the rents and profits of the estate, for the slaves that I have set free, and others that I hope to set free hereafter. The estate has been a good while in my hands, and I have hesitated to fulfill my brother's injunction, and free all the slaves, for a good many reasons, prominent among which is the fact that I could not fully determine what to do with them afterwards. The funds accruing from the property I have used for the following purposes :—First, a moderate sum yearly has been devoted to the care of Alida and her daughter; second, a larger sum has been expended in searching for the boy Hugh. As I had nothing to guide me except a peculiar birthmark, it has been entirely unsuccessful. I have also freed a portion of the slaves, and have accumulated a fund to be used in freeing the others, my design being to secure from the estate a fair support for Alida and her child or children as if they had been the lawful widow and children of my testator, and then to use the balance to effect the manumission of his slaves. I am satisfied that this was the purpose for which he made me his sole devisee.

Now, if the will be held invalid in the suit already begun by the collateral heirs, I must not only make good all these amounts, but Alida and her children become assets of the estate, unless her marriage can be successfully set up. It was undoubtedly legal in New York, and very probably illegal in Carolina. If, however, her claim were set up in the United States Court, it is the opinion of my counsel that she would prevail, and herself and children be declared heirs of the estate. This would, of course, relieve me and save them. I will provide for all the expense of such a suit, and, indeed, will perform the will of my brother if it require the bulk of my own estate to do it.

In the event of my death, also, it might be very important that some one should hold the key to the identity of Alida's daughter. According to her father's expressed desire, I have so well disguised her existence that even her mother is. in doubt with regard to it. On the other hand, it may be necessary to conceal and protect her. She may be either a slave or an heiress, and in either case there might arise occasions when it would be necessary to establish her identity. This is all the more necessary, as I shall take with me upon a voyage I am contemplating my old servant Jason, who is the only one who knows all the facts attending the transformation of the child from what she was to what she is.

I do not think it will ever become necessary to use this knowledge, and I am most desirous to avoid the revelation for the sake of the girl herself. He may have been wrong, but Mr. Eighmie was especially anxious that his children should never know that there was any suspicion of taint upon their lawful birth or Caucasian descent. Of course, its unnecessary revelation could only excite the keenest anguish. I feel that I can safely intrust both the business and the secret to your honor and discretion. I would prefer that you should remain yourself uninformed except in certain emergencies. I, therefore, desire, with your permission, to intrust to your care a sealed statement of all the material facts, which shall only be opened by you under circumstances which, in your judgment, shall dictate such a course ; this package, with your own suggestions in regard to it as well as mine, to be transmitted to any one you may select to act with like discretion in case of your death.

Please let me know whether you will accept this trust, and thereby confer a favor of the utmost importance, not only upon the unfortunate sufferers from the evils of slavery, but also upon

Your humble servant,

MERWYN HARGROVE.

To this epistle, when the servant who bore it returned upon the morrow, Jared Clarkson returned the following answer :

MY DEAR FRIEND : My own affairs press upon me so heavily, both as to time and strength, that I seem forbidden by common prudence to add to it the burden of other people's business or care. The matter which you present is of so peculiar a nature, however, and I am already so deeply interested in those whom it most nearly concerns, that I have decided to make an exception to my rule and do whatsoever you require. Humanity, justice and liberty commend the course you have taken. I do not think the requirement of secrecy as to the descent a wise one, though all must admit that the fact of being an African, even by the slightest admixture, has become through the wickedness of our nature and life, a most terrible evil. This is not only foolish but wicked. It is a fight against God. Yet it is none the less a fearful curse to those who bear the knowledge in their hearts that in their veins is but one drop of richer blood than the Caucasian. I, myself, have seen a man in whom it was hardly possible to trace a sign of admixture, curse God with a bitterness that knew no remedy, for the evil that rested on his life. I have seen a woman, as fair as any in the land, and as well endowed, intellectually, whose descent was clouded by a taint that might show upon her children's brows—I have heard her declare that she would willingly be flayed alive if thereby she could feel herself exalted to the level of the white race. I can conceive of nothing more horrible than the sensations of one thus situated who has grown up with all the exclusive assumption of the white race, and you may be sure that I would be as loath to scathe any soul with the curse of a body akin to the despised and persecuted African as you can be. I have always made it a rule to do whatever lay in my power to remove the evil of slavery. I have bought the slave from his master and set him free; I have aided the fugitive to escape; I have defended him from the claim of an unrighteous law; I have endeavored to alleviate the poverty it entailed upon its victims when set free by liberal gifts, and now feel that your request that I should aid in alleviating the worst of all the ills that flow from this most fearful of all iniquities is one that I can by no means refuse.

Please inform me of all that it is necessary for me to know and I will discharge the trust you impose, if not so self-forgetfully as you have done, yet at least with an equal desire to do what is right and just and merciful to all concerned.   Yours, very truly,

JARED CLARKSON.

The answer to Mr. Bartlemy's letter directed him to enter an appearance and prepare an answer for Merwyn Hargrove in the suit in equity brought against him by the collateral heirs of George Eighmie, and enclosed a power of attorney from "Jared Clarkson, the guardian of Alida Eighmie, a lunatic, and her two children, Heloise and Hugh Eighmie, infants of the ages of sixteen and eighteen years respectively," authorizing and directing him to bring suit against Merwyn Hargrove for the recovery of the estate of George Eighmie, deceased, the husband of the said lunatic and father of the said infants. Then the retinue at Sturmhold was reduced, the shutters were closed and the master departed; only the weak, chattering woman and her watchful care-takers remained in the deserted home.

CHAPTER XXIV.

BY AN UNPRACTICED HAND.

It was a few days after the events of the last chapter that Martin Kortright, now in the first term of his senior year at college, received the following letter, much to the detriment of his record in the recitations of that day:

Dear Martin :—I do not believe I ever can write a love-letter. I told Amy so when I wrote last, and she wanted to read my letter, but I wouldn't let her; though there wasn't a word of love in it, was there?

I do not see that it makes one bit of difference having you for a lover. I have always told you everything I knew or thought or felt, and now I cannot do any more. My heart has always been open to you ever since we first met, and it would be absurd for me to pretend to have any more affection for you now than I had before. Of course, I am glad we are to be married some time, and are never to be separated all our lives; but truly, Martin, I had never dreamed of such a separation as possible, until your letter came demanding so impetuously what had long ago been conceded without any request. I am afraid I am not a proficient in this matter of love. Amy, who is such a proud, self-reliant creature, says she is quite ashamed of me for owning that I loved you just as much before as after you asked me to be yours. She says she would never admit that she had loved one who had never asked her love. I cannot see why. I did love you; it was right that I should love you; and so, why not admit it? Whether you were playmate, brother, friend, lover—it was all one to me. I loved you just as much under one name as the other, and could never love anybody else as well, no matter what name they assumed.

Papa has told me all about the queer interview he had with you, and I laughed till I cried over it. Oh, you dear old blunderhead! couldn't you think far enough to know that if you must have your sister transformed into a sweetheart you must treat for her in due and proper form? Dear me! what fun it must have been to see you! I made papa tell me over and over again just what you said and how you looked, and all about it. And then to think you had forgotten all about poor me! No, I know you had not forgotten—only just put me aside for a little time while you did a man's part. I will not be jealous, dear. Indeed, I am glad to know that the man I love can put away that love which is a part of himself long enough to think good thoughts and wish to do good deeds for others. I expect my lover to do great things. You won my heart when a boy by your courage, and I could never love a man less brave. I would have you be a true knight, and do noble devoir for truth and righteousness. I cannot bear to think that you should sit still and look upon wrong without striving to undo it. I would rather you should die in battle than live while the conflict raged and shun its dangers. But I suppose the time has not yet come. I would not have you seek danger merely for its own sake, but if there should be any need for your aid to overthrow slavery, I should gladly give you up, even forever, in such a holy cause.

I am almost sorry you are not going to Kansas with that strange Mr. Brown, whose words and looks still thrill me when I think of them. I do not wonder that you were fascinated. I am sure if I were a boy I should go with him, even if I lost my sweetheart. But *you* must not do it. That would be very naughty, you know. Besides that, you have promised, and so cannot go now even if you would. Papa is no doubt right—of course he is right—but then Mr. Brown is right, too.

What do you think, Martin? Papa told me a secret last night—but, dear me, I haven't even told you that papa was here, have I? Here I have been going on just as if you knew all about it, and you didn't know a word. Well, he says I may write you just as long letters as I choose— that the closer our intercourse now the sweeter will be our love hereafter. Wasn't that kind of the dear old bear? Do you know, Martin, I am sure it hurts him terribly to give me up, even to you. You know I am all he has had to love for so long—except you, who are indeed more like a dear foster-brother than anything else—that he seems as if he were to be left quite alone if your claim is to be allowed. It seems strange that he has so buried himself away from the world. He must have worshipped my dear mamma, and yet he hardly ever speaks of her; but when he does, his eye grows moist and his voice husky in an instant. I asked him yesterday why we never saw any of our relatives, and were such a very hermit's lodge there at Sturmhold. He only looked at me very tenderly and said, "Don't be impatient, little one. You will know some time—unless" he added sadly, "unless, indeed, God spare you the knowledge, as I hope He may."

What can he mean, do you suppose? It must be something dreadful. It made me cold with terror when I heard it, but I cannot imagine what it can be. Indeed, I am not going to try. I am sure he has had a very sorrowful life, and am glad I have been able to give him some pleasure. He has been the dearest, best papa to me that such a naughty girl ever had, I am sure. He never would scold me, nor let anybody else, do what I might.

But I have not told you about his coming. I suppose you knew he meant to come, but I did not, until he dropped in upon us here two days ago—he and Jason— all equipped for travel, as if they were going around the world; as, for that matter, they may be, since he never knows how far he will go when he starts out. We have had just splendid times while he has been here. All the girls went wild over my distinguished-looking papa, and I teased him about it until he blushed—well, almost as badly as you did, I suppose, when papa reminded you that he had a daughter. Even Amy, who is so very high-toned and exclusive, approved him entirely, until he happened to admit that he thought slavery was a very great evil. Then she would no more of him, but declared it treason to her "dear native South" ever to hint such a thing. Papa only smiled in his grave, sad way, and said: "My dear young lady, you are certain to learn how weak and vain are your words. The time is not far distant when every slaveholder will echo the wish of one of the bravest and best of them: 'I would to God that the foot of the slave had never pressed the soil of our American continent.'"

You ought to have seen how scornful and proud she looked. You see she is an immense heiress, though she knows nothing of her estates or people. Her guardian sends her money, and she thinks the South is just the gate of Paradise, as indeed it must be, even in spite of slavery.

By the way, papa says—and that's the secret I started to tell you away back—that he is going to free all the slaves he owns. He says it will cost a great deal, and may leave him very poor. He hoped we—you and I, dear—would not mind that. Only think, Martin, as if we cared whether he was rich or poor, as long as we had him to love! I just sprang into his lap, put my arms about his neck and kissed him over and over again, and told him he ought to be ashamed to hint such a thing. I knew you would be glad of it, and he said he believed you would. Oh, I tell you, Martin, he is a papa worth having; and I do believe he loves you almost as much as he does me. He started for New York this morning, and the matron gave me a holiday to get over my grief at parting; so I am consoling myself by writing to—to—my boy-lover—brother—I declare, Marty, I don't know what to call you. I am afraid I haven't a bit of sentiment, aren't you? I don't see why I always have so much to write to you about. But now I have no one else to write to, you must expect to wear out your eyes reading my scrawlly letters. You know the teacher says my handwriting is the worst he ever saw, and growing no better every day, which I am sure is his fault, for I practice a great deal, as you know.

Papa says I may not hear from him in as much as six months, or perhaps even more. What an age to wait! Besides that, I cannot write to him after this week, as he does not know where he will be; so that no mail will reach him, and it would be just awful, you know, to have one of my letters going all round the world hunting for him. So I am to wait, and be patient and good until he comes back. If he does not come by vacation I am to go and stay with your mamma, and let her get used to having a daughter, I suppose. At least, I am to do so if I choose. If it does not suit my royal pleasure, I am to stay in stately solitude at Sturmhold, subject to your father's direction and control. Papa says he has given him strict charge during his absence, to look after me, keep me out of mischief and see that I am not allowed to cry after the moon. When I told him that Mr. Kortright was too busy with all his factories and mills to look after such a midget as I, he pinched my cheek, kissed me, and said, "Ah, well, he can make his son his agent then!" So it seems you are to be my guardian, by proxy at least. I suppose I shall have to be very good, and always make obeisance to you and say, "Please, sir, may I take a drive?" every day, or you will shut me up in the tower-room and sit like a great dragon at the foot of the stairs, mounting watch and ward over my donjon-keep. By the way, he says you are studying too hard, and will be sure to kill yourself, as so many of the good boys do, before you have a chance to accomplish anything worthy of a strong man, unless you give yourself time to think and rest and grow as well as merely to acquire. I do think that is the foolishest thing in the world, and I mean to be real bad, so that you will have to look after me all the time and not study a bit while I am at home.

Isn't it sad about poor Lida? I shudder when I think of it. Poor, dear, broken-hearted creature! Papa says she was a beautiful woman when she was young. Ever since I can remember she has been the same sad-faced, tearful creature you have known, paying little attention to any one but me. She used to go about the house and weep and moan whenever papa was away, so that I was half afraid of her even then. After a while she seemed to be afraid of him, and for a time before she ran away and brought us together so strangely, she used to talk and act so wildly that I was really terrified. Then I think papa must have talked very plainly to her, for she never did so any more. Indeed she very much changed, being just quietly sorrowful instead of boisterous and frenzied in her grief. I never heard her say a word about herself except to promise that she would some time tell me all. She used to utter terrible things about some one—she did not say who, but I was sure she meant papa—but has never done so since that time. Indeed she has rarely said a word against any one since, unless slavery was inadvertently mentioned, when she invariably went wild at once. Oh, yes, there was one exception. She always disliked you, and seemed from the very first to have a positive spite against you. Poor woman, I suppose she was jealous of the love her pet gave to her boy-playmate. It is almost a mercy that she cannot realize our love now. I am sure it would grieve her nearly to death. Just to think how her whole life has been burned up with sorrow because of slavery! It cannot be that anything is right from which comes such wrong. Papa says it has all been because she does not know whether she is black or white. I do not see how that can be, since she was Uncle George's wife. I asked papa, but he only said, "Do not ask me, child—do not ever try to know."

I am sure it is too horrible to think of. No wonder the poor tear-blanched creature became insane. I should think she would hate everybody. I believe I would rather die than meet such a terrible doom as hers. Poor thing! I think I shall stay at Sturmhold all the time when I come home, just to soothe her if I can. I am glad I am to graduate next summer, so that she can have something better than a hired care-taker, though I know that the servants papa has left will do all that they can for her. I shall write to your mother and tell her so, in order that she may not expect me to stay at Paradise Bay. Poor Lida! my dear old "Mammy," deserves all the consolation she can gather from the presence of one whom she has served with such a foolish fondness.

Wasn't it kind in your friend Mr. Clarkson to look after her when her mind gave way so suddenly at the meeting? Papa says he is one of the noblest men in the world, and that you and I are to go and see him, or at least write to him, on the day after I graduate, if he should not return before that time—which I am sure he will. I would rather never graduate at all than do so without him to witness my triumph—I mean over the susceptible hearts of the young men of Burlingdale, not over my classmates in the studies of the "Sem." There are twenty-three in our class, and I shall be at the very top of the list—when it is turned upside down! You see I leave all the scholarship and intellectual eminence to you. I only yearn for nice things and—admiration. I am determined to break more hearts here in Burlingdale than all the other girls together, in revenge for having surrendered my own heart to my old playmate at the first summons. So you had better look out. Do not think that your too easy victory is secure, or the first that you know some young Lochinvar will carry me away over these brown hills, and you will be "left lamenting." You see the danger of being made my guardian by a too trustful papa. I am sure to find my St. George, just because I shall have a dragon to be delivered from, you know.

I declare, it is dark. If you cannot find time to read this long letter during the week, being so engaged with Greek and Latin and other more attractive and important things, you can keep it until Sunday, and use it as a sedative for an afternoon nap, which you will no doubt greatly need before you finish it.   As ever,   HILDA.

P. S.—9 P. M.—The bell will ring for the lights to be put out in a minute and I must give my letter to the teacher, who comes around to see that it is done, in order that it may be mailed in the morning.   I have only time to say God bless the naughty boy that "wants to be my lover."   H.

CHAPTER XXV.

A PUNIC PEACE.

A THIRD of a century before the time of which we write, a strange treaty had been ratified between Liberty and Slavery. Out of the territory then recently acquired from France it was proposed to erect a new state. Should Slavery or Freedom prevail within its borders? This was the question that, in 1820, arose in the minds of people and legislators when it was proposed to make out of the vast, unbounded territory that lay beyond the Mississippi, the new State of Missouri.

The circumstances attending this first actual introduction of the slavery question into national politics are worthy of something more than a passing notice at the hands of the student of the great movement which for more than forty years thereafter gave tone and color to almost every event of our political history. It should be noted, first of all, that the political instrumentalities of that day were entirely different from those with which we are now familiar. The country was in the transition period, when personal power and individual popularity, as means by which political bodies were made to cohere, were about to give way to the organizations which have since been known as parties. Up to that time such a thing as a party, in the modern acceptation of that term in America, had been unknown. It was a development that grew out of the established facts in our history, however, as naturally as the oak is evolved from the acorn. Such a thing was not contemplated in the original plan of our government.

English political writers are wont to sneer at our Constitution because it is a written one. They declare it to be inelastic, rigid and not adaptable to circumstances. They claim that it is an invention and not a growth; that it limits progress instead of being shaped by events. This charge is not only fallacious but absurd. Yet it has been very generally admitted by political writers. A written constitution is only the formulation of previous growth. All that the English people had acquired of civil and religious liberty, as well as all that the colonies had learned before the Revolution and during the battle-heated years of that momentous struggle—may be found in the weighty provisions of our organic law. Not only does it mark the antecedent growth, but experience has shown that a written constitution is far more easily amended and improved than an unwritten one whose first distinctive feature is the absurd declaration that it is already the perfection of human wisdom and universal justice. The written form supplies to a healthy degree the place of that reverence for rank and tradition which in England counterbalances the progressive tendency of the people. Lacking this inherited check upon the impulse of the moment, the barriers of our Constitution were designed, and have proved themselves sufficient, to restrain the popular impulse until the passing sentiment has grown and ripened into a mature conviction. Then they are swept away. A written Constitution, while it is the bulwark behind which conservatism rallies its forces to prevent sudden and ill-advised change, yet lends itself to well-considered amendment with a readiness that the unwritten Constitution of England has never displayed. The one is changed by the will of a requisite majority of voters in two-thirds of the states. Public opinion has only to express itself with sufficient emphasis to transform at once the written Constitution into perfect accord with the popular will. The unwritten one, upon the contrary, despite the fact that its chief boast is its flexibility, must wait until a generation of judges have grown up under the influence of some new thought before its domains can be enlarged. The one permits an immediate expression of the public will; the other only a remote reflection of it.

Our Constitution is no stranger even to that unconconscious change which comes only by a modified public sentiment with regard to specific provisions. Of this peculiar adaptability of our fundamental law to varying conditions and unanticipated development, without awaiting the process of formal amendment, there could be no better illustration than the growth of that political machinery which we call party.

In the Constitution devised by the fathers no provision was made for any such instrumentality for ascertaining the will of the people as a political party. Indeed, it was not anticipated that the popular will would be directly appealed to for a decision of public questions. It was intended that the people should choose *rulers.* It was believed that men would be elected to legislative and executive positions, not by reason of any previously expressed opinions upon specific questions, or because of their known inclination toward any particular line of public policy, but simply because of their capacity, integrity and general fitness for the duty of framing or executing laws. These men were not expected to perform the people's will, but to secure the general welfare by the exercise of their own discretion, irrespective of what their constituents might desire. It was believed that the populace was not always to be trusted to know what was good for itself, much less what would truly subserve the interests of the future, and could only be allowed to choose men to think and act for it. The idea was a beautiful one, but from the very first it was an absolute failure. The people had taken up the notion of self-government in dead earnest. They construed the "Declaration of Independence" literally, and insisted upon governing themselves in their own way. They rebelled against the idea of sending men to represent their power merely, and demanded that they should represent also their will. Almost before the new government had been put into operation it had been so extended by the force of universal construction as to change its whole character. The people insisted upon deciding all important questions for themselves and in advance of their determination by the law-making power. Instead of selecting a man purely because of his personal fitness for the task of legislation, they also inquired if his opinions upon questions likely to arise for his action were in harmony with those of the majority whose servant they persisted in considering him. Instead of choosing for their chief executive the man who was deemed the greatest, wisest and most patriotic of his time, they began to prefer this one or that because of his peculiar views in regard to the construction of the Constitution, the limits of state and federal power, and the relation of the executive to the legislative and judicial branches. This was neither intended nor foreseen by the framers of the Constitution. Indeed, its forms were expressly designed to forestall such a contingency. But the people were not to be balked of self-government. The electoral college, which was devised as a bulwark against any such ultra-democratic tendency upon the part of the masses, lent itself to their will as readily as the intersecting streets and avenues of the capital, originally designed to promote defensive operations against anticipated popular tumult, lend themselves to-day to peaceful adornment.

Out of this irrepressible inclination of the people for the immediate exercise of the functions of government grew the American idea of party. In order to make the electoral college the simple recorder of the will of the majority, concert of action became necessary. Men who were pledged to vote for certain popular favorites were at first presented in groups by voluntary promoters of the interests of the aspirant in order to secure for him the popular support. Thus the elector, instead of being such in fact, became simply an agent of those by whom he was chosen and was bound in honor to do their will, even though his own judgment and inclination pointed otherwise. To apply the same method to all other offices was but a natural step toward the seizure of all power by the people. When this was effected only one thing more remained to be done, and that was to select the candidate for whom the consolidated vote should be cast by some concerted action. The convention of delegates chosen by voluntary associations of voters, authorized to prepare a declaration of principles, and select candidates for the support of those who approve the doctrines of the platform, was then unheard of. This was all that was needed for the complete development of the American party as it now is, and the transformation of the Constitution from an instrument designed to prevent concert of action among the voters into a plan of government that renders unorganized political action the height of individual stupidity. Party organization, while it has in a measure made the exercise of individual choice impossible, has rendered the will of the majority much more effectual. The voter loses something of free will, but the people gain immensely in power by this growth, which fastened itself upon our Constitution in defiance of the intent of its framers, and in accord with the genius of a people bent upon carrying the principle of self-government to its legitimate end.

At that time slavery had not yet developed into a national question. Public opinion had not yet crystallized for or against it as an institution of the future. Here and there, throughout all sections, were found men far-seeing enough to dread its continuance and growth. Its abolition in the states of the North had been accomplished with very little agitation. The proportion of slave-owners was too few, and the general tone of the public mind too evidently hostile to make the struggle either prolonged or doubtful. Perhaps this very fact tended to divert the public mind from the importance of the institution in those states where this condition of affairs was reversed. The ease with which it had been banished from Northern States led to the belief that it would gradually disappear even from its Southern strongholds. It was generally supposed that the growth of these communities in population, in commercial and manufacturing enterprises, would sooner or later so overpower the agricultural slave-interest that the mere fact of its false economy and baneful influence upon the white race would secure its voluntary extinction. It was believed that if confined within specific limits it must sooner or later die from the action of its own exhaustive forces. A constant accession of new territory, a fresh supply of virgin soil, was looked upon as an essential element of its continuance. It was for this reason among others that not a few of all parties throughout the country had been opposed to the "Louisiana Purchase." For the first time in our history public attention was directed to slavery as a national question by the acquisition of this territory, and the inquiry at once arose, Is it to be "free" or "slave"? Were the already exhausted areas of slavery to be enlarged by newer and richer domains? Was the over-crowded slave population of Virginia to find a profitable outlet in the fertile fields of the far Southwest? Was the market value of the slave, which had already begun to depreciate, to be at once enhanced by opening up fresh fields in which his labor might be profitably employed ? Was the young republic to give a still greater proportion of its area to slavery ? Was slave-breeding and slave-trading to become as much a part of our internal economy as stock-raising or sheep-farming ?

These questions had but vaguely shaped themselves in the public mind when it was proposed that still another state should be carved out of the "Louisiana Purchase." Of the aspirants for presidential honors at that time there was perhaps but one who did not look with dread to the agitation of this question. Whatever its results to the nation at large, its immediate effect upon their individual prospects was of so uncertain a character as to render its discussion at least unadvisable so far as they were concerned. As it chanced, the most strenuous advocates of slavery among these presidential aspirants—at least those having the most direct personal interest in the subject—looked for the bulk of their support to those states of the North in which the feeling in regard to slavery was already becoming most clearly defined and evidently hostile ; while, on the other hand, those whose sentiments had hitherto been most outspoken upon the question of personal liberty and right looked for much of their support to the states of the South in which slavery was most strongly seated. Oddly enough, the Southern slaveholder was, in theory, the most rampant of personal-liberty-loving republicans. Of their own individual rights no class of men were ever more jealous. Not one iota of the right to rule would they abandon on any consideration. The flexing of the Constitution from its original purpose and intent was very largely their work. The barriers which stood between the citizen and the citadel of federal power they labored with angry vehemence to tear down. The very imperiousness that made them masters led them to prize the privilege of being co-equal rulers of the nation. Counting the "all men" of the Declaration as intended to embrace only the white race, and indeed only such individuals of the white race as might be given the privilege of participating in the government, they were untiring in their efforts to secure and possess this privilege. Regarding human chattelism as a divine institution, they were yet peculiar champions of individual right in the direction of the government. Denying the African's claim to the meanest of human rights, they were ever ready to fight to the death for the most insignificant of individual privileges for the Caucasian. Even when they doubted the policy of slavery, they would not yield the right to enslave.

Thus it came about that while the tide of public sentiment in the North was already setting quietly but strongly against the extension and perpetuation of slavery; while the legislature of Virginia was seeking to find some method by which the increase of slave population within her borders might be checked—these tentative movements had not yet assumed sufficient form and consistency to justify any of the presidential aspirants in making this question a material part of the canvass then commencing. It was well understood that if once seriously broached, it might produce results which no one could foresee. There were men, even at that time, who were willing to undergo persecution in order to awaken the public conscience to a thorough comprehension of what they deemed an evil of unparalleled magnitude. The slaveholding element was always fierce and impetuous—jealous to the extreme of everything that bore the guise of interference with what they deemed a right conceded and guaranteed by the federal compact.

When the territory now known as Missouri, in which slavery had already taken up its abode, and where it had during the period elapsing since its acquisition been tolerated and protected by the laws of the land— when this territory applied for permission to assume organic form as a state of the American Union, this troublesome question threatened to assume definite shape and become a national issue. Everyone was aware of a strong undertow of feeling throughout the Northern States which was hostile to the extension of the territorial limits of slavery. Everyone knew that the South would rise *en masse*, without regard to political affiliation or preference, to demand the admission of this territory as a slave state. Threats of secession were freely made should this not be conceded. That there were some who desired to precipitate the conflict which afterwards occurred, there is no doubt. There were many upon both sides of the question who believed it was unadvisable to delay a final determination of it, there can be no doubt, but—as is nearly always the case with a matter the result of which is so momentous and doubtful—the policy of delay prevailed. The advocates of slavery and the champions of freedom among the people's representatives in Congress assembled, fixed upon a compromise, satisfactory to neither but serving for the time being to keep the main question in abeyance. It was agreed between these self-constituted plenipotentiaries that all of the untrodden West, north of a certain line prolonged until it should strike the shores of the Pacific, should from and after the passage of that bill be solemnly dedicated to freedom, and that all south of said line should constitute the undisturbed domain of slavery. It was a negotiation made by those who had no power to treat ; a dedication made by those who had no right to grant; a compromise by which it was proposed to bind two powers which had given no authority to those who assumed to act for them. Nevertheless, the treaty was concluded, and the solemn farce was heralded throughout the North as a triumph of liberty, and at the South as a victory won for slavery. Two little sections of an act of Congress passed into history under the name and style of the "Missouri Compromise." It was said to be morally binding upon the North, as the especial representative of liberty. It was claimed to be a guarantee in behalf of the South, as the impersonation of slavery. It was accounted by almost all a final determination of a vexatious, and possibly dangerous, question.

For a third of a century this fiction was maintained. Slavery and freedom mustered undisturbed on their respective sides of this imaginary line. Freedom occupied without objection the far Northwest. Slavery laid its hands upon the farther South. Again, at the period of which we write, the hostile forces, now more definitely defined and thoroughly organized approached the flimsy barrier which had been erected to keep them apart. The territory now occupied by the States of Kansas and Nebraska was the tempting bait that invited to a renewal of the conflict.

CHAPTER XXVI.

THE struggle between the two opposing ideas, as we have seen, had grown more and more intense, until it had culminated in the victory of the Southern idea in the passage and enforcement of the Fugitive Slave law. Their triumph seemed to have made drunk the opponents of the Abolition movement. The insignificance of the vote polled by the " Free Democracy " in the Presidential struggle of 1852, as well as the overwhelming success of the declared exponent of the policy on which that law was based, no doubt did very much to induce the friends of slavery to believe that any demand they might make would not only be conceded by their party but submitted to by the nation. When the " Missouri Compromise" was adopted, it was not generally believed that the region west of the west line of Missouri and north of 36° 30′ north latitude would ever be of any value. Its distance from the great markets of the world, under the conditions then affecting the problem of transportation, was supposed to render it unavailable even for stock-raising. The great Northwest was then a wilderness. Where the garden of the world now is, there was silence. Illinois was just born into the sisterhood of States. Where now sits the Queen City of the West—a miracle of busy life, there was only a slender stockade and a little cluster of huts. The seats of empire that lay beyond were hardly deemed habitable. The prairie was thought to be bleak and untamable ; the forest dark and impenetrable. What lay to the south-

ward of the line of compromise was known to be fertile;
what was to the northward was believed to be sterile.
So Slavery exulted in the bargain that was made, believing that the rich domain it secured to her would
easily counterbalance in power the possibilities of what
had been surrendered.

This contest between freedom and slavery for the
power to be derived from the statocracy of the national
domain is an interesting and instructive chapter of our
history. Of the thirteen original States, six were either
free or soon became so, while the others retained the institution of slavery in the territory belonging to them.
The first State to be created out of the unorganized territory of the nation added still another to the prepondera-
ting power of slavery. It was Kentucky, in 1791,
counterbalanced, in the same year, by Vermont, which
had never known slavery in its limits. Tennessee followed in 1796, with the "institution" inherited from
her mother, North Carolina. After a furious struggle, Ohio, with a free Constitution, was carved out
of the public domain in 1802. In 1812 Louisiana restored once more the original preponderance of slavery.
In 1816 Indiana added another name to the roll of
freedom. Mississippi restored the former condition in
1817. Illinois took her place on the other side in
1818. Slavery brought forward Alabama in 1819, and
freedom, after a desperate contest, secured a place for
Maine in 1820. Thitherto the two hostile forces had
achieved alternate advantages. Then Slavery increased
her lead by two—Missouri, in 1821, and Arkansas, in
1836. Michigan offset one of these in 1837, only to be
counterbalanced by Florida in 1845, the twin of Iowa,
admitted upon the same day—the result of a bargain
between the two great powers. Texas, conquered for
the express purpose of preserving the balance of power
in favor of slavery, was admitted in 1845, and balanced

by Wisconsin in 1847. Then came California in 1850, the people taking the matter into their own hands and coming to the national legislature with a voluntary constitution framed and adopted without specific legal authority, but expressly excluding slavery from her soil. With this in their hands the freemen of the new El Dorado demanded admission to the family of States and could not be refused. Then the roll of the slave states was complete. This alternation was by no accident of growth. By long continued yielding it came to be regarded as a sort of common law that the equipoise should be thus maintained. In sixty years nine slave states and eight in which bondage was forbidden had been added to the list of constituent commonwealths. That portion of the public domain which had been assigned to slavery by the Compromise, so far as it was then available, or was likely soon to become so, was exhausted. On the other hand the Northwest was already gravid with new states. Minnesota and Oregon were clamoring at the national portal. The tide of civilization had poured across the Mississippi, following the footsteps of the modern Argonauts. The desert trail was found to be lined with flowers. The prairies proved to be rich with the mould of the ages. Where the buffalo had wandered undisturbed the smoke of the settler's cabin arose. The church and the school-house, the infallible insignia of a New England civilization, were almost hidden by the giant growth of maize. The boundless meadows lay laughing in the sunshine. The riches of the East were poverty compared with this. Liberty discerned its worth, and sent her sons to enter in and occupy. Along all its creeks and rivers; in the little belts of woodland, wherever thrift and foresight could discover especial excellence, there the hardy Northern pioneer built his sod-cabin or lighted his camp-fire and staked his claim. Already this territory

was swarming with settlers and would soon be ready
for admission as a State.

Under these circumstances, Slavery turned its eyes
eagerly upon the fertile plains.   Only the Compromise
of 1820 stood between it and this gem of the national
domain.   Frail barrier !   Hitherto it had been permitted
to stand because there had been no desire to go beyond.
Now that the lust of possession tempted, it must be
swept away.   Upon this question the South was not a
unit, but she had so often triumphed by threats that
she never doubted their potency.   So she demanded
flatly that the clauses excluding slavery from the territories west of Missouri and north of its southern line,
should be absolutely repealed.   The North, which had
sullenly submitted to the Fugitive Slave law, burst into
a strange fever of wrath at this demand.   The Compromise, which had been always thitherto the weapon of
the South, they now seized in their own defense.   No
one had the hardihood in serious earnest to claim that
it was not repealable.   The power that debarred had
also an undoubted right to admit it.   Some did claim
that the act of 1820 was, in some sense, a consecration of
the soil to freedom, and therefore, by the common law
of liberty, inviolate ; but the theory was worthier of the
domains of sentiment than the forum of reason.   The
South, exultant in her late success, pressed for her legal
right to clear from the path of every citizen all obstacles
to his occupation of the common national domain.   The
course of reasoning she adopted upon this question may
be summarized, thus :

1. The Congress of 1820, was not, and could not have
   been, authorized to make a permanent 'exclusion of
   slavery from any part of the national domain.

2. Every citizen of every state has a right to carry with
   him into the unorganized territory of the United States

all the rights and privileges with which he is clothed as a citizen of such state.

3. He has the right to take with him any property he may possess in the state from which he migrates, to hold and enjoy the same in the territory, and to be protected in such enjoyment by the federal law.

To this the North offered :

1. The answer of the Abolitionists : Slavery being an evil if not a crime, if the Constitution recognizes it at all it is only to permit its existence in those states where it was at the time of its adoption, and gave no right to establish it in territory not embraced in their original limits.

2. The response of the more conservative Northron, who recognized slavery as a legal fact in the slave states but regarded it as an evil to be fought with every lawful weapon, and to be eradicated peacefully and legally, as soon as possible : that the South, having assented to the Compromise of 1820, and received benefits thereunder in the creation, practically without opposition, of eight slave states morally bound by its conditions.

To these the South rejoined :

1. We have, both as citizens and as states, the same rights in the public domain as you. You are not shut out of any part of it ; neither should we be. Your rights of property are secured to you in Texas ; in like manner ours should be secured to us in Kansas.

2. The Compromise of 1820 was a simple exclusion. We were barred from an empire. You suffered no detriment therefrom. The non-slaveholder—the free laborer—was not excluded from an inch of our soil. Because we have submitted to this injustice for thirty years and more, we are not barred from reclaiming a right, the resumption of which can injure no one. We do not object to your entering the territory ; by what right do you seek to exclude us and our possessions?

These objections were not fully met. The North was hardly in a mood for argument. The hostility to slavery which had spread and smouldered year after year, now burst all bounds. By some strange process the institution had become queerly personified in the Northern mind. It was almost entirely disassociated from the Southern people as individuals. It was a reality, a thing, a material existence which they looked upon as doing, claiming and resisting quite independently of its mere instruments and agents—the people of the South. Against this intangible yet conscious essence the heart of the North was aglow with wrath. The Fugitive Slave law had been looked upon as a step of defiant aggression on the part of the hated institution. Their instinctive love of law and the inherited reverence for the Constitution had endured even this exasperating strain; but underneath the calm exterior there were sullen murmurings that should have warned the friends of slavery that they could go no further. Unfortunately the people of the South had never idealized the institution of slavery so as to disassociate themselves from it. It was their right—their institution—and hostility thereto not only implied but actually covered and concealed a positive animosity against all who were beneficially interested in it. So opposition to slavery meant to them hatred of the South, and they urged their right to carry slavery into the territories all the more fiercely because of the unreasonable prejudice against themselves which they believed to lie at the bottom of opposition to it. They were undoubtedly right in their claim so far as the Constitution was concerned. The better reasoning was in favor of their claim for equal enjoyment of the public domain; but the hostility to slavery had reached that point where one more act of aggression on its part was sure to provoke a conflict, and when the conflict came slavery was certain to go to the wall.

The act was consummated. The South won, and her victory accomplished the ruin of the institution in behalf of which the battle was fought. The Missouri Compromise was repealed. At once throughout the North there ran a flame of indignation. "Free Kansas or fight!" rang from mountain and valley. In an instant the past was dead. The political issues of the day grew stale in an hour. The ghost of the old Whig party wandered still here and there. The secret ritual of the "Know Nothings" was not sufficient to hold men to their allegiance to the American party. The question that had been thrust aside so often had at length found entrance into national politics, and Slavery and Freedom stood face to face, not only on the plains of Kansas but in every village and hamlet in the land. A band of citizens of Michigan called for a convention to form a party in the state, to be composed of "all who were opposed to the *aggressions* of slavery." The word was fitly chosen. Many thousands who would not have uttered a word or lifted a hand against slavery in the states, were ready to fight to the death against what they deemed its "aggressions."

The new party was called Republican. It sprung into life like Minerva. In a day it had swallowed up, like Aaron's rod, all parties except its one great enemy. The lightning spread the contagion. State after state made haste to furnish its contingent. Men woke in the morning Whigs or Know Nothings and slept at night Republicans. The past was rolled away as a scroll. The present filled the earth.

The shrieker for freedom—the professional Abolition orator who had shouted for so many years apparently in vain—found himself now upon the crest of the wave. The "aggressions of slavery" had suddenly vivified all his old arguments. He stood a prophet justified in his own day. Where he had met revilings before, he heard only plaudits now. The abstraction of yesterday had become a reality to-day. The spirit of liberty was mustering its hosts for the Armageddon with slavery. Kansas was the advance post of both. Here came the first skirmish.

The South has never been backward in maintaining what it conceived to be its right, nor has it ever stopped to count the odds against it. No matter how much of boasting it may have done ; no matter how mistaken its views, it has always been ready to vouch for them with blood. The South believed it had an abstract right to carry slavery into Kansas, and it was not slow to assert that right. It sent its voluntary representatives to take and hold. They came from far and near. Missouri overflowed with typical plantation-grown, slave-nursed, slave-holding and slave-raising Americans, who counted the right to enslave inalienable in the freeman and were willing to fight for it as an inestimable privilege. They were called, north of the mystic line that separated the realms so strangely bound together, "Border Ruffians."

The East and North mustered their forces at once to hold the territory against all attempts to establish slavery in its borders. Money flowed like water. Tools, provisions, arms were furnished all who would go and settle there. The anti-slavery societies sent out armed colonies. In the section where slavery held sway they were called "Jay-Hawkers."

A reign of rapine, blood and plunder followed. The fury of the South for the first time met the sturdy resolution of the North. While a desultory warfare was waged upon her plains Kansas was the watchword of a more important conflict in the national arena.

Names are things in the world of politics, and epithets become weapons of offense or defense in every struggle between conflicting dogmas.

In the presidential election of 1856, slavery came for the first time to be the question at issue between the two great parties of the country—not its rights, nor yet its policy, but its "aggressions." It was the trial trip of the new party. It was hardly a year since its banner had been unfurled. It was cumbered with fears and fossils. Many of its members still called themselves by other names. Very few had forgotten the idols they had worshipped. There was the hazard that attends all new ventures—the half-heartedness, the distrust, the thrifty inclination not to go so far as to make retreat impossible. The man chosen to lead was one who had nothing to lose. Fortune favored him even when it marked him for disaster. The young giant did not overcome its veteran antagonist, but the struggle was so close that any unprejudiced observer might easily have seen that the death-grapple had begun. A party that had never cast a presidential vote before had brought the best trained opponent the country had ever known—the victor in many a conflict—to the very edge of defeat. The "aggressions of slavery" had healed all dissensions in the ranks of its foes. It had won in the first skirmish; the reconnoissance in force had been repulsed, but over against it was an enemy devoted solely to its destruction.

CHAPTER XXVII.

NOT WITHOUT HONOR.

DAWSON FOX was about to return to Skendoah. It was a long time since he had gone forth, a sturdy child of poverty, to do a man's work and win a name for himself that he might come back and woo pretty Mattie Ermendorf to share his labor and his fame. It was twenty-five years and more since he had learned that the dream of his youth was not to be fulfilled. The little hamlet had never missed the barefoot boy who went away ; and it listened with something of wonder and a little self-gratulation to the sermon of the high-browed earnest-eyed young man who had returned. And now again the thriving town that had grown up where had been only the "Drovers' Wayside Home " and the few straggling houses of the old-time corners was about to honor itself by reclaiming an interest in a long-lost son. The town was full of it. The dead-walls were placarded with it, and the village newspaper, edited by a man who had come to the village hardly a year before, teemed with glowing accounts of the "gifted and eloquent son of Skendoah," who was said to be "remembered with peculiar pride and affection by all our old citizens." The " old citizens " were very numerous, too, considering what the town had been before Harrison Kortright had restored the lost lake Memnona, and turned its prisoned powers upon the dripping wheels below. Dawson Fox was in everybody's mouth. Almost every man and woman in whose hair there showed a thread of silver, was sure to have some memory of the returning celebrity, or at least some tradition derived from the specially intimate associates of his youth. Men stopped each other on the street to tell tales of his boyhood. Laborers in the factories allowed their machines to run idly on while they talked of the returning prodigy. This is what the handbills said of him:

BLEEDING KANSAS !

A Meeting of the Citizens of Skendoah

WILL BE HELD AT

KORTRIGHT HALL

Next Wednesday Night,

TO TESTIFY OUR SYMPATHY

AND

DEVISE MEANS FOR SENDING AID

TO THE

Settlers in Kansas, who are Suffering from the

Ravages of Border-Ruffian Hordes,

WHO SEEK TO

Drive Every Freeman from Her Borders.

Hon. Harrison Kortright will preside. Rev. Dawson Fox, the celebrated Orator and Missionary, who is known as the "Apostle of Freedom" in Kansas, where he has labored unceasingly for three years, will address the meeting. The distinguished orator is a native of Skendoah, and will be warmly welcomed in his former home, where he has never been forgotten.

The company of emigrants who have been fitted out from Skendoah and vicinity will leave on Thursday. They will be accompanied to the station by a grand procession of all the citizens who favor Free Speech, Free Labor, Free Soil and Free Kansas. Their outfit is not quite as complete as is desirable, but every man has his Sharpe's rifle and plenty of ammunition.

The water will be shut off at 12 o'clock on Thursday, so that all may take part in this demonstration.

By order of the Committee.

Dawson Fox had been a missionary, and had labored faithfully among the people to whom he had been sent, but not with any notable success. All who knew the man, and how he had toiled in his distant field, wondered at this fact. His associates and superiors in the foreign mission work said, after a while, that he was a most brilliant and devoted man, but not suited to that work. It was suggested that he should marry, but it only excited a strange petulancy when he was urged to do so. At length labor and loneliness and the terrible climate brought him a release. His health was broken, and it was decided that only the homeward voyage and home scenes could effect a cure. He had not spent all these years pining for a lost and hopeless love. So he told himself, and he spoke truly when he said so. He was not the man to destroy himself with regret. Few men in his position had ever given so much time to study; but that had not brought him forgetfulness. The long years of self-sacrifice and unceasing application, in which he had dreamed only of Mattie Ermendorf, had burned her image into his heart beyond possibility of eradication. If he had won her he would have become a part of the world, for she would have led him into it. Without her, however, he was fitted only to be a hermit. His studies were a cell where only he and his love came in those years, and when his hope had died he hid there with his dead, which was more precious than all the living. He wrought in the learning of the land he was sent to enlighten, but came not near the hearts of its people, because his own heart was the sealed sepulchre of love.

When he returned he had half hoped that during his absence time might have wrought some miracle in his behalf; but when he sat at Jared Clarkson's hospitable board and heard from his lips of the prosperity that had fallen on Skendoah·through the man who had married the woman he had loved, and learned that Paradise Bay, now in the outskirts of a thrifty town, had been transformed into an elegant mansion, whose mistress was the good angel of every sorrowing heart within its busy limit, he simply said to himself, "It is well." He felt that the life he would have bound to his own had been made richer in blessing to them that needed, perhaps, and had no doubt been fuller of joy than if he had had his will. So he did not venture near to witness her joy, lest even then he should mar its completeness, but finding a work ready to his hand which ran with his inclination, he gave himself to it, as soon as restored health would permit, and for many years he had been one of the most noted of that class of peripatetic missionaries who were known as Abolition orators.

Of these there were two classes—men who had nothing else to do, and men who did little else. The former class too often became mere ranters, spouters for a single idea. Their sense of fitness and proportion was destroyed, and to their minds the world seemed swinging round a single thought. Dawson Fox was not only too large a man to be thus bounded and absorbed, and life had also brought to him too wide an outlook to permit such subjugation. He felt that the world was not all bounded by the nation whose travail had just begun, though he sincerely believed that here the question of individual liberty was to be fought out for all times and for all peoples. It was that portion of the great world-conflict that filled the present. It was to him also a part of that religion to the promotion of which he had been dedicated—the one element of Christianity which it was given unto our day and times to illustrate and construe for the edification of the ages. To him this idea was a part of a far greater whole. Liberty was a foundation-stone, but the edifice built above was far more worthy and beautiful than that on which it rested. Man was greater, in his eyes, than any of his attributes; God infinitely above the laws by Him ordained. He felt the work of establishing freedom to be only another

form of missionary labor. In his view, religion was
made for man, and not man for religion. He had been
unable to do a laborer's part in one portion of the Lord's
vineyard, but in that which he had now entered his
powers had full play, and he found himself strengthened
by knowledge and experience for the work. So, it was
no wonder that the disappointed foreign missionary became famous as an advocate of liberty and a home missionary on the plains of Kansas. He had crossed its
border almost with the first settlers, drawn thither by
that fine instinct of its strategic importance in the great
conflict, that so often seems more like prophecy than
forecast in natures that are strung to a higher pitch of
observation than the common herd. Regardless of sect,
he had constituted himself at once a pastor of the scattered people, keeping alive, at the same time, the spirit
of religion and of liberty in their hearts. He had shared
their dangers and sufferings, and had more than once
been their emissary to the rich and populous East, whose
outpost they defended.

More than once had Mr. Kortright, meeting him at
various assemblies of this character, sought to induce
him to revisit the home of his boyhood; but it had been
in vain. The large-hearted, busy-brained manufacturer
had no suspicion of the reason why. He had something
more than mere regard for this man of a double life.
They had been boys together—not exactly playmates in
any familiar sense, but they had known each other—and
he fully realized the disadvantages under which Dawson Fox had labored, and honored the success he had
achieved. Strangely enough, he did not stop to measure
it by any material standard. Perhaps strong natures
rarely do. The fact of success is of more weight with
the man who has wrought his own way upward than
the mere accident of wealth. Dawson Fox had succeeded; so had Harrison Kortright, and they two, in a

sense, towered alone above those with whom they had
played and fought and with whom they had been wont
to compare themselves in the old days. It mattered not
that one was rich and the other poor. Both had honored the native soil, and each was willing to accord to
the other the meed of credit for his exertion and success.
The magnate of Skendoah was no aristocrat. No man
had ever accused him of that; but he must have been
more or less than human not to have been proud of himself and his work. In a single decade he had transformed
the silent hamlet into a busy city. Lake Memnona was
his monument—his appeal to the ages—the attestation of
his manhood. His life before that had been nothing.
So he said, and so every one else believed, forgetful that
it is in silence and repose that Nature ripens her best
fruits. The years of silence had been years of growth
with him. He did not know it; yet he regarded with
peculiar pleasure whatever there was of worth and value
in those years. The friends of that time were of especial
delight to him now. One by one he had found a place
for several of them in connection with his various enterprises, and all regarded him still as "the 'Squire." They
said of him—everybody who knew him—that old Kortright had not forgotten what he had come up from. It
was a mistake. He was simply unconscious that he had
come up. He felt his later life to be no better or worthier than his early manhood. It was only broader and
stronger—that was all. The people who wrought with
him were not beneath him. They were not his work-
people, but his neighbors. The little church had grown in
size but not in magnificence. Kortright Hall, as the
people had insisted that it should be called, was the
property of the citizens and for their use. All sorts of
gatherings were held here in which the citizens, or any
considerable number of them, were interested. Its platform was free. Its seats were free, unless the people

by a general ballot put a price on them for any specific purpose.

It was here that he desired to welcome Dawson Fox, and with that purpose, in order both to gratify the expected guest and his old friends, he had procured the committee to be made up of men whose names he believed the orator would still remember. Among these were our old friend Shields, still the positive, independent, keen-minded farmer, whose estate had felt the impetus of Skendoah's growth until he was now, in his later years, a man of affluence; and Van Wormer, the stirring head of a valuable business that the waters of Lake Memnona had brought into life.

"It's a pity," said Shields, running his hand over the thin, gray hairs that framed his sharp features on either side, when they had met to draft the letter of invitation—"it's a pity old 'Squire Ritner ain't here to take a part in this. It's my notion that he's about the only one that had any special liking for Dawson when he was a ragged boy round here. He did take to him, and I guess he helped him arter he left here."

"I'm sure I don't know," said Kortright, "but there never was a man more likely to do another a good turn than Ritner. We lost a *man* when we buried him."

"That we did," said Shields. "I've heard him talk about Dawson more'n once since he began to make a figger in the world, and it was easy to see he'd always had a high opinion of him."

"He was always ahead of all the rest of us in finding out good things to be done," said Kortright, with a sigh.

"Except in finding water-power," laughed Van Wormer, with his old propensity to tease.

"Well," said Kortright, "Josiah Ritner wasn't the sharpest man in findin' pennies or dollars that's ever been within a hundred miles of Skendoah, but I've never met a man that knew quite so well how to use 'em. The time was, gentlemen, when that man took me out of about the worst rut I ever got into."

"How was that?" asked Van Wormer.

"Well, you know, I wasn't exactly used to handling as much money as I had to use in starting these things, and I was pretty nervous about the outcome for a time. I worked mighty hard for a year or two, and didn't think of much else day in and day out, till the factories were up and everything running as smooth and easy as water through a pine 'trunk.' Then the habit had got so fastened onto me that I never thought of giving attention to anything else. One day 'Squire Ritner came into the office, and as I was too busy to talk he just sat and watched me for an hour or so. We'd always been fast friends, but I should think it had been two years since we'd said much more'n 'How d'ye do?' in passing. After a while we were alone a minute and the 'Squire came up and put his hand on my shoulder in that sort of petting way he had with everybody, you know, and said:

"'Seems to me, Kortright, you're a' forgittin' that you ain't nothing but a trustee.'

"I never was so scared in my life, for I thought he'd got hold of something I didn't care about being known; but when I looked up I saw his meaning at once. I got up and took his hand and shook it as if he'd been my brother, as he surely was, and said, 'So I had, 'Squire; but I promise you I won't any more.'"

"Oh, ho!" said Shields, with a twinkle in his eye, "that's what Mis Kortright laughs about yet as your 'second conversion,'—eh?"

"Exactly. I bought a new span of horses and a new carriage, and went home at four o'clock and took her out riding. It was about the first time I'd done such a thing since our courting days, too."

Kortright laughed at the recollection, and it was evident that his friends understood what his "second conversion" meant.

"And, by the way," said Shields, "that reminds me that Ritner once told me that Fox took it very much to heart, your marryin' Mattie Ermendorf."

"Crossed in love, eh?" said Van Wormer gleefully. "Well, well, 'Squire, I had no idea you were bringing an old rival back here to exult over his misfortune."

"Sho, sho," said Kortright, with a little impatience, but with the hint of a blush on his fine, honest face. "That is just one of Shields' jokes."

"Not a bit on 't," said Shields, combing his thin locks with his hand; "it's what Ritner told me—and told it in dead earnest, too."

"Why, man," said Kortright, with an amused smile, "Dawson Fox hadn't been in Skendoah for years before we were married. I don't 'spose he'd seen Mattie since she was a little girl."

"That's jest what Ritner said," persisted Shields. "He said they were great cronies as boy and gal, and he'd sot his heart on marryin' her before he went away to school, an' he was mightily broke down when he come back arterwards an' found matters all arranged for her to marry you."

"He did come back just before we were married," said Kortright musingly.

"Jest so, jest so," said Shields. "I thought Ritner wa'n't likely to be very far out of the way on 't. He wasn't given to talking what he didn't know about."

Kortright's head dropped thoughtfully upon his breast. A new light had come into his mind. The cryptomerias that still flanked the pathway to his door; his wife's tender care of them; the fact that she had scarcely spoken of Dawson Fox, notwithstanding his own eulogies, all confirmed this story of an early attachment between them.

"I declare, Mr. Shields," said Van Wormer, with a wink toward Kortright, and a shrug of his shoulders meant as a rebuke to Shields for his indiscretion, "I believe you 've made the 'Squire jealous."

"'Tain't possible," said Shields in surprise, for the first time realizing that it was possible.

"Poor fellow," said Kortright, looking up and smiling gravely at their banter; "poor fellow! I know what he lost, gentlemen, and can't but think how lonesome the years would have been if I had been in his place and he in mine."

There was a tender light in his eye as he spoke, and his lips trembled even as he smiled. The knowledge of this romantic episode in her life clothed the wife of his bosom only with a tenderer reverence. How had he been blessed in her love, while this other better man, this brilliant orator, who had sought it, had been left empty-hearted in the world! The man was too brave and self-forgetful to feel a twinge of pain or have a hint of jealousy.

"We must do all the more," he continued, "to make him feel that we haven't forgotten him. That is, if he will come. I 'm afraid he won't; but if he does we 'll give him such a welcome as a man don't often get when he comes back to a place he hasn't been in three days since be was a boy."

"Well," said Shields sententiously, "you know there ain't many such men as he."

"Nor many such as 'Squire Kortright," said Van Wormer with a peculiar warmth.

"Oh, of course," said Shields, with a reproachful earnestness that brought a laugh from both the others.

"Thank you, gentlemen," said Kortright; "but we are not getting on with our business. You just write the letter, Van Wormer, and we will sign it—if it suits us."

The letter was written more than once, and finally sent on its way. When Harrison Kortright met his wife, an hour afterwards, there was a soft light in his eyes and a tenderness that astonished the good woman as he put his arm about her waist and kissed her still fair lips. It was a most lover-like scene that followed, when he told her all that he had heard, and listened to its confirmation from her lips. They were old lovers, and married lovers, too, whom our modern analysts of the human heart count only worthy of sneers and jests ; but it was really beautiful to the angel eyes that looked down on Paradise Bay that afternoon and saw the wife, in whom the romantic girl had never died, who had hungered all the years of her married life for the blandishments and caresses of love, cast herself into her husband's arms, kiss the pale, worn face, fondle the gray whiskers tenderly, and declare how she had been blessed above all other women in his fervent devotion. She was a silly old woman ; he a weak, feeble old man, whose step still betrayed the touch of disease ; yet methinks it were a prettier picture and better to look upon than if love had not been there. It certainly cannot be counted artistic in our modern sense, because there was nothing vile or degrading in it. However, that night there went out from Skendoah another missive to Dawson Fox, full of the fragrance of the girl-love of long ago, which, though it had never ripened into woman-love in the heart of Mattie Ermendorf, had never faded from the memory of Martha Kortright.

In answer to both missives Dawson Fox had said "Yes," and on the morrow he was to come, to be for two days a guest at Paradise Bay, and then to speak at the great meeting to be held in aid of "Bleeding Kansas,"

CHAPTER XXVIII.

BRIDGING THE CHASM.

UPON the day when Dawson Fox was to arrive, Mr. Kortright was unusually busy. He requested the other members of the committee to accompany Mrs. Kortright in his carriage to the station, two miles away, to welcome their distinguished guest to his old home. Only the wife fathomed the subtlety of this maneuver. To her the silent, reserved man had year by year become more and more transparent. She saw through his loving artifice when he told her that morning how he had planned for the day.

"And I shan't be home till supper; so you must take care of him, and not let him wear himself out talking to everybody. You'd better keep him quiet here at home, or perhaps take him out riding toward evening."

The comely dame looked at him with a loving smile, and said:

"I didn't know much about you when we were married."

"Not know me?" said the 'Squire in amaze. "Why, we were boy and girl together."

"Yes," meditatively.

"And you knew all there was to know about me."

"It takes a long while to learn a man."

"There's where you're mistaken. One sees clear through us at first sight. It's you women that are deep. Only think how long we had lived together and I never knew—"

"There wasn't anything to know," interrupted the

349

matron, with a blush that swept like a wave over her comely face and up to the line of her soft gray hair.

"And there isn't anything to know now," laughed the 'Squire, as he put his left arm about her, and with the cane dangling by its crooked neck over his right, lifted her chin and looked lovingly down into her face.

"Oh, yes, there is," she said, as she laid her head on his shoulder. "I shall never learn all your kindness and thoughtfulness for others—"

"There, there," said he, with a sudden moistening of the eyelids. "Don't let us be a couple of old fools. I just thought the poor fellow mightn't feel quite so bad if he got used to seeing you again without having me around to remind him of his loss."

"And my gain," said the quick-witted woman, looking up at him archly and proudly.

"See here, I 'm a-going," said the 'Squire, as he limped quickly away (he had always limped and always carried a cane since that first day we saw him). He turned as he reached the door, shook his head at his wife, and went away with a warm light upon his thin gray face and in his deep gray eye.

There was a light in her face, too—a love-light that deepened its matronly beauty and made the soft, silvery crown above seem like a refulgent halo to the weary-looking man who came down the platform between Shields and Van Wormer and was introduced to her as the Rev. Dawson Fox. There was a half-startled look in his eye, his lip trembled under the grizzled moustache, his hand clasped hers half-nervously. Then he looked into her eyes; saw the light there, read the earnest, quiet welcome before it fell from her lips, and, taking the seat beside her, felt a strange sense of rest. There was no spurious sentimentality about the man. He had loved Mattie Ermendorf, and had never loved any other. But that love had been pure and unselfish.

His ceaseless prayer had been for her happiness. The older and broader he had grown the deeper and tenderer had become his devotion to his youthful dream. He had dreaded to be awakened from it. He feared to read in her eyes something he would not wish to see—the evidence of a life not altogether complete and perfect. He feared to find the trace of sorrow, tears and discontent. Instead, he found only the ripe fruitage of peace and love. He was content. He saw with languid interest the young city through which they drove. He heard the rumble of the water-wheels and listened to the story of Lake Memnona's subjugation. He noted here and there a remembered object—asked dreamily after this and that half-forgotten name. He had lived here once—or some one like him—but it was in some previous state of existence. He had wandered over the hills—he had known the woods and fields; yet he hardly realized that it was himself who had once dwelt there. His life lay between—a life of labor and disappointment and ill-success—in another world. He tried to go back to that old time, but he could not. What there had been he dimly remembered; for what there was he hardly cared. The world had gone away and left him. He was dead already save where he touched the world's life at one vital spot. He laid himself back on the cushions, closed his eyes, and tried to think whether he were dreaming or waking. His face was pinched and worn. The long tawny beard only half hid its ghastliness.

"He's just about tuckered out," said Shields in a whisper. The younger man assented with a nod. The woman watched him keenly, and knew better than they the secret of his weariness. He roused himself in a moment and begged pardon for his incivility. The committee stopped at the store of the younger, and Dawson Fox and his hostess drove on alone across the

new bridge, past the old school-house to the mansion of
Harrison Kortright. He reached out and took her
hand. A soft, contented smile passed over his face.
He was at rest. Then they came to the end. Two tall,
drooping evergreens flanked the doorway—two glimpses
of the orient. He saw them ; guessed their origin in
a moment, pressed the hand he held fervently and
turned dewy eyes upon his companion. He was satisfied. The past had been suddenly bridged. The boy
was alive again. Weariness, pain and defeat were all
forgotten. He had been remembered—kindly, tenderly,
truly. Happiness had not induced forgetfulness. The
love which shone in her eyes for the man she had
married had not led her to cast aside the memory of
the lover whose passion had been unveiled too late.
When he had been shown to his room he fell upon his
knees and asked that a blessing might rest upon the
home he had entered. The broken life had been re-
united, and when in the afternoon Mrs. Kortright took
her guest to ride, hunting up the old scenes and pointing out the changes that had been wrought, there was
no longer any apathy or weariness. The man had become a boy again. His eye beamed ; his voice was full
of glee. The woman and the man touched hands across
the chasm of the years and were once more boy and
girl together. Their route led by Sturmhold, and the
fond mother proudly told the story of her son's love and
its return by the bright, gifted heiress. As she showed
him through its rooms and chattered of its history, the
master's life and the prospects of her son, they came
suddenly upon Lida. The poor woman gazed a moment
vacantly into the bright face of Mrs. Kortright, then,
with a cry of recognition, sprang toward her and seized
her hand. Mrs. Kortright was surprised. She had heard
that the woman had sane intervals and that they were
becoming more and more frequent, but she had never

seen one of them before. In her surprise and ignorance she uttered the very worst thing she could have said.

"How do you do?" she cried, warmly clasping the other's hand. "How pleased Hilda will be to know that you are well again. I shall write and tell her."

"Hilda?" said the other with a startled look. "Hilda? Oh, yes—I know—Hilda." Then her look changed to one of mortal hate. She snatched away her hand and said impetuously, "You need not trouble yourself, madam; I shall write to Hilda myself."

Then she turned and stalked angrily away.

"That woman looks too dangerous to be at large," said Fox, watching her retreating figure.

"Oh, not at all," said Mrs. Kortright. "Her attendants are very careful, but she has never shown any inclination to do mischief."

"She glared at you very angrily."

"Yes, indeed. She seems always to dislike me since her misfortune, and that is as near being violent as she ever gets."

When they returned home Mr. Kortright came out upon the porch to receive them. There was a thrill of rapture in the heart of the still fair woman, who stood by and watched their hearty greeting at the thought that these two men had loved her—aye, loved her still. A blush came to her soft cheek with this last thought, and then as the two men turned to the old times, each evidently full of admiration for the other, she laughed as she followed them within at the thought that her Martin, if present, would be as full of the future as they were of the past. They were not old men. Both of them were progressives, who counted the present but the stepping-stone of to-morrow; but they had reached the age when retrospect grows pleasant as the background of to-day. She almost wished that Martin were there, as he would have been but for her fear that the excitement of the morrow might awaken his longing to take part in the struggle then going on in Kansas and stir his enthusiasm to a pitch which might defy even his word of honor plighted to the absent Captain Hargrove. As this name floated through her mind, she wondered where he was and what had befallen the master of Sturmhold. The time was drawing near when, in obedience to his request, if he were not heard from, her husband was to take charge of his affairs and act upon the presumption of his death. Her heart stood still with foreboding as she sat down in the unlighted sitting-room. The two men's voices sounded far away, though she could almost reach them with her outstretched hand. She was nervous, she said to herself, as she went out to see that the evening meal was in readiness.

CHAPTER XXIX.

A HARD BARGAIN.

SKENDOAH is full of life, yet strangely silent. The wheels stand idle. The water ripples peacefully over them, trickles through the mossy trunks, overflows the silent flumes and runs in a sparkling current down the rocky channel. The mills are silent, and the rows of windows in the factories only give back the light that shines from the public hall, or reflect the beams of the moon as it wades through fleecy autumn clouds. The water had been shut off at four o'clock, and when the water was shut off Skendoah was dead. The head-gate by which the race below was fed was the great aortic valve of the village life. When that was closed all its activities ceased. The pulleys, belts and spindles were still. The cogged wheels ceased to grind and gnaw. The trip-hammers hung poised and motionless. The breath of the forges failed. The anvils grew cold and silent. The din of warfare betwixt man and matter ceased. The laborers had left their stations. The dust was settling slowly within, even as the silent dew without.

It was two hours since the autumn twilight began, and more than an hour had passed since the glare of torches, the beating of drums and blare of brazen instruments, with the tramp of many feet, had sounded in the streets. The town had gathered in its council hall. The miniature republic had assembled its witanagemote, where rich and poor and high and low and old and young—male and female—considered of the nation's

355

weal. One of the prime integers of republican power took counsel as to the country's future and its part therein. The people, in whose hands was the sceptre of authority, had met in the town hall to decide as to how it should be exercised.

They were not all agreed. The struggle of parties in the little town had been very fierce. Yet in that free-working, free-thinking community the majority had daily grown stronger and the minority weaker, as the contest between liberty and slavery approached its culmination. At first there had been little rancor. Among the scattered farmers of the hill-sides political thought and controversy had been, in a great measure, a diversion. The conflict of parties had seemed like a great national game, in which all took a part and all felt an interest, as in any other game; but very few took the result seriously to heart. As one or the other side achieved success the jest of defeat was shifted back and forth, and Whig and Democrat exchanged condolence or congratulation with only enough of chagrin or exultation to give zest to the recurrent conflict. When, however, the question of human right came to be actually and directly involved in the contest, it gradually took on a more serious cast. The line of demarcation was more sharply drawn. Neighbors grew cool to one another. Friends began to abate something of customary warmth. Business followed in the wake of preference. Churches were divided. Families were sundered.

In Skendoah these rules had suffered no exception. So there were some who were by no means pleased at the demonstration that was taking place. There were some who took no pride in Dawson Fox, and no interest in the cause he represented. Or rather, there were some who contemned him because of the cause he represented. They were not many, however, and the limit of their opposition was silence, or, at the utmost, sneers. Those who indulged in these were generally considered to be largely moved by jealousy of Harrison Kortright and envy of his remarkable success. Except these few, who sulked at home, and those others whom care or illness kept away, the town had emptied itself into the great rectangular hall, whose platform, from its first dedication to popular use, had been a veritable tribunal of liberty. Save for its flashing windows and a few feeble lights here and there, the town was dark. But for the regular shouts of applause, the steady rhythm of an orator's full and animated tones, a burst of song or a snatch of martial music, the town was silent. The horses of those who had driven in from the neighboring county were hitched around the public square. A few of the shops were yet open, in the hope of catching a penny from some belated purchaser. The long rows of factories that lined the water's edge were dark and desolate. There was something weird in the contrast between the abundant life and light within the hall and the silence and darkness without.

Dawson Fox was telling the dwellers of his boyhood home the story of Kansas—"bleeding Kansas," as it was then the fashion to style the territory on which the skirmishers of the two great hosts were encamped, and not unfrequently engaged. The crowded hall showed a sea of earnest faces. All types and nationalities were gathered there. Almost every part of Europe had its representatives. A half-dozen colored men and women were there, some with the watchful, hunted look of the fugitive, and others with a self-importance which naturally arose from a consciousness that their race was in fact the bone of contention, the cause of war. But the most noticeable in numbers and in evident preponderance of character, were they of that type of face we call American—keen, watchful, scru-

tinizing, almost skeptical in its attent earnestness. They
were jurors in the greatest assize of earth—knights and
barons, holding *in capite* under the Great King, and
accountable to Him alone.   Dawson Fox was the advocate, not of himself or of the Free-State settlers of Kansas, but of the principle they represented— of the cause
that underlay their occupancy of the boundless prairies.
He had entirely lost his worn and haggard look of the
day before.   The inspiration of the orator and the fervor
of the prophet had overborne his physical infirmities.
His thin face was flushed, his spare form erect and full,
and his step upon the platform was as proud as that
of a conqueror.   His faith discounted the ages, and the
triumph he foretold was of the far millennial days. His
audience listened calmly.   The crow's feet about the
keen, watchful eyes grew deeper and plainer.   The
sharp, worn faces—men's faces and women's faces—on
which the struggle of life had carved lines of care—the
indices of self-reliant, independent natures — followed
his words with keen, curious looks of questioning or
approval, until little by little their language became
unanimous, and the orator led them without dissent to
his conclusions.   Then his eloquence grew more fervid.
He had not only to convince them that he was right,
but to inspire them to act on that conviction.   He
sought not only to awaken faith, but to secure the
works that testify belief.

The night without grew dark.   The clouds that swept
across the moon's face were denser.   The autumn wind
arose and moaned pitifully around the nooks and angles
of the building.   The signs upon the streets below
creaked and clattered.   The horses fastened to the rail-
ing along the public square looked wistfully about for
their masters, and shifted their positions to avoid the
wind and the clouds of dry dust which it whirled before it.

The orator became more and more impassioned; the audience more enwrapt. The chairman, the Hon. Harrison Kortright, leaned forward, his keen white face aglow with interest. His deep gray eyes flashed fire, and his sharp, firm mouth was closed with almost angry determination. He had no need to be convinced, but only to be awakened. By his side sat Shields, one of the vice-presidents of the meeting, and the oldest of the orator's youthful acquaintances. His thin features seemed thinner than ever before, as little by little he drew forward his chair until it stood almost at the speaker's side. His narrow bald head shone in the light of the overhanging chandelier, while his scattering gray locks were thrust back upon one side, and his left hand, encircling the upturned ear made surer that he should lose no word the speaker uttered. And those words came thick and hot. Mrs. Kortright listened with a pale, wondering face to the story which he told of struggle in that new western land. She heard how the legions of slavery overran the border; how homes were ravaged and burned; the stock driven off and crops destroyed. Oh! many a heart stood still as the tale of murder was told—cruel, unprovoked, save by the advocacy of free thought and free speech. He told how, under the forms of law, men were arrested, torn from their families, exposed to every privation and torture; and even women and children made victims by infuriate bands to whom slavery seemed fair and sacred, and liberty—the liberty of the colored man—foul and unmeasurable wrong to the white man. The audience listened breathlessly. Mrs. Kortright thanked God in her heart that Martin was not present. She was sure that no power could restrain him should he hear this impassioned plea.

The light poured out of the windows and shone with a red, fitful glare upon the windows of the factory op-

posite. The clouds shut in the moon. The wind whirled
in boisterous gusts through the unpaved streets. How
the factory windows glowed! It was almost ghostly the
red reflection from the lighted hall. One could almost
fancy the usual night work in progress. What a row
of glittering panes! Two hundred and forty feet of
shafting in one line! Ah! what a forest of belts and
pulleys and wheels! How the floor was studded with
wondrous combinations of wood and iron! How many
polished forms, now cold and dead, would wake to life
when the water was turned on upon the morrow! Windows! Ah, the whole front was studded with them!
Light is as important to the work done in this mill,
which is the pride of Harrison Kortright's heart—the
crown and climax of his success—as the great wheel
which gives power to the polished shaft and life to the
flying belts! Ah, what an array of windows! How they
glow in the reflected light. How clear the sashes show
between the panes!

Harrison Kortright, looking past the speaker, sees
them through the windows of the hall. His bosom
swells with self-reproach as he thinks of the wealth
those gleaming windows represent, and remembers
how little he has done for the cause the orator is pre-
senting. He turns his eyes again with admiration and
resolve toward the speaker. He will give liberally to
aid the Kansas pioneers. As God has dealt generously
with him so will he deal with his oppressed and needy
fellows. Then he remembered how plainly the sashes
showed in the windows a hundred yards away. It was
queer. He had never thought the whole front of the factory would be so lighted up with the glare from the hall.
It was so red, too. It must be on account of the darkness of the night. He looked again. The windows
were still brighter than before! and—what a silly
dreamer he was—he could almost swear that he saw

the polished shafts and idle belts! No—the machinery was in motion! He almost laughed outright as he thought what a silly fool he was. He had studied it so much that he saw it, as it was by day, even through the night and the distance. It was queer. It must be one of those optical delusions which we are all subject to at times. It was strange that he could see only the windows of the second story, too. He remembered that they were just on a level with those of the hall. He had sighted across the sills one day while they were putting them in and ascertained that fact. So the angle was just right for him to catch the reflection. Yet it was strange the first and third stories were so dark. And the second was growing lighter! It was—could it be? He shaded his eyes with his left hand to look the closer. The right, which grasped his cane, grew rigid as he gazed. His face could not be more colorless or inscrutable, but the light went out of his eyes—the lines about his mouth grew deeper.

There was a cry without.

The orator paused.

Harrison Kortright was at his side in a moment and whispering in his ear, "There must be no alarm. If there is a rush a hundred will be trampled to death."

The speaker understood, and pressed his hand in silence.

"Fire!"

One shrill, wild cry, that the winds took up and whirled away into the night. The audience looked from one to another in questioning surprise. Thank God, the windows were too high for them to see what was visible from the the platform. The door was upon the opposite side of the building, too.

"Fire! Fire!"

There were two voices now, but the wind whistled and mocked at them. Some of the audience started from their seats. The speaker held up his right hand, the palm toward them. The buzz of alarm subsided instantly.

"This," said the orator, "is no doubt a trick of the enemy."

"Fire! Fire! Fire!"

There were three voices now, and the wind could not drown them. Kortright whispered in the speaker's ear. Shields looked from the speaker to the audience in surprise.

"It is not," said the speaker, "the first time that an alarm of fire has been raised to break up an Abolition meeting!"

The windows of the mill were light enough now. The wheels were turning, the belts flying, the empty arms of the machines clashing and flashing against the red flames that lighted up the panes.

"Fire! Clang! Boom! Fire!"

The alarm-bell joined its terrors to the voices of shouting men without.

"Keep quiet!" said Kortright sternly. "They've probably made a bonfire on the public square."

"It is just time to close our meeting, anyhow," said the orator, consulting his watch.

A few started toward the door.

"Don't be in a hurry," said the speaker pleasantly. "The band will now play 'The Star-spangled Banner.'"

The band played. The audience was uneasy. Very many started to go out.

"We will meet here to-morrow at twelve to see our boys off for Kansas!" shouted Kortright in a pause of the music. "Don't forget it."

The blare of the trumpets filled the hall. The people, reassured by his words and manner, moved quietly toward the stairs; Harrison Kortright watched anxiously, clasping his friend's hand as if in congratulation and speaking to him with careless animation,

They stepped toward Shields and turned his attention another way. The hall was half emptied of the unsuspecting hearers, when up the stairway came the roar of many voices:

"Fire! Fire! Kortright's mill is on fire!"

Outside, the rush of many feet, the clamor of unnumbered voices and the clang of the alarm-bell mingled on the breeze. The three men on the platform turned toward the window and saw the red flame and dense clouds of prisoned smoke burst through the flashing, crashing panes and roll upward around the doomed building.

"Thank God!" said Kortright, "no life has been lost."

Then he rushed off the platform, spoke a word of cheer to his white-faced wife, who, standing upon a chair, was gazing at the scene of desolation, and in a moment more was out of doors directing and stimulating the efforts of the people to control the fire.

From end to end the great factory was now wrapped in a sheet of red, leaping, smoke-tipped flame. The whole second story was ablaze. The fire leaped out of the windows on either side; ran up the wooden walls; climbed upon the roof; burst through the floor into the third story and ate its way downward into the first. The wind tossed the flames about in wild mockery. It caught up burning fragments and bore them here and there. It swept the flames down upon the pallid multitude, who gazed helplessly on the havoc that was being wrought, and scattered them with its fierce breath. The light flashed up against the clouds and painted their darkness with lurid colors. A hungry roar went up from the devouring flames as if an insensate demon asked for more.

The firemen tried in vain to save the nearest building. The factories stood thick along the banks of the narrow rivulet. The hill rose sharply just behind them and across the narrow street stood thick and close the houses of the workingmen. The wind blew from the south-westward. In front of this factory was the public square and the hall beyond. Mrs. Kortright, with her face pressed against the window, saw her husband, his gray hair and white upturned face lighted by the flames, stop the firemen who were trying to save the mill above, which was his own, and lead them down to that which stood below, in which he had no interest. But this lay in the path of the flames, between the blazing factory and the people's houses—between it and a score of other mills and factories below. Side by side with him was Daw-son Fox—the self-constituted leader of the men he was addressing but a moment before. She saw the fire-light shine on his flushed face. His long, light beard floated on the wind that was now a gale. His eye flashed as he half turned his face toward her and waved his hand in the direction of the houses on the exposed hillside below. She knew all in a moment. They were going to aban-don the factory in the attempt to save the dwellings.

Already the people had divined their danger, and the panic-stricken crowd rushed each to his own threshold. Men, women and children were stripping the houses in hot haste. Whatever was deemed most precious was seized first and carried to a place of safety or aban-doned for something more valuable. It was a mad, raging crowd, and in their terror they despoiled them-selves almost as much as the fiend that followed hard upon their footsteps would have done.

She started to go. Her husband had bidden her to wait there in safety. She paused; then laid aside her wrappings; tied a red scarf about her head; flung her India shawl about her chest scarf-wise, and went out to aid in bringing order out of confusion—to cheer the men who stood in the pathway of the flame and bade defiance to its lurid wrath.

Dawson Fox, with a gallant band who followed his lead without question, was at the apex of the flame that crept swiftly and fiercely toward the factory below and was already scorching with its hot breath the first of the tenement-houses across the street.

"Only hold it back a little," Kortright had said to him hoarsely, "until I can get this wild mob organized so that we can fight it inch by inch. Of course, Smith's factory must go; but we may be able to save the houses— some of them at least. Those who own them cannot afford to lose them."

Fortunately the flumes were full. The little hand-engine—the pride of the village on its holiday parades— sucked the water from the race that ran in front of the mill and threw it on the flame through only a single length of hose. Strong arms manned the brakes, and as one dropped off wearied with the terrific exertion, another took his place. The men's faces glowed with excitement and perspiration. They dipped water from the race to slake their thirst. The water cracked and spluttered as it left the nozzle; hissed weakly as it struck the flame-wrapped building, or was transformed into clouds of vapor that showed soft and fleecy against the red light and dense up-rolling billows of smoke. Then the wind swept the flame down into their faces. The smoke and soot choked them. The heat singed their eyebrows and blistered their arms and faces. They fell back along the canal a few steps, and renewed the conflict. Nearer and nearer crept the flame to the doomed factory below—nearer and nearer to the doomed dwellings across the narrow street. Fainter and more hopeless grew the struggle of the puny engine with the mighty conflagration.

But every moment Kortright was educing order out of confusion. Already the corner house, which was most threatened, was swathed in dripping blankets from sill to ridge-pole. Ladders were placed at the farther side, up which buckets were passed to men upon the roof. They knew that it must go eventually, but while they held it the movable belongings of other homes were being rapidly and systematically removed to a place of safety.

All at once the race began to overflow. The engine was with difficulty dragged across a narrow bridge, whose planks were already floating away. The mill below was abandoned to its fate. Its upper gable was hardly ten yards away from the blazing pile. Already the flames seemed about to leap across the intervening space.

The owner of the imperiled mill had wrought like a Hercules for its preservation.

" It 's no use !" he said, when it was proposed to carry the hose across the race and keep up the struggle. "It 's no use. Forty such engines couldn't save it."

" I 'm afraid that 's so," said Kortright. "If there was a chance we 'd take it. The only thing now is to save the houses if we can."

" Yes," said the owner dejectedly. Then suddenly, as if a new thought had occurred to him, "How came the water to be turned on to-night, 'Squire ?"

" How came the water to be turned on ?" echoed Kortright angrily. "How came that mill on fire ?" he asked, pointing to the flaming pile.

" Really, I don't know. Some accident, I suppose," said the other, somewhat abashed by his impetuosity.

" Accident ?" said Kortright scornfully; "the gate was raised and the machinery was running when the fire broke out ?"

" So ? I remember now," said the other; "though I had not thought of it before."

" You can hear the wheel now ?"

The other listened.

"That's a fact," with a look of horror. "It must have been set on fire."

"Unquestionably."

"By whom?"

"God only knows!"

"You have not an enemy in Skendoah."

"Not that I know of."

"Then why—?"

"See here, Smith," said Kortright, turning on him fiercely, "if I have not an enemy in Skendoah, liberty has!"

"You don't mean—?"

"Aren't you hurt as well as I?" pointing to the exposed gable that was already beginning to smoke.

"Ruined, ruined, sir," shaking his head hopelessly. "Every cent lost, and a load of debt beside."

"Where were you an hour ago?"

"In the hall."

"And those people?" jerking his thumb over his shoulder toward the dwellings in the rear.

"At the hall, too."

"Don't you see who the man meant to strike at that lighted that fire, started my machinery and lifted that gate?"

"My God! you don't mean—?"

"Of course I do!" hissed Kortright through his set teeth, "but, God helping me, he shall fail."

"You don't expect to save anything below here," with a wave of the hand taking in half the town.

"I will," fiercely.

"How?"

"I don't know."

"I guess not. It can't be done."

"Hark! What is that?"

A dull, heavy sound was heard as he spoke. It was not the rumble of the wheel beneath the fated mill

or the rush of the devouring flames, but a muffled roar
that shook the earth beneath them. Every one stopped
and listened in amazement. Then a man who stood
upon the bridge that spanned the stream a hundred
yards below, looked up toward the great dam, and saw
a strange white Something leap out of the darkness, out
of the very base of the great wall which had so long
imprisoned the waters of Memnona, and rush down the
old bed of the torrent. He saw it swell and rise until
it filled and overflowed the narrow channel which had
been almost closed up and built over since the waters
had been shut up behind the great wall of earth and
stone. He beheld its white crest flash beneath the red
rays of the burning mill before he half comprehended
what it meant. Then he rushed across the bridge
toward the breathless, waiting crowd and cried :

" The dam 's broke ! The lake 's coming !"

" Impossible !" said Smith, incredulously.

"Impossible !" said Kortright, decidedly, remembering the foundations on which it rested.

" Impossible !" echoed every one who heard.

All waited breathlessly.

The roar grew louder. The earth trembled beneath
their feet. The flames burned unheeded. Dawson Fox
stepped to the side of Mrs. Kortright, as if apprehensive for her safety. She had been one of the most active. Her example had done much to quiet the panic
which had at first seized men as well as women. Her
eyes were fixed on the white-haired man in the middle
of the street. He stood listening, wondering. All at
once he raised his head, and, with uplifted hands,
shouted :

"Thank God ! Thank God !"

Those who heard him thought Harrison Kortright
had suddenly become crazed.

" Mr. Smith !" he cried. " Sejanus Smith !"

" Here !" answered the proprietor, who had stepped back a few paces in apprehension.

" What will you take for that mill ?"

The fire was already curling up the smoking clapboards.

" In addition to the insurance ?" cautiously.

" Yes, in addition to that."

" Ten cents," contemptuously.

" I will give you ten thousand dollars !"

" What ?"

" I will give you ten thousand dollars."

" It is sure to burn."

" Of course. Will you take it ?"

" Certainly, if you mean it."

" All right ! Shake hands !"

The two men clasped each other's hands in the street. The bargain was confirmed. The hot breath of the flame swept over them. They were almost alone on the bank of the race. The crowd wondered what it meant.

The flame leaped across the narrow space, and, with a roar like that of artillery, the gable of the mill Kortright had just purchased burst into a blaze from sill to cornice.

CHAPTER XXX.

A GOOD INVESTMENT.

A GROAN that was heard above the roar of the flames burst from the crowd who were watching the conflagration. The last faint ray of hope had disappeared. Up to that moment it had seemed possible to prevent the spread of the flames. The factory that was already half-consumed was farther removed from the other buildings of the town than any of the others, because of the open square in front of it. It is true that the wind drove the fire directly toward the corner of a block, but the street with the overflowing race was between them, and it was believed that with the most strenuous exertions it might be saved. For this Harrison Kortright had abundantly provided, and for a quarter of an hour—an interval that seems nothing less than an age at such a time—the efforts of all had been directed to that end. Smith's factory, however, which was now on fire, owing to a bend in the stream which was followed by the street was thrust like a wedge into the most thickly-built portion of the town. Its lower end, with hardly the interval of a yard, overlapped for half its width another monster mill, whose destruction was inevitable if the flames consumed the one they had now attacked. Along the whole front of these, dwellings and business houses were thickly built just beyond the narrow street. These the demoralized crowd were about to attack in the hope of saving whatever could be borne away. Already they had begun to break open the doors and windows, when the voice of Harrison Kortright was heard exclaiming :

"I want fifty good men to help me save Skendoah. Every man who is willing to obey me, step forward !"

More than a hundred were about him in an instant. That he might be the better heard, he sprang upon a box, which had been carried half across the street and abandoned.

"Gentlemen, if you will follow my directions, I will save the town."

There was an incredulous silence.

"I see you do not believe me. You did not believe me when I set out to build the town, either."

There were cries of "That's so !" "Go on !" "Hurrah for 'Squire Kortright !" It was a vote of confidence—elliptical but sincere. The man who had created the town out of nothing might surely be trusted to save it if possible. The crowd gathered closer and listened attentively.

"I am not surprised that you hardly believe it, but I mean what I say. You all know me, and you know I am not accustomed to give fancy prices for anything. Isn't that so ?"

"That's truth. No doubt of that !"

"Well, I've just invested a little more in Skendoah property. You know I sold Smith his water-right and land a few years ago for three thousand dollars. Well, I've just bought it back for ten."

"Ah, the divil ! It'll be many a long day afore ye'll see the money back, I'm thinkin'," said a quick-witted Irishman.

"I never shall see it back unless we save the town, and we can do that if every man will act as I direct. Will you do it ?"

"Aye ! Aye !"

"Then we must organize. I will name a few whom

all must obey. As I call their names, let them come
forward and receive orders."

He glanced sharply over the crowd, and by the light
of the fire quickly selected his lieutenants. As they came
up he gave one after another his instructions, and the
crowd was soon dispersed to their execution, except half
a dozen who remained grouped around their gray-haired
leader. It was evident at once that the confidence which
had been expressed by those about him was shared by
all to whom Kortright's determination was conveyed.
The panic was quickly suppressed, and the crowd quietly
urged back by those whom he had detailed for that purpose. Then he spoke a few words to the men who remained, laying his hand impressively upon the shoulder
of the man he had chosen to be their leader.

"I know," said he, "that it is a dangerous duty, and
I have selected you men because I know you will not
flinch. If you succeed, the town is safe. If not, Harrison Kortright will be with you. I never ask a man to
do what I would shrink from myself."

"We 'll 'tend to it, boss; you never mind," said one.

"No," said Kortright, decidedly. "You bring it here
and I will do the rest. Remember, you have promised
to obey."

"Yes, but—"

"Make haste! There is not a minute to lose!"

He waved his hand imperiously and the men started
off at a run.

Dawson Fox stepped forward and took Kortright's
hand. He had heard every word.

"Let me do this," he said, looking up into the other's
face.

"You cannot," decidedly.

"But I—"

"You know nothing of the premises. The man who

is to do that must have every foot of that mill as clear in his mind as that fire is in your eye."

"Then I think I ought to be the man," said the recent owner hesitatingly.

He had stood by and heard the plan which Kortright had devised. The firelight shone on his face. It was pale, but his lips were shut tightly and his voice was steady.

Kortright gave him his hand.

"You are a young man, Smith, with a young family. Besides," with a smile, "it is my mill, you know. By the way, Fox, you will remember if anything happens to me that I owe Sejanus Smith ten thousand dollars."

"And what shall I do ?" asked Smith, huskily. There must be something—"

"Yes, certainly. Get your men ready and some of Tanner's, and, as soon as it is over, cover the gable of Tanner's mill with wet blankets and throw up an embankment at the lower end of your mill. It would be a good thing if you could dam the race, too."

"All right," said Smith, as he started off. "It shall be done !"

"And I," said Dawson Fox, looking reverently upon the white-faced man who stepped down from the box and glanced sharply round at the flames, "What shall I do ?"

Harrison Kortright looked swiftly up and down the flame-lit street before he answered. The engine had been driven from the race by the heat and was now plying from some well or cistern on the exposed corner. Men were on the roofs along the whole row of buildings, supplied with buckets, to put out the coals and cinders that might fall upon the shingle roofs. Others patroled the street similarly equipped and watched the fronts of the buildings. The crowd had disappeared. Kortright's eyes beamed with satisfaction as he saw how readily his instructions had been carried out. At the entrance to an alley almost opposite he saw his wife watching him with a countenance full of anxiety.

"What can I do?" repeated Dawson Fox.

"You," said Kortright, solemnly, "You will look after Mattie!" His lip quivered and the clasp of his hand was like a vise, but his voice was firm.

"But I would rather—"

"You cannot do what is to be done. If you stay with me she will be alone. If you are with her I know she will be safe."

Dawson Fox bowed, wrung his hand and turned away just as the men who had been sent away returned bearing between them through the heated street a number of kegs, each of which was marked:

"*Powder.*"

Placing himself at the head of these men Kortright crossed the race and entered the building he had so recently purchased, the upper end of which was already aflame, while the heated currents of smoke rolled through the upper stories, scorching and searing like the blast of a furnace. Dawson Fox re-crossed the street and took his place by the side of Mrs. Kortright in the shadow of a brick building where she stood. An instant afterward all but one of the men returned, and, running up and down the street, cautioned every one to retire to a place of safety. After a moment Harrison Kortright and the foreman of the mill, who had remained with him, came out, and seeing that all were out of danger, the former, after some protestation on the part of his companion, went again into the mill. The foreman stepped nervously toward the narrow foot-bridge that crossed the race. The shouting was hushed. Only the sound of the flames was heard, and the roar of rushing waters. Around every corner peered an anxious face. Presently Harrison Kortright rushed out through smoke that was now pouring from every door and window. He staggered, half-blinded, toward the foot-bridge. Seeing the foreman waiting there he cried out:

"Run! Run! It is all right."

The man turned and fled. Harrison Kortright rushed upon the bridge as fast as his lameness would permit. Half-way across he turned as if to see that the train he had lighted was burning properly. As he did so his foot fell upon the end of a loose board; the other end flew up, and in an instant he was struggling in the water. As he fell a shadow darted out of the shaded alley opposite, and the lookers-on saw Dawson Fox fly across the street toward him. Just as he reached the bank of the race there was a dull roar that was heard above the tumult of the waters and the rush of the flame that towered above the doomed building. Then the walls of the lower factory trembled. The whole structure seemed to be lifted up. The blazing gable was thrown back upon the pile from which it had caught the flame. The windows bulged outward. The roof parted at the ridge-pole, and then fell inwards. A vast cloud of black smoke and dust shut out the whole from sight, and shot upward against the white, fleecy clouds that just then had opened around the cold, full moon. Then there was another and a sharper explosion. The earth shook with the force of the concussion. A thousand pounds of powder had been exploded beneath the mill. The vast pile rose and crumbled. A bright flash shot upward from the centre. Then the whole sank down into a shapeless mass. The air seemed full of broken fragments. Pieces of the shattered building rattled like hail upon the roofs of the houses opposite. Mrs. Kortright started to rush to her husband through the shower of fragments. A strong arm held her back.

"It's no use, Mrs. Kortright," said Smith, as he refused to release her. "You cannot help them. The water is not deep. If your husband is not hit with the falling pieces he is safe."

A moment after a hundred feet were hurrying to the place where Kortright had disappeared. Dawson Fox had halted for an instant when the explosion had occurred, and then had leaped into the race. Those who came to the rescue saw a man struggling in the water. A dozen hands seized him and drew him forth. Strangled, gasping, dripping, they bore him to the middle of the street. The light of the burning mill fell on the white, drawn face of Harrison Kortright. For a moment all else was forgotten. Mrs. Kortright sat in the dusty roadway with his head upon her lap. The crowd rushed forth from their hiding places and pressed around with anxious faces. Some one brought a torch of blazing fragments and held it near him. All else was forgotten in the danger of the founder and benefactor of the town. The village doctor made a hasty examination. The patient lay pallid and gasping. A thousand suggestions were made. His breathing grew stronger and more regular. The richly-dressed woman wiped his face with her white handkerchief, and held him tightly to her breast. Presently he opened his eyes and tried to speak. The physician rose and said cheerfully :

"He is not hurt ; only strangled and confused."

Then there was a shout. They took him in their arms to bear him to a place of comfort and shelter. He shook himself loose; sat up; gazed wildly about, and chokingly exclaimed :

"Fox ! Fox ! where is he ?"

Where, indeed ! In their anxiety for their friend and neighbor they had forgotten the stranger.

Instant search was made, and from the swollen race was soon dragged forth another form. This one was silent and limp. No stertorous gasp gave promise of life. When his face was turned toward the fire-light a deep red gash showed upon the temple, and the hands of those who held his head were deeply stained with blood. The physician placed his thumb upon the wound and felt a harsh, dull grating answer to his pressure. He shook his head hopelessly, and wiped the blood from his hand. Dawson Fox was dead. A fragment of the building had struck him as he stood over the man he sought to rescue. He had saved the husband of his boy-love by yielding up his own life instead. There were many tearful eyes that marked a sad, sweet smile upon the cold dead face as it lay there in the dusty roadway lighted by the raging fire.

Harrison Kortright heard the sad tidings and offered no more resistance to those who would bear him away. He realized as no one else could the sacrifice that had been made for him. He remembered the brave, set face lighted by the lurid glow of the explosion, that for a moment hung over him. He remembered the strong arms that for an instant clasped him close, held him above the strangling current and then relaxed their hold, tremulous and weak, while he who had come to rescue fell prone across his breast and bore him again beneath the water.

As the crowd started on along a narrow street that led up the hill-side from the bank of the stream with their sad burden, there came a cry from those whom Smith had rallied to protect the mill below:

"The water is rising! The bridge has gone!"

At the same time the flame that was springing up in the debris of the explosion began to hiss and splutter.

"The sluice-gates are open," said Kortright feebly. "It is all right. The channel is too narrow and the water will back up so as to overflow the lower story. Thank God! the town is safe."

He was right. The long unused channel of the mountain torrent had been so obstructed by walls and piers that when the tide poured out of the sluice-gates there was not space for it to flow off, and it choked and fouled until it overspread its banks and poured into the lower story of the mills that stood thick along its course. By this means the fire was prevented from spreading, and Skendoah was saved from a disaster which for a time seemed to be unavoidable. Yet the tale of destruction was not yet ended. As they bore the living and the dead up the hill to the shelter of a friendly house some one uttered an exclamation which caused all to look around. Upon the dark hill-side beyond the roaring torrent that boiled between, a sheet of yellow flame shot up, lighting the whole surrounding region. Mrs. Kortright saw at a glance what it meant.

"Move on, move on!" she cried hastily to those who bore her husband. She dreaded, above all things, lest his dull eyes should learn the truth. Paradise Bay was wrapped in flame.

CHAPTER XXXI.

SKENDOAH was not in ashes, but a black, smouldering gap in the row of factories along the bank of the stream greeted the eyes of its people on the morning succeeding the events of our last chapter. The rush of water along the tortuous channel had subsided. The prisoned lake had escaped from thralldom. Only a sparkling rivulet ran along the muddy bottom of the great reservoir, bustled through the open jaws of the huge waste-gate, and foamed and flashed in the long-unused channel below. Flood and fire had both despoiled the little town, but the former had put an end to the ravages of the latter. By what means the gate had been opened, and whether as an act of good or evil purpose, no one knew. At any other time, the flood would have been an absolute misfortune. Coming as it did, it was an inestimable blessing. Yet it had left rueful marks as well as the flame it quenched. The street across which the battle with the flames had been fought had been submerged a few moments afterwards. The water pouring through the gate, impelled by the weight of the accumulated store behind the dam, would have soon overflowed the channel had it been straight and unobstructed. But it was neither. Little by little factories and bridges had encroached upon the domain of the mountain torrent, until, when it suddenly burst loose, it was to find its way choked and impeded at every turn. It tore away one obstruction after another, only to heap up in a bend just below the village the debris of its fury, until its tumultuous rage was, for

the time, effectually checked. Then the waters began
to rise in the town, sullenly and silently heaping up
behind this temporary barrier, until they crept into
the lower windows of the factories, caught the hissing
cinders that fell from the flaming buildings, passed
beyond the farther walls, stole across the street, and
choked in rising vapor the conflagration that raged
above its dark and angry surface. Lake Memnona was
empty once more. The fire was extinguished. The
flood had subsided. Dawson Fox was dead. Harrison
Kortright was chained to his bed with the shackles of his
old enemy newly fastened on his overwrought system.
On the hill-side beyond, a black smouldering mass lay
among the scorched and blighted trees where the prett-
iest and richest of the mansions of Skendoah had
stood.

"Who did it?" was the inquiry which each one asked
of himself and his neighbor. The idlers who gazed at
the ruins, loitered about the streets and met in the
doorways, talked of nothing else. The water being
turned off, the remaining mills were shut down, some of
them that the damages by the flood might be repaired,
and the others because there was no inclination on the
part of any one to labor. The boys played up and down
the stream, clambered in and out of the broken windows
of the mills, burrowed among the debris of the overflow
for flotsam, or waded about upon the slimy bottom of
the pond in search of finny prey which had been left
among the ooze by the sudden decadence of the waters.
But all the time they were wondering, like their elders,
as to the cause of the calamity.

In the town-hall, on a plainly-draped bier, lay the
body of Dawson Fox. At that time the people of the
little country town, despite its sudden dash at prosperity, had not learned to decorate the place of the dead.
Flowers at a funeral would have been regarded almost

as a sacrilege, and no one even thought of draping the banner that hung listlessly above the platform, the coffin across. All was cold, dull black, save the fixed white face, with its framework of white satin, that lay within. Solemn-faced and noiselessly the people passed in and out. A jury of inquest was impaneled in the room below, and came up in a body to view the corpse. There needed to be no autopsy. A thousand knew the cause of death. The real inquiry was as to the cause of the fire.

The examination was a profitless one. Many witnesses were called, many questions asked and very little learned. A few facts were made plain :

1. The gate which supplied the common race by which all the mills received their supply of water, had been closed at four o'clock on the day previous, by general consent of the owners and operatives.

2. The water had been turned off the wheel in Kortright's mill and the machinery stopped, by express order of the owner, an hour earlier than the time mentioned.

3. When the fire was discovered at about a quarter to ten o'clock in the evening, the wheel was running and the machinery of the mill in motion.

4. The waste-gate was not opened until more than an hour after the breaking out of the fire. It had never been opened before since the building of the dam. It was reached by a frame of timbers that extended above the dam some forty feet or more, into the deepest part of the original channel. It was worked by a large iron screw, which itself was operated by means of a wooden lever which passed through its head. To open these gates to their fullest extent, as they were found the next morning, with a head of forty feet of water or thereabouts resting against

them, was a task requiring no little time and strength for its accomplishment.

5. Paradise Bay was discovered to be on fire something more than half an hour after the rush of water through the waste-gate was first noted.

From these facts the jury concluded that Kortright's mill and Kortright's house were set on fire by some person desirous of doing him an injury, and utterly reckless as to those who might share in the calamity. There were some other incidents which served more to confuse the jury than to aid them in prosecuting the inquiry beyond this point. Just here two very troublesome questions arose :

1. Why was the machinery of the mill put in motion ?
2. Why were the waste-gates opened ?

To the first, the most evident and general response was that it was done through sheer wantonness of malice. To the second, there was an inclination to reply that the incendiary, terrified at the result of his work, had hit upon this plan to extinguish the flames, and repair, to some extent, the evil he had done.

In seeming contradiction of this theory, however, was the fact that the wooden lever used to open the gates was found in the road half way to Kortright's residence. If the two fires were regarded as the work of one incendiary, it was evident that after kindling the first he had passed along the top of the dam, opened the sluice and then lighted the second. This was the general belief. Some dwellers in the upper part of the town testified to having seen a dark form pass and repass along the crest of the dam while the fire was at its height. A boy who had come from a farm-house upon the east side of the stream to witness the conflagration that was raging beyond, had been terrified by a strange shape that rushed at him with an uplifted bludgeon not far from where the gate-lever was found. He had not waited for further inquiry, but fled homeward across the fields and fences, inspired by a terror that took little heed of obstacles. His story was so confused and absurd that little heed was paid to it. As to two points all were agreed:

1. The fire was the work of an incendiary.
2. The said incendiary was moved and instigated by a particular malice toward Harrison Kortright.

Whether this malice was based upon a more general antipathy to the cause of human freedom, which Kortright at that time especially represented, was a question in regard to which there was great difference of opinion. The majority—and it was a turbulent and loud-speaking majority—believed this to be the case. The minority—a subdued and apologetic one—pointed to the opening of the sluice-gates and the firing only of Kortright's property in support of a contrary view. The majority sneered at this as absurd. To them the acts referred to were only part of a preconcerted plan to escape detection.

So the jury returned a verdict which was true in one sense no doubt, though hardly reasonable in a legal sense, that Dawson Fox came to his death by the unlawful and incendiary act of a certain person or persons to them unknown. The people of Skendoah and of the country round, by a large majority, had already decided, however, that the burning of Kortright's mill, the destruction of his house, and the death of Dawson Fox, were all of them acts of the opponents of personal liberty—outrages of the pro-slavery propagandists. Of those who entertained this belief Harrison Kortright was among the most undoubting and sincere. His love of Skendoah and his desire for wealth and success were at once swallowed up in a burning zeal for justice and revenge. He saw little prospect of detecting the actual perpetrator of the crime, but he was sure that he knew its motive. So he lay upon his sick bed, silent but alert, and planned with firm-set lips and flashing eyes how he would strike back at that hated institution whose minions he never once doubted had given his property to the flame and shed the blood of his friend. He had been a firm but quiet opponent of slavery up to this time. The dead man who rested upon his bier in the town-hall, the "flaming apostle of liberty in Kansas," had been dull and mild when compared with what this calm, gray-haired man of business resolved that he would be thereafter.

Jared Clarkson, who had come to sympathize with one friend and bury another, fierce as was his hatred of the "institution," shrank in something of terror from the burning zeal of this man who seemed inspired to avenge the death of his friend, not upon its immediate perpetrators, but on what he deemed the remote cause. Martin, summoned by news of the disaster, was devoted in the very moment of his arrival to the purpose that filled his father's heart. Instead of five, it had been decided that Skendoah should send ten men to uphold the right in Kansas; that they should leave upon the morrow, and that Martin should go with them. They should be *bona fide* settlers, too, sworn to make the virgin territory free soil. He himself would be answerable for one-half their expenses for the first year. The mother sobbed placidly and helplessly. The crippled magnate was a king whose imperious will brooked no denial. The son, fired by the events which had occurred, took his father's command as a consecration. Already his heart was eager for the conflict. He was impatient of the days that must intervene before he should stand upon the prairie and enter the camp of "Old Brown." He saw, with his father's eyes, that slavery must be destroyed. No matter what it might cost—war, blood, death—anything were better than the one thing he was called upon to aid in sweeping from the earth. In his zeal he forgot his promise to Hargrove. He even forgot for the moment that sweet presence in the New England seminary, who was to be his other-self—*dimidium meæ*, he had already begun to call her in the stilted Latin phrase of the college.

The funeral was in the afternoon. Jared Clarkson stood by the open bier, and in noble words and fervid accents told the story of his life and death. Happy the dead who had such an eulogist! The people listened quietly but sternly to his words. When the funeral was over there was a meeting in the town hall. Only men attended it, and they were stern-faced and angry-eyed. The women stayed at home and wondered beneath their breaths what would be done. There was very little speaking. They adopted resolutions which seemed tame to them, but were regarded as incendiary and revolutionary by all the world which saw not the charred ruins, and the cold, dead face. Jared Clarkson wrote them. While his life was full of charity his pen seemed always tipped with venom. The people of Skendoah declared thereby that Dawson Fox died a victim of political hate; that the hand that held the torch which had disfigured and all but devastated their beautiful village, was that of the great enemy of man and liberty, the slave-power of the South. This was recited at great length, and with sundry ingenious rhetorical flourishes. It will be noted that there was not a particle of evidence to support this conclusion, yet upon it the popular heart rested with the most undisturbed confidence. Of the ultimate cause there was not a doubt; of the immediate instrument, not a suspicion. There was not a human being to whom any inhabitant pointed in his thought even and said, "I believe that his hand did this deed." There were a few of whom all men said, "They are responsible for this evil." They were those who had sneered at his enterprises, and carped at the political faith of Harrison Kortright—the stubborn, irreconcilable minority which is to be found in every community, men born in the opposition and condemned by temperament to be envious, if not malignant. A committee of public safety was also organized, whose duty it was to take every possible means to ferret out the crime. This was needless. From his sick bed a far more potent spirit was already at work. Silently and coolly, but with a determination that never faltered, Harrison Kortright set himself to discover the hand that had smitten him in the darkness. Like the populace, he was without suspicion of any one. Like them, too, he was affected with distrust of many. He was actuated not less by a desire for public safety than by a sense of personal wrong, but most of all by an intense desire to bring to punishment the malefactors whose act had resulted in the death of his friend. Mrs. Kortright alone did not believe that the accepted theory of the crime was the true one. Without opposing his plans, she insensibly modified her husband's resentment and disarmed his distrust. She had no pet hypothesis. To her the events of that night were only a sad, insoluble mystery. She cared little for the loss of property. The death of the man who had been her lover and had come back after many years in the guise of so sweet a friend, while sorrowful enough, was not without its consolation. His death had been worthy of himself at his best estate. If there had been a shade of weakness in his life, it was removed by the manner of his death. The hint of failure, the flavor of ill-success, could never pass this crowning act of self-sacrifice. His was a memory to be cherished, not only with affection, but with pride. The loss of her home had cut her to the heart. She reproached herself with the thought that it brought more sorrow than the death of her friend. It was natural that it should. The home upon the hill-side had bounded her whole life. Whatever change had come in their condition, while it left its marks upon their surroundings, expanding and enriching the homestead from time to time, until to the eye of the stranger its identity seemed destroyed, yet to her it had always remained the same. It was her home. Her personality fitted into every niche along with that of her husband. In losing it she seemed to have lost a part of her very being. It was the background on which all her existence had been projected. These feelings, however, were swallowed up in two all-absorbing sources of gratification—her husband lived, and the town had been saved from destruction. She did not believe, she would not believe, that any hand within its limits had been lifted to strike at him. She could not believe that any political animosity would induce any one to peril the safety of the town, and especially to aim a blow at her. So she smiled at the resolutions that went far and wide throughout the land. The letters of condolence which poured in upon her husband, all assuming that he was a martyr to a great cause, both amused and annoyed her. Once he had laughed at her hostility to slavery; now he was almost angry that she would not account it the sole cause of their misfortunes. They had yet to learn the lesson which Time so often teaches to those who disagree, that both were right and both were wrong.

It was because of this conviction that Mrs. Kortright, for perhaps the first time in her life, offered a serious objection to any project on which her husband had decided. She did oppose the sending of her son to Kansas. Five good men and true had readily been found among those thrown out of employment, for a time at least, by the fire, to go with the other five, as Free State settlers, to Kansas. Their departure had necessarily been delayed beyond the time which the impetuous sufferer had fixed upon at first. There had been a subscription started to rebuild a little frontier church in which Dawson Fox had ministered, and which had been destroyed by a gang of Missouri raiders, as a memorial to his memory. During this period of delay Mrs. Kortright did not fail to urge as gently as she could upon her husband's attention that their son had given his word to Hargrove, which it would be bad faith to ignore, except in case of some great public crisis.

"And is it not a great crisis," the sick man confidently asked, "when slavery, not content with having invaded our homes to search for the fugitive, and compelled us by law to return him into bondage, comes also and applies its favorite methods for repressing free speech here in the midst of us ?"

"Admitting this," his wife would say, "you cannot deny that we are not only bound to regard Mr. Hargrove's wishes ourselves, but that Martin is under especial obligation to do so. Can you claim that there is any more need for him to forego his preparation for life's duties and engage in the conflict going on in Kansas now than when you gratefully thanked Captain Hargrove for preventing his departure ?"

To this view no answer could be given, but it is probable that his wife's importunities would have been of little avail to restrain the exasperated father and hold back the son, whose martial ardor was at fever heat, had it not been for certain items of intelligence which arrived while they waited for the day fixed upon for their departure.

The first of these was a letter from Hilda, to whom Martin had found leisure, even amid the excitements of the time, to write a full account of all that had occurred, including the fact that his father had determined that he should go to Kansas with the others. Upon this topic he had dilated with much earnestness and enthusiasm. The young girl, dwelling in the quiet of the Blankshire hills, knowing nothing of the mental atmosphere of Skendoah, save from his letter, and withal influenced not a little by the selfishness of love, took a view of the situation which effectually dampened the ardor of the would-be knight-errant of liberty, and staggered the positiveness of the father's conviction. She wrote:

"My Dear Martin: I was glad to get your long letter, though it made me very sad indeed. I would come to you at once, for I am sure you need me, but a letter which I have just received from Papa—the first after so many months—says that he will follow in a few days, and will take me home for a vacation that is not set down in the catalogue. As this is the last year, and the principal is sure of her pay anyhow, she does not care so very much about absences as she otherwise would. I look for him every day, and may be with you as soon as my letter. I may even get there in time to read it to you. That would be nice, wouldn't it? Just think of a young gentleman getting a letter from his lady-love by word of mouth—her mouth, too! I think it would be capital sport, only you would have to promise very solemnly not to—to—interrupt, you know.

"Oh, my dear Martin, you must forgive me for seeming to be gay when you are in such serious trouble at Skendoah. I am sure I am sorry—very sorry for poor Mr. Fox, whom I did not know at all, you know (and whom I am sure I should not have liked if I had known), and for your papa, who suffers so much, and your dear mamma, who has lost her beautiful home. Poor dear Aunt Mattie (I shall never learn to call her anything else), she must feel as if her life had been cut right in twain and the best part of it thrown away, leaving her only the evening years to call her own."

"And that is just the way I do feel," sobbed Mrs. Kortright, interrupting the reading of the letter; "but who would have thought she would have understood it? I wish she were here, the dear child; I do indeed."

"But then I am so glad that *you* are safe, your father alive, your mother well, and my papa coming home, that I cannot be sad a bit and hardly manage to be serious. I am just as happy as a bird, and wish I were one to just fly to you for one little minute and then back here before Papa could have a chance to come and find me gone. That would be awful. I do think it would break his heart if he should come and not find me watching for him. I know I should never get over crying about it. I am sure you need me there very much, too. What in the world are you all stopping at that little hotel for? I hope you don't mean to stay there while dear old Sturmhold stands vacant and just aching for a population. What difference does it make that it is ten miles away? Your father ought to get as far from business as he can, and you are going to Kansas. So you say at least. Now, you know that Papa would not allow you to stay there an hour, nor would I if I could have my way. I have written to the servants at Sturmhold to put everything in order and send the carriage to you at Skendoah. You did not tell me whether the barn and horses were burned or not—which was very careless of you. Now, if you *are* going to Kansas— which I do not at all believe—"

Martin smiled and Mr. Kortright frowned at this,

—"the very first thing you should do is to put your father and mother where they will be perfectly comfortable while you are away, and Sturmhold is just the place. Besides, Papa and I will be there in a few days, and you know we shall all want to be together, except you, who will, of course, prefer to be—in Kansas. I am sure your father would like to go there, because he will want me to nurse him. He knows what a capital nurse I am, because he has tried it. I remember being left alone with him when he was sick before. I suppose he was busy thinking of what he would do when he got out again, for he answered my questions at first absently, and then with more and more of irritation, until finally your mother came in and he exclaimed : 'Good Heaven, Mattie, can't you think of something that this child can ask a few questions about?' I don't need any help now. So if he will come to Sturmhold I will ask questions enough to keep his mind off his business, and then he will get well, only just taking a rest now and then while Papa tells his adventures. He has been away so long that I am sure they will be many and well worth listening to. However, if you will not go at my invitation, I will leave Papa to settle all that when he comes.

"By the way, Martin—you will excuse me for saying so, but speaking of your father's business brings it to my mind—I remember hearing Papa say that the work Harrison Kortright did every day was enough to kill two or three ordinary men. Even such a little dunce as I am can see that it must be enormous. Why, even my little business matters almost bring on a collapse when I undertake to straighten them out. Once a month or so we girls always get leave to go into the town shopping, and I am sure to be laid up for a day or two afterwards. Miss Hunniwell says it is caramels and the like, but I know it is the cares of business. Then, too, Papa gave me a bank-book and a check-book before he went away, and you have no idea of the trouble I have trying to find out how much cash I have in the bank. I know there must be a good deal though, for I haven't used up more than half the checks in my book yet.

"Now Marty, dear, don't laugh at me. I know I am nothing but a silly little girl ; but it does seem to me that instead of going out to Kansas 'to help on the good cause,' as you say, you would help on a great deal better cause, and the one you mean a great deal faster, too, by staying at home and taking that great business off from your poor father's shoulders just as fast as you can. You know I

want you to do right, and I would not have you shirk
your duty, or what you think to be your duty, for anything in the world. When you first thought of going you
know I was half sorry that Papa discouraged you from
doing so. Now, it seems as if he must have been a prophet
and have foreseen this very day. I have just read over
your letter where you tell me what he told you—that
Kansas was at best only an outpost, and if there was to
be a great conflict between freedom and slavery it would
not be fought out by little squads of partisan rangers
fighting and plundering on the prairie. Cannot you recall his language and see if it is not as true now as
then? If you think you ought to go, and your father desires it, of course you must pay no heed to what I say. I
am only a weak-hearted school-girl. Besides that you
know I—I am in love, and don't want you to go away just
when I am coming home. It has been an age since I saw
you, and nothing less.

"I hate to speak of it, Marty, dear, but—you won't be
angry, will you? Didn't you—it seems as if you wrote that
you did—or maybe it was he—didn't you give Papa your
word of honor that you would not engage in this Kansas
melée, or trouble, whatever it is? You know he is a
Southerner, though he does hate slavery so awfully, and
is very punctilious about any agreement made on honor.
What shall I tell him, Martin, dear, if he says to me
'Hilda, your betrothed promised me on his honor not to
do this thing, and yet has done it, and done it in my absence, too?' You must tell me how to answer him, because
my father even must not impeach in my hearing the honor
of my husband that is to be. I will uphold his honor as
I would have him defend mine—even with life itself. ·

"Good-by, my dearly beloved. Give my love and duty to
your parents, and implore them to grant my requests so
far as they may count it right to do so, and no farther.
May Heaven bless and guide you is the constant prayer of
your   HILDA.

"P. S.—Do not think I pity the slave or hate slavery any less than I always have done; but it seems to me that— that it is hard to tell just what is being done or ought to be done in Kansas. They tell horrible stories about 'Old Brown,' as he is called. I don't believe they can be true; but it seems to me very hard to tell how many patriots there are and how many freebooters, even among the 'Free State men.' Some of those we call the best men in Kansas say that John Brown is hardly any better than the worst. They say that he burns and pillages and even kills unarmed people in the night-time. I do not expect that men placed as they are—fighting against the law for what they believe to be right—can always be blameless; but it would hurt me terribly, Martin—I think, indeed, it would kill me—if there should be any doubt about the righteousness and honorableness of any act that might be attributed to you either directly or indirectly.   H."

Harrison Kortright was lying on a couch in the best room of the tidy little hotel that had succeeded the Drovers' Wayside Home which once stood at the Skendoah cross-roads. Mrs. Kortright sat at the head of the couch, and Martin sat near the fireplace opposite the foot. He still held the letter in his hand, and his flushed face showed that its contents had touched him deeply. The early winter evening had come suddenly on, and the wood-fire lighted up the group.

"Well, father," said Mrs. Kortright anxiously, "what do you think of what Hilda writes?"

Mr. Kortright turned his eyes from the fire, on which they had rested, to his son's face.

"She is a brave girl," he said.

"And a good one," added his wife.

Martin's face flushed with pleasure.

"A brave girl and a good girl," repeated the father slowly, "and has a way of thinking for herself that isn't altogether common. I'm glad of it, too, and glad she is going to be Martin's wife. She'll make a daughter you'll always be proud of, Mattie."

Tears sprang to the son's eyes, and the mother leaned over and kissed the pale brow of her husband. There was a suppressed moan as he shifted his position a trifle, and continued, not noticing the caress:

"She shows the right spirit. Any one can see that she is just as honest as the day. Marriage won't make a particle of difference with her. She has begun to be a wife already, and no more thinks of separating her interest or her life from Martin's than if they had lived together for ten years."

"Well, so they have, pretty nearly," said Mrs. Kortright, smiling.

"That is so," responded he, "and we have almost forgotten that they were growing up. I am afraid I was a little hasty in urging Martin to go, but it's just as well. I've been so given to having my own way that it's time I learned that Martin is not a boy any longer, but a man, who must act for himself. We are right betwixt two generations—on the divide, as you may say. We haven't finished our work exactly, and he hasn't begun his. We must go on in the old way, but he must take his own way and cut out the channel in which his life must flow. As it was our duty to keep him with us up to this point, so it is now our duty to let him go. You must decide this matter for yourself, my son," he added, reaching forth his hand, "and write Hilda what you will do. Let me know your decision in the morning."

The son shook his father's hand, and was about to withdraw from the room, when the landlord rapped at the door, and said that Mr. Clarkson wished to know if Mr. Kortright was able to see him on a matter of importance.

"Of course—of course; let him come in," said Kortright, resuming at once his usual alert and eager manner.

"I must beg pardon for troubling you at such an unseemly hour," said Clarkson, entering at once, "but—"

"No excuses," said Kortright, with brusque courtesy. "Jared Clarkson can never come where Harrison Kortright is, at a wrong time."

"Thanks," said Clarkson, taking his hand with a tender heartiness that testified better than words could have done his thoughtful remembrance of his friend's affliction. "I would not have come at this time, but the business that brings me will not admit delay."

"Something about our Kansas boys, I suppose," said Kortright.

"No; it affects especially you and me," was the reply.

"Is it anything private?" asked Mrs. Kortright, rising as if to retire.

"No, no," said Clarkson hastily. "Pray be seated, ma'am. It affects us all. I am only doubtful as to whether I ought to tell you, in your present condition, Kortright."

"It is bad news, then."

"Very sad news, indeed."

"Brown? Has he—?" asked Kortright, with a look of quick intelligence.

"It has nothing to do with Brown," said Clarkson, smiling in spite of his grave mission. "I have not heard from him in a long time. But I received a telegram to-day which—well, read it for yourself."

He drew a dispatch from his pocket and handed it to Kortright as he spoke.

"Let me light the lamp," said Mrs. Kortright, rising as she spoke, and taking from the mantel a glass lamp filled with camphene, which she placed upon the table, and, removing the extinguishers from the wicks, lighted with a match. Meantime Kortright had held the telegram up to the firelight and read ·

"JARED CLARKSON, Esq., Rockboro :

"Deliver testament. Executor must act at once. Testator dead.　　　　　　　　　　　　　　M. B."

It bore date from a Southern city.

"Well," said he, with a puzzled look, "what does it mean ?"

"It means that I must deliver this into your hands," said Clarkson, handing him a folded document.

"And this— ?" asked Kortright, beginning to open it confusedly.

"That is the will of Merwyn Hargrove, in which you are named executor," said Clarkson impressively.

"And Captain Hargrove ?" queried the sick man anxiously.

"Is dead !" responded Clarkson.

CHAPTER XXXII.

POSSESSIO PEDIS.

DEATH is a fact that never becomes common. No period of hourly apprehension makes us ready for the announcement. Come when it will, it brings a tremor of surprise. Like the crash of thunder near at hand, or the rumble of the earthquake, one is never quite prepared to hear it. It may not alarm nor even startle, but it always hushes. There are, however, instances in which it is heard with a peculiar thrill. We expect the old to die and the young to live as a universal rule. The demise of those who have long been afflicted with disease or are of peculiarly frail and weakly habit is, of course, regarded as more probable and therefore is less startling than that of the active and strong. The temperament of the decedent, too, is a distinct element in the effect that death produces. There are men who are neither young nor vigorous, but whom we never associate with the idea of death until the fact stares us in the face, and we wonder at it. We are never able to realize that they are not as they always have been. We are forever thinking of them as alive, and recalling with a start our error. Such a man was Merwyn Hargrove. He was not especially robust, but his life for years had been one unvarying round of re-duplicated days. What yesterday had been with him, to-morrow was sure to be again. His personality was self-sustaining. He neither leaned upon his neighbors nor held them up. He neither talked of himself nor listened when another broached the subject. Griefs and pleasures were alike to him so far as others were concerned. He had become a fixture, as it were, in the eyes of all who knew him. He did not come very close to their lives, but yet he did not drop out of them, and there was probably no one in that whole region whose life seemed so much a matter of course as that of Merwyn Hargrove. There was an amazement, therefore, that for a time forbade any speech on the part of the little group who heard Mr. Clarkson's announcement. Kortright looked steadily at the speaker. His wife, after the first start, watched her husband carefully, as if to note the effect of this unexpected news upon him. Martin stood at the foot of the bed transfixed with horror. Mr. Kortright at length spoke, holding up the telegram as he did so.

"You think there is no mistake?"

"I am very sure there is none."

"This ' M. B.'—who is he?"

"Matthew Bartlemy, Captain Hargrove's attorney in the South."

"You have no idea how or when— ?"

"You know all that I do."

"You say I am the executor?"

"Yes."

"What do you suppose this man wishes me to do?"

"I am aware that Captain Hargrove anticipated a struggle in regard to his property, and it is probable that the object of this haste is to have you enter into possession in order that you may the better hold for his devisees."

"I will do it," said the sick man, with his accustomed decisiveness. "What is the first thing to be done?"

"We will offer the will for probate as soon as possible," said Clarkson; "but it is better that you should take possession immediately. Bartlemy evidently fears a hostile entry."

"Martin shall go to Sturmhold to-night, and I will follow to-morrow. Will that do?"

"That is the very best that can be done," answered Clarkson. "Captain Hargrove certainly made no mistake in choosing you for his executor," he added as he nodded approval.

"Merwyn Hargrove has a right to command me and mine, whether alive or dead," said Kortright with emotion. "Martin," he added, "you must make no delay."

"But, father," said Martin hesitantly, "do you remember—there is Hilda—ought we not to inform her of this?"

"True; I had forgotten," said Kortright thoughtfully. Clarkson looked quickly from one to the other.

"Hilda," said Mrs. Kortright, noticing this look of inquiry, "Captain Hargrove's daughter, is to be Martin's wife."

"I ought to go for her at once," said Martin.

"Better wait till we are sure," said Kortright cautiously.

"You may serve her even better by going to Sturmhold," added Clarkson with sympathetic assurance.

Martin still hesitated.

"Do not seek to be the bearer of evil tidings, my son," said his mother. "Let Hilda be happy as long as she may."

"I will do as you wish," said Martin, with evident reluctance, "though I think she ought to know of this and come here at once."

How true is love's prescience!

An hour later Martin was on his way to Sturmhold, full of sad forebodings.

CHAPTER XXXIII.

A NINETEENTH CENTURY BUCCANEER.

THE next day the air was full of rumors. Captain Hargrove was dead and 'Squire Kortright was his executor. That everybody in Skendoah knew. The manner of Hargrove's death was variously guessed. It was believed that in some way or other slavery was answerable for this, as well as the burning of the mills. There were especially strange reports in regard to Sturmhold—its young mistress, and poor Madame Eighmie, as the crazy woman was called in the neighborhood. There was talk of kidnappers and fire-eaters and violence.

"They'd better not be tryin' any of them tricks," said the old man Shields. "'Tain't so long since the Anti-Rent war here, that the people of these parts have forgot to take care of themselves, and their neighbors, too. The fact on 't is there 's been just about as much man-stealing and land-stealing done in this region as we care about sitting still and looking on at. I 'm an old man, but if any nigger-hunter comes into this country a-tracking after a runaway or a stayaway, I 'm ready to be one of a crowd that 'll give him all the pond-water he 'll care about takin' aboard at a time."

He was not alone in these sentiments. A company of citizens waited on Mr. Kortright as he was about to enter his carriage to be driven to Sturmhold, and offered to watch the premises night after night, in turn, as long as he might think a guard necessary. It was even reported that suspicious movements had been observed about the place during the previous night by

Martin. That young man did not return, as his parents had expected, but sent a short note of excuse by one of the servants. This fact troubled Harrison Kortright, and hastened his departure. He declined, however, the good offices of his neighbors, and only arranged for the man who had been watchman at the mill to go with him to Sturmhold and remain for a short time.

One of the New York papers received that day contained the following :

"A DOUBTFUL RUMOR.

"There is a report of a wholesale kidnapping affair upon the coast of Carolina, in which a well-known citizen of one of our interior counties is said to have lost his life. Great excitement is reported in that region, and the affair is denounced as an 'Abolition outrage' of unprecedented magnitude. The tendency to exaggeration on the part of the 'chivalry' in regard to anything affecting in the remotest degree the 'peculiar institution,' leads us to anticipate that this will prove to be a great stir over a very small matter. It may even prove to be a flurry started to cover up one of those knife and pistol affairs to which Southern hospitality so often appeals when the Northern creditor goes there to enforce his demand. At all events we shall refrain from further comment until we obtain fuller information."

Another referred to it under the heading

"A QUEER COMPLICATION.

"The report comes from Washington that a special messenger from the governor of one of the Southern States arrived in that city yesterday, and laid before the President a request that he would dispatch at once a swift-sailing man-of-war to intercept a schooner that cleared from this port, about ten days ago, for Kingston and San Domingo via Newbern, Wilmington and Charleston. It seems that instead of touching at either of these ports, or proceeding on her voyage, the schooner hove to, somewhere off Hatteras, and took on board some forty or fifty slaves which were brought outside the bar and transferred to the schooner by a fast-sailing yacht which is well known in this harbor and up and down the Hudson. It is supposed that the intention is to take the slaves to Hayti, or, perhaps, to one of the British West Indies, for the purpose of freeing them. The President referred the matter to the Attorney-General, and the Secretary of the Navy was ordered to have a vessel in readiness should it be decided to attempt the pursuit. It is not probable that anything will be done, as it is not thought that the government has any power to act in the premises.

"The *Sea Foam* is reported to have passed up the river last night, but this is not credited. It is rumored that she has been engaged in such kidnapping excursions along the rivers and sounds of that region before. Her owner is said to have been outlawed and a price set upon his head for seducing slaves to run away, more than a year ago. It is generally believed that the whole story is a canard, and intended as a set-off to the absurd stories of Southern outrage in Kansas."

That evening Jared Clarkson drove over to Sturmhold. Harrison Kortright was on a couch in the library. His wife was with him when Clarkson was admitted. Kortright gave him a swift glance as they shook hands, and said in a calm, steady tone :

"It is true, then ?"

"Too true."

"You have learned the particulars ?"

"I have a letter from Mr. Bartlemy," said Clarkson, taking it from his pocket.

"Wait a moment," said Kortright. "I want Martin to hear it. He will have to act for me in this matter, and I want he should know it all. I can only lie here and plan. He must do the work."

Mrs. Kortright withdrew while he was speaking and

soon returned with their son. Martin had a troubled, anxious look as he shook hands with Clarkson and sat down beside his father's couch. Mr. Clarkson, with the delicate sense of perception which always characterizes men of his temperament, recognized at once the development which a single night of suffering had wrought in the young man's nature. His tone revealed respect and consideration as he said:

"I have a letter from Mr. Bartlemy which I was about to read."

Martin bowed and Clarkson continued:

"It is written from Richmond, Virginia."

"My Dear Sir : I have just reached this point, having come here post-haste in order that I might communicate with you without awakening suspicion. I learned of the death of your friend and my client, Captain Hargrove, just before leaving home. He was killed two days ago in an attempt to remove the slaves of his late brother, George Eighmie, from Mallowbanks, the plantation formerly belonging to the said Eighmie. You will probably learn the particulars as soon as I, through the public press. I am so well informed as to the purposes of the heirs of Eighmie—who may also prove to be Hargrove's heirs, though they are only of the half blood—that I think we should take immediate measures to prevent their stealing a march on us by taking possession of the premises at Sturmhold. If you carry out my instructions as given by telegraph, Mr. Kortright will be on the ground before you get this, and I judge him to be a man not easily frightened or driven."

A smile came over Clarkson's face as he read the old lawyer's estimate of the man before him. Kortright's pale face flushed a little as he said:

"He did not know his letter would find me as I am."

"I don't think he would have changed his opinion if he had," said Clarkson. Then he read on:

"Nevertheless—and this I want you to impress upon him seriously—he must keep a sharp watch. Our Southern people have not in all respects the same regard for the mere forms of law as you of the North, and Gilman has a long head. In the fight they intend to make, possession of the realty in your state would be of the utmost importance. So too is the discovery and identification of Lida's children. I have just learned that the boy Hugh ran away from his master, who lives near Harper's Ferry in this state, some three or four years ago. He had a peculiar livid scar that looks like a cut, extending from the nose almost back to the ear on the right side of his face."

"Oh, Mr. Clarkson," exclaimed Mrs. Kortright, "do you remember the young fugitive that was rescued from the jail?"

"Sure enough," said Clarkson with a start. "The description fits him exactly."

"And Lida—" said Mrs. Kortright. "You remember how she ran after the carriage, calling out, 'My baby! my boy!'"

"And we thought her crazed," said Clarkson bitterly, as he rose and walked back and forth across the room. "Oh, vile and terrible institution, what evil hast thou not to answer for—a lost child, a crazed mother! How long, O Lord, how long?"

There was a moment's silence. The veins stood out on Clarkson's brow, and his hand was clenched with the excitement of his thought. His eyes burned so fiercely, when they flashed upon the auditors without seeing them, that it seemed as if there might be danger of his own mind losing its proper balance.

After a time, Kortright said quietly:

"Well, what more has Mr. Bartlemy to say?"

Clarkson at once resumed his reading:

"The girl I think we shall not find it hard to discover. By the way, if Unthank, Hargrove's body servant, turns up in that region, by all means keep him in concealment, but do not lose track of him. Even if we are unable to use him as a witness, his information will be indispensable to us. He is the only one living who really knows anything about Hargrove's life for the last twenty years. But don't let him be seen about there under any circumstances—at least until after you hear from me again. By the way, I learned while hunting for the boy Hugh that the man who owned him has the only one of Unthank's children whom he has not managed to run off. This may help you to keep him in sight if you let him know it."

"My God!" exclaimed Clarkson. "How heartless slavery makes the best of men!" Then he resumed his reading:

"I am going direct to Mallowbanks to-day, and will attend to the burial of our friend and whatever else needs to be done there. Do not relax your vigilance, and tell Kortright he must not leave the plantation for an hour until the danger is past. It would be better if he did not leave the house. Those who are against us are very determined men. We will teach them, however, that they can't fool with a client of Matthew Bartlemy or I'm mistaken. I've got my heart set on straightening out this tangle, and I'm going to do it, if I live long enough, even if I have to give up all the rest of my practice. Bob Gilman shall not have a chance to brag that he has got around the old man, if there's any way to circumvent him. I leave in an hour.

"Yours hastily,

"MATTHEW BARTLEMY."

There was a moment's silence, when Kortright remarked:

"Is that all?"

"No," answered Clarkson; "I have a copy of the *Clayburn Register*. I only glanced over it hastily on my way here. It contains a full account of the killing of Captain Hargrove. Shall I read it?" he asked, glancing at Mrs. Kortright.

"Of course," answered Kortright for himself. "We must know it all some time, and the sooner the better."

Clarkson glanced down the column and said:

"There is no need to read the head-lines. It was evidently a godsend to the editor, and he makes the most of it. It is a horrible tale as he tells it. This is what he says:

•   "A STARTLING OCCURRENCE.

"We stop the press to insert a hurried and imperfect account of the most infamous abolition outrage ever perpetrated on the soil of a Southern state. The people of Clayburn county have long been aware that a renegade born upon her soil, but for many years a resident of a Northern state, had become one of the most dangerous and pestiferous of that gang of nigger-stealing fanatics who seem to have no purpose in life except to disturb the peace and harmony of Southern society. This man, himself born a slaveholder, and of a family noted for cruelty and harshness to their slaves, became by accident the executor of an eccentric half-brother, whose will has for many years been a subject of litigation in the courts of the state. Almost a generation of lawyers have passed away since Eighmie *vs.* Hargrove was first entered upon the docket. Several minor suits have grown out of it, all of which would probably have been dismissed for want of prosecution, since the heirs of George Eighmie were also the natural heirs of Merwyn Hargrove, had they not learned that it was the intention of the latter not only to divert the property entirely from his family and bestow it upon the base-born children of a mulatto woman, with whom his testator sustained illicit relations, but also to deprive them of a chance of recovering it at his death by freeing and removing the slaves. Already the plantation of Mallowbanks had suffered severely in its productive capacity by the loss of about one-fourth of the requisite working force, which Hargrove had freed and colonized at the North. Although he is reported to be a man of large means, it was evident to every one that no estate could stand such wholesale depletion as he contemplated, and yet be sufficient to reimburse the heirs for losses sustained through his misfeasance. Under these circumstances an injunction was obtained to prevent his removing the slaves during the pendency of the litigation. This was some two or three years ago, and he has shown no inclination to carry out his original purpose until a few months ago circumstances that came to the knowledge of the claimants put them on their guard, and they arranged to have Mr. Alfred Iddings, a poor but respectable man, who lives on an adjoining plantation, keep watch of matters at Mallowbanks, and let them know of any attempt to remove the slaves, or, in fact, of the coming of Hargrove. It should be stated that about two years ago Hargrove was indicted for kidnapping and seducing slaves to run away from their masters; and, in accordance with the law, as he constantly evaded arrest, coming and going in the night time, on his swift-sailing yacht, the *Sea Foam*, he was formally outlawed by the proper authority. The claimants were determined to assert their rights at all hazards, and were fully sustained by the popular sentiment of the vicinage, which was kept in a constant state of alarm by this descendant of old Hargrove of Hargrove's Quarter, who seemed to have inherited all the thieving propensities of his buccaneer ancestor.

"Nothing came of these precautions, however, until this morning about three o'clock, when Mr. Iddings, being awakened by the barking of his dogs, became aware of some unusual stir about the negro quarter at Mallowbanks. The morning being foggy, he could not at first make out what it was, but running along the path that skirts the shore he soon came to the inlet, where he found the *Sea Foam*, with her sails furled and an armed desperado sitting in the stern, evidently awaiting the arrival of some one on shore. The moon was at the full, and Iddings was able to see everything upon the deck as plain as if it had been midday. For a little while he was thoroughly astonished. Then he thought that if the craft was there the master of it could not be far off. Stealing back along the path, he ran quickly through the corn-fields to the house of Major Sherwood Eighmie, one of the claimants. As soon as Iddings communicated what he had seen to Major Eighmie, that gentleman seized his conch and blew a blast that awakened the whole neighborhood. The coming of the yacht had been foreseen, and upon Major Eighmie giving the signal agreed on, all the gentlemen of the neighborhood seized their arms and started for the landing. About this time a fire was seen in the direction of Mallowbanks, and the general belief was that the crowd of ruffians, with Hargrove at their head, had pillaged and fired the Eighmie homestead. Shots were heard in the direction of the landing, and also of the house. Owing to the fog, and the uncertainty as to the number of the marauders, it was necessary to advance upon them with caution. It was, therefore, some considerable time before the band of armed neighbors reached the fire, which they found to be not at the mansion, but at the negro quarters, which had been deserted and set on fire. When this fact was ascertained, the whole infamous plan burst on the minds of the pursuers. It was a great kidnapping scheme! The negroes had been partly corrupted and partly coerced into flight. At once a cry was raised, 'To the landing! To the landing!' Major Eighmie called upon them to follow him, and the enraged neighbors responded promptly to his appeal. They started down the path to the landing, but had not advanced more than a hundred yards when a perfect volley was fired at them out of a clump of wood that intervened between them and the inlet. The bullets that whistled over them showed that Hargrove had a strong and well-armed party to aid him in his nefarious enterprise. The citizens then advanced carefully, firing every time they caught a glimpse of the enemy. At length they reached

AT BAY.

Unthank, raising his gun, drew a bead on the advancing party, but Hargrove forbade him to fire.—p. 409.

the brow of the hill above the landing just as the fog
lifted and a sharp breeze sprang up from the west. There
was the yacht, with every stitch of canvas set, loaded to
the gunwale with frightened negroes, who were crying
piteously at being driven away from their home and
friends. The wind filled the sails and straightened the
hawser, that was fastened to a tree on the bank. Half way
down the slope was Unthank, the desperate negro villain,
who has served Hargrove as his body-servant for twenty
years, and who has been his confederate and agent in all
his recent villanies, supporting his master, who was evidently wounded. The yacht was hardly twenty steps
away, and the black scoundrel was making desperate
efforts to get him aboard. Hargrove was perfectly helpless. He must have been wounded somewhere about the
spine, as he seemed unable to use his limbs at all, though
he was quite conscious and able to use his hands very
freely, as he afterwards showed. The neighbors at once
opened fire on the precious pair. Hargrove looked around,
and, seeing that escape was hopeless, spoke a few words
to the negro. A black-bearded scoundrel, who stood in
the stern of the yacht with a knife raised ready to cut
the rope, called out to them to make haste. Unthank
laid his master on the ground at the foot of a large water-
oak, and raising his gun drew a bead on the advancing
party. Hargrove, however, forbade him to fire, and taking
a packet from his bosom gave it to him and ordered
him aboard the yacht. The negro refused to obey. Hargrove again commanded him to go. Upon his refusing a
second time, Hargrove ordered the man in the stern to
cut loose. The rascal did so without waiting for further orders. Unthank, seeing it was his last chance, ran
down the slope and jumped from the landing just as the
yacht swung out into the wind. The neighbors rushed
forward to prevent the escape of the slaves, but before
they had advanced ten steps were fired upon by Hargrove.
As he was known to be a desperate villain and was un-

doubtedly well armed, besides being protected by the tree, it was not a safe matter to advance upon him without cover. While those in front fired upon him steadily, some others of the party crawled through a little belt of bushes above where he lay and sent a bullet crashing through his skull. He was undoubtedly saving his fire, expecting a rush to be made on him in front. Strangely enough none of the attacking party were hurt, though Hargrove is known to have been the best rifle-shot ever seen in these parts. By that time the day had broken, and the yacht was dancing over the water before a twelve-knot breeze half a mile away.

"It was discovered afterward that the *Sea Foam* had a consort outside the bar to which her cargo was transferred. She had evidently made one or two trips before the one on which she was discovered, as more than fifty slaves are missing from the plantation. Documents that were found upon the person of this daring robber show that he intended to remove every slave at Mallowbanks. It is perhaps but fair to say that he claimed these slaves not as executor but as legatee under the will of his half-brother. The court was unable to try the question of his right by reason of his refusal to come forward and reply to the interrogatories of the complainant. Being a non-resident the court had no jurisdiction over him except to enjoin him from removing the property. The neighbors were so enraged that the dead body was treated somewhat roughly, until the overseer at Mallowbanks took it in charge. The coroner has been informed, and a jury will probably be impaneled who will thoroughly examine into the affair. Major Sherwood Eighmie starts North to-day to take steps to secure remuneration from the estate of the dead kidnapper for the loss sustained. The community. are probably indebted to him for ridding the coast of a most dangerous enemy. It is said that the deceased was such an insatiable negro lover that he took his brother's favorite wench and her mulatto children to his palatial home among the Catskills and introduced them into the selectest circles of Northern Abolition society as his own wife and daughter!

"This is altogether the most daring piece of villany the abolitionists have yet attempted. The recent expulsion from our soil of the Massachusetts attorney who came to the state expressly to gain a residence in order to test some points of our slave code before the Federal courts, must now be recognized as a wise and prudent measure. The letter of the law is not always to be relied upon. Perhaps, under the circumstances, the act in which Hargrove was engaged would not be held to be a felony, but it was certainly very natural that men who saw themselves about to be robbed by an armed marauder should not be over-nice in their conduct toward him. A number of shots are said to have taken effect upon him, and it would probably be impossible to ascertain who fired the one that actually caused his death. There was nothing found upon his body to implicate any other parties in his act. Indeed, there was an explicit disclaimer, and a declaration written in his own hand, and dated the day before, affirming that he only did it in the assertion of his lawful ownership of the property. No reliance can be put on the declarations of such an outcast from decent society, and it is exceedingly improbable that it is true. The whole body of abolitionists of the North are undoubtedly responsible for this invasion of our soil and violation of our rights. We counsel our people to exercise moderation, but vigilance. Every Yankee craft that comes into our waters should be thoroughly overhauled for stowaways, and not one should ever be allowed to leave her moorings without being so thoroughly fumigated as to drive out or kill every living thing under her hatches. The South must protect itself and its institutions against the envy and greed of Northern hypocrites and fanatics."

So the descendant of the buccaneer, who had risked his life in planting slavery in the colony, was slain in the attempt to restore the children of those slaves to freedom.

As the people of Skendoah attributed their misfortune to slavery, as an ultimate cause, so the citizens of Clayburn county accounted the abolition fanaticism the disturber of their peace. Distrust was paving the way for strife.

CHAPTER XXXIV.

A CHANGE OF BASE.

THE time had come when he who should untie the Gordian knot of slavery was to appear. Thousands of the best and bravest had grappled with the problem in vain. Many a gallant knight had graven "Liberty" upon his helm only to find himself sooner or later doing battle for slavery. The high and the low had been baffled. What seemed at the beginning an insoluble enigma had grown daily more intricate and difficult. Slavery, which had grown from a little speck to cover half the political horizon, had from the first falsified all theories. Instead of dying it had flourished; instead of losing strength it had gained power; instead of yielding to the sentiment of the world it openly defied it. It ruled not only the states where it existed, but those which fattened on its results. The great industries of the North consumed its raw material and supplied its demand for manufactured articles and bowed to its behests. Cotton was king, and slavery was the suzerain of cotton. In pride, in power, in wealth, it had grown with every decade stronger and stronger, until now it seemed that the nation was under its absolute control. The sentiment of the North had grown year by year more pronounced, and the opposition to slavery more and more determined, yet the way to its extirpation seemed hourly to grow more difficult, and the desired end to be farther and farther away. Before the wave of sentiment uprose forever the barrier of the Constitution. The fundamental law of the nation's life stood between slavery and the onslaught of its foes.

Amendment in the manner prescribed was hopeless.
Around or behind this instrument there seemed to be
no feasible method of going. To trample it under foot
was to destroy the nation based upon it. The life of
the Republic was pledged for the life of slavery. "The
irrepressible conflict" still held on its triumphant way
in the hearts of the American people, but none could
see any way to victory. Some there were who demanded
the forcible removal of the obstacle. One man who had
not ceased to declare for many years that only blood
could wash away the evil was preparing to make good
his prophecy. He looked forward to a day when the
slave should win his way to freedom by force. There
were many who agreed with him that there was no
other method. Some listened to his plans and vaguely
indorsed his designs. To many they were partially disclosed, but none knew their details. He had one
thought only: slavery must be destroyed. He cared
little for the Constitution, or the nation builded thereon.
Laws, customs and institutions were nothing to him;
only the men who were subject to them were sacred in
his eyes. For him the universe held but two facts—
God, who created all things, and man, made in His
image. That slavery was an evil was all he needed to
know. That it was doomed to destruction was, by the
mere fact of its unholiness, rendered certain beyond
question to his mind. How it should be destroyed he
he did not know—he did not care. That men should
die in compassing its destruction he did not doubt;
whether one or ten or millions it mattered not. He
counted liberty as part of the revealed Word, which
he devoutly believed, and to him it was of infinitely less
moment that men should die than that its lightest syllable should fail. So, too, while he lived for humanity,
he thought it far better that a nation or a race even
should perish from the face of the earth than that they

should live to suffer wrong. Righteousness and wrong were his two abstractions. To overcome the one was to do the other. He regarded the nation only as a means for achieving a specific end. If the end was not completely achieved he thought the instrument should be at once discarded. On the plains of Kansas, in the swamps of the South, among the snows of the Adirondacks, and in the mountains of Virginia, he thought of but one thing—how he might redeem the slave from the wrong of servitude. Without selfishness or malice or greed, hating with undying bitterness the sin of slavery, he could see no obstacle in the way of liberation of the slaves, except the insincerity and inertness of the people. John Brown represented one extreme of thought. Few even of those who agreed with him had the courage and self-denial to adopt the methods he espoused. He represented the sentiment of the most active and ultra portion of the anti-slavery element. The destruction of slavery at once and at all hazards was their controlling motive. These people had done the better portion of the work of awakening public sentiment upon this question. They were the pioneers without being the leaders of popular belief. There was little need, at the time of which we write, of laboring to convince the Northern masses of the desirability of the result they desired to accomplish. How to obtain it without overthrowing the national fabric was the sole question.

It is a strange fact, and shows a queer phase of our American character, that many of those who were willing to violate the statute law in aiding the fugitive slave, who would even imperil life and liberty in securing for the bondman the means to escape, and were ready to defend and protect him in such unlawful acts, no sooner perceived that a movement involved the subversion of the Constitution, or actual defiance of its authority, than they at once refused all connection therewith. They were willing to violate the law—to become felons, perhaps, but they could not contemplate with composure the abrogation of the great contract that constitutes the charter of our liberties. Of these there were very many. It mattered not how deep their conviction of the right of liberty and the evil of slavery, they were ready to endure the evil a while longer rather than antagonize the basis principles of our Constitution by assailing the citadel of the state's right, within which slavery was entrenched. This was the feeling of the great mass of the people. The fanatics, who were ready and willing to do and dare anything, were few, very few, in comparison. It was evident that only an absolute conviction of the direst necessity for such a course would induce the American people even to put itself on guard against the institution of slavery. To move against it openly was regarded as treason; to combine against it secretly was accounted sedition.

Besides all this, and after all that could be said, no matter how deep their abhorrence might be, there were very many people of the North who excused their inaction by the declaration :

"It is not a matter for us to consider. The sin of Slavery does not lie at our doors, nor the danger. The institution belongs to the South. Our hands are clean. If they desire to invite the curse it must entail, well and good. We cannot hinder them."

Many strove to overthrow this delusion and prove that every man of the North was, morally, at least, responsible for the act of his fellow-citizen of the South. But in this they made little progress, as it seemed, until there came one to whose homely sentences the people listened as if he spake by inspiration. So clear and cogent were his reasons that no one gave him credit for uttering any new truths. They seemed so plain and simple

that the dullest listener conceived that he only heard
a re-statement of his own thought. He was a man
born of the people, as are all in whom the spirit of the
Deliverer dwells. From Mary's son till now the Messi-
anic spirit has ever appeared beneath the lowliest
lintel. The Deliverer comes always from the plain.
The middle class—above the abject poor, and below the
soul-dwarfed rich—is that which gives the world the men
that overturn its institutions, relieve its people from
the bondage of their past and open the gateway of the
future. The greatest of our mighty men was one who
stood among us in such simple guise that even those
who sat at meat with him dreamed not of his greatness.

By birthright he was of the South, and, as such,
cursed by its destiny. Father and mother, smitten
by poverty and ignorance, dwelt in the shadow of
the Kentucky "knobs." The destiny of the "poor-
white" brooded over their united lives. Slavery which
made few rich and many poor counted them among
its victims. The shame which passed by the slave
because of his irresponsibility, lighted on the freeman,
compelled, like him, to toil. So that labor became
a badge of degradation; and need, which elsewhere was
the spur to increased endeavor, there became only a
whip to sting and to debase. Labor was degenerated
into a badge of servitude—the mark of a subverted manhood. Only idleness was honorable. He whose hand
was forced to toil for self-support was kindred to the
slave and even less esteemed. Even the slave's contempt was visited on such. "Poor-white!" How the
name stuck and stung and dragged downwards! What
a world of humiliation in its two syllables! Com-
miseration, contempt—despair! "White trash!" Ex-
pressive synonym! The fringe of a race of princes!
The débris of a people whose prerogative it was to rule,

and whose distinctive privilege it was to be served by
another. It was a sad estate, full of shame and self-
abasement, and all the more degrading because their
only pride lay in the fact that they were allied in blood
to the class who ruled and contemned them. Such was
the genesis of the Deliverer. The poor-white birth-
mark was his sole inheritance.

Yet not in his own person did he feel this degradation. Across the narrow river that skirts "the dark
and bloody ground" upon the Northward, a younger
sister state, with a happier destiny, had been established. His Bethlehem was on the Sangamon. Yet the
brand of the "poor-white" was stamped upon his soul.
Poverty and ignorance and hopelessness rocked his
cradle. Laughter and tears were strangely mingled in
his nature. Little by little he came to know himself.
More than thirty years he served before he knew that
he had a mission to perform. He was always a dreamer.
He did not fast in the desert nor flee to the caverns for
inspiration; but the forest and the stream and the
prairie—silence and solitude and distance—nourished
the dream of power, revealed to him himself. He had
few books and no teachers. Man and nature were the
volumes which he read most easily and studied most
assiduously.

He was not profoundly versed in the lore of the past,
but the facts of the present were indelibly stamped upon
his mind. His philosophy was direct and simple. He
did not waste time in elaborating systems for the future
or reasons for the past. How things came to be as they
were he was at no trouble to explain. What should
be the ultimate outcome of the mixture of good and
evil which we call life, he gave little thought to deter-
mining. The duty of the present and its relations to the
nearer future he perceived with the utmost clearness.

The accident of stature first opened the way to leader-

ship. The desire to be foremost spurred him to renewed
exertion. Slowly he awoke to the knowledge of power.
Uncultured of mind and uncouth of limb, none looked
to him for a leadership in thought. Yet his words were
like winged arrows. He used the simple dialect of the
people, and spoke directly to their hearts.

The peril of the near future rested like a shadow
upon his life. To him the nation was the sum of all
excellence. Flaws in it were like spots in the sunshine.
He revered the Constitution no less than its most devoted worshipper. To him it was the guarantee of all
that made liberty desirable. He hated slavery as an
enemy of the dominant race. He felt himself wronged
through generations by its blight. It was not pity for
the slave that moved him to oppose the system, so
much as dread of the system itself and its paralyzing
and debasing effects upon every grade of society exposed
to its influence. He felt its injustice, not merely to those
who served without reward, but also to those who, by
its influence, were shut out of the struggle of life—the
fair competition for its rewards.

He did not profess to be more profoundly versed in
the philosophy and history of this question than others.
On the contrary, in this respect he followed gladly
where others led. He seconded rather than directed
in any considerable degree the efforts to awaken interest in the character of slavery and to combine the
people of the North in philanthropic movements in
behalf of the slaves. Justice rather than pity marked
his attitude toward them. By the most fanatical he
was even regarded as lukewarm in the cause of which
he was destined to become the one immortal leader and
exemplar. He was no impassioned advocate of mercy.
It was not his mission to deal with the philosophy of the
primary cause or resultant effects of social movements.
The function reserved to him was to perceive with

unequaled clearness the consequence of admitted facts, to impress them upon the popular heart as no one else had ever done, and then to find a way to avoid the peril that impended. Sprung from the people, his reverence for their will and belief in their ultimate decision were so great that he was sometimes deemed a demagogue. He was not one, however, that bowed to the half-formed will of the masses, but one who sought to bring them up to his own conviction — not with reproaches and sneers, not with arrogance and scorn, but with unceasing humility, a never-failing good temper, and a familiarity and sincerity of statement that in the end always won his way to the popular heart. As a philanthropist he was inferior to thousands; as a student of the facts of history and politics he was easily distanced by scores of his contemporaries; as a fervid and impassioned orator he was excelled by many; but as one who realized the peril of the hour and had power to make the voice of the people in very truth the voice of God, he was easily foremost. In capacity to devise a way of escape from peril, and to lead the people willingly and gladly along the narrow path by which alone safety was possible, he was unapproached by any man of his day.

The party representing the anti-slavery idea, which had been based on the declaration that "the repression of slavery" was desirable, recoiled from its first conflict with the slave-power less demoralized by defeat than amazed at the near approach to victory which it had accomplished. Yet this result had been achieved, as we have already shown, more by the accidental co-operation of discordant elements than by the harmonious action of a consolidated and homogeneous party. No sooner had it demonstrated its power than incongruous elements began to develop within it. Not only the strife of ambitious leaders, but the radical divergence of factions animated by mutually antagonistic

impulses, promised not merely to prevent a complete
and stable organization, but also to render futile all
hope of future victory. What was needed was a mor-
dant that should cause all these factions to adhere to a
common purpose—to remain faithful to a common end.
This solvent of hostile ideas was first obtained when the
uncouth backwoodsman was chosen by his party associates to represent them and uphold the principles of the
yet inchoate party in an oratorical conflict with the
subtlest, strongest, ablest of the champions of state sovereignty and the peculiar institution which flourished
under its protection. All unconscious that his words were
the master-key of the situation, Abraham Lincoln rose at
once from an obscurity which is all the more remarkable because it contained no appreciable hint of the
eminence that awaited him, to the very front rank of
his age, when he put forth as the basis of the momentous struggle in which he was about to engage this proposition :

"A house divided against itself cannot stand . . .
The American nation must be all free or all slave."

On that issue the battle was joined anew. From
that hour the conflict was waged on no other ground.
The most fanatical and the most conservative elements
of the free state civilization met here upon a common
level. Thenceforward Abraham Lincoln was the unquestioned leader of the movement for the overthrow of
slavery—the generalissimo of all the forces mustering for
its destruction. For the first time a means had been
found to harmonize all differences of séntiment and secure the utmost unity of purpose and action on the part
of all who were opposed to the "peculiar institution,"
which held in its degrading touch one half the land, and
threatened with its demoralizing influences the other
moiety. The great dilemma—"all free or all slave"—
stared the American people in the face as the unavoid-

able fact of the near future.   To the people of the North it came like a revelation sustained by irrefragable proofs. The disruption of the treaty which the slave-power had itself proposed; the seizure of Kansas through the co-operation of the established government; the Fugitive Slave law, and the aggressions upon personal liberty thereunder, all pointed to the dilemma which this clear-sighted child of the people placed before them for con-sideration.   It needed no argument and admitted of no hesitation.   There was· but one question: If free or slave, which?   In every man's consciousness it became a ceaseless refrain.   To the objection that nothing could be done except through a violation of the Constitution, there was but one answer: "Free or slave?"   There was in this no attack upon the "compact made between the states," or "the sacred pledge which the fathers gave."   It was no appeal to a "higher law," and yet there was no farther room for the excuse: "It is no concern of ours."   "Mason and Dixon's line" was no longer the boundary of evil consequences resulting from slavery.   "All free or all slave" stood at the threshold of every Northern home, and compelled father, brother and son to decide upon the dread alternative before they crossed the lintel.   All who regarded slavery as an evil, an injustice or a sin were by this one thought mar-shaled under the banner of this new leader.   From this text he never swerved.

Undoubtedly the contest between Lincoln and Doug-las was the most momentous oratorical struggle that ever occurred.   Both men were firm believers in the views they advocated, and each represented a new idea. The one idea was a subtle evasion, a specious make-shift, designed to avoid apparent objection to the ex-tension of slavery, and, under the guise of absolute impartiality to all parties, sections and ideas, to render possible its peaceful establishment on the plains of the

West. It was a measure which no Southern champion of slavery could ever have devised. It was noteworthy for its subtle appreciation of the spirit and genius of the North. As a piece of mere political shrewdness it is almost without a parallel in history. Those in whose behalf it was conceived and put forth could only half appreciate its specious strength. Against argument it stood well-nigh impregnable. The distinctions on which it was based were so subtle, its discriminations were so keen, that it was hardly susceptible of popular refutation, except from the standpoint of its consequences. But the proposition which Mr. Lincoln put forth, while offering the most perfect possible reply to the theory of "squatter sovereignty," was also one which put not only the expounder of that doctrine but even the man who was merely tolerant of slavery, on his defense. It was at once a parry and a thrust. It was like a turn of the wrist of the expert swordsman. It seemed so easy that we forgot the power, the skill, the intellect that lay behind its elucidation and its application. It set over against the perils of slavery the blessings of liberty. Through the dread of slavery it impelled, and by the love of liberty it induced co-operation in any movement that should most readily and easily destroy the one and establish the other. It was a trumpet-call that mustered at once all the forces of liberty against the life of slavery.

From that moment all else in the struggle of parties was forgotten. Whether the whole land should be free or slave was the only question worthy of consideration—an issue that overbore all minor differences. The South recognized it as the summons to the last great battle. They perceived the power of the new leader even before his own associates became aware of it. To the latter he was known simply as a valiant soldier who had met the champion of slavery on his chosen field, and in the face of assured defeat had planted deeply and securely the seeds of ultimate victory. They thought of him only as one who, single-handed and alone, had won from the enemy an important stronghold. The chiefs in the anti-slavery movement had no thought of acknowledging him as their leader. Seward and Sumner and Wade and Greeley and Chase and Giddings and Gerrit Smith and Wendell Phillips, and a hundred more almost, would have laughed at the idea of this uncouth child of the prairie stepping up before them and occupying, before all the world and for all time, unquestioned preeminence as "the great Emancipator." Even now the especial admirers of each are fond of putting their names before that of the unpretentious giant of the Sangamon country as leaders in the great anti-slavery conflict. But the force of a blow must be judged by its results, and the power of the man who gives it by the ease with which it is delivered. Judged by this rule, Abraham Lincoln established an unquestioned right to the foremost place as a leader when by a single sentence he made victory not only possible but inevitable—fused a thousand discordant motives into one, and brought the anti-slavery struggle down from the domain of humanitarian theory to the level of tangible universal interest. He discovered nothing, but he transmuted weakness into power.

There are those, too, in whose minds the feats of knight-errantry eclipse the splendor of victories that change the face of history. To such minds the glory of the partisan leader vastly outshines the laurel of the unseen and undemonstrative director of mighty forces. To these the anti-slavery struggle presents as heroes and leaders the names of certain gladiators—combatants of the press and forum, who stimulated public thought, pricked the public conscience and did yeoman work in tearing down the citadel of established dogma. They

were men without whose aid the public sentiment on
which the great strategic movements of the day were
based could never have existed. But having done that
they could do no more. Prophets and forerunners and
pioneers—pathfinders who pointed out the way of liberty
—their day had almost passed—their work had all but
ended when the practical genius of Lincoln combined
the forces they had raised and marshaled them for the
grand assault. To some the bright swords and waving
plumes hid the calm, grave face of the leader.

The South, with surer prescience, saw its enemy afar
off. It recognized the master-stroke aimed at the
corner-stone instead of the outworks of the citadel.
It perceived in him the leader of the grand assault
upon the position which slavery occupied, and stubbornly refused to credit any denial that was made
of the purpose of those who stood with him. When,
shortly afterward, he was made the head of the party
organization, they did not hesitate to consider it a
declaration of war against their pet institution. And
they were right thus far at least. Abraham Lincoln
was chosen to be President because the Republican
party had determined to do all that might be done,
without actual violation of the Constitution, to destroy
slavery. To deny that fact is to re-echo a quibble
which, while it might not be reprehensible in a heated
controversy, is unworthy the attention of the student
of a mighty revolution. It was from an impulse of
self-defense, therefore, that the press and politicians of
the South leveled their batteries of invective, of ridicule, of infamy against him, in the vain hope of de-
stroying him before his power was understood and
appreciated by his friends. So the great, kindly, pure-
hearted Saul became a "monster," a "baboon," a
"clown," a "beast"—all that was infamous and foul,
and remains such to this day to many thousands to

whom his life was a most beneficent providence.   In
nothing did his greatness show more clearly than in
the fact that nothing provoked him to anger, and he
made answer to no aspersion.   Unfaltering in his devotion to the principle that liberty and slavery could not
co-exist, unswerving in his faith in the wisdom and
fidelity of the people, he trod alone the pathway which
his genius first discerned, along dizzy heights, through
fateful fens, in the darkness and in the light; never
going too fast to enable the whole people to follow
his course, and never moving too slow when once assured of the support which was necessary to success;
undaunted by fear and unblinded by ambition, until
the end was reached and his work was accomplished.
Slavery avenged itself through him.   The child of the
"poor-white" of the Kentucky knobs liberated not
the slave only, but those whom the slave had been
made the instrument to degrade.   Not Emancipator
only, but Liberator, will he be hailed when the centuries look back upon him.

It has become the fashion in these later days to look
upon Lincoln as the accident of an accident rather than
as the man of the age—the greatest of all who have
borne the name American.   Little souls who came near
his great life—who viewed his nature as the insect scans
the bark of the oak along the rugate surface of which
he creeps, with a self-satisfied contempt of the rude
strength and solid core that lies within—have been
winning for themselves a sort of immortality and an
infinitude of contempt by trying to paint the man
whose perfections they could never apprehend.   Our
literature has been overrun with a horde of puny
drivelers made purblind by the glory of a life whose
light was so serene and steady that they counted it but
a reflection of the lurid conflict amid which he lived.
It was not because one man schemed or another

paltered that Abraham Lincoln came to the leadership
of the hosts of freedom. Neither was it through the
merit of any or all of his advisers that he succeeded in
accomplishing the task set before him, but chiefly through
his own consummate genius and unmatched power.
It was not luck but intellect that brought him from
obscurity to the forefront of the greatest movement in
history. The men who stood beside him were pigmies
in practical power when compared with him. He was
so great that he needed no padding, and was careless of
his fame. As he came from the people so he left himself fearlessly in their hands. It has been customary,
while admitting his prudence, sagacity and self-control,
to depreciate his intellectual power. The change of
position which he effected by a single phrase, was so
easily done and seemed so evident when once put forth,
that few have stopped to think that the intellect of
Sumner, the prophetic grasp of Seward, the foresight of
Chase and the brain of a thousand others who seemed
his compeers, had been thitherto utterly unable to form-
ulate a common ground of opposition to slavery, which
should commend itself to the mind and conscience
of the people. He alone, of all the men of that time,
had the sagacity to discover the key of the position, to unite all the discordant elements in the attack
upon it, and to hold them up to the conflict until the
victory was won. By that thought he fused all the
discordant elements into one. It was one of those
strokes of power which mark the highest genius. By
this alone he would have established his claim to
rank as much above his associates in intellect as he is
admitted to have stood, in sagacity, devotion and self-
forgetfulness. Standing on a level with the lowliest, he
towered conspicuously above the greatest. Those who
saw the apparent ease with which he achieved these
results only half realized his greatness. Their regard

was dissipated by a thousand insignificant details. Only the future can properly estimate the brain that consolidated the opposition to slavery, held the nation to the work of putting down rebellion, and called his cabinet together only to consider the wording of a proclamation that was to change the status of a race forever. He bestrode our land like a Colossus, all unconscious of his own power, frankly esteeming others at their just value—incapable of detraction or envy, and trusting his fame, with a magnificent unconcern as to the result, to the future. Pure, simple, unassuming, kindly, touched with sadness and relieved with mirth, but never stained with falsehood or treachery, or any hint of shameful act; his heart as tender as his life was grand; he stands in history a little child in his humility, a saint in purity, a king in power. Offspring of the sadly smitten South; nursling of the favored North; giant of the great West—his life was the richest fruitage of the liberty he loved! His name is the topmost which a continent has given unto fame!

CHAPTER XXXV.

BLINDFOLD AND BAREFOOT.

BEECHWOOD SEMINARY stood just without the pur-
lieus of one of the busy little towns that are hidden
among the New England hills. The ceaseless groan
of water-wheels, the breath of wheezing engines, the
hum of lathes, the whir of spindles, the ring of pulsing
hammers and the hiss of glowing forges filled the steep-
sided ravine along which the village was builded. It was
a goblin's cave set in a quiet, peaceful scene. Its people
were slaves who worked for the gnomes of trade. Motion
and force were incarnate in their lives. They wrought
with dull hands magical transformations. Earth became
crystal beneath their touch. The misty fibre that the wind
blew here and there became the snowy web that wrapt the
limbs of beauty or the cable that bade defiance to the
storm. Nature shrunk away from her busy, boastful rival.
Where she had ended her work, science and art began
theirs. They mocked at her tardy processes, and scorned
her incomplete results. They stole her secrets; scattered her treasures; prisoned her forces, and made of
the once silent glen a busy, bustling, throbbing hive of
crowded, wearied, weighted life. On either side the
hills rose sharp and stern. From base to summit they
were clothed with a garment of verdure that even in
winter hid half their ruggedness. The laurel thrust its
contorted limbs across the gray cliffs and softened their
outlines with its verdure. The spruce and hemlock
screened the savageness that the birch and maple would
have left uncovered when the summer departed, so
that the beholder almost wondered that civilization

was content with the narrow stretch which it had conquered for itself along the banks of the boisterous
torrent. Less than a mile away, where the mountain
swept down into a broad plateau, not only overlooking the bustling town but also commanding an outlook up and down one of those noble valleys that the
icy rivers of the north cut through the granite ledges
in their pathway to the steaming sea, stood Beechwood
Seminary. By what chance this glaring three-storied
caravansary, with its green blinds only breaking the
vast parallelograms of white with which it faced the
four cardinal points, came to be located in a spot of
such surpassing loveliness, no man knoweth. It was
just far enough from the town to feel its life, near
enough to the mountain to partake of its solitude,
and high enough above the valley to command all its
beauty. With true Yankee disregard of nature, the
original forest had been cut away in front, and the
grounds of the institution "adorned," the catalogue
said, "with rare and elegant shrubbery"—some stunted
evergreens and a few hardy decidua which clung to the
wind-swept terrace, doubtfully enough in winter, and
leaved and bloomed in summer, weakly and sadly attempting to remedy the violence done to nature in the
silly conventional attempt at improvement. A white
picket fence enclosed the rectangled lawn known as the
seminary grounds. At the back of it, however, nature
had held her own. The quaint old farm-house which
once occupied this classic spot had not been torn away,
but rose up by successive steps from the very midst
of the old orchard, beyond which was a narrow belt of
rocky pasture land skirted by a gray-lichened wall half
hidden under the brown-leaved undergrowth, and above
and beyond the dark resinous woods where the pine
cones and needles lay thick beneath, and the light was
tempered by the inlocked foliage above. Thrift had done

all that could well be done to mar the face of nature, but its beauty still survived.

It was upon this scene that Hilda looked the morning after the events described in our last chapter. She stood at one of the back windows of the seminary and gazed upon the mountain glowing in the sparkling splendor of a wintry morning. The season was a late one, and the snow had not yet come, but glistening rime rested on fence and wall, and transformed the white birch limbs into stems of silver filigree. The blades of grass and the brown leaves which the autumn winds had piled here and there were touched with points of light. The background of evergreens was strengthened by the contrast and enriched by the sharp shadows that the newly risen sun threw over it.

Hilda was now almost eighteen. She had grown lithe and graceful in form, and her girlish impetuosity of manner had been tempered by four years of training at Beechwood. Yet in her great dark eyes was the same unshrinking directness, and her quick decision of movement showed that she had inherited not a little of her father's steadfastness of purpose. Unfailing health had left its matchless impress on her ruddy cheeks, and given to her eyes a light that was almost saucy in the revelation that it made of buoyant vitality. Her soft, liquid eyes glowed with evident enjoyment as she gazed upon the bright scene without, though a far-away look in their depths showed that her thoughts were wandering. Yet the little trace of care that was in them as she glanced out upon the sunlit mountain, was so foreign to her wont that it hardly tempered their vivacious brightness. A rich, warm-tinted morning robe encompassed her shapely figure, and her wealth of soft dark hair was wound in a shining coil behind, save only a fringe of rebellious ringlets that escaped control and clustered about her wide, full brow. There

was a careless ease of manner that told better than words
could, that she had slept on roses. Life had brought
neither trouble nor care. A cloud had appeared on its
horizon, but it was only a little one, and so very far off
that she hardly felt its shadow. There was something
in form and gesture that recalled her father. Bright
and sunny in temperament, she had yet enough of his
thoughtful coolness to constitute a nature not easily
moulded, or likely to be turned aside from a purpose
once conceived.

She had kindled in the open grate a fire of materials
that had been placed ready for her hand the night before
—snowy bits of pine, long, slender splints of creamy ash
and heavy pieces of maple, with closely-curling cones of
rich birch-bark for kindling. The flames roared up the
chimney and awakened her from her revery. She went
and stood before the fire, stretching out her shapely
hands to catch the grateful warmth. Then she drew
back her robe, and held one slippered foot after the other
toward the flame. After a few moments she looked at
her watch, and stepping lightly across the floor to a half-
open door, said softly:

"Amy!"

She listened until she heard the regular breathing of
a sleeper, then glanced quickly within, and, with a
smile, closed the door and withdrew.

"Heigho!" she said, "I do believe I am the only girl
at Beechwood that likes to see the sun rise, and I am
not sure that I would if it did not give me such a nice,
quiet time to write to Martin. Poor fellow!" she added,
"he must be having a very sad time."

She drew a little stand before the fire, and, arranging
her writing materials, sat for a moment gazing at the
bright flames as they leaped up the chimney's black
throat, ere she began to write. This was her greeting—
her orison to her absent lover:

"My Dear Martin : I have risen very early to write to you, for it seems to me that you are anxious and troubled, though I cannot tell why you should be. Surely your father's loss cannot be so very great as to be any good cause, and I cannot think that his illness is really serious—in the sense of danger, I mean. Of course, it is painful and unpleasant, but you will be able to do for him so much more than you would otherwise be allowed to undertake, that you must really enjoy showing him how well and willingly you can serve him. I wish I could be with you, and I would come at once if Papa had not enjoined me to stay until he came to fetch me. Dear Papa, how thoughtful he has always been, and how careful of my happiness! But he will come soon. I know he will, for I have dreamed of him every night for almost a week; and three successive nights, you know, is a *sure* sign, or all the wisdom of the witches goes for nothing. You used to call me a witch, and so cannot deny me the power of divination. It is odd, the repetition of this dream. Every time I see Papa in the stern of the dear old *Sea Foam*. The sails are set; she is standing in through the breakers along a narrow channel. The wind is abeam, brisk but not heavy. The moon is at the full, and makes it as light as day. Papa holds the tiller, and keeps her head in the track the moon makes on the waves. Beyond a narrow point the sea is as smooth as glass, and the glimmer of the moonlight on it is steady and full. It seems as if the *Sea Foam* were going to sail right on into the moon itself. I know the place very well. I have heard Papa and Unthank tell of it so often that I could not fail to know it. It is the old inlet—Hargrove's Inlet—where the buccaneers used to go in and out in the old days. Papa used to say that he was prouder of having found that narrow passage through the breakers, by which his rugged kinsmen used to come and go upon their lawless errands on the main, than almost anything else that he had done. It seems that he and Unthank are the only ones that know

it now, though I have heard him tell the bearings over so
often that I almost think I could take the *Sea Foam* in
there myself.

"That is all there is of it; but every night I see the same
—the brave old boat; the shining, seething sea; my father
holding the tiller as easily as if he guided a toy, and
watching the course with the moonlight shining on his
dear face. I am sure he will come pretty soon, not because I dream about him, but because I think of him so
much. Oh, he is sure to come to me, and then we will
both come to you. I keep my trunk all packed up, so
that there need not be any delay, and twenty times a day
I go over the pretty little things I will say to him when he
comes in, when we start off and all along through the sunset hills as we fly quickly on our way to dear old Sturmhold.

"Why have you not written me? It has been just an
age since a letter came. Oh, I know! Of course you are
so busy you have hardly time to breathe. I don't wonder
that you have no time to write. Then, you are expecting
me every day, too. Tell your father how sorry I am for
him, and kiss your dear mother for me. I want them to
think as well of me as they can before I come, for I am
sure to impair their good opinion by some prank ere I
have had time to outwear the freshness of their welcome
home. I wonder why Papa was so particular to charge
me to stay here till he came or until I heard from him?
He never did so before. However, I shall stay. He knows
that, and he will come here the very first thing.

"This is Saturday, and is a holiday. I am going to post
this after breakfast, and then go for a stroll in the woods.
It is cool this morning, but when the sun is well up, the
open nooks among the evergreens will be warm and cosy.
At any rate, I am going, just to be alone, and smell the
pines. It is just the sweetest place in the world to sit and
think—to paint pictures and dream dreams. Amy says it
is sombre and lonesome among the rocks and under the

trees, but I do not see how it could be improved—unless one's lover could be there, too.

"Well, good-by, dear. Amy has waked, and come like a half-frozen ghost and curled herself up between my red wrapper and the fire. I never saw such a cold, bloodless creature as she is. She has the most wonderful eyes, and hair that is as black as jet. She is very proud of it, and well she may be, for the great shining coils lie like a crown upon her small, shapely head, and make her slender neck seem slenderer still. Her dark olive skin has not a trace of flush, and its dull pallor contrasts so strangely with the great black eyes and mass of jetty hair that it sometimes makes her look almost weird. This effect is no doubt aided by the smallness of her features and the thinness of her lips. She seems like a child almost, and yet they call her 'Queenie,' because of her haughty and dignified bearing. She is a strange compound of pride and passion —strength and weakness. She is thin-blooded, and, I fear, cold-hearted, yet I cannot help loving and pitying her. We have always been great friends, yet I should almost doubt that she had any real affection for me were it not for her terrible jealousy of you. It is funny that my best friend should be my lover's worst enemy. Of course, I count it no hardship to choose between you; though it does make me feel very sad to think that I shall be with her only a few months more, for I am really the only friend she has, and I am afraid she is not likely to find new ones. Poor girl! I cannot but think how much happier is my lot than hers. Good-by. She will not let me write any more, and I do not think I ought to write such long letters, when I do not get even a line in reply. Remember me to the servants, and think of me often when you visit dear old Sturmhold. How I long to be there with you—yours always and altogether.   HILDA."

For more than four years the cosy corner room, from one window of which she looked down the river, and from the other out upon the mountain, had been Hilda's habitation during the term-time at Beechwood. It was on the second floor, opened on the roof of the old farm-house, and had been chosen by her because the view reminded her of home, she said. Her father had stipulated that she should not be removed from this room, nor on any account debarred from the privilege of wandering at will on Saturdays in woods and fields, on foot or on horseback, wheresoever she would. This privilege had been accorded with hesitation; but Hilda had soon become such a prime favorite, not only with the principal and teachers, but also with her mates, that it soon ceased to attract attention, the more especially as it came to be applied to many of the other scholars as well. The room which opened off from Hilda's had been occupied for the same time by Amy Hargrove. Between these a very singular friendship had arisen. While both were brunettes, the dull pallidness of Amy's complexion was in strong contrast with the ruddy bloom that tinged the cheeks of Hilda. Both were considered beauties—one bright and cheerful, and the other cold and haughty. The one had many friends, the other few. They were alike in but one thing—they were both excellent scholars, and rivals for the honors of their class. Everybody wondered at their intimacy. They seemed to have so little in common, and yet they were almost inseparable. The fact was that their friendship was based as much upon the accident of contrasting physical conditions as anything else. Hilda's abounding vitality seemed almost a necessity to the meagre, thin-blooded little creature whom she took under her charge and petted and cared for almost like a child. She laughed at her whimsicalities, submitted to her pretensions, and when it was necessary, disregarded her fantasies. She had none of that self-consciousness that made her jealous of any of the really brilliant parts of her friend. She pitied her from her heart; for, despite her arrogance and assumption, she was alone in the world. She had no near kindred, and the one vexation of her life was the fact that her guardian paid no heed to her existence save in providing amply· for her comfort. She, too, had been secured special privileges at Beechwood. Her pony was not inferior to Hilda's; but she loved far better to have the two harnessed together and driven through shady lanes by another, than to mount and ride, as Hilda delighted to do, over the steep mountain roads. Despite these dissimilarities, there was rarely any difference between the friends. The one was happy to subserve the other's pleasure; the other was careful not to try her good nature too far. It was the everlasting puzzle of the strong and the weak; the broad and the narrow; the great and the small. Their natures were complementary, and for that very reason perhaps had so long harmonized.

The day of which we write was one of the rare occasions when the occupants of the two adjoining rooms did not agree. Ever since Hilda's engagement to Martin, Amy had been jealous of the young man's share in her companion's affection. It always put her in a pet to have Hilda write to him, and she spared no opportunity of manifesting, as far as she dared, her disapproval. On this day she had made up her mind that Hilda must drive with her to a town some miles down the river, to visit a friend whom she had met the summer before. As we have seen, this did not comport with Hilda's plans, and the result was that before the wayward little creature had dressed for the day she had worked herself into a fever of fretfulness. Hilda laughed at her angry expostulation, and when she stamped her little foot in rage, reminded her of a sheep at Sturmhold which was addicted to the same impatient gesture. The result was that the fiery little queen retired to her

own room, closed and locked the door between, and
when the bell for breakfast rang the excuse of a raging
headache which she gave for non-attendance was by
no means without foundation. She was prostrated by
that curse of natures in which the nervous far predomi-
nates over the physical—a sick-headache. Her room was
darkened, and she became a solitary prisoner for the
nonce. Hilda, reproaching herself for her refusal to
comply with her friend's wishes, would have become
her nurse, but the spoiled creature would not permit
her to even enter the room.

She, therefore, rode into the town to post her letter,
meeting the country mail upon the way, and wondering
whether it contained any messages from her loved
ones. As she passed along the narrow busy streets
that led to the post-office she found herself curiously
watched by those she met. The postmaster, a fussy,
important man with spectacles and thin gray hair—
a deacon in the church and one of the social and religious lights of the little town —drew her into conversation as she handed in her letter, and, on some
artful pretext, kept her waiting while more than one of
the townspeople came in and regarded her with a
strange eagerness. Dropping into a store to make some
slight purchases she noted the same unusual watch-
fulness on the part of all. There was some whispered
conversation between the proprietor and a few men who
stood near the stove, accompanied by meaning glances
in her direction. She caught the clerk who waited on
her telegraphing with his eyes, evidently in response to
their looks of inquiry. The hot blood rushed to her
face as she became conscious that she was the object
of observation and remark. Thinking there might be
some disarrangement of her attire which was attract-
ing attention, she turned full upon the little knot at
the stove with an angry light in her eyes, and then

deliberately walked past them to a mirror which hung against the wall at the back of the store. Save her flushed face and flashing eyes the glass showed nothing unusual in her appearance, and the picture that was flashed back at her was certainly not one that need object to scrutiny. She was used to admiration. She had received it all her life. Her father had petted her and praised her beauty always, and every one who came under his rooftree soon found that the shortest path to his approval was unstinted praise of his daughter. Since she had been at Beechwood she had been the belle of the little town. Everybody in it knew her. Her favor had been a matter of competition with several of the young men, even after it was generally understood that she was already engaged. She was probably better known through the country by her long walks and rides than any other girl at Beechwood. She knew admiration, and rather liked it. But this was not admiration. What could it be ?

As she left the store she encountered a knot of men on the sidewalk. They tried to seem not to be noticing her. She knew them. They were a lawyer, a doctor, an editor and the son of a wealthy mill-owner. As she went toward her horse, which she had hitched near the post-office, they all gazed after her, and at once engaged in an animated conversation. Could they be talking of her ? For the first time, she was allowed to lead her horse up to the platform that ran in front of one of the stores, and mount without aid. It was no inconvenience. She had as soon do it as not. She was so expert a horsewoman that only the slightest advantage of surface was needed to enable her to leap into the saddle. She did not care about the attention, either. She was too sincere by nature to desire to be a flirt. She loved Martin too earnestly to even seem to favor another. She liked attention ; she desired to please, and was glad to be thought beautiful and attractive. It gave her father pleasure. She was glad to be dowered with beauty for Martin's sake, too. Besides that, she enjoyed seeing others happy, and was glad to be the cause of their happiness. Yet she had never sought such attention, and would not have missed it had it not been universally accorded up to that time. Almost every week for four years, saving the vacations, she had ridden at least once into the town, and never in all that time had she been without a knight to offer his hand for her foot when she mounted to ride away. Indeed, it had been an honor for which there had more than once been sharp competition. Now she mounted alone. Yet a half a dozen familiar faces were at the windows of the shops peering out at her. Not one of the men who stood scarcely ten steps away had ever allowed her to do so before. The young mill-owner seemed quite to have forgotten her existence. Yet he had lately been so pronounced in his attentions that she had wondered if it were not her duty to tell him of her relations with Martin, so that he need have no excuse for continuing them. What could be the matter? There must be something wrong with her attire. She looked herself over nervously, as well as she could. Lifted her habit to see if by chance it failed to fall properly. Wondered if a glimpse of her skirt had shown beneath its border. Her face burned with shame at the thought. She leaned forward in the saddle and breathed freer when she found that was not the cause. Yet what could it be?

She turned her horse's head, and, with a sharp stroke, started on a swift gallop for the seminary.

Hardly had she gone a hundred yards when she saw the good pastor of the village church beckoning to her and calling after her. She reined in her horse and he came out to her — into the middle of the street — the good man who had only bowed and smiled as she had ridden past him hitherto. There is trouble in his face, but he is kind—very kind, indeed. She almost weeps as he takes her hand, raising his hat with scrupulous politeness, and looking anxiously into her face as he asks many questions, all very kindly and gently, of her father, of the fire at Skendoah, and all the other things that bear on her life. It is very strange she thinks. But meantime he talks on. What a sturdy, resolute face he has! As he talks, he rests his arm over the horse's neck. Is the whole town watching them? She thinks so. He does not see it, however. He is not reproving her for her gayety, either, as he has done sometimes, but is telling her how trials should be borne. What can he mean? And when he has finished and shaken her hand once more, and she is about to start, he turns again and enjoins upon her anew to come to him if she ever needs a friend. "Come right to my house, my dear," he says, with his honest face aglow, "at any time of night or day. You will always be welcome— just as welcome as if it were your home. Remember, now." What a strange injunction, and how solemnly yet kindly given! What an odd look of inquiry and embarrassment was in his eyes, too! He really seemed oppressed with sympathy for her. Yet she needed none. Ah, could it be? Her father—had anything happened to him? Her heart stood still with terror as the thought struck her. But no, it could not be. It was not sorrow that she had seen in the eyes that stared at her. Sympathy is sweet and tender and kind. This was hard and furtive and mean. It was a low, jeering, hateful stare, that meant—oh, what did it mean? Anger and pride and shame repeated again and again the futile question. Her eyes flashed; her face flushed and paled by turns; her hands clutched the reins nervously, and she bit her nether lip until the blood started forth in her vexation.

Then she gave her horse the rein and dashed over the frozen road to the seminary.

Had the world gone mad? From every window the faces of her schoolmates were peering forth with the same curious expression. Some were lit with furtive sympathy, and some bore the same sinister leer she had met in the town. The very servant who took her horse as she dismounted scanned her face and figure curiously as he did so. She ran up the steps and entered the hall. A dozen expectant faces were turned upon her with the same indefinable, searching glance. She rushed up the stairway and flew to her room. She saw them peeping at her from the rooms, and was conscious of opened doors and watchful observers after she had passed. Was she bewitched? Was there any strange thing in her appearance—any horrible gaucherie of dress or manner—that caused her to be observed and talked of in such an unaccountable way? Had she been transformed in a day?

She rushed to her room and ran at once to the mirror to find, if she could, a clew to the mystery. Her attire was faultless. She caught a hand-glass from the drawer, and turning from the mirror inspected her dress from top to toe. She walked away from the glass; she turned one side and then the other; raised one arm and then the other; lifted her trailing habit, inspected even her shoes—but could see nothing that should cause remark. Amy was passing back and forth in the room. By a side glance in the mirror she detected on her face the same speculative look she had seen on others; only in her case it was linked with something she had not seen elsewhere. There was a cold, hard look—anger, almost disgust, upon her proud, regular features. Her thin lips were surely half parted in a sneer. Hilda dropped the glass and sprang toward her friend. Amy drew back and raised her hands, as if to avoid her touch. Hilda noticed that she held some books and trifles of her own that in their community of use had been usually kept in this room rather than her own. She glanced around and saw that everything belonging to her companion had been removed—books, pictures, bits of needlework, trinkets which they had hung upon the walls or laid upon the tables, in girlish attempts at decoration. On the bed in careless confusion was heaped a mass of like trifles belonging to herself, which had in the same manner found lodgment in Amy's room. Slowly it dawned upon her. Amy had returned her trinkets and was taking away her own. Her amazement was increased a thousandfold. She grew faint and dizzy with mysterious apprehension. Was the world slipping from beneath her feet? Was mankind flying from her presence? Did she bear a leper spot that all should shun and jeer or hate? She could not think—only feel and fear and dread. Every nerve seemed burdened with indefinable agony. The blood tingled in every vein. Her heart thrilled with pain. Her head was a crucible of fire. She must, she would know what it meant.

"Oh, Amy, Amy!" she said in the shrill, wiry tones which only intensest agony can give, "what is it? Do tell me what makes you look at me so strangely—and the others—the girls—everybody?"

Amy pointed coldly to the glass, her lips now parted in an unmistakable sneer, showing the small white teeth close shut beneath them, while her eyes flashed with angry fire.

Hilda shot one more glance of inquiry at the mirror.

"What is it?" she cried in despair. "Do tell me! I can see nothing."

"Yet it is very plain to others."

Again Hilda looked.

"Oh, what is it? Please tell me! Do you not see

you are killing me ?   Why does everybody shun me to-
day ?"

"Because they have only just learned the truth, I
suppose," said the other coldly.

"The truth ! What do you mean ?" The question
was asked in open-mouthed wonder. "What have you
learned—what has anybody learned, that they did not
know before ?"

"Really one would think you did not know !" said
Amy with a mocking laugh, as she entered her own
room.

Hilda sprang forward.

"Amy, speak ! What is it ? I know nothing !"

She was entering her classmate's room, as she spoke.
Amy turned upon her as she reached the threshold and
pushed her violently back.

"Stand back !" she cried. "Stand back ! Do not dare
to come into my room ! Do not touch me ! The very
sight of you is contamination !"

"Oh, Amy—Amy !" wailed the poor girl. "What do
you mean? What has happened? Why are you so
angry with me ?"

"Why ?" shrieked the friend, now transformed into
a demon of hate. "Why ? Because I do not choose
to associate with such as you! Because I am a lady !
Because you have imposed upon and outraged us ! Because the man you call your father—"

"Stop, Amy Hargrove !" The frenzied girl was transformed into an angry goddess in an instant. "Stop !"
she repeated and strode toward the venomous little figure
with an air of menace that made it shrink away in fear.
"Say what you please of me, but do not dare to utter one
word against my father."

"Your father ?" sneered Amy, still retreating.

"Yes, *my father!* Is it anything strange that I should
refuse to hear my father defamed ?"

"Meaning, I suppose, Captain Hargrove !" lisped the white-faced vixen, while her eyes gleamed like burning coals with hate.

"Of course. You know my father. Everybody knows him !"—wonderingly, but yet defiantly.

"Everybody *thought* they knew him," replied the other with a shrug. "Now they know better."

"What !" exclaimed Hilda, with a surprised, hysterical laugh. "Are you crazy, Amy ? Pray, who is my father, then ?"

"Ah, indeed ! That is not important now. Your mother is known !" meaningly.

"My mother ?"

"Oh, yes ! Your mother ! Don't try to put on that look of innocence. The game is played out. We know who your mother was—or rather what she was ?"

"What she was ? My mother ? What *do* you mean ?" cried Hilda, her hands clasped before her and her voice quivering with wonder and dread.

"What do I mean ? I mean that we know now that your mother was a slave—George Eighmie's negro wife !"

There was a shriek—a fall ! Amy sprang quickly forward, closed and locked the door, braced herself against it, and stood shivering and pallid, with chattering teeth and eyes upturned in terror. Did she fear something that lay inanimate and still upon the other side, which the thin panels hid ?

CHAPTER XXXVI.

BEECHWOOD SEMINARY had a wide reputation. It not only afforded exceptionally fine advantages for the education of young ladies, but it was eminently respectable. To have been admitted to its classes was of itself a certificate of social rank. To have graduated from Beechwood was to hold a master-key to good society everywhere in the land. Twenty years had passed since the Misses Hunniwell began with three boarders, whom they taught in the parlor of their father's house, upon the front of which the seminary building proper now abutted. Their father had been a merchant who had saved from ruin, in the "crash" of '37, only this old homestead and the little hill-side farm, whose chief value was that it furnished firewood and shelter. His daughters had been well educated, and were too proud to descend from their former high social position to any menial avocation, and too "capable," as the saying of that region is, to be dependent upon others. Their mother was dead. So between them they managed the household and the scholars, and managed both so well that their fame soon came to the ears of others — parents and pupils.

Then the father died. Their pupils filled the house, and some even obtained board at the neighbors'. They builded a separate school-room; it was soon more than full. Then a small legacy fell to them. They borrowed what was really a large sum in those times, and erected the comfortable structure that now bore the name of Beechwood Seminary. In a few years the

debt was extinguished. One of the sisters died, and
the other wrought with still greater pride and devotion because of her memory. It was a high-priced and
high-toned institution; but it was a thoroughly good
one. Its founders contemplated their own advantage,
yet they were strictly honest, and would have scorned
to take pay for anything without giving a fair equivalent
for it. They were, above all things else, ladies. They
were descended from one of those old families of the
colony whom the age of vulgar shops and factories
overtook and drove in upon themselves. They were
types of that aristocracy which somehow or other grew
up and stood, proud and cold and self-respecting, among
the barren hills which mechanic art invaded with its
army of hand-workers—men and women—whose labor
was to build the foundations of the aristocracy of to-day.
The Hunniwells were an old family. Their blood was
very clear and very blue. The chilly purity of that
creed whose great expounder had once dwelt almost in
sight of the seminary, had left its impress on their
hearts. To "be a lady forever" was a Scriptural injunction that followed hard upon the decalogue in their
minds. To be in all things "under the breath of good
repute" was a prime pre-requisite to favor with them.
They pitied the poor. They would cheerfully serve the
humblest. Suffering never cried to them in vain. Conscience and sincerity were to be seen in their soft,
refined, yet sharply cut faces, as clearly as the blue
veins that showed through the silky skin. The calm
gray eyes were full and strong, but they were kind
and, in a way, tender. They were interested in their
neighbors of the busy borough that had grown up so near
the old farmhouse by them. They patronized the public schools which nestled about among the hills. Rarely
did one of these close a term that one of the sisters
with a few of their pupils did not honor the closing day

with their presence. The white slender fingers pointed out errors on the blackboard or the slate. The silky brown curls that framed the calm, refined faces and softened their serene severity, rose and fell with the little nods of approval which they gave for the encouragement of merit. Their aristocracy was not one of scorn or self-assertion, but of infinite self-respect. They did not like new things or take kindly to new ideas. The proprieties of the olden time ruled their convictions. They kept aloof from "isms" that smacked of question of the old doctrines. As the delegated guardians of the pupils intrusted to their charge, they held it a sacred doctrine to see that these imbibed, while under their care, no doubtful dogma. They were not ascetics. They did not shut their pupils away from the society that surrounded them, but required them to attend church upon the Sabbath, encouraged them to attend the prayer-meetings, and with the parents' assent allowed them sometimes to attend social gatherings and to receive, with scarcely a show of restraint, the visits of the young men of the neighborhood on certain specified evenings. The Misses Hunniwell were ladies and had no young ladies at their school whom they could not trust. So, too, they were not unreasonably severe in regard to girlish escapades, recognizing that young life must break from its leading-strings now and then. Their picnics, "recreation evenings" and holidays were festal occasions full of sweet innocent pleasure, not only to their pupils but to the favored youths who were deemed worthy of admission to this hill-side Eden.

Since the death of the elder sister, and especially since the coming of Hilda and Amy, even the former seemingly light discipline had been somewhat relaxed. Hilda, especially, had become a prime favorite, despite her apparent disregard of some of the minor

proprieties. Much was forgiven, because of the free,
untrammeled life of Sturmhold. The privileges which
Captain Hargrove had demanded as the condition of
her coming had been granted with some reluctance.
Perhaps no man of less evident gentility — certainly
no man whose Southern birth and lineage did not
entitle him to ask such a thing as a concession to the
home life and custom of his daughter—could have obtained the consent of the lady principal of Beechwood
to the keeping of a pony for his daughter's use. It was
with no little misgiving that it was granted. After a
time it seemed to prove so innocent a pleasure, and Hilda's abounding health as well as her frank good nature,
cheerful application and marked superiority in her studies
had so thoroughly overcome the good lady's fears, that
more than one sleek pet stood in the stable of the institution. She was not at all averse to the added income,
though no temptation of gain could have induced her to
lower, in the least degree, the standard of excellence or
the tone of exclusiveness and propriety which clung
around this pride of her lonely life. Since these innova-
tions had come she had even allowed herself a pleasant
luxury, which she had never before dreamed of indulging.
Having now to keep an assistant for the man-of-all-
work, who spaded the garden, milked the cows, prepared the wood and did the purveying for the institution, she had set up her carriage in a modest way,
instead of relying on the village livery when she needed
a vehicle for any purpose. So it happened that Beechwood had come to be regarded as not only a respectable and exclusive institution, but even in a sense a
luxurious one. All this added to its prosperity and
popularity until the number of pupils who were refused
admission, year by year, almost equaled the number
accepted.

Yet let it not be supposed that there was any lack of

wholesome discipline at Beechwood. Woe to the young lady who transgressed in any really important feature its regulations. She found that beneath the gentle nature of the principal there was a will of iron. Concealment of any fault or evasion of any duty was certain to receive merited reproof and humiliation. Falsehood in word or act was the most heinous sin. The unworthy, incorrigible or persistently neglectful were weeded out with the most summary firmness. She was tender in her care but inflexible in her requirements. Among the things most rigidly prohibited was all mention of the question which had grown to be the absorbing topic of the day. Holding herself to be the parent *pro tempore* of her pupils, she considered it a sacred duty to see to it that the home teachings of each were not perverted while under her care. Having pupils from the South, as well as the North, she counted it needful, both for her own interest and as a trustee of their interests, not only that discussion and dissension should be avoided, but that ideas which might be repugnant to the respective parents should not be imbibed by them while under her control. So while the life about her became a seething mass of heated controversy, Beechwood felt none of its influence. To this fact Miss Hunniwell owed no little loss of prestige among the people of the town. She was said to be bitterly proslavery in her views, and the seminary was regarded by some of the most rancorous of the abolition fanatics as a nursery of the most pestiferous doctrines.

This opposition naturally inclined this self-reliant woman to a more positive and pronounced hostility to that sentiment which had gradually worked its way into so many of the institutions of the North. So, when a family of colored children found their way into the schoolhouse of the little village, she ceased her customary visits there, and so far overstepped her own rule as not only

to speak somewhat bitterly in reference to it in private
conversation, but also to refer to it in her customary
Wednesday afternoon talks to her pupils. She did not
like slavery. She even regretted its existence, and was
truly sorry for the slave's hard fate. But, on the other
hand, she did not like the negro. She thought he had
a right to the proceeds of his own labor—to be a man
and have a home—but that did not make him white,
or entitle him to be the equal of the white man. She
gave liberally to the Colonization Society, and hoped
the day would come—indeed, she prayed for it daily—
when Christianized slaves would be reshipped to Africa
by the million as missionaries, who should convert their
barbarian kinsmen to Christianity. She took no note of
probability or possibility. She never stopped to consider of their fitness, and it did not once occur to her
that the untaught slave was, at best, a queer emissary
to bear the message of Christian freedom to the continent whence Christian hands had ravished slaves for
centuries to minister to Christian greed. Her only feeling was that they ought not to have been taken from
thence, and, being here, ought to be gotten rid of as
soon as possible. There were very many who sympathized with these views, but in the region where she
dwelt the antipathy to slavery as an act of personal injustice to the slave was fast overcoming the antipathy
of race and color.

It was to this community and to this woman that the
report had come, so well supported that none could
doubt, that a favorite pupil of this exclusive institution
was a threefold social leper—illegitimate, the daughter
of a slave—perhaps a slave herself—and cursed with
that befouling taint, the blood of Africa. The metropolitan journals had brought the news, now fully confirmed, of the death of Captain Hargrove in the attempt
to remove the slaves from Mallowbanks, together with

the further information, derived from papers found upon
his person that removed all possible doubt, that the
daughter of George Eighmie and Alida had been entered as a pupil at Beechwood. The village paper,
which was rampantly Abolitionist in its tone, had referred
to it with a sly touch of gratification at the position
in which the principal would find herself, combined with
a really sympathetic allusion to the young lady herself.
Another journal, of opposite proclivities, published in a
village a few miles away, had discoursed upon it at
considerable length, taking occasion to express its entire confidence that Miss Hunniwell had been imposed
upon by the accomplished kidnapper and the girl whom
he had represented as his daughter. It added that the
latter was said to be gifted with that rare beauty which
the quadroon sometimes possesses, but was easily recognized as having colored blood when the fact was once
suggested to an observer. Three letters had also come
by that morning's mail to the lady principal, which
brought vividly before her mind all the horrors of the
fact she had learned. Two of these were from Southern patrons. They were bitterly indignant at the fact
that their daughters had been made the victims of such
an infamous fraud, and demanded their instant return
to their homes. They denounced her in unmeasured
terms for the very sin she hated most—deception. She
felt that their anger was justified. She was angry herself
at the imposition which had been practiced upon her,
and utterly appalled at the disgrace which must ensue
to her beloved seminary. The other letter was from
Mr. Robert Gilman, in his capacity of attorney for the
heirs of Eighmie, informing her that they had positive
information that "a certain negro girl, belonging to the
estate of said Eighmie," was kept and harbored at the
seminary under her charge, under the name of Hilda
Hargrove, having been entered there as the daughter of

Merwyn Ha grove, deceased, who had the said girl in
his possession, claiming to be the testamentary heir of
said Eighmie, ough in fact held only to be an administrator *de son tort* of said estate. A reward of one thousand dollars was offered if she would hold and detain the
said negro girl until the duly authorized administrator
could take measures to reclaim the same as the property
of the estate. He added that the administrator would
arrive in a very short time—perhaps nearly as soon as his
letter—fully prepared to substantiate his claim and take
the necessary steps to recover possession of the slave.

A cry of horror escaped the lips of the teacher as she
threw the letter from her, almost before she had finished
its perusal.

In an instant she was transformed. The anger of her
patrons, the pecuniary loss, the shame that would at-
tach to Beechwood and its loss of prestige—all were
forgotten in the horrible vision that rose up before her
of the fate that impended over her favorite pupil. Till
that moment she had not been conscious of any exceptional fondness for Hilda. Her beauty, her winsome
frankness and her affectionate disposition had made her
a favorite with all; but this foster-mother of twenty generations of *alumnæ*, this *alma mater* of a thousand spotless girls, would have counted herself unworthy of her
trust had she admitted in her heart an hour before that
she could love one of them in any great degree more than
another. She would have dismissed from her employ at
once any teacher who had manifested a like partiality
for any particular pupil. All her life she had been as
impartial as Rhadamanthus, and had fixed her pride
upon and given her care and tenderness in almost equal
degree to all. Now, the heart of this gray-haired, childless woman burst the bound of habit, and cast aside all
the wisdom and pride of her life. She forgot every one
that was under her charge save this lone child of a law-

less union—the hopeless Pariah, the incurable leper, before whom waited only a life of shame and suffering—this nameless waif of the Dead Sea of Slavery. She saw it all—the chains—the block—the mart—the life of shame—the death long waited for and welcomed because an end of life. Within her breast the mother sprang to life. Born of this spirit-travail Hilda became at once her child—her one ewe-lamb—her very own. Her father's death had given her back the mother she had never known.

"Oh, my darling! my darling!" cried the childless woman, as she clasped her arms across her bosom and walked back and forth across the study floor. "My child! My Hilda! What shall I do? How shall I save you?"

That moment she caught the fire of the enthusiasts. In that hour she became a fanatic. The one thought which was seething in the heart of the people had found entrance to her own, and drove out all others. No argument, no exposition of theory had ever touched her calm, conservative nature; but the very thought of this Nessus robe, which must forever encase the fair young form in the room above, overturned at once her life-long convictions, destroyed all thought of prudence, and set her in battle array against an institution of which Hilda's peril was but an incident—rare, perhaps, but possible. With her nature it was not enough to feel or believe. She must act. She ceased her rapid walk across the room, took the letter of the attorney from the floor, and carefully read it again. Her soft cheek burned and her eyes flashed with anger. She sat for a long time with her head resting on one hand, her lips close shut, and the letter crushed in the clinched fingers of the other. She was thinking—thinking what she could do, what she must do. She had decided without thought what she ought to do. She hated this attorney who could speak so coolly of the fate that impended over her favorite. Yet he was a good man, an honest man; a loving, tender-hearted father and a conscientious attorney. In writing this letter he had performed a simple duty which the law imposed upon him. If he had known her thought, he would no doubt have been surprised. He would have felt that she was unjust, and he, in his turn, would also have been unjust. Cruelty was as foreign to his nature as to hers. He was only the product of a system she could not understand, as she was the creature of a development of which he knew nothing.

She heard the shriek and then the fall in the room above. In an instant she comprehended what had passed. She knew that the fatal message had reached Hilda's ears. She sprang to her feet, rushed out of her study, ran along the hall and up the stairs with the crumpled letter in her hand. The curious pupils, who had come from their rooms at the sound of the shriek, shrank away from her as she passed them in amazement. She did not speak to them nor look at them. No one had ever seen her manifest excitement before. A teacher, with a white, terrified face, met her at the head of the stairs, and asked her a question. Miss Hunniwell thrust her rudely aside without reply, passed straight on to Hilda's room, turned the knob without knocking, entered, and closed the door behind her. Without there were pale faces, quivering lips and hushed, wondering whispers. The premonition of a sad, mysterious tragedy that was being enacted in the midst of them had hushed the chatter of an hour before.

CHAPTER XXXVII.

THE FREEMASONRY OF THE OPPRESSED.

MISS HUNNIWELL was for a moment half-bewildered at the sight which she beheld on entering Hilda's room. She had pictured to herself when she heard the shriek, and as she flew along the hall and up the stairway, a crowd of curious, chattering girls, whose witless tongues had brought to Hilda's ears the knowledge of calamity. She expected to find them standing about their fainting companion, themselves pale and tearful over the result of their own thoughtlessness. But they were not there. The room was still and empty save for Hilda, lying insensible upon the floor, still clad in her riding-habit. The little jaunty cap she wore with it, which had become familiar to every wayfarer on the mountain roads for miles around, had fallen off, and her wealth of dark hair, released from its coil, was trailing on the carpet by her side. In falling she had caught the coverlet, and had dragged it half off the bed. It was the last unconscious effort at self-protection. Her arm now lay relaxed and motionless. Her white face was upturned, and the fitful, stertorous sobbing which shook her frame was the only sign of life about her. Kindly nature had given way, and the over-strained heart was for a time unconscious of its agony. But she was entirely alone. Could it be that her tormentors had fled? The teacher did not deem it possible. She had come at once on hearing her cry. There was no time for any one to have escaped from the room. After a moment she became aware of something unusual in the appearance of the room. She could not at first determine what it was.

456

She glanced quickly about to make sure of the change she felt rather than saw. The wardrobe, bureau, bed—all were in their accustomed places. The table in front of the fireplace and the little desk of bird's-eye maple, with trimmings of wild cherry, at which Hilda always wrote her letters, was in its accustomed place beside the window that looked out upon the mountain. Yet there was something strange and unexpected—something that disquieted and surprised her. What could it be? It was not the pale face and relaxed form upon the floor. She had anticipated that. All at once she noted with surprise that the door that opened into Amy's room was closed. She had not seen it shut for years—not since the two girls had become intimates. She had not looked for this, but in an instant she comprehended what had occurred. She had not been for a score of years teacher and confidant of all the girls that thronged the halls of Beechwood without knowing the innermost nature of every one of them. The clew to the situation was in her hand. She divined instinctively the scene that had taken place. She saw, as it were, the cowering, hateful presence beyond the close-shut door, as well as the white-faced form upon the floor. A smile of sorrowful contempt parted her thin, soft lips as she thought what hand had struck the blow, and realized how doubly harsh arrogance and pride must have made it.

"Poor child!" she murmured, "she has had a bitter foretaste of what is in store for her."

Then she tucked the gray curls behind her ears, a quick, instinctive gesture of preparation, and addressed herself to the task of restoring the prostrate figure to consciousness. A fainting girl was no new thing to her. She had seen scores of them, and knew exactly what was to be done. In an amazingly short time Hilda was sitting upright by the bedside, her teeth chattering, the dripping locks thrust back from her brow, her riding-cap hanging upon one side, and the long coil falling down her back, and slowly untwisting, while her great wondering eyes sought those of the teacher, full of fear and full of questioning. But no questions were permitted. The nurse who had her in charge was both skillful and tender. Silence was imposed before she could open her lips to frame an inquiry. Very soon her habit was removed, a light wrapper substituted, and Hilda was lying on the bed watching the teacher as, with housewifely care, she shook out and hung up the clothing that had been cast aside. Then Miss Hunniwell went out into the hall. She knew the advantage of leaving the dazed brain to work its way out of the mists of unconsciousness alone. She closed the door behind her, and stood upon the landing at the head of the stairway, gazing down into the sunlit hall below. Several of the pupils took occasion to leave their rooms, cross the hall, or descend the stairs as she waited. All of them stole quick, curious glances as they passed. Miss Hunniwell did not heed them, though with the teacher's instinct she saw them all. Then she pulled a cord that rang a bell in some distant part of the house, and, after a moment's waiting, gave an order to the servant who answered her summons. When she returned Miss Hunniwell took from her hands the tray she brought and re-entered Hilda's room. She saw at once that reason had resumed its sway. She judged that Hilda's memory had, in part at least, come back. The teacher wondered how much she remembered — how much she knew. She feared the effect upon her reason if all the sad truth were told at once. She knew that it was a case demanding all her care and pity. Love and duty were all enlisted in behalf of the fair victim of untoward fate. Hilda looked at her with surprise as she locked the door and came toward the bed with the tray in her hand. She seemed struggling to recall the events of the day. When she was bidden to partake of the simple fare set before her, she looked up and said:

"Oh, Miss Hunniwell, please tell me what has happened!"

"Hush, my dear, hush!" said the teacher, as she lifted a warning finger. "You must keep still now. By-and-by I will answer all your questions."

The calm voice and composed look soothed the excited girl at once. So she ate and drank obedient to the teacher's behest, somewhat languidly, it is true, but not without relish ; for, despite the rebellion of her over-strained nerves, Hilda was young and healthy, and such natures not only quickly recuperate, but feel the demands of appetite all the more keenly for the burden they have borne. So she ate the toast and drank the tea, and wondered what had happened that she should be thus attended as an invalid. The teacher said nothing, but her manner was so tender and caressing that Hilda even found herself wondering at it, and the tears that filled her eyes were tears of gratitude. She knew that some evil impended over her. She remembered dimly the curious glances she had encountered in the village. She half recalled some terrible words that Amy had spoken. She had scarcely comprehended them at the time. She had only vaguely felt that she had become —she knew not what—a something terrible—so terrible that even her best friend regarded her with aversion. She was conscious that she was not as she had been the day before. The world was now her enemy. Henceforth she was to be an outcast. She could not state the cause, but she felt the fact. All the world would stare at her hereafter as the men in the village had done that morning.

The pity in the teacher's eyes confirmed all this. She knew that her unwonted tenderness meant that she had no other friends. She thought dimly of Martin as lost

—separated from her forever. She did not blame him. Why, she knew not, but she felt that she had become a leper, and that even her teacher waited on her thus at the risk of mortal contagion. She was very grateful to her. She wished that she might die then and there, and not live to know the agony she felt was in store for her. It would be so sweet to die with the knowledge that some one still loved her. She remembered that when the darkness came on she had felt herself all alone in the universe. The world had seemed to be slipping away from her, and she herself falling away down into darkness—unfathomable, boundless. She had come back —back into the world. No, not into the world—into the light—into life—her world—her narrow life, into which no one else might ever come. Even this gentle-hearted teacher might only approach its dim, intangible border. No loving presence could share with the desolation in which she must hereafter dwell. The best could but give her sympathy and pity, where everybody had given love and honor hitherto. She did not understand it, but she accepted it as a doom of which she had somehow become conscious. It seemed like a terrible dream, but she knew it was a more terrible reality. She could not define it. The words that Amy had used had slipped away from her; but they were terrible words, and her look of hate and disgust had been still more terrible. She wondered if the teacher loved her. That good lady had taken away the tray, and now stood by the window gazing out upon the mountain. She was trying to decide what she would say to Hilda—what she would tell her of all that she had learned. Hilda raised herself on her elbow and looked at her. Would she— would anybody love her hereafter? Would Martin?— Ah! how her brain reeled. She remembered now. That was the question she had asked herself when the darkness fell upon her. It was of him she had thought in that moment ere she fell into the abyss of silence. She must give him up. Love could only be to her a name. It had been a matter of course hitherto. She had not known how bright the sunshine was until the eclipse had come. Could it have been only a terrible dream?

She glanced at the door that led into Amy's room. It was shut close. Her eyes swept about the room. All that had been Amy's was removed. Ah! how terrible must be the contagion with which she was smitten so suddenly. Her eye fell upon the heap of trinkets Amy had cast in reckless disorder upon the bed. Everything confirmed her fear. It was—it must be—all too true. Only her father was left her now. Her father! What was this horrible fear? What had she heard? What had Amy said about her father?

Hilda uttered a moan, and the teacher sprang to her side. She saw that memory had now fully returned, and her cheek blanched at the thought of all that this fair child must face. She threw her arms about her and kissed her again and again—not without a thrill of terror at what she did. Could it be? Was this fair thing——a groan came from her lips. Even the guard which years of discipline had set upon them could not repress her anguish. Hilda heard—saw—felt the truth. Her very lips grew white. Her nostrils quivered and her eyes glared with terror, but not for herself. She had forgotten her own woe. Her father alone filled her consciousness. He was in peril—perhaps suffering, dying.

She caught the teacher by the shoulders; held her fast at arm's length, and gazing into her frightened face cried in tones of fierce, threatening agony:

"My father! My father! What about my father?"

There was a moment's silence. The teacher could not answer. She could only wonder dimly, how much the girl knew—how much she guessed. Hilda's fingers buried themselves in the soft white shoulders of the

slender, gray-haired lady. She even shook her like a
child as she said in hoarse, terrible tones

"Speak quick—my father!"

The teacher recovered her self-control with an effort.
She looked calmly into her questioner's eyes and answered:

"He is dead!"

The glaring eyeballs grew glassy in their fixed stare.
The strained muscles relaxed—

"Dead! Dead!"

A dazed, incredulous expression succeeded to the
strained glare in her eyes. "Dead! Dead!" she repeated dully and vacantly, as if she could not comprehend the meaning of the words.

Then the teacher with gentle force bore her back upon
the pillow and kindly and tenderly told her all that she
knew of her father's death—carefully avoiding all allusion to what she had learned in regard to Hilda herself.
Tears came to her relief very soon. Sorrow succeeded
to terror. She turned her face to the pillow and
wept in an agony of grief. After a time the teacher
left her, hoping that her overwrought system might
find relief in sleep. She was not mistaken; after an
hour of silent weeping Hilda slept. The teacher had
locked the door as she passed out, to secure her from
interruption. Once the door of Amy's room opened,
and she peered in with a sinister look upon her thin,
pinched face. Close beside the bed she saw a letter.
With stealthy steps she crept forward, seized it, and re-
treated to her own room. A half-hour afterward she
came again. There was a glow of malignant triumph
on her face as she crept forward and deposited the letter
where she had found it. Then she closed and locked
the door, and threw the key as far as she could out of
the window. The letter was that which Mr. Gilman
had written to the mistress of Beechwood.

Two hours had passed when Hilda awoke. The terror of the morning had all departed. Sorrow for her father's death had swallowed up all other thought. She had forgotten Amy's words. She remembered dimly that something had separated them, but she cared little for it. The world was nothing to her if her father was not to be in it. She thought of Martin, and wondered dimly why he had not come to her. She did not care very much. It would hardly have been a consolation, yet she wished he had come. Then her thoughts wandered away to the scene of her father's death. She felt an unconquerable desire to see the place where he had fought and died in defense of his honor. She knew that he had not engaged in the removal of the slaves from any especial regard for their well-being. Indeed, she knew his almost savage aversion to the victims of slavery, as well as the institution itself. He had done this simply to redeem his pledge to his dead brother. She could not help exulting, even in her sorrow, over his steadfast devotion to the pledge he had given. She must see the scene of his sacrifice. She must go and weep upon his grave. She had given him up. She knew he was dead. Of that she had not a doubt. Yet his presence seemed still to fill the world. She rose to bring his portrait from a frame on which it rested on the little bureau. As she did so her foot crushed a paper lying at the bedside. She stooped and picked it up. Without looking at it she went to the bureau, and resting her arms upon it, gazed long and lovingly at her father's face. Then she pressed the picture to her heart— kissed it again and again—dimmed it with her tears —wiped the cold, bright surface of the daguerreotype with her handkerchief, and watched the beloved features as they emerged again from the misty film that overspread the plate.

By-and-by she noted the letter which she still held.

She saw her father's name. She did not stop to ask to whom it belonged, but read on, line after line, until her cheek blanched with terror. The old horror of the morning had come back—no longer vague and indistinct, but clear and tangible. The terrible truth was here revealed without the shadow of concealment. She was not only bereaved, but debased. The father she had adored was not her father. Could it be? She would not believe it. And yet it seemed as if there could be no mistake. It had been learned from documents found on his person. Had his own lips bidden her to disbelieve his life? She could not. She would not. And then, what was that about herself? It mattered very little now that she was doubly fatherless. Yet it was terrible to contemplate.

She pushed back her hair, and gazed long and anxiously at her reflection in the mirror. She scanned the clear white of the eye—pearly to the very edge of the dark iris. Then she thrust back her sleeve and noted the texture of the soft white skin—traced the course of the blue veins through its transparent whiteness—the nails pink and pearly to the very base—caught the mass of hair that trailed down her back, and held it betwixt her eye and the light, noting its soft, silken texture and the rich brown tinge that it gave forth. Was it possible? Had her father deceived her when he told of her mother—of the orchards of Italy and the russet-coated pears of Piedmont, for which she moaned so piteously when the touch of death was on her wasted frame? Was the ivory miniature that hung in her bosom a lie? She drew it forth and gazed upon it—held it up beside her face and scanned the reflection in the glass—placed it beside the little frame, and asked herself, could he have dealt falsely with any one—least of all with the memory of the fair wife whose love never lost its potency? "Never! never!" she said to herself, and her dark eye flashed

with pride. Falsehood could not inhabit that citadel of
honor. Then she *was* his daughter — the daughter of
that fair woman whom he loved—and this foul taint—
it was all a lie—a terrible nightmare—a horrible mistake! Yet it was he that said it. It was his cold, dead
lips that had sent to her the message of dishonor. It was
he who had left as his sole heritage, perhaps, the knowledge of illegitimacy—the curse of servile parentage—
the horror of a tainted blood! How she loathed herself
as she thought of it! She tore open her robe and
gazed upon her palpitating bosom. She wished that
she might tear out the heart that throbbed beneath it.
She would willingly pour out her very life if the one
drop that corrupted its red tide—the one drop of darker,
baser blood—might only flow forth and leave her dead
body undefiled. Oh, it was terrible! At once bereaved
and debased forever! Even the fair white breast seemed
foul and loathsome as the tettered leper's skin. But if
there should be a mistake—a doubt? Ah, that were
more terrible still! A doubt! With the suggestion
came the thought of Martin. A doubt—only a doubt,
perhaps, but a doubt so terrible that it stabs love to
death! She walked back and forth across the room.
Her stockinged feet gave forth no sound. The moan of
her unsyllabled agony dies upon her lips. She must
give him up, too! Father, mother, lover—even her own
identity—gone at one fell swoop of fate! Ah, she can
never come to his arms now! All the bright visions of
love-crowned life are swept away. Doubt is as bad as
certainty. Even if she could hide it fate might reveal
the hideous fact. The brand she had escaped a child
might bear! No! no! no! Love was not for her!
Midnight had fallen on her morning.

A knock at the door startled her. She stood and
listened in silence. A strange terror seized upon her.
Then the knock was repeated, and a note was thrust

under the door. She gazed at the white missive in
affright. After a time, half smiling at her fears, she
picked it up and read:

"DEAR MISS HARGROVE : You are in great peril, but
you have friends who will help you. The bloodhounds are
on your track. Meet me at the back gate of the seminary
at the time of evening prayers. Do not leave your room
on any account during the day. You are surrounded by
enemies. Trust no one. Prepare for a long journey, but
take as little as possible. Dress warmly, plainly. Remember, you promised to trust me. God bless and strengthen
you. Yours hastily,

"GILBERT ANDERSON."

The letter was scrawled hastily in pencil. It was
from the minister in the village. Thank God, she had
one friend—yes, two. Yet, stop; they were friends
only from pity. It were better she had none. What
did it mean? In danger? What peril could threaten
her? At once it flashed upon her. She caught up the
lawyer's letter and read its woful sentences again. Ah,
it was plain now! The administrator had arrived. He
had come for her. She was a slave. The law would
give her to him. What mattered her past life—her
present surroundings! They only served as a background to make the future more terrible. The law knew
her only as a slave—a chattel—a thing. The law was
her enemy henceforth.

And now a new, overmastering terror got hold upon
her—the terror of the hunted fugitive. Bereavement,
debasement, the loss of love, friends, everything was
forgotten in one idea — how the terrible doom of the
future might be avoided. Strangely enough, she did
not once think of death as a refuge. Flight, escape,
was all that filled her mind. She ran to the window
and gazed out upon the mountain. The dark evergreens seemed to offer shelter. If she could only get

among them she would be safe. "Surrounded by enemies." Whom did he mean? Who could be her enemy?
Not Miss Hunniwell, certainly. A slight noise in the next
room caused her to start. Ah, he was right! She had
enemies—one at least, and if that one, why not many?
She threw up the window and leaned far out to see if
she could not discover anything that betokened peril.
Was the house guarded? How would the law lay its
hand on her? Would all her pretty little keepsakes be
torn from her? Would they put shackles on her wrists?
Would she be sold in the market-place? Would her
charms be bartered for gold? Of course. She was a
slave, and a slave can have no right. All that she had
—aye, all that she *was*—the law would give to a master! She felt as if she could not wait until the night.
She must leap out and fly at once. She remembered
how she had climbed down from the roof that lay
just below her window. She clambered unconsciously
upon the window-sill. A quick, shrill whistle startled
her. It was from the copse upon the hill-side, hardly
a bow-shot away, but above the level of the casement.
She glanced hurriedly along the dark belt of ever-
green. Nothing. Another whistle—soft, quick, furtive. It fastens her glance upon one spot—the darkest
covert on the hill-side. Out of the thick verdure flashes
a gleam of white—a token, a signal—quickly withdrawn. She gazes where it was in sickening terror.
There is a motion of the branches. Fear keeps her
still. She watches the opening, paralyzed with horror.
While she looks a face appears, framed in the green
foliage. It looks into her eyes, but she is not afraid.
The freemasonry of slavery has already taught her its
signals of distress and succor. The hailing-sign of universal brotherhood catches her eye. She knows that
the face is that of a friend. It beckons to her. She
shakes her head. It importunes with eager eyes. She

still refuses. It gesticulates wildly, it pleads, it begs. She slips off the window seat, writes a hasty note, ties it about a bit of stone she has brought in from one of her rambles, and throws it as far out upon the mountain-side as she can. She sees the Face run toward it cautiously; pick it up; read it; nod assent, and then suddenly steal away. She wonders at its strange caution, but she trusts the Face implicitly. Degradation had begun its work. To her the Face meant fellowship, fraternity. Between them was a tie the sword could not cut asunder. The fire could not burn nor many waters quench her trust. *The face was black!*

CHAPTER XXXVIII.

OUT OF THE TOILS.

As Hilda turned from the window a new view of the situation flashed upon her. The hour of passive suffering had gone by; the time for active resistance had come. She walked across the room and tried the door. It was fastened from the outside. She was a prisoner. At first she rebelled at the thought. It occurred to her to burst it open and defy the world. She was not afraid to do so. The blood of the Hargroves surged into her face, and as she caught sight of the reflection in the mirror she knew that the look of fierce determination painted on it had come from the brave man she had been wont to call her father. It was all a base lie, and she would yet crowd it down the throats that uttered it. But how?

That was the question. She was in danger. They would take her for a slave. She must escape from her pursuers. Not only her own future but her father's honor demanded that. Her father's honor! He had given his life for it, and she would give hers to save it from taint. All else was naught to her. All? Her hand pressed her heart as the thought of Martin swept through her brain. Then there came for the first time a terrible, sickening fear. Could it be that he had heard this story of unutterable shame, and had cast her out of his heart? She tried to spurn the thought, but it would return. Why was he not here? He must have heard—he must have known. And yet, why should she blame him? If he were at her feet beg-

ging for her consent, she would not unite her destiny
with his—no, not for worlds. The dread shadow that
hung over her should not rest upon another life by any
act of hers. And yet she would have been glad to
know that "in evil as well as good report" he loved
her still. She did believe—she would believe that he
did. Some terrible calamity must have kept him away
—some accident—ah! there were a thousand things
that would account for it.

She caught a daguerreotype case from the table, gazed
upon it eagerly, kissed it and hid it in her bosom. She
would keep it forever—the shadow of a love that might
never be renewed, but yet full of bliss in its memory.
She went and opened the little desk at which she had
spent so many happy hours in writing to this playmate-
friend—this brother-lover of hers. She would write one
more—the last. She brushed the dust from the purple
baize cover; touched her pens and paper tenderly;
thought again of the refined and delicate surroundings which she had always enjoyed, and wondered
vaguely what her life would be like thereafter. It did
not matter. She would do what honor dictated, and no
cowardly thought should make her weak. Across her
memory flashed the picture she had seen in her dream
—her father standing at the tiller, and the moonlit
track that led to death. She could die or live, she said
to herself; but, dying or living, she would be worthy of
that memory.

Then she drew forth the paper and wrote. It was the
thin tinted paper, which was accounted the very finest in
that day. It was made in the old mill in the village beyond, the rumble of whose wheel she could almost hear.
The genial owner was very proud of his best "laid
paper," and had presented her with a generous store of
it one day when she went to visit his daughter, in that
happy past that was already so far away that it seemed

to have belonged to some one else. She put away these soft memories and wrote:

"My Dear, Dear Martin."

She had never doubled this tender epithet before. She paused a moment and looked at it. Then she drew her pen through one of them. A moment after she obliterated the possessive. "Not mine," she said to herself. "Only the Martin that I thought was mine, but still dear." Then she tore the sheet into little fragments and began again. Her pen did not rest until the sheet was finished:

"Dear Martin: You of course know what has happened, or soon will know. True or false, it must separate us; unless, indeed, its falsity can be clearly shown. Even then it may well be that you would shrink from uniting your life with one on whom such a cloud had rested. I do not believe you would. I do not think you would hesitate to stand beside me and brave even the worst that fate may have in store for me. I know you are noble and courageous. If you had not been I could not have loved you, and my father would not have trusted you. But because you are all that I love and honor, I must not bring you shame—no, nor even the shadow of it. Strong as is my love, I could not endure the possibility of distrust; and you would not ask me to do violence to my own sense of honor even at the dictate of affection. Besides, I will not hide from you my fear that what I believe will never be proved. You know the mystery my father always preserved in regard to Alida and her children. I even shudder at the fear that my trust in him may itself be broken. Ah, poor crazed Alida! If it should be that she is in truth my mother, then indeed—but it cannot be! Yet, now that I am bidding you good-by, Martin dear, let me ask you to be kind to her, to shield and protect her, as if, indeed, she were my mother. You know I cannot do it. I must even fly for my own safety. The law—they say so, at least—

the law claims me as a slave. Ah! how often we have thought of such things, little dreaming they would ever come near us. I remember now all the stories I heard when that strange Mr. Brown was here. How long ago it seems, and I wondered then if they could all be true. And now I am one of those strange things myself—a slave—a soulless mortal, an irresponsible immortal. I am another's property to have and to hold, fast bound and fast held by the riveted chains of the law. This hand that writes to you is not mine. You have called it yours, but it can only be yours by purchase now. These lips that you have kissed—I suppose their beauty only adds to my value in dollars and cents.

"But do not fear, Martin. I shall never be a slave. Death is a bridegroom who is always ready. No fear and no force can keep me from his arms if I must go to them to save myself from dishonor. Do not be afraid. She who has loved you—who always will love you—has not a drop of blood in her veins that would not run gladly out to save herself from such a fate.

"Yet, Martin, I would almost as soon live or die a slave, as to remain even in luxury and ease knowing that he whom I have worshipped as my father had deceived me—was not my father—and that the shame they seek to fix upon me now, was mine to bear forever and to give with my life, unto my offspring! No, not that! Sooner than that, I would bury shame and suffering in a shameful grave. No other life shall take such blight from mine.

"But I must say farewell, Marty. The dear old days come back as I write—when we were boy and girl—brother and sister—soul-wedded lovers from the first. God bless you, Marty! We shall never meet again I fear—we dare not meet—unless—unless a hopeless hope prove true.

"I am going away—how or where I do not know, and you must not seek to know. Do not follow me—do not try to find me. If the sunshine ever falls upon my life again, I will come to you. Till then—or forever, as it may

be—as it must be, unless—ah, why will I hope! Farewell,
Marty! Say farewell when you read this, as if, indeed,
you kissed my dead lips—to know me forever after only
as a sweet memory. I cannot tell you, dear love, how I
suffer; yet, even now, it is more for you than for myself.
Again, and always, let me say—adieu.   HILDA."

She bowed her head upon the desk, and drowned her
dead love in tears. Her frame shook with sobs; and
love that knows not laws, nor customs, nor constitutions, nor the sacred "rights of things" for a time took
tribute of her fair young life. Then she started suddenly
and dried her tears unconsciously. Fear came upon
her once more. The sun was wearing westwardly. She
sealed her letter hurriedly. Hardly had she done so
when there was a knock at the door. She tried to say
come in, but the words died on her white lips. The
key turned in the lock, and the teacher entered. She
bore a waiter on which was a bountiful repast. She
closed and locked the door, set the waiter on the table,
and came and stood beside Hilda, gazing at her search-
ingly. She stooped to kiss her, but Hilda drew away
from her, while a hot tide surged over cheek and brow.
The teacher read the address of the letter on the desk,
and then glanced quickly around the room. Her eye
fell on the lawyer's letter. She tried to seize it, but
Hilda was too quick for her and snatched it away.

"You have read that?" asked Miss Hunniwell, her
voice shaking in spite of her boasted self-control.

"Yes," said Hilda sullenly. She had risen, and was
standing defiantly in the corner by the window.

As she spoke, she saw a man wearing a broad-
brimmed slouch hat pass along the carriage-way to the
rear of the house. She saw, too, the black face watching him from the thicket above.

"You know then?" said the teacher inquiringly,
with her hands clasped tremblingly before her.

"I know it is a lie!" said Hilda vehemently.

"Oh, no doubt, no doubt," said the teacher reassuringly; "but you know that—that you are in danger?"

For answer Hilda pointed to the figure approaching the carriage-house. Miss Hunniwell uttered an exclamation of indignant surprise.

"The wicked wretch!" she exclaimed. "Does he think that he can prevent your escape by prowling around the premises in that style? If he thinks he is going to take you away from Beechwood and into—into —Oh! I beg your pardon, dear."

Hilda had cast herself into her arms, and was weeping on her shoulder.

"Hush! What is that?" exclaimed the teacher.

Hilda looked up in surprise, but followed her gaze as well as tears would permit.

The stranger stood in the driveway scanning curiously the rear of the seminary. As Miss Hunniwell spoke a small white packet fell at his feet. He glanced around in surprise; then picked it up, unfolded it, and seemed to be reading. He looked toward the window near which they stood, nodded his head in that direction, and then walked quickly away. The teacher stood for a moment thoroughly amazed. Then her face lighted with intelligence and scorn, as she nodded toward Amy's room and said:

"Enemies without and spies within! Poor girl! poor girl! But they shall not get you. That man has been here twice to-day. He is the man referred to in that letter—the administrator of somebody, who wants to get hold of you. But he shall not. He has no warrant, and cannot get any before morning, and you will be far enough away before then or I shall miss my guess."

"What will you do?" asked Hilda.

"Never mind, dear. Eat your dinner while I send away the spy," said the teacher, shaking her head wisely.

She left the room. Hilda heard her knock at Amy's door, and a moment after heard them both leave the room and pass along the hall. Soon the teacher returned, smiling at her own shrewdness.

"I have informed one of the teachers that she is to keep Miss Amy Hargrove in her room until after prayers," she said. "Now we can lay our plans, and there is no time to lose. I have already telegraphed for a lawyer and Mr. Jared Clarkson ; also to Mr. Kortright."

"Martin ?" asked Hilda, turning pale.

"Yes, certainly. He will be here by to-morrow night at the farthest."

"Oh, Miss Hunniwell, why did you do it ?"

"Why, I thought you would want him here, above all," answered the teacher in surprise.

"Oh no, no ! I cannot see him ! He must not come ! Do you not see," she continued, and a deep flush had taken the place of pallor in her face ; "if—if—it should be—as they say ?"

"Ah, poor child ! but it is not," said the teacher positively.

"But—but can we prove it is not so ?" asked Hilda plaintively.

"True, true," said the teacher, walking back and forth and wringing her hands distractedly. "Oh, what an infamous thing ! What a horrible, wicked law for a Christian people to obey ! But we will not obey !" she exclaimed hotly, as she stopped suddenly before her pupil. "We will take you away from them ; we will defy the law. Did not Mr. Clarkson do it last year? We will do it here ! I will do it. I will appeal to the people. I will go myself. I will help tear down the jails. We will defy the world if need be ; we will rescue you. You shall go to Canada, where people are free. Thank God, there is one place they may be !"

The delicate woman was transformed into a fury by the sense of injustice and wrong. Her hands were clinched, and the blue veins showed through her soft, fair skin, while her eyes burned with a strange, wild light that no one had ever dreamed could slumber in their blue depths.

"Thank you a thousand times," said Hilda, as she clasped the teacher in her arms and kissed her, while her tears fell on the hot, red cheeks. "You are very kind and good, but I must not risk such chances."

"What can you do?"

"I must go away."

"But how? You saw how the house is watched?"

"It must be done," said Hilda. Then she showed the note from Anderson and told how she had received it.

"Aye," said the teacher bitterly. "He distrusted me. They thought I would give you up. Even the servants are truer than I have been to the right and liberty."

Hilda soothed her self-reproaches, and after a little the woman's wit coupled with the teacher's experience perfected a plan very much more feasible than the one the minister had devised. Hilda donned her most serviceable garments. Her bank account was turned into bank-bills by the teacher; a valise was hastily packed, and she was ready. Miss Hunniwell stood at the door of the dining-room and noted that all the pupils entered. Then she closed the door and a muffled figure stole down to the side entrance. The principal's carriage happened to be waiting there. The driver stood carelessly by. While the pupils sang the usual hymn that preceded the evening repast at Beechwood the muffled figure came out of the door and entered the carriage. The driver closed the carriage door and strolled carelessly along, leading his horses by the bit to the front entrance. After a short time Miss Hunniwell, equipped for a drive, came down the wide steps with a market-basket in her hand. She entered the carriage; the driver took his place on the front seat, and just as the daylight faded from the sky, drove leisurely through the streets of the little village, turned northward at the end, and with a chuckle brought the snug roadsters down to their work as if they had a long trip before them.

  . . . .

Ten miles away there was a busy town, at which two trains met at ten o'clock that night—the one going eastward and the other westward. A young girl left a carriage which was standing by the platform and entered one of them just as it moved away. The driver was busy with his horses. A gray-headed woman watched her anxiously from the carriage-door as she went along the platform, passed the dimly-lighted station and was then lost to view.

Evening prayers at Beechwood came at eight o'clock. Then all met in the chapel, the organ pealed forth its notes, and soft, young voices uttered songs of praise. The day's record was made up, announcements for the morrow made, and then the day at the seminary was at an end. Each pupil retired to her room; an hour was allowed for preparation for repose, and then silence settled on the throng of white young souls beneath its roof. Until evening prayers, Amy Hargrove was kept a close prisoner in the teacher's room to which she had been sent by Miss Hunniwell; returning then to her own room she found all still in the adjoining apartment. She applied eye and ear to the key-hole. She could only see the flicker of the fading firelight; she could hear nothing. She tried to open the door, and then first remembered that she had locked it. Then she took the key from her own door, and after some trouble turned the bolt. She opened the door and entered cautiously. The firelight showed that the room was empty. Hilda's

things were scattered about. The door was locked. So
was the wardrobe and the trunk. So, too, the little
desk. Amy moved carefully about, examining everything. Then she sat down upon the rug by the
hearth and thought. It was evident that Hilda had
fled, but where?—how? She could not understand. Of
course Miss Hunniwell would not like to have her arrested there. No doubt she pitied her. Indeed, she
pitied her herself, or would have done so, but for the
fraud that had been practiced on her. She could almost
forgive that and pity her still but for the envy in her
heart. Why was it that everybody loved Hilda, and
seemed only to distrust and avoid her? Even the Southern girls in the school were all sorry for Hilda now,
and were angry at the man who had come to assert his
right and do his duty as an officer of the law. Of course
it was a pity that Hilda had been brought up to think
herself free and white; but it was silly to make such a
fuss about her now that they knew that she was neither.
While she thought of these things Amy was startled by
a slight noise at the window. Some one was quietly
forcing an entrance. The sash was pried up; a hand
was thrust in. Her heart stood still with terror. She
understood it all in an instant. She had never dreamed
when she wrote the note she had thrown to the man
in pursuit of his slave, informing him that "the person
he was seeking was in the room adjoining," and, in
answer to his look of inquiry, had motioned toward
that window, that any one would try to enter except
by the door and with lawful warrant. She had been
instigated by envy, and a meddlesome desire to have
her own ingratitude justified after a fashion by the
capture of this slave-girl, who had outstripped her
in the regard of her fellows, as well as in the
studies they had pursued together. Now she feared
that her interference would be revealed. What if the

kidnappers should be discovered and themselves arrested? Then she would be exposed, covered with infamy—perhaps held guilty with them. She would warn them now, and have them go away as quietly as possible. She was terribly frightened. The sweat stood in drops on her forehead and her limbs refused to move. The window was raised now, and a man stepped lightly within. She noticed that he wore coarse woolen socks over his boots to lessen the sound. She looked up at his face, and saw that it was strangely muffled. At length she found strength to rise. She must warn them at once. Suppose Miss Hunniwell were to return? She ran quickly across the room, and laid her hand on the man's arm. She had no fear of him. It was her information that had brought him there.

"Hush!" she said in a low whisper.

She started, however, when an arm was thrown about her waist, but before she could cry out something soft was pressed against her face; there was a pungent, choking odor; a strange sweetish taste in her mouth; the world seemed suddenly to grow dark and close about her; then as quickly to grow light and expand to infinite distance. She felt herself slipping away from existence, and then—she knew no more.

CHAPTER XXXIX.

THE CHURCH MILITANT.

THE administrator of George Eighmie was very far
from being a bad man. He considered his cousin's
relation with Alida, and the attempt to free his slaves
and devote the proceeds of his estate to the benefit of
the children resulting from that union, an outrage, not
only upon society in general and the peculiar institution of the South in particular, but especially upon his
own kith and kin. This feeling at least was but natural,
and simply represented the general sentiment of the
community in which he dwelt, intensified somewhat by
that feeling of personal resentment which the heir-ex-
pectant always feels when his hopes are blighted by
unanticipated claimants. He bore no ill-will to Alida
or her children, but he believed them to be legally and
justly the slaves of his long-deceased relative, and, as
such, rightfully subject to the claims of the heirs. This
belief was an inherited one. He had been little more
than a boy when his cousin died, and the sentiment had
grown stronger and stronger in his breast with every
succeeding discussion of the subject in the family councils. He had been selected for his present position, after
the long years of litigation, because he was cool, courageous and intelligent. He was a man of substance,
though not of great wealth—thrifty, energetic and respectable. He was a member of the church, consistent,
earnest and devout. He would no sooner have committed what he deemed a wrong than the saintly-faced
Miss Hunniwell herself. Nay, he would have resisted
what he thought to be injustice just as stubbornly, and

with the same immutable conviction that he was doing right thereby. He was a law-abiding man ; upright and fair in his dealings with others, and no more desirous of securing his own rights than of rendering righteousness to others. It was his duty, as he was instructed and believed, to reduce to possession the assets of the estate he had sworn to administer. It was especially his duty toward the rightful heirs to reclaim Alida and her children, because they had been advised that it was possible that complications might arise through the suit already begun by Jared Clarkson, as the guardian of Alida, which would be entirely avoided if the children of Eighmie were brought within the jurisdiction of the courts of the state in which he died. He had no doubt that Hilda was the daughter of Alida, and he had determined to obtain possession of her person, and take her to Carolina before Clarkson or others of her friends could have an opportunity either to place her beyond the reach of the law or to interpose any legal barrier to her removal. He did not regard Hilda as having any rights at all, except the slender one of personal defense which the law allowed the slave. He was ready to admit that it would be hard for her to come down from the luxurious position she had occupied as the petted daughter of a wealthy and refined gentleman to a state of servitude, and he would have felt no little pity for her on that account. Were her state of subjection once clearly acknowledged, and her claims as the heir of Hargrove abandoned and extinguished, he would willingly have consulted her happiness by consenting to release the claims of the estate upon her person for a nominal consideration. In short, Sherwood Eighmie was an honest, upright, Christian gentleman, who had no more doubt of the righteousness of slavery than of any other tenet of his faith. He did not wish to secure the girl from any motive of cruelty or revenge.

He would have treated her kindly, according to his ideas of kindness, had she fallen into his hands; but he did not regard it as any injustice or inhumanity on his part to perform to the letter the duties his position devolved upon him. He was a just man even to his own slaves, treating them fairly rather than indulgently. He expected and exacted service, and he held himself bound as a Christian master to give good support, attention in sickness, and a reasonable amount of relaxation to those who served. He would have fought for one of his slaves only less readily than for his children, and would have resented their ill-treatment by another to the limit of the law or the extent of his power. He would have done this, however, not so much out of consideration for the slave himself, as because he regarded it as the duty of the master, and also because any interference with his servant was an infraction of his right as master. In short, he was a good, fair, average man, shaped and fashioned by one set of ideas, as Harrison Kortright had been by another. Submitted to the same influences, the two men would not have been unlike in character. Growing up as they did, they seemed to stand at the very antipodes of thought.

The fact was well known both to himself and his lawyer that Miss Hunniwell was not inclined to the extreme doctrines of the Abolitionists, and from this it was inferred that perhaps the best method to secure his end was to speak her fair, and obtain if possible her co-operation in getting possession of the "person held to service or labor" whom he sought. He could not understand, nor could his counsel, why any one not a rampant Abolitionist should object to rendering to him what the law not only gave him the right to have, but commanded him to take and keep as a part of the estate of his intestate. He had arranged it so that his attorney's letter should reach her just at the time it did.

In fact, he had himself brought it the day before and mailed it in the village. He had been at slight pains to conceal his identity, and had brought with him from Baltimore two men who were ready to perform his bidding in all things. They were men of experience, too, for they had more than once been engaged in the recapture of slaves in several of the border states.

As regards Miss Hunniwell, both he and his legal adviser had made the common mistake of the Southerner in estimating the Northern character,—by supposing her to be entirely mercenary in her impulses. That anything beside her material interests would affect her action in the matter he never once dreamed until he stood in her presence and heard her indignant refusal to accede to his request. Even then he was unable to appreciate the motive that controlled her action. He accounted her show of indignation as resulting from a careful balancing of profit and loss, and sought to convince her that refusal would be far more disastrous to her school than assent to his demand could possibly be.

When her soft cheek flushed and her clear blue eyes flashed at this, and she requested him to leave the premises without delay, he simply thought he had blundered in the method in which he had broached the subject. It was not until his second visit, when he came armed with his proofs, which were merely received as evidences of a wicked purpose by the mistress of Beechwood, that he mistrusted that her refusal arose from the fact that she, too, had imbibed the pestiferous notions of the Abolitionists. When she openly avowed not only her purpose to harbor and maintain the slave without regard to his demands, but also declared that she would do all in her power to prevent his getting hold of his property at all, then he first perceived that, like all the rest of "the Yankees," she was at heart an enemy of "the South," and thoroughly determined to obstruct the execution of any law designed to protect the interests of her people. Thereupon he had at once determined to use any means short of actual violence to secure possession of his slave. He had a good idea of Hilda's appearance, for she had been pointed out to him in the town that morning as " the daughter of that poor Captain Hargrove that was killed by the slaveholders lately."

He at once took measures to apply for a warrant, and set his men to watch the institution to prevent the escape of the fugitive. He had strolled restlessly about the building, not so much with the idea of securing the prize as to see what avenues there were for her escape. The note which Amy had thrown at his feet first put in his mind the idea of forcibly seizing and carrying away his slave. He knew he was in a community intensely hostile to his purpose, who would spare no pains to outwit, delay and thwart his plans. In a legal struggle he dreaded their activity, shrewdness and fertility of resource, especially aided, as he saw it would be, by an almost universal public sentiment; but he thought that a bold, quick stroke would meet with little or no resistance, and estimated that he would be able to remove the girl should he once get her in his power without serious inconvenience. Like most Southern men of that time, he counted all Northern men as cowards, and had no doubt that himself and his two assistants would present a show of force that would effectually prevent all attempt at a rescue.

Upon mentioning the matter to these worthies he found them entirely of his opinion. They at once proceeded to reconnoitre the rear of the seminary, and announced their readiness to undertake the enterprise that very night. Their plans were quickly matured. One of them had noticed a ladder lying beside the carriage-house which was all that was needed to give access to the roof below Hilda's window. A carriage was easily obtained, which one of the assistants was to drive, while the other, with the aid of Eighmie, was to secure the girl. It seemed a very simple matter. None of them had any fear as to the result. Indeed, they thought it more than likely there would be no resistance or pursuit, but Sherwood Eighmie hardly relished the idea of a stealthy entrance into the house. He would much have preferred to go in by the front door, regardless of all remonstrance, and carry away what he was entitled to take. The entry by the window smacked to him of burglary; but his two assistants, with whose lives this method was more in harmony, overruled his objection by dwelling on the obstacles he was likely to meet with from a hostile community and the very slender prospect of obtaining justice by strictly legal methods. Besides, they argued that a bold and dashing movement of this kind would greatly increase the prestige of the South, and as they could easily be beyond the state line before any pursuit was made, there was really only a show of danger in it—just enough to make it enjoyable. This advice was not altogether disinterested, since these worthies would be able, as they well knew, to demand a much greater sum for engaging in such an adventure than if they should merely follow their employer about as an unnecessary body-guard while he awaited the slow process of the law to put him in possession of his own. To climb a ladder, crack a window or forcibly remove an unwilling slave-girl from a harbor of refuge, were none of them acts that they regarded with any especial horror. So they ridiculed the hesitancy of their principal, made light of his objections, piqued his vanity and appealed to his prejudice until they carried their point, and it was decided that the capture should be made an hour after evening prayers at the seminary.

A little after dark two vehicles moved out of the village toward the seminary. In the first of these was the worthy pastor, whose face glowed with the anticipation of doing a good act. The man and horse were oddly matched, and yet there was not lacking a sense of fitness between them. The divine, a great broad-shouldered, Saxon-visaged man, sat in the light, covered buggy, his soft felt hat pulled well down over his ears, the robe tucked close about him, and urged forward the staid, shambling bay with an occasional cluck, which had no effect upon that animal, which merely kept on at the same steady pace. Yet a close observer could see at a glance that there was good material both in man and horse. The broad, firm jaw and cool gray eye bespoke a man who, if somewhat slow in making up his mind, would never waver from a decision once made. The firm grip of the bare broad hand that grasped the reins showed that even in a physical contest he would be no mean opponent. The horse was a dark blood-bay, whose powerful shoulder and long, sloping quarters showed that his stride was capable of being quickened until it reached a rate by no means despicable even among frequenters of the turf. In his careless way the dominie was a horseman, and, despite his seemingly careless driving, was not accustomed to take anybody's "dust" on the country roads he traveled. His horse knew all his moods, and would not only endure his perpetual nagging, but when his master was in serious earnest, pricked up his ears, stretched out his long neck, and threw the dirt in a style that made urging superfluous. He was a sagacious beast, too, and at the word of command backed from the stall into the shafts, and, with the buggy attached, out of the barn into the little yard behind the parsonage. He was even trusted to trot round to the front door without a driver, there to wait while the dominie changed his clothes and prepared for the road. Left unfastened by his absent-minded master on the highway for a time longer than he deemed needful for a pastoral call, he sometimes trotted leisurely home and waited at the stable-door for his master's return. In short, Mr. Anderson and his horse were well suited to the plan he had devised, which was nothing less than to take Hilda twenty miles and more across the country before sunrise to a state that had never felt the foot of a slave except on his way to freedom—the only state of the North from which one never was returned to bondage.

He had laid his plans with great care. The man-of-all-work at the seminary he knew to be good and true, and a member of his church. To him he had revealed just enough of the facts to enable him to understand Hilda's danger and his pastor's desire to avert it. Through him he had conveyed to her the note she had received, but he had neglected to inform him of the means he intended to take to thwart the designs of the enemy. For this reason he had received no intimation of the change of heart of the Principal, and the change of the plan of escape through her co-operation. The coachman thought he was simply carrying out the design of his pastor when he drove through the town, in open day almost, with the prize which the slave-master coveted. So the good-natured divine's eyes shone with the warmth of benevolence behind his gold-bowed glasses as he clucked to his bay horse, and imagined himself a knight-errant bound to the relief of a sore-distressed damsel.

As he drove on down the river road that ran in front of the seminary, he heard the rattle of wheels behind, and looking around he saw a two-seated carriage containing three men. He could not see very well at a distance, but he knew the team with a horseman's instinct, and wondered where it could be going in that direction at that time of day. Half unconsciously he drew rein, and scanned the occupants of the carriage more closely as they came near. He recognized them instantly. They were enemies—enemies of all that was good and tender in humanity—traffickers in human flesh —man-slayers, women-stealers—the enemies of God, because they were the enemies of His poorest poor.

These thoughts went through the good pastor's mind as he looked through the little window at the back of his buggy into the face of his brother in the church, Sherwood Eighmie, deacon of the church at Rawdon, in Clayburn County, Carolina. Strange that a few degrees of latitude should put honest men so far asunder in belief as to what constituted righteousness!

The dominie did not think of this, however, but began to wonder what their mission in this direction could be. Little by little the essential elements of the plan of the kidnappers dawned upon him. Both were after the same game, he thought, but he had the advantage—he knew them and they did not know him. He would foil them. Then it occurred to him to wonder how they expected to get possession of the prize. It did not take him long to conclude that she was to be betrayed by the teacher. It was common report that Eighmie had been twice to the seminary on that day, and as nothing was known of the result of his visits, this conclusion, though it seems to be harsh to us who know the truth, was by no means unnatural to one in his state of knowledge. That Hilda was to be betrayed he felt assured, and that he must save her he felt still more convinced.

It was now quite dark, and they were more than a mile beyond the seminary. Once or twice the party behind had halted. Then the dominie had stopped, too, and watched them through his little window. The others had not been unmindful of this maneuver.

"That old duffer's a-watching us, Colonel," said one of the assistants, speaking to Eighmie.

"What makes you think so?"

"Think? I know. When we go fast, he throws out a leg and gits away from us; when we slow up, he shuts off steam, and when we stop altogether, he anchors just ahead of us."

"Oh, pshaw! you're too suspicious, Barnes. How do you suppose that man knows any more about us than we do about him?"

"I don't know *how*, Colonel; but I'll lay a fiver that he knows us, knows our business here, and guesses, if he don't know for certain, that there's some sort of devilment brings us this way at this time of night."

"Really, Barnes, you're getting nervous. You seem to think these Yankees know everything."

"Don't you have any trouble about Jim Barnes. He never showed no white feather yet, and he ain't likely to now."

"But you were so eager for this plan—"

"So I were, Colonel; so I were—not exactly as hot for it as Bill Marsden, but I thought it a heap better 'n the one you had in mind."

"Of course it is," said the one called Marsden, sullenly. "I'd rather have a hundred men after me than a lot of screechin' gals at my heels."

"There ain't no doubt about this bein' the best way," said Barnes; "but they ain't neither of 'em clear of difficulty. You see, Colonel, I've been on this sort of expeditions before, and I tell ye what it is, these Yankees are mighty knowin' folks."

"They are said to be very inquisitive," said Eighmie, laughing, "but they haven't troubled us yet."

"That's just where our Southern folks make a mistake about the Yankees," said Barnes oracularly. "It ain't so much the number of questions they asks as 'tis the amount of things they'll find out without askin' questions, thet makes the Yankee different from the rest of mankind. Now, here we've been in this little town two days, and there hain't hardly been three questions asked all on us, but you can jest bet your bottom dollar there hain't a boy in Blankshire don't know who we are, where we come from, and thet we 're atter that gal they call Hildy Hargrove up there at Beechnut Seminary, or whatever its name is."

"That 's so," said Marsden. "You can read that in their faces, men, women and children, when we go 'long the street. Ye see, Colonel, we 're three strangers in a little 'huddle,' as they call it, where strangers ain't over-abundant as a rule, so they put things together and find out all about us while a Southern man 'ud be gettin' an introduction."

"That may be," said Eighmie; "but that 's no reason why the man in that buggy ahead should be watching us now."

"It may not be any reason," said Barnes, doggedly; "but they 're nigh about all against us here, an' when you 've got sech a thing on hand as we have to-night, it 's well enough to be lookin' out for accidents."

"Well, what do you propose?" asked Eighmie.

"We 've got to throw that fellow off his guard some way, and I think the best plan is to go by him. It may make us a little late, but we 've got to chance that; and, mind you, we ain't any worse off if this plan falls through in that way than if we hadn't started out on it."

"Well, go ahead," said Eighmie.

Barnes touched the horses with his whip, and almost at the instant they broke into a trot; the dominie's horse did likewise, and for a quarter of a mile, despite a constant acceleration of speed, the two vehicles kept at about the same distance apart, until finally the bay turned sharply into a lane leading up to a farmhouse on the hill-side, in whose window a bright light was burning.

"What do you think now?" asked Eighmie with a quiet laugh.

"Mebbe you 're right," said Barnes; "but I 'm always suspicious of a Yankee, and you 'll find, Colonel, that the safest way of dealing with 'em is to credit them with knowing all that you know and a little more besides."

The others laughed at Barnes' justification of his caution, and dismissed all farther thought of its cause.

Hardly had the other vehicle passed the opening of the lane, however, when the bay horse again slackened his speed to a walk, and the dominie, peering out at the side, watched the carriage until it disappeared from sight around a little hill that effectually hid from view the road along which they had come. Then he stopped the bay, listened a moment to make sure that he was not mistaken, reined his horse to one side of the narrow lane, backed until the near wheel touched the wall, gave the bay the word, and in a moment was whirling along the road they had come at a gait anything but ministerial. In five minutes he was in front of the seminary. It was considerably past the hour when he had hoped to arrive. The evening prayers were over, and the pupils had dispersed to their rooms. Many of them had retired, as the darkened windows showed. It would not do to drive up the frozen avenue. Still less would it do to go on a hundred yards and take the wood-road that led up to the rear of the building. He knew every inch of ground. The wood-road was narrow and rocky. If he had abundance of time, the sagacious bay would pick his way along it almost noiselessly, but haste was necessary now. Hilda must be waiting. At any moment the enemy might return. He passed through the gate, turned out of the avenue upon the lawn, crushing an *arbor vitæ* beneath each wheel as he broke through the scanty hedge, drove noiselessly along the turf until

he reached the opening between the carriage-house and
the kitchen, looked hastily about, and, seeing no one,
let the horse take its way to the rear of the premises,
and turned him down the wood-road to a clump of evergreens half a dozen rods away. By this thicket the
horse and buggy were completely hidden. He lowered
the top of the buggy, threw the robe over the dash-
board, twisted the reins about the whip, stepped quickly
down, and hurried back toward the house.

The night was a cool one, and he swung his arms and
stamped cautiously upon the turf by the roadside to restore the circulation as he went. The stars shone
brightly, but there was no moon. As he neared the
rear of the building he moved more cautiously. He
fancied he heard a step in the bushes at his left, and
thinking it might be Hilda waiting for him, he stopped
and called her name softly. There was no answer, but
he was sure he heard a suppressed breathing.

"Hilda—my child—Miss Hargrove—don't be afraid.
It's I, Mr. Anderson. Are you there?" he said in a half
whisper. Then he listened. No answer. He could
hear his heart beat. The stars seemed blinking in
mockery at his anxiety. He was sure a human being
was crouching near him. A thrill of terror swept
through his frame. Could it be that the kidnappers
had an accomplice watching outside? Had the poor
girl been seized because of his delay? A thousand possibilities occurred to him ere he had breathed twice.
Then a touch of fear came. It was a strange position
for him, a minister of the Gospel, to be in. Suppose he
should be set upon and overpowered? Suppose he
should get into a conflict with these Southern despera-
does? Suppose— He shook his broad shoulders and
threw away his fears. He would suppose nothing. He
had come to do right—God's right—and he would do it
whatever the result. His hands shut tight and his teeth

met under his tawny beard like the jaws of a vise. He was no child to be frightened at a shadow. He marched with the step of a grenadier to the corner of the carriage-house and stood there listening. A solitary pine growing just at the corner of the stable screened him from view in all directions. There was no light at the back of the house except in Amy's room, and a soft flickering one in Hilda's. Presently the former was extinguished. Then he watched the door expecting Hilda to appear. He was afraid to approach the house and knock lest he should destroy her chances of escape. Then he remembered her girlish escapade of climbing down the roof, and thought perchance she might have recourse to the same method again. He heard the horses munching their food in their stalls, and wondered if it could be that, not finding him at his post, she might not have saddled her horse and fled without waiting for his aid. It was like her to do so. She was not the girl to sit quietly and meet an evil fate. The cold stung him as he waited and speculated on his strange position. Should he go or stay ? He had forgotten those whom he had come to circumvent; he thought only of the girl whom he meant to succor. He had almost lost hope, but still he waited. Something had evidently gone wrong ! He did not know the time, but it was past nine o'clock, for the lights were all extinguished. He had just decided to wait no longer when he heard a sound that put all thought of leaving out of his mind.

There was a step upon the gravel walk beyond the carriage-house—soft and stealthy, but a man's step— then another. Then two men came from beyond the carriage-house bearing something between them. Very cautiously they passed through the open gate within a yard of where he stood, and went round the rear of the building to the other side of the wing. What was it they were carrying ? He could not imagine. He waited till they had passed out of sight, and then stole softly along and peered around the corner of the house. Not twenty feet away two men were raising a ladder to the roof beneath Hilda's window. The whole scheme flashed upon him at a glance. The other man was waiting in the carriage. These were to bring the girl, and before morning poor Hilda would be on her way to servitude without hope of rescue. It all depended upon him. He was one to two—aye, one to three, and unarmed at that. But then he had been a champion wrestler at old Bowdoin in his youth. He had grown up a fisherman's son on the coast of Maine, and had matched his muscle against wind and tide in many a storm. He would do what he could. But for his remissness Hilda would have been beyond danger now. He had no idea what he would do. A thousand plans flashed through his mind. He did nothing—only waited.

One man was half-way up the ladder when a stone fell from the orchard wall not a rod from where he stood. There was a rustle in the bushes, too. The man upon the ladder paused. The watcher at the corner could hear their words as they whispered to each other in the chill night air.

"What 's that, Colonel?"

There was a moment's silence.

"Nothing, I reckon—a stone loosened by the frost, or a cat, maybe."

They waited a moment more, then the man ascended. "Now," thought the minister, "is my time," and yet he hesitated. He felt a stone beneath his foot, and reached down and picked it up. He clutched it eagerly in his right hand. It made a deadly weapon in that brawny fist. He felt himself a match for the man at the foot of the ladder, however he might be armed. He took a step forward, then paused, holding his hand before him irresolutely. "No," he thought, "I will not subject myself to temptation. Only as a last resort will I use a weapon." He dropped the stone in the pocket of his overcoat.

There was a low, tremulous moan. The man at the foot of the ladder ran quickly up to the eaves. The minister sprang forward and saw the other one step out of the window of Hilda's room with a limp, white figure in his arms.

"She's all right, Colonel," he heard him say. "She won't make no more fuss. You jes' steddy the ladder while I bring her down."

The minister stood spell-bound. The horror of the scene overpowered his faculties. He could neither move nor cry out. One man was at the foot of the ladder and the other half-way down before he awoke to the necessity of instant action. Colonel Eighmie heard a step, and turned his head quickly over his shoulder, still keeping his grasp upon the ladder. The minister took five steps like a whirlwind, and his fist fell with the force of a sledge-hammer at the base of Eighmie's ear.

"Scoundrels! Kidnappers!" he hissed through his set teeth.

Eighmie staggered and fell, half overturning the ladder as he did so.

"No ye don't," said the voice of Barnes, as he sprang up the ladder with his limp burden.

It was too late. Hardly had he reached the eaves when the ladder, disturbed by the fall of Eighmie, slipped, turned, and the top began to slide slowly along the tin gutter against which it rested. Barnes saw that he must drop the girl or fall with her to the ground and into the hands of he knew not how many enemies. It did not take him long to decide between a negro girl and himself. In an instant his arms were free; and, clutching the ladder with one hand and the spouting with the other, he threw his feet against the upright

portion of the building and swung himself lightly upon
the roof which he had lately quitted. Gilbert Anderson
looking upward, saw the white figure as it fell, and
springing forward, caught it before it reached the
ground. The shock brought him to his knees, but he
rallied and started to run toward where his horse was
waiting. As he did so, Barnes, who began to realize
the weakness of the attacking party, and who, even
when engaged in an unlawful enterprise, was, as he had
quietly declared, "no part of a coward," swung down
from the eave-spout and dropped to the ground. Anderson
had just turned the corner when he started in pursuit.
He was a little shaken by his fall, and not noticing the
ladder which lay in his way he stumbled over it, and
fell heavily to the ground. By the time he reached the
corner of the house Anderson was almost out of sight.
Only a flutter of white down the lane served to guide
him in his pursuit.

Even with the burden which he bore Anderson would
have found it easy to outstrip his pursuer had he gone
up the hill instead of trying to utilize his buggy as a
means of escape. The time occupied in placing the
half-unconscious girl in the vehicle enabled Barnes,
who had no idea of yielding peaceable possession of his
booty, to approach almost within striking distance before Anderson could back his horse out of the bushes and
take his seat in the buggy. He stood holding the reins
in his left hand, which also supported the young girl
upon the seat. His right hand clasped the stone in the
pocket of his overcoat. He could just see the outlines
of the man's figure as he stood in the shadow of the
pines. The right hind wheel of the buggy was between
them.

"Halt!" shouted Barnes. "Give up that gal or I
fire!"

The hand flew from the pocket; the stone whistled

through the air; there was a flash, a shriek; the minister sprang into the buggy, and the sparks flew out of the cold rocks along the wood-road as the frightened bay sped homeward. The figure that lay across his lap, hidden by the robe, moaned and shivered, but never once replied to his repeated assurances of safety. When he reached the highway Anderson raised the cover of the buggy but did not check the speed of the excited horse until the wheels rattled up the entrance to his own barn. Then he leaped out, looked carefully around, and, taking the girl in his arms, he bore her into the house. As he laid her upon the lounge in the cosy sitting-room his wife saw that his hands were stained with blood. As he stood looking at the ominous stain she sprang forward, and, lifting the bowed head, they gazed into the thin, pinched face, now bloodless and pallid, of Amy Hargrove.

"Why, husband!" cried the wife, "this is not Hilda! What does it all mean?"

"I—I—don't—know!" said the minister in amazement. Nor did it matter. A physician who was soon called pronounced the wound dangerous, and prescribed silence, darkness and the strictest care. The bullet of the slave-catcher had just missed the heart of the informer.

· · · · · · · · · ·

Ten o'clock brought the southward train and the full moon. Other strangers came likewise to Burlingdale. The battered sign that hung at the door of the unpretentious inn creaked on its hinges in surprise as they passed beneath it. The rooms were full for once, and the smiling landlord thought to himself, as he looked over his register, that a fugitive slave was almost as good for an inn-keeper as a circus. Two of the newcomers were evidently officials. They had that unmistakable uniform of self-importance that leads one to consider whether life would be worth living should reform at length fix the limits of life as the measure of official tenure. They inquired for Mr. Eighmie, and when told that he was not in looked knowingly at each other.

They were the United States marshal for the district and his deputy. They had a warrant under the broad seal of the District Court running in the name of the Chief Justice of the United States, commanding them to take the body of a certain slave-girl Hilda, otherwise known as Hilda Hargrove. They evidently understood the situation, or thought they did, for after some refreshment they started out on foot toward the seminary. A young man had taken the same direction a few minutes before. He turned off into the wood-road ; they advanced straight on, and, turning into the grounds, walked up the avenue to the house. Just as they reached it they met Marsden and Eighmie. There was a hurried consultation, not altogether pleasing to the officer of the law as it seemed. After a moment he said angrily :

"So it seems, gentlemen, that instead of waiting for the assistance of the law you have attempted an abduction and been roughly handled."

"We found the girl was about to escape, sir," said Marsden.

"Very likely," said the marshal, incredulously.

"Oh, but we did, sir !" said Eighmie seriously.

"Well, even if you did, it is no excuse for your violation of the law. I can have nothing to do with it."

"But the girl, sir," said Eighmie, "and the rascals who set upon us ?"

"I understand you took the girl out of the house, and she was then taken from you ?"

"Yes ; and there was a shot fired, and we believe Barnes must have been killed."

"Very likely. People who will insist on being kidnappers must expect to get their necks broken. I will have nothing to do with it. There is no use of disturbing the seminary people any more. Indeed, you have disturbed them too much now for your own good. I should advise you, gentlemen, to make yourselves scarce before morning."

"Just what I've been telling him," said Marsden quickly, "but he won't take any advice."

"I will not go until I know the fate of Barnes," said Eighmie stubbornly. "I may have acted imprudently. If I have violated the law, I am ready to suffer for it; but I will not desert a man who shared the danger at my request."

"Help! Murder! Help!" came from the wood-road as he spoke.

They all ran quickly in the direction of the sound. In the middle of the lane, by the little clump of evergreens near which the minister's horse had stood, a man was kneeling and supporting on his arm the head of another. The moon was shining full upon the face of the prostrate man. They scrambled over the wall, the marshal and his deputy ahead, the others following.

"Barnes!" said Marsden, as soon as he caught sight of the face. He knelt down and put a hand upon his breast. "Dead!"

The man who was supporting the other had no hat. His face was pale, and his teeth chattered as he looked from one to another of the observers.

"What does it mean?" he asked.

"It means murder, young man—that's what it means!" said Eighmie excitedly.

"Murder?"

"Yes, murder."

"Who could have done it?"

"You were the first that found it out it seems," said Marsden, with a sneer.

"I?"

" Yes, you !"

" But I know nothing about it. I stumbled over him as I came along just now."

" Just now ?" said Marsden, still sneering. " This is a pretty time of night for a stroll, ain't it ?"

The young man laid the dead man's head carefully upon the ground, and, rising, folded his arms, and said with dignity :

"Gentlemen, if any one has any suspicion of me, I am willing to answer to the law ; but I will not endure such remarks from any but an officer of the law."

" You are right, too," said the marshal. "I am an officer—the United States Marshal. When did you find this body ?"

" Just a moment ago."

" What were you doing here at this hour ?"

The young man's face flushed, and he stammered as he tried to answer.

" Tell the truth," said the marshal, " or do not speak at all. Where is your hat ?"

"I don't know," he answered confusedly. "It must have fallen off when I stumbled."

"Quite likely," said Marsden, with a sneer. "Perhaps this is it ?"

He drew a crushed and battered hat from under his knee beside the dead man as he spoke. The other assented silently by taking it, brushing off the dust and striving to restore it to its original shape. It was sodden on one side. His hand was moistened as he brushed, and he carelessly wiped it against his sleeve.

The marshal watched him keenly.

"What is your name ?" he asked.

" Martin Kortright."

" That is he," said Eighmie excitedly. "I knew he was one of her friends. He did it, you may be sure. He 's her lover, sir."

"Hers—whose?"

"Hilda's—the girl we're after—the one we had when we were attacked."

"What of her? Where is she? What do you mean?" said Martin, striding over the prostrate form and clutching the arm of Eighmie.

"Stand off!" said Eighmie. "Stand off! Oh, you know where she is! And you know about this, too," pointing to the body of Barnes. "Why don't you arrest him, Mr. Marshal? Are you going to let him escape?"

"I am sorry to say I must arrest both him and you, gentlemen. This is a matter for the state courts; but, as a felony has been committed, if not two, I must take you into custody and deliver you to the state authorities. Come."

As he turned there was a rush into the undergrowth at the road-side, and Marsden fled up the mountain-side.

"Never mind," said the officer to his deputy, "we will hold these two. The fool thinks he can get away, but he hasn't a ghost of a chance."

He laid his hand on Martin's shoulder as he spoke, and the deputy in like manner took hold of Eighmie.

"You need not hold me," said Eighmie. "I will go wherever you wish."

"So will I," said Martin.

"Come on then, gentlemen," said the marshal; "but let us see if this poor fellow is really dead. Take hold, and let us carry him to the seminary."

The officers and their prisoners bore the inanimate form carefully around to the front of the building, and laid him down upon the broad, white steps just as a carriage drove up, and the mistress of Beechwood alighted.

CHAPTER XL.

"DEAD? Impossible!" was the exclamation of Miss Hunniwell, after a hurried explanation by the marshal. "Who could have killed him?"

"We have felt bound to hold this young man, who was found with the body," said the marshal almost apologetically.

The lady glanced keenly at Martin and asked, with that mixture of command and interrogation which the successful teacher is sure to acquire:

"Who found him with it?"

"Well, I and my deputy—that is, he gave the alarm and we ran to the place and found him supporting this man's head."

"And you—where were you when he called?"

"We were just entering the grounds."

"Just entering these grounds! Why, how long ago did this happen?"

"Only a short time—perhaps twenty minutes."

"And pray, sir, what were you doing on my premises at this hour of the night?"

"I am the United States Marshal for this district," said the official, somewhat pompously.

"Well?" ejaculated the unrelenting inquisitor, as she looked down upon him from the steps.

The moonlight showed a flush upon his cheek as he answered:

"I have a warrant for the arrest of a certain fugitive slave, and was directed by the claimant to meet him here upon the arrival of the train."

" And this young man—who is he ?"

" I am Martin Kortright, ma'am," said he, answering for himself, and removing his hat as he did so.

" Ah ! I am very glad to meet you," she said, stepping forward and giving him her hand. " You came upon the train in answer to my telegram ?"

" Yes, ma'am," he replied.

" And you came out here—why ?"

" I was somewhat alarmed by your dispatch, and thought I would come and look at the place without waiting for morning."

" I see ; and in so doing you fell among thieves," said the lady severely. " I do not understand what has taken place in my absence," she continued, " but whether this man be dead or alive, this is not a fit place for him to remain. Bring him in."

She had rung the bell on her arrival, and a teacher with a pallid face that told of the terrors that had afflicted the gentle flock at Beechwood during the absence of the mistress, now answered her summons. Miss Hunniwell took the candle from her trembling hand, and, standing beside the open door, motioned to the men to enter. As they ascended the steps she directed her coachman to drive at once for a physician and an officer of the law.

The latter portion of her message was altogether needless. The anger of the good minister had grown into a flame when he learned the gravity of Amy's hurt. How the mistake should have arisen, or whether it was a mistake, he could not tell. The more he thought upon it the stronger grew his suspicion that Hilda was yet in danger. He lost no time, therefore, in letting certain of his neighbors, including the officers of the law in the village, know that a crime had been committed. The fear which he had entertained for a time as to the result of his own action had passed away, and he now only felt a renewed anxiety for the safety of Hilda and the capture of her abductors. The atmosphere of the little village was already charged with explosive material. The presence of the slave-hunters and something of the nature of their errand was well known in the town, and in many a household the evening prayer that night had contained an especially earnest petition for " them that are in bonds." The whole village seemed to rest in anticipation of exciting events. Men and women were awake and eager to know what had happened. Almost before he knew it the good minister found himself returning to the scene of the night's adventure with a band of resolute men, whose action was all the more significant because there were no threats or boasts to be heard among them. The constable had a pistol, or was supposed to have one, but except for walking-sticks and extemporized clubs wrenched from picket-fences or cut with the ever-ready pocket-knife from the overhanging elms that lined the streets, very few of them were armed. As they approached the place where the road leading to the seminary turned off to the left the sound of a vehicle rapidly driven over the frozen ground reached their ears. Then the hoof-strokes of a double team were heard upon the bridge. Some boys who had pushed on ahead of the main company gave the alarm.

" That's them !" " It's Bassett's grays !" " The kidnappers !" and other like cries were heard as the boys leaped the fences and sought shelter from attack. Instinctively the men formed a line across the road, and as the wagon rolled out of the darkness of the covered bridge into the moonlight, Marsden, who was the sole occupant of the carriage, could distinctly see their earnest faces and the hurried preparations that were being made to obstruct his course. For an instant he half-checked the horses in their sweeping trot. Then he saw that it was too late. There was no room to turn. He might burst through. At all events it was his only chance. The obstruction was forty yards away, and once past that barrier it was only twenty miles to the state line. Behind him was—he knew not what of danger. He drew the reins tighter, and gave the lash to the sprightly grays. As he neared the line the men wavered. It was no light matter to stand in the way of the infuriated team. Marsden rose up, lashed the horses, and gave a shrill yell of defiance. Just before he reached the corner a new barrier suddenly arose across his way. Two men had lifted a white picket gate from its hinges, and now held it suspended between them above the roadway. Seeing their purpose, a dozen sprang to their aid. It was impassable, reaching high above the horses' heads, and shifting to this side and that as their course seemed to vary. The only chance was to try and break it down. He headed the horses square against it. The pole burst through the narrow palings. The men who held it were thrown down, but the frame of the gate was against the horses' legs. Their feet were caught between the slats. They stumbled and fell. A dozen hands seized the wheels before they had ceased to revolve. Marsden, thrown forward and half-stunned, was a prisoner before he had time to draw a weapon, and was marched off, with his hands tied, to the town-hall under charge of a trusty guard.

His attempt at escape had failed. After climbing the hill-side a short distance, he had realized the futility of trying to escape in that manner, and stealing back to the road, had sought to use the method which had been decided upon in case of success, without waiting to ascertain any more definitely the fate of his companions.

After this the company, now much diminished in numbers, moved on. Meeting the coachman from the semi-

nary, the minister asked him a few hurried questions, to
which the man gave most confusing replies. All that he
could gather from him was that some one was dead, or
at least badly injured, at the seminary, and he had been
sent for the doctor. Directing him where the physician might be found, they proceeded. Before they
reached the grounds the carriage passed them on its return. Then they halted for consultation, and it was
determined that the better way would be to quietly sur-
round the building, after which the constable and a few
others should go forward to reconnoitre. Nothing could
be done, that worthy said, until a warrant was issued.
This the justice would fill out upon the minister's information as soon as he could procure the names of the
kidnappers from the register at the hotel. All they
could do in the meantime was merely to prevent the
escape of the offenders. So the mob waited in patient
silence for the ponderous wheels of the law to move
round.

While these things were occurring in the village an
equally strange scene had been enacted in the seminary. Following the direction of Miss Hunniwell the
men bore their unconscious burden along the hall and
into one of the reception-rooms, leaving a row of crimson drops from the door to the side of a low settle on
which she directed that he should be placed. Wondering eyes and pallid faces peered over the banisters
above at this strange procession. Water was brought
and a sponge; and Miss Hunniwell, tucking back her
lace-edged sleeves, took the basin and washed the blood
from the coarse pale face. As she did so she noted a soft,
uncertain breath. The marshal found a dim pulsation at
the wrist also. The left temple was crushed and torn.
Out of the severed fibres came a slender, fitful stream
of red. Martin pressed his finger hard upon a point
just in front of and above the ear and it ceased. Then

they poured a little brandy down his throat. His res-
piration became more regular and decided. Then the
surgeon came—a gruff, fearless man, with the freedom
of speech and positiveness of manner that the old country practitioner gets. He examined the wounded man
carefully; tried the skull, to find any fracture or depression; caught up the severed artery and dressed the
wound.

"He'll get along," said he grimly, when his examination was completed. "A concussion of the brain with
a considerable loss of blood. That's what saved him
probably, though it has left him weak. It was a close
call—would have killed most men; but these cattle never
die when they ought to."

"Can he be removed?" inquired Eighmie anxiously.

"When, to-night?" asked the physician, looking keenly
at his interrogator.

"Yes."

"No indeed!"

"When do you think?"

"Well, I should say fully as soon as his employer
will be likely to have any use for him."

"I don't understand you, sir."

"You probably will before you are through with to-
night's business."

"I am ready to answer for all my acts, sir," said
Eighmie somewhat defiantly.

"Oh yes!" sneered the doctor, "we've heard of your
Southern bravado before, but you'll need something
more 'n that this time, or I'm mistaken."

"Come, come, gentlemen," said the marshal, "this
is no place to discuss these things. What we want to
know and what Miss Hunniwell wants to know is, what
we had better do with this man."

"If you ask my opinion *as a man*," said the doctor
savagely, "I would say pitch the carrion out-doors and

cheat the gallows by letting him die, before he has a chance to be hanged."

"That is the humanity of which the Yankee is forever prating," said Eighmie sneeringly.

"A fair match for the chivalry of which you boast," hissed the doctor in reply. "If I ain't mistaken you 're the man that came here to drag a young girl into slavery after killing her father."

"The man who claimed to be her father was killed."

"Yes, shot in the back without being allowed to surrender."   .

"But that was in the heat of passion, sir. All our good people regret it now."

"And do you suppose that we have no heat of passion? Damn it, sir!" cried the doctor, white with wrath and striding toward Eighmie, "I 'd be very glad to help hang the whole of your hellish crowd to a tree without judge or jury."

"See here, doctor!" said the marshal, stepping between them; "what is the matter? I never saw you in such a mood as this before. I thought you were a moderate, reasonable man."

"Don't talk to me of reason. Everybody knows I 've never been an Abolitionist or anything of the kind, but I 've seen that to-night that makes me actually bloodthirsty. I 'm a law-abiding man, but, as certain as God lives, if the girl dies, I 'm ready to make one of a crowd to hang every scoundrel that had a hand in this business higher than Haman."

"Doctor, you are raving," said the marshal, pushing him back.

"Oh, I am, am I?" said the doctor. "Well, let me tell you, sir, I mean every word of it, and I don't draw any distinction between a Southern slave-hunter and a Northern nigger-catcher, either."

"If you mean me, sir," said the marshal angrily,

"I came here to perform a sworn duty. I am just as much bound to execute the law as you are to obey it. I have no more interest in this matter than you."

"Except double fees in case of conviction," sneered the doctor.

"I didn't make the law," said the other doggedly.

"No, you only volunteered to do the dirty work that was cut out for you."

"What do you mean by murder, doctor?" asked Miss Hunniwell, laying her hand upon his arm, and looking into his face with anxious solicitude.

"Where have you been to-night, madam?" inquired the doctor, turning sharply upon her.

She stammered, and her face flushed. She was not used to prevarication, and yet she dare not reveal the truth.

"I—I—have—been out with a friend—I have just returned."

"Oh, I see!" he said incredulously. "So you don't know what these gentlemen have been about here at Beechwood in your absence?"

"I can only imagine that it must be something very terrible."

"Terrible? Yes, I should think so. Well, I don't know all about it myself, but I do know that these nigger-hunting gentry have made it just about an even chance whether one of your girls lives to see the sun rise or not."

"Is it Hilda—Hilda Hargrove?" asked Martin, impetuously grasping the doctor's arm as he spoke.

"No, it wasn't Hilda—'twas the other one—the little black-eyed creature that was always with her."

"Amy?" asked the teacher.

"Yes, that's her name."

"But Hilda—where is Hilda then?" persisted Martin, keeping his hold upon the doctor's arm.

"That I can't tell you, young man, if you shake me all night. Perhaps this gentleman can give you some information," jerking his thumb toward Eighmie as he spoke. "Whether they made a mistake, or thought it just as cheap to kidnap two girls as one, I don't know, but I guess they'll have a chance to explain before they've done with it."

Martin turned toward Eighmie, but as he was about to speak he felt the teacher's hand upon his arm.

"Do not be troubled," she whispered hastily ; "Hilda is safe."

While this was passing footsteps were heard advancing along the hall. The constable entered, and said:

"I have a warrant for Sherwood Eighmie."

"That is my name," said Eighmie, stepping forward.

"Also," said the constable, "for James S. Barnes."

Eighmie pointed to the wounded man.

"Not able to be moved?" asked the constable of the doctor.

"Not under a week—more likely a fortnight," said the physician.

"Well, come on, then," to Eighmie.

"Wait a moment," said the other. Then, turning to the doctor, he produced a roll of bills, and said earnestly: "Doctor, I don't know how this thing is going to end, but I want you to see that this man is taken care of. He was injured in my service, and I must not desert him."

"Oh, I will see that he is cared for," said the doctor, though he isn't worth it. Give the money to Miss Hunniwell, sir. She will need to get nurses and delicacies. Never mind me. I wouldn't work a bit better for all the money in your purse. After it's all over I'll put in my bill. But you may rest assured that I will do my very best for the poor devil professionally, though, personally, I honestly think no man ever needed hanging worse than he.''

"What he did," said Eighmie, "was at my instigation. I won't shirk any responsibility, whatever the result."

"Well, I will say that is a manly thing," said the doctor heartily, "and I do hope that we have seen the worst side of this night's work."

"Thank you," said Eighmie simply. "I would like to ask a favor of you if I might."

"Anything I can honestly do in your behalf you may rely upon my doing. Professionally, you need have no fear that I will not do my best for the patient."

"It is not that," said Eighmie hesitantly, "but would you mind—the young lady—I don't suppose you know how I feel about it. Of course, I am sorry for the hurt she has received, but I would rather die—I would even rather she would die—than have it thought —than have her think—that I would kidnap a free white girl in order to make her a slave."

"Yet you intended to abduct one as white as she."

"Yes, a slave."

"No," said the doctor, shaking his head solemnly; "I can't understand it. To my mind the evil that is done, even if the worst result, is less than the evil you intended. Nevertheless, I will tell Miss Amy how much you regret the mistake, though I doubt if she will understand your feeling any better than I do."

"Perhaps not," responded Eighmie; "yet I should be glad to have her know I did not intend her any harm."

Then they went away, leaving only the doctor, Martin, the mistress of Beechwood and the still unconscious man upon the settle.

It was necessary that the doctor should return, as Amy needed close attention. He had just begun to give

directions for the care of Barnes to Martin, who consented to watch with him that night, when the minister
entered and declared his intention of caring for the sick
man, avowing his own responsibility for his condition.
After this explanation, Miss Hunniwell gave Martin
Hilda's letter, and he returned to the village only to
learn that the shadow which had seemed to lift from
his pathway so unexpectedly had only closed about it
more darkly than before.

For the teacher this eventful night had still another
surprise. As she left the reception-room to go to the
chamber a dark form stepped out of the shadow of the
stairway and addressed her in tones of respectful entreaty:

"Please, ma'am, will you tell me where our Miss
Hilda is, and if she's got safe away?"

"Who are you?" asked the startled lady, in a low,
cautious tone.

"I'm Marse Hargrove's ole servant, ma'am. Jason
they call me—sometimes Jason Unthank—'kase my ole
marster's name was Unthank, you know."

"I have heard Hilda speak of you frequently, Jason."

"Of course yer has, honey. Why I brought her up,
mostly—Marse Merwyn an' me—atter the young missus
died."

"You knew Hilda when she was a child, Jason?"
said the teacher, with a new interest in her tones.

"Knew her! Lor' bress yer, yis. Wasn't I down
there in the Indies when she was born? I 'spect I
seed her 'fore she was a day ole, an' hain't hardly
hed my eyes offen her sence dat time—only when I 'se
been off on a v'y'ge with Marse Captain, or something
of that sort, yer know."

"Oh, Jason, if we had only known this before, all
this trouble and bloodshed might have been avoided."

"Please, ma'am, what's it all about? What's Marse

Eighmie an' his crowd a-pesterin' Miss Hilda 'bout, any-how?"

"They claim she is a slave."

"Who says dat? It's a lie! My Miss Hilda a nig-ger! Bress her heart, dat she ain't. Jes' let me know who says dat, ma'am, an' ole Jason 'll settle wid him for it. Dam rascals! I couldn't understan' what 'twas all about, but I seed she war in a heap of trouble. So I waited roun', an' when dey tried to carry her off, yer know, I was jis' a gwine ter lay Marse Eighmie out wid a rock when in rushed dat other feller, grabbed Miss Hilda 'way from 'em an' run. Den I was all struck in a heap, an' hardly knowed which one ter lite on; but I knowed that Marse Eighmie an' his crowd didn't mean her no good, an' 'lowed dat 'tother man couldn't be any wuss. Besides, I heard him callin' to her ez ef he wuz friends with her. So I didn't stop to ax no questions, an' when one of Marse Eighmie's men begun shootin' at him I jes' turned in on him myself. That 's the reason yer had to send fer the doctor fer him, I 'spect," he con-cluded coolly, with a sly nod toward the room where Barnes was lying.

"Hush, Jason, you must not speak so loud," said Miss Hunniwell, herself hardly able to control her con-flicting emotions. "Come in here; I must talk with you."

"Yes, ma'am," said Jason as he followed her with the peculiar noiseless tread of the well-trained body-servant, which, without being stealthy, seems always to come and go without any appeal to our consciousness. She opened the door of the little library or office that adjoined her own room. A fire was smouldering upon the hearth, which Jason deftly coaxed into a cheerful blaze. The mistress of Beechwood plied the old ser-vant with questions until fully convinced that he was able to relieve Hilda not only of the fear of enslavement

but of the still greater horror of a corrupted lineage. It
was with no little difficulty, however, that she restrained
his impatience to learn the whereabouts of Hilda :

"You see, ma'am, I'se got ter find her. Marse Captain jes dat las' minute 'fore I jumped abo'd de sloop,
when he jes made me put him down an' leave him 'kase
'tweren't possible for both on us ter git off—though I 'd
a heap ruther staid an' died with him thar, I would,
ma'am, an' no mistake—that very minute Marse Hargrove tuk out ob his bosom dis yer package I'se got
here,"—striking his breast pocket as he spoke—"an' he
says to me, 'Jason, don't you miss givin' dat into Miss
Hilda's own han's yourself. It 's my last words, my
will an' test'ment, Jason ; my last blessing to my darling, Jason, which she must have or she won't be happy
no more as long as she lives.' An' I swar to him right
thar, ma'am, jes' a minute afore I seed him shot dead,
dat I wouldn't let no man's nor woman's han' tech dat
ar letter till I give it into Miss Hilda's own dear han's ;
an' I won't nuther. So yer see I'se *got* ter see Miss
Hilda, an' right away too."

The man's excitement had made him forget the better
language of his later years and brought the dialect of
his youth to his tongue.

"Why didn't you come and give it to her before ?"
asked the woman tearfully.

"I was afeared to, ma'am. You know this trouble I
was in with Marse Merwyn, an' I was afraid de law
might take hold on me, yer know. Some of de papers
do say we 'd all be took back dar to be tried yet—
which jes' means hangin' straight out in sech a case yer
know. Then thar was Marse Eighmie. I seed him
a-hangin' round here, an' I 'lowed he was atter me,
never once dreamin' he was tryin' to git my pore Miss
Hilda to make a nigger on her. Ef I 'd only knowed
that, ther' wouldn't been no trouble 'bout him an' his

crowd now. Jason would hev settled with the las' one of 'em a heap better 'n he did with dat mean white critter in yon, too.''

"Jason, Mr. Anderson thinks he is the one that injured that man ? He feels very badly about it," said Miss Hunniwell.

"Mr. Anderson—that's the man that thought he was helping Miss Hilda. I remember hearing him speak his name now. He's a perfect gentleman, that man is; but, pshaw ! that rock he threw wouldn't a-stopped that low-down cuss a quarter of a minute ef Jason hadn't a tuk a hand in 'bout dat time.''

" But you ought to let him know, so that he will not feel so badly. He's nursing him now, because he thinks it his duty to help restore the man he has injured.''

" Certain, ma'am, certain. I'll do that, and I'd be glad to do the nussin', too, after I've seen Miss Hilda, you know. I hain't a doubt I'd do it a heap better than Mr. Anderson. I seed him when he come in, an' he don't look like he was cut out for a nuss, nohow.''

" But I don't know where Hilda is," said Miss Hunniwell.

" You don't know ? Didn't this man, Mr. Anderson, take her away in his buggy ?''

" No, that was another young lady they got by mistake.''

" Then whar has my young mistis gone ?''

" I took her away in my carriage just before dark.''

" An' yet don't know where she is ?" suspiciously.

"Just so, Jason. I took her to the depot, and saw her take the train.''

" Where was she goin' ?" asked Jason, picking up his hat, that was lying at his feet, as if about to start in pursuit.

"I don't know," was the answer.

"Don't know? Didn't she tell yer whar she was goin'?" asked the man almost angrily.

"She not only did not tell me, Jason, but she positively refused to do so."

"Den I mus' find her," said Jason, with a long-drawn sigh. "I promised Marse Merwyn, an' I'll do it ef I don't nebber hev ary other day's rest while I live."

"But, Jason," began Miss Hunniwell.

"Don't talk ter me; don't talk," said Jason shaking his hand toward her and turning away his head. "I'll jes' keep a-trampin' day an' night till I find dat ar gal— dat Miss Hilda. Dat I will, an' dar ain't no use in talkin' 'bout it. I'm much obleeged to ye, ma'am, but I might jes' ez well be gittin' 'long. Dar ain't no sense in waiting heah."

He started toward the door as he spoke.

"But where will you go, Jason?"

"Oh, it don't matter—anywhar. P'r'aps de Lord will kinder show me de way for de pore chile's sake. I don't take much stock in de Lord myself, kase it 'pears to me He's mighty onreliable. Take Him up one side an' down de other, an' I can't see ez it makes more 'n about a good average—fair to middlin' ez they say about cotting."

"Jason," said the teacher sternly, "you must not speak in that manner."

"Can't help it, ma'am; I p'intedly can't. What the Lord let that low-down, poor, way-off Eighmie crowd kill Marse Hargrove for?"

"I cannot tell, Jason; but you know He had some good purpose in it, and He will guide you in your search for Hilda if you will only follow where He leads."

"It may be, ma'am, but I don't see ez He's a-doin' any leadin' now, nor anything else, only mixin' matters up so that it looks as ef they'd never git straight agin."

"That is because you will not wait and trust Him, Jason. You want everything done in your own way."

"I wants dat little gal got outen her trouble. Dat's what I want, ma'am; an' I wants it done right away, too."

"That is all right for you to wish, Jason; but you must follow God and not try to lead Him. Just think, now. The whole world is before you. You don't know whether Hilda has gone east or west or north or south."

"I reckon *you* knows which way the train was goin' that she got on, don't yer?"

"I don't even know that, Jason. I was so fearful for her, and so flustered by the danger she was in, that I could do nothing but watch and see that she was safe upon the train, and then close my eyes in grateful prayer. There were two trains at the station. When I looked again both were going out. Which Hilda was on I don't know."

"She's done gone back to Sturmhold, dat's whar she's gone," said Jason, after a moment's pause.

"That's where she has not gone," said the teacher. "You forget that she was hiding—hiding away from Mr. Eighmie, and hiding away from Martin Kortright."

"What's she hidin' from young Marse Martin for?"

"Because she was afraid that—that what they said about her father might be true."

"I see," said Jason, "I see. She was afraid there might be jes' one little drap of colored blood in her veins, an' she'd rather die than see Marse Martin agin ef ther was. I don't blame her nuther—I don't blame her. It's the cuss of Cain, shore, an' it's no wonder that blessed chile should feel like hidin' away when she thought she hed it jes' like ole Cain hisself when he hear de Lord a callin' atter him. Yis, you're right. She's hid jes' ez safe ez a young partridge. Marse Martin 'll try powerful hard, but he won't find

her—never! Miss Hilda's too peart for dat. She's
her pappy all over, Miss Hilda is, only she looks powerful like her ma, pore dear. He won't never find her
ez long ez she keeps on hidin'; no mo' will Jason
nuther. Ther ain't no give up in that gal more 'n ther
was in her pa—not a bit. When she's once sot her
head on anything she'll stan' to it till the very last.
We won't never find her, none of us, ma'am, unless the
Lord *does* take hold an' show us whar she's hid. Pore
gal! pore gal!"

The faithful servant sank down upon the floor,
thoroughly crushed with disappointment. Miss Hunniwell arose, and, putting her hand upon his shoulder, said :

"There, there, Jason. Don't be cast down. There
is a chance, a hope, which we must not lose sight of.
She has promised to write to me."

"Yer don't say," said Jason, raising his head.
"When ?"

"At least within a year. Sooner, if she is in trouble
or need of any kind."

"An' will yer let ole Jason know where de pore
chile is ?"

"Just as soon as I hear."

"Bless God, ma'am, I'll stay right here an' wait.
Don't ye want ter hire a boy, ma'am ?" said he, with a
quick rebound from grief to joy, peculiar to his mercu-
rial race, as he sprang to his feet and bowed laughingly
before her, like a slave-boy seeking a home at the
Christmas time. Though past middle life Jason retained
the activity of youth and like all his race defied the
closest observer to determine his age.

"Yes, I do," said Miss Hunniwell, entering into the
humor of his request, and catching at once at this
means of serving Hilda most effectually. "I want
some one to nurse this wounded man, and after that to
help about the stable and the house."

"Anywhar, ma'am, anywhar. There's mighty few things Jason can't do, and it'll need a power of work to keep him contented till he hears from Miss Hilda. But there's one thing I'd like ter know, ma'am."

"What is that, Jason?"

"Ef that warn't our Miss Hilda they were tryin' ter git away with, who was it?"

"It was a young lady that occupied the room next to hers," said the teacher, "Miss Amy Hargrove."

"Yer don't say?" exclaimed Jason in astonishment.

"Yes, and the man in yonder shot her, so that there is great danger that she may die."

"Yer don't say?" repeated Jason in open-mouthed amazement. "Yer don't say? An' it warn't our Hilda at all but that other one that was run off with an' hurt. An' yer say she's like ter die, ma'am?"

"So the doctor fears."

"Wal now, ma'am, p'r'aps I might as well take back what I said about de Lo'd a while ago. 'Pears like He must ha' knowed what He war about atter all," said Jason with a peculiar solemnity of tone and manner.

Gilbert Anderson, walking back to his snug home in the gray morning, with the sense of blood-guiltiness lifted from his soul, uttered the same sentiment in more refined language.

CHAPTER XLI.

THE PROOF THAT HEALETH DOUBT.

JARED CLARKSON was greatly disturbed by the dispatch from Miss Hunniwell—"Come at once for Miss Hargrove's sake." Accustomed as he was to accept responsibility, he had somehow shrunk in an unaccountable manner from the trust imposed on him by Merwyn Hargrove. The sight of the sealed parcel lying in his safe had more than once filled him with apprehension. Every time that he had been required to act under the instructions Hargrove had given him he had done so with peculiar reluctance. It was as if he had a premonition of evil connected with them. More than once he had determined to shift this burden upon Kortright, and but for the invalid's condition would no doubt have done so before this time. Even as it was, he hesitated to comply with the teacher's urgent request, and instead of taking the train at once drove over to Sturmhold for consultation with Kortright, taking with him the sealed package and Hargrove's letter in regard to it.

The two men talked long and anxiously of the events which had occurred, and speculated not a little as to what the trouble that threatened Hilda might be.

"I am sure I cannot imagine," said Clarkson, "nor why they should have sent for me. That they should telegraph for Martin is very natural."

"I suppose to seek your advice because you were her father's friend, and are, in a sense, his representative now," answered Kortright.

"I have thought of that," said Clarkson, "but it

520

seems improbable that her father would have intrusted her with the peculiar character of our relations."

"Well," said Kortright, with decision, "Hilda evidently needs your aid, and you must go, and go at once, too."

"Then, if that is settled," said Clarkson, "I think it best that this parcel should be opened, and I do not wish that to be done except in the presence of another trustworthy friend of the deceased besides myself."

He took the package from his pocket as he spoke. It was indorsed in the handwriting of Hargrove:

"This package will be opened by the person to whom it may be intrusted only when such person shall, in the exercise of a sound and honest discretion, believe that the time has come when it is absolutely necessary for him to know the exact truth in regard to the children of the late George Eighmie and Alida, his wife. If no such occasion arises previous to the marriage of Hilda, or before she attains the age of twenty-one years, it is my desire that this parcel be placed in her hands with its seals yet unbroken.

    Signed,   Merwyn Hargrove."

It was sealed with his monogram and the bristling boar's head crest which the old buccaneer had adopted as a boastful emblem of lowly origin and dangerous strength. Clarkson handed the parcel to Kortright, who read the superscription carefully, and remarked doubtfully as he returned it:

"You are sure the time has come?"

"I am very sure," answered Clarkson. "I cannot act intelligently in any matter touching Hilda without the knowledge this envelope contains."

"Perhaps not," said Kortright, "though I don't exactly see why. It doesn't impress me that her present trouble is in any way connected with the Eighmie children."

"Oh, it must be, directly or indirectly, else I should never have been summoned," said Clarkson.

"I cannot understand why you think so," Kortright replied.

"Well, let me show you," said Clarkson, settling himself for one of his favorite monologues. "You know that there were two of these children—the Eighmie children I mean. One of these Captain Hargrove, in conformity with the desire of his half-brother, deprived of her identity, hid, 'transformed' he calls it in his letter. The other he tells us he could not trace. The latter I have found. I am now, as I fully believe, able to lay my hands on the son of George and Alida Eighmie. He having been born before the emancipation of his mother and the second marriage of his parents in this state, even though formally legitimatized by the father under our laws, it is somewhat doubtful what his legal *status* might be adjudged to be. This being the case, I have already taken steps to extinguish the title of the man who recently claimed him as a slave by taking a bill of sale to myself. You see," he added, smiling at his own conceit, "I am getting aristocratic. I come of a slave-holding stock and am now a slave-owner myself. It is no wonder that Southern gentlemen are partial to one having so much in common with them, despite my fearful reputation as an Abolitionist, is it?"

Kortright's only reply was a smile, and Clarkson went on:

"The proof that the young man to whom I refer is the veritable Hugh Eighmie for whom Captain Hargrove sought so long and unsuccessfully, is almost perfect. I had hoped to present him to Hargrove on his return, when, no doubt, he could very soon have made the chain complete. Before the opportunity came, however, he was stricken down in the performance of his duty. Ever since that event I have been in great trouble as to what I ought to do in reference to this young man. He and his sister are unquestionably the true heirs of George Eighmie, unless illegitimate. I am the more troubled because of the fact that I was enabled to identify Hugh by his mother's instant recognition of her son when she had but a passing glimpse of his features, and that, too, by a very imperfect light."

"Indeed, you surprise me!" said Kortright.

"Yes," said Clarkson, "we have been accustomed to regard Alida as a poor, feeble creature, whose wits are not to be relied on, ever since you brought her to my house in the big snow-storm—let me see, now just about ten years ago, isn't it?"

"Ten years and a few days," said Kortright, solemnly shaking his head. "Ah, Mr. Clarkson, there have been great changes in that time."

"Yes, indeed," returned the other, "wonderful changes. It is hardly possible that another decade can bring the like."

There was a moment's silence, full of thoughtful retrospect to these men to whom the sunset of life was drawing near. They were not old men, but the era which they spoke had taxed their lives with burdens and activities no other past had ever known. After a time Clarkson continued:

"Well, as I was saying, we have never looked upon Alida as altogether right in her mind since that time."

Kortright nodded, but made no other response.

"Hargrove himself thought her thoroughly demented even before, and attributed her insanity solely to grief at the loss of her children; but it was not until the recognition of her son in the person of a hunted fugitive, that she came to her present hopeless condition. Since that occasion I suppose she has manifested no evidence of sanity, or even of active intellection, at all."

Kortright glanced uneasily at the door, and said:

"I don't know about that. Would you mind turning the key in the door, Clarkson? I have something to tell you that I would not have Mrs. Kortright know for a good deal."

Clarkson opened his eyes with surprise, but did as he was requested. When he returned Kortright motioned to him to sit down in the invalid chair by the side of the couch so that he could lay his hand upon his knee, and said:

"Do you know, I cannot understand that woman— Alida? She has evidently always been given to hallucinations. No proof could ever satisfy her, for a great while at a time, that Hargrove, who literally sacrificed his whole life to carry out her husband's fancies, was really her friend."

"That," said Clarkson, sententiously, "was because he had no real sympathy with her or her race—at least with the race the taint of whose blood has blighted her life. Besides that, he never reposed any confidence in her."

"Whatever the cause, that was the fact, but it could not be for any such reason that she took an incurable dislike to us."

"Has she done so?"

"Yes, indeed. You see I am such a victim to this rheumatism now, that day and night have lost their normal relations so far as I am concerned. I wake by night and sleep by day, or *vice versa*, as the case may be. Sometimes I am awake for two or three days and nights in succession, and then perhaps I sleep almost as long. For this reason, I stay here in the library all the time. It's the only part of this great house that ever seemed home-like to me anyhow. I lie upon my couch here, or crawl into my chair, and think or read, sleep or wake, without disturbing any one. Martha occupies the bedroom adjoining, but she is a sound sleeper, and hears nothing unless I call her name. Well, it wasn't long after we came here that I found that this woman, Alida, was a very different creature at night from what she seems to be or is in the daytime. I was lying here on my couch one night when she came in, went straight to that desk there—the one the Captain used, you know—raised the lid, and appeared to be hunting around for something which she could not find. Then she went to the shelves there, took down one or two books, and seemed to be searching through them for something that she expected to find between the leaves. Failing in this, she came here to the grate, warmed her feet one after the other, in the meantime knitting her brows, and seeming to be in great distress, as if unable to recall something she had once known. She paid no attention to me, not appearing to be aware of my presence. Of course I was very much surprised at this manifestation, and fully intended to have spoken of it the next day, but something drove it from my mind, and her visits soon came to be so frequent that I became interested in them, and even looked forward to the night, when my ailment was very painful, with a sort of enjoyment. It was not always the same, this novel entertainment, and I soon found great relief in trying to decipher the causes of her varying moods. By careful watching I came to understand much that she does, or, at least, to form a good idea of what it means to her. She rarely speaks, but now and then uses an exclamation that aids me in arriving at a conclusion with regard to her thoughts.

"It is very strange," said Clarkson. "She is evidently a somnambulist."

"No doubt," assented Kortright, "but do you not see this strange thing beside—the waking woman is weak and silly, almost dead to what is going on about her; but the sleeping woman is active, alert and evidently alive to circumstances, sentiments, antipathies and preferences which are of the past or which she fits into a past which is the present to her. She is not always unconscious of surrounding objects, but always mistakes them, when she does notice them, for something connected with the train of thought she seems pursuing."

"It is very remarkable," said Clarkson.

"The scene with the desk and books is the one most frequently enacted. I have been through the desk again and again, and turned over every book upon the shelf to which she always goes. A queer thing about it is that if I disarrange the papers at the left of the desk she seems at once worried and disturbed, and will not leave it until she has placed the packages back just as they were. Those at the right hand she seems to pay no attention to at all. It is queer, too, that one volume of the set of books she always examines is missing. One time I had them changed and other books put in their places. She was greatly excited by that; pulled the books out, threw them on the floor, and finally seemed to half awake, or rather to assume her ordinary waking condition. There is this strange thing about her condition, she is most awake when she is soundest asleep. She sees, hears, thinks; but she sees and hears and thinks only with reference to a state of facts that exists but in her memory or imagination. The silly, furtive leer she has in the daytime came into her eyes; she looked cautiously at me, and finally stole out on tiptoe, turning every now and then to glare back at me. It seemed to distress her so that I had the books restored the next day."

"You amaze me," said Clarkson. "Do you think it safe that she should wander about unguarded in this manner during the night?"

"Candidly," said Kortright, with an amused smile, "I do not, but what would become of my entertainment if she were confined? I assure you it is of great advantage to me. I always forget my pain while she is here, and usually fall asleep afterward trying to unravel the charades she has acted."

"Have you ever succeeded?" asked Clarkson curiously.

"Oh, yes, indeed; and I have thus learned some very strange things," answered Kortright. "It was by that means that I discovered her antipathy to my family, especially toward Martin. When I am very bad, sometimes, one of the family will insist upon watching with me, as they say, which usually results in their going to sleep and my watching them. As I am on this side the fireplace," he continued, "they naturally sit on the other, which brings them directly in her path when she comes to lean upon the mantel to warm her feet at the fire and recall what she has forgotten. Martin was the first one she found there one night when he was comfortably sleeping on his watch. When she had peered around the back of my invalid chair in which he sat, in the half-awake manner that any interruption of her wonted routine produces, and seemed to recognize who it was, she became so terribly excited that I really feared she would attack him. However, she left the room without awaking him, and that night, for the first time, returned again. It was perhaps an hour afterward. I had wakened Martin and sent him to bed, on the false pretense that I was more comfortable. When she re-entered the room the impression of his presence was evidently still fresh in her mind. She shook her fist at the empty chair, gnashed her teeth, and then suddenly burst into a laugh. I was afraid she would wake Martha, but fortunately she did not. Then she went through a pantomime that I could not understand, and which yet seemed to have a regular order, and to be connected in her thought with Martin, for at the end she ran quickly to the door, stopped and listened as if fearing pursuit, shook her hand at the chair again, and stealthily disappeared."

"This is really astounding," exclaimed the listener.

"Wait a moment," said Kortright. "The next night, as it happened, Martha had insisted on sitting up with me, and was asleep in that same chair. Alida discovered the intrusion as before. After a while she seemed to recognize my wife's identity, and for a time a look of hesitation, almost tenderness, passed over her face as she stood in the firelight gazing into the placid face of my watcher. Finally she exhibited toward her the same evidences of aversion, however, she had shown toward Martin the night before. As she went out, I made haste to awaken wife and get her to bed, so that I might have a good opportunity to watch Alida's conduct should she return. She did return, and went through the performance of the night before without varying a movement. After this she frequently returned, especially if anything interfered with the usual routine of her first visit, and went through this same mimicry of an event that has evidently left a most vivid impression on her mind, until I have learned to interpret every gesture, and know as well what she is thinking of as if she uttered articulate sounds instead of using this strange pantomime. She sometimes does utter a word or two, but even without that I think I should have solved the riddle finally since the subject of it was most intimately connected with my own life."

"No!" exclaimed Clarkson incredulously. "What is the subject of this strange hallucination, do you suppose?"

"She lives over again her own experience on the night of the burning of the factory and Paradise Bay."

"How can that be?" asked Clarkson; "she could hardly have seen the flames from here."

"She set the fire herself!" said Kortright earnestly.

" You do not mean it ?"

"There is no doubt of it. She performs all the acts
the incendiary must have performed : turns on the
water ; sets the fire under the stairway ; watches the
flame ; turns the lever of the waste-gate ; flees and turns
in to do still another act of vengeance at Paradise Bay."

" Are you sure you are not mistaken ?" asked Clarkson. " Is your brain in good working order, or do your
own fancies color what you see ?"

" I am not fanciful, and I have worked too long over
this riddle to question its solution now," said Kortright.

"What could have been her motive ?" asked Clarkson.

" It could only have been a blind jealousy of Martin,"
responded Kortright. " I have recalled since this began
the fact of her aversion for him even as a boy. It was
probably due to her insensate jealousy of all those for
whom Hilda manifested any attachment."

" Well, what is your conclusion ?" asked Clarkson
after a moment's thought. " Do you think her an impostor ?"

" Not by any means," was the ready response. " I
am no scientist, but I have heard that the brain is really
two brains and that certain parts of it may act without,
or even in opposition to, the action of the remainder.
Now my explanation is that the woman is crazy beyond
all doubt. Every part of her brain is diseased and ab-
normal ; but one part may be said to sleep during the
day, and the other, weaker and duller, during the night.
During her somnambulistic state the most active and
positive elements of her nature are at work, and she
loves and hates with all the intensity of her earlier
days. I am inclined to think that she acted the incendiary in this half-unconscious state. Only a little while
before Hilda had been home for her vacation. The
young people had been together here a good deal, and
had probably been very lover-like. This had fired her

weak brain to frenzy, and had intensified all her former hatred for my son."

"What is her feeling toward you ?"

"She has never seemed to recognize me fully. I could not account for this at first, but finally concluded that it was because of my reclining position on the couch. Then, again, I have sometimes thought that she half mistakes me for Hargrove, who was himself accustomed to occupy a couch here in the library a good portion of the time instead of the bed in the room adjoining. Indeed, it was that fact that first suggested to my mind the advisability of doing so myself."

"You think she has sane and lucid intervals, then?"

"Well, I should hardly want to say that, but I think she has intervals when certain past facts are very clearly recalled to her memory," answered Kortright.

"Ah! that indeed," said Clarkson meditatively, as he rose and pressing one hand upon his neck threw his head quickly back as if to relieve an accustomed pain. Then he walked up and down the room in deep thought, his hands behind him and his head bowed on his breast, but with a step as nervous and elastic as if the years had not touched his frame nor care bowed his spirit. Kortright, chained to his pillow by disease, followed the footsteps of his friend with a look akin to envy. Presently he stopped at the foot of the couch, and looking down at the wan, keen face before him, he said:

"Squire Kortright, do you know it is very strange that we should come to speak of this woman and her mental status at this time ?"

"Why so ?" asks the other.

"Because," answered Clarkson, "it is the strength of one of her impressions that makes me feel it incumbent upon me to open this package."

"How is that ?" asked Kortright, with a languid interest.

"Do you know that she has always claimed that Hilda is her daughter?"

"Oh, yes," said the sick man, laughingly; "everybody here knows of that crazy notion. She even goes farther, and declares that her name is Heloise—sometimes Heloise and sometimes Marah. It seems that her own child was known by both of these names—the first bestowed by the mother, and the latter by the father, who, at her birth, had begun to taste the bitterness of his folly. In her quieter days she will stand gazing at Hilda's picture, painted when she was a child, you know, and will go into a fearful rage if any one calls it Hilda."

"Well, Kortright," said Clarkson firmly, "I believe her."

"You believe her? You believe what? I don't understand," said Kortright, with a puzzled expression.

"I believe that Hilda is Alida's child!"

"The devil you do!" exclaimed Kortright, springing up with an alacrity he had not known in many months, and gazing into Clarkson's face in unfeigned astonishment. "I beg pardon," he said presently; "I haven't used such a word before in forty years, but will you allow me to ask, Jared Clarkson, if you are insane as well as Alida?"

A flush passed over Clarkson's face which Kortright was too much amazed to note. There had been rumors at one time and another afloat in the community that the brain of this gifted man was at times somewhat disordered. The inquiry of Kortright was therefore a barbed arrow, which struck home all the more surely because it was evidently not intended to do mischief.

"Nevertheless," he answered quietly, "I do believe it, and have long believed it. Alida has always asserted it with the utmost positiveness, and, so far as I know, Hargrove never denied it."

"Denied it? Of course he never did. Would you

think it necessary to deny a crazy servant's claim to one of your children? The thing is too ridiculous even to be laughed at!" exclaimed Kortright with indignant scorn.

"And yet I do believe it," persisted Clarkson. "You must admit, Mr. Kortright, that it is hardly an argument to compare one of our quiet households with one so full of mystery as this at Sturmhold."

"Mystery? Yes, mystery enough; but none of his making, Mr. Clarkson. He was a man as open as the day save where others were concerned—so simple and faithful that he never once thought of peril to himself or his child in the trust he undertook for the sake of that miserable, slack-spirited half-brother that was enslaved by this woman's pretty face."

"You are warm in your praise, and it is commendable that you should be," answered Clarkson; "but if what you say is all true, why was Hilda so constantly mixed up with this mysterious trust? First, she is provided for by the contract with you. Why should that be when his will made her his sole heir?"

"That is easily explained," said Kortright.

"Explained! Oh, yes, I know. But why the need of explanation?" demanded Clarkson. "Then, too, this very parcel is to be delivered into her hand, under certain contingencies."

"Of course, in order that she may continue her father's watch-care and benefactions, no doubt."

"That is the most reasonable explanation that can be given, if we exclude Alida's claim," said Clarkson; "but the fact is that no explanation—no hypothesis of a probable cause—nothing but the plainest and barest proof can prevail, in my mind, over the maternal instinct of this woman, who, at all times, whether sane or insane, has steadily and stubbornly asserted the fact."

"Well, then, in Heaven's name, break the seal and have the proof!" exclaimed Kortright, pointing to the envelope on the table.

Clarkson lifted the envelope with a trembling hand. Taking a sharp knife from his pocket he carefully cut around the seals, leaving them still unbroken, and after opening the whole length of the packet, drew forth two smaller parcels from within. He read aloud the indorsement of the first:

"To be delivered to Hilda, without delay, whenever the accompanying package is opened and examined by any person authorized so to do.   M. H."

"That looks a good deal as if Hilda and the other were one and the same, doesn't it?" said Kortright in a sneering tone.

"Wait," said Clarkson, as he raised the other and read the superscription:

"The papers herein contained will sufficiently establish the identity of the daughter of George Eighmie and Alida, claiming to be his wife. They are all originals.
                (Signed)   MERWYN HARGROVE."

"Open it! open it!" Kortright exclaimed impatiently.

Clarkson did so and drew out a bundle of papers. Hastily glancing at the filings on the backs, he opened them one after another. At first his face showed only surprise. Then it grew pale.

"Well, what is it?" asked Kortright, reaching out his hand.

Jared Clarkson made no answer, but extended the papers to him, and sitting down by the table, buried his face in his hands. A sob that was almost a groan escaped him. Whether his conjecture was right or wrong, what he had found occasioned him only sorrow.

Harrison Kortright took the package, searched about the pillow for his glasses, put them on and looked through the file of papers carefully, one by one. There were ten of them—all alike.

" Pshaw ! what is all this nonsense ?" he said at length ; but his hand trembled and his voice quavered as he spoke.

The papers were term-bills, and read :

"CAPTAIN MERWYN HARGROVE,

In acct. with Beechwood Seminary,

To Board and Tuition of Hilda Hargrove."

CHAPTER XLII

HILDA rode out of the station unconscious of the direction she was taking—not knowing nor caring whither she went. She was going away hardly expecting ever to return. The cloud above her seemed impenetrable. She could not keep the touch of her old life. She must bury herself. This was her only refuge, not so much from the danger of enslavement as from the scath of scorn and debasement. She did not know where or how it could be done. She only knew that she must flee away from present peril. She must have opportunity to transform herself—to bury her identity—to begin a new existence.

It was a foolish notion, but Hilda did not know the world. She only knew what she wished to do, and like the father of whose name they sought to rob her, she counted not the obstacles. She looked out of the car window, saw the fields and woods fly past, in the weird winter moonlight. Surely she was safe. The desert of life would hide her. She did not hear the conductor when he came through the train, and, spying a new face, stopped at her seat and said:

"Ticket!"

She only saw the white, ghostly world without, flying by and standing sentinel between her and a dreaded fate.

"Ticket!" touching her shoulder lightly.

She started, turned and glanced up at him quickly, as if she thought he suspected her. She wondered if they could telegraph ahead and have her detained at the next station. She had heard of such things being done in case of criminals. She wondered if she would be considered a criminal because she was fleeing from the law.

"Ticket!" repeated the conductor, extending his hand.

"I—I forgot to get one," she said faintly. Then she caught nervously at her pocket-book and handed him a bill.

"Where to?" inquired the official, bending down an ear.

Where, indeed? She had no idea where she was going or which way the train was moving. She stammered, flushed, and was sure she was betraying herself.

"Straight through?"

She bowed her head. He had a roll of bills between every two fingers of his left hand for convenience in making change—ones, twos and fives, all separate. He thrust the ten-dollar bill she had given him into his vest-pocket, gave her a two, a one, and some change, handed her a check for Boston, and went on. She was rather pleased with her destination. By-and-by the horror began to wear away. The danger from which she fled was momently receding. She began to feel more comfortable—almost bold. After a time she slept, but uneasily, and with frightful dreams. As the sun rose they came into Boston. The city was still asleep. The hoar-frost was thick upon roof and spire, and the sunshine gilded every pinnacle. She took a carriage to the Revere. How bright and clean the crooked, rough-paved streets seemed to her! This was Boston —the seat of culture and the cradle of liberty. What a mockery the title was! The blue smoke rose sharp and clear against the sky from thousands of happy homes, but she was a fugitive. Against a cloud to the northeastward she dimly saw the top of a gray column once. She guessed that it was the monument on Bunker Hill, and there flashed through her mind all that it commemorated. The city was very proud of that gray granite shaft. The commonwealth boasted itself the possessor of the blood-stained soil on which it stood. The nation pointed to it as a memento of the struggle that gave it birth. The world accounted it a pillar of liberty—the memorial shaft of a new civilization. Yet under its shadow she was a fugitive, fleeing from bondage and degradation.

"Revere House, ma'am!"

The driver opened the door, and stood waiting for his fee. A servant came and took her modest bag. She was ushered into the reception-room—narrow, stuffy, with furniture that seemed as if once it had been new. The servant placed her bag on the table, and asked if she would have a room. She turned to look out of the window upon the funny triangle that is called a square in Boston. The clerk came and inquired her name. She started, flushed and paled. Her name? What was it? What should she say?

The clerk waited. He thought he had startled her by his abruptness.

"I beg pardon, ma'am—what did you say was the name?"

"Oh, yes; my name, of course." She smiled, opened her portemonnaie, and seemed to be seeking for a card. "Well, never mind. Louise Amis, Springfield."

"Miss?"

"Of course," with a smile.

"A-m-y?"

"No—A-m-i-s."

"Oh, yes—Amis. Any baggage?"

"Not now. I shall be here only a short time. Will you let me know the precise address of Miss Fanny Goodwin? It is somewhere on Rutland Square, but I have forgotten the number."

" An acquaintance ?" asked the clerk carelessly.

" A school friend."

" Indeed !"

He started off. Just as he reached the door she
called him back.

" How very stupid of me !" she said.   " I suppose
you want pay for your room in advance ?"

" That is our rule where guests have no baggage,"
politely.

" I ought to have known; but I never traveled so
far alone before," she said innocently and truthfully.

She took out her portemonnaie, carelessly showing it
to be well lined with bills—thanks to Miss Hunniwell's
foresight. She gave him twice as much as he asked.
He went away, and the servant came and showed her
to a room.   Her first lesson in dissimulation was over.
She was safe, and had time to breathe before taking
another step.   She read the morning paper.   There
was a brief notice of some excitement in Blankshire by
reason of an alleged attempt at kidnapping.   There
were not more than ten lines, and only a vague allusion
to herself.   It seemed strange that what was of such
importance to her should be of so little moment to the
world.   She ate her breakfast, went out and wandered
about the narrow streets, bright and quiet, with the
Sabbath hush upon them.   She saw Faneuil Hall, the
Common, the quaint old graveyard full of headstones
whose names are an epitome of history.   She wandered
into a church.   The notes of the organ soothed her.
The accents of a grand old hymn whose echoes seemed
burdened with greetings of good cheer from the brave
hearts of the past strengthened and consoled her spirit.
Then she returned to her room in the hotel with a
dazed, unreal feeling, as if she were not herself but
another.   She laid down upon the bed to think.   She
did not know that she was at all fatigued, but hardly had

her head touched the pillow when she fell asleep, wondering even in her dreams how she could be an outcast in a city founded as a refuge and consecrated to liberty and equality.

When she awoke the day was already declining. A boy was calling an "Extra." She looked out and saw the crowd buying with avidity. She opened the window and listened. "All about the kidnapping!" she heard him cry. She called a servant and procured a copy—a small, square sheet printed on one side only. Could it be that her flight was sufficient to stir the drowsy Sabbath quiet of the city? Had fate pursued her so quickly? Would not the world give her sanctuary in its great throbbing heart? Must she indeed flee into the wilderness? Sure enough, it was all there. The world had waked to the terror that haunted her life. She read it all—a whole column by telegraph, with staring head-lines, and another of editorial remarks. She read all about herself—some of it truth and some of it queer conjecture. Her father's life and death were commented on. Her position, supposed wealth, accomplishments and beauty were all stated. The description given was very accurate. She almost feared she might be recognized. Then she read—what was this? Amy, Mr. Anderson, Martin! Wounds! Bloodshed! Great excitement! Talk of lynching! Jared Clarkson to arrive to-morrow!

Her head swam as she read, but she still read on to the end. Then she bathed her hot face, combed her hair, putting up the curls she had been accustomed to wear, and throwing it out upon each side by the use of puff-combs which she had never used before. She was Merwyn Hargrove's daughter still, she said to herself, and she would not flinch from anything that might impend. She surveyed herself in the glass, and smiled at her own apprehension as she read over again the concluding statement in regard to the events described: "It is believed that Miss Hargrove has fled to Canada or is still hidden in the vicinity. Her complete disappearance is certainly a mystery."

When she went down to dinner her flushed cheeks and bright eyes enhanced her usual charms. More than one glance of admiration followed her as she was shown to a seat. The tables were full. Two gentlemen and a lady sat at the one with her. The gentlemen were reading the little "Extra" and discussing the news from Blankshire. A great many in the room seemed to be engaged in like manner. She heard some at a table back of her talking upon the same subject. At first she was frightened. Then she saw that every one was too absorbed in the event to suspect her of being one of the actors in it.

"This is horrible!" said the young man who sat opposite.

"It is a very aggravated case, as far as concerns the rank and station of the intended victim. Otherwise it is no worse than a hundred cases that have occurred under this infamous law." The speaker was a gray-bearded, grave-faced man who sat at the end of the table.

"Well, I am glad the girl got away, anyhow," said the young man.

"So am I," said the lady heartily.

Hilda felt her cheeks burn and tears come into her eyes. She wished they knew how grateful the fugitive was for their sympathy.

"And I am very sorry," said the grave elderly man in a soft, earnest tone.

Hilda started and turned a pale, frightened face toward him.

"I beg your pardon, young lady, I am not so cruel as you think me."

The color came back to her face, and she bent her head over her plate to hide her confusion.

"Yet I cannot but regret," he continued, "the escape of the kidnappers' intended prey. I know enslavement would have been unutterably sad to her, but it is only by such shining examples that the nation can be awakened to the enormity of slavery. What I say seems heartless, no doubt, but I verily believe that the application of this infamous law to just such a case as this would do more to arouse the land, to awaken conscience, to weaken slavery and promote the cause of liberty, than the return to bondage of a thousand men and women who have fled from oppression, and are at the best only toilers who have rebelled against an untoward fate. In this case it is different. We see one snatched from a home of luxury, from the most polished society, from friends and love, and sought to be thrust into nothingness. I admit that it would be terrible to her—death itself would be preferable—but I certainly believe that her sufferings would be worth ten thousand lives in the beneficent results that would flow therefrom. We mourn the virgin martyrs of the arena and the catacombs, but none the less we know that their blood was in truth the seed of the church, and thank God that it was shed. I meant the young lady no harm, but I wish the slave release from bondage. The loss of one life is as nothing to the evil that keeps a race in degradation."

Hilda gazed into the soft gray eyes, and seemed to feel a new light in her soul. As she listened to his words she forgot all feeling of apprehension for herself. She gazed at him in a fixed, absorbed manner, which he mistook for inquiry, and resumed, addressing himself unconsciously to her, while the others listened with respectful attention.

"You see," he said thoughtfully, "the world is ruled

by great examples. Influence is only the power of example; but if the example be petty the influence will be weak. Religion itself is but the force of the highest example. The power that thrills the life of eighteen centuries is not the word of God. The Logos of the Apostle was weak and vain until it was framed in the life of Jesus Christ. The cross and the crown of thorns gave vitality to Christian truth. Without the MAN Christ Jesus the written word would have been naught to us. The sacrifice of Virginia overthrew the tyrant. Jeanne d'Arc led and triumphed through the unfearing intensity of her devotion. Always it has been an example that has moved the world forward and overthrown evil. By-and-by slavery will demand a sacrifice—so notable, so cruel and so needless—that the whole land will be smitten with horror, and the institution will disappear in the blaze of public wrath. It is not abstract truth that moves men's hearts, but always the concrete. This young woman's father might have been a shining example, and his death would have done a vast injury to slavery, but no one seemed to understand just the cause of it. While he seems to have been bitterly opposed to slavery he was yet animated by a feeling of angry defiance, rather than of sacrificial offering up of himself for the good of another."

"I think he was animated by a sense of duty and of honor," said Hilda quietly.

"There can be no doubt of that," rejoined the stranger, in the same persuasive tones, and with the same clear light in his great gray eyes; "but a sense of duty may impel to acts which, although meritorious, are yet not impressive. I may eat my dinner from a sense of duty, but others will wait for an appetite before they follow my example. Honor, too, is apt to be tainted with selfishness, and it is only the example of self-sac-

rifice that lives and moves the world to noble deeds.
This man—what was his name ?"

"Hargrove," said Hilda absently.

"Yes, Hargrove, Merwyn Hargrove—I remember
seeing him once a few years ago—was of the type that
heroes are made of, but he was too self-bounded, too
oblivious of the world outside of the tasks he seems to
have set himself to accomplish, to make a good martyr.
He perhaps released more slaves than any man living,
and actually sacrificed more money to do it than any
Northern philanthropist has ever thought of doing. He
did his work thoroughly, too. He took the slaves to
Hayti and purchased for them there a tract of land of
which each had his due share in fee. He freed them,
and provided for their safety and support. At the
same time, he did this, not because of his love for the
slave, nor even because of his hatred for slavery—
though that was no doubt intense—but for some reason
noble and chivalric enough perhaps, but applicable only
to himself. He was a hero, but not a martyr."

"A hero but not a martyr," murmured Hilda. "You
may be right."

"The distinction is a fair one," continued the stranger.
"Moreover, the martyr will yet appear. The encroach-
ments of slavery are daily coming home to our Northern
life. The blood that furnished martyrs under Bloody
Mary runs in our veins, and the day is not far distant
when the Martyr will appear. He will testify of the
truth in such a way that all men will believe."

"I think I know the man," she said absently.

The stranger gazed at her a moment in silence, and
then remarked slowly and solemnly :

"I also have seen one whom I have sometimes thought
might bear testimony of the truth for us all. Whether
one shall suffice, or shall only be a forerunner of

many whose blood must purge away our sin, God
knoweth."

"Why do you say *our* sin?" asked the younger man.

"Because," replied the other, "it *is* ours. We make
a grave mistake when we seek to cast the blame of
slavery on the South. A cancer does not belong to the
limb on which it appears, but to the whole body that
suffers from the poison that it generates. We of the
North are even more responsible for the evils of slavery
than they of the South, because we perceive and admit
them and they do not."

"But do they believe it right?"

"Unquestionably. They not only believe it right,
but they believe it to be the only way in which the two
races can co-exist upon this continent."

"But why should they attempt to get hold of this
young lady in this manner? Her friends would no doubt
have raised more money than she is worth as a slave."

"You forget that Hargrove was a very wealthy man.
This is probably an attempt to induce her to release all
claim on his estate."

"Indeed!" said the young man in surprise.

"I merely judge that from the fact you have mentioned; but if she is Hargrove's daughter, they have
made a mistake."

"You knew him?"

"No, but I have heard Jared Clarkson speak of him
more than once. He came of fighting stock, and if she
has his blood they may have caught a tartar."

"I hope the Lord they have!" said the young man
fervently.

"So do I," said the lady earnestly. "They might
have waited till she was out of mourning for her father,
anyhow."

This feminine view of the situation provoked a burst

of laughter, in which Hilda could not help joining despite the sad thought it evoked.

Then the conversation drifted off into other channels. Hilda finished her meal without feeling any fear of detection. Indeed, she thought she would have felt rather glad to be recognized. Her fear seemed so petty and foolish. She blushed as she tried to fancy what her father would have thought of her cowardly flight. But he should have no more cause to blush for her. She felt the blood of the Hargroves coursing through her veins, and she would show the world that she was her father's daughter and worthy of his name, as he had said in his will. When the meal was over, she went to her room to think of the future in the new light the hour had cast upon it.

CHAPTER XLIII.

THAT NOTHING BE LOST.

SOME of the events that occurred in and about Burlingdale during the week that followed the attempted abduction are worthy of record, though they may not seem directly to concern the chief characters of our story.

. . . .

Beechwood Seminary was in a tumult after the enactment of a double tragedy at its very doors. The crimson drops along the hall and down the steps were cleansed without delay from the polished ash, but in a hundred tender hearts they were ineffaceably fixed. Not a slippered foot crossed where this line of horror had been without a thrill of fear. The broken ladder, the battle-ground beneath the window, the blood-stains in the steep wood-road, the recollection of the companion who had been ravished from their midst, just missing a bloody death; the mystery surrounding the fate of that other schoolmate, who had vanished out of their life and left no trace—these were too fertile themes for girlish imagining to permit the routine of task and recitation to go on from day to day with any profit. Indeed, the principal was soon convinced that it would be at the risk of very serious peril to the health of her pupils should they remain during the balance of the term. The nervous strain to which they had been exposed began almost immediately to show itself on some of the more susceptible of them. The conscientious teacher did not hesitate an instant when the health of her pupils was set over against her own advantage. Within a week the shivering brood were scattered to their homes, and the tragedy of Beechwood was rehearsed over and over again at a hundred distant firesides by pale-faced narrators, who shuddered as they boastfully declared, "I was there, you know." There were none left at the seminary save a few scholars whose homes were most remote, two or three teachers, the slowly-recuperating invalid and his dusky nurse. For the first time in a quarter of a century the routine of Beechwood was broken up. In the midst of term-time its halls were silent. The vacation antedated the Christmas holidays that year by almost a month. To each of her patrons Miss Hunniwell forwarded a brief statement of the causes which led to this decision on her part, discounting the term-bills which she sent out in accordance with the abbreviation of the school-year resulting therefrom. In a vain attempt to hold what it deemed its own, Slavery had thrust its ghastliest shadow into a hundred households. Every family altar seemed violated by the invasion of Beechwood. The sanctuary of the vestal virgins had been invaded. The treasury wherein a hundred families had placed their most priceless jewels had been broken, and one had been reft thence by force. Many a mother shuddered as she pressed her loved one to her bosom, and thought that she might have been the victim. Many a father's look grew stern as he considered the danger his child had shared, and uttered to himself again the question which the prophet of the prairie had propounded to his countrymen, "All free or all slave?" Many a brother's heart was consecrated by the blood of one innocent beautiful victim to do knightly service against the monster that lived on human lives.

.   .   .   .

Upon the second day after the abduction Jared Clarkson arrived in the little village. The excitement, which was already intense, was greatly heightened by his presence. He seemed worn, depressed, disheartened. To the swarm of friends and co-workers in the cause of liberty, who crowded around him and hailed his coming with delight, his language and manner were most unsatisfactory. He had come solely upon private business, he said. Instead of gladly lending his presence and eloquence to give *éclat* to a demonstration intended to improve the occasion and deepen the anti-slavery sentiments of the community, he pleaded fatigue, headache and important and burdensome engagements. He finally compromised with the committee by agreeing to attend the meeting if not asked to speak. To this they readily assented—a compromise made only to be broken. The result was a speech so full of sorrow and despair that they who heard it wondered if they really were listening to that ever-jubilant prophet of victory whose optimism nothing had been able to daunt until that hour. They knew not that Jared Clarkson spoke with a burden of sorrow he had never known before— a burden to which he dared not refer lest some unguarded expression might enhance the woe of an innocent victim. He knew full well the curse that rested over the fugitive girl. To him all classes and conditions of men were alike. To him the Gospel message had come with the force and vitality it bore in that earlier time, when, in one day, it melted the chains of five thousand bondsmen of a noble Roman. Race or color were no disabling conditions of his favor. He knew that there were some like him—but, oh, so few! He well knew that if the One Divine should come to earth clad in the livery of a dusky skin, while there were thousands, aye, millions, who would give Him charity—the dole of condescending pity—there were almost none who would or could make Him welcome in home and heart. He knew—none better than he—how the brand of color made its possessor an outcast in the land of his birth. He knew how it barred the way to rank and station and opportunity—how it paralyzed the hand of friendship and blighted the heart of love. He knew, too,—oh, the bitterness of that knowledge!—how his heart burned as it throbbed against the papers in his pocket—for he dared not part with them lest another should learn the fearful truth. He knew that, somewhere in the dark, cold night, somewhere in the cheerless, crowded, crushing world, Hilda, the child of luxury and love; Hilda, petted and beautiful and bright; Hilda, the daughter of the dead friend, who had trusted him with the cursed secret of her birth, in order that he might shield her from sorrow and harm; Hilda, his ward in Heaven's Chancery, was fleeing none knew whither or to what—refuge or death! No wonder that his voice faltered. Of all the slaves the earth had known there was but one that lived in his memory in that hour—the one for whose safety he was surety to a dead friend. No wonder his brain throbbed with agony! No wonder his heart was bursting with despair! The woe he was charged to mitigate was beyond human power to assuage. Already it had borne fruit in the heart of its victim. The leper had fled into the wilderness, crying back with the agony of blighted hope and shattered love, "Unclean! Unclean!" Is it any wonder that he forgot slavery in pity for the one slave whose life was in his hands? The prophet of denunciation forgot to curse, and uttered only a wail of hopeless woe. The public were disappointed. His friends were disgusted. They had come for blood, and received instead only an oblation of tears!

. . . .

Martin Kortright was disappointed also. He had waited, chafing liked a caged hyena for two days, because a telegram from his father bade him wait until Jared

Clarkson came. Already he had lost a day in the search to which his life must be given. He felt strong and confident. There were two things he would do. He would first disprove the lie.. His Hilda—his love, his lily—he had no fear of stain upon her birth. He would trace her lineage. He would prove her purity. And, when that was done—ah! then he would find her, would give the record into her hand, and offer up his life for a kiss—a smile—aye, for the bare knowledge that she was no longer to be an outcast among men. He was not cast down. He did not *hope*—he was confident—he was sure. His only sorrow was that he did not know where Hilda was, so that he might assuage her grief. He was only anxious to begin his labors, that he might by a day, by an hour, hasten his triumph and shorten her woe. To him came Jared Clarkson at length, with his look of despair and the confirmation of the tale of horror. But love did not falter.

"It cannot be," said Martin. "There is some mistake. I shall unravel it."

Then he gave the lie to all his vows, and started off to seek, not the truth he boasted that he would discover, but the love he longed to comfort. He laughed at her behest that he should wait until she came. He would defy her will—so bold is love! He would overturn the world, he said—so strong is love! He would find her wheresoever she might hide—so sure is love! He would rest from his search only when he might fall into the grave—so true is fond young love!

. . . .

Martin's incredulity as to Clarkson's conclusion was based first upon an invincible determination not to believe, and second upon the testimony of Jason whose story he had heard. To him he referred this trustee of a woeful secret, and sped away exultantly to Sturmhold to make such preparation as was needful for the search he had already begun—for mail and telegraph had already conveyed his messages of inquiry to every conceivable place where the fugitive could have sought shelter. Jared Clarkson heard the story and hoped. He visited the seminary and talked with Miss Hunniwell. He believed in woman's intuition, and her buoyant faith strengthened the hope he sought to cherish. He even tried to forget the damning testimony already in his possession. He was a man of business habits, however; prudent, sagacious, painstaking, though over-credulous when once he had accepted any hypothesis. He cross-examined Jason carefully:

"You remember when Hilda was born?"

"Perfectly, sah."

"It was in the West Indies?"

"At Kingston, sah."

"Do you know the name of the house at which they were stopping?"

"It was a private house, sah; a minister's. I stayed on the sloop, but went up to the house to see if anything was wanted nigh about every day."

"Did you see the child christened?"

"That I did, an' one of the man's daughters where they lived was its god-mammy, too. She did look powerful nice, all in white, wid the little baby in her arms."

"Was the child healthy?"

"Powerful puny, sah; an' Miss Retta were poorly, too. Atter it war a few months old we took 'em both aboard the sloop, an' tried cruisin' roun' for a spell, but they couldn't stan' it nohow—not even to go roun' the island, you know. So we put back, an' Marse Merwyn an' me come to the States for a while to look after some of that pesky Mallerbank business, that hain't never been nothin' but trouble an' trouble, an' no good comin' out on 't. When we went back Miss Retta warn't no better, an' the doctors an' all hands persuaded her to leave the baby wid Miss Rickson—that was the name of the family, sah—while she come back with Marse Merwyn."

"The child remained with Miss Rickson how long ?"

"Wal, it must have been nigh onto two years—p'raps more. She hadn't been back so very long when Miss Retta died."

"Were you with Captain Hargrove when he brought his daughter away from Kingston ?"

"He didn't bring her !"

"Who did ?"

"Miss Rickson were on her way to England, you know, wid her folks, an' she brung de little lady on to New York. Leastways dat 's what I heard."

"You did not see Miss Rickson when she brought the child on, then ?"

"No, sah. The Captain went down a few days afore. I stayed at Sturmhold 'kase he was just packing off all de ole servants dat he 'd done set free an' settlin' ob 'em in de West, an' hirin' new ones. Dat was de time he brung Miss Lida back wid him."

"Who had the care of the child after it was brought to Sturmhold ?"

"Wal, pretty much everybody. Bein' the only one she ruled the whole house ; but, of course, Miss Lida was the nurse."

"Was she as fond of the child then as afterward ?"

"Law, yes, sah ; an' that jealous of Miss Retta she 'd stan' an' glare at her while she was pettin' that chile like she war ready to eat her up."

"When did you first hear Alida claim that Hilda was her child ?"

"Wal, it must have been a year or two atter Miss Retta died."

"What did you say to her then ?" '

"Told her I 'd slap her mouf ef I ever heard her talking such a thing again—ef she did set up for a white woman."

"What did she say in reply?"

"Oh, nothin' at all. She's jes' a pore, no-'count, silly creetur', anyhow. Marse Merwyn was powerful put out that I'd threatened to slap her mouf, an' told me I warn't never to pay no 'tention to anything she said."

"She had a child about Hilda's age, did she not?"

"There was some few months difference atwixt 'em. I don't mind which was the oldest now."

"Did Alida's child resemble Hilda?"

"Well, it did have dark eyes an' hair, but not such eyes and hair as our Hilda—not by any manner of means."

"Now, Jason, tell us honestly, what became of Alida's daughter?"

"Lida's gal! Lida's gal!" exclaimed Jason, springing from his chair. "I hain't got no right to tell you anything 'bout her, Marse Clarkson. I knows yer don't mean no harm, but I promised Marse Merwyn I wouldn't never mention the lightest word 'bout that gal 'cept I had his written orders ter do so, or Miss Hilda axed me wid her own sweet mouf atter he war dead. An' I can't break no promise ter Marse Merwyn, no-how."

"Well," said Clarkson, "I have here his written appeal to you to enlighten me upon this point." He drew forth Hargrove's letter and read the passage referring to Jason.

"Dat ain't givin' me no leave," said Jason, skeptically. "It says I can tell, but don't once say I shall tell."

"Jason," said Clarkson solemnly, "Captain Hargrove left a parcel with me which he said would inform me of the identity of the daughter of George and Alida Eighmie."

"Then you don't need to ax Jason," said the man shrewdly.

"The information is not direct, but yet it is entirely conclusive to my mind. The package contained only the bills for Hilda's tuition here at Beechwood."

"That's queer!" said Jason, with a puzzled look.

"In other words, your old master says to me this paper will tell you who is Alida's child, and hands me one of Miss Hunniwell's bills for Hilda's board and tuition. What do you say to that?"

"Wal, Marse Clarkson, 'tain't my place to say nothin' 'bout it, 'cept I has Marse Merwyn's orders, an' I ain't a-goin' to, nuther; but ef I *should* say anything," he added slyly, "I'd say that 'cordin' ter my notion, there'd been a mistake somewhar or somewhar else."

"And you refuse to tell me what you know?"

"Unless yer has Marse Merwyn's orders."

"Then I must follow the light I have and regard Hilda as the daughter of Alida."

"'Pears like yer all mighty anxious to make a nigger outen the pore gal," said the old servant sullenly. "But Jason's had his orders, an' he ain't a-goin' ter break 'em for no man's foolishness, dat he ain't."

This conversation had the effect to confirm Clarkson in his previous belief, and to cause the teacher to appeal anew to God for a solution of the mystery.

．　．　．　．　．　．　．　．　．　．

The wound which Amy Hargrove had received proved to be less serious than at first supposed. The shot had glanced around, instead of passing through a vital part. Upon the second day the doctor was able to announce that the hurt was not a serious one. Eighmie and Marsden were thereupon released on bail, so heavy, however, that they were compelled to remain in the village in order to satisfy the apprehensions of their bondsmen. The injured girl was at first the object of unbounded sympathy; but her conduct was not altogether what those who came to condole with her ex-

pected. Some very uncharitably declared that she was
rather proud than otherwise of her part in this midnight adventure. She had no word of blame for the
men who had been guilty of lawless violence, or of the
institution at whose doors all seemed anxious to lay the
blame for her suffering.

"It was all a mistake," she said in a quiet, matter-
of-course tone. "They are gentlemen and did not
intend me any harm. They would have brought me
back as soon as they found I was not the slave they
were seeking."

Indeed, she seemed to blame only two people for the
harm that had befallen her—Hilda and Mr. Anderson.
Of the former she would say nothing. No expression of
sympathy for the unfortunate girl, nor any burst of indignation against her intended captors could elicit a
word of regret or disapproval from the quiet figure that
occupied the bed in the dimly-lighted guest-chamber of
the parsonage. Those who watched her at such times
could only note that the little weazened face grew a
trifle whiter and harder in its outlines; the narrow
brow contracted and the black eyes rolled from side to
side under the half-shut lids with suppressed excitement. Of the minister she only said that he no doubt
meant well enough, but his interference at that particular time was very unfortunate for her. The message
which the doctor brought from Eighmie gave her evident pleasure, and she insisted on being given a pencil
and a sheet of paper that she might reply. The doctor
protested angrily, but she had her way, and wrote :

"SIR: I am by no means sure that I am not more in
fault than you. Of course, you would never have made
the attempt but for the information I gave. In doing what
I did I had no thought that you would try to obtain possession of the impostor from whose pretensions I had been
an especial sufferer by such means. I was angry at the

fraud practiced upon me and others, and intended simply to notify you that the girl you sought was still in the house. I am sorry, on many accounts, that I did so, but beg to assure you that I entertain no unkindly feeling toward you because of the result.

"Respectfully,   AMY HARGROVE."

The grim old doctor carried the missive to the man to whom it was addressed, after having perused it carefully, who inquired in astonishment:

"Who is this young lady?"

"One of your own sort, I suppose," answered the blunt physician. "She comes from the South, is an heiress, and probably sympathizes with you in your disappointment."

"She is a lady, anyhow," responded Eighmie with severe emphasis; "and anything that I can do to compensate her for the injury I shall cheerfully do."

After the first day Amy was undisturbed by visits of condolence. Miss Hunniwell came once or twice, but she was a poor dissembler, and knew enough of Amy's treachery to her friend to feel a profound disgust for her, which if not expressed could hardly be said to be concealed. She was kindly cared for by the minister's household; a few formal inquiries were made each day, but by some means or other the idea had gotten out that if not actually concerned in the plot to abduct Hilda she was by no means averse to its success.

For herself, she asked no questions. If she noted the unfriendly coolness that came to pervade the manner of all who approached her, she made no sign. She obeyed the instructions of the physician to the letter—remained absolutely quiet, avoided all conversation, and before the excitement attending her injury had subsided was pronounced able to be removed to the seminary. Then, for the first time since her injury, she burst into tears, and begged to be allowed to remain for a few days

longer. She gave no reason, nor was any asked. Her
distress was too apparent not to awaken the sympathy
of the good parson and his wife. Their hearts were
touched by her grief, and they not only assented to her
wish, but sought to make the days of her convalescence
as pleasant as they could. As soon as she was able she
wrote a letter, to which she began to inquire for an answer almost before it had been mailed.

. . . .

The people of Burlingdale and its vicinity felt a certain proprietary interest in the attempted abduction.
The town had in no way been celebrated above its
neighbors thitherto. Its people had been good and bad,
rich and poor, notable and insignificant, in the due proportion of the average New England village. One
murder away back in the time of Shay's war had made
the whole region where the house had stood more
famous than the muster of the rebels. It was only a
vulgar murder of the meanest sort, however. There
had been a fair average of suicides and accidents,
some big fires and a "pretty sizeable" dam-breaking,
but nothing to compare with this affair at Beechwood
in the elements of a first-class sensation. In less than
forty-eight hours after it became known every inhabitant of Burlingdale felt that it was an honor to dwell
in a town that was the scene of such a tragedy. Every
man, woman and child had seen all that was visible,
heard all that could be found out, guessed until their
powers of invention were exhausted, and waited in dignified and expectant silence for what the morrow would
bring forth. But the morrow was wretchedly barren.
So was the next day and the next, until the people
began to murmur. Before the week was ended, public
indignation could no longer be restrained. Not only
the people but the local press declared that the course
which had been pursued by all those who might reason-

ably be supposed to have any knowledge of the affair had been most extraordinary.

In all that had occurred since the commission of the crime, it was universally declared that the public had been treated very shabbily. There had been a reserve, almost a mystery, attaching to the actors in the tragedy which was regarded as nothing less than an attempt to defraud it of prescriptive rights. A thousand questions had been left unanswered, and the most persistent inquiry in every quarter had failed to throw light upon them.

It was high time, everybody felt, that such persons should understand that the public had some privileges which they were bound to respect. A crime was a matter in regard to which the people had a right to be informed. The officers of justice were but the servants of the people. Jared Clarkson should remember that fame was inconsistent with secrecy. As a public character he was bound to render an account of what he did and what he knew to those whose approval made him famous. So, too, with a minister of the Gospel. There should be no mystery in his life. A doctor should remember also that the suspicion of complicity with crime was a debasement of his profession. The public clamored for knowledge, and all were warned that those who stood in the path of its desire would find that they were standing in their own light also. Each and all of those having any knowledge of the crime or the parties thereto were exhorted to enlighten the public in regard to it, under penalty of its displeasure. These were some of the questions to which categorical answers were demanded day by day but not vouchsafed :

" What had become of Hilda ?"

" Who shot Amy ?"

" Who was it that came so near killing Barnes ?"

" Why had Martin Kortright left as suddenly as he had come ?"

" What interest had Jared Clarkson in the matter ?"

" Why should he be closeted with Sherwood Eighmie for hours at a time ?"

" What had he in common with the slave-hunter ?"

" Why did the prosecution of these notorious offenders lag ?"

" Why had the prosecuting attorney been more than once in private consultation with Clarkson and Eighmie ?"

" What were the documents drawn up between Clarkson and Eighmie, witnessed by the State's Attorney, and acknowledged before a notary ?"

" Had Jared Clarkson bought up the unholy claim of another slave-owner to his chattel ?"

" Was the peace of individuals to be purchased at a sacrifice of public justice ?"

" Did a crack-brained philanthropist propose to cure the evils of slavery by constantly interfering to protect its emissaries from the penalty of violated law ?"

" Why did not the Doctor tell what he knew ?"

" Was Miss Hunniwell a party to the conspiracy to defeat the ends of justice ?"

" Why was Gilbert Anderson so strangely silent, and how did he chance to be driving on the unused road in the rear of the seminary that night ?"

These and very many other questions were asked by press and people, far and near, and a myriad of guesses were hazarded by the gossips in reply to each ; yet none the less did the public feel itself aggrieved, and all the more busily did it seek to penetrate the mystery that hung about the strange events.

.   .   .   .

Jared Clarkson had made up his mind as to the duty that lay before him even before his arrival. Painful to any one, it was especially repulsive to him. He knew that in a free government there were but two remedies for bad laws—their strict enforcement or absolute defiance. He hated all that smacked of slavery, or rather he abhorred it with a vehemence that made simple hatred pale. Wrath and disgust swept through his heart like a whirlwind whenever he thought of this Minotaur, for whom a labyrinth had been builded in the fairest portion of our land. He hated the worship of this beast of blood only less than he pitied the victims. He knew that he would be blamed for what he proposed to do, but he had never shrunk from duty because of public clamor. The reprehension of friends and foes had been alike insufficient to deter him from the path his conscience had marked out. But even if he had been the veriest coward that ever shrank from disapproval, he could not then have hesitated. Had not Merwyn Hargrove committed to his charge the trust in which he himself had been faithful unto death? He could not shrink while the picture Jason had painted of that last moment was yet fresh in his memory. His exemplar was sleeping under the shadow of the water-oak by the Mallowbank landing in an unmarked grave. He was calling to his representative to do even as he would have done under like circumstances. What would he have done? That Jared Clarkson determined to do, whatever the risk of blame! What would he do—Merwyn Hargrove—were he then and there present? It needed not much study to decide. So thought the sorrowful heritor of his wretched secret.

. . . .

The public rumor was not without foundation. Sherwood Eighmie and his counsel had conferred with Jared Clarkson and the State's Attorney. There had been much skillful fencing, and the diplomacy of the profession had been exhausted upon each side, in the attempt to learn what hand the other held without disclosing their own. This was continued for a long time in vain.

At length subterfuge was apparently thrown aside, and Eighmie's counsel made specific answer to Clarkson's oft-repeated question :

"What reason have you for believing that Hilda Hargrove was the daughter of your intestate?"

The answer was :

1—There was no evidence of the birth of a daughter to Captain Hargrove and his wife. Kingston had been ransacked for evidence of the birth and christening in vain.

2—The introduction of Hilda to the household at Sturmhold was exactly contemporaneous with the disappearance of Heloise Eighmie.

3—Lida had always claimed her as her own child.

4—The former servants, except Jason, were discharged, and he was a party to the substitution.

5—Hargrove well knew of Lida's claim upon the child, and never denied it.

6—In a letter written by himself to Jared Clarkson, which was found upon his person after death, Captain Hargrove had stated the fact that he desired his executors to expend all that might be derived from the estate of George Eighmie, or so much thereof as might be required, in discovering and freeing Hugh Eighmie, and that the balance of said estate, together with a sum equal to what had been expended in rearing the daughter of George and Alida, in all respects as if she had been his own child, including her expenses at Beechwood Seminary, "where she now is," should be paid to the said Hugh Eighmie in some manner so as to conceal from him all knowledge of the source from whence it came. "As to the daughter," the writer remarked, "she is already amply provided for by the operation of my will."

7—The will thus distinctly alluded to contained no name or reference to any one except the executors appointed thereby and "Hilda Hargrove, a daughter, who has never failed in duty or affection, to whom I

leave my whole estate, well knowing that she will
honor my name and memory by wise use thereof."

And now said Eighmie's counsel, not without evident
apprehension :

"What do you rely upon to rebut this chain of circumstances ?"

Jared Clarkson responded with equal frankness :

"The presumption of legitimacy, and the open, constant and unmistakable acknowledgment of the father."

"And nothing more?" asked the counsel, with ill-
concealed anxiety.

"That is enough," responded Clarkson evasively.

Neither party underestimated the strength of the
other. Eighmie was fettered by the fact of crime committed. Clarkson was weighed down by fear of the
truth. Neither party dared defy the other.

CHAPTER XLIV.

WHEN Hilda reached her room it seemed as if the world had taken on a new aspect. Every nerve tingled with indignation. Fear had been swallowed up in anger. There was a tinge of shame, too, in her thought as she remembered how she had fled at the first hint of danger. She wondered what her father would have said had he witnessed her flight. Then the memory of her dream came back and she saw him again with the light of the moon upon his face as he held the sloop upon her course and went calmly on to meet his cruel fate. As the shadows gathered above the city and she heard the bells ring out the invitation to evening worship she seemed also to see the face of that strange Mr. Brown, which was so fixed in her memory that she could never forget it. Very sad and very stern it seemed, as if it looked in pitying scorn upon her weakness. Then she thought of all who were behind her in the struggle —true-hearted Harrison Kortright and his wife; Martin, whom she could ever command, though she must never love him any more; Jared Clarkson, whom even her father trusted; Gilbert Anderson, who would even have taken life in her defense; the prudent and devoted teacher; and Jason, who had come, no doubt, to warn her of her danger. Oh! she had a host of friends, and it was weak and silly of her to flee from them. The tears flowed fast as she thought of them, and she wondered that she could ever have been so distrustful. The world, which in the morning had seemed so barren of all friendship or truth, now seemed overflowing with sympathy and devotion.

Then the thought of her duty came. Duty to whom? First of all, to her father and his memory. She had pledged herself, even in the first gush of her agony, to do honor to his name. How should she do it? By displaying the same spirit. None should ever say her acts belied her parentage. She paced back and forth across her room in the deepening gloom, her hands clasped tightly and her veins throbbing with defiant exultation. The future seemed to open before her a vista of light as she thought. If indeed it should—a shiver of dread passed through her frame at the thought—if it should be that she were not *his* daughter—if she were, in fact, the daughter of George Eighmie and of the poor weak creature who aimlessly wandered about the corridors of Sturmhold—why then, indeed, a still grander duty lay before her. In that case she owed even more to that man who had given her his name, his filial love—aye, even his life. Then, too, she would owe a broader duty to that people whose misfortune had put its taint upon her life—whose primeval curse had blighted her love. The sacrificial spirit took hold upon her. Perhaps, she thought, it might be her destiny to become one of the great examples which should help to alleviate the thralldom of a race and lift a shadow from a nation's life. Whatever might be the truth in regard to herself her duty pointed still in one direction. She must return and face her destiny. Bond or free, rich or poor, it should not be said that the daughter of Merwyn Hargrove, or the daughter of that friend for whom he rendered up his life, failed to do honor to his memory.

But what was the first thing to be done? How should she begin to act the worthy part for which she had been cast? She wished that she might fly back to her room in the seminary. She wondered if it were empty, or had another occupant already. Then she began to think how she might return and reach it unperceived. She knew not why, but somehow it seemed as if she must begin her new life in the very place where the old one ended. Where the old one ended? Had it ended? She smiled as she thought how she had buried the Hilda of two days before. Even Martin—dearly remembered as he must ever be—she had given him up. She had no hope that the doubt would ever be cleared away. In fact, she half expected that it would be confirmed. She could hardly help believing that her life had been grafted upon that little life which had exhaled almost as soon as it was begun. She had vague memories of a tropical home—was it memory, or was it the weird necromancy of that loved story-teller who had painted for her so many pictures of the lands his eyes had seen? She could not tell. She only knew that the sweet, unruffled life she had led had given way to one full of woe and suffering perhaps, but one that she did not shrink from facing. The ordeal was prepared. The smoking plowshares lay along her path. The judges were in waiting. Yes, her old life was ended—cut sharply in twain, but she longed to graft a new one upon it. She would join and unite them so that the point of severance should hardly be perceptible to other eyes. The luxury, the ease, the freedom she had enjoyed, what were they but a preparation for the duty that lay before? She must go back to her old haunts and begin anew.

But how? Again and again the question recurred. She wished she had the gray-bearded man she had met at dinner to advise her. Then she remembered having heard her father say that advice was a good thing when one already knew what he meant to do. She thought what he would do were he in her place— the dear wise father, who had always left her to decide for herself. Surely he had not done this without a purpose. He meant that she should decide, and not only decide, but act on her own judgment in the future, as he had encouraged her to do in the past. Ah, it was cruel! The lady at the table had only half stated the rapacity of her pursuers. Not only had they not waited for her to take off her mourning, but they had not even allowed her time to put it on. The tears flowed at the memory of her affliction. She reproached herself that even the sorest trouble had caused her to neglect to testify her grief to the whole world. Henceforth her garb should bear witness to her sorrow. She would wear only weeds all her life long. Sackcloth should enswathe her form even as woe must overshadow her life.

All at once she forgot her despondency. She was young, and her buoyant nature laughed at trammels. Her tears were none the less bitter because they were so easily wiped away. She sprang to her feet, laughing, softly and quietly. Then she made haste to light the gas; searched in her bag and brought out some black stuff; combed her hair smoother still upon her brow; plaited the dark stuff along her cheek, which had grown pale with the woe of the last two days; smiled contentedly, and then sat down at the table to examine the contents of her purse. She found that they were ample for all her present needs. Miss Hunniwell, more prudent than herself, had foreseen her need, and had transformed the larger portion of the deposit her father had made in her behalf into ready money, in anticipation of the need of a prolonged concealment. It was strange what a change had come over her. Calmly, even smilingly, she prepared for her couch. She slumbered peacefully, and on the morrow was astir early among the city shops, cheapening, buying and directing, as if danger and sorrow were unknown to her. Nevertheless, her cheeks were strangely pale, and her demeanor quiet and subdued.

A few days afterward a lady in widow's weeds got off the train at Burlingdale. She was fair and young—that much might be seen through her heavy veil. She asked to be driven to the seminary, and handed the hackman her check, for which he received a trunk unusually large and new, on which a name was stamped in large letters. Many read, but none seemed to recognize it. There was an unusual crowd at the station, but no one paid any attention to the new arrival. The people were so excited over the affair at Beechwood that they had no time to notice any one not specially connected with it. The lady was alone in the hack, and on the way to the seminary the driver told her all about the matter—all that was known, at least, as well as some guesses of his own at the unknown. The stranger seemed much shocked, and at one time appeared almost inclined to retract her order and go to the hotel. The driver, in his rough way, was very sorry for his fare — she was so young and tender, and yet wearing widow's weeds. She seemed entirely broken down with sorrow, and never raised her veil nor spoke above a subdued monotone during the trip. He made some cautious inquiries regarding her affliction, but a quick sob and the sudden thrusting of a white handkerchief under the gold-bowed glasses which she wore told the good-natured fellow that his inquisitiveness was very painful. So he desisted, and gave his attention to his team. Arrived at the seminary, she sent her card to the principal, and waited in the reception-room until she came. Many of the pupils, who were busy with preparations for departure, glanced in at the door half curiously. She did not look at them, nor once lift her veil. Miss Hunniwell came with a look of mild surprise upon her face and the card of the new-comer in her hand. As soon as she had entered the room the strange lady rose

and closed the door. Then turning to the teacher, she
raised her veil. The teacher regarded her with a puzzled look, as if seeking to bring back to her memory
some half-forgotten face. Then she shook her head
almost imperceptibly.

"Don't you know me?" asked the stranger.

The teacher started, came closer, and peered anxiously into the pale face framed in the dull black of
the widow's weeds. The stranger took off her glasses.
Miss Hunniwell started, and would have screamed, but
a plump white hand was clasped firmly over her mouth.
Then there were tears and embraces and anxious inquiries, as when friends long parted meet again. The
door was opened after a time, and Miss Hunniwell and
her guest passed along the hall together. The stranger's
veil was down, but the teacher's agitation was clearly
perceptible. She took the stranger to her own room,
where she soon left her to attend to her own duties. It
was a matter of great surprise when she directed the
lady's trunk to be taken to Hilda's room; but she explained that it was an old pupil who once occupied that
room, and had now come back to seek seclusion in her
deep affliction. She had explained to her, she said, the
unfortunate associations of the room, but she did not
seem to mind them at all. No other room would seem at
all homelike to her, and she especially desired that she
might be allowed to have that. So the strange widow lady
was soon duly installed in the room Hilda had chosen
when she came, hardly more than a child, to select the
place in which she would pass the years of her school-life.

After a time the teacher brought Jason to the room.
The lady had put aside her widow's veil and removed
the glasses she had worn. Her hair was brushed
smoothly down upon her forehead, and only a faint line
of white about the throat relieved the sombre depths
of the mourning which she wore. She advanced and

offered her hand to Jason. Her lip quivered and her eyes filled with tears as she did so.

The faithful servant gazed at her a moment in astonishment. Then he suddenly seized her by the arms, peered keenly into her face, and exclaimed:

"If it ain't Miss Hilda! Bless God, our little Miss Hilda!"

Before she could prevent, he had seized her in his arms, and was carrying her about the room, as if she had been a child, tears rolling down his face, and his lips uttering half-incoherent bursts of gratitude.

"There, there, Jason," said she, gently releasing herself at length. "I am very glad to see you again, but you must not try to toss me about in that fashion. I am not as light as I once was."

She gave him her hand as she spoke, which, with the characteristic freedom of the old servant of the plantation, he kissed and fondled, while his eyes seemed to devour her features.

"Ah, Miss Hilda," he exclaimed, "I thought I wouldn't never git a sight of you no more. You jes' run off, nobody knows how nor whar, an' leave Jason here without a word—jes' bound to wait till you comes back in your own way, whenever you gits ready, for all the world like your pa. I declare, child, you're his own gal, sure. Here 's Marse Eighmie comes a-tearin' round atter ye, an' all at once, jes' when he thinks he 's got yer safe, whar is yer? Then, atter a little, when everybody thinks yers done gone an' hid, jes' as ef yer 'd been a sure enuff nigger, as all on 'em tries ter make out, why, here you is!"

Despite the fact of Hilda's evident sorrow, and that he had not seen her since her father's tragic death, he could not repress his joy. But his mood changed instantly, as he saw her lip tremulous with grief at this allusion.

"There, there, honey," he said soothingly; "don't you go to feeling bad now. You know there ain't nothin' that would make Marse Merwyn gladder 'n jes' ter know what his little gal 's done—come right back here into the jaws of the lion that 's a-huntin' atter her, as you has, chile. Bless yer dear heart, you 's yer pa all over again, that yer is, an' Jason knows it. That was always the way with him, you know—here one minute an' there the next, axin' nobody's advice, an' tellin' nobody what he was gwine ter do till it was all over an' done. There, there, dear, don't take on so—please don't, honey," said Jason, as she snatched away her hand, and, sinking on a chair, sobbed aloud with a sorrow she had before had no opportunity to indulge.

After a time she checked her grief, and said with a choking voice :

"Have you no message for me, Jason, from — from my father ?"

"There, now, what an old stupid he is !" exclaimed Jason reproachfully. "Here I 've been a gwine on about nuffin', an' this dear chile jes' a hungerin' for dem las' words her pa sent her. 'Clar it does seem as if Jason was gittin' to be a straight-out fool an' no mistake."

The faithful servitor had opened his vest as he spoke, and from an inside pocket now drew forth a letter which he handed to Hilda with an air of reverence that could not have been greater had she been a queen and he an humble liegeman kneeling at her feet.

"There, Miss Hilda, that 's what I ought to have given you before, only I was that glad I done forgot all about it. Marse Cap'n give me that jes' the las' minute 'fore he made me come away. De Lo'd knows, Miss Hilda, I didn't want to do it nohow, an' I wouldn't if he hadn't jes' forced me to. There warn't no sort of use on 't—none in the world. If he 'd jes' have let me take a crack or two at that crowd in dead earnest in-

stead of firin' all round 'em as we'd been a doin',
there'd a been plenty of time to have got him aboard
an' off before they'd have rallied up to stop us. But
he wouldn't do it, Miss Hilda—he p'intedly wouldn't—
but jes' give me this letter an' told me not to let no
man or woman catch so much as a glimpse of the least-
est corner of it till I put it in your hands, Miss Hilda.
And I hain't. Now, there 'tis, an' Jason's filled his
last orders. There ain't nothin' more for him to do
now—nothin' more.''

''Thank you, Jason,'' said Hilda, as she took the letter and glanced at the superscription. ''You are a
good, faithful fellow,'' she added, as the tears streamed
down her cheeks. She pressed the letter passionately to
her bosom, as if to still with its touch the beating of
her heart. She reached out her other hand and patted
the cheek of the faithful servant. He caught it and
covered it with kisses.

''You must not say there is nothing more for you to
do, Jason. Papa sent you away, no doubt, that you
might take care of me. He knew I would need you
when he was gone.''

''I'll do it, Miss Hilda—anything you want in the
wide world I'll do. If you'll jes' let Jason serve you
like he did Marse Captain, that's all he wants.''

''You shall always do that, Jason.''

''Thank ye, Miss Hilda, thank ye; but you must
promise not to run off an' leave me no more,'' said he,
half doubtfully.

''Oh, never fear!'' said Hilda, as she turned to the
window and broke the seal of her father's letter. Hardly
had she glanced at its contents when an expression of
surprise escaped her lips. She read a little farther, and
a cry of pleasure came bubbling from her heart. An
instant after she rushed across the room, with the
crumpled letter close clasped to her bosom, fell upon

her knees beside the bed, and cried, as the tears rolled down her cheeks :

" Thank God ! thank God ! Poor Papa ! Dear Papa ! Thank God ! Thank God !"

The teacher stole away and left the faithful servant alone with his young mistress, to tell the story of the father's tragic death.

. . . .

Martin Kortright returned to Sturmhold burning with zeal in his lady-love's behalf. To his parents he told over and over again the story of what had occurred at Beechwood. He laid before them all the plans his ardent brain had devised for discovering whither she had flown. Already he had secured the co-operation of detectives, and he proposed before a week had passed to put her likeness and a full description in the hands of the police of every city in the country. To all this Harrison Kortright imperatively objected.

" If she were a runaway servant or a lost child, that would do. But you must remember, my son, that it is Hilda Hargrove of whom we are speaking. Just read that letter of hers once more, and you will see that the girl who wrote it doesn't need to be hawked around the country like a lost poodle. She means to do something, and wants to be left alone to do it in her own way. Heaven knows she has people enough hunting after her already, and you would only add to her troubles if you began a pursuit. Let her alone, my son. Let her have time to get over her grief and terror, and determine on the course she will pursue. She has sufficient for her present needs, and knows very well that she has only to indicate a want in order to have it gratified."

" But she will think I have no spirit if I sit down and wait for her to clear up this mystery all alone," said Martin. " If I could only let her know what Jason is able to prove, she would come back at once."

"I am not so sure of that," rejoined his father. "She is not running away from the slave-catcher so much as from the fear that she may be something worse than a slave herself."

"Jason's testimony settles that also," interrupted Martin.

"I am afraid Jason's story is hardly conclusive," said the father. "Jared Clarkson knows that I don't put a particle of confidence in the inference he draws from the papers in his possession. I am sure that Hilda is Merwyn Hargrove's child. Not only did he acknowledge her as such, but she resembles him as closely as one person can another. She has all his coolness and courage, as well as his quiet candor and undoubting self-reliance. Even he could detect nothing of her mother about her except in appearance. Now, if Clarkson put the same reliance in Jason's story that you do, he would have telegraphed at once to relieve my anxiety. I heard from him twice yesterday, but nothing to indicate that he has changed his impressions in the least."

"But Hilda ought to know what Jason says, and have the letter he refuses to give to any one else as well as the package Clarkson has for her."

"That is true," said the old man, "but you are not the one to take it to her. If she knew you were on her track, can you not see that she would just rush deeper and deeper into obscurity? It is you and your love that she dreads more than all the slave-hunters in the world. If you should pursue her before this doubt is settled, she would not hesitate to destroy herself in order to escape from you."

"My God!" exclaimed Martin, "what shall I do?"

"Do?" said his father reproachfully. "You are the last one to ask that question. If ever a woman had a right to demand obedience from her lover, that woman is Hilda Hargrove at this time."

"She doesn't expect me to obey and leave her to suffer, does she?" asked Martin impetuously.

"She expects, and she has a right to expect, that you will obey her wishes when they are fair and reasonable ones."

"But hers are not reasonable," said the son, with some show of irritation.

"Let us see," said the father. "She tells you frankly that she would die before she would marry with a doubt upon her birth. You, in your impetuous love, might at first think otherwise, but there could be no surer way of securing the unhappiness of both than by overcoming, if you could, this objection. You are as sure of her love as if you looked into her heart, but you know also that you can never change her determination."

"But I cannot wait in idleness while she is in trouble —perhaps in peril," protested the young man, as he strode back and forth across the room with clinched hands and a brow knotted with agony.

"Wait you must, my son, because she bids you. If there were no other reason at this time, you are bound to regard implicitly her lightest wish. But you do not need to be idle. Your waiting and separation may continue for many a year, but whenever the cloud is lifted, as it will be some time, you may be sure she will keep her word. You should remember that she may need a good deal of money to carry out her plans, and we must be ready to meet her requirements. We are her trustees—you and I. You must continue to do the work I am no longer able to perform."

"There is nothing to do about the estate. It is all in good condition, and almost taking care of itself."

"You speak of her father's estate, my son. It is time you learned that Hilda has even a closer relation to us. One half of all that stands to-day in my name belongs to her."

Harrison Kortright then explained the facts which the reader already knows.

"Does Hilda know this?" asked Martin, drawing a long breath, when his father had concluded.

"I do not know," was the reply, "but I take it for granted that she does. You know her father always had great confidence in her. I doubt if he kept anything from her except that miserable matter of his brother's children."

"You think, then, that she wishes me to stay here and look after her interests as you have done hitherto?"

"It is reasonable to suppose that she would desire to have her matters in such shape as to yield whatever funds she may require, is it not?"

"I suppose so," answered Martin moodily; "but how shall I know her wants, or she know that I am obeying her request?"

"I suppose she will expect that without any information, but I see no reason why you should not communicate with her," said the father.

"How?" asked Martin, stopping short in his walk.

"By advertisement," replied his father. "You may be sure that Hilda will see it. She will not miss a line that concerns any one connected with this matter."

So the father and son devised some brief personals which Hilda only would understand, and know that they were messages from home.

CHAPTER XLV.

A MASKED BATTERY.

HILDA'S first thought after having secured unsuspected refuge in her old quarters was to find out exactly what had been done, in order that she might determine what she ought to do. She no longer felt any apprehension on her own account. Her father's letter had entirely relieved her mind as to that, but it also devolved upon her the continuance of that task which had cost him his life. The son and daughter of George and Alida Eighmie were not only commended to her care, but she was especially charged to discover, if possible, the former, and to see to it that the latter remained in utter ignorance of her birth and origin, unless circumstances made such a disclosure imperatively necessary. On the next day, therefore, Mr. Clarkson came to the seminary at the request of Miss Hunniwell. After his first surprise at the presence of the young lady whose guardianship had been so unwillingly thrust upon him, he bethought him of the package he was charged to deliver into her hands, and returned to his hotel for it. Having delivered it to Hilda, he seemed at once to be relieved of a great burden. After she had glanced over its contents, he began to tell her what he had done, or rather what he had determined to do. Very fortunately for her, he said, the enemy had made a false move. Instead of trusting to the law, they had gone outside of it, and had tried to assert their rights with a strong hand. This fact he proposed to utilize in effecting a compromise, by which the collateral heirs of George Eighmie should release all claim upon the children of Alida.

"'I suppose," said Hilda thoughtfully, "that it will be best for me to remain concealed while you are engaged in this negotiation ?"

"Oh, of course," exclaimed Clarkson. "Your absence was the most fortunate thing that could have occurred."

"Have they discovered the strange mistake they made ?" she asked.

"Mistake ?"

"Yes—in regard to the identity of the daughter of George Eighmie ?"

"I do not understand your meaning," said Clarkson, with a puzzled look.

"I mean, do they know who she is ?"

"Well," said Clarkson with some embarrassment, "they suspect the truth, of course, but they really know no more than when they came."

"Indeed," said Hilda, "that is very fortunate. Then I should suppose the best thing to do would be to throw them still farther off the scent."

"Of course ; but how ?" asked Clarkson.

"I might show myself," suggested Hilda.

"Show yourself, my dear," he cried, starting up in alarm. "It would disarrange everything. It would be fatal. Do please remember that the warrant for your arrest is still in the marshal's hands."

"Well, suppose it is, what then ?" asked Hilda in surprise.

"You would be seized in an instant if they knew of your presence."

"What if I were ?" persisted Hilda. "They can do me no harm."

"Perhaps not," said Clarkson thoughtfully, "but what good can result from it ?"

"The legal proceedings would take some time, I suppose ?"

" Several days, at least."

" They might be delayed, protracted ?"

" Of course."

" How long ?"

" For some weeks, probably."

" Well, in the meantime—"

" In the meantime, you would be in jail."

" In jail ?"

" Yes ; that is, you would be in custody, unless released on a writ of *habeas corpus.*"

" Well, it would be all right in the end."

" Probably, but is it not better to relinquish all claim to the estate of Eighmie, and thereby put an end to their pursuit ? By that means, too, the facts remain solely in our possession."

" I see. I must guard against that. It was Papa's last wish that I should conceal the facts, if possible, forever."

" If you will allow me," said Clarkson, " I think there has been entirely too much concealment in this matter."

" That may be, but we must still continue it for her sake."

" For her sake ? Whom do you mean ?"

" Why, the one we have been speaking of all this time—George Eighmie's daughter."

" I was in hope," said Clarkson scornfully, " that when she was once out of danger she would have the moral courage to avow the truth."

" How can she, when she does not know it ?" asked Hilda artlessly.

" But she does know it," said Clarkson impatiently. " Miss—Miss Hilda—I—I must say that I am disappointed in you. I will gladly do all in my power to rescue you from your present peril, because of my promise to your—to Captain Hargrove, I mean—but after that you must understand that I will have nothing to do with any false pretenses."

" But how can I help it ?"

" You will be your own mistress."

" Well ?"

" You will have an ample fortune."

" Well ?"

' Why not stand up and defy this infamous race-prejudice ?"

" What would you have me do ?"

" Nothing now; but when the danger is over, and you are in the secure possession of what you will receive, I would have you repay the debt of gratitude you owe to Merwyn Hargrove, not by keeping up the miserable sham he urged upon you, but by showing the world his noble conduct in its true significance."

" I do not understand you, sir," said Hilda, shrinking from his vehemence.

" You do not understand ?" he said angrily. " Say you will not, rather. I mean that you should be brave enough and strong enough to avow the truth—to say to the world, ' This man was so true and noble that he conquered every prejudice in order to fulfill his pledge. He even took to his heart one cursed with the blood of a despised race—gave her a daughter's place and a daughter's love.' In other words, I would have you avow your own parentage."

" My parentage ?" cried Hilda in amazement.

" Yes, I would have you reward the devotion of a poor, crazed mother, and acknowledge with pride the heroism of that brother—" the speaker paused, looked hastily about, and then added in a lower tone— " that brother who has devoted his strength to the service of the race whose degradation has blighted his life."

Hilda shrunk from him as he spoke in undisguised dismay. Then she turned impetuously upon him :

" Why, Mr. Clarkson," she exclaimed, " what do you

mean by such language? Do you think my father was
a liar? Do you think his solemn declaration to you
was a falsehood? Do you impeach his dying message
to me?"

"It is because of his declaration that I speak thus!"

Hilda looked as if she doubted his sanity. Finally
she opened the packet in her hand, ran over its contents
hastily, and said:

"Mr. Clarkson, my father tells me here that he has
informed you of all the facts concerning the daughter
of Alida."

"So he did, by means of the parcel accompanying
that which you hold."

"Will you be good enough to allow me to examine
that parcel?"

Clarkson looked at her half-suspiciously; then drew
the package from his pocket, and after showing the superscription, handed her the bills it contained. She glanced
at them carelessly, and extended her hand for more.

"That is all," said Clarkson.

"All? Was there nothing more, absolutely nothing?"

"Nothing but this wrapper, which had evidently
been used to inclose other papers."

He handed her a sheet of paper loosely folded to inclose others. It was indorsed in her father's distinct
and positive hand:

Inclosures.

1. Letter from A. E.
2.   "   "   S. M.
3.   "   "   W. K.
4.   "   "   M. H. to W. K.
5. Affidavit of J. U.
6. Statement of acct. of W. K.
7. Letters H. E. to W. K.
8   "   M. H. to W. K.
9. Letter of instructions to W. K.
10.   "   Bills of M. H.

"And nothing more?" asked Hilda, with a perplexed look.

"Nothing more," said Clarkson wonderingly.

Hilda sat down and rested her head upon her hand in thought. She turned the papers over and over, as if seeking to unravel some mystery. In the meantime, Clarkson sat watching her with a curious, pitying look. Once or twice he half started, as if he feared she were about to destroy the papers he had given her. After a time she rose, crossed to where he sat, and handing him the package she had received from him which was addressed to her, she said quietly :

"Will you please read that?"

When he had concluded she gave him the letter she had received by the hand of Jason.

"And that also, if you please."

The effect on Jared Clarkson was astonishing. Incredulity, amazement, joy, and finally mortification, were depicted in turn upon his countenance. After a time he rose, and with a deep blush upon his fine, frank face, extended his hand and said :

"I crave your pardon, Miss Hargrove. I am sorry to have been so poor a counsellor."

Then Hilda broke down and wept passionately. The long struggle was over, and nature would have its way. She had passed the dread ordeal and must fain weep over her deliverance. Clarkson stood by, absently patting her head and smoothing the masses of her hair, to soothe her agitation.

"I very greatly regret having caused you so much pain, my dear," he said in a low, fatherly tone.

She looked up into his face half smiling through her tears, and said :

"It only shows how true a friend my father chose to aid me in the task he left unfinished."

Clarkson stooped and kissed her forehead.

．　　．　　．　　．　　．　　．　　．　　．　　．　　．

After this there were some grave consultations in the widow's room at the seminary. An eminent lawyer came more than once; Jason was carefully examined, and before another day had passed Sherwood Eighmie and his confederates found a legal network woven about them which portended unexpected difficulties. Actions for conspiracy and libel were brought against them in the name of Hilda Hargrove, based upon affidavits sworn to by her, and requiring very heavy bonds on the part of the defendants. In the meantime the demeanor of Clarkson underwent a change that no one could account for. Instead of depression and gloom his mirth was almost hilarious. There was no longer any display of anxiety, and the compromise which he had set on foot was entirely neglected. The strange widow lady after two days' sojourn found that the associations of her old room were not so soothing as she had expected. Besides that she had received a great many visits for one seeking seclusion, and it was a matter of little wonder to the remaining pupils of the seminary that she had concluded to seek a more tranquil home. So she was driven to the station and took the train westward. By some strange chance Jason left upon the same train, but he rode in the second-class car and paid no heed to the young widow whose veil fell in decorous folds almost to her feet.

CHAPTER XLVI.

THE news of the attempted abduction at Beechwood awakened the utmost excitement at Skendoah. A thousand things had contributed to produce this result. While Squire Kortright might be termed the tutelary deity of the place, yet there was a sort of traditional belief, very largely due to the significant winks and nods of the old man Shields, that the master of Sturmhold was associated with Kortright in the enterprise out of which the town had grown. Moreover, Merwyn Hargrove had been a sort of lion in the region where he lived. There was something very attractive in the half isolation which he maintained, as well as in the mysterious tales that had from time to time connected his name with both good and bad achievements. But whatever his life had been, the manner of his death would have fixed his place in the esteem of his neighbors beyond all cavil. Coming as it did upon the heels of their own great calamity, and being allied to it still more closely in cause, they gladly looked upon him as a martyr in whose name and fame they had each a sort of proprietary interest. Added to these facts was the farther one that the relation subsisting between Martin and Hilda was very well understood throughout the region, and we shall not find it hard to realize the excitement which the story of Eighmie's attempt and Hilda's flight aroused in the little village. Martin and Hilda for their own sakes were well-beloved. The villagers had seen them grow up from childhood, sustaining to each other always the most intimate relations. Their mutual affection had been a matter of pleasant jest and kindly gossip long before either of them had suspected its existence. Hilda's beauty and Martin's staunch sincerity had deepened this impression until almost every villager felt as shocked and outraged by the news as if his own heart's dearest treasure had been ravished from his possession. Their sorrow and anger had manifested itself in every conceivable form. Since the return of Martin, the office, which was now wholly under his control, had been thronged almost all the time with sympathizing friends and visitors.

A public meeting had been held, and in speeches and resolutions the people had testified at once their loyalty to principle and also their determination to make the most of their own local celebrities. A band of young men had been organized whose purpose was declared to be the rescue of Hilda should she ever be so unfortunate as to fall into the hands of her persecutors. To say that the story of her origin was disbelieved in Skendoah, but states the truth too mildly. It was scouted at as a transparent fraud by every man, woman and child in Skendoah and vicinity. No one there had any more doubt of her right to inherit as the daughter of Merwyn Hargrove than of the fact that he had named her sole legatee in his will. This universal feeling was intensified still more by the knowledge that Jared Clarkson had become her champion and defender. However poorly they might have esteemed her cause, the fact that he had espoused it would have secured for her their sympathy. When this was added to the other causes mentioned we can well believe the statement of the local press, that "Skendoah was ablaze with excitement." Had volunteers been called for at any hour to go to her rescue the town would have been almost depopulated of its male inhabitants.

It was in the middle of the afternoon—the very busiest

hour of the day in the office where Martin Kortright
was at work—the office from which his father had so
long directed those operations that had linked his name
forever with the town's prosperity. The plain black-
lettered sign, "Skendoah Mills," that hung over the
door had never been changed. Though the son was in
charge of the great interests embraced by this propri-
etorship, it was understood that he was as yet only the
right hand of the father. In fact all business papers
were still signed "Harrison Kortright," though executed by "Martin Kortright, Attorney."

Despite the hum of labor upon all sides, the young
man's thoughts were busy with Hilda. As he gave directions in regard to the purchase of supplies, the sale of
stock, the rebuilding of the burned factories, now well
under way, and a thousand other details essential to a
great enterprise, he wondered where she was, and
whether she would approve the course he had decided
upon. He had yielded to his father's views chiefly because he could really see nothing else to do, but also very
largely from a conviction that Hilda would realize how
much harder it was to obey her than to follow his own
inclinations and seek to discover whither she had flown.
He had an impression, too, that spies were on his track,
and that if he should succeed in finding her it would
be only to increase her peril. So he worked on with the
sad, pale face that had haunted him ever since he heard
of her flight coming between him and the paper when
he wrote, dimming his eyes and dulling his brain.

To the people of Skendoah this conduct on Martin's
part was the subject of unstinted praise. They would
not for a moment admit that he did not know her
hiding-place. That notion was to them absurd. They
believed that he knew, and kept away in order that she
need not be traced through him.

"They won't ever git that gal by follerin' up his

tracks,'' said Shields, pursing up his thin lips and
glancing approvingly over the razor-like edge of his
nose at Martin through the office window. "Both of
'em are too much like them they 're named after to be
caught in that way. Here he is pokin' 'round here as
innocent and careless as you can imagine, and Hilda
nowhere in the world that anybody knows on. Now,
mark my words—the first you know that young man 'll
take it into his head to travel and drown his grief,
and the next thing you 'll hear there 'll be a wedding
somewhere over the water, and they 'll snap their
fingers at slave-catchers. And Skendoah 'll stand by
'em, too, and furnish them the money to have a good
time—furnish it regular every week, and lots of it, too.
Bless their hearts, if anybody ever deserved it, it 's just
them two.''

There was a suspicion of moisture about the old man's
eyes as he spoke. He had hardly gone a hundred
yards from the office when he heard a tumult in the
street leading toward the depot. What could it mean ?
A carriage was coming slowly along the street, beside
which walked and ran and shouted an ever-increasing
crowd. Hats and handkerchiefs were waving in the
air. Men forsook their shops and women their houses
to join the cavalcade. Crowds poured out of the factories, and all was clamor and confusion. At length
the driver whipped his horses into a quick trot, the
crowd was left behind, and the carriage drove up to
the office door. Jason sprang from the driver's seat
and assisted a lady in deep mourning to alight. As she
touched the ground she threw aside her veil, and
showed a bright soft blush upon her cheeks. She ran
up the steps, pushed back the door that stood ajar, and
saw Martin gazing blankly upon the page before him.
His pen was idle, and his thought was not of business.
In the room beyond she could hear the clerks busily

calling to each other from the books they were posting. The clamor outside came nearer while she paused. The blush grew deeper. She held her breath, and stole on tiptoe up to him. Looking over his shoulder she saw the page before him held but one word, "Hilda." There was a rustle — the perfume of a remembered presence — a pair of soft hands were about his neck, warm lips pressed his own, and a voice whispered:

"Martin!"

There was a quick uprising and a fond embrace. After a time the blushing, tearful face, framed in dull black and translucent white, smiled up from its resting-place upon his breast and said:

"I have come!"

The clamor swelled louder and louder without. Some one had bethought them of the town bell, and its deep, sonorous peal rang joyfully out over the excited town. The water was shut off. The wheels were still. The square in the middle of the town was alive with eager faces. After a time Martin appeared in the office door with Hilda upon his arm. Then the crowd went wild. Cheer after cheer went up. The one piece of ordnance in the town was dragged forth from its dusty hiding-place beneath the stairs of the town hall and mingled its reverberations with the clangor of the bells and the shouts of the people. Harrison Kortright, in the library at Sturmhold, heard its echoes faintly. For almost a week sleep had hardly visited his eyelids. He started up on his couch, listened for a short time to the recurrent shocks, smiled peacefully, and said to the plump matron by the bedside:

"They 've heard from Hilda."

Then he laid his head upon the pillow and slept.

CHAPTER XLVII.

A FLICKERING LAMP.

IT was a boisterous cavalcade that set out for Sturm-hold that afternoon. The Father, it is true, had been but a short time dead, but the Daughter was alive again. She was like one risen from the dead. She had come through the ordeal unscathed. The hot plowshares she had been called upon to tread beneath her feet had not scorched even the tender soles. When they were ready to leave the village, they found a procession ready to escort them. Men, women and children, almost the entire population of Skendoah, with the brass band in the lead, discoursing triumphant music, marched out of the little square down the narrow street, across the bridge and up the hill beyond. The blue waters of Memnona glittered in the sunshine. Hats and handkerchiefs and banners waved adieu. Shouts and laughter and tears spoke their well wishing. Smiles and tears testified the pleasure that even in her sorrow Hilda gathered from this good-will. A few carriages and a gay group of horsemen escorted the lovers homeward. The air was chill, but the December sun was bright; the roads were hard, the pace was brisk, and, despite the trace of sorrow, jocund Love led the procession. Sorrow for the dead could not quench the joy of the living. The old life was ended ; the new begun. Trustor and trustee were of the past ; the *cestuis que trust* had come into their own. All that the past had sown, the present had come to reap.

As they drew near the gray-turreted mansion, one by one the friends who had borne them company thus far bade them farewell with cheerfu' words, bright smiles
588

and wind-blown kisses. Despite their joy at her return, they felt that only Love might accompany the bereaved daughter within the home made sacred by the memory of one who would not come again, despite her prayers and tears. Leaning upon Martin's arm, and shielded by the veil which had been her refuge from peril, Hilda entered again the temple filled with her father's memory. Oh, how divine the fragrance that clings about the home where love hath dwelt! The dim, faint memory of a mother's waning life mingled here with the abounding richness of a father's love. His presence was everywhere—upon the graveled walk, beside the gate, within the door—wheresoever she turned her eyes she beheld *him*—her loved, her lost. She saw the servants through her tears—those who had served him. She thanked them with gentle obeisance for the greeting which they gave his daughter. She half resented the presence of Harrison Kortright and the gray-haired dame who greeted her with motherly effusion in the hall. Even Martin seemed to be almost an intrusion at that hour. She broke away from them and rushed along the hall to the great stairway. Then she turned quickly, threw her arms about Martin's neck; kissed him through her tears, as if she would do penance for her thought; hid her head upon his breast and wept in his embrace. As she turned away she saw a head thrust out of a door beyond, and a quick, furtive look of surprise and hate shot past her and rested upon Martin. She recognized her old nurse and went forward and spoke pleasantly. A dull, vacant stare was all she received. Then she fled away to her own room, locked the door, and, for the first time since her bereavement, gave way to the sweet, sad luxury of sorrow.

Of the great house which he had builded, three rooms had almost bounded the solitary life of Merwyn Hargrove—the room in which his wife died, that in which his daughter slept and the library where the treasures

of his unfortunate brother's life were. These constituted his home—ah, how empty now that he would
fill it no more with his strong life ! This had been her
childhood home. What pleasures had not thronged all
the familiar nooks ! Safety, repose, love—home. All
good things had come to her within its walls. Without,
sorrow and danger and unutterable horror ! Love had
met her on this very threshold. In this room she had
bent down from her father's arms to press the first kiss
on his lips who was now her lover.

The room adjoining—if the unclosed folding-doors
could be said to have separated them—was her father's
—the holy of holies, into which she had come each
morning since her recollection—a white-robed worshipper—a welcome priestess, with her morning greeting, to receive her morning kiss. From the tower
adjoining this—her mother's sunny boudoir it had been
in her life, and nothing there had been disturbed—a narrow stairway led down to the library, opening with curious art behind a case of books that seemed only to have
been thrust out from the wall to make room for the volumes upon its crowded shelves.

How often in her childhood she had risen in the
night and sought her father in the library ! How her
bare feet pattered down the lonely staircase, and bounded
across the warm tufted carpet to the outstretched arms !
How often she knew nothing of the return until she
waked to find her father's arms about her in the morning ! Oh, tender, strong-armed father ! Oh, watchful,
loving heart ! How his presence thrilled her memory !
How his absence chilled her heart ! She knelt by his
bedside and wept and prayed. How grateful was her
heart that he had been ; how disconsolate that he was
not ! Ah, how passionately she kissed the white, cool
pillow—kissed it because his head had pressed it, because it would press it no more !

After a time they called her to the evening meal. She begged to be left alone. Then Mrs. Kortright came. She would not see her. Jason came afterward, and, with the privileged persistency of the old servant, knocked until she answered—knocked until she wiped her tear-stained eyes, and opened the door a little way that he might speak to her. He did not ask her to eat— he did not try to persuade, but told her that on the stand before the hearth in the library he had placed a lunch. There was a good fire there that would last all night. If she should get cold or hungry in the night she would re- member the stairway in the tower. The fire made it look "mighty cosy" there, he said, "most as if Marse Merwyn himself were there." She thanked him grate- fully for his deft attention. Then he went away and left her to live over again the life the dead had shaped and blessed. It was not until long afterward, when the night had grown still and her limbs were numbed and chill as if with long embracement of the dead, that youth and health conquered her sorrow, and she stole down the stairs to the library.

No sooner had Hilda arrived at Sturmhold than Harri- son Kortright, with subtle forecast of her wishes, di- rected everything to be removed from the library that could in any manner suggest its occupancy by another since her father's death. During the short time he had been there he had often thought that she might be an- noyed at his presence. Yet he had remained because it seemed his duty to occupy the mansion, and no other room was so home-like and comfortable to him. In truth he seemed to be nearer to the man whose interests he had undertaken to guard there than elsewhere. As soon as she came, however, his couch was taken away, and the lounge that Hargrove had used substituted in its place. His easy-chair and all that could betoken his presence was removed. So when Hilda came softly down

the stairway, opened the half-concealed door and stepped
into the room, she almost felt as if her father would step
forth from some dim alcove to give her welcome.

The wood-fire had burned low, but a great mass of
glowing embers dispensed a comfortable warmth. An
easy-chair sat beside the hearth. A shaded lamp cast a
soft radiance through the room. She sat down and
warmed her chilled hands. After a time she lifted the
snowy cloth and began to eat the luncheon that had
been provided for her. The keenness of her sorrow had
passed away. A sweet drowsy mood, full of tender
memories, came over her. Little by little consciousness
receded, and she slept. Thought shaped itself into a
dream. She was still sitting by the fire in the library,
but now she was waiting for her father's coming. She
watched the door, expecting every moment that it would
open and admit him. She grew weary with delay, and
wondered why he did not come as she dreamed that he
had promised. She fancied that some great danger
beset him. She thought that he was calling to her, but
she could not go. Her limbs were leaden, but each sense
was marvelously keen. The wall of the library seemed
to open, and she saw beyond. Gradually the personality
of her dream changed. Her father faded from her
thought, but the sense of peril still remained. Now it
was Martin over whom it impended. She was still in
the library. He was in his own room—the room in the
tower that matched her mother's boudoir. She knew
that he had chosen that since he had lived at Sturmhold,
because it had been their play-room in childhood. How
strange our dreaming fancies are! She dreamed that
the fire rolled out upon the hearth and spread—a livid,
seething torrent—to the foot of the stairs that led up to
her lover's room. It charred the floor, curled about the
steps, caught the banisters, blistered the wall, and gnawed
its way slowly upward.

Then she saw a figure—who could it be? It seemed that she ought to recognize it, but she did not. A figure with wild eyes, disheveled hair, and garments strangely disarrayed. She saw it steal along the hall, burst into the library, rush to her father's desk, tear open the lid, grope nervously about for a while, and then, with a sudden, eager cry, snatch something from within, and press it to her bosom. The dream had merged into reality. Hilda was wide awake. She saw a woman standing by her father's desk whom she did not know. She had forgotten for the moment that he was dead. She thought a robbery—a wrong to him—was being committed, and sprang forward to prevent it. She clutched the woman by the arm and shrieked for help. The startled robber turned on her assailant. A brand had rolled out upon the hearth and burst into a blaze. Hilda's pale face and black robe stood revealed by its light. A strange look of terrified recognition flashed across the woman's face. The wild, frenzied glare died out of her eyes. She ceased to struggle, shivered, and shrank away.

"Rietta! Rietta!" she said in a voice hoarse with terror. Then, with a shriek of mortal fear, she sank down upon the floor a shivering, chattering, shapeless mass, and Hilda recognized her old nurse, the crazed and pitiable Alida.

.   .   .   .

Hilda's cries brought the household to the library. When they raised Alida to bear her away, a curiously-wrought key dropped from her hand. As they went past the room in the base of the tower the smell of fire began to pervade the house. The door was locked. They burst it open and found the flame, half-smothered by its own hot breath, creeping slowly up the stairs. It was soon quenched, and the unconscious sleeper above knew not how near the stealthy foot of death had come to him, until he heard a terrified voice calling at his door; and when he answered he heard a fervent "Thank God," as Hilda tripped across the hall to her own room and was back in the library almost before Mr. Kortright had noted her absence. Martin soon joined them. Hilda told the story of the night, and Mr. Kortright of many other nights. Then Jason came with the key that had dropped from Alida's hand. He said it was the key of the strong box that Merwyn Hargrove had built into the wall of Sturmhold. He had lost it just before he went away, and had more than once bewailed the fact. Then they wondered how Alida came to have it at that time, and Mr. Kortright went to examine the desk. Upon the left a secret drawer lay open to his gaze ; what seemed the framework of the desk, having turned inward on a hinge, disclosed a tiny recess in which a bundle of papers still lay. Mr. Kortright took them up, and, after merely glancing at the indorsements, handed them to Hilda. There were ten of them, and the indorsements corresponded with those upon the wrapper in the possession of Jared Clarkson, as Mr. Kortright noted at once. In the meantime Jason was searching among the same books Alida had been wont to examine, for the missing volume. Hilda remembered having seen it in her father's room. When she had brought it, Jason turned it over until he found a blue mark drawn around the paging. This was the combination on which the safe was locked He drew the heavy desk away from the wall, and quickly threw back a panel of the wainscoting and revealed a small vault filled with papers. A brief examination showed that this hidden store-house contained neither deeds nor bonds nor any evidence of debt or thing of appreciable value, but only the records of love—letters and mementos of the wife he had never ceased to mourn—the letters they had exchanged as lovers, and afterward as husband and wife. There were some letters in a cramped Italian hand from Hilda's grandfather, and a large package of them from Miss Fanny Errickson, in regard to the little nursling which had been left in her care. This was the name which Jason had persisted in calling Rickson. By these, Hilda's history might be traced almost day by day from the hour her mother left her, in Kingston, until the good lady, then on her way to England after her father's death, had written : "I send this by Captain Hargrove, who has been laughing and crying by turns for an hour, over the sturdy little girl I have brought him instead of the puny babe he remembers. She is indeed a beautiful child, and I hope that in the happy life before her she may not quite forget her volunteer nurse, who only wishes she might never part with her little Hilda."

"It is strange," said Martin, "that Alida should have known where the key was hidden."

"Good reason why she knew," exclaimed Jason. "She put it there herself. I could most take my oath Captain Hargrove never knowed of that little till. I never heard of it, certain. Besides, he told me himself the key was lost."

"But how did she know where to find the combination ?"

"Jest watched till she found where he kept it," replied Jason. "I told Marse Merwyn that woman was always spyin' round. But he said it didn't make no sort of difference. There was nothing for her to find out, and she was a poor, no-'count creature at the best, and could do no sort of harm to any one. It seems she did find out something, though, and might have done a power of harm."

"What do you suppose was her purpose ?" asked Hilda of Harrison Kortright.

"It is hard to tell," said he with a sigh, "just what she meant to do. She had undoubtedly watched your father at his desk, and was perhaps aware of the nature of his communication to Clarkson. Her malady, perhaps, was less serious then than now. She had dwelt upon the idea that you were her daughter until it had become the controlling idea of her disordered mind. She probably removed these papers from the envelope and substituted others, not, perhaps, thinking of the character of those put in their places so much as the abstraction of these."

"But why should she wish the key to this vault?" inquired Hilda.

"For the same reason, probably," said Kortright. "She seems to have thought that if she could destroy the evidence that you were the daughter of Merwyn Hargrove, you would of necessity be considered as her child."

"So you think her purpose was to destroy them?"

"Originally that was her design, without a doubt. Of late, in her nightly intervals of semi-lucidity she seems to have had a distinct purpose. Her crazed brain remembered that there was something at the left of the desk that she wanted. She had half-forgotten what it was and where she had hidden it. She dimly remembered, also, that there was something in that set of books that was somehow connected with her general design. I doubt if she knew what it was. She no doubt opened the drawer to-night by accident, or the sight of Martin may have stimulated her memory so that she recollected where it was. The possession of the key may, perhaps, have enabled her to recall what it was she wished to find in the book she was accustomed to examine on her nightly visits to the library, or it may be that she only knew that your father always looked at the book before opening the safe, and had no distinct idea what it was she sought."

"Poor Alida!" sighed Hilda.

Aye, poor indeed! Her life had exemplified the fearful possibilities for horror that a system destined to swift destruction held. After a life of shame and sorrow and misery her poor crazed brain was soon to be at rest. When one came searching for her a few days afterward, in order that a mother's crime might be in part atoned, he was just in time to gaze upon a still, cold face, note a birth-mark, which the abundant iron-gray hair had hid, and stand by her open grave.

"Poor Lida," repeated Hilda, as she thought of the woes that had beset the life of one whose worst fault had been an unreasoning love for her. Tears fell fast as she thought what Alida had suffered and she herself had escaped.

Aye, weep gentle heiress of sweet memories! The last plowshare is overpast. Ah, not the last! The children of George Eighmie, whom your father has given you in charge to watch over—what of them?

CHAPTER XLVIII.

AMY HARGROVE had at length an answer to her letter. It was very brief, merely referring her to a letter which the writer had sent to Miss Hunniwell. So, in response to her request, the teacher visited her convalescent pupil, taking with her the letter alluded to. It was from the president of the Bank of the Metropolis, and was in response to one of the circular letters she had sent out announcing the discontinuance of the school for the time being, and inclosing bill for Amy's board and tuition.

She had also suggested that because of the injury Amy had received she might require more than her usual allowance for the term. It was in this manner that all of Amy's bills had been paid, and all communication with her guardian had been made through the president of the bank. To this letter Miss Hunniwell received the following reply:

"MADAME: I have yours of the 8th inst., and inclose draft for the amount of your bill. In response to your farther suggestion, it may be well for me to state that the remainder of the sum deposited with me for the benefit of Miss Amy Hargrove amounts to $674.43, which will be paid to your order or to hers. In case she should desire to draw on us, however, we should require your indorsement as a guarantee that the money actually reached her hands.

"I deem it proper to state here that no farther responsibility will be assumed on account of the young lady by the person who made this deposit. It is needless, therefore, to advise prudence in its expenditure. It will probably suffice to carry her through the next term, when it would be wise for her to seek some means of self-support.

"To avoid needless inquiry, it may be well for me to add that I am strictly prohibited from disclosing the name of the party who provided this fund, save upon his written request or that of his legal representatives.

"With the utmost sympathy for the young lady and yourself, I am your obedient servant,

"WILLIS KENYON, *President.*"

Amy's pinched, cold face became ashen in its pallor as she read this letter, and tossing back her curls looked up at the teacher with a wild terror in her great black eyes. Her lips grew white, and a shiver passed through her frame as she asked huskily:

"What does it mean?"

"I do not know," said the teacher kindly.

.   .   .   .

There came to Jared Clarkson, while yet at Burlingdale, by the hand of a brisk young attorney, a letter from Matthew Bartlemy to this effect:

"MY DEAR SIR: I can hardly make out what you are all doing up there in Blankshire. Why you haven't put Eighmie where he can have a chance to cool his heels in solitude before this, I cannot imagine. However, I suppose you know. I'm almost sorry for the man, too. He wouldn't have been half the fool he is if his counsel, Bob Gilman, was not so powerful sharp that he can't use the little sense the Lord gave him. He was just possessed with the idea that Hilda was George Eighmie's child, and had been adopted by Hargrove as his own in order to conceal her identity. I don't know why he took up the notion unless it was just because that was a thing no human being that had a grain of sense would ever think of doing. I knew Gilman had that idea years ago, and I must say I was foolish enough, one while, to be a little afraid it might be true. I even went so far as to sound Hargrove on it myself. But, bless your heart, I never was more ashamed of a thing in my life. Why there wasn't a quiver in his eye nor a flush on his face as he spoke of it. A half-amused, half-pitying smile stole round his mouth as he referred to it, evidently not dreaming that any one but a crazy woman could entertain such an idea. I didn't say anything about it when I came back, because I had a notion that some time or other Gilman would burn his fingers with it, just as he has. That letter to you that was found on Hargrove's body clinched this notion in his mind, and I must say it did squint that way mighty strong. If I had not known better I might have weakened then. But I knew a man had better try to walk on water than think of standing on that hypothesis. So I only laughed to myself, and watched to see where I could put in to advantage in Gilman's game. I had no fear for Hilda, though I cannot quite understand that letter. Hargrove was a mighty careful man about his papers, and I have no doubt you have the whole riddle at your fingers' ends before now. What has become of Hilda, though, it puzzles me to make out. It isn't like the girl to run away. She don't come of running stock, and always seemed to have spirit enough to do credit to her blood. From what the papers say it looks as if there was something you were afraid of. Knowing it cannot be Hilda, I have wondered if it could be that Eighmie's mistake was nearer what he wished than the game he expected to bag.

"However, I will not try to make any guesses at this distance, but tell you why I send the bearer to you now. He brings almost conclusive proof—indeed I think it is conclusive—that the mother of Alida was never a slave, consequently Alida was not a slave, and Eighmie's marriage with her was valid. This evidence consists of the sworn confession of a woman who has lately died, to the effect that she was delivered of an illegitimate female child at the house of Dr. Gant, which she left in his care—or rather to his pity—for, though she gave him a hundred dollars more than he stipulated for his services, she made no conditions about the child. Indeed, she avers that she never saw it but once, and expressly told him she had no desire to see it again. She had been sent to Dr. Gant under an assumed name, in order to conceal her disgrace, and never informed the doctor what her real name was. She thought little of the matter until many years afterward, when, a childless widow, she began to mourn for the babe she had so inhumanly cast away among strangers. Before that, however, the doctor had died, and her agent could get no clue to the girl's identity. He happened to strike on me, and told me enough of the story to awaken my suspicion that the daughter was Alida. As the woman was still alive, at that time, and was not exactly ready to admit the whole truth, however, I only hinted at what I knew. At the same time, I made up my mind that if I heard of Salathiel Jenkins being in this state I would get the truth out of him so far as he knew it. There were one or two old things hanging over Jenkins that I knew would incline him mightily toward truth-telling if he could hope thereby to keep me from hooking on to him. After a while I got hold of Jenkins sure enough, and he gave the affidavit which Mr. Torrens will show you. I ought to have said before that the bearer is Alfred Torrens, Esq., of Gleason, Torrens & Torrens, Attorneys, Washington—a most respectable firm. You probably know the old man Torrens, as he is very much of an Abolitionist, though not quite as rank as you. This affidavit closes up the gap pretty closely. The dates agree with the woman's confession, and the doctor's letters, to which he refers, give the name by which the woman was known while under Gant's care. It evidently lay on the doctor's conscience, for Jenkins says he tried repeatedly to find the girl, but he always blocked the way by telling him that he had forgotten what he did with her. I suspect there was some blackmailing, if not some kidnapping done by Jenkins in the matter. The woman has left property, I think, to this daughter, or her descendants, under some sort of impossible conditions which Mr. Torrens will explain to you if he sees fit. I infer that the gist of them is that the beneficiaries shall take the testatrix's name, and that her youthful frailty shall be entirely concealed. Whether you can aid him or not depends, I think, on whether you understand Hargrove's letter to you. If you do you probably have the clue in your hand. If you do not, the Lord only knows where the young man will have to go to find that necessary bit of thread.

"My chief interest in the matter is that it cuts Gilman's folks out of all chance to recover Mallowbanks or mulct Hargrove's executors in damages for his spoliation of the estate in manumitting the slaves. We can close the whole thing up now, and when the little girl Hilda comes of age or marries, she can step right into an unincumbered inheritance, which I hope she will enjoy, as her father had trouble enough over other people's folly. By the way, please give the child my regards, and tell her that when it does come off—her marriage, I mean—old Matthew Bartlemy will expect an invitation, and is going to come all the way to Sturmhold to drink her health and dance the first set with the bride. Though I suspect the son of that clear-headed Dutch-Yankee, Kortright, will find the gal and marry her before you find even which way she has gone.

"Please write me all that you think would make me feel good about your experience with Gilman's clients. He's so sick of his relief expedition now that he has taken to his bed. I don't allow that he shall forget it while I live either.

"I suppose the suits here might as well be closed out now. You might get a power-of-attorney out of Eighmie, allowing me to enter judgment. If you have him by the wrist, as I suppose, he will no doubt be in a 'disposing mind,' as the law phrases it, and let you have about anything you choose to ask for.   Yours faithfully,

"M. BARTLEMY.

"P. S.—I will send in my bill against the estate as soon as I have everything completed. I suppose this matter will set you against slavery worse than ever, and I admit that it is a pretty hard thing. After all, it is not fair to judge an institution by its worst features or its accidental results,

One might just as well denounce the town-meeting because there are paupers in New England, as declaim against slavery because such cases as Alida's are possible. Such fool business as running all over the North hunting niggers, whether it is lawful or not, will soon end the whole matter. The fact is that slavery only exists now by the tolerance of the North. They have the power and a constantly-increasing numerical predominance.. Our fire-eaters laugh at this, but when the tug comes, it is the most men and the most money that wins. I think that in less than twenty years this question will be decided. If it ever comes to an open rupture with the North, likely niggers will not be worth fifty cents a head when the controversy is over. The whole political atmosphere seems to me feverish and excited. If the Secessionists and Abolitionists could all be hanged, we might have peace long enough for those that are left to die of old age. That would be hard for you and your friends, but I don't see any other way. By the way, what do you think of that fellow Jason? Do they ever raise such servants anywhere except in a state of slavery? That man only cost Hargrove about six hundred dollars, and he's worth his weight in gold. Tell Miss Hilda never to let him go out of her service under any circumstances.   Yours,

"M. B."

.   .   .   .

Gilbert Anderson, before he attempted the rescue of Hilda, was an unknown country minister. Ten years of honest work among the New England hills, though not without results of which we need not be ashamed, had certainly been barren of fame. Within a week thereafter the East and the West were engaged in clamorous rivalry for his possession. His unquestioning manhood had struck a chord in the hearts of the people that was to make him welcome throughout the land. Without knowing it he had become a hero. Telegrams and letters poured in upon him at a rate he had never dreamed of. It was evident that this-modest yet self-reliant expounder of the Divine Word would ere long leave the little hamlet in the New England hills to take part in the endless Armageddon within the walls of some great city.

Jared Clarkson was charmed with the manly earnestness and simplicity of this country clergyman. The more he saw of him the deeper grew this favorable impression, and, with characteristic heartiness, he neglected no opportunity to speak of him in his letters in terms that were certain to enhance the regard of those who read. During his entire stay in Burlingdale the good pastor's library was his favorite resort. Upon the last of his accustomed visits Mr. Torrens accompanied him, and while Clarkson disputed with the pastor about theology in the library, the young lawyer conversed with Amy Hargrove in the parlor.

Of what they spoke none ever knew, but when, two days afterward, Mr. Torrens started on his return, Amy Hargrove went with him. From that day none who had known her ever heard her name again. A few months afterward Gilbert Anderson received a draft almost equal to a year's salary. It was mailed in New York, but there was no clue to the source from which it came. He was greatly troubled about accepting so large a sum from an unknown donor. His wife insisted that it was meant as payment for what they had done for their strange, involuntary guest, and, considering the facts, not at all excessive. As it came at a time when such a windfall was peculiarly acceptable in making preparation for the new field of labor in the far western city, his objection was at length overruled and the draft was cashed. After all, the good woman's speculations were more fanciful than real.

. . . .

The affair at Beechwood is one of those mysteries that are never cleared up to the satisfaction of the public. There were many guesses at the truth, but none ever knew whether they were right or wrong. The data on which they were based consisted chiefly of these facts: Sherwood Eighmie and his confederates were allowed to depart on merely nominal bail. This bail was forfeited, and the suits, public and private, were allowed to die of sheer indifference on the part of the prosecution. When Eighmie returned to his home the litigation between "Eighmie *et al.* and Hargrove's executors" was dismissed on the plaintiffs' motion and at their cost. From these facts the people in and about Burlingdale concluded that public justice had been bargained for private right. They could only have been half right at best, but those who held these views were stimulated thereby to a more active antagonism to slavery. These facts occasioned much comment also in the region where Sherwood Eighmie lived, but he kept his own counsel. There it was generously believed that public sentiment in Blankshire had balked the law, and that, in order to save himself and his fellows from troublesome and endless prosecution in a hostile community, he had agreed to surrender his rights, and had chivalrously kept his word. In the minds of all who accepted this view, it tended not a little to fasten the conviction that the South could not look for any justice at the hands of the North, but only envy, chicanery and hate. Not long afterward Eighmie entered into possession of Mallowbanks, by what right no one knew; but, as nobody appeared to dispute his possession, he continued to hold it. Years afterward there was found upon the Register's books of Clayburn county the record of two quit-claim deeds of the plantation known as Mallowbanks, situate in said county, properly described by metes and bounds, one executed to Hilda Hargrove by Heloise Eighmie, and the other to Sherwood Eighmie by Hilda Hargrove. As these constituted color of title in him, his possession became, in the course of years, an indefeasible right.

CHAPTER XLIX.

THE HARVESTING.

ANOTHER year had passed. The Man and the Hour had come. The culmination of half a century's thought was at hand. It was a bright day in October. Where a majestic current bursts its way through solid granite walls, nestling in the shadow of overhanging mountains, was a little hamlet turbulent with wild excitement. The pomp of war was strangely interspersed with the garb of peace. Turmoil and frenzy, bravado and fear, were curiously mingled. A piebald soldiery mimicked with quaint oddity the duties which the veteran performs unconsciously. A little squad of men in blue uniforms, under direction of a grave-faced man of middle age, constituted the centre of attraction. A cordon of sentinels was drawn around an open space near the river-bank. A long low building, with a double doorway that occupied almost the whole front, stood at the end of this space. Outside this line of sentinels pressed the populace, citizen soldiers and rustics, old and young, crowding upon each other to see what was within.

It was not much, yet none who saw it—aye, none who read of it in the journals of that day—will ever forget it. Within that narrow space an old man lay upon the ground. A blood-stained blanket underneath his helpless limbs. A son upon his right hand dying. Upon his left another, dead. The sun beat upon his bare head. Eager crowds questioned and jeered. The blood oozed through the matted hair and ran slowly down his neck. A wound upon his forehead was half hidden by a handkerchief, grimy and discolored. Sweat and dust and blood were upon his face and hands. The surgeons said he could not live.

This old man, with less than a score of followers, had startled the world from slumber. In every Southern state the call to arms was heard. Patrols were doubled. Slaves were watched. Terror came to every home in a dozen states. The sunshine hid unnumbered perils. The womb of night was big with horrors. Thousands were in hourly fear. Millions slept in terror many a night thereafter. He had fallen. His insane attempt had failed. The magazine on which the South had builded was yet un-fired. The insurrection of a day was at an end. The flags of two states waved triumphantly over him. The Stars and Stripes proudly attested the supremacy of the Constitution and the laws. A few dead bodies were in sight. Here and there others lay upon the public way—within the shattered building, on the rocks in the turgid river—some black, some white. Even death could not protect them. Insult pursued their poor still clay. Men shot the dead. Pools of blood were about the streets.

Even in his weakened, broken plight the old man was leonine in look and gesture. A word of comfort to the dying son, of pity for the one already dead, but of his own sad hurt no word. No murmur of complaint, no moan of pain. To those who stood over him plying his ebbing strength with fierce inquisition, his replies were clear and calm. To those who uttered curses, he found breath to administer reproof. Even cowards were compelled to admire his courage, and those who hated most to admit his sincerity. "The bravest man I ever saw," said one whose own courage many a bloody field afterwards attested. "No man ever lived before who was at all like him," said another, who bent over him that day and sought to drag from his lips the story of some great conspiracy—some Catilinian revolt against "the best government the sun ever shone upon." In vain. At the top and bottom,

the beginning and the end, there was but one man—one
thought, one name—John Brown. Not boastful nor ambitious; not seeking power or wealth; not looking to
overthrow a nation or found a dynasty—the one man
"unlike all other men" had drawn unto himself a few
whose hearts were fused with the fervor of his own high
purpose, and had undertaken a movement perilous and
rash beyond any in history.

The Martyr had appeared. Self-immolated he lay
upon the soil of Virginia. The world knows the story.
That "strange Mr. Brown," as Hilda had called him.
"Old Brown, of Ossawatamie," as his enemies named
him. "Old man Brown," as the most friendly of the
metropolitan journals of that day termed him. "Captain John Brown," as he modestly avowed himself upon
his capture—the incarnation of a thought that already
colored with its fervid glow the life of one-half of a great
people—John Brown had offered himself and the poor
lives that clung to his a sacrifice for liberty and a protest
against slavery. "Guilty," said they who saw only the
blood that flowed. "Mad," said they who pitied. "A
fool," cried those who measured his act by their own
weak spirit. "Unlike all other men," said the statesman
who saw and wondered. "John Brown," is all the world
has yet found to say of him. Uncomprehended, because
the world has so few standards by which he might be
measured. Revered as a martyr through one-half the
land. Execrated as a monster by the other. Looked
upon with reverence in many thousand Northern homes.
A name of terror at every Southern fireside. To the
North the forerunner of justice and liberty. To the
South the incarnation of bloodshed, rapine, woe! To
the one his act meant aggression. To the other his execution meant defiance. When he died, throughout the
North the church-bells tolled and prayer was uttered for
the passing soul. In the South thanksgiving was offered

for deliverance from evil. John Brown! Monster and Martyr; Conspirator and Saint; Murderer and Liberator; Cause and Consequence! Animating one-half the land to emulate his example; stimulating the other to meet aggression; inciting both to the shedding of blood!

Brave, humble, single-hearted, simple living. Seeking not his own gain. Cruel in the scathing intensity of his hate for wrong. Grand in the impossibility of his attempt. Sublime in his faith that through his death the purpose of his life would be performed. The climax of one age and the harbinger of another!

Upon the bridge that spans the river stands a restless crowd gazing at a half-naked body that lies upon a rock midway of the rushing stream. It is long since dead, but many a shot is fired at the bare breast and cold, set face that overhangs the eddy that boils beneath.

"D'ye see that mark upon his face?" said one.

"For all the world like 'Lathiel Jenkins," answered his fellow, curiously.

"Don't you know him?"

"No."

"Why, it's that boy 'Lathiel used to own—the one that run away."

"You don't say?"

"Yes; I knew he'd go to the bad. He was always saying he'd '*rather die than be a slave.*'"

"Well, he's had his choice," said the other carelessly.

"Yes," was the reply. "It's a pity, too. He was a right likely boy if he hadn't been so high-strung."

.   .   .   .

Skendoah has a holiday once more. The wheels are still; the looms silent; the factories closed. The houses are decked with flags. Martial music echoes through the streets. A thousand bayonets catch the sunbeams. The tread of serried ranks is almost drowned by the clatter of attendant feet upon the sidewalks. There are moist eyes and quivering lips. Mothers and wives and sisters are sacrificing to the sentiment of freedom. Skendoah has given of its best and bravest. A thousand households have yielded up a chosen life—a first-born or a best-beloved. In the front rides one with grave, flushed face, still young. The end of preparation and of waiting has come at length. He is not one man but a thousand. Behind him are the ripening years. The labors of a generation have brought forth fruit. The lost lake yields up its treasures. The busy years have transmuted into gold the waters of Memnona. Skendoah sends its heroes forth, equipped for the soldier's work, and Martin Kortright leads them.

The train is filled; the engine puffs and shrieks; the crowd cheers lustily; the tears are hidden and the sighs are drowned. In an open barouche stands a fair young wife whose eyes are bright and dry, waving a farewell. So long as the train is in sight the spotless signal of her love waves good cheer to the departed. When the last glimpse of it is lost she bows her head upon the shoulder of the gray, decrepit man who sits beside her, and utters to the coachman the one word, "Home!" Ah! how sobbingly weak and vain it sounds! Sturmhold once more has lost its master. As they drive through the thronged streets—past the silent factories, across the bridge above the empty channel, and see the soft spring sunlight kissing the blue waters of Memnona, Harrison Kortright waves his hand toward the quiet lake, the clustered homes, the silent caverns where the gnomes of · labor sleep, and says:

"This day cometh the Harvest!"

The nation faces the ordeal the Past has prepared. HOT PLOWSHARES lie along her path and she is led blindfold and barefoot to the trial. The ages wait to sit in judgment!

[THE END.]

BULLET AND SHELL.

War as the Soldier saw it:

CAMP, MARCH AND PICKET; BATTLE-FIELD AND BIVOUAC; PRISON AND HOSPITAL.

By GEORGE F. WILLIAMS,

OF THE 5TH AND 146TH REGIMENTS NEW YORK VOLUNTEERS, AND WAR CORRESPONDENT WITH THE ARMY OF THE POTOMAC, THE ARMY OF THE SHENANDOAH, AND THE ARMY OF THE CUMBERLAND.

Illustrated

WITH ENGRAVINGS FROM SKETCHES AMONG THE ACTUAL SCENES

By EDWIN FORBES,

PICTORIAL WAR CORRESPONDENT; AUTHOR OF "LIFE-STUDIES OF THE GREAT ARMY;" MEMBER OF THE FRENCH ETCHING CLUB.

FORDS, HOWARD, & HULBERT,

Publishers, 27 Park Place, New York.

A CONCISE HISTORY

OF THE

American People.

BY JACOB HARRIS PATTON, A.M.
Author of "*The Natural Resources of the United States*," etc.

Twenty five years ago, Prof. PATTON, then a teacher of history, began collecting materials and casting into shape this important work, very much on the plan later adopted in "Green's History of the English People." The complete work, in two volumes, is a *History of the United States* from the discovery of the continent to 1882 ; a *History of American Politics*, divided into successive Presidential terms ; and a historic presentation of the *Life of the American People*, comprising the beginning and growth of industries, the formative force of religious ideas, the results of widely different systems of education during six generations and their influence upon public opinion, the causes and the course of the several wars, including much that is *new and valuable*, in a full, succinct, and impartial record of the Civil War.

A distinct portion of the work is devoted to "*How We are Governed*." Prof. PATTON concludes that every citizen, and especially every voter, should have a practical knowledge of this subject.

It is the aim of PATTON'S AMERICAN PEOPLE to embody all the elements of *true history*—the essential facts, the underlying causes and principles, the drift of events, the force of ideas, and the parts men play—and to set before the reader a moving drama of real, vivid forms. History, thus presented, becomes the most fascinating and instructive department of literature.

"PROF. PATTON approaches much nearer to the Ideal Historian than any writer of similar books. His work must be given the highest place among short Histor:es of the United States."—*Christian Union* (New York.)

"We take great pleasure in commending it for general reading and reference, for use in c· lleges and schools, and for all the purposes of a complete and accurate history."—*N. Y. Observer.*

The Portrait Illustrations, with Autographs and Biographical Diction-ary of Eminent Men, serve to represent the leading departments of progress —Law, Literature, Theology, Science, Music, Invention—the Soldier and Statesman, the Discoverer, Explorer, Frontiersman, etc.

Complete in 2 vols., 8vo, 1160 pages, postpaid to any address for $3 per vol.

www.ingramcontent.com/pod-product-compliance
Lightning Source LLC
Chambersburg PA
CBHW021931110726
47901CB00003B/793